VERTICAL
COFFIN

VERTICAL
COFFIN

STEPHEN J. CANNELL

ST. MARTIN'S GRIFFIN ⚇ NEW YORK

www.stmartins.com

ISBN 0-312-33190-8

The Tin Collectors was originally published by St. Martin's Press in
January 2001.

First Edition: January 2004

10 9 8 7 6 5 4 3 2 1

This one's for my old friend, Chuck Bowman. As young men we shared far-fetched dreams and now we're actually living them.

ACKNOWLEDGMENTS

As always, there are many people to thank. Without the help I get from my friends in law enforcement, both city and federal, I would be lost. Bill Gately, U.S. Customs (Ret.), has been a great friend and a constant source of information and realistic detail. I dedicated *The Viking Funeral* to him because that novel was based on one of his cases. This time around, as always, he supplied valuable insight and advice. Dick Weart, ATF (Ret.), an old friend, hooked me up with several people at Alcohol, Tobacco, Firearms, and Explosives—most notably, Joe Dougherty, ATF Baltimore. Lieutenant Eric Parra of the L.A. County Sheriff's Special Enforcement Bureau welcomed me and gave me a tour of the facilities. He introduced me to a heroic bunch of guys who spent hours talking to me with the tape running. Thanks to Sergeant Phil Barth and Deputies Jeff Riggin, Mark Schlegel, Carlos Parga, William Robert, George Cramer, and Willie Robinson. I would also like to thank Stan White, LASD (Ret.).

Any mistakes I made in portraying either the operations or the tactics of ATF Special Response Team or the Sheriff's SEB are mine alone.

As always, I have great help in the office. My mop-and-pail crew of crack assistants unscramble my dyslexic spelling and work tirelessly, running down info, checking facts, and doing endless manuscript cleanups. I owe them a huge thanks. Grace Curcio, my friend and assistant for twenty-five-plus years, has retired, but she still types my weekend pages. Kathy Ezso is now on point and makes this work go smoothly, juggling more details than would seem possible. Jane Endorf is tireless and without peer. Thanks, guys. Jo Swerling is the first one to see the manuscript after it's ready. I hand it to him with shaking hands and he does the first cold read with an expert but gentle eye.

Thanks to my new agent, Robert Gottlieb at Trident Media. He has helped me redesign my thinking and career. Robert, we're on a roll.

I would like to thank all my friends at St. Martin's, especially my editor, Charles Spicer, who has been a constant source of strength, and my publisher, Sally Richardson, who has not hesitated to step up for me. Also a big thanks to Matt Baldacci, Joe Cleemann, and Mathew Shear.

At home is where my real strength lies. My children are a constant source of joy and wonder. Tawnia, you have made your dad a happy man. You are a magnificent mother and it has been a joy for me to watch you work your way up from gofer to sought-after television director (without my help). Your gifts are personal and professional. Chelsea, you continue to grow and become more awesome. Your life choices and sense of fairness signal a wonderful spirit and true heart. You are all a father could hope for. Cody, you have proven what can happen when you work for a goal and don't give up on your dreams. I have watched you mature and see that success in life comes from the inside out. You have made me proud. My wife, Marcia, holds my circus together, keeps the family on course, and changes the air in my head when it gets too full of helium. You have made all our dreams come true, babe.

VERTICAL COFFIN: A term used by SWAT teams to describe any threshold. When clearing a house, police are most vulnerable to gunfire while passing through doorways.

VERTICAL COFFIN

JULY 14
THESE COLORS
DON'T RUN

THEY SWUNG WIDE off Trancas Canyon, thirteen bikes clutching down to make the turn; high-octane Harley engines growling loudly, tearing an ugly hole in the still afternoon. Right ear down, one by one they all finished the turn and straightened up on the Pacific Coast Highway, the old Camino Real. They were ten miles northwest of Malibu, hurtling along the four-lane, timing their moves to roar around slower-moving traffic. Thirteen Harley V-twins in formation. Metal locusts growing larger and more dangerous as they swarmed, the two-second rule be damned.

They called Emo Rojas "Maniac." He was prez, so he was out front, riding point. Emo's giant shoulders reaching high to grab polished ape hangers that stretched like chrome wings over his black Harley Softail. His four-stroke roared angrily: intake, compression, combustion, exhaust. A growling black-and-silver she-devil.

Next was the ride captain Darren Zook, called "Goat" Big, with sleeveless black leathers and arms from Gold's Gym. Hard to tell where his arms stopped and the vest began—he was that black. Outrageous wraparound, chrome-rimmed darks hugged his square face like clip-on bug filters.

Behind Goat was Jabba the Slut. She'd arrived just minutes before the ride, patched in club colors. An American flag do-rag wrapped her head while ink-black shades the size of welders' goggles hid her porcelain-white face. She was club treasurer and had the ride money, so she rode third. Bulging biceps and man-sized thighs straddled the 95 V-twin of her yellow-and-black Screamin' Eagle Deuce; scuffed boots thrust forward on highway pegs.

After Jabba the Slut came the two-by-twos. Blam-Blam, on a chrome-and-black Harley Super Glide. A tub of guts in too-tight leathers with vibrating love handles. Next to him was Drill-Bit, then Johnny Bravo and Pebbles, Wart and Shooter, Mean Mike and The Rooster.

Then came Chooch and Shane Scully. Since they were not patched members of the club, only guests, they rode last: tail-gun charlies. Chooch on Emo's backup bike, a red Harley Fat Boy with a dry clutch. Shane rode Swede Petersen's modified Road King. They came out of Trancas Canyon at the end of the line, completed the turn and accelerated, hurrying to close ranks, bunching tight again, until they blocked both southbound lanes like scurrilous outlaws—riding four across, lane splitting, the throaty animal rumble of all that horsepower redefining them, the exhaust; a self-induced steroid.

You could see awe and revulsion in the eyes of the Sunday drivers they passed. The beach crowd in their SUVs looked over and saw thirteen thugs on custom choppers with mean-looking, radical fork rakes. They saw the head wraps and greasy leathers and quickly looked away. The club patch—the colors—rode their leathers defiantly. Across the shoulder blades in a death font was their name: IRON PIGS. Under that the logo: a fierce warthog with curling tusks and fire blowing out of its nostrils. The bottom rocker said "California."

Only the baddest club in the state was allowed to wear a bottom rocker. In the eighties that was the Hell's Angels. Then the Mongols blew in and changed all that. They shot a few Angels, ripped the bottom rockers off the dead bikers. The Mongols said you wore the California patch at your own risk. It had been the rule ever since. All bikers knew that if you were caught by a Mongol with a bottom rocker under your colors, you were dead. Mongols alone wore the patch.

Mongols, and of course, Iron Pigs.

The thirteen riders snaked down PCH. The Pacific Ocean glittered on the right, the Malibu Mountains dressed in dry, beige summer colors framed the left. Finally they turned on Mulholland Highway, climbing into the hills. Now the roar of bored pistons and straight pipes bounced off mountains, pinging loudly in the granite canyons. Another left turn off Mulholland took them to Las Flores Road, the hawgs slowing as the road wound dangerously. The late afternoon sun glinted off polished chrome and lacquered paint. A few people heard the deafening rumble and came out of their houses to watch them pass. Then up onto Puma Road, two-by-two, a growling metal centipede making its way slowly along the narrow highway.

Shane looked over at Chooch and saw him grinning. Hard not to feel the rush of all that energy and power. They were nearing the end, rolling in, loud and dangerous. Around the corner, up ahead, was a biker hangout high in the Malibu Mountains.

They rounded the last curve and saw The Rock Store. The parking lot was full. Almost a hundred bikes lined up like soldiers at parade rest, all dressed right, leaning on metal kickstands. Mostly, it was American iron, Harleys and Indians, with a few Japanese rice-burners. The Rock Store was Mecca for Southern California bikers. It was the high church—hawg heaven.

Maniac pulled in and, one by one, the Iron Pigs backed their bikes into a line, then shut them down. Silence filled their ears, laid tight against their skulls. Goat dismounted and turned to face the Pigs.

"Ride captain buys the beers," he said. A cheer was followed by a round of vicious insults.

"I got your ride money, Goat. Right now, you couldn't buy a Hoover Street hooker," Jabba the Slut scoffed. Then she threw a canvas bag full of cash at him. The Iron Pigs whistled and hooted.

Chooch and Shane climbed off their borrowed bikes. "I'll buy you a beer if you don't tell your mother," Shane whispered, instantly realizing he sounded like a Boy Scout at a truck stop.

"I own you now, Dad," Chooch teased. "If I tell Mom about this, you'll be in honey-do jail until Christmas."

"You gotta take a few chances in life," Shane grinned, and threw an arm around his son's shoulder as they all walked toward The Rock Store.

Shane heard a bike start up and looked around just in time to see Jabba the Slut pulling out on her custom Softail. Then he remembered she said she was on the mid-watch and had to get to work. She deep-throated the yellow-and-black Harley, roaring down the road, laying rubber, kicking ass on her way back to L.A.

"I wonder what she looks like under those goggles and do-rag?" Shane pondered.

The Rock Store had been a stagecoach stop in the early 1900s. Ed and Veronica Sazko owned it since the sixties. They made it into a convenience store. The rock foundation was responsible for its name. Two old red-and-white gas pumps sat out front dinging off the gallons like antique slots. In the seventies, the Sazkos had added a dining room and bar. They'd sold one hell of a lot of beer since then. Most L.A. bikers eventually hit the Rock Store. Everybody from Jay Leno to old-time, bee-in-the-teeth Harley roughnecks hung there. Shane, Chooch, and the remaining Iron Pigs found three open booths, crowded in, and drank beer as the roof shadows grew long, stretching across the porch into the dirt yard. The place started to clear out by seven. By seven thirty most of the Iron Pigs had left. Maniac, Goat, Chooch, and Shane hung on stubbornly, not wanting the ride to end. Alexa was in Chicago at a police convention so Shane and Chooch were spending some guy time together. Maniac and Goat took off their head wraps and the cool biker handles disappeared with them. They were back to being Emo and Darren.

Chooch was explaining the Wing-T offense he quarterbacked at Harvard-Westlake High School, finger painting plays on the table using the moist condensation from their beer cans. Emo watched closely as the play was diagrammed on the sawed wood.

"Don't you run any options off that formation?" Emo asked. His overdeveloped shoulders and muscular build made him look like a linebacker, but Shane knew he'd once played quarterback at Cerritos Junior College.

"Yeah." Chooch drew another play as he talked. "You can fake to the halfback, coming across like this; or do a naked roll-out pass run option. We also have a pitch to the trailing back."

Emo leaned over and looked down at the diagram painted in water on the chipped cedar table. Then he added a play of his own.

"You should tell your coach to put in a Z-Option off the roll-out. You throw back to the wingback on the far side." He drew the pass pattern and Chooch looked carefully at the play.

"Countermotion," he said, and Emo Rojas nodded.

Shane thought this was just about perfect. He and his son

were making the important, but difficult, transition from parent and child to buddies.

They heard the four Harleys pull in, but nobody paid too much attention. Darren Zook went to the restroom to tap a kidney. Shane went to get another beer from the bar. He had just paid when he heard angry voices coming from the other room.

"Do I look like I give a fuck?" he heard somebody shout.

Shane moved out of the bar and stood in the threshold of the dining room. He saw four scruffy looking bikers leaning over the booth where Emo and Chooch sat. Shane knew at a glance these were outlaws. One-percenters. Chooch was trying to get to his feet, but one of the large thugs had his hand on the boy's shoulder holding him in place. Hard to do because Chooch, at eighteen, had grown into a six-foot-three, 225-pound college football prospect. These four outlaws were patched. When one of them moved, Shane saw the Mongol's colors riding his back like a dangerous insult.

"This ain't gonna work, dickhead," one of the Mongols said to Emo. He was big. At least two hundred and fifty pounds, with a red beard and deep-set eyes. He looked mean, but slow.

"Hey Rainman," one of the other Mongols said to red beard, "this kid ain't patched. Maybe he's a prospect."

Rainman leaned in and glared at Chooch. "Then you're prospecting for dead people." He turned and growled at Emo. "You wear the bottom rocker in our state, you eat shit and die."

Chooch was still being held in place. But then without warning, he bolted up, spun, and shoved the Mongol behind him hard, using a forearm shiver. Suddenly everyone was moving at once. Emo Rojas ducked under Rainman's wild right and bolted out of the booth. Chooch scrambled out beside him.

A hard-eyed Mongol with GEEZER stitched on his pocket was holding the door. He pulled a cut-down out from under his three-quarter-length coat—a shotgun with a four-inch barrel.

Cut-downs were illegal in California, but these guys made their own laws. Geezer chambered the piece and everybody froze.

"You got one way outta this place," Rainman said to Emo. He was smiling through his red beard, but his slit eyes offered little humor and no hope. "You get down on your belly and ya crawl out the door. I'm gonna break you up, rip that bottom rocker off, and stuff it up your ass. Then if you suck this prospect's dick, I might let you run."

Now a slight smile appeared on Emo's face. Adrenaline, or some form of street insanity. Chooch was on the balls of his feet and ready.

Shane left the bar threshold and moved quietly along an adjoining wall, then looped right and ran through the service door. Geezer didn't see it coming until it was too late. Shane dove over a table and hit the gunman between the shoulder blades, right in the middle of the ugly, snarling Mongol logo, taking the man to the ground. The shotgun flew from his hands, discharging into the air. It landed, then bucked out the door into the dirt.

How long the fight lasted was a topic of dispute for months. Darren Zook, who heard the shotgun blast and ran out of the can, said he thought he was only in the brawl for about thirty seconds. Shane and Emo felt it had lasted over three minutes— but to be honest, fish and fight stories always get bigger with each telling.

Most dustups end up on the ground, so the LAPD and the L.A. Sheriff's Department teach a version of Brazilian jujitsu, which is a ground-fighting technique. Tough guys and heroes like to stand toe-to-toe and trade punches, but Emo, Shane, and Darren all took their guys down fast, wrapping them up in arm locks and leg holds. Geezer screamed as Shane applied too much leverage and broke his right wrist. Rainman hit Chooch, who shook it off and countered with two sharp left hooks that dumped him.

Whether it took a minute or an hour, the end result was the same. Shane, Darren, Emo, and Chooch were standing over the four dazed Mongols. It was a moment that would bond them forever.

"Los Angeles Sheriff's Department. You're under arrest," Emo said, as he flashed his deputy's star and cuffed Rainman.

Shane flashed his LAPD badge, then grabbed his cuffs and hooked Geezer up. Darren and Emo cuffed the other two, who called themselves Crash and Nasty, then went through the bikers' pockets and finally found enough meth in their saddlebags to add Possession with Intent to Distribute to the charge sheet. Afterwards, they escorted their captives outside and waited for the LASD transport van.

The Mongols shook their heads in dismay. "You guys are cops?" Rainman asked. "I thought you were outlaws."

Darren said, "Iron Pigs don't ask if they can wear the bottom rocker, because you gotta be a cop to join." Then Emo reached out and tore Rainman's California rocker off his leathers and stuffed it in the trash can out front. He tapped his own club logo. "These colors don't run."

When the sheriff's van pulled away with the four Mongols, it was almost dark. Shane and Chooch said good-bye to Emo and Darren then walked back to their borrowed bikes. As Chooch turned to get on his Fat Boy, Shane saw that he had a cut on his eyebrow trickling blood. His lip was also beginning to swell.

"Your mom's gonna kill us," he said.

"We didn't run, Dad," Chooch said proudly.

"Yep. We hung solid," Shane agreed. As he started his Harley he thought this boy had surely been sent to him by God.

VERTICAL 1 COFFIN

I T WAS MID-SEPTEMBER, hot and dry, the kind of hot that makes you think of frosty cans of Coors and long swims in the ocean. I was standing in a small, burned-out shack ten miles east of Palmdale in the high desert. There wasn't much left—a rock chimney and some blackened footings. My shoes were already covered with soot from kicking at scorched rocks and the remnants of charred furniture. It was ten on a Tuesday morning and the lizards had already abandoned their flat rocks to slither into the shady crevices between granite outcroppings.

This had been a Palmdale P.D. crime scene a month ago. Now it was mine. I'd driven out here in a primered Ford Bronco along with Sonny Lopez. The truck was his privately owned vehicle, known in police circles as a POV. Sonny was a sheriff's deputy working L.A. Impact, a multijurisdictional law-enforcement task force located in Los Angeles County, in Lancaster. The TF was a bad pork stew made up of LAPD and state cops, LASD, and a smattering of feds from the FBI, Customs, and ATF. All of them pretending to be a kick-ass unit, while at the same time trying to get past their deep jurisdictional prejudices.

Sonny Lopez was in his mid-thirties, tall, and movie-star handsome. He was working meth labs for L.A. Impact. This one had exploded and burned to the ground. At first it was thought to be a gas leak, but the county fire teams had learned to call the cops if they saw chemistry glassware in the ashes. When they were raking the debris cold, too many test tubes came up in the furrows. Since crystal kitchens tended to explode more frequently than Palestinian suicide bombers, the Palmdale P.D. did tests on the soil and found high quantities of methamphetamine. In fact, the dirt was so laced with amp, the site started to get nightly visits from local crankheads. They hauled away the soil, taking it home to mine it for meth. A dirt lab is what we called it. L.A. Impact did a lot of meth investigations, so they were called in.

I came from a far more depressing direction.

Two kids had starved to death in a house in Fullerton; fourteen-month-old Cindy and her four-month-old brother, Ben. Their mother, Paula Beck, was a crystal addict with half a dozen meth-cooking busts in her package. Paula was currently in the Sybil Brand Institute facing two involuntary manslaughter charges. The D.A. wanted to boot it up to murder two and had asked Special Crimes at LAPD to look for extenuating circumstances. Since my partner, Zack Farrell, was on a temporary leave of absence to be with his ill mother in Florida, and since it was mostly a background check, which required no partner, I got to work on that grizzly little double homicide. The D.A. thought if he could file the bigger charge against Paula he could get her to roll on her ex-boyfriend, Paco Martinez, a high-profile drug dealer. Paula had been banging him until a month ago, when she'd finally gotten so tweaked and crankster-thin he kicked her out.

Once Deputy Lopez determined that this burned out hacienda had been Paula Beck's pad, the sheriff's and LAPD crime computers played "Let's Make a Deal" and that's how we ended up in Palmdale together. Because Paco Martinez was such a major player, I'd been expecting to find a big crystal plant. But now that I was here, I knew I'd wasted the trip. This was just a user lab, a Beavis and Butt-head kitchen where poor, strung-out Paula Beck cooked her own personal bag of crystal, then fried her brains. I wondered if little Cindy had crawled in the dirt out front while Ben lay screaming in soaking diapers watching his mommy shoot the moon. I wondered if she'd gotten so tweaked in Fullerton that she just forgot she had left her two babies locked in their room till they starved to death.

So now Sonny and I were standing in Paula's kitchen, both silently wondering, if somebody had taken notice sooner could this whole terrible tragedy have been avoided?

But crystal is the oxymoron of narcotics. Technically, methamphetamine is the artificially synthesized version of the body's natural adrenal hormone. Cook up a good batch and it makes you feel beautiful, sexy, attractive, and alert. The problem is that it also takes away whatever it was that you wanted from it. If you use it for sex, you can't have an orgasm. Take it for work, you become totally inefficient. And very quickly it goes negative. You start to get so drowsy you need to load up just to keep your eyes open. It's a nightmare drug. I've seen recovered heroin users, but not one recovered meth addict. They all check off the ride at the first possible stop.

Cindy and Ben had paid Paula's trip ticket and now I was out here trying to cash her in for a D.A. who really only wanted her boyfriend. It was part of an endless cycle of death and destruction.

More and more I was finding it difficult to do this job. All I saw was human wreckage. Even when I succeeded in doing something that felt right, more often than not, I'd been cursed for it. People didn't want cops around. Even my victories produced confusion. I had been fighting these feelings by not thinking about them, pushing them aside like bad food, knowing that if I ate much more it would soon make me sick. But you can't run from moral dilemmas, and I knew my days in law enforcement were numbered unless I found an answer.

"This lab burned a month ago?" I asked, jerking my ruminations out of this deep rut and back onto Paula's cratered family.

"Yep." Sonny looked around the flat, dry desert, his dark good looks clouded by his own elusive thoughts.

A hawk wheeled high overhead, a black shadow against the cobalt sky. The bird called softly to me. A mournful sound: too late . . . too late . . . too late.

"You gonna write any of this up?" Sonny asked. "I got the PFD reports. I can burn you a copy if that'd help, but there's nothing much here. It's been baked and raked. Whatta ya say we head back?"

"She's out here cooking up a batch, gets so amped out, she burns her own place. It's a wonder those kids lasted as long as they did."

Sonny nodded and looked up at the sun. "Man, it's hot. How did my ancestors put up with this heat?" He wiped his face with a handkerchief, anxious to get moving.

"Let's roll," I said.

We trudged back to the Bronco. Sonny cranked the air up, but it blew hot for almost three minutes before things got better. We took the Grapevine over the hill and in less than an hour dropped back into the Valley. My car was at the Agoura sheriff's substation where we'd met. We rode in silence most of the way.

Finally, somewhere near Sunland, Sonny looked over and

shook his head angrily. "How do you get so wired you forget your own kids?" he grumbled. "It's bummin' me out."

"We both shoulda gone into retail," I replied.

When we arrived at the substation all hell was breaking loose. Sonny almost hit a black-and-white Suburban that was careening out of the parking garage. I could see the wide-eyed, adrenaline-charged face of the uniformed driver as he bounced the vehicle out of the lot and squealed away up the street.

"That's our technical command vehicle," Sonny said. "The area commander uses it to roll on hot calls." Seconds later, ten sheriff's deputies ran out of the station carrying shotguns and Kevlar, trying to buckle into their Tac vests as they ran.

"This don't look good," Sonny said. He squealed into a parking spot, jumped out, and ran toward the substation.

I was LAPD and this was an L.A. Sheriff's Department roll-out. As I picked up my briefcase and headed toward my black Acura, I told myself, leave it be, I've got enough action on my own beat.

The joke in LAPD is that the sheriffs are just rent-a-cops on steroids. The reason is that LASD sells their services to any unincorporated city in L.A. County that needs them. They contract out, just like the square badges who work the malls. The rip is they wear stars not badges, and that *star* is just *rats* spelled backwards. Of course, that's just a sleazy, jurisdictional cheap shot. The LAPD, gods that we are, are paid by the almighty taxpayers, giving us superior placement in the jurisdictional universe. All of which is worth about what you paid for it. Nothing.

I was unlocking the Acura when Sonny Lopez ran back into the lot with four deputies and a lieutenant. The "LT" was cradling a Tactical Operation Tango 51, which I'd read was their new Remington 700 Action sniper rifle. It was an extremely accurate long gun that fired a 168-grain Boattail .308 hollow point. Huge stopping power. Something big was definitely going down. The deputies and their watch commander piled into a new sheriff's Suburban with a Mars Bar, hit the cherries, and squealed out fast. Sonny never even glanced back at me. He was that pumped.

I reached into my car and switched to the Impact channel on my police radio. The LAPD and LASD work on completely different radio frequencies, but since I had worked with L.A. Impact twice before on overlapping cases, I had put their TAC frequency on my scanner. This was a major scramble and I figured some of the Impact crew was undoubtedly rolling on it. If so, I'd be able to crib their transmissions. They used Tactical Frequency 4. I switched it on and immediately heard somebody screaming:

". . . Deputy down! Thirty-Mary-Four is down! He's layin' up on the porch right in the door. Every time we try and get to him, the sonofabitch inside starts pourin' lead out at us." You could hear the adrenaline in his voice.

Somebody else came back yelling an order. "Forget Emo! We can't get him out of there—not yet. Set up your fire lines. Cover the back. Get a secure perimeter and somebody run over and tell those fucking SRT SWAT guys not to canister the place with hot gas. I don't have their frequency. Tell 'em we can't take a fire. This neighborhood is too dense and the brush is too dry."

Emo? I thought. *Emo Rojas?*

I pulled out of the substation parking lot as I triggered my mike. "This is LAPD Sergeant Scully. What's your location?"

"Get the fuck off this channel," somebody barked.

"Where is this?" I yelled. "What's the Twenty?"

"Hidden Ranch Road," someone else answered.

I don't ride that much in the county and had no idea where that was, so I pulled over and programmed the street and city into my Acura's GPS. A map appeared on the LCD screen. It was the main road in a housing development called Hidden

Ranch. The street dead-ended at a cul-de-sac in the foothills of Agoura two miles behind me. I swung a U, put the hammer down, and made it there in two minutes, with my on-line bitch goddess screaming directions. *In two hundred feet turn right,* she ordered.

You could hear the gunfire from almost half a mile away. Not the flat popping sound of 9 mm handguns, or the hard crack of an Ithaca pump, but the BLAPBLAPBLAPBLAP of an AK-47, or some heavy-ordnance machine rifle on full auto.

When I reached Hidden Ranch Road I saw a residential area full of two-story builder houses in the mid-to-expensive range tucked up against the dry San Gabriel foothills. Fifteen LASD's cars were already on the scene. At least twenty-five deputies were fanned out hiding behind garden walls and parked squad cars. Some were pouring 9 mm rounds into a house at the end of the cul-de-sac.

Just then a shooter appeared in one of the downstairs windows and let loose with an AK-47. The weapon tore holes right through the sheriff's van parked in the center of the street. Then the gunman ducked back out of sight. Two sheriff's air units and a TV news chopper added to the wall of noise as they circled relentlessly overhead. I rolled out low from the Acura, hung my badge case open on my jacket pocket, grabbed my Beretta and ran toward the sheriff's vans and the Suburban TCV parked in a semicircle in the middle of the cul-de-sac.

The shooter's house was a phony Georgian with fake trim and Doric columns. Sprawled across the threshold of the front door was a uniformed deputy. He wasn't moving. But I recognized those shoulders, that short black hair. It was Emo Rojas. Flat on his face, lying in the vertical coffin.

BARRICADED SUSPECT 2

As **I** **APPROACHED** I heard a uniformed sheriff's captain screaming into his cell phone.

"The shit just jumped off! We got an active shooter and a deputy down. I need an incident commander and a Special Enforcement Bureau team on site now! There's an SRT unit here, but they're pinned down across the street. They're not on our frequency, so I can't communicate with them."

Just then, a four-vehicle sheriff's SEB convoy rolled in, sirens wailing, flashers on. The SWAT van squealed to a stop near the three sheriff's vehicles already parked in the center of the cul-de-sac. Two deputy cars and an armored rescue vehicle, an ARV, followed. I had done some cross-training with the LASD at their facility in Spring Ranch, so I knew how they were set up. Special Weapons Teams were comprised of a team leader, usually a sergeant, the second in command was a scout, who did the onsite tactical operation plan. A back-up scout assisted him. The fourth man stayed at the truck to gather intelligence. The fifth and sixth men were responsible for equipment. There were two snipers, called long guns. The weapon of choice for the long guns was a Tango 51 or its predecessor, the 40-X. Both rifles fired armor-piercing .308s. Each long gun had a spotter with him to help isolate targets and to give him tactical support and cover.

The team leader unlocked the SWAT van and the long guns swarmed inside to grab their weapons while the backup scout started passing out flash-bang grenades.

The fourth man opened the office on the side of the truck where the incident board and the weapons team roster hung. He pulled out a graphed Lucite desktop, grabbed a piece of paper, and started to diagram the house and the cul-de-sac, eyeballing it from where he stood, doing a rough but reasonably accurate layout, including all the vehicles parked on the street.

"Get in touch with the city planning office and see if you can get somebody to fax us the plans of this house," the fourth man said to the fifth.

Just then the barricaded suspect popped up again in an upstairs window, firing his AK-47. From where I was hiding, it looked like the weapon held a hundred-round drum mag. The slugs started tearing up the police cars out front and blowing holes in the brick walls where deputies were proned out trying to take cover.

The team leader grabbed his shoulder mike. "All deputies on this channel, get back! You aren't safe. This guy's using lead core rounds. You can't hide behind walls or car doors. Get behind a house, or at least find an engine block."

He opened an ammo box and started handing out .308 mags. His two long rifles and spotters jammed the clips home, then deployed quickly, running low, looking for a good place to set up shop. I ran up to the SWAT van, took cover, then glanced at the team roster clipped to the door. This was the Gray team. The team leader, Sergeant Scott Cook; scout, Rick Manos; first long gun, Gary Nightingale; and spotter, Michael Nightingale. *Brothers?* As I was reading the board the fourth man spun me roughly around.

"Who the fuck are you, Chester?"

"Scully. LAPD."

"Get lost. This ain't your rodeo."

I held up my Beretta. "This guy's in Kevlar. My nines are useless. Can I borrow some Teflon rounds?"

"Shit," he said, but turned, grabbed a box, and tossed it to me. "Stay behind something dense. Those lead cores he's using are brutal."

"Right."

I moved away and ducked down behind the engine compartment of a sheriff's car. The deputies pinned behind the brick wall were trying to retreat, but every thirty seconds or so the shooter would appear in another window of his house and start firing. His twenty-round bursts tore up everything they hit. I knelt and thumbed the useless, standard 9 mm Winchesters out of my clip, then started feeding in the Teflon mag rounds. Once I had all thirteen loaded, I slammed the clip home, chambered the gun, then peeked up over the hood of the car. Emo was still up on the porch. It didn't look like he'd moved at all. Nobody had the stones to try and go up there. If you made a run and timed it wrong, it was pretty much suicide. You were gonna get chopped in half by that AK.

I told myself that even though Emo wasn't moving, it didn't mean he was dead.

Ten yards away I spotted Sonny Lopez crouched down behind a squad car with another deputy. Both held shotguns at port arms. Their Ithacas were useless in this situation, and you could tell from their strained expressions that they knew it. I moved up from behind and tapped Sonny on the shoulder.

He jerked around to look at me. His face was pulled tight. "Scully, whatta you doin' here?"

"Not to be a critic, but shouldn't we go get our guy off the porch?"

"Can't. The perp's got armor-piercing shit. He's blowing holes right through car doors. We're calling for more backup."

"Why doesn't somebody get him on a cell phone, try and cool this down?"

"The lieutenant tried talking to him. Guy won't come out. An incident commander's on his way. Captain Matthews wants to sit tight and wait for him."

Then, in an attempt to explain why all these cops were on their faces eating dirt, Sonny added, "This asshole's nuts," which was more or less obvious.

"Look, that's Emo Rojas up there, right?" I said.

"You know him?"

"Yeah. If we could get one of those two SWAT teams to work the right side of the house, maybe they could draw the guy over there and you and I could make a run and pull Emo off the porch."

"You outta your mind?" Lopez said.

"Probably," I answered. "Wanta try it?"

He thought about it for a moment, looked skeptically toward the house.

Just then the shooter popped up again. He was upstairs this time, and let go with a five-second burst, aiming at the squad car we were hiding behind. The black and white rocked hard with the impact from a stream of lead that sliced through the door panels like they were plywood. Windshield glass and side mirrors shattered and flew. Then the man ducked back down. It seemed to help Sonny make up his mind.

"Let's go," he said hotly. "Lemme get my Loo to sign off on it." He moved off to find his lieutenant.

There was walkie-talkie madness all around me. People

screaming, shouting counter-instructions, stepping on each others' transmissions. While all this was happening, I decided if I was going to try to get Emo off that porch, I was going to need some better intel. I looked up and saw that there were now three news helicopters swirling overhead. Pinned down, I couldn't really risk rising up to case the situation. I looked behind me. The neighbors' houses across the street had all been evacuated. I waited until the shooter popped up and greased off another burst. After he finished I sprinted across the street to the nearest house. Luckily, the front door had been left ajar. I hit the front porch, crossed it in two steps, and kicked the door wide, entering the house.

I ran through the downstairs and collected two small portable TVs, one in the kitchen and one in the office. Then, carrying one in each arm, I ran through an Early American–style living room into the den, where I found a big-screen TV. I turned it on and plugged in the two portables. Every thirty seconds or so, the AK cut loose out front. Bullets whined and ricocheted in a deadly concert of tortured metal. I couldn't hook up all three sets to cable, but I was able to pick up the local news stations with the rabbit ears on the portables. I flipped around the channels, stopping at three different stations that were carrying the shootout. KTLA had a bird up. So did KTTV and KNBC. For the first time, I could see the entire scene.

The sheriffs had the house completely surrounded, front and back. The long lenses from the news cameras kept zooming in tight, and now, when the shooter appeared and fired, I got a pretty good look at him. This asshole was dressed head-to-toe in black body armor and was wearing a gas mask. He would pop up, looking like an extra in a Steven Seagal movie, and squeeze off a five-second burst, then disappear. His window choices seemed random.

I took off my watch, set it on the table in front of me, and started to time him. First he worked the downstairs. He'd shoot through three or four different windows at random, then move upstairs. After watching for about three minutes I could see the pattern.

Downstairs, he was all over the place shooting short, twenty-round bursts. But he always ended at the window on the far left side of the house. He'd fire a long stream of lead from that position, and then be gone for thirty to forty seconds before reappearing upstairs. He'd shoot randomly out of the upstairs windows, then be downstairs again. But his last firing position on the ground floor was always that same window on the far left of the house. My guess was that the staircase was over there.

It took him thirty seconds to get upstairs and start shooting again. He was triggering off five-second bursts, which I estimated at about fifteen or twenty rounds. He probably needed another ten seconds to change C-clips at the top of the stairs before again going to work in the upstairs windows. The time for me to make my move up to the porch was after he shot the long burst through the far left downstairs window.

I turned off the TVs and decided to test my theory. Moving to the front door, I waited for him to shoot out of the last window downstairs, then ran out of the house and across the street. I settled down behind the same squad car where I had been earlier, easily beating the next burst of gunfire from the upstairs window.

Sonny was already there and turned when I arrived. "Where were you?" he asked.

"Watching TV."

Sonny gave me a strange look, so I said, "Are we good to go?"

"Loo says no. The captain wants to wait for the incident commander from the downtown bureau."

"What is he, some kinda desk commander?" I said.

"More or less," Sonny agreed.

"Then I say screw him. Emo could be pumping dry. He could be dying. We can't just leave him up there."

Sonny didn't speak, but after a second he nodded.

I told Sonny my plan. We both tried to watch the shooter take one more lap around the house so Sonny could see for himself. But in truth, it was damn hard to keep your head up while he was pouring those lead cores down on us.

"Next time, after he does the last downstairs window on the left, we go," I said. "Okay?"

Sonny licked his lips and nodded grimly.

We waited until the shooter finished his last downstairs pop-up, then both of us exploded out from behind the car and ran low, heads down, across the lawn and dove under the porch. I don't think the shooter saw us, but then I wasn't looking either. The minute we started our run there was a lot of yelling from the sheriff's troops behind us. Somebody started screaming and calling us assholes.

Once we were under the porch, Sonny pulled his transmitter off his Tac vest and spoke clearly into it. "We're gonna pull Emo off there," he said. "Lay down some cover fire, but aim high. Don't hit us! Get our SWAT van up here on the lawn. Give us a place to take him. This is going down after the next time he shoots."

A few seconds later another lead burp ripped the air: BLAP-BLAPBLAPBLAP! Fifty sheriffs and two SWAT teams responded, pouring lead into the house as Sonny and I rolled up simultaneously and grabbed Emo by the ankles. Bullets thunked and glass shattered from the sheriffs' volley as we started pulling Emo off the deck. He streaked a wide stripe of bright red blood and brown stomach matter on the porch behind him before flopping down onto the lawn with us. As soon as he hit I knew he was dead. There was a huge hole in his gut, another in the center of his chest, his pants were messed. His bowels had let go; urine soaked his leg.

I held his head anyway.

Just then six SWAT guys who were all tricked out in black jumpsuits opened up with grenade launchers, mortaring hot gas canisters through half a dozen windows in the house: THUNK-THUNK-THUNK. A few remaining windows shattered. Smoke billowed.

"Who the hell are those guys?" I asked Sonny. "That's hot gas. They should use the cold canisters. They're gonna set the house on fire. The whole hillside could go."

Sonny shook his head. "Don't know," he said.

They looked like SRT to me.

Two minutes later the house flamed. Black smoke billowed out of the upstairs windows. But the barricaded suspect had a gas mask, and kept shooting, popping up, firing short bursts. Sonny and I were trapped under the porch.

After about ten minutes we heard on the radio that the man had stopped shooting out of the upstairs window and was now running back and forth downstairs. The roaring fire covered the sound of everything but the occasional high, shrill wail of a late-arriving fire unit and the short, choppy bursts from the AK-47. Eventually, as the fire raged, his gun went silent.

It was getting so hot where Sonny and I were that we had to pull back or be incinerated. The shooter hadn't fired for more than two minutes, so we grabbed Emo's body and dragged him across the lawn to the SWAT van. The sheriff's department SEB long rifles covered us, firing a deadly volley into the raging fire and billowing smoke. The heat from the blaze seared my back as we dragged Emo's body behind the van and laid him down.

When I turned I wasn't at all prepared for what I saw. Every room in the house had flames and black smoke pouring out of the windows. The roof was on fire. Ten minutes later the entire second floor collapsed. Then, one by one, boxes of ammo started going off in the garage. Armor-piercing .308s and .223s whizzed through the neighborhood like deadly hornets. Without warning, huge explosions rocked the cars we hid behind. Whatever just went up, it wasn't conventional ordnance. It was some kind of high-grade explosive. Everybody out front hit the deck and stayed down until it was over.

Finally, when they were sure that whatever caused the explosions had detonated, the fire units moved in, concentrating on keeping the dry brush in the foothills from going up, and working to keep the sparks from igniting the houses next door.

I found out from one of the deputies that Emo Rojas, who was a sheriff's motorcycle officer, had volunteered at roll call that morning to serve the warrant at end of watch.

Apparently, one of the home owners, a guy named Vincent Smiley, had been walking around the Hidden Ranch neighborhood flashing a badge and impersonating a sheriff's deputy. The neighbors called the department and found out that Smiley wasn't a sheriff. A warrant to pick him up was issued. Emo borrowed a D-car at the substation and came out here with his partner, Dave Brill. It was a nothing bust. A class-B felony. So Emo just walked up and rang the front doorbell with the arrest warrant in his hand while Brill stayed in the car filling out the incident report. Nobody was expecting trouble.

Then Smiley opened the front door and shot twice.

Emo was probably dead before he hit the ground.

CRIME SCENE

A FTER EMO'S CORPSE left in the ambulance I tried to disappear. I wanted to hide in some dark place and check my psyche for damage, to see how I really felt about this, before something I couldn't fix broke inside me. The Agoura substation's area commander, Captain Matthews, was still in charge because the incident commander from LASD headquarters didn't make it to the site until Vincent Smiley had changed categories, going from an active shooter to a crispy critter. When the IC finally showed up the site was already Code 4. He didn't want any part of it and gave this disaster a kiss and a wave, leaving a dead deputy, a smoldering house, and angry neighbors for Captain Matthews to deal with. Naturally, Matthews was pissed. He recognized career leprosy when he saw it.

He grabbed my arm and stopped me from leaving. "Gonna need your statement," he growled.

"Right, Skipper. Solid," I said, trying to sound hard-boiled and competent.

"Wait in that patrol car by yourself," he instructed. "I don't want you talking to anybody, changing your story around to fit somebody else's account."

So I sat in a sheriff's car alone, and watched the rest of the place burn to the ground, fueled by the hot gas grenades and Smiley's illegal explosives. It didn't take long either. The place burned down faster than a Skid Row hotel. The fire crews kept the hill from going up and managed to keep the structures next door wet. Even though those houses didn't catch fire, the adjoining walls were scorched from the intense heat.

I tried to think about the brand of insanity that had made Vincent Smiley, whoever he was, strap on all that body armor and trade rounds with half the uniforms in the Valley. He'd stayed inside his burning prefab Georgian, raining death indiscriminately out the windows, endangering his entire neighborhood until he was buried in a collapsing inferno. Was he trying to get the sheriffs to kill him?

Suicide by Cop was the new hot category in law enforcement. It covered situations like this, where the perp's actions defied conventional rules of behavior. I thought hard about it, because I was trying to keep my mind from sinking into a painful memory of Emo Rojas. I wasn't sure I could face where that would take me yet.

I had really liked Emo. He was one of those cops who could wear a badge without letting it change what he weighed.

The fire crews hosed down the smoldering remains of the house, then raked the embers cool. When it was over there wasn't much more left than at Paula Beck's shack out in Palmdale. Just a chimney and a mound of steaming ashes.

I watched the neighbors gather in little knots, looking on with wide, blank expressions—staring at the charred ground that hours ago was a fancy, two-story Georgian.

The M.E. and SID arrived shortly after the smoke monkeys knocked down the flames, then stood around and waited. Once it was cool enough, a team of CSI techs started sifting through the ash and bagging brass, while the coroner's people began searching for Mr. Smiley's remains. They found him in a bathtub. He'd been parboiled, then charbroiled. When they tried to get him out of the tub, he was so cooked he broke into pieces. God knows how hot the fire had been downstairs, but it sure didn't leave much for the coroner to identify. They loaded him into three rubber body bags and rolled him out on a gurney. The neighbors watched him leave with tight expressions of fear and relief. Teenage girls clustered together chewing the sides of their thumbs, muttering platitudes.

"How does this happen?" whispered a young mother who was standing near the car I was in.

It was my question, too.

"You Scully?" a voice asked, interrupting these thoughts. I looked through the side window and saw a tall angular man in a tan suit. Old-style Ray-Ban Aviators were perched on his face with fifty-mission swagger. The plastic nosepiece had yellowed years ago. He was chewing a toothpick, his hair was one week past a buzz cut, and his face had the weathered, no-nonsense look of somebody who'd spent a lot of time squinting down a barrel at big game.

"Yeah," I said. "Shane Scully, LAPD."

"Right." He looked me up and down—a quick, professional appraisal. "Sergeant Bob Dodds. I'm running point on the shooting review for SEB. We got a division commander and somebody from the D.A. headed out here. Gonna do the OIS review at the Agoura substation." OIS stood for Officer Involved Shooting. "I'm gonna need your preliminary statement now."

He climbed in the back seat with me, turned on a tape

recorder and held it between us. "This is Sergeant Robert Dodds and I'm conducting a post-incident statement given by Sergeant Shane Scully, LAPD. It's one forty P.M. September fourteenth." Then he turned to me.

"So what's the story here, Scully? Can't get enough action in town, you gotta jump out on county calls?" It was an old interrogation technique. Start with an insult, see what happens.

I smiled back at him. "Are you planning to ask me what I saw, Sergeant Dodds, or would you rather just chew on that toothpick and act like an asshole?"

We sat looking at each other, breathing in that funky squad car smell. They all smell pretty much the same: Lysol, vomit, warm plastic. The M.E.'s Black Mariah rolled past, taking Vincent Smiley to the morgue for his last earthly checkup. Dodds and I both watched him leave, then he looked back at me.

"This is a mess," I said. I pointed out the window. "That SWAT team over there, the men in black, hit this hood like Rommel's Africa Corps. Nobody stopped to call for a qualified negotiator. Half your Valley day watch and an SEB team also rolled, everybody's cranking off rounds. . . ." I motioned again toward the black-suited SWAT team that had fired the gas grenades. "That bunch starts lobbing hot gas canisters while we're still up under the porch. Almost turned this neighborhood into a mini-Waco." He said nothing. I could see my warped reflection in his Ray-Bans. "This isn't my jurisdiction," I continued. "I'm a non-sheriff and a potentially friendly witness, so what I say will carry a lot of weight. I can tell this two or three different ways." I smiled thinly. "Now, how we gonna play it?"

Bob Dodds took off his shades. "Why don't we start over?" he said, then put out his hand and we shook. "Emilio Rojas was a friend of mine," he added.

"Me too. It's why I came up."

Dodds picked up the tape recorder, rewound it and hit record, reslated it, then began recording over our false start.

"Begin with why you came up here," he said in a much friendlier voice.

"I heard it on TAC-four. Heard somebody say Emo was down, lying up on the porch. Since I knew Emo, I came. Got here and basically hid behind a car."

"The lieutenant says you and Sergeant Lopez disobeyed his direct order not to attempt to pull Rojas off that porch. He's a little torqued about it. 'A foolish stunt,' is what he called it. You could have been killed rescuing Rojas, who was already dead."

"Here's how that story tells," I said. "I don't work for the lieutenant, don't even know his name, so, in a strict command sense, he can't order me to do anything. On the other hand, if I'd heard his order, I certainly would have obeyed it in the spirit of interdepartmental cooperation."

"You would, huh?" Dodds frowned. "Am I gonna need to roll up my pant cuffs here?"

"I'm a book guy," I said. "But here's what happened. Nobody knew then if Emo was alive or dead. I saw him lying up there, and since he was a friend, I kinda freaked. I took off without asking anybody . . . I can see now it was a big mistake. Sergeant Lopez was just trying to stop me. Chased me right up the lawn. Next thing you know, we were both under the porch. Once we were there, seemed like there was no reason not to pull Emo down."

Dodds shut off the tape again.

"Is that the way Lopez's gonna tell it?"

"It is, if you give me a minute to explain it to him first."

Sergeant Dodds smiled. "So it's like that, is it?" he said.

"Yep. How 'bout we cut this brave deputy a little slack?"

Dodds smiled, and after a moment he nodded. "Okay," he

said. "If you get to him before I do, I guess there's not much I can do." He turned the tape back on.

"So who's in charge of those trigger-happy kazoonies in the cool black jumpsuits?" I asked.

"They're feds," Dodds answered, confirming my guess. "An SRT unit from Alcohol, Tobacco, Firearms, and Explosives."

SRT stood for Situation Response Team—federal SWAT. The media-conscious feds had stopped using ballsy acronyms for their urban assault team, preferring nonviolent handles like SRT or SWT. Even after all the flack that the LAPD had taken of late, we still cling stubbornly to kick-ass unit designations, preferring names like CRASH or SWAT. It seems some lessons are impossible for us to learn.

Dodds handed me his card. "You better call your watch commander and tell him you'll be here most of the afternoon. Drive down to the substation and check in with Jan Micklyn. She's with our Internal Affairs Shooting Review Board. She'll find a place for you to hang out. We'll get your complete statement, wrap you out fast as we can." He snapped off the tape.

I started to get out of the car, then turned back, "A Situation Response Team from ATF? They're located downtown. What were they doing way the hell out here?"

"It's a good question. Their team leader says they were doing range work, practicing clearing houses at their training facility in the foothills. They were driving back and heard it on the L.A. Impact frequency."

"Sounds good." I shot him a little smile. Even though we were buddies now, my smile didn't seem to warm him much. He squinted at me with that weathered shooter's expression, making me feel like game in a laser sight. Then, without saying anything else, he got out of the car and walked away.

I found Sonny over by the van, sitting on a curb looking at the burned-down house. He had soot and Emo's blood on his shirt, a frown on his face. I filled him in on my statement to Dodds and he looked up at me and nodded. "Thanks, Shane. I owe you for that."

"No you don't. We did the right thing. Why let a bad order and a dumb section in the rule book change it?"

On the drive back to the substation I called and checked in with Lieutenant Jeb Calloway, who was a twenty-year LAPD vet and my new boss at Special Crimes. Cal, as everybody called him, was a big African-American with a shaved head who looked like he should be working event security at a rap concert.

"That shoot-out is all over the news," Cal said after I explained where I was. "Sounds like the IC up there got froggy and pulled the string early."

I told him the incident commander didn't make it and that Captain Matthews, the area commander, got caught wearing the hat. After I explained the rest of what happened he just grunted. He'd seen enough CYA in his career to know everybody was probably ducking.

When I arrived at the substation the ATF SRT truck was parked in the secure lot in a visitor parking stall. As I walked past it I banged on the side to see if anybody was home. Nobody answered. The back was a locked box that contained all their high-tech toys and deadly ordnance. But I didn't want what was in the back. I walked around to the driver's side and checked to see if the alarm was set. All SWAT vehicles have very sophisticated alarms, and the trucks were never supposed to be left unattended without that alarm set. However, this one was open, the alarm light off. Probably, with all the adrenaline overload, the cherry in charge of team security just forgot. He was going catch a ration of shit later, but I didn't care. I stepped up on the running board, opened the door, and jumped in. Then I turned on the police scanner and started flipping through channels.

The unit didn't have TAC-4. I knew that channel had to be

specially programmed by a communications tech, because I'd had to have it done on my scanner.

So who was kidding who here? If these guys didn't hear the call on TAC-4, how the hell did they know a shooting was in progress?

OIS

I FOUND SERGEANT Micklyn setting up shop in the substation. She was a dark-haired, no-nonsense member of OIS and had taken over two I rooms for interviews. She said she wasn't ready for me yet, but settled me in an empty office in the back where I put in a call to DSG at Parker Center.

"My God, Shane," Alexa said after I told her what happened, sounding for a minute more like my worried wife instead of the acting head of the LAPD Detective Services Group.

Alexa and I had an easy, professional relationship on the job. That was because I always did what she said. She wasn't my direct supervisor; she was five layers above me on the command structure. But she was my division commander. If one wants a career in police science, one does not give one's division commander any substantial grief.

At home it was different. We had a completely open and balanced relationship, although I had always suspected that in most complicated, emotional, or political situations Alexa could out perform me. Of course, I could beat her at arm wrestling. She is also the most beautiful woman I have ever known. Tall, with an athlete's body and a face that belongs on the cover of a glamour magazine: black hair, Irish eyes, and strong cheekbones that ride high above the flat plains of her face and frame a strong but sensuous mouth.

I, on the other hand, look like something you'd find in the center ring at the Main Street Boxing Gym. My hair is always ruffled and unkempt, no matter what I do, so I keep it short. My body language is the trademark shuffle of a street brawler, which for a while in my teens I'd been. It always surprised me when women found all this nonsense intriguing. But the only thing that mattered was that Alexa had bought the package.

After I told her about Emo and the shoot-out, she remained quiet for a minute. "But you're okay," she said again.

"Yeah, physically I'm fine. Not a scratch. But emotionally I'm having trouble with it. Emo's dead. He was serving a warrant on some guy for impersonating an officer. Got hit standing in the perp's doorway."

I didn't tell her I'd exposed my scabrous hide to gunfire in an attempt to pull him out and had only managed to rescue a corpse. Hopefully, that detail would be confined to sheriff's department internal documents, and she wouldn't be copied.

"I'll be back as soon as I can, but they're cooking a three-layer cake out here. Active shooter, lotta deputies at the incident, all of 'em cheesing off rounds. Sheriff's SEB had a SWAT team on the scene, ATF rolled a truck. It's gonna take some time for OIS to get all the stories coordinated so it plays okay for the six o'clock news."

"Don't be such a cynic," she said. "I love you. Call if you get outta there in time to meet someplace for dinner."

"Right." I hung up and stood out in the waiting room where I practiced trying to be invisible, which is hard to do when you're in a sheriff's substation wearing a sports jacket with a dead deputy's blood and stomach contents spattered all over it.

I finally got a chance to make my statement at four o'clock. I was led into one of Sergeant Micklyn's I rooms and seated at a wood table in front of a tape machine. Captain Matthews sat in a chair across the room and kept quiet. He glowered as a young lawyer from the D.A.'s office took notes. Sergeant Micklyn ran the interview, Sergeant Dodds stood against a white concrete wall and listened. I started telling my story, adding my one embellishment to keep Sonny Lopez straight with his lieutenant. After I finished I looked at Dodds, who still had on his Ray-Bans, even though we were inside. He had been leaning his thin frame against the wall, chewing his toothpick, looking like a cowboy in a Bull Durham commercial. He finally pushed away and straddled a straight-back chair facing me.

"You sure you didn't fire your weapon at the scene?" he asked. "Even though you got them rounds from SEB?"

"I didn't fire," I answered.

"You have any psychological misgivings here? You and Emo were friends. You got the heebie-jeebies? You want me to call your supervisor, get you some time off . . . arrange for a visit to a psych?" It was a standard post-interview question, asked after all shootings to protect the department from a cop's lawsuit, in case he cracked up later.

"No, I'm fine," I said.

Captain Matthews, who had said nothing, got up and walked toward the door. Then, without warning, he swung back.

"Tell me something, Sergeant. Did you see that fed SRT truck parked at the scene when you were coming up Hidden Ranch Road?" he asked.

"I think they got there ahead of me, Captain," I said.

"That's not what I asked you."

"I didn't see them until after I was there. Then later they started lobbing hot gas, like I already said."

"So you didn't see them arrive?" he said.

"Excuse me, Captain, but why don't you just go ask them when they got there? They're still in the station."

"Because they won't agree to be interviewed," he said, repressed anger bubbling to the surface like toxic waste.

"They were on the scene at your shooting," I said. "They fired shots. They gotta sit for your internal review."

"Tell *them* that," he said. "They're saying they'll only talk to their own Internal Affairs."

I thought that might be the new low in interagency cooperation, but I didn't say anything.

Then Sergeant Micklyn, whose first name was Jan, officially closed the interview, picked up her tape recorder, snapped it off, and popped out my cassette. She labeled it, then set it in a stack with some others.

"Since that tape is off, maybe I can help you with one thing," I said.

"What's that?" Dobbs said.

"You told me that ATF arrived quickly because they were coming from a training day and heard the cross talk on the L.A. Impact channel."

"That's their story," Dobbs agreed.

"Kinda hard to do when you don't have TAC-four on your scanner." Dodds let one eyebrow climb his forehead. "On the way in here I looked in their truck. Not on there," I said.

Dodds glanced at Captain Matthews. Neither said anything or changed expressions, but a lot was going on between them. Then someone knocked on the I room door. Dodds opened it. A uniformed deputy was outside.

"Captain, I've got the ASAC from ATF outside. Name's Brady Cagel. He wants to talk to the incident commander. Guess that's still you," the deputy said.

Matthews groaned. Dodds took off his sunglasses and carefully wiped them with a handkerchief, not looking at Matthews, who moved to the door and said, "Where's SRT? They still in my office?"

"Still there," the deputy said, and both of them left.

Dodds turned to me.

"I'm done with you for now, Scully. We'll get this typed up and you can sign it in a day or so."

"Okay." I got to my feet and walked back into the substation. You could feel the tension. Everybody's nerves were frayed and sparking. Dangerous energy was arcing around like loose bolts of electricity.

Brady Cagel was your standard-issue fed in a suit. He was in the waiting area alone. Medium height, with a tight build. His regular features, short hair, and square jaw made him look rugged, not handsome. But he was angry. His eyes, like lasers, were zapping around, peeling the paint off walls in the under-furnished lobby.

I wasn't about to miss this, so I ducked into the coffee room and started searching my pocket for quarters to feed into the vending machines. After a moment a lock buzzed and I heard Captain Matthews come through the electric door into the waiting room.

"Agent Cagel?" I heard him say. "I'm Matthews, the CO." There was a pause while I guess they shook hands.

Then Cagel said, "I'm the ASAC for SRT. I understand you're keeping my people here."

"I need your unit to all make statements. I can't close our shooting review without it. We need an account from everyone who discharged a weapon on the scene."

"You'll get statements. We'll just do it over at our shop, is all. We're gonna use our review apparatus. I'll shoot everything over to you after it's done."

"They'll have to make the statements in my presence," Matthews said, his voice getting hard.

Then I heard feet shuffling and it got quiet out there, so I went to the coffee room door and took a peek. They had gone to the leather club chairs in the waiting area and were now seated, leaning toward each other. I couldn't quite hear what they were saying, so I crossed to the vending machines, bought some candy, then moved back to the door and looked out again. I could now hear them again, because their voices were raised in anger.

"We're not going to sit for your shooting panel, get used to it," Cagel was saying.

"Your guys were firing Parabellums and hot gas without coordinating with me. It was my incident. You were operating out there without even being on the same radio frequency," Matthews said. "Your guys set the house on fire. I have a lot of questions. I wanta know how they got to our crime scene less than three minutes after the shooting started."

"I talked to my team leader. He says they were coming back from a training exercise, heard it going down on the Impact channel."

"Only their truck doesn't have the Impact frequency on its scanner," Matthews said.

"You're mistaken," Cagel replied. "Now, where are my people? I have an IAD inquiry convening downtown. We're already keeping a lot of people waiting."

Matthews was losing this one. He had no way to force SRT into his review if they didn't want to do it. They worked for a separate agency.

"There was a lot of armor-piercing ordnance stored in that house," Matthews finally said. "Grenades, at least fifty thousand rounds of three-oh-eights or two-twenty-threes. We had some big explosions, which could have been dynamite, or even C-four. You sure ATF wasn't already teed up on that guy for some illegal firearms complaint, and that's how you got there so fast?"

Brady Cagel stood. "Look, Captain, we're going to do a thorough investigation. I haven't interviewed my team leader yet, but we will pursue everything by the book. Once our IAD says the investigation is completed, we'll make sure you get a copy. Then you can add it to your review. Now where is my team? I'm not going to ask you again."

"They're in my office," Matthews said tightly.

I didn't need to see him to know he was seething. I heard the ASAC move past the coffee room and ask the desk sergeant to let him into the rear area.

I waited until I heard the electric lock buzz, then went into the bathroom and tried to get Emo's blood and guts off my jacket. I scrubbed with wet paper towels but wasn't having much luck. The sports coat looked like a complete loss, but I stripped it off, folded it over my arm, and carried it out with me anyway.

In the parking lot I found Sonny Lopez waiting by my car. He still had Emo's DNA on his uniform. We stood looking at each other for a long moment, not sure how to wrap this up.

"Thanks for helping me get him down off the porch," I said. "If he'd stayed up there, we woulda lost the body."

"I was waiting out here to tell you I shoulda suggested it first. He was my *carnal*, my station mate. I kinda froze."

"Not when it counted," I said, and put a hand on his shoulder. I could feel his nerves and muscles twitch under my hand.

"This is really fucked, huh?" he finally said.

"Yep."

"SRT just rolled out of here in their new LAV." The feds called their SWAT van a light armored vehicle. "I've never seen Captain Matthews so jacked up. He's usually pretty mellow."

"That's 'cause SRT won't sit for your shooting review. They're doing a parallel investigation. His ass is on the line. He lost a deputy, the perp is barbeque, the house in ashes. There's gonna be beaucoup legal trouble over this," I said.

"It's even worse than that, Shane. I just found out from the desk sergeant that ATF called us. They got the initial complaint, but since Smiley was impersonating a sheriff's deputy and lived in the county, ATF handed us the collar. The neighbors up there told me an hour ago that Smiley had been wandering around, showing his neighbors a sheriff's badge for months. He'd been telling 'em he works for our antiterrorist division. They said last week Smiley took some of the guys who live up there into his garage and showed them his armory. Boxes of ammo, grenade launchers. They said he even had plastic explosives up there, some C-four."

"That's what blew the roof off the garage," I said.

Sonny nodded. "The neighbors called ATF and reported it because they didn't want some spook in their neighborhood with a garage full of explosives. Matthews thinks after they gave us the impersonating charge they were parked nearby, waiting to see what would happen about the guns. That's how they got there so fast."

It didn't sound right to me, then Sonny's handsome face contorted.

"The feds didn't want to serve a warrant on a guy with an AK-forty-seven and a garage full of C-four so they sent Emo up there thinkin' he was arresting some ding on a class-B nothing, and he walks into a bullet. All the while ATF was waiting down the road to see whether he got the cuffs on or not." Lopez was shaking with anger.

I knew part of it was just a post-shoot-out adrenaline burn, but I didn't like the dangerous look in Sonny's black eyes. His chest was rising and falling as he took deep breaths to calm himself down. His heartbeat pulsed a vein on his forehead.

"Listen Sonny, I think you need to go end-of-watch, hit a heavy bag or something, then get a beer and chill out."

"I'm gonna go get a fucking riot gun and chill out the ATF building downtown . . ."

"Good idea. Real smart," I said softly.

"Damn it, Shane, they might as well have just killed him themselves."

"Sonny, let their shooting review panel deal with this. If there's a problem, their Internal Affairs guys will flag it."

He dropped his head and looked at his shoes. When he glanced up again he was crying.

"I know his wife and kids," Sonny said. "I help him coach Pop Warner football. He was my *carnal*. My amigo . . . Those fucking guys . . ." He couldn't finish, overwhelmed with emotion.

"Get outta here, man. You need to get your feet under you."

"I loved him, Shane."

"Me too," I said softly.

GETTING 5 READY

I T WAS TEN o'clock on Saturday morning six days later, and Emo's funeral was scheduled for two that afternoon. I was sitting in the backyard of my little house in Venice, California. Our adopted marmalade cat, Franco, lounged at my feet, taking in the view of plastic reproduction gondolas floating in two feet of brackish seawater and narrow, arched, one-lane bridges spanning shallow saltwater canals. Venice, California, had been built in the twenties by Abbott Kinney, who had designed it to resemble a scaled-down version of Venice, Italy. It was an architecturally challenged throwback to the fifteen hundreds. Run down now, and a little sad, the neighborhood still clung proudly to its tacky, old-world heritage like a stubborn drunk refusing to get off a barstool. I don't know how Franco felt about it, but I loved it for its corny pride.

Chooch was inside doing his homework. Delfina, his girl-friend, whom we had taken in after her cousin, American Macado, died last year, was now living in Chooch's old room. He had willingly moved into makeshift quarters we'd set up in the garage. Delfina was proving to be a great addition to the family. She was a beautiful, black-eyed Hispanic girl who usu-ally brought a soft, relaxed point of view to our mix. This morning she was off at a rehearsal at Venice High School where she was now enrolled. They were putting on a production of *West Side Story*, and Delfina was playing Maria. All week she had been rehearsing songs, her slightly thin, true voice floating through the house. She had left an hour ago, visibly nervous because they were doing the first run through with music.

I was stretched out on my patio furniture reading a disturbing follow-up article on the Hidden Ranch shoot-out in the morning edition of the *L.A. Times*. It was under the same grainy photo of Vincent Smiley the newspaper had been running all week. In the shot the dead killer appeared young and expressionless. A vacant smile split his lips like a poorly drawn line that didn't foreshadow his violent end.

He looked small. Small eyes, small neck, small life. It was hard to think somebody like Vincent Smiley could have killed a man like Emo Rojas. But all of society has come to understand that guns in the hands of idiots are mindless equalizers. I was trying to get a handle on my emotions and prepare myself for the funeral ahead.

I hate cop funerals. After the Vikings case, and Tremaine Lane's over-the-top grave site production, I had promised myself that I would never attend another brother officer's burial; that I would try and find a quiet place to say my good-bye alone. But there wasn't much I could do about ducking this one. In fact, to be blunt, it was my second cop funeral since making that hollow promise. So it seemed I was just blowing off steam and lacked the courage of my own convictions.

I steeled myself to get through it. It had been six days since the shooting on Hidden Ranch Road. The incident was still a front-page, above-the-fold feature in the *L.A. Times*. The fickle electronic media had played it big for three news cycles, then returned to their endless fascination with celebrity mischief. But new facts kept rolling out on the pages of the *Times*. Since I wasn't part of the active sheriff's investigation, I was getting most of my information from the unreliable rumor mill downtown, and from the morning paper.

In a profile of Smiley earlier in the week, the paper revealed that he had once been a member of the Arcadia Police Department. He'd been on the job for about ten months in 2002, made it through their academy training, but had been rolled out as a probationer shortly after he hit the street. Apparently his training officer observed some critical flaws in his psyche and submarined him. The Arcadia police had not shared the reason for his dismissal with the press, saying, since Vincent Smiley was dead and not being tried, his psychiatric records would remain locked up in his 10-01 file.

The county coroner couldn't do a standard print or dental match on Smiley's corpse because the body was too badly burned. His teeth had turned to dust from the intense heat, but the M.E. had positively identified the body, using DNA. Apparently Smiley had given a sample to the Arcadia P.D. when he was still on the force—something I found very unusual, if not downright strange. Police unions were adamant against letting their officers give DNA, citing a list of probable cause and Fourth Amendment statutes. But for some reason Smiley had voluntarily given up a sample. It made me wonder if his dismissal might have stemmed from charges of sexual misconduct, and he had given the sample voluntarily in an attempt to beat the rap.

As far as anybody knew, Smiley didn't have any family that was still alive, so he was to be held in the morgue for the required two weeks. In another eight days, if his body wasn't claimed, he would be dumped in a pauper's grave, courtesy of the county, destined to spend eternity in a ten-foot hole full of the very homeless miscreants he had once hoped to police.

The crisis had lurched along for almost a week, like a cartoon cowboy with a slew of arrows in his back. On Friday, the L.A. County Board of Supervisors, headed by a broken steam valve named Enrique Salazar, got into the act. Salazar had picked up the sheriff's fallen shield and was charging the hill at Justice. He repeated the charge that ATF had not shared all the pertinent details of the arrest before sending Emo out to serve the warrant, speculating that this probably happened because Emo was a Mexican. Of course, nobody at ATF could have possibly known that a Mexican-American sheriff would serve the warrant, so that was just Enrique playing to his Hispanic base. But he also reasoned that ATF had not told the sheriffs about the illegal weapons cache, because, had the sheriffs known, they would have said, "Serve your own damn warrant." The Salazar piece was this morning's front-page ticking bomb.

Far more troubling than that was the fact that the temperature between these two law enforcement groups was at slow boil. Only the LAPD had managed to stay neutral.

Alexa came out, sat on the metal chair beside me, and took my hand. I showed her the front-page article in the *Times*.

"Saw it," she said. "Two thousand of Emo's friends and coworkers gathering this afternoon to cry over his body, and Salazar picks today to say ATF thought he was just another dumb Mexican. Guy needs a new public affairs consultant."

"This isn't going to go away," I said. "Salazar is going to make it an election issue. He'll go to the governor."

"In that case, he won't have to go far. The governor is going to be at the funeral. My office was notified that his security detail was going to need special parking at Forest Lawn."

"Great," I said.

She turned and looked at me carefully. "Shane, we need to talk about this."

I thought we had been talking about it, but apparently Alexa had something else on her mind.

"This whole thing with Emo—it's been eating at you. Even Chooch asked if you were okay."

"Yeah, I'm okay, it's just . . ." I stopped and let it hang there, not sure how to phrase what I was feeling.

"Just what?"

"I just wish I hadn't been up there. I wish I hadn't seen it. I can't get the memory of his blood off my skin."

"And?"

"And I hate cop funerals. I'm dreading this thing this afternoon. Bring in a TV camera and every publicity-seeking asshole in the state shows up. The governor comes, the city council, all the chiefs, sheriffs, and undersheriffs—even you and Tony. No offense intended."

"None taken." She cocked her head, thinking for a moment, then smiled. "I think."

"You saw what happened when we buried Tremaine. It'll be just like that. All the department ass-kissers who didn't even know Emo swarming like flies on garbage. All telling the brass what a great guy Emo was, how they were in the same foxholes with him, all spinning their dumb war stories. Most of the people making speeches this afternoon will be strangers. The ones who really loved him will get pushed to the back. We'll all be listening to guys like Salazar turn Emo's funeral into a campaign issue. Once they're done, down Emo goes into the hole, awash in crocodile tears and bullshit. Then everybody leaves, hoping the governor will remember they were there."

"Then why are you going?"

"I don't want to go, but I have to. How do you not go to a good friend's funeral?"

"Why is Chooch going?" she said, hitting me with a blind shot that I hadn't seen coming. I looked away to buy time, gather my defenses.

"Huh?" Not much of a response, I admit, but I'm not too good at dodging her.

"He's in there finishing his homework so he'll be able to go."

"Oh. I guess that could maybe be because I sorta told him he could go."

"He didn't even know Emo."

"Yes he did." I heaved a sigh. Once again I was going to have to bust myself. I took a deep breath. "He knew him because he went on an Iron Pigs ride with us two months ago."

"Right. Sure he did. He doesn't even know how to ride a Harley."

"Last July—the week you were in Chicago, I borrowed two bikes. We practiced every night for five days. Got him licensed Friday afternoon. I swore him to secrecy because I knew you wouldn't want him riding a hawg."

"You're damn right I wouldn't." She fell silent and let go of my hand. "And he sure doesn't need to go to this funeral."

"Let him go. He wants to. It's part of growing up. People you know and care about die. It's a bitch, but it happens. He liked Emo. They're both quarterbacks."

"When cops die, you know he puts you in the coffin, Shane. Emotionally, he sees you in the box."

"I suppose."

"No suppose about it. It's true." She was mad about the Harley ride but had the good sense not to bang me around about it now. Instead, her anger was coming out over Chooch and the funeral.

"Look, I'll talk to him, okay? I'll make him understand," I said.

"Make me understand," she challenged.

"You already do, sweetheart. It's why I love you." I gave her a hopeful smile.

She looked at me and her eyes softened. "Damn you, Shane. I'm really pissed off here. Acting goofy and sweet is no fair." Then she got up and went in to get Chooch.

GODSPEED, THIRTY-MARY-FOUR

DELFINA WOULD BE at rehearsal until six. Chooch went to the funeral on crutches, because he had a broken foot.

Here's how that happened. About a week after the Iron Pigs ride in mid-July, during the first week of two-a-day football drills, he tried to escape a blitz, spun right, and rolled over on his right foot, cracking one of the small bones on the outside. Chooch was being recruited heavily by half a dozen big Division 1 universities and was afraid that the tiny bone break in his foot was going to cost him his entire multimillion-dollar pro-football career.

I gave him my "Life Is a Journey" speech. Net effect, zero. I gave him my "You Only Grow from Adversity" speech. Nothing. Finally, Alexa convinced him that his football career wasn't as important right now as his academic career, and he'd better make sure he kept his grades up; because, if he didn't get the athletic scholarship he'd need to get into college on pure academics. She reminded him he could always walk on if he didn't get the ride. This made sense to Chooch, and he had a 3.8 going into midterms. All of this is noteworthy only when you realize that, as usual, Alexa's pragmatic approach had carried the day.

It was a bright, cloudless Saturday afternoon as we drove to Forest Lawn. The San Gabriel Mountains were almost purple against the cobalt sky. A light Santa Ana wind had cleared the basin of smog for Emo's funeral. As we neared the off-ramp to Forest Lawn Drive, I could see this was going to be a mob scene. Traffic was already piling up on the 210 Freeway before we reached the L.A. River. You could tell it was for Emo, because even the people who weren't in squad cars were wearing uniforms with black ribbons pinned diagonally across their badges.

I wanted to drop Chooch off as close as possible. I've spent my share of time walking with birch under my arms, and I know that handling crutches on grass is a bitch. I managed to sneak up next to the chapel where the hearse and limos were parked. When I dropped Chooch and Alexa off there were already more than a thousand people milling in front of the church, most in tan deputies' uniforms. A smattering of LAPD blue punctuated the crowd. A sound system and some video screens had been set up for the overflow crowd that couldn't squeeze inside the church.

The LAPD white hat working traffic at this event turned me around and sent me back down toward the mortuary office. Forest Lawn was inside the city limits of Los Angeles, so, even though 80 percent of the attendees were county deputies, we were working the event. I found a parking place down by the office and wedged the Acura into a no-parking zone, putting two wheels up on the grass. I didn't think our traffic control officers would be handing out too many greenies at a cop's funeral.

As I was locking up I heard the loud, familiar rumble of straight pipes. I turned and saw almost a hundred Iron Pigs from different chapters all over the state making their way solemnly up Forest Lawn Drive, riding two-by-two. They had their uniforms on. Green from the Highway Patrol, tan and brown from the Sacramento P.D., tan and blue from the L.A. sheriff's and Orange County, blue and white from Los Angeles, Pacoima, Newhall, and San Diego.

The bikes were all custom Harleys, and both men and women alike wore their lightweight summer colors, most stitched on sleeveless jean or leather vests, worn over police uniforms. The club motto stitched on some of the jackets now seemed a dangerous threat: "Cut One and We All Bleed." They snaked up the drive as everyone stopped talking and turned to watch.

Darren Zook, the local chapter's ride captain, was out front leading them. He slowed to a stop in front of the church, then turned and backed his bike against a sixty-foot stretch of curb that had been coned off in preparation for their arrival. One by one the officers dismounted, kicked their stands down, leaned their bikes, and stepped away. The lacquered yellow, orange, and candy-apple red paint jobs dappled colored sunshine against polished chrome manifolds. Then the Iron Pigs moved silently toward the church.

I finished locking the Acura and followed. I was almost up to where Alexa and Chooch were standing when I heard a voice raised in anger. The tone made my adrenaline kick. An angry curse uttered with deadly sincerity. I moved closer.

"You fucking people don't belong here!" I heard Darren Zook say. He was near the concrete steps of the old church glaring at six guys in dark suits. At first I didn't recognize them, but as I approached I knew who they were. Men in Black—the ATF Situation Response Team from the Hidden Ranch shootout. They were standing in a group on the church steps, unsure how to handle this.

"We came to pay our respects," one of them said. I'd seen most of their pictures in the newspaper for a week, and I think he was the one named Billy Greenridge.

"You paid your respects on Hidden Ranch Road. Now get the fuck out of here," Zook said.

The feds started to look around for backup or support, or maybe just for a friendly face, but the Iron Pigs quickly closed ranks around them.

"Get out or get thrown out," Darren Zook growled dangerously.

"Look, we feel—" Greenridge began.

But Darren cut him off. He and three other Iron Pigs grabbed Greenridge roughly by his arm, spun him around, and started to march him down the walk to the cars. Then a dozen more of the police bikers grabbed the remaining ATF agents and quickly hustled them out behind him.

Before they reached the parking lot, the ATF ASAC, Brady Cagel, pushed through the crowd and blocked the path. "You people are way out of order," he said.

"Get these assholes out of here," Darren said. "And you go with 'em. I won't have you guys at Emo's funeral."

Two more sheriffs grabbed Brady Cagel. Then they half-pushed, half-dragged the entire SRT unit, plus their ASAC, down the steps and pinned them against some parked cars across from the church.

"Get out," Darren Zook repeated. His voice thick with rage.

"I'm going to write this up," Cagel said.

"Get out or get thrown out!"

"Let's go." Cagel motioned his team to follow. Then he and his brother agents walked down the road to their cars, while almost two thousand pairs of eyes glared holes in their backs.

Emilio Rojas Jr.'s funeral started late. It was two thirty before the organ in the big church began to play. There were more than a thousand people who couldn't squeeze inside and were watching the service on two big-screen TVs. Alexa and Chooch had managed to get in and save me a seat near the back.

The LASD Chorus sang "Ave Maria." Emo's brother Miguel spoke about his brother as a boy, mentioned his sense of humor and how he always had a smile for everybody. His widow, Elana, sat quietly and listened, dabbing her eyes with a handkerchief. Emo's six-year-old son, Alfredo, was beside her, ramrod straight, eyes brimming with tears, but somehow he kept them from running.

The service was a Catholic mass that seemed endless to me. After the coffin was blessed and sprinkled with holy water, ten Iron Pigs from the local chapter carried the box out of the church and slid it into the hearse for the short trip up the hill.

We followed the winding road to the grave site. Then the crowd gathered on the hillside while the family sat under sun tents for the political speeches. The governor, who hadn't known Emo, told us what an exceptional officer he had been, how bright and friendly. He said Emo was the gold standard by which all others would be judged.

Supervisor Salazar, who never knew Emo, talked about his courage on the job and how he represented the Mexican-American dream, how he had made a difference to his family and to his people, and how he would always be remembered.

Next came the command structure. Sheriff Bill Messenger, the diminutive head of LASD, spoke of valor under fire. Next to him stood Tony Filosiani. He was wearing his dress-blue LAPD chief's uniform. Four command stars gleamed on each of his wide shoulders. At five foot seven, two-hundred plus pounds, the chief of the LAPD was shaped like a blue lunchbox with medals. Because this was a sheriff's deputy's funeral, Tony had elected not to speak. The undersheriff spoke next. Then Captain Matthews offered a personal apology, because he had been in charge the day Emo died. His voice was choked with emotion. One by one they all came to the mike, standing erect in starched

uniforms, their rank emblems glittering. They said Emo represented the brightest and best. Some of them searched for poetic
metaphors. One commander from Ad Vice actually said that
Emo reminded her of a California cactus: tough and dangerous
on the surface, but sweet inside.

It was hot, and sweat started running down the back of my
shirt. I couldn't help but think that Emo was up there shitting
bricks over some of this. The cactus simile was priceless. Most
of these testimonials were from people who wouldn't have
taken the time to have coffee with him when he was alive.

Six officers on black-and-white police Electra Glides came
over the hill in the Missing Man motorcycle formation, a V with
an empty space in the corner. They rode across the grass slowly.
Somebody released six white doves. A man I didn't know
walked over to Elana and handed her the seventh. She kissed the
dove on its back, then released it into the sky. We all watched as
it flew away.

Next, the LASD Helicopter Air Unit did a flyby. Four Bell Jet
Rangers passed low over the grave, then peeled off and climbed
away in separate directions.

After Elana was handed the folded American flag, it was supposed to be over. People were starting to leave when Emo's last
backup, Dave Brill, decided he had something to say. He had
not been asked to speak, but stepped up and took the mike anyway. He looked frayed and empty, like a man whose soul had
been leaking slowly out of him. He cleared his throat and the
sound system barked loudly.

"I just wanted to say . . ."

He stopped and looked around at the politicians, who had
turned back to face him but were stealing impatient looks at
their watches—meetings to take, flights to make.

"Emo . . . Emo was . . ." Then Brill broke down and started
crying. He sucked it up and tried again. "Emo . . . I . . . I'm
sorry. I . . . Y'see, we . . . At the academy, we . . ."

He couldn't continue. He faced the grave, his face contorted in pain. As he turned toward the speakers, the microphone squealed feedback. Dave Brill looked at the coffin, unsure now of how to get off or how to say what he felt. What he really wanted to tell Emo was how sorry he was that he hadn't been able to protect him. That he'd been sitting in the D-car doing paperwork, with his gun in his holster, when his friend died.

Overcome with grief and emotion, and using Emo's police call sign, he finally said the only thing he could think of: "Godspeed, Thirty-Mary-Four."

Then Brill laid the microphone on the coffin and walked away from the grave. The governor and most of the brass were already ten steps ahead of him.

God, I hate cop funerals.

WAKE

THERE WERE SEVEN of us wedged in a back booth at the Pew and Cue on Barham Boulevard, four blocks north of Forest Lawn Drive. It was an hour after the service. We were supposed to be Emo's "tights"—the guys who loved him most. Two were fellow motorcycle officers, Darren Zook and Dave Brill. Next to them, were Gary and Mike Nightingale from SEB. The Nightingale brothers were on the sheriff's Special Weapons Team that had been at Hidden Ranch Road. Their expressions were grave, carved from granite. I remembered the mission board I'd seen on the side of the truck. Gary was a long gun, Mike his spotter. In the corner was a deputy named Christine Bell and, across from her, Sonny Lopez. I sat at the end.

The Pew and Cue was small, dark, and crowded. Wooden

tables and straight-backed wood pews lined the room. The barroom adjoined a pool hall, but none of our little group of mourners was shooting eight ball. We were there to drink and brood. Alexa had driven Chooch home. I was going to catch a ride back to Venice with Gary Nightingale who, it turned out, lived less than a mile from me.

Emo's last backup, Dave Brill, was pounding down scotch shooters, leading choir practice, telling an Emo war story. "There was this time in the hills," he was saying, "him and me, up there cruising the twisties on Angeles Crest. We'd been riding for hours and were both getting sorta iron-assed, so we decide to go ten-ninety and crib for a while. So Emo turns and rides down this dirt road. We round a corner and, lo and behold, here's this fucking meth lab and fifteen armed shitheads with Harleys doing a drug deal outside a beat-up motor home. And I think, 'That's it, we're dust.' Y'know? But Emo just looks at these stringy haired SOBs, gets off his bike, walks up, smiles, and starts pitching them tickets to the Sheriff's Inner City Fundraiser, the kid's concert thing. Acting like that's the only reason we rode down there in the first place. These guys don't know if they're busted or not. But it's only ten bucks a ticket, so they figure it's cheaper than the grief they're gonna get shooting two deputies. Sold 'em two hundred dollars worth. Then Emo, he turns to this one ink-strewn asshole with an eye patch and he says, 'Hey, partner, this concert is gonna be Barry Manilow and elevator music. You guys are probably into bands like Tool or Rage Against the Machine, and won't go. But ya want, you can donate your ticket back. That way, we can send extra kids to the concert.' Then one by one, all of these guys are giving their tickets back. We ride out of there with two hundred dollars cash and we still got all the fucking concert tickets. Come back with twenty cops an hour later, hook 'em all up. The guy was amazing."

The stories went on like that. Little by little, they were working the ache of Emo's passing out of their souls.

Gary and Mike Nightingale started talking about the shoot-out. "That guy, Vincent Smiley," Gary said, "it really sucks when these suicides ain't got the balls to just do it. Gotta get us to fire the bullet for 'em. He can't do the Dutch, so he dumps Emo to get a shoot-out going. What bullshit."

Darren Zook got up to go to the bathroom. He wandered into the pool room, which is where the restroom arrow said the men's can was. I was drinking beers, trying to be part of this, but not finding much solace either. War stories about dead cop buddies never made me feel better. I was thinking instead of Emo at the Rock Store, leaning over the table with Chooch, both of them drawing football plays in water with their fingers.

Then I remembered Sonny had told me that Emo coached a Pop Warner team. Pop Warner was tackle football for kids in the nine- to fifteen-year-old age brackets.

"Who's gonna take over and coach his football team?" I asked, as a thought tickled the back of my brain.

"My kid plays on that team," Christine Bell said. "Sonny, you helped him coach, you should do it."

"Not me." Sonny Lopez slowly brought his head up. He'd been looking down into his beer, as if the answer to life was floating in there. "I coach blocking and tackling, that's my thing. Emo was running some kind of Veer offense. I wouldn't know a tight-end from a chorus boy. You need somebody who understands that offense."

"Somebody'll step up," Brill said, emotion bending his voice. "Emo had friends, man. People were always standin' in line t'carry that man's flag."

Darren Zook came back to the table. His face was tight, his black skin stretched white around his jaw. "Those fucking guys are in there," he whispered, pointing to the pool hall.

"What guys?" Christine asked, but everybody else at the table knew. SRT had come here, just like us, because it was the closest bar to Forest Lawn.

Darren turned and started towards the poolroom. I scrambled out of the booth, grabbed his arm, and spun him around.

"Whatta you doing?" I said.

"I got some things to say to those assholes," he snarled.

"No you don't. Sit down."

"Hey, fuck you. Who are you anyway? You came on one ride with us. You're blue, we're tan. You're not even in our tribe."

He yanked his arm away from me and started into the pool hall. I looked over at the booth. Four sheriff's deputies all sitting there trying to decide if they wanted to stop it or join it.

"This is no good," I said softly. Then I turned and followed Darren into the poolroom.

There were two SRT commandos shooting a rack on the far side of the room. The other four members were in a booth drinking. Brady Cagel must not like hanging with his troops, because he wasn't around. I looked over and saw Darren Zook by the cue rack, carefully selecting a weapon. He was making a big deal out of running his hand over the stick, checking it for cracks. Then he pulled it down and headed toward the six SRT agents. I cut between pool tables and intercepted him.

"Darren, you're drunk. This ain't it," I said, holding one hand against his chest. Now the SRT agents looked up and saw us for the first time.

"Hey Billy," Gordon Grundy, a big, square-headed federal SWAT commando said, "Yer fucking moolie's back." All the feds looked up at us. The vibe was so nasty that the four civilians playing pool at the next table laid their cues down on the green felt and just walked out of the bar. On the way they passed the four sheriffs from our table, who now stood in the threshold: Brill, the Nightingale brothers, even Christine Bell.

"Here come the rent-a-cops," a stocky, Hispanic fireplug fed in a black suit said. I thought his name was Ignacio Rosano. He stood, and as he did, three other feds rose with him. Now everybody was on their feet.

"Let's cool down," I said. "We don't need this, guys."

"Get the fuck outta here, Scully," Zook said. Then, without warning, he pushed me hard to the right and swung the pool cue. It hit Rosano on the shoulder and bounced up hard, into his throat, landing with a loud *THWACK*.

The dance was on.

Bar fights, like bad parties, are no fun and hard to remember afterwards.

I paired up with Billy Greenridge. He was a SWAT-trained commando about my same height, and had good moves. I tried my Brazilian jujitsu, but he was fast and I couldn't take him to the ground. We traded right hands. I caught the first few body shots on my elbows, then one slipped through and cracked a rib. *This is not the way police officers are trained to behave,* I whined to myself as I covered up. Then I saw his square jaw loom into view—a clean shot. I swung hard, but he spun and I missed, catching his shoulder and throwing myself badly off balance in the process. Out of the corner of my eye I saw people wheeling and trading punches. Darren and one of the SRT guys were doing some kind of *Quo Vadis* thing with pool cues. Christine Bell seemed hard pressed to find an opponent. The feds kept ignoring her, turning away and going for one of the guys, until she stepped up and kicked Grundy between the legs and brought him down like a bag of sand.

The worst part of this fight was that it was so stupid. Our side was also going to be shamefully easy to identify afterwards, all in our nice police dress uniforms, complete with name plates.

Two of the feds were now lying on the floor. As I turned to find a new opponent, I caught it from behind with a pool cue. The next thing I knew, I was on my hands and knees under the table trying to remember what continent I was on. That's when one of the feds put me out of my misery. I caught a shiny, black brogan with the right side of my head.

I was done. Down for the count. Gone.

Oh well.

BUSTED 8 AGAIN

WHAT THE HELL happened to you?" Alexa asked. It was
eight fifteen the next morning. As soon as I stepped out
of the shower I put on a baseball cap to cover the six emergency-
room stitches in the back of my head. But I guess the shower
had opened the edge of the cut, and blood was running down
the back of my neck.

"Take off that silly hat," she ordered.

"Oh, I don't think . . ."

She reached out and snatched the hat off. Then we did a little
circle dance where she kept trying to get around behind me.
"Shane, have you been fighting?" Sounding now like the horse-
faced nun in those old Mickey Rooney movies.

Busted again.

Chooch had just hobbled out the door with Delfina, both of

them on the way to school. He dropped her at Venice High each morning, then drove out to Harvard-Westlake in the Valley. We were alone, so I couldn't even use the kids for cover. I brought us both mugs of coffee and handed one to Alexa. She sat at the kitchen table and looked unhappy. I knew she couldn't stick around long, because she had a nine o'clock meeting with Tony Filosiani. They were reviewing some detective crime scene tactics in Vernon, where the department had a big public relations problem pending on a bad arrest.

"Who hit you?" she demanded again.

"What makes you think I got hit? This was a . . . I fell off a whatever—a thing." *Great, Shane.* "I was leaning back and tipped over in a chair, hit my head." *Better.*

"I can spot blunt force trauma. Don't forget who you're dealing with," she said.

She was right. It's pretty hard to BS a trained street detective. When it came to skirting the edges of the truth, this was not your normal marriage.

So I told her about the fight that took place the night before at the Pew and Cue. When I finished she was very quiet.

"Well, say something," I said. I hated it when she went quiet. That was always the worst.

"What do you want me to say, Shane? We've got major problems going down between sheriffs and SRT. Lawsuits are bound to get filed, so how do you help? You and a bunch of sheriffs go out after Emo's funeral, get plastered, then get into a fight with SRT. Let's see . . . What should I say? How about this: Was it fun?"

"Would it help if I told you I tried hard to break it up before it got started?"

"That might help."

"I tried really, really, really hard to break it up before it got started."

"Y'know, Shane, I love you, but you still have a lotta spots left that need smoothing off."

"And you're slowly sanding them. I want you to know I'm extremely grateful."

"Did the LAPD roll on it? Is this disaster gonna show up on a department green sheet downtown?"

"One of our black-and-whites was called, but Darren talked 'em out of doing anything."

"Darren. Not you."

"I was . . . in the toilet throwing up."

"Shit." Now she looked worried. "You got knocked out?"

"I don't think I was puking because of a concussion. I think it was bad chicken wings. I feel really good this morning. Tip-top. The E.R. docs didn't even want to hold me."

"Because you didn't tell them you were throwing up."

"A lot of it is kinda vague. I've got blank spots."

"Really." She leaned back, tipping in her chair, still watching me.

"Be careful," I said. "I wouldn't want you to go over and hit your head, like I did."

"Shut up, Shane."

But I'd turned the corner, I could already hear a smile in her voice.

"It was just bad luck. We didn't know they'd be in there."

She heaved a sigh. "Look at me. Right in the eye." She leaned forward and started checking my pupils. "You're okay, I guess."

She got up. I stood with her, but got a little dizzy when I did. To be honest, I might have picked up a mild concussion, but the less said here, the better.

She kissed me without passion; still angry, but she was late. "Be home for dinner?" she asked.

"I think so. I'm trying to wrap up the Paula Beck thing today. Once the D.A. files and Zack comes back from Miami, we can move on to something else. I'll be on the fourth floor. Lunch?"

"I don't break bread with lawless brawlers," she said.

"I was not brawling. I barely hit anybody."

"Noon at the Peking Duck," she snapped.

We left in separate cars. I drove my Acura, following her new blue Lexus until she sped up around the 10 Freeway and lost me in the heavy traffic.

I spent most of the morning on the fourth floor at Parker Center wrapping up the Beck investigation. I didn't think I had come up with enough on Paula for the D.A. to file the double-H. Even though the case was tragic, it really was just involuntary manslaughter. The D.A. could try and run his bluff, but if her public defender wasn't a complete moron he'd know it was a stretch. I finished the investigation report and handed it in to Cal, who glanced it over, then smiled at me.

"What happened at the Pew and Cue?" he said, his black, shiny, chrome-dome glinting purple in the overhead fluorescents.

"I wasn't there," I said.

"It's all over the department. Somebody said you got knocked cold." I kept my six-stitch lace-up turned from his view.

"Me?" I said. "Wasn't there. Bum rumor."

I had lunch with Alexa and we didn't say much. She picked at an avocado plate, which I could have told her was a bad menu choice at the Peking Duck. Stick to the Oriental dishes in that joint, the egg rolls and dim sum.

The rest of the day went slowly. I searched through our files on predicate felons, looking for a new target Zack and I could work when he got back. By six I was getting ready to pack it in, when my phone rang. It was Sergeant Ellen Campbell, who works as Alexa's administrative assistant.

"The skipper wants to see you," she said brightly. The skipper was Alexa.

"On my way."

I closed up my desk, logged off my computer, and rode the elevator up two flights to the sixth floor. I figured Alexa was going to suggest we make up over dinner. There was a Greek restaurant called Acropolis, in the Valley, she'd been wanting to try.

I walked down the thick, sea-foam green carpet that covered the corridors of the command floor, entered Alexa's outer office, and found Ellen, a perennially happy, freckled blonde sitting behind her desk. Most lieutenants aren't staff rank officers and don't have private secretaries, but Alexa was an acting division commander, and head of Detective Services Group. She reported directly to the Office of Operations, which was right below the Chief, so she was way up on the department flowchart.

DSG supervised all the detective bureaus, from Forgery and Missing Persons, to Special Crimes and Robbery-Homicide. Normally the head of DSG would be a captain or a commander, but Alexa had taken over the XO position a year ago as a lieutenant. She was made acting head by Chief Tony Filosiani after her boss, Captain Mark Shephard, had been shot and killed. Chief Filosiani liked her and was willing to leave her as acting head until she made captain, which, the way she was going, would probably be in another year.

Ellen was facing her computer as I crossed the office. "Storms blowing. Wear your raincoat," she said without looking up.

Alexa's digs were small. One window, no view. She had portable bookshelves on every wall. Tony Filosiani was a law enforcement junkie and read everything from student doctoral theses on criminology to medical volumes on forensic science. Alexa had picked up the trait. She had books and manuals piled everywhere. It was the new department. The rubber hose was in the Hall of Fame. Now we forced confessions with drops of DNA, luminous light, and blood-spatter evidence.

"Shane, sit down," my wife said, looking harried. She glanced at her watch and I instantly knew we weren't going to dinner.

"What's up?" I asked.

"Big problems. ATF Internal Affairs just sent us over a copy of their findings on the Hidden Ranch shoot-out. They found SRT innocent of any wrongdoing."

"What'd you expect?"

"Sheriff Messenger's in with Tony right now. He's pissed. The mayor is coming over with Enrique Salazar from the Board of Supervisors. The area SAC from ATF is on his way, too."

"Look, Alexa, it's . . ."

"No. Stop talking for a minute and listen. We're going into a meeting on this in seconds. The ATF finding claims that they told the sheriff's warrant control office about the automatic weapons in Smiley's garage. Of course, the WCO denies it, and of course, there's no paperwork substantiating what ATF says."

"Of course."

"But Brady Cagel says they never write any paper on stuff like that when they give over a bust to another agency, and the fact is, he's right."

"But what does this have to do with us? It's a sheriff's department–ATF spat."

Her intercom buzzed. She picked up the phone, listened, then said, "Right. Thanks, Ellen." She hung up and said, "Come on. Mayor MacKenzie's here. We're on."

"Alexa, whatta ya mean *we're* on?"

"We've been ordered by the mayor to reinvestigate it." And she was out of the office and down the hall.

I hurried to catch up, finally grabbing her arm before she got to Chief Filosiani's huge double doors. "You're giving this to me?" Duh . . . Finally getting it.

"Look, Shane, I need you. This is the ultimate red-ball. Either way this goes, nobody is going to come out a winner. The best we can hope for is some kind of mitigating circumstance. But we probably won't get that lucky. The mayor doesn't want ATF to reinvestigate. He's not happy with their current finding and doesn't trust their objectivity. He also can't trust the sheriff to be unbiased. He knows there's going to be multiple lawsuits on the shoot-out from the neighbors and from Emo's family, so he came to us. We're your classic uninvolved third party."

"Why me?"

"Three reasons. One: you're a great cop and you're fair . . ."

"Stop it. You'll make me vomit."

"Two: you're the only L.A. cop that Sheriff Messenger will accept. He liked the way you handled the Viking case."

"What's the third?"

"You're the only person in this building *I* can trust not to leak. We're gonna do this together."

The door to the chief's office opened and Tony was standing there. His round Santa Claus face was red, but his cheeks were not ho-ho merry. He motioned us into the outer office.

The chief's waiting room was fronted by a secretarial area. Bea, his battle-ax with a heart of gold, was sitting behind a large desk, a murder-one scowl already on her hawkish face. She nodded at Alexa and me as the chief led us into his office. You had to be very observant to spot the twinkle in her eye.

Mayor Richard MacKenzie, known around town as Mayor Mac, was standing by the window. He was a tall, skinny, hollow-chested man with riveting blue eyes and a ridiculous blond comb-over. His double-breasted suits all fit like hand-me-downs. Also in the office, looking like he wanted to throw an ashtray, was Bill Messenger. Half Armenian, half Egyptian, he was a second-generation deputy who had been elected county sheriff two years ago.

Across the room, wearing charcoal stripes and a purple tie, looking exactly like what he was, a slightly overweight politician working on a sound bite, stood Enrique Salazar.

Tony closed the door behind us. "Shane, you know Mayor MacKenzie and Sheriff Messenger," he said.

"Yes," I said, shaking hands.

"And Supervisor Salazar."

Enrique didn't cross the room. He waved a ring-laden hand at me instead.

The office was strangely underfurnished. Chief Filosiani was a no-nonsense commander, known by his troops as the Day-Glo Dago because of his New York Italian demeanor and his penchant for flashy pinky rings. He had stripped out the expensive antiques and artwork that was the legacy of his predecessor, Burl Brewer, then sold them at auction and used the money to buy new Ultima Tac vests for his SWAT teams. He had installed utilitarian metal office furniture in the room, but there was damn little of it.

"Have you filled Shane in?" Tony was saying.

"A little," Alexa said. "I've explained the—" She stopped when Bea opened the door and admitted a sandy-haired, brown-eyed, compact man in a tan suit who looked like a carefully tailored gymnast. Behind him was the ATF ASAC, Brady Cagel.

Tony shook hands with the first man, then introduced him to the room. "Garrett Metcalf is the new SAC area commander. He and Mr. Cagel are here to make sure we don't blackjack ATF. Supervisor Salazar is looking after the county's interests."

"We're already late for a briefing at Justice," Metcalf said. "We can't stay but a minute. What's so important here, you had to demand an emergency meeting?"

Mayor Mac turned away from the window. "We have the IAD shooting review you faxed over," he said. "You guys should scare up a literary agent and start publishing fiction."

"Whatta you want, Mr. Mayor? You want me to lie?" Cagel snapped back. "Want me to fire shots at my own people when they didn't do anything?"

"They sent one of my deputies up to Hidden Ranch without all the pertinent details," Messenger said.

"I'm not going to argue this with you, Bill," Metcalf responded. "Our ASAC told your warrant control office there was a possibility of automatic weapons up there. Your guys didn't act on it or include it in the warrant. What am I supposed to do?"

"You're just whitewashing," Messenger said. He looked like

he was on the verge of throwing one of his well-known Egyptian conniptions.

Garrett Metcalf said, "Your warrant guys dropped the ball. We're not gonna pay the freight."

"I'm asking LAPD to reinvestigate," the mayor said. "Detective Scully is a neutral party. I've asked him to rehang the investigation."

"He can investigate all he wants," Metcalf said. "It won't matter. It's closed. This is it as far as ATF and Justice are concerned. Not to get pissy, but a municipal investigation just isn't gonna cut it. This is a federal finding from Justice. It's over."

"Municipal crimes are tried in municipal courts," Salazar said, speaking for the first time. "The federal government can't change that." His words flew across the room like chips of ice.

Metcalf walked to the door and turned: "You people are looking at lawsuits on your dead deputy. Some of those neighbors are probably also gonna file. You turned that block into a fire zone. I sympathize, but it's not our problem."

"*You* turned it into the fire zone," Salazar said. "Your guys fired the hot gas. The L.A. County Supervisors are holding hearings, not only into the death of a Mexican-American sheriff, who looks like he was just sent in there and wasted, but into the entire behavior of the Justice Department on cross-jurisdictional matters."

"We're not gonna be scapegoats," Cagel said. "In case you haven't read your own county codes, an incident commander is responsible for everything that flows down from his scene. Your guy Matthews was in charge, so he's wearing the hat." He threw the LASD Manual onto Tony's desk. "Section thirty-one, paragraph eighteen. Great reading." He turned, and both feds walked out of the office.

"You've got to get this investigation done and a report written in less than two days," Tony said to me.

"I want a deputy on it with you," Messenger said.

"I agree," Salazar added.

"Nothing doin'," Mayor Mac replied. "I want only LAPD. They've got no stake in it. No axe to grind. Enrique, you know better than anybody what the press will do if this looks like a cover-up. We need an independent finding."

"We'll get right on it, sir," Alexa said, and led me out of the office.

Moments later we were standing in the hall.

"Alexa, I'm hardly uninvolved," I said. "I got into a fistfight with that SRT weapons team. There're already rumors about it circulating in the department."

"Shane, I know it's not perfect, but I need you, okay? Something tells me this isn't over yet. Not by a long shot."

Boy, was she ever right about that.

FOOTBALL

IT WAS 10 P.M., and I had been reading crime scene reports for
three hours. Alexa was inside going over the ATF shooting
review. I needed to get my mind off the Hidden Ranch mess for
a while, so I took a break and got together with Chooch. We sat
in the backyard talking football.

"I'm not hearing from as many coaches as I thought I would.
We're already in our second game, and I'm just standing on the
sidelines with a clipboard. I'm gonna lose the chance for a scholarship," Chooch complained. He was sitting next to me on the
patio under a quarter moon.

The narrow Venice canals were picturesque, the arched
bridges and shimmering water tinged silver in the pale moonlight. Venice was a haven for nonconformists and throwback

hippies, and I could hear Led Zeppelin leaking from one of the houses on Grand Canal.

Chooch started banging on his cast with the rubber tip of his right crutch, the injured foot his new mortal enemy.

"C'mon. You go back to the doc in a week. Maybe he'll take the cast off. You've still got a chance to get into the last few games, as well as the CIF playoffs."

"College recruiting trips are in December. I'm screwed, Dad."

"You just got another call from Coach Paterno."

"Yeah, I know."

"He saw your video from last year's games. He still seems interested."

"Penn State wants to move me to defensive-back," he said sadly. "I wanta be a quarterback. I know the position."

"You got four recruiting letters. You're gonna have coaches' visits from Arizona, Oregon, Tulane, and Miami of Ohio. The SMU scout wants to talk to you when he comes through next month."

"Dad, I'm not playing. They're not gonna give a full ride to some guy holding a clipboard."

"They understand injuries, son."

"No they don't. I'm missing almost a full year of experience. They're gonna think I'm just some green, two-year high school player. I'll probably do better going to a junior college, where I could at least start as a freshman, then transfer to a D-one school my junior year."

"Chooch—life isn't just about football. What's important is your education."

He sat quietly, looking at his offending foot. He was really in the dumps.

"I had an idea the other day. You know Emo coached a Pop Warner team? The Rams, I think."

"Yeah, you told me."

"With him gone, they're probably looking for a new head coach."

He didn't say anything.

"Sonny Lopez is coaching defensive linemen and linebackers. They need someone who knows how to run a Veer Offense."

"I don't know anything about a Veer. We run a Wing-T."

"Not much difference. They're both option offenses."

"There's a lot of difference, Dad."

"Okay, but you know fundamentals. You could teach the quarterbacks the reason for a three-step drop as opposed to five—how to do defensive reads, or look off a defender, stuff like that."

"I can't coach a buncha twelve-year-old kids. What good is that gonna do me?"

"This was Emo's team. You were his friend. He cared about these boys. Sometimes you gotta do things for other reasons than just, 'What's in it for me.'"

Chooch sat quietly for a long minute.

"Hey, I don't even know if I can get you the gig. I didn't want to ask Sonny to float the idea past the league if you were gonna say no. But it might get your spirits up, give you something else to focus on."

He was still glowering at his foot.

"Son, most of the mistakes I've made in my life, I made because I've been a loner. I started out an orphan, and it's been hard for me to let my guard down, invest in other people."

He still wasn't looking at me.

"You and Alexa have helped me understand that life is about more than just survival, but I don't always share my feelings, and there are times when I feel so desperate and alone I don't think I can stand it. Sometimes I'm not always the best partner, husband, or dad, because some part of me is always holding back. I don't want you to be like that. It's important that you learn how to give parts of yourself to others without wanting something in return."

He didn't speak, but he had a puzzled look on his face.

"Give it some time. Talk it over with your mom and Delfina. Think about it for a day. Will you at least do that?"

Yeah, sure," he said. Then he got up, grabbed his other crutch, and lumbered back into the house.

I rubbed my eyes. I felt I hadn't said it right. Then I went back to the shooting reviews. But it took me a while to get into it.

I had Vincent Smiley's Arcadia P.D. application, which was dated June 15, 2000. I'd already read it twice, now I looked again at the same vacant picture the *Times* had used. It was clipped to the top of the form. There wasn't much in his police application that helped. He went to middle school in Glendale. There was nothing listed for high school, except a note that said he had done home schooling from grades ten to twelve. He got his GED in '95, then two years of junior college at Glendale Community. His mother and father died in a car wreck in '95. I read a short essay that was attached, where he detailed his reasons for wanting to be a police officer. It was filled with the kind of vacuous nonsense that beauty contestants utter. *I want to be a policeman to help people and foster peace among diverse segments of society.* ZZZZZ.

An hour later, Alexa came out and handed me a cold beer. She plopped down in the chair Chooch had vacated, and we clinked bottles.

"Where you gonna start?" she asked.

"Out at the crime scene. Hidden Ranch Road, first thing in the morning."

"Shane, far be it from me to tell you how to do your job . . ."

"But?"

"But the guy is dead. Smiley is gone. His DNA is patched and matched. What's the point of starting out there? The neighbors have been interviewed. There's nothing much in their state-ments, except he acted like his elevator got stuck between floors and he was storing illegal weapons in his garage. We already know all that."

"I always start with the inciting incident, then work out from there. That's the way I was trained to do it."

"Except, we only have two days. Maybe you should take a shortcut."

"No shortcuts in a thorough investigation, babe. You know that."

"But . . ."

"You can always get another detective," I said, and sipped my beer, looking out at the water. "Okay with me, if that's what you decide."

"Nope. Can't get out of it that easy. You're my guy. Do it your way. Now take me to bed and give me a party."

"Thought you'd never ask."

ROTTWEILER 10

THE NEXT MORNING I drove out to Hidden Ranch. On the way I kept thinking about the incident reports I'd read the previous night.

At the beginning of every investigation I start by looking for coincidences and inconsistencies. In police work, you quickly learn it's never wise to trust a coincidence, because coincidences are often caused by criminal lies or mistakes. Inconsistencies occur when two people have conflicting opinions about a shared event, and there is often a lie or a misunderstanding at its core. In both of these circumstances it is generally profitable for an investigator to take a closer look.

After reading the deputies' statements, it seemed that almost all the sheriffs at the scene agreed that Vincent Smiley was a suicide, that he had staged it so the police would be forced to kill him. Death by cop. Even after shooting Emo, Smiley had plenty of chances to surrender. He could have thrown down his weapon, come out and saved his life, but instead he chose to barricade himself inside the house and shoot it out with the police until there was no possible solution but his own extinction.

I had to agree that on the surface it looked like a manufactured suicide. Except for two things. First, the guy had been wearing Kevlar. From my perspective, you don't wear Kevlar when you're trying to get the cops to kill you. It was inconsistent, but not unheard of.

The second inconsistency occurred in two of the neighbors' post-event statements. According to a neighbor named William Palmer, who lived four houses away on Hidden Ranch Road, Smiley had spent most of the previous summer building a bomb shelter in his basement. A woman down the street named Katie Clark had also mentioned the same thing. So the question is, why does someone who is so afraid he might die in a nuclear blast that he builds a bomb shelter in his basement commit suicide, and why was he wearing Kevlar? Those two facts didn't seem to fit in the same emotional quadrant with the Death-by-Cop theory.

I called Katie Clark, and her baby-sitter told me she was out of town on business until next Friday. That left William Palmer. He agreed to stay home and wait for me until 9 A.M.

As I turned back onto Hidden Ranch Road I remembered the bizarre insanity of my last visit here. I was still shaken by that bloodstained memory. I pulled up and parked in front of William Palmer's two-story colonial. White with dark green trim. Bright purple bougainvillea trellised off the front porch. Birds sang in the sycamore trees. A welcome contrast to the memory of that chattering AK-47.

I trudged up the walkway and rang the bell. After a moment Palmer opened the door. He was a tall, thirty-plus man with short hair and laugh lines framing a friendly smile. I liked him on sight. After I showed my creds, he shook my hand and led me into a large, well-appointed living room.

As we sat down he asked me to call him Tad. "Everybody does," he said, adding that he sold insurance for Aetna and had a meeting with his district manager in an hour, a not-too-subtle hint letting me know he didn't have much time. So we got right into a discussion of Vincent Smiley.

"The guy was always kinda nuts," Tad said, shaking his head at the memory. "Like, he'd walk his dog early every morning. If you went out to pick up your paper or were even backing out of your driveway late to work, he'd always want to stop and talk. And it was always about nonsense. Like, why didn't you plant out your hedge line? Or, your pool house would look better painted pale yellow. . . . I don't know how he afforded that house of his. Somebody said it was from the life insurance after his parents died. He just hung out, giving dumb advice and getting on everybody's nerves. Since he didn't work, he had no sense of anybody else being on a schedule."

"Nobody said anything about a dog," I said. "That wasn't in any of the statements I read."

"Yeah, a big, slobbering, black Rottweiler. Mean son-of-a-bitch. I was always worried he'd get loose and maul somebody's kid. I know it's not right to be glad he's dead, but it was no fun having Smiley in the neighborhood."

"And he told you about the weapons in his garage?"

"Showed 'em to me. He was all, 'Don't you love this?' Then he'd pull out a grenade launcher or something, and break it open, show you the breech, show you a box of ammo for his AK-forty-seven. Then he shows us boxes of plastic gunk and tells us it's C-four."

"How would a guy like Smiley acquire C-four? That stuff is impossible to get. The government restricts its distribution so terrorists can't get it."

"I don't have a clue," Palmer said. "But I've got kids and a wife. I don't need that shit four doors away. Claire is taking the kids to school right now, but you can ask her when she gets back. She thinks he was one of those antigovernment survivalist nuts. He had this computer in his garage. He bragged about hacking into some military training site called Cactus West. It had all kinds of acronyms like MCAS, Yuma, or TACTS. He showed it to me."

"You have any idea what that stands for?" I asked, writing this down.

"None at all. I tried to find it on my computer, but I couldn't. Like I said, it was a secure military Web site. Add that to the automatic rifles, C-four, and a phony sheriff's badge, and we all knew we had a huge problem."

"Tad, you said in your statement he was building a bomb shelter?"

"Yeah. June, July, all last summer, basically. Said it was in his basement. He was hauling dirt outta that house right through the back door. Had it piled up in the backyard. Took truckloads away at the end of each month."

"And you're sure it was a bomb shelter?"

"That's what he said." Tad was beginning to sneak looks at his watch.

"I'll be just a minute more," I said. "So, if he was building a bomb shelter, what's your take on the idea that he shot that deputy so the cops would come up here and kill him?"

"I agree with my wife. The guy was a survivalist. I don't think he had a death wish. He told me once he went to a camp for training on how to survive in the wild. He was always flashing that badge, but he was also terrified of authority. He said he hated cops."

"He hates the cops, and at the same time he's telling everybody he is one."

"That's why me and Claire, and the Bellinghams, got together and decided to call the sheriff's department and check him out. He didn't seem like a cop to any of us. The sheriff's office said he wasn't on their roster, so we knew the badge was a phony."

"If you had to characterize him for me, how would you describe him? Just a general impression."

"The thing about Vince was he was kinda—y'know, outta sync. He didn't act right. He laughed at stuff that wasn't funny. His vibe was wrong. When he showed us all the stuff in his garage he'd kinda caress it. It was more than just ammo, it was like—manhood."

"And you called ATF, not the sheriff, right?"

"That was because a lot of that stuff in there was illegal. The automatic weapons and the grenade launcher. Chuck Bellingham said we should call Alcohol, Tobacco, Firearms, and Explosives because illegal weapons are their beat."

He looked at his watch again and I stood up to go. "Thanks," I said. "Do you have a card, in case I have any more questions?"

He pulled one out of his wallet and handed it to me as we walked to the front door. After he showed me out I got back in my car, picked up my cell phone, and dialed the LASD bureau downtown and asked for the forensics lab. A criminalist named Robyn DeYoung was in charge of the Hidden Ranch shoot-out. Once I had her on the phone, I identified myself, and asked, "Did you guys find a dog's remains out there?"

She sounded guarded. "No, but you're LAPD. What's your interest? This is a sheriff's investigation."

"You can check with Sheriff Messenger's office. He'll verify my involvement."

There was a long pause.

"I'd like to have somebody go out and rake through the ashes and look for that dog's remains," I continued.

"Why?" she asked.

"Because it's a loose end. There's supposed to be a dog. If you didn't find a dog, then where is it? It's a Rottweiler. They aren't all that cuddly. If he's out and running around loose up in the foothills, we should probably know that, don't you think?"

She didn't respond.

"Also, there's supposed to be a bomb shelter in the basement. We need to dig down and try and find it." She got very silent. I could tell I wasn't scoring many points with Ms. DeYoung.

"I'll check with Sheriff Messenger," she said after another long pause, not happy about having to go back out and sift through all those ashes again, or dig out a ton of soggy rubble looking for a bomb shelter. I had the feeling my request was going to get assigned a very low priority. I took down her direct-dial number and rang off.

My next stop was Smiley's burned-down house. I wanted one last look. I drove up the street and pulled to the curb on the east side of the cul-de-sac. There was already a green Suburban parked there. A blond woman was wandering in the ashes where the house had once stood. She was muscular, with short, spiky, white-blonde hair. As I walked closer I could see the powerful slope of a weightlifter's shoulders. Almost five-ten in low heels, she was wearing a tan miniskirt and a sleeveless cotton blouse. Her arms were cut, her legs were sinewy and tanned. I wouldn't call her exactly beautiful, but she fit into that unique category of strong-faced women who can accurately be called handsome. When she turned and focussed a level stare at me, another unique feature became apparent. Her right eye was blue, her left one green.

I stepped into the still damp ashes, crossed the distance between us, pulled out my badge and showed it to her. She studied it carefully. "LAPD?" she said. "I thought this was a sheriff's investigation."

"Let's start with who you are." I was trying not to sound badge-heavy and territorial, but I hated having civilians wandering around up here, even though the sheriff's yellow crime scene tape was down.

"I'm Kimmy Fox." She smiled at me. Her smile was dazzling, her square teeth, bright and even as a row of porcelain tile. "I live right down the road. The two-story Regency on the right." She pointed at a house with a manicured yard.

I looked down and saw that she was holding two, ash-dusted brass cartridges. Evidence that sheriff's CSI had missed. "Looking for souvenirs?" I said as I reached for the shell casings. She handed them to me reluctantly.

"I still can't believe all this happened," she said.

"Did you know Mr. Smiley well?"

"As well as you can know somebody like that. He was kinda strange. He had this way of looking at you. Like you were a thing . . . or just property. It was very off-putting."

"You see him with his dog? I understand he walked a dog every morning."

"I'm sorry?"

"A black Rottweiler."

"Oh, yeah. Everybody knew that dog. Vicious. I'm a mom, and I was always worried he'd get loose. I have morning carpool this year, so I saw him out walking that beast a lot when I was heading out." She smiled again. "My kids are on midsemester break. Little rascals conned me into two days at Disneyland this morning." She looked at her watch. "Guess I should get going."

"You ever see mounds of dirt piled in the backyard in June or July? I understand he was building a bomb shelter last summer."

"How could you miss it? Who builds a bomb shelter anymore? That was a sixties thing." Then she smiled at me. "Could I have those back?" she said, looking at the cartridges in my hand.

"Sorry. It's evidence."

"Oh . . . okay. I was just going to show them to my husband. He was curious about all that stuff in Vincent's garage—the guns and boxes of ammo." She started to fidget. "I'm sorry if I did anything wrong coming up here. They took down the crime tape, so I figured it was okay. The guy lived just down the street from us. Then last week, he goes completely nuts, starts shooting up the neighborhood. It's just—I needed a way to close the door on it, is all."

"I understand."

She nodded. "Well, better get going, I have teacups to ride."

"Ride carefully," I smiled.

She walked away from me, picking her way out of the ashes, then down the walk on strong, muscular legs.

There was something about her that seemed familiar, but I couldn't pin it down. I watched as she drove her Suburban up the street and parked in her driveway half a block away. I turned back and surveyed the burned-out house, wondering how the mindless insanity that had caused all this could live in such a peaceful neighborhood.

THE ARGUMENT 11

Y ou're coming at it from the wrong direction," Alexa said. "You're wasting precious time investigating Vincent Smiley's death. He's not the problem anymore."

We were finally at the Acropolis restaurant in the Valley, sitting at a patio table, but our plates of moussaka were untouched and cooling as we argued.

"Honey, if I don't start there I won't even know what questions to ask."

"You've only got two, or possibly three outcomes. Either ATF knew about the automatic weapons and C-four in that house, withheld information critical to the safety of the deputy serving the warrant, and they're lying, or they shared the information with the sheriff's warrant control office like they said, and the sheriffs are lying."

"What's the third?" I asked, because I sure couldn't see it.

"ATF was just on their way back from a training day like they claimed, and heard the shoot-out on the radio and nobody's lying."

"They couldn't hear it without that TAC frequency in their truck."

"Right. And you can't prove it's not there, because you can bet by now that truck has the frequency installed. Besides, you didn't have a warrant to search the damn thing."

"Picky, picky, picky."

"Hey, Shane, no kidding. You're on the wrong path here. Vincent Smiley isn't the problem."

"He had a dog—a Rottweiler, and the sheriffs didn't find the remains."

"So what?"

"It's a loose end. I don't like loose ends."

"It's nothing."

"If he had boxes of C-four, where did he get them? It's so regulated by the government there's not even a black market for that stuff."

"I don't know Shane, but it's not what you're supposed to be investigating."

"He wore Kevlar and built a bomb shelter. He was hacked into a secure military computer called Cactus West. People who wear Kevlar and build bomb shelters do it because they want to stay alive. I don't think Smiley was trying to get the cops to kill him."

"We have death-by-cop suicides wearing body armor all the time. Look at the North Hollywood bank shoot-out. Those guys knew they were gonna die. Smiley built his bomb shelter almost ten months ago. Things change. Maybe he took a bad hit of acid. Maybe he was dusted on PCP and went off the rails. Look, the only reason LAPD is on this thing in the first place is because the ATF shooting review cleared their SRT, and the mayor thinks it's a bad finding. Stick to that."

"If it's a bad finding, then give it to our Professional Standards Bureau." Our new, media-friendly name for Internal Affairs. "They're good at scoping out OIS mistakes." I continued. "What the hell am I doing with it anyway?" I was raising my voice a little, and the people at the adjoining tables were beginning to look over at us with annoyed expressions.

"I can't give it to Professional Standards. It's not an LAPD shooting. And you're the only one Bill Messenger will accept. Don't make it more than it is. Just do the job."

"Is the moussaka not to your liking?" the maitre d' asked. He had drifted over to our table, displaying an elegant presence. His manner and tone made it clear that he thought we were destroying the restaurant's classic ambience.

"It's fine," I snapped.

"Bag it," Alexa barked.

The maitre d' waved a waiter over. He cleared the plates while both of us tried to calm down. After he left I leaned toward her and lowered my voice. "Alexa, you've been a cop for almost as long as I have."

"Are we gonna start comparing pedigrees now?" she hissed.

"In all those years, how many times have you seen somebody who wants to be a cop start by filing applications with the Arcadia P.D.?"

She was silent for a long time. "So?" she finally said.

"So, my guess is that Smiley started out by applying to the LAPD or the sheriff's department, then, once he failed those entrance requirements, he worked his way down the list to the smaller departments. Santa Monica, Pasadena, Glendale, Arcadia."

"Again, so what?"

"Since Arcadia wouldn't give us their psych package on him,

how about we look in our own academy apps? We do preliminary psychological tests. Maybe he's in there."

"Why do you keep coming back to him? For God's sake, Shane, do you think he's still alive or something?"

"No. I trust the DNA match. What I think is, maybe a sheriff or ATF agent knew something about Smiley, or maybe Smiley had something on one of them. He gave the Arcadia P.D. a DNA sample, maybe he raped some cop's sister and this was disguised payback. Maybe he had knowledge about some cop's misdeeds and needed to be silenced. Somebody is lying about that warrant, and I'm looking for the motive. I just want to keep my options open."

"Maybe ATF just screwed up and that's why they're lying," she said, voicing the solution both the LASD and LAPD were rooting for.

"I still want to see if he ever applied to our academy."

"Shane, don't make me order you to do this my way."

"And don't force me to disobey my division commander's direct order. At the center of this, something's very wrong. Smiley hates cops, but he's walking around pretending to be one? He has boxes of C-four, nobody knows where it came from. The vest, the bomb shelter, it's all inconsistent. It needs to be looked at."

She studied me for a long moment. "I'm standing on top of a land mine here. I don't need you to tell me how much powder is in the mine. I need you to disarm the damn thing."

"Honey, you're coming at this from a totally parochial position. You already have a theory and you want my investigation to confirm it. That's not the way to go about it."

She sighed and her expression softened.

"I'm through investigating Hidden Ranch anyway," I said to mollify her. "I'm now working my way from the center out. Sheriffs are still in control of all the lab and CSI evidence. I talked to a labbie in their forensics division named Robyn DeYoung. She's the evidence tech for Hidden Ranch and she isn't too eager to follow through on any of my requests. That has to change. I want them to look for the dog and the bomb shelter."

"Okay. I'll make you a deal. I'll unstick that, and I'll see if Smiley's in our academy apps, but you have to start concentrating on whether ATF or the sheriffs are lying."

We both sat back in our chairs and stared across the linen tablecloth like fighters who had gone into neutral corners.

"I can't promise you anything," I said. "I gotta take this where it leads." Then I smiled and said, "Still love me?"

"Jesus!" she snarled.

"An easy mistake. But no, I'm Shane," I teased.

We got home at ten and found Chooch studying in his makeshift room out in the garage. "Have fun?" he asked.

Neither of us answered.

I got a beer while Alexa went to work in her office, answering e-mails. I was sitting in the living room, trying to focus on the eleven o'clock news, when Delfina came in and stood in the doorway.

"Shane?" she said, and I glanced over at her. She had her hair pulled back in a barrette and was holding our adopted cat, Franco, stroking his orange and white fur softly.

"How you doing, Del?" I said. "Thought you had a big chemistry test tomorrow." She was a junior, and chemistry was definitely not her best subject.

"I do," she smiled, "but I need to talk to you about Chooch."

I grabbed the remote and turned the volume down.

"Come on."

I led her out onto the patio. She followed silently behind. We settled into two chairs in my favorite spot overlooking the narrow canals with their Disneyesque bridges. She put Franco down and immediately the marmalade cat began to wind around my ankles.

"I've been talking to Chooch about that job coaching kids," she said.

"What's he think?"

"A lot of things are bothering him right now. He's afraid if he doesn't stay with his own football practices at Harvard-Westlake his coach will get angry and not play him, even when his foot heals. I told him that is not so. He is much better than his replacement. But he is unsure. He's also afraid if he takes over Mr. Rojas's team and doesn't do a good job you'll be disappointed. He wants you to respect what he does, but he is torn. He's afraid to make a decision. I'm telling him no decision is the same as a decision, because they'll get somebody else to be the coach. He needs to make up his mind."

"What do you think?"

"I'm worried about him, Shane. He's not like before. He's not the happy person now. I think it's very important that he does something to take his mind off his troubles."

"It's why I suggested this in the first place."

"I think I can get him to say yes," Delfina said softly.

"How?"

"I'm his *chavala*." She gave me a knowing, worldly smile. "I think, if you tell them now that Chooch will coach the team, I can get him to say yes in a day or two. Then we will have done a good thing."

"But we will have done it behind his back."

"He is *un marvillo*, you know that. But he is also sometimes acting the spoiled little boy. This will be good for him and for others. Sometimes with boys you must give them just a little push to help them decide. You get the job, and I will get the coach."

I smiled at her. Franco looked up and meowed loudly. So, of course, with both of them so vocally on the record, there was nothing much I could do but agree. *"Yo te acuerdo,"* I said.

It was late, but I took a chance and called Sonny Lopez. He was still up. When I threw Chooch's name at him he thought it was a great idea, and said he'd check with the league office and get back to me.

An hour later Alexa and I were slamming around in our bedroom, getting ready for bed. Finally she got in on her side and I got in on mine. We pulled the covers up and I snapped off the lights.

"Yes," she said.

"Yes, what?"

"Yes, I still love you." Then she rolled over and looked at me, propped up on one elbow. I could just barely see her in the ambient light coming through the window. A beautiful, dark-haired vision. "It isn't about you and me, it's about tactics," she said.

"Honey, I know you're getting pressure from Mayor Mac and Salazar, as well as Tony and Bill. I know you think I just wasted one whole day reinvestigating things that didn't need to be investigated. But this is how I do it. If I don't put all the jigsaw pieces on the table, I'll never solve the puzzle."

She scooted over, put her arms around me and held me tight. "I just hate arguing with you," she said softly, "even when you're wrong."

I held her, smelled her hair, and felt the soft textures of her body. I decided I'd rather make love than war.

So that was what we did.

POLICE MADNESS

WHEN WE GOT there Billy Greenridge from SRT was dead in a vertical coffin. His feet were still inside the living room, his large body spilled headfirst across the threshold, half in and half out of the front door of his house. The back of his head was a pulpy mess, dripping blood and brain matter onto the oleander bushes that grew just under the railing.

It was nine-fifteen the following morning.

The house was a small, wood-shingled, California Craftsman in the Rampart Division. Rampart is inside LAPD jurisdiction, so, although Greenridge was a fed, for now it was an LAPD crime scene. However, if they pressed, I knew ATF could take it away. He was their murdered agent.

Alexa and I arrived in separate cars from Parker Center. We parked and found three LAPD tech vans already on the scene, along with four LAPD black-and-whites. There were two unmarked cars with federal license plates. I recognized the ATF ASAC, Brady Cagel, already up on the porch looking down at his dead agent. Eight LAPD blues and two other men not in uniform formed a choir around the body. As I approached, I realized that the two non-uniforms were also members of SRT. Gordon Grundy was on Cagel's right, tall, square-headed, and rawboned. His stoic face looked like someone had painted a straight-line mouth and gunmetal eyes on a block of granite. Next to Grundy was stocky Ignacio Rosano, whom I remembered from the bar fight. I'd learned he was called Nacho. The LAPD uniforms were trying to get the three feds off the porch, but the Justice Department agents didn't seem inclined to cooperate.

"Here's our division commander." One of the LAPD blues said, pointing at Alexa as we walked up.

Brady Cagel pulled out his shield and badged us. "You guys don't belong here," he said, "I'm claiming the crime scene."

"All my uniformed people who don't have a reason to be up here right now, get off this porch and secure the street out front. One of you stay here and start an incident log. The rest of you tape off a staging area, then wait by your cars." Alexa issued instructions and seven uniformed officers turned and left the porch. One of the cops remained behind, opened a notebook and started the crime scene attendance sheet. The CSI techs faded back into the house.

Brady Cagel and his two feds held their ground. "This is a dead federal agent," he said. "That makes it our investigation, according to Title Eighteen of the U.S. Code of Crimes and Criminal Procedures. I have somebody from our homicide division on his way."

"It's in our jurisdiction," Alexa said. "There's also a strong possibility that this is connected to the death of Deputy Sheriff Emo Rojas, which we've been ordered to investigate by Mayor

MacKenzie. Until you file a jurisdictional claim and get a favorable ruling, it's gonna stay our case." Alexa looked right at Cagel. "So, for now, you three guys get off this porch, or I'm instructing my officers to come back up here and arrest you for interfering in an active homicide investigation and obstructing justice."

"What horseshit," he growled.

"Get moving or face the consequences," she warned.

Cagel gave it a moment's thought, looked at the eight LAPD officers twenty feet away, realized he was badly outnumbered, then motioned to his two teammates and they stepped back and headed to their cars.

Alexa watched as they walked across the street. But they didn't leave. Cagel was already on his cell phone, probably calling the U.S. Attorney for a legal opinion. Just then, another unmarked vehicle with government plates pulled in. I recognized two more members of SRT: Bill Wagner, who was nicknamed "Ringo," and Bob Zant, called "Happy." This collection of catchy nicknames stood across the street in a tight huddle, looking like a terrorist cell getting set to run a play.

"The case will end up getting transferred, unless I can get the U.S. Attorney to block the Title Eighteen," Alexa said softly.

"How's he gonna come down on our side?" I asked. "We're municipal. He's federal."

"Mayor Mac has to convince him we have a potential SWAT war going on here." Alexa for the first time put into words what everyone feared. "We need a neutral homicide team working this, and right now we're it. So let's do it right. If we do end up transferring the case, I don't want a lot of complaints about the way we handled the preliminary investigation." Then she looked around the crime scene. "Where the hell *is* my homicide team?"

"Rampart homicide dicks and the M.E. are en route," one of the crime techs said.

An LAPD crime photographer was already inside taking pictures. I could hear his motorized camera firing off frames. I took a quick tour of the two-bedroom house. It was furnished with bad art and vinyl furniture. It looked as if Greenridge lived alone. No female accessories in the bedroom, bath, or shower.

Finally, a Rampart Division homicide car slid to the curb and the last cop I wanted to see working this murder hauled his obese, 280-pound ass out of the D-car and started to waddle up the walk. Lou Ruta was fat, red-faced, and out of shape. He'd gained at least twenty pounds since we'd tangled at Carol White's murder scene last year. He struggled up the front steps gasping like a torn windbag, until he finally caught sight of me.

"What's going on here, a boy scout meeting?"

"That'll be enough of that, Sergeant." Alexa said, stepping out from behind the front door into his view. Ruta's face whitened, then darkened. Last came a ghastly expression where fleshy jowls pulled away from tobacco-stained ivory in a gargoyle's smile.

"Sorry, Lieutenant, didn't see ya back there," he muttered, then kneeled and studied the corpse.

The bullet had hit Greenridge in the forehead, leaving a delicate, dime-sized hole positioned like an Indian caste mark right between his eyes. Then it blew the back of his head off, leaving bone chips and gore all over the porch.

"Somebody look for the bullet," Ruta told the CSI techs, who were now standing nearby waiting for instructions. "Looks like a drive-by. Guy was comin' out his door. If the shot came from the passenger seat of a car parked down on the street, we got an upward trajectory, so start looking high in the walls across from the front door and in the living room ceiling."

The techs jumped into action.

I pulled Alexa aside, leading her down off the porch. "This guy's a joke, Alexa. The vic fell forward. How's that an upshot? Ruta's gonna screw this up."

She looked troubled. Her problem was that, as head of DSG, she couldn't favor one detective over another. Since Ruta had been next up on the homicide rotation at Rampart, she couldn't just pull him off without cause. He'd go to the union, file a complaint, and he'd win. She also couldn't admit she had a bad detective out here working active shootings. But the truth was, Ruta had lost interest years ago, and everybody was holding their breath until he got his twenty in and pulled the pin in March.

Just then, two sheriff's units roared past the LAPD squad cars blocking the end of the street and chirped to a stop. Four deputies got out and started toward the house, but the LAPD officers stationed there stopped them. The deputies gathered back by their cars. It didn't take long for ATF and sheriffs to start giving stink-eye to each other.

"This is going to the dogs," Alexa said, observing the cliques of angry agents and deputies gathering out on the street.

Happy Zant had picked up the microphone in his federal car and started talking to someone, probably calling in reinforcements.

"You gotta move some of this meat outta here before we have another fistfight," I told Alexa.

She nodded, looked at the street, then turned back to me. "Okay, here's how this is gonna work. As of now, I'm reassigning you to Rampart homicide. You're gonna be the primary on this shooting. Work it with Ruta and his partner, but you're on point."

"What about the Hidden Ranch investigation?"

"This *is* the Hidden Ranch investigation. That's your case, so as far as I'm concerned, all crimes that flow from it are yours. You work this hit, while I try and keep us from getting shot down by Title Eighteen."

Then she turned and addressed the blues who had wandered back up toward the porch. "Get enough police presence out here to move the sheriffs and ATF guys out of our staging area and down the street." One of the uniforms hustled to his car to make a call.

I crossed to where Lou Ruta was standing over the body, peeling a cigar. He let the wrapper fall and it blew away in the morning breeze, landing in the bushes by the far end of the porch. I walked down the steps and picked the cellophane off the oleander. I took it back up onto the porch and handed it to him.

"Got your fingerprints, Sarge. CSI finds it, you could get busted for this murder."

He glowered, but stuffed the wrapper in his pocket, then jammed the cigar into his mouth and started searching for a match.

"And if you light that stogie and spew ash on this site, you're gonna be smokin' it out of your ass."

"Big tough guy," he said. But he pocketed the unlit cigar as well, then started looking out at the street. "Where the fuck's my split-tail partner?"

A few minutes later Alexa took Ruta aside and gave him the news that from now on he was reporting to me on this homicide. His face contorted when she told him, but he said nothing. Then Alexa left to try and cut a deal with the U.S. Attorney.

Five minutes later Ruta's partner arrived. She was a nervous-looking honey-blonde with too-big hair. Her name was Beverly King, and from the way she looked at him, I could instantly tell she hated his guts.

CRIME SCENE 13

ATF DIDN'T WORK many homicides. Their beat was illegal party favors—guns, booze, and stogies. Because we worked hundreds of murders a year, normally on homicides that fell in their jurisdiction, they'd send us an agent to help out, but would leave us on point. After the Hidden Ranch shoot-out, that obviously wasn't going to happen.

Ruta was pacing in the living room shooting off orders at everybody. "Get me a phone dump on this hard line and don't forget his cell calls," he barked at Beverly King.

She nodded, her face pinched tight with stress, her body language a concert of uncertainty. She took off through the living room toward the phone.

"Not through the crime scene, you idiot!" Ruta yelled. "Go

out the front door, around to the back porch. After it's dusted, use the phone in the kitchen. Who the fuck taught you crime scene tactics, Katie Couric?"

Beverly King muttered an apology and scooted out the front door on her errand.

I walked over to Ruta. "Why don't you cut her some slack?"

"Why don't you suck my dick? Or can I say that to the husband of our division commander?"

"Hey, Lou, you can say anything you want, just don't piss me off, or I'll drag your sorry ass outside and disconnect your dome light." I smiled benignly. "Besides, how would I ever find your dick in all that blubber?" He reddened but didn't respond.

All around us, CSIs were doing their thing. They were getting ready to flip Billy Greenridge, after bagging his hands. In my opinion, there wasn't going to be any DNA under his nails. This didn't look like it was done from up close. He looked like he was shot from a distance with a high-powered round, probably from a sniper's rifle.

Everybody was more or less thinking that someone from the sheriff's enforcement bureau had done this, but nobody wanted to say it because of where that would take us.

Beverly King found the bullet hole in the living room wall. It had punched through a copy of that corny painting of dogs playing poker. The picture hung opposite the front door, the bullet passing right through the head of a fox terrier holding five spades in his paw. Apparently not a winning hand. Then the slug went through the laundry room and back porch, blasting out into the backyard, where it was lost somewhere in the open field beyond. It had to have been a big round, like a .308, to go through Billy's head, three walls, and keep going. Hunting for it in the field behind the house was going to be an iffy project. The bullet would probably never be found.

When the M.E.s were finally ready to transport the body I

went over and watched them load Billy onto the gurney, his bloody remains now all zipped up neatly in a rubber coroner's bag. I walked out with the M.E.'s assistant, an Asian man named Ray Tsu, helping him push the gurney. Tsu had a pipe-cleaner build and long hair parted in the middle and pushed behind his ears like black tieback curtains.

We struggled, pushing the load up to the coroner's van. The front wheels of the gurney folded under and we slid the body into the back. Before he shut the van doors, I stopped him.

"Can I take one last look, Ray?"

"Sure." He unzipped the bag and Billy's pasty, white face came into view. I examined the bullet hole in the center of his forehead. An ugly red cyclops.

"Up or down?" I asked, referring to the trajectory.

"Ruta says up," Tsu dodged.

"Yeah, but whatta you say?"

"Depends on the attitude of his head when he got hit," he hedged again. "I'm just a tech. You should get all that from the M.E."

Just to keep the conversation rolling, I said, "Bullet fired from some shooter sitting in a car parked out front would be slightly up, right? An upshot would knock his head back. The head's responsible for what? A little over a tenth of a person's gross weight?"

"Eighteen percent."

"Right, eighteen. So it's like a fulcrum, whichever way the head goes, so goes the body. An upshot should blow him back, but he fell forward, head toward the street. How come?"

"There's no rules on this stuff, Shane," Ray said, smiling now, despite our ghoulish subject matter.

"Take a guess," I said. "You see a lot of this. I won't hold you to it."

"Well, two ways it happens, maybe. One, if he was shot up

close, like from a few feet away with a big round. The muzzle velocity on a three-oh-eight or a two-twenty-three is so great coming out of the barrel, it maybe blows out the back of his skull without much recoil. So he doesn't fall back, but his head rebounds slightly from the exit kick and that throws him forward. Or it was a down-shot from a ways away, and the shot takes him to his knees. From there, depending how he hit, he could fall anywhere."

"Any other way it happens?"

"I've seen hundreds of drive-bys the last few years. Sometimes there's no reason why a body lands the way it does. Bullets ricochet off bones, change directions. The rules of physics on this can get skewed. He could have even bounced off the door frame and got knocked forward."

Ray Tsu rezipped the bag and closed the van door, then paused before leaving. "Ruta's got his full, fair share of mean, don't he?"

"In our business, it's real easy to go sour. It's something to watch out for."

Tsu nodded, then got into the van and pulled out. The rest of the preliminary crime scene investigation went right down departmental guidelines. We drew a grid of the place, graphed everything, vacuumed for trace evidence, hair, and fiber, in case the shooter had been in the house before he pulled the trigger. A long shot, but you never know. We looked for brass out front. Didn't find any. Photographed and dusted, taped up and backed out. Textbook.

Out on the street Ruta was hovering. I wanted some time alone to run my theories and thoughts, so I told him I was done. He grunted, walked to his car, and pulled away. I saw Beverly King sitting on the curb having a cigarette, trying to get rid of some anger. I walked up to her. Her hands were shaking as she took a drag.

"Good going in there," I said, referring to the fact that she had found the bullet hole in the painting. It wasn't a huge victory, but she needed something.

"Right. Mrs. Columbo saves the case." Her tone was bitter. Angry.

"Detective King, some things we can change, some things we can't. The secret is knowing the difference."

"I guess," she said, looking up and snapping the butt away. It scattered sparks in the street where it landed. "The guy just gets me froggy. Once he starts selling his wolf tickets, I end up getting tentative and start making mistakes."

"Ruta can't define you. Only you can do that. You let him get into your head, you're finished. The trick is to ignore his flack and stay focused. You're in charge of your game; he's in charge of his. Don't get the two mixed up, just because he's got two extra stripes and some attitude."

"Easy to say."

"Think of it this way. You're a homicide dick. A specialist. A lot's at stake when you get a call. You're the last hope the vic has for justice. Billy Greenridge is your client now. Don't let exposure to negativity cheat your client out of the best you have."

She frowned. "Who are you supposed to be, Deepak Chopra?"

"I'm just a guy who's done it wrong too many times and had to pay for it."

Finally her look softened and she smiled. "Thanks, Shane," she said softly.

SIGHTING 14

I DROVE ACROSS town to the new County Medical Examiner's office located on the southeast corner of the L.A State College campus. They had recently broken ground on a high-tech, state-of-the-art crime lab facility next door and as I pulled in I could see the growling bulldozers working in the adjoining field preparing the site. The coroner's unit was already up and had been in business for about a month. It was a modern three-story building with mirrored glass. I pulled into a slot in student parking, put my handcuffs over the steering wheel—the universal signal to all cruising traffic control officers and parking police that this was a cop car—then I entered the air-conditioned, sterile confines of the new facility.

I was there because I needed some time to pass. I wanted to let things settle down before going back to Billy Greenridge's little house on Mission Street. There was a good chance that the sheriff's black-and-whites and ATF cars would cruise that neighborhood for hours. It was going to be the latest "Whatta-buncha-bullshit" gripe for both agencies.

I didn't want to get caught standing on the front porch chewing my nails with a dumb look on my face, so I came here to satisfy one little detail that I probably already had the answer to.

I badged my way down to the second subbasement floor and found a county M.E. named Lisa Williams, who had done the DNA match on Smiley. She was a thirty-year-old African-American wearing a blue medical smock, slippers, and hair net. A surgical mask was hanging around her neck.

"Sure," she said after I told her what I wanted. She led me down a hallway into a quarter-acre-sized, windowless room full of fluorescent-lit workstations and cubicles. We arrived at her desk and she turned on her computer and waited for it to boot up. "The DNA sample we got from the Arcadia P.D. was taken by their medical officer in 'oh-two. It's a legally obtained sample, witnessed with double signatures. We matched it to the DNA we got off the corpse at Hidden Ranch."

Her computer had loaded, and now the two DNA strands were side by side in the center of her monitor. She started scrolling.

"On the right is the 'oh-two Arcadia sample. The left is the one we took from the charred body last week. It's a perfect match. No variables, intangibles, or dropouts. These strings of base pairs line up perfectly. That corpse in the morgue is definitely Vincent Smiley."

"Thanks."

I left with nothing new learned. Okay, maybe it was a waste of time, but I'm a stickler about this stuff. I looked at my watch. I'd been gone an hour. Time to head back to the house on Mission.

I parked up the street, then walked back to the wooden Craftsman. Ruta was sure that the shooter had been in a car, but according to the location of the bullet hole in the living room, my trajectory estimate put a shot from a car on the street too low. Of course, the doer could have opened the car door, stepped out, fired from a standing position, then picked up his brass and left. That would have more or less lined him up with the bullet hole. But if he did it that way he was risking exposure and identification by a neighbor.

Ray Tsu had said a down-shot might have knocked Green-ridge to his knees and pitched him forward with his head toward the street.

I remembered Billy from the bar fight. He and I had stood toe-to-toe trading body shots. We were about the same height. I had measured the height of the bullet hole in the living room two hours earlier, using my arm. When I pointed at the hole, it was about three inches below my shoulder. So now, facing the opposite direction, centered in the doorway where I thought he had been, I extended my arm to about head high, pointed it straight out and raised it three inches. It was now, more or less, pointed up at an apartment building across the street. If the shot hadn't come from a parked car, then maybe the bullet had come from that building.

I knew it was an outside chance, because most street assassins like to have a set of wheels under them when doing a drive-by. Disregarding that logic, I sighted along my arm at the four-story apartment complex. It was an old, sixties-style building. Con-crete boxes. Ugly. In my opinion, the sixties had been a decade of architectural blight. I counted windows and realized that, if the shot came from over there, it would have to be from the third or fourth window at the end of the building, second floor.

I walked up the street so I wouldn't be seen by any of the peo-ple living in the apartments, then doubled back and came down the sidewalk, hugging the buildings on the other side. I entered the apartment complex and took the elevator to the second floor. It was a groaning, creaking ride. The door finally wheezed open and I exited into a dark hallway. I knew approximately how far down the hall the window I had sighted would be. When I reached the spot, I looked at the closest door. It was ajar. I pulled out my Beretta, and with my toe, pushed it open a crack and looked in.

The apartment was carpeted but had no furniture or drapes. Standing on the east side of the room, looking inside an empty bookshelf, was a woman. I knew those muscular legs, cut arms, that spiky white hair. I stepped inside. She heard me behind her and turned.

"Aren't you supposed to be riding teacups at Disneyland?" I asked.

"Hi," she smiled at me. The smile really was a dazzler. I'm sure it had gotten her out of a lot of tight spots, but not this one.

"Listen, I can explain," she said.

"How?" I replied. Then I moved forward and snatched her purse off her shoulder and went through it. I found her wallet, opened it.

"Look—okay, I'm not Kimmy Whatever. I'm . . ."

"Nancy Chambers?" I said, reading her California driver's license. The picture was definitely her: weight lifter's neck, mismatched eyes, white-blonde hair.

"First you're at Hidden Ranch digging through that crime scene, trying to remove evidence, now you're poking around up here. This needs to be an excellent explanation, Nancy."

"I'm a newspaper reporter. My press card is in there. I work for the *Valley Times*, the crime desk. I'm doing a series of articles on urban violence. The Hidden Ranch thing is this Sunday's Op-Ed piece."

"How's that get you over here?"

"I have a police scanner in my car. I was monitoring federal frequencies. I heard them talking about this. I knew Billy Greenridge was on the ATF SWAT team that was up at Hidden Ranch, so I came over."

By then I had found her press card for the *Valley Times*. Under her picture it read "Nancy Chambers, Reporter."

"People call me, Nan." She smiled, again giving me the Pepsodent Challenge.

"Whatta you think you're doing here?"

"Investigating my story. Greenridge was hit by a sniper. I think this might be the firing position. Look at this."

She stepped aside and pointed down at something under the window. I looked down and saw a tripod mark, three little indentations in the carpet next to the window.

"He sets up a shooting stand right here," Nan said, really into it now, "and when Greenridge comes out of his house, kapow!" She turned to face me. "This could be where the killer shot the rifle," she announced triumphantly. "I was just looking around for his brass."

"I hope you didn't already steal the cartridge casing, like you tried to yesterday."

"I'm a reporter, not a criminal," she said, "but I don't think it's here. I already looked."

I glanced around the room, then turned and faced the window. "Unless they're specifically made for lefties, most rifles port to the right, so when the brass ejects, it should be over here on the right side of the room."

We both started searching, looking up on the empty shelves, in the moldings around the carpet edge. Then I glanced down and saw a floor heating grate. It was a large, old-fashioned, cast-iron number fastened down with brass screws. The opening was big enough for a cartridge case to drop through, and if it had, my hope was that in his haste, the sniper would have left it there. I took out a pen knife and, while she watched, loosened the screws and lifted the heavy metal. I saw it before the grate came off—a spent casing from a .308. I took out a pen, reached down, and sticking the point in the open end of the case, lifted it out. Sometimes my detective skills astound even me.

"We found it!" she said, beaming.

I was frowning. I knew that now our tool marks section in the ballistics lab would have to go out and test fire all of the long rifles at sheriff's SWAT. Under the circumstances, not an easy request. But if this cartridge casing matched one of their Tango 51s or 40-Xs, we were off on a horrible misadventure.

"I think this could be terrific," she grinned.

"I think it could be terrible," I replied.

FUMING

I CLOSED UP the apartment using the button lock, wondering how many prints Nan smudged on the way in. I had been careful not to touch anything, but I was pretty sure she had left prints everywhere.

"Whatta you doing?" she asked, as we walked across the street. I still had the cartridge casing upside down on my pen tip. I fished out the key to my Acura and opened the trunk, withdrew a small crime scene evidence kit, then headed toward the back door of Billy Greenridge's house where I knew Beverly King had found the hide-a-key under a pot.

"Aren't you supposed to put that in a bag or something?" she said, dogging my footsteps.

"Latent prints typically fall into two categories," I told her, showing off a little, "porous and nonporous."

"You mind if I get this down?" She fished a notebook and pen out of her purse, flipped to a clean page, and started writing. "I might be able to use some of it." She was scribbling: "Nonporous—okay, go on."

"Porous prints appear on soft surfaces like paper or cardboard, unfinished wood. You can bag a porous print because the finger oil has sunk into the material, basically setting it. If this shooter wasn't wearing gloves when he loaded this cartridge, then any prints he left on here will be nonporous. Nonporous is any hard surface. Nonporous prints are fragile. Anything can wipe them off, even the evidence bag, so I have to fume it first, to set the print before I transport it."

"This is fascinating. Fume it. Okay . . ." She was scribbling in her notebook. "So our bullet is nonporous."

Suddenly it was *our* bullet—of course it wasn't a bullet, it was a cartridge case.

I unlocked the back door of Billy Greenridge's house and walked into his kitchen. She was hot on my heels, writing as she went. I handed her "our bullet."

"Hold the pen like that, don't touch the brass," I instructed.

I removed a pair of latex gloves from the kit and snapped them on, then moved around the kitchen, taking what I needed. I took a coffee cup out of a cupboard, filled it, and put it in the microwave, setting it to boil. Next, I found some aluminum foil in a drawer.

I reached into my evidence kit, removed a tube of superglue, and dabbed about a nickel-sized glob on a square of foil. Then, I shut off the microwave and put the foil inside, next to the steaming cup of water, took the pen with the bullet casing out of Nan's hand, and carefully placed it tail down in the microwave. The microwave was acting only as an enclosed space to hold the superglue fumes and the steam from the cup of boiling water. I closed the door and looked at my watch.

"This is amazing," Nan gushed. "But what on earth are you trying to do?"

"Harden the print. Superglue is basically a chemical called cyanoacrylate. The fumes get heated slightly by the cup of boiling-hot water. They float around in there—attach themselves to the amino and lactic acids, the glucose, sweat, and peptides that are the print residue. You can see the white ridges from the fumes starting to form on the cartridge already. Looks like maybe we got something."

She leaned down and looked through the glass of the microwave door, smiling. "This is so cool," she said. "You're like Bill Nye the Science Guy with a badge."

I groaned at that, then looked at my watch. Long enough. I opened the door, and with my gloved hand removed the cartridge case and held it up to the light. We had a slightly smudged partial print. It looked like an index or middle finger. Besides the print were some striated action marks, which had been left when the casing ported. They could also prove helpful.

"Not a clean print," I said, "but maybe the lab can raise it some more. At least now it's hardened." I took out an evidence baggie and dropped the casing with its preserved print inside.

"I never knew you could do that."

"Easier than getting a crime tech out here, waiting for an hour, and getting the same result. Let's go."

I cleaned up the mess in the microwave, placed the coffee cup back in the cupboard, then took everything else with me as I exited the house and locked the door. I walked Nan Chambers over to her green Suburban parked on a side street and watched while she unlocked the car and opened the door.

"What was your name, again?" she asked, turning back and smiling. "Scully or something?"

She started to write it down, but I took the notebook out of her hands. "Don't bother. It won't be good if we see each other again, or if my name shows up in your paper."

I started thumbing through her notes. Aside from my lecture on latent prints, she had a page on each of the ATF SWAT members.

Date of birth, education, time in service—with background information: married, how many kids, etc. She also had a few other statements from the neighbors at Hidden Ranch—and notes from an interview with William Palmer. We had covered a lot of the same terrain. I finished flipping through the book. It looked legit.

"Isn't this illegal search and seizure?" she said, interrupting my thoughts.

"Probably, but it doesn't matter unless I arrest you for this crime and try to get your book submitted as evidence in court. But since I'm in a charitable mood, I'm gonna let you take a pass. Unless you ignore my warning, we should have no problem."

She was pinning me with those strange mismatched eyes. Her expression had hardened. "I haven't committed any crime."

"The crime is interfering with a police investigation, breaking into that apartment without permission, and the possible destruction of evidence."

"What crime scene?"

"That apartment. If it's the shooting position, it's a secondary crime scene."

She didn't look handsome now. She looked pissed and a little frightening. "I went to the manager, got his permission to look inside," she said. "He opened up for me. I didn't see any crime scene tape and I don't need your permission to go inside an a place I'm thinking about renting when I have the manager's permission."

"Ms. Chambers—"

"It's Miss. I'm not much on feminism. I do okay without it."

"You are not an uninformed bystander who is interested in renting an apartment, you're a newspaper reporter. You pushed into a room that you knew might be connected to a homicide, possibly disturbing fingerprints or trace evidence. Now I'm going to have CSI contact you and get a set of elimination prints. I'm not going to put up with any more of this from you. If I ever see you again, I'm filing those charges." I handed her notebook back. "Good-bye."

She got into her Suburban and drove out of my life—I hoped.

On my way back to the Glass House, I got a radio call instructing me to switch to TAC-2 for a message from my C.O. Cal came on and told me that I had a "forthwith" from the chief to meet him and Alexa at the U.S. Attorney's office.

"What's cookin'?"

"Your ass. Twelfth floor, Office twelve eighty-nine."

FORTHWITH

I T TOOK A full forty minutes to get there. Two of L.A.'s enduring myths are that it's a tropical paradise and that you can get anywhere in the Basin in twenty minutes.

The U.S. Federal Annex is on Spring Street. It's a large, turn-of-the-century Greek monstrosity with a roof fresco decorated with frolicking satyrs. The winds had died down and the flags out front hung like dead pelts. I parked in the underground garage, stowed my gun in the trunk, and cleared security in the basement. Then I rode the elevator to the twelfth floor.

Federal buildings always feel musty to me. Maybe it's all that in-line thinking. The tile halls were polished, the doors dark mahogany or oiled maple, I'm not sure which. The only woods I'm good at identifying are peckerwoods.

I found Suite 1289. When I entered the reception area I heard arguing coming from the inner office. A vanilla-flavored male secretary looked at my credentials and pointed at the door. He didn't speak. Why waste your breath on lower lifeforms like city cops?

Inside the high-ceilinged room was a crowd of angry, misguided people. It was Cole Hatton's office, the U.S. Attorney for the Central District of California. He was a good-looking, dark-haired fifty-year-old with a country club tan who wore his clothes so well that I instantly distrusted him.

Bill Messenger and his area commander Paul Matthews stood on one side of the room. Garrett Metcalf and Brady Cagel were next to the windows in nicely fitted, gabardine suits, easily winning the fashion competition. Tony Filosiani and Mayor MacKenzie looked uncomfortable in the center of the room, while Alexa hovered nearby.

"This is Sergeant Scully," Tony said. I shook hands with Cole Hatton, who barely looked at me before he turned back to the mayor.

"I don't see any rationale for overturning a federal statute," he said. "The Bureau of Alcohol, Tobacco, Firearms, and Explosives should be allowed to investigate the death of one of their own. According to your own criminalists, there was C-four residue on the ashes. Illegal C-four is a mandated statute of ATF. That's basically it, unless the FBI deems that its own absence from the case would materially affect the interest of justice. That's the way the statute reads." His voice was booming in the high-ceilinged room. Everybody winced at the mention of the FBI.

"We've got a dead sheriff's deputy and some very strange circumstances surrounding the service of a warrant given to us by ATF," Messenger said. "Their Internal Affairs investigated and found no wrongdoing, but our IAD sees it differently. The county will undoubtedly face lawsuits. Since the mayor ordered the LAPD to reinvestigate, our opinion is that these cases are related, and that gives Sergeant Scully standing to investigate the Greenridge murder."

"How is the murder of William Greenridge related to Emo Rojas? That's nuts," Garrett Metcalf said hotly. "Unless you're suggesting something pretty damn unfriendly."

"Can we all calm down?" Hatton said, then crossed to his desk. "I'm going to bifurcate the investigations. LAPD can go ahead and reinvestigate the Hidden Ranch warrant problem, but ATF is going to handle their own agent homicide and the investigation into how the hell this nut got his hands on so much C-four."

"And if the two investigations overlap?" Alexa asked.

"Try and keep that from happening. Build a Chinese wall," Hatton instructed.

"Hey, if they overlap, Cole, they overlap." Now Tony was getting mad. "How'm I gonna build a Chinese wall? That's total bullshit."

"Hand over all of your tapes, photographs, forensics, ballistics, and trace evidence from the Mission Street crime scene to the ATF homicide investigators," Hatton said to Tony. "Do it before close of business today. That's it."

We all filed out of his office. The feds looked smug, the cops looked pissed, Mayor Mac, Tony, and Alexa looked dazed.

Technically speaking, the crime scene we had been ordered out of was Greenridge's house on Mission. Nobody had said anything about the apartment across the street. Of course, to be fair, they didn't even know about that yet. But if I played it carefully, and if Nan Chambers didn't blow me in on the pages of the *Valley Times* tomorrow morning, maybe I could keep us in the game. I had to call her and set up a meeting to make sure she'd play along.

The brass casing from the .308 was burning a hole in my pocket as we walked into the underground garage.

DRINKS

W E NEED TO talk," I said, stopping the two top cops before they got into their cars. Alexa had stayed upstairs with the feds to work out the details of handing over the evidence from Mission Street. I pulled out the .308 casing and showed it to Tony. He studied the brass in the cellophane evidence bag. "Looks like it's been fumed."

"It has."

I told them about finding the secondary crime scene and how I discovered the cartridge casing with Nan Chambers, then hardened the print in Billy's microwave. I finished by saying, "I locked up the apartment, but I didn't call it in or bring our crime techs out there yet. I was just about to when I got the forthwith."

Messenger was now holding the cellophane baggie with his

thumb and index finger, glaring at the casing like it was a dead cockroach he'd found in his salad. It wasn't hard to figure out what was going through the sheriff's mind. If that partial print on the shell casing matched one of his SEB SWAT members, then his department was hip high in trouble.

"We got a big problem," Tony said, his Brooklynese bubbling up. "You turn this over to ATF, first they're gonna demand you print-check all your guys, then they're gonna wanta test-fire them Tango Fifty-ones and Forty-Xs you got at SEB to see if one matches the breach and ejection striations on this brass. The sheriff's police union is gonna start throwing bricks. They'll say you got no probable cause to test those weapons, and this turns from a petty jurisdictional squabble into a shit sandwich."

Bill Messenger was still holding my cellophane evidence bag. "Okay, Tony, how do you wanta do it then?"

"It's your department, Bill. We're only investigating the warrant problem at Hidden Ranch. You wanta take on a U.S. Attorney, have at it."

"I got a compromise," Bill said. Tony listened, rocking back slightly on his heels.

"You let me put an investigator next to Shane and I'll get all my SEB long rifles tested. There won't be any union trouble. I'll do it under the radar, have the range officer take them all out for sight adjustments or something, then we'll collect the brass and look for a match. If this casing fits one of those rifles, or this print is from one of my guys, then I'll find a way to get past the union. I got no room in my outfit for killers. I'll bust 'em myself and hand the whole thing over to ATF."

"I don't want some deputy looking over my shoulder," I said, seizing only on the first thing he said and ignoring the rest.

"Shut up, Shane," Tony commanded. Then he looked at Messenger. "Okay. You get a print run started and have your SEB long guns tested and checked against this brass, and in return, Shane works with one deputy of your choosing."

"Deal," Messenger said. "And as long as all the Hidden Ranch forensic stuff is already at our crime lab, I'd like to suggest we leave it there. My criminalists are as good as yours. It'll save time."

Tony nodded his agreement. Then Bill Messenger turned to me. "Your partner is going to be Sergeant Brickhouse, one of my crack IAD investigators. You two can meet over at the sheriff's main building this afternoon at four."

"No. Your office is too far away, and I have a bunch of stuff to do on this side of the hill. Let's meet at Denny's restaurant at five. The one on Lankershim in the Valley."

"Done." Then Messenger turned, and carrying the brass casing, walked to his car.

After he drove out, I looked at Tony. "How the hell's this gonna work? I'm really supposed to investigate the Rojas shooting with some biased hump from the sheriff's rat squad?"

Tony unlocked his car, took off his coat, and threw it over the seat. "Yeah, because if I was in Messenger's position I'd feel just like him. I'd want my own investigator looking out for my interests, too. He's in a deep crack." Tony settled into his Crown Vic and turned to look at me. "We've gotta turn that secondary crime scene over to ATF," he said. "Why don't you get somebody to rediscover it? Then call the feds and give it to them."

"But we don't give 'em the shell casing I found in there? How's that work?"

"I don't know. I'll think about it and we'll reevaluate all our options as things progress. In the meantime, put this thing down fast, Shane. I don't like where it's going. If SEB and SRT are gunning for each other after work, we're all gonna end up in the bag." He put his car in gear and drove out.

I still had two hours before my meeting with Sergeant Brickhouse. As soon as I was on street level where my cell would work, I needed to make two calls: Lou Ruta and Nan Chambers. The first was going to be Ruta. I finally had a use for that angry asshole. I pulled up the ramp into a smoggy L.A. afternoon and reached for my phone. It rang before I could open it.

"Hello?" I held the unit to my ear as I drove.

"Shane? Sonny Lopez." He sounded a long way away, or we had a bad connection.

"What's up?"

"I got Chooch the coaching job. But there's a league guy you have to talk to. He's got some questions. Like, is Chooch eighteen?"

"Not quite."

"A Pop Warner head coach has to be eighteen, but I can sign up for that job and he can be what they call a demonstrator. Demonstrators in Pop Warner aren't coaches, they're guys who demonstrate to the kids how to do stuff. Technically I'll be in charge, but he'll do the head coaching job. We just don't tell anyone. There's other stuff you need to sign off on. We're meeting with this guy at six tonight."

"I can't. Got an appointment. How 'bout in the next hour or so, for drinks?"

"I'll have to call you back," Sonny said.

We hung up and I dialed Ruta. "Yeah?" he growled.

After I told him we were off the case, I told him about the windows across the street from the murder scene, and that somebody should tell the feds to check the apartments over there in case it was the shooting position.

"Whatta buncha shit," he said and hung up. I wasn't sure if he was talking about my theory or us getting bounced. Then I called the *Valley Times*. Nan Chambers was out, but I left my name and number and the message that I wanted to see her immediately.

Sonny Lopez called back fifteen minutes later. "Okay, the guy will meet you at the Boar and Bull on Ventura for drinks. Be there in twenty."

"Deal," I said.

The place was almost empty when I arrived. I moved through the darkly colorful restaurant. Stuffed boar and bull heads with glassy eyes were mounted over the bar, gazing down like hairy drunks hung on the wall to dry out.

I found my way into the back room where four members of the sheriff's department were sitting in one of the red leather booths under a big-screen TV that was playing a tape of last Sunday's Chargers game, with the sound off.

"Hey, Shane," Darren Zook called out.

I walked over. I knew them all. Darren was at one end of the booth. Next to him was Sonny Lopez, then Gary Nightingale. Rick Manos, who I remembered from their mission board was an SEB scout, sat on the far end. This was obviously not going to be about football.

Sonny said, "Want a beer?"

"Not till I know what's going on." I pulled up a free chair and straddled it, sitting at the end of the horseshoe booth so I was facing them. "So let's just get to it."

"Okay. You were Emo's friend. Word is you're the one looking into all this, so I guess we're looking to you for some cover," Sonny said.

"Cover, or cover-up?" I asked.

Rick Manos leaned forward. I'd heard about him before. Big street rep. His silent jacket said he was not a guy to mess with.

"We know you got the Greenridge homicide," Manos said. "We also know ATF is gonna try and force you to put it on my people. SEB didn't kill that guy, piece of shit that he was."

"Okay, here's my take on that," I said. "I don't know whether SEB popped Billy Greenridge, or if he was shot by some old peckerwood bust of his who crawled out of the woodpile at Vacaville, looking for payback. But it doesn't matter what I think anymore, 'cause ATF Title-Eighteened us. They've got it now, so if you got a problem talk to the nutsacks over at Justice. But I'll tell you this much, if I was still involved I'd put your request on the record and you'd all lose pay and grade."

"You're taking this the wrong way," Lopez said.

"How is that, Sonny? You guys just asked me to throw an investigation."

"We didn't kill Billy Greenridge," Manos said. His voice was soft, but I could hear the anger. "We just look good for it and everybody wants this thing put down fast."

"I'm sure if you lay back everything will turn out fine." I started to get up and Rick Manos and Gary Nightingale stood with me. Each took one of my arms to keep me from leaving. "You sure this is the way you want to play it?" I said softly.

They hesitated, then let go.

"Shane, they killed Emo," Sonny said. "They sent him up there without knowing what he was walking into. Why isn't anybody investigating that?"

"They are," I said.

"Yeah? And just who's doing that?" Manos said.

"Me. I'm looking into it for Sheriff Messenger and Mayor Mac."

"LAPD?" Nightingale said, but his face clouded with disbelief, as if I'd just said the Girl Scouts of America were working the case.

"I'm not gonna bend the warrant investigation either," I went on. "I'm gonna do it straight up, and my advice to you guys is to back up and hit neutral. Proactive behavior is just gonna make things worse."

"What if their SRT team decides to even the score?" Gary Nightingale said. "We didn't pop Greenridge, but they think we did. What if they snipe at one of us next?"

"That's why you guys get the extra-thick Kevlar," I said, and stepped back from the table.

"You were supposed to be Emo's friend," Lopez said.

"I was his friend, and I know if it had been one of us up there on the porch instead of him, Emo would never be asking for stuff like this." Then I looked directly at Sonny. "And thanks for using my son to lure me out with all that bullshit about Pop Warner. Next time you want to have a police meeting, call my office and make a regular appointment."

"Here." Sonny reached down on the seat beside him, picked up a thick blue binder, and slid it across the table toward me. "That's the play book for the Rams and the rule book for the league. The guy you've gotta call's number is in there."

As I reached for it Rick Manos grabbed my arm and held it. When he looked up at me, his eyes were as dark and empty as two gun barrels.

"If the shit jumps off, be sure you've got a side to be on," he warned.

RATS

A**T FIVE O'CLOCK** I was waiting for Sergeant Brickhouse in a back booth at Denny's, the Pop Warner binder sat unopened on the seat beside me. I was still angry about the meeting at the Boar and Bull. I'd expected much more from those guys. I sat with a cup of coffee, trying to calm down while a growing dissatisfaction with my role in police work festered.

I guess what pissed me off most was how over the years situations like this had forced my expectations down and made me question everything I had once believed in. When I joined the force we were Blue Knights, protectors of the innocent. Centurions. I had worn my uniform with pride, but without realizing why, things had started to change, and I had slowly lost my point of view.

I remember the first time somebody spit on my black-and-white. I was only about three years on the job, still in a uniform, working a neighborhood car in Van Nuys. It was a heavily Hispanic area and a ten-year-old *vatito* ran up while we were at a stop sign and hocked a lugie. It hit and ran down the squad car's windshield. The boy flipped us off, then took off running. My partner said the next time he saw that *flaquito,* he'd slap him silly. I had another reaction. I was angry, sure, but also I wanted that boy to know I was out there in the streets for him. If he needed me I was his backup. Instead, he only saw somebody to despise.

The same thing happened again six months later, when I was working an L-car in Carson. I had parked the unit, and this old African-American woman with her arms full of groceries spit on the windshield of my empty Plain-Jane. I came out of a coffee shop just as she did it and caught her. She started yelling curses at me. If somebody had tried to mug her, I was prepared to risk my life to stop it. She didn't understand that my job was to protect and serve *her.*

Of course, I also knew that in her eyes I didn't exist. As a man, I was invisible. All she saw was the uniform, and it was a symbol of something she hated. What distressed me was that this virulent hatred spanned fifty years and two ethnic boundaries, from that ten-year-old Hispanic boy in Van Nuys, to the black grandmother in Carson.

Rodney King and the O.J. case were part of it. The Rampart scandal put it in overdrive. We were not Blue Knights to some of these citizens, but a gang in blue—thugs with life-and-death power, who kicked ass, took names, and didn't care if we got it right, as long as we got it down. Hook'm, book'm, and cook'm. A bad bust probably just takes another guilty asshole off the street, so don't sweat it. It was the total collapse of an idea I once treasured.

Years ago I thought I should make a difference. Be a one-man cleanup crew. One afternoon I spotted the same old woman carrying groceries in Carson and I followed her home. I guessed her age was about sixty, but she looked almost a hundred. When I knocked on her door she opened it to the length of the chain lock. Our emotional and intellectual view of each other was as narrow as that inch-wide slit.

"Go away," she said, seeing my uniform. "They all dead." Then she slammed the door.

Two days later, while I was patrolling the same area, I saw her again. She was struggling with an especially large armload of packages. Her ankles were swollen, her face shiny with sweat as she toiled along. I rolled up beside her, got out, and opened my squad car door. "Can I give you a ride home, Ma'am?" I asked.

She stood at the side of the curb and looked at me with contempt. "I told you, they all dead," she said, exasperated. "You killed ever' one. Now you think I be gettin' in dat damn *po*-lice car?"

"But I didn't kill them," I said. "I never met them."

"You *po*-lice, ain't ya? Two boys and one baby girl—my grandchildren, all dead, shot by *po*-lice." And then she spat again, this time on me. I felt it spray across my face and run down into my collar.

I got back into my car, drove half a block away and parked. I was shaken by the incident. I didn't know why the police had shot her grandchildren or even if they had a valid reason. But I knew it didn't matter. A valid reason or a legal justification wouldn't change the hatred in that woman's ancient, yellow eyes. I could have carried her groceries twice a week for the rest of my life and it wouldn't begin to make up for those three dead children.

Protect and Serve. I tried to live up to that increasingly difficult motto. But I was flawed. I was vulnerable to anger and ego like everyone else. I had emotional prejudice and a parochial moral view, which I tried to overcome. On the street, I tried to be color-blind and situation-neutral. Yet, with each passing year I became more fatigued by the effort.

I would have given a year's pay to have that old woman forgive me for the deaths of three children I never even knew, and that puzzled me. Why should it be so important? Why should I invest so deeply in something I wasn't a part of and couldn't change?

But I did. I guess somewhere deep down I still needed my uniform to validate me. Maybe I needed it for identity or for a sense of belonging. Maybe I had chosen to be a cop because I respected the values in the manual; and when all those values got skewed I didn't have the guts to get off the ride. I still wanted to do the right thing. I still wanted the people I served to know I cared. But more and more, nobody cared if I cared. I had been absorbed into the mix, unable to rise above the perceptions of others. Now I feared SEB and SRT were on a course that would only make it worse, and that was what was darkening my mood and ruining my day.

I looked up as Nan Chambers walked into the restaurant. She saw me and headed in my direction on those strong muscular legs, her cut arms swinging, spiky hair bristling, turning heads all over the room as she crossed toward me.

"Your office told me you were going to be here," she said, answering my unspoken question like a gypsy mind reader.

"We need to come to an understanding," I said. "You can't write about that crime scene we found across the street, at least not yet. That's gotta stay between us, Nan. And if you left any prints at that apartment, get ready for a visit from the feds."

"I didn't leave any prints," she said, and slid uninvited into the booth across from me.

Then she reached into her purse and pulled out a leather wallet, opened it, and slid it across the table. I read:

SGT. JOSEPHINE BRICKHOUSE

LASD

Pinned under the creds was a star.

BRICK SHITHOUSE

DON'T TAKE IT so hard," Jo Brickhouse said. She had just repacked her badge and was leaning her muscled forearms on the table. "Besides, from what I've seen so far, you could use the help."

"I don't want any help. At least, not from you."

"Scully, we live in a democracy. Tony, Bill, and I say yes. You say no. This was voted on. Three against one. You lose. Get over it."

"That's not a vote, that's three coyotes and a poodle deciding on what to have for dinner."

I put a dollar down for my coffee, then got up and headed out of the restaurant. I didn't see her green Suburban parked in the lot, so I turned and looked through Denny's front window. She was still inside buying something at the counter. I got into my

Acura feeling completely sandbagged. I'm generally not this damn gullible. I guess my feelings were hurt, or my pride—something.

She came through the swinging door of Denny's, opened my passenger side, and slid in carrying a caffe latte to go.

"Take your own car. I'm not a taxi service," I snapped.

"I was dropped. Don't have wheels. That SUV was a department plain-wrap. Vice needed it back, so I'm with you. You can drop me at the L.A. substation at EOW."

She closed the door, slamming it harder than I like, then started to pour about six packets of Equal into her latte. "Okay, Scully, we need to get something straight before we partner up. I have some issues."

"I'll bet lying isn't gonna be one of them."

"I'm gay. I don't sleep with guys, and you're not the priceless piece of ass that's gonna change that, so put your fantasies away, stay on your side of the car, and we'll do fine."

"Then a blow job's out of the question?"

"You can stow that sarcastic bullshit. I've been in law enforcement for over ten years. I've learned it works a whole lot better if I get this out of the way, up front. I pack a nine-millimeter Glock with thirteen in the clip. I'm a range-qualified sharpshooter and I have two black belts, one in karate, one in tae kwon do. Just because I'm a woman doesn't mean I'm a pussy. I don't want to be your backup. We can take turns on cover, or flip for it, whatever. But I'm not your CHCO."

"My what?"

"Coat-holder and communications officer."

"In case you're interested, you're coming off like a complete asshole."

"I can be that, too. But deal straight and you get the best. Pull any horseshit, and you can go ahead and bring it on down, frog-boy, 'cause I won't put up with it." Then she shot me that dazzling smile and took a sip of latte. "These are good. Sure you don't want one?"

I put the car in reverse and backed out a little too fast, but she was really pissing me off. Male pride. I mean, I'm happily married, but come on—you shouldn't knock what you haven't tried. I turned onto Lankershim and drove toward the sheriff's forensic lab.

Jo Brickhouse was looking around the front seat and up on the dash. "Where's your murder book on Greenridge?" she asked. "You didn't give those goat-fucks from ATF your notes, did you?"

"No murder book."

"You're the primary on a homicide and you don't keep a murder book?" She sounded stunned.

"Yeah, I would've been keeping a murder book, but I was pulled off the case before I had time to get most of my evidence back from your slow-as-shit crime lab."

"You don't have to take that tone, Scully. I wasn't criticizing. I just like to keep everything written down: keep a good event timeline, evidence records, crime scene photos, background. I'll get one going. For now, we can use my notes." She pulled out her spiral pad.

"But you're not going to be my secretary, I bet."

"Sure, I've got no problem pushing some pencil lead. But let's do it right." She opened her notebook and tore out three pages. "This lecture on latent prints was simply fascinating. You want it, or can it go in the file?"

"I know a better place you can stick it."

"Temper, temper," she said, and wadded up the papers and dropped them in the back seat.

We drove in silence for six blocks. I snuck another look at her. There was a lot of animal magnetism there. In retrospect, I could see why she needed to get her personal proclivities on the line up front. She'd undoubtedly had to deal with her share of squad-car Romeos. I tried to settle down, make the best of it. Finally she finished her coffee, slurping the last drop, then she just pitched the damn cup into the back seat with the three wadded-up sheets of notebook paper.

"This is not a department car. I'd appreciate it if you didn't throw your litter in the back."

"Sorry."

She hitched herself around and leaned over the seat. She was in a miniskirt, and for a minute she was poking a well-developed ass up in the air, nearly mooning the next car over. The driver did a double take. For my part, I almost hit a taxi. She sat back, put the cup on the seat between us, and stuffed my dumb-ass fingerprint lecture in her purse.

"Sorry about the short skirt. I was doing field interviews today. Sometimes it helps to show a little leg. Tomorrow I'll be in class-C stuff."

"Whatever that is."

"Sheriff's department dress code for plain clothes dicks. Excuse the expression."

We drove in silence for another minute or two. "So, Scully," she finally said. "Where the hell are we going?"

"Bill Messenger took our bullet, that three-oh-eight casing, out to your forensics lab for a print scan and tool marks. I figure, since you pack a star you can get the techs out there to give us a sneak peek."

"This is probably good thinking," she said, then settled back in her seat.

But to be truthful, even the way she said that was pissing me off—like she was validating a surprising idea from a total blockhead. Then she hitched sideways on the seat, snapping her short skirt down. All her movements were athletic and a little too big. She was a muscular girl who took up slightly more space than I was accustomed to.

"So, I had time to check you out before Messenger sent me to meet you," she said. "You're married to your division commander. I've seen her on the news and once at a cross-training day for detectives, out at our SWAT range at Spring Ranch. Damn fine package."

I looked over, not sure what to make of that. Finally I nodded and said, "I think so."

"Look, Shane, I'll give you the keys to the kingdom here, the Rosetta Stone for our partnership."

I waited. What do you say to shit like that?

"I have no hidden agendas, no back-channel dog wash. Like Popeye, 'I yam what I yam.'" Then she smiled. "So don't get your shorts in a bunch just because I want to lay out some ground rules. You got any stuff you want out there, let it fly."

I didn't have to ask my friends at the sheriff's what Sergeant Brickhouse's department nickname was.

Had to be Brick Shithouse.

I found out later I was right.

THE "OLD" CRIME LAB

THE SHERIFF'S SEVENTY-FIVE-YEAR-OLD crime lab is just east of Hollywood in a run-down three-story building near Elysian Park. The place is on its last legs. Since the department has already broken ground on its new, $96 million forensics facility next to the M.E.'s building on the L.A. State campus, this pile of bricks was not getting much attention. When I pulled into the parking lot I spotted deferred maintenance everywhere I looked. The cream-color paint was peeling off brick siding. Cracked asphalt and faded, white hash marks lined the parking lot. Weeds grew in the landscaping.

But this was still where most crimes were solved. The ultimate revenge of the nerds, where geeks caught cheats. It encompassed all the major crime sections: firearms, biology, DNA, trace evidence, and identifications. In this high-volume facility,

LASD criminalists juggled seventy-five thousand pieces of evidence each year, as the criminal justice system chugged merrily along. Getting moved to the head of the line was normally a futile exercise in this overworked battleground of egos and priorities, but our shell casing had been personally hand delivered by the big boss, Bill Messenger, so my guess was, under these circumstances, we'd be first up.

Jo and I had not spoken for almost half the ride over. She sat beside me, looking out the side window, content to say nothing. Silence can be a weapon in the front seat of a police car. I wasn't sure what game we were playing yet.

I parked in a visitor's space. We got out and she pushed ahead of me through the double glass doors into the crime lab.

"You have an evidence number?" she demanded.

"No, but it came in here through Bill Messenger."

"That oughta have Doctor Chuck E. Cheese sitting up pretty straight," she said, then went to a visitor phone in the empty lobby and dialed a number.

I looked around while she talked to somebody in the back. The place really needed help. The linoleum had turned black and was peeling up across the room, exposing the wood flooring underneath. It looked like somebody delivering a gallon of acid base had dropped the load. But I guess it's hard to spend money on a building that you know is going to be bulldozed in twelve months.

"Scully, you're with me," Jo barked, sounding like my old Marine Corps drill sergeant. A security lock buzzed and she held the door open as we entered.

"Latents got a four-point hit," she said. "They already sent the brass up to tool marks to graph the striations and impressed action marks. When we found that casing yesterday it looked to me like it also had some pretty good breech and pin impressions."

She was showing off now. I was tempted to say "Fuck you," but, gentleman that I am, I only muttered, "Bite me."

She smiled, pushed past, and led the way. "Latent Prints is down here."

We walked down a narrow corridor, past the weapons library and lab. Through the glass doors, I could see thousands of rifles and handguns of every known manufacturer locked behind metal bars in the armory. These guns could be used to match firing patterns on weapons seized or placed in evidence. They could also be shown to witnesses for the purpose of firearm identification.

We continued past the GSR and footprint lab, a notorious grunt station for newbies. The youngest criminalists were stuck in there doing footprint analysis or using the electron microscope to perform gunshot residue tests. Then we passed a room housing the protein base analyzer that charted DNA profiles, also known as electropherograms. Next, down the hall was a trace evidence lab devoted to hair and fiber. There was a lot of state-of-the-art equipment in this crumbling facility.

At the end of the corridor Sergeant Brickhouse swept into the fingerprint bay. The room was empty. Blown-up photographs of fingerprints were pinned up everywhere. Two long benches containing print photographs in labled boxes were pushed against the walls. There was a large, overstuffed chair in the corner. Jo turned around and glanced out into the hall, looking for the criminalist.

"Chuck oughta be down in a minute. On the phone a minute ago, he told me he was just going to check on our print upstairs. They ran our latent through the federal print index."

We stood in the lab with the silence between us growing painfully.

"Answer me one thing," I said to break the awkward spell.

"Shoot."

"Did Bill Messenger instruct you to investigate the Hidden Ranch thing? Is that why you were up at Smiley's burned-out house poking around, and over in the apartment on Mission Street?"

"I've been sworn to secrecy," she deadpanned.

"Only, when I partner up with somebody there can be no secrets."

"Scully, grow up. I'm not telling you what I've been ordered not to, but use your imagination."

"Okay. So Messenger had you up there even after he promised the mayor and Tony he'd leave it in my hands?"

"I don't wanta talk about this. Let's just move on, okay?"

I was about to tear her a new asshole, when into the room waddled the fattest, baldest, young man I had ever seen. He even made Ruta look svelte. His appearance was made even worse by his wardrobe. He had on an oversized, bilious, lime-colored Hawaiian shirt that flapped around the thighs of his frayed, tent-like jeans. The effect was startling. His head looked like a pale, medicine ball sitting atop a mountain of green Jell-O.

Jo said hi and introduced me. "Shane Scully, meet Doctor Charles Gouda."

Charles Gouda—Dr. Chuck E. Cheese. Got it.

He lowered himself carefully into the overstuffed chair, letting out a long sigh as he dropped.

"Just got back the run from the federal print index," he said. "Nada. But it was pretty thin to begin with. Only four identifiers."

He leaned over and picked up a photograph of the print, then showed it to us. "Whoever fumed this thing saved the print, but with round surfaces like shell casings we rarely get a full ten point match anyway." Chuck pointed to the photograph with his pen. "What it comes down to is, you got two pretty good typicals here, a good core and an okay whorl, half an isle up here. This tent arch ain't too bad. Basically, it's pretty low-yield. Call it four and a half points to be generous. Since it's a sole index finger, there's not enough here for the federal computer. If I had a comparison print to put next to it I could get some eyeballs on it and give you an opinion, but nothing you'd want to take in front of our awesome denizens of justice. In court, you need at least six out of ten identifiers or the defense is gonna feed it to you."

Then, to make that gastronomic point absolutely clear, he belched.

"How long till tool marks is finished?" I asked.

Doctor Gouda belched again, this time more delicately, catching the burp in his baseball mitt of a hand. He opened his desk drawer and took out a half-eaten sandwich. It looked like tomatoes and anchovies, which, in my opinion, ranks right up there with shit on a bun. He took a bite, frowned, then threw it in the trash.

After all that I really wasn't expecting an answer, but I got one anyway.

"Beats me," Doctor Chuck E. Cheese said through an ugly mouthful of chewed fish.

MIJARES RESTAURANT

I MET CHOOCH, Alexa, and Delfina at Mijares Restaurant for dinner. Chooch's sports-injury doctor was in Pasadena, and Mijares is one of the best Mexican restaurants on the east end of the L.A. Basin. I arrived last and was led to their table out on an enclosed patio. Chooch was wearing a new white cast and a glum look.

I kissed my wife, said hi to Chooch and Del, then dropped into a wood-backed chair and ordered a double margarita. Long day, so screw it. In the other room was a ranchedo duet, two guitarists in traditional dress, picking *Malagueña Salerosa* on humpbacked Martins.

"I see you didn't get the plaster off," I said.

"Nope." Chooch was staring morosely down at a Coke on

the placemat in front of him. Delfina reached out and took his hand.

"But the doctor said in a week, maybe," she explained. "It's coming along good. The bone is almost healed."

Chooch nodded bleakly, as if the idea that his foot would ever mend was just too far away to grasp.

I had the Pop Warner League book with me, and I looked at Delfina and gave her a little eyebrow raise. A silent question. She nodded, so I laid the blue binder on the table, then pushed it over to him. I had called the league on the way over and had received some additional information.

"What's that?" Chooch asked.

"Pop Warner League rule book. You're good to go if you want the gig. Emo's team, the Rams, is in the Junior Bantam division." Chooch was looking down despondently at the binder, so I added: "That's twelve through fourteen. The kids can be in the hundred-fifteen- to hundred-sixty-pound range at the beginning of the season, which was August, but nobody can weigh more than one-sixty-nine by the end of the season in December. As of late, they've been holding workouts, but with no head coach they had to forfeit their last game."

Chooch opened the book and stared at the front page. Then, with no enthusiasm, he started flipping through it. Delfina frowned, as Alexa and I traded looks.

"*¿Que haces tu?*" Delfina said angrily. "We talked about this. You said you wanted to do it for Emo Rojas. Now your father has made it happen and you sit here like a troll on a rock."

"Okay, okay," he said and put the book on the floor by his feet.

"Honey, if you don't want to coach the team, don't coach it," Alexa said. "It's not going to help these kids to have a coach who doesn't want to be there."

"You guys—you don't . . ." Chooch stopped, then put his head down. "Forget it."

"Do you want me to talk to your coach?" I asked. "Make sure it's okay with him? Is that what you're worried about?"

"No, Coach Norris said it was fine. He even said he'd look at the playbook and help me with some revisions if I wanted."

"So, what's the problem?"

"It's like . . ." He paused, then took a deep breath. "It's like, by agreeing to do this, I'm saying my season is over. Maybe my college career with it."

"These Pop Warner teams play on Saturday or Sunday. Harvard-Westlake plays Friday nights. Once your foot heals, you go back on your team and set the Pop Warner practices to fit your schedule," I said.

"I know, it's just . . ."

"Then, don't do it, son," I interrupted. "Mom's right. You have to want to."

"I'll do it, okay? I said I'd do it, so I will."

But he sure didn't sound happy about it.

Then our conversation turned to Delfina's *West Side Story* rehearsals. She was excited and animated as she told us about the full run-through with music. Chooch remained strangely quiet while she talked.

■ ■ ■

When we got home I went to my office and booted up my PC. Then I typed in Cactus West.

A few seconds later a welcome screen came up. There was a window for a password. I punched in: *MCAS Yuma TACTS*

A message popped up:

> Access denied. This is a U.S. Marine Corps secure site. Your computer will be scanned if you attempt to reenter.

I logged off and was still frowning at the screen when Franco yowled to tell me he hadn't been fed. I took him into the kitchen and fixed his dinner while Chooch and Delfina sat in the back-yard. She was talking hard at him.

Alexa and I decided to take a walk around the neighborhood to avoid the fallout of what looked like the beginnings of a teenage quarrel. We strolled along the walkways that bordered the canal. The wedge-cut quarter moon hung low in the night sky. It lit the water and turned the mist-wet edges of the houses and garden gates silver. A late-feeding hell-diver took off out of the water, startling us. He beat his wings savagely, disappearing into the sky.

"I talked to Tony and Bill this afternoon," Alexa said. "Bill is going to free up your request with his people at CSI. They're going out to Hidden Ranch sometime tomorrow afternoon to look for the dog's remains and check on that basement bomb shelter." She said it like she thought it was a complete waste of county time.

"I'm not scoring too many points in this family tonight, am I?" I said.

"It's just, you know how badly this is setting up. The sooner we clear it the better. I won't lie to you. I'm getting a lot of pres-sure, and I think checking Smiley's background and that house isn't going to get us anywhere, but I'm through arguing about it. It's your investigation, so it's your call."

"In that case, can I get you to find out what's on this Web site?" I handed her a slip of paper with 'CACTUS WEST MCAS YUMA TACTS' printed on it. "It's some kind of Marine Corps secure site that Smiley hacked into. If we can't find out through the mayor's office, maybe the geeks in our computer division can see if they could hack into it." She didn't say anything, but wrinkled her nose and put the slip in her pocket.

We walked over and stood on one of the arched bridges that spanned the main canal. I told Alexa that we had a partial print on the shell casing from the apartment, but that it was smudged, with maybe only four identifiers, and that tool marks would look for a match on striations after Sheriff Messenger had his SEB long rifles fired.

She nodded and we both looked across the water at our house. Delfina and Chooch were still sitting in the yard, heads together, talking earnestly.

"So, how's your new partner Joe Brickhouse?" Alexa finally asked, changing to a better subject.

"She's—different," I said.

"She? *Joe* is a girl?"

"Not in the traditional sense."

"Is she pretty?"

"Very. But she kills that impression effectively, because she's the most opinionated, in-your-face partner I think I've ever had. Present company excluded."

"I don't like this. I know how drawn you are to strong women," she teased.

"And she's gay," I said. "Apparently, I'm not the priceless piece of ass that's going to change that, either."

"I feel better already," Alexa said and held my hand.

"But *you* might qualify. She thinks you're 'a damn fine package,' or something to that effect. She's also a control freak. I'm biting my tongue trying to keep from tangling with her, but it may require more self-discipline than I possess."

We stood quietly for a long moment. Suddenly a fish surfaced. It's tail slapped the water as it swam away. Both Alexa and I looked down at the spot below us, but our scaly eavesdropper was long gone.

"Look, Shane, this is what Sheriff Messenger wants, so having her for a partner is a small price to pay. If he can test fire his SEB long rifles and prove that the casing didn't come from any of their firearms, then we've gone a long way toward settling all this down."

"Right," I said. "And if it did come from one of his long guns, then I have only one question."

"What's that?"

"Who do I have to fuck to get off this damn case?"

"Me," she said, then smiled sexily.

PAYBACK

IT WAS FINALLY cooling off in Los Angeles. By evening the temperature had begun to dip down into the fifties, but around midnight, with an abrupt barometric change, the hot Santa Ana winds had started up again, blowing out of the desert, flaring allergies and tempers. Alexa and I were both sprawled on top of the blankets as the pre-dawn temperature in our bedroom climbed into the mid-seventies. Alexa had been restless, constantly turning over, unable to sleep. The ringing phone brought me up out of a semiconscious steambath. I fumbled it off the hook and glanced at the bedside clock. A few minutes past three in the morning. Alexa said something unfriendly and turned over again as I pushed the receiver against my ear and muttered my name.

"Scully? We're on," a female voice commanded. It took me a minute to get there, but then I realized it was Jo Brickhouse.

"It's three A.M.," I snarled. But as consciousness returned I began to realize she probably wouldn't be calling at this hour unless it was pretty important.

Just then, Alexa's beeper went off and shot a bolt of adrenaline through me. *Uh-oh. Something was definitely up.*

Alexa grabbed her pager off the bedside table. "Damn," she said, reading the LCD screen, "Tony."

"What's going on, Jo?" I asked, pulling my head further out of the vat of oatmeal I keep it in when I sleep.

"Spotter on the SEB Gray team just ate a round. Guy's name is Michael Nightingale. Same basic deal. Vertical coffin—dead on the back porch. This should be our case, 'cause he's a sheriff, and there's a damn good chance now it's connected to the Rojas killing, but the way this is falling, who knows? The FBI could even claim it."

"Right. Title Eighteen. 'Unless the FBI's absence from the case materially effects the course of justice,' or something."

"Get your ass out to two four six Sherman Way, Van Nuys. It's LAPD turf, so for now, we're up. Take the Cahuenga off-ramp, it's quicker. And let's see some smoke. I'm already rolling."

"Right." When I hung up Alexa was on the cordless phone with Tony and was walking into the bathroom, talking as she went. I scissor-kicked out of bed and followed her. As I walked in Alexa finished her call and pushed the hang-up button on the handset. She grabbed her hair brush, ran it through her hair once, then threw it on the counter. So much for grooming.

"Nightingale?" I asked.

"Yep. Michael. Spotter for his brother Gary on SEB."

"I know."

"Tony wants me downtown. Since Nightingale's a sheriff, he's got Bill Messenger on the way in. It's in our jurisdiction, so unless Messenger says otherwise, it's our one eighty-seven. Yours, Sergeant Brickhouse's, and Ruta's."

I was already in my Jockeys. Alexa scooped up her panties and was hopping on one foot as she put them on. Then she grabbed her bra and headed into the bedroom. I skinned into a pair of dirty jeans I had thrown into the laundry hamper, stepped into some loafers—not bothering with socks—then went into the bedroom and threw on yesterday's shirt and jacket.

"Do I really have this, or am I gonna go out there, stand over a corpse, and wrestle with a buncha feds over whose case it is, like last time?"

Alexa had on a mismatched outfit. She was taking no care with her appearance, which was unusual. Suddenly, she stopped buttoning her blouse and turned to face me. "Shane, I don't have to tell you, this is the worst thing that could have happened. Amps up everything. It's going to be a national news story now. No way to stop it. There'll be reporters hanging from the trees. Geraldo will be on the front lawn interviewing neighbors."

"Look, Alexa . . . I—"

"No. Listen. If this is two SWAT teams going at it, we've got to stop it now. You've gotta find some physical evidence, the bullet or the cartridge casing, a print, something. In the meantime I'm gonna search these two SWAT houses, bring ten or twelve sheriffs and ATF agents into custody, and hold 'em until this is sorted out."

"You can't do that without a helluva lot more evidence than we have now."

"Stop arguing with me," she said hotly.

"Alexa, you're not thinking straight."

"You want these people out on the streets after work, rolling around in SWAT vans, trying to pick each other off?"

"Of course not. But you can't arrest people without evidence."

"I can hold them for forty-eight hours without charging them."

"Cops? No chance. You try that and the U.S. Attorney will take this right out from under us and give it to the FBI. Plus, you're gonna fire up all the rank and file from both agencies. Then come the lawyers, the unions, and the network news."

"Then get me something I can use. Fast."

As I looked at her I saw something I'd never seen before. She was frightened. Unlike me, Alexa had never had a crisis of conscience on the job. She believed in a set of rules that had always served her. But this didn't fit any of them. Nobody had ever seen fit to spit on my beautiful wife. But now she was living her worst nightmare. She believed in the system, and the system was spinning out of control. This was the total collapse of another treasured idea. She wasn't thinking straight, she wasn't sleeping, and I could see confusion in her eyes. She wasn't sure how to deal with it, or even if she had the skill. It worried me.

"You gonna be okay?" I asked.

"Just get me something. I need some leverage," she said, and turned around looking for her shoes.

I grabbed my gun and tin and took off toward my car, pausing in Chooch's makeshift bedroom to tell him that his mom and I were being called out. He rolled over in bed, rubbed his eyes, and nodded. He'd seen this before. Then I exited through the side door, jumped into the Acura, and peeled out.

God only knew what would happen next.

NIGHTINGALES

THERE WERE FOUR police cars and three media vans parked in front of the neat, one-story ranch-style house in a *Leave It to Beaver* neighborhood in Van Nuys. Nobody had bothered to tape off a staging area yet. The street was wide open, and as I got out of my car another news van rolled in and three crew types hit the street and started unpacking video equipment.

The crime scene was alive with spectators. I saw a lot of strained looks and hidden agendas. If Jo Brickhouse hadn't been screwing up her end so badly I would have enjoyed watching her trying to handle this angry mess, but there were already half a dozen people on the porch standing over the body. I saw two TV news teams and a print photographer walking around inside the house shooting tape with their sun-guns on. Like the Morning News with Ken and Barbie needed to be in there handling evidence and getting shots of the widow crying in the den.

Adding to the emotion and hyperbole were Rick Manos, the SEB Gray team scout, and his long gun, Gary Nightingale, who was sitting on the corner of the porch crying, holding his dead sibling's hand. To her credit, Jo Brickhouse was trying to move all the extra people out, but this thing had already lifted off. Brady Cagel and his band of feds hadn't put in an appearance yet. *Interesting,* I thought. *Why not?*

I pulled Jo Brickhouse aside. "You're missing a sure bet here. You should be selling tickets."

"What am I supposed to do, physically throw these assholes off the porch?"

"Exactly. You're a woman, not a pussy, remember?" While she was turning a few more shades of red, I stepped up and took Rick Manos by the arm.

"Get your people off this porch," I ordered.

"This isn't your case, it's ours." He snatched his arm back.

"I'm through with that shit," I replied. "You're SWAT, I'm homicide. You don't know how to work a murder. Look at the mess you've already got here. Besides, this is inside L.A. city limits, and Sergeant Brickhouse from your department is on it, so get your people out of here."

"We told you this was gonna happen, but you wouldn't listen!" Rick said hotly.

I didn't like the way he was facing me, too ready, too close to the edge. He killed people for a living and wasn't used to getting pushed around. I decided the best way to handle him was to put him to work.

"You wanta do something worthwhile, get those damn newsies out of the house. Who let them in?"

Manos looked at me, trying to decide if he was going to answer. Finally he shrugged. "I don't know. Barbara Nightingale probably. They were here when we arrived." But he still didn't move—not sure he wanted to take an order from me, even a good one.

"If you want me to solve Michael's murder, get all the civilians out of there. We gotta bolt this puppy down. Come on, help me out. You know this is fucked."

He nodded and started inside.

"Hey Rick," I said, and he stopped. "Take Gary with you. Give him something to do other than leak DNA all over his brother's body."

Rick looked down at the SEB long gun, who had tears streaming down his face. Then he went over and gently took hold of Gary's arm.

"Let's go Gar, okay? We gotta help clear out this house," he said. "Then you should go sit with Barbara."

The two of them went into the house and I heard voices raised in anger, but the blow-dries inside weren't a match for Manos and Nightingale.

Just then two more of our black-and-whites and a fourth TV news van rolled in. Jo Brickhouse was heading toward me, shaking her head in frustration. I stopped her.

"Get a patrol car blocking each end of the street and move all those news vans and press cars at least a block away. Tape off a staging area out front."

She took off and I grabbed one of our uniforms. His nameplate identified him as S. Berg. "You wanta help me, Officer Berg?" He nodded. "Get a notebook and start an incident log and crime-scene attendance sheet. Nobody gets past you without signing in. Start with me. I'm Scully, three forty-five A.M."

He pulled out a spiral pad, wrote my name down, and I signed it.

"Get everybody who was inside, including civilians. Depending on how this goes, we may need to contact all of them later for elimination prints."

It took us almost ten minutes to clear the house. It really

pisses me off when news crews arrive at a crime scene ahead of us, but the midnight stringers and late shift newsrooms ride the police frequencies. Because they have mobile units all over town, they can often get to the meat ahead of us.

I had a murder once, right after I joined South Bureau Homicide, where I arrived at the crime scene and couldn't find the body. There were twenty people in the murdered guy's apartment: neighbors, friends, TV, and print news. I'm looking all over the place, and I can't find the vic. Finally I asked the person who called it in where the body was. "In the bedroom," this guy tells me. So I go back in there and I still can't find it. I start thinking *I don't believe this! Somebody stole the damned corpse.*

Then I hear a news photographer in the bathroom firing off stills with a motorized camera. So I go in there and ask him, "You seen the dead guy anywhere around?" And now I'm feeling like a complete yahoo.

"Yeah," this asshole tells me. "I finished taking pictures in there and the body was kinda grossing me out, so I rolled him under the bed."

Amazing.

Finally I had the crime scene locked down and Officer Berg taking names at the door. Nobody could find Lou Ruta. He wasn't answering his pager, but Beverly King called in and reported that she was five minutes out, so I waited for her before I started.

When she arrived Jo kept the other cops off the porch, while Beverly and I took Mrs. Nightingale into a spare bedroom. After we calmed her down we took her preliminary statement. She told us that Michael had been on call last night, so she had taken the kids out to a movie. When she got home she came in the front door, didn't see her husband, and figured he was still at work. She went to bed, but woke up at two. Michael was still not home, so she called the squad and found out that he had gone EOW three hours earlier. She started to worry and began looking around, and finally found him head-shot on the back porch. She managed to get the kids to a neighbor, then called it in.

Basically, she knew nothing. Heard and saw nothing.

It's SOP in all homicides to regard the spouse as a prime suspect until the facts prove otherwise. But the truth was, Barbara Nightingale looked and sounded legit to me. Still, I couldn't let my suspicion that this was done by a bunch of angry commandos at SRT color my thinking. I had to keep all options open; collect information and evidence with no preconceived bias.

Alexa was right. This was going to be huge—a media frenzy. I had only Jo and Beverly to assist me, and neither had much homicide experience. I could use more help.

When I walked back into the living room I asked Beverly King, "So, where's Ruta? Think he's ever gonna show?" Even though he was a jerk, at least he was an experienced one.

Beverly shrugged, probably relieved that her partner was MIA, but came to his defense anyway. "Maybe his pager batteries are dead." Which is sort of the adult equivalent of the dog ate my homework.

Sergeant Brickhouse was starting to direct the forensic techs onto the porch, so I went outside to stop her.

"Let's just hold off on all that for a minute. I don't want anybody to touch anything for a while."

"Why?" she argued. "We need to get on this. Bag and tag the vic, get a liver temperature to establish time of death, search for trace evidence."

"Just calm down for a minute, okay?"

"I don't work for you, Scully," she said angrily. "You don't outrank me either."

I pulled her off the porch, holding her muscled arm. She was hard to move—big and strong. I led her out of earshot of Beverly King and the CSI techs. We stood in the backyard, ten or twelve yards away.

"Let the fuck go of me," she said. "I don't . . ."

"Work for me, I know. But how 'bout working *with* me?" She glowered, but I charged ahead. "How much time did you spend in homicide before you went to IAD?"

"That's not the point. I'm here at the direct request of Sheriff Messenger, Enrique Salazar, and the county supervisors. My department has a lot at stake now. This dead officer was ours. I'm your jurisdiction on this shooting," she said hotly.

"This isn't the time or place to have it out, but I'm damned tired of fighting with you for control of the wheel. We need some guidelines."

"Here's a guideline! Stop trying to tell me what to do."

"I've done over a hundred homicides. I have a way I do it. Why don't you take advantage of that, instead of resenting it?"

She looked at me, anger still flaring. "Okay. This should be fascinating. So why don't we start with the body, since the body is the reason we're all here?"

"The body isn't going to get up and leave, so there's no need to rush."

"You don't even want SID to get started? That's nuts."

"While you and the sheriffs were on the porch holding Michael's hand, half the city desks in town were wandering around inside, screwing up the evidence. We can't change that now, but I want to take a minute and work out an operational theory. The crime scene might have been altered. I wanta think this out for a minute."

"The porch *is* the crime scene," she fired back, then added defensively, "I kept it as clear as I could."

Then the second L.A. myth made an unscheduled appearance. "Where the hell were you? I called you at three A.M. It doesn't take forty minutes to get here from Venice."

I took a deep breath to control my anger.

"We don't know what the crime scene is. Since I don't see a bullet hole in the back door or porch, we don't know where this happened. He could have been shot inside and dragged out here. The biggest mistake that is usually made in a homicide investigation is prescribing too small an initial crime scene area. If I could rope off the entire block, I'd do it. Now let's just back off for a minute and try to work up a shooting theory."

She was looking at me, her chest, rising and falling. Hyperventilating. Pissed.

"Look," I said, "this is bad form standing out here arguing. We'll have this out later. For now, let's do it my way."

She turned and walked off, leaving me standing there.

The truth was, I always stretched the edge of the crime scene to the farthest point out, and walked that area first, marking anything that looked out of place. After I had the immediate scene under control and the body was secure, experience had taught me that it's extremely hard to keep people from prowling the edges of the site. Neighbors, and even other cops, patrol the border, and if it's a large area it's easy for some well-intentioned schlub to pick something up or leave a footprint. We could find some cop's bootprint, plaster it, then start running off in the completely wrong direction of looking for a killer wearing size-ten combat boots.

Once I spent two weeks working a hair follicle our CSI techs found at a murder scene. The lab reported that the hair had undergone an amber tint dye job. It also had traces of an expensive French shampoo and a special French conditioner. A good potential lead. I put it out on the news that we were looking for an upscale killer with tinted amber hair who uses an expensive, French shampoo and conditioner.

A week later, I'm looking in Alexa's bathroom cabinet and I see all those same products in there. It turned out that the hair had fallen off my own coat and belonged to my wife. It's very hard to protect a crime scene, so I always start at the far edges first, and work in toward the body.

I walked the perimeter carefully, examining the ground, looking down, shining my police flashlight. The sun would be up in a few hours, but I couldn't wait, because I had seen the anger and pain in Gary Nightingale, the deadly resolve and violence in Rick Manos. I had also promised Alexa I wouldn't let this investigation drift.

The projectile had entered Michael's head from the front, the same as Billy Greenridge. The slug caught him square in the forehead, right between the running lights. He had fallen where he was shot and since the bullet had not hit the house or the door behind him, that meant it probably came from the side. To miss the house completely, the shooter had to have been firing from either the far right or the far left portion of the back yard.

I started walking around out there, searching for the shooting location. About forty yards away, behind an old lemon tree, I saw footprints. Boots. Big ones; size thirteen at least. The lowest limb of the tree had a fork about five feet up from the ground. A perfect place to cradle a rifle barrel. I called the crime techs over and showed them the footprints and the tree limb. They started photographing and getting ready to plaster the impressions.

I kept looking around on the ground on the right side of the tree. About forty feet away, lying under a small hedge, I spotted the casing.

I called Jo Brickhouse over and pointed it out to her. Beverly King followed. It was an ArmaLite .223, the kind of ordnance common to AR-15 assault rifles.

It didn't escape my notice that the long guns SRT had been using up at Hidden Ranch were AR-15s. The .223s were very fast rounds, with a muzzle velocity of over three thousand feet per second. The projectile is designed to tumble and break into smaller pieces on impact. After we photographed it, I leaned down and retrieved the brass, again using my pen tip. I held it up and we all stared at it.

The casing was a deadly calling card, and all three of us were thinking the same thing. Finally, Beverly King put our thoughts into words: "This seems way too easy."

WARRANTS

THE STRONG SANTA Ana winds whipped September leaves off the elm trees that lined Sherman Way, driving the temperature up further, scattering trash from overflowing garbage cans, and blowing down our yellow crime scene tape.

Michael Nightingale's body rolled out in a coroner's van at eight-thirty that morning. Barbara Nightingale left ten minutes later in the back seat of her sister's yellow station wagon. I caught a glimpse of two children with her, young boys, little, towheaded versions of their father. Their faces tight, blank with confusion.

"The only good thing that's happened here so far is SRT hasn't shown," Jo Brickhouse said.

"No need to come out and watch, if you already know what happened," I answered.

The thought scored. I saw a silent curse cross her face. Anger followed. She hated not coming up with that herself.

Before we took off, Beverly, Jo, and I huddled on the back porch and divided up responsibilities. "We need to have that two-twenty-three casing checked and matched for tool marks and possible fingerprints. Not to jump to conclusions, but SRT's long guns are AR-fifteens, so we need to test fire all their carbines."

"The feds are never gonna cooperate," Jo said. She was probably right.

"The three of us can't make it happen, but maybe your chief and mine can talk some sense into ATF. Failing that, maybe the mayor or Supervisor Salazar can force it down. We have to play this straight up, with no favorites. Test fire and match the brass from both SWAT teams—"

I stopped because both Jo and Beverly had wrinkled their noses. My idea obviously stunk. "Let's just hope for the best," I added. "Hope they don't put agency loyalty above common sense."

Beverly and Jo remained skeptical. To be fair, so was I, but a little positive thinking never hurts.

"Jo," I said, "could you walk that casing and the footprint cast through your lab, get us squared away down there as fast as possible?"

She glanced at Beverly checking out her reaction to having me give the orders. Detective King seemed to have no problem. Finally, Jo nodded and said, "Okay."

"Beverly, you stay with the body, go to the autopsy. Hopefully, that slug broke on impact and we can retrieve a bullet fragment for lead content comparisons. Also get us a full blood panel. I'd like to know if Mike was drinking last night. If he was at a bar we need to find out. Tell the M.E. to get us a liver temp ASAP. We need a close time of death to start our pre- and perimortem timelines."

Jo made a frustrated noise in the back of her throat.

I ignored her. "Check with the vic's SEB team leader," I continued saying to Beverly. "The guy's name is Scott Cook. See when Mike left work, if there were any unusual circumstances."

"I'll call Sergeant Cook," Jo interrupted, "If we keep it inside the sheriff's department we'll get more." It was a good suggestion.

Beverly offered, "Why don't I get a team of cadets from the academy to start hunting around this neighborhood, looking for what's left of the bullet?"

"What're the odds of ever finding that? A two-twenty-three? It's probably in a zillion pieces," Jo said.

"But we gotta try."

"What're you gonna do?" Jo asked me.

The question rang with accusatory overtones, as if, while they were out doing all the real police work, I was going to be in Beverly Hills enjoying a Turkish steam and a hot oil massage.

"I'm gonna see if I can get these warring agencies on the same side." I bowed my head in sarcastic theatricality. "May justice be served. Amen."

We broke our huddle like college athletes and headed to our cars.

I called Alexa on the way back to the office and told her what I wanted. She said the chief was way ahead of me. Everybody was meeting in his office at ten. My presence was required.

"Brady Cagel gonna be there?" I asked.

"Brady, Cole Hatton, Garrett Metcalf, Supervisor Salazar— the whole *mishpucha,* but this time everybody's gonna have a chief legal counsel in tow."

"Don't you love this?" I muttered.

"Sucks," she said.

I found out later that the meeting was being held at the Glass

House because Tony had a budget meeting at eleven. Always nice to know who's picking the playing field.

There were enough lawyers in Filosiani's big office to set a quorum for the local bar association. Tony and Bill had just informed Cole Hatton that LAPD had found a .308 casing across the street from Greenridge's house. His reaction to that wasn't friendly.

After a heated argument over withholding evidence from the primary agency investigating the homicide and half a dozen threatened lawsuits, that problem was put on hold and the argument quickly came down to whether there was enough probable cause for searching both SEB's and SRT's armories. The different agency lawyers were all circling that scrap like hungry reef sharks.

Then the door opened and Enrique Salazar entered, arriving late. He waved off the formal handshakes and took up a position next to his cops. Sheriff Messenger leaned over and whispered in his ear, filling him in.

"Look," Tom Neil, the mouthpiece from the sheriff's union said, "any way you cut this, everybody knows you're not asking these SWAT officers for their help. You're looking for a murder suspect. This is an active homicide investigation, so you've got to follow the normal rules of evidence. If you want to search our armory you're gonna need a warrant. That means you better come up with adequate probable cause for the search. You've got nothing that ties either of these casings to SEB or SRT."

I looked at Enrique Salazar. He was staying quiet. No good politics could come from this. Bill Messenger was rocking back on his heels, a worried look on his face. The police unions didn't care about his need to wrap this up quickly. They were only interested in the legal rights of the rank-and-file deputies and agents. I suspected he'd already tested SEB's long guns without a warrant, and now, if we couldn't shoot his police union lawyer down, he couldn't use anything he'd found without risking the court case later.

Tony didn't want to let the meeting degenerate into legal haggling, so he cut it off fast. "I have a municipal judge on standby. He already agreed to sign the search warrant, on the grounds that these cops are officers of the court and, as such, have a sworn duty to provide evidence and enforce the law."

"Reversible error." Neil said. "When you pin on a badge you don't give up your rights as a U.S. citizen under the Constitution."

"Who's gonna work up the search warrant preparation list?" Cole Hatton asked. "Is this warrant going to be delivered by LAPD SWAT?"

The warrant prep list uses a number scale to determine the level of risk assigned to the warrant's delivery. The warrant control officer checks twelve categories. A total of five risk points or more out of twelve mandates that the warrant be served by a SWAT team.

Normally warrants were served on criminals, but as I mentally ran through the warrant prep list, I saw the dilemma that serving SEB and SRT presented.

1. Was it a barricaded location?—Yes.
2. Were automatic weapons believed to be on the premises?—Yes.
3. Are the perps suspected of committing an assault on a peace officer?—Yes.
4. Were hostages believed to be at the location?—No.
5. Were assault weapons, body armor, or ballistic protection present?—Yes.
6. Were there barred doors or windows?—Yes.
7. Was there countersurveillance, closed circuit TV, intrusion devices?—Yes.

8. Guard dogs?—Yes.
9. Third strike candidates?—No.
10. Did the suspects have violent criminal histories?—No, but SWAT officers were certainly accustomed to violence.
11. Did handguns exist at the location?—Yes
12. Had there been threats by suspects against police officers?—More or less.

By my math, nine out of twelve points were present here, which technically put the serving of this warrant at the highest risk possible and mandated a SWAT team.

You could see the indecision in the room. Everyone was asking themselves: *Isn't this different? These are cops, not criminals. Should a strict adherence to the prep list be observed? Isn't it unnecessarily provocative to serve a SWAT team with a SWAT team?*

Nobody said anything.

Alexa finally spoke: "Let's low-key it. Do it with a warrant control team; but we should recognize the risk and keep SWAT in reserve."

"No." Tony overruled sharply. "That's nuts. We do it by the book."

Alexa stiffened slightly, but she put up no further argument.

"If we serve our people, you gotta serve yours," Salazar finally spoke.

Brady Cagel and Garrett Metcalf, with their tan gabardine suits and styled hair, stood stone-faced, looking like window mannequins, or an ad for genetic engineering.

"We don't have time to argue about this." Cole Hatton stepped up, grasping the gravity of the problem.

"I can convince a friendly federal judge across the street to paper the warrant on our guys. Tony, you get the municipal judge for the sheriffs."

Metcalf and Cagel didn't like it, but what could they say? Their own U.S. Attorney had just jumped the fence.

The meeting broke up. A lot of unhappy faces crowded into the elevator for the ride down. I walked with Alexa back to her office. She was quiet most of the way. Once she was behind her desk she picked up a folder and handed it to me.

"What's this?" I asked.

"You were right about Vincent Smiley applying to the LAPD before Arcadia," she said stiffly. "We turned him down in April of 'ninety-nine. He flunked the preliminary psych interview. I made a copy of the written denial by the academy, but I haven't had a chance to read anything, except the summary. He looks like damaged goods." She seemed distracted, tense—wrapped tighter than the inside of a baseball. I was about to say something when her phone rang, so I waved good-bye and left.

When I reached the lobby I was paged. The LCD readout said: Jo Brickhouse. I found her number and called back. She was still out at the sheriff's crime lab when she answered.

"Me," I said. "What's up?"

"The crime techs have done both casings. Good striation marks and pin impressions on both. If we can get comparison casings, our lab says they have enough here to make a match."

"Good. Sheriff Messenger just covered his ass with a search warrant. He can't use the first batch—illegally obtained. He'll have to stick with the cover story, say the range captain was just adjusting sights, and do it all over again. Get in touch with Messenger's office and have him send the second batch of brass over to the lab as soon as he gets them. I'll let you know when the SRT long guns have been tested."

"One more thing . . ." she said.

"Go."

"Robyn DeYoung, the CSI for Hidden Ranch, just rolled out of here with an evidence team and two vans full of academy cadets. She's on her way back up there to search for a dog and a bomb shelter. What's all that about?" She sounded suspicious.

"Try to reach Messenger and make arrangements to get his brass out to your lab, then meet me out there as soon as you can. I'll fill you in when I see you."

DIGGING

WHEN I GOT back to Hidden Ranch Road there were two parked sheriff's academy vans and at least two dozen academy cadets up by the burned-out house, dressed in grubbies and yellow fire slickers, leaning on shovels. They seemed glad to be working on an actual case, instead of running laps and doing pull-ups at the Academy. They were eagerly looking at the large dig site, anxious to begin.

I spotted a slightly plump female criminalist with wire-rimmed glasses and red, curly, Orphan Annie–styled hair. She looked to be in her mid-thirties and was wearing a crime tech windbreaker, sweatpants, and a white T-shirt that said: *Get Off My Fucking Crime Scene.* Had to be Robyn DeYoung.

Jo hadn't arrived yet, so I walked up to Robyn, who was

standing a few feet past where the front porch had once been, just about on the exact spot where Emo Rojas had bled to death. She was holding an open set of builder's plans and was issuing instructions, dividing the cadets into four teams and assigning them to separate quadrants of the dig site. When she finished, she turned to me.

"Don't tell me. You're Scully," she said.

"Guilty," I replied. "DeYoung?"

She nodded. Aside from the curly red hair, she also had freckles across the bridge of her nose and was attempting a disapproving scowl. But she possessed an instant likability, an infectious demeanor. She was mad at me for sending her back out here in all this damp ash and rubble, but for her anger wasn't a durable emotion, and it was already burning off like predawn mist.

"Sorry to put you through this again," I said, trying to soften her up.

"If you wanna grab a shovel, I have a fire slicker in my trunk that might fit you."

"Gee—me with a shovel. Now there's a heady concept."

"Didn't think so," she said. "Okay. Always good to have another supervisor." She opened the plans and studied them.

"Building department?" I asked.

"Yep. Pulled 'em this morning. No architect on these homes. Builder contracted. They all run between three and five hundred K. They seem nice, but when you look close they're just two-story, hollow-wall deals. Probably why it flashed over so fast."

"Right," I said. "The hot gas grenades and all that ammo in the garage probably didn't hurt either."

She let it pass, then asked, "What am I looking for again?"

"Rottweiler."

"Okay, have a seat and get started on your ice cream. If he's here, we'll dig him up."

I returned to the car, then opened the manila envelope containing Smiley's LAPD academy records and started to read.

The person who did the psychological profile was Doctor Hammond Emerson IV. I always love it when people put Roman numerals after their names, like inbred New England dilettante French royalty. Doctor Emerson had conducted three interviews with Smiley in 1999. He found the subject to be evasive and secretive. He felt that Smiley clearly had parental issues, particularly with his mother, which the doctor surmised could have stemmed from child abuse. Emerson noted in his summary that Vincent exhibited some gender confusion and a sense of hostility toward women that most probably also stemmed from the deep-seated problems with his mother, Edna Smiley—currently deceased.

Doctor Emerson concluded that Vincent Smiley demonstrated sado-sexual tendencies combined with latent rage. Emerson also surmised that these problems would create great stress when interrelating with females, both in the department as well as in society.

The LAPD academy employed a point system for applicants. Out of a possible one hundred points Smiley had scored forty, well below the seventy required to be considered for admission. Not even a close miss.

I closed the file, tapping it with my thumb. Was the AK-47 a deadly penis substitute? Was Smiley trying to make up for his sexual confusion by going postal and shooting up his neighborhood?

Just then Jo Brickhouse pulled to the curb in a sheriff's black-and-white. We both got out of our cars and met halfway. I handed her the file. "What's this?" she said. She still seemed angry, but maybe it was me, and I was just projecting.

"Smiley's LAPD academy app. He applied to us before Arcadia. Probably took a shot at your department, too. You might see if they turned him down and if they have a psych profile on him."

She took the file, opened it, and skimmed it while I watched the cadets moving ash and charred lumber off the site.

"Gay?" she said raising an eyebrow.

"Hey, come on, take it easy. That doesn't necessarily make him a bad person."

There was a moment while two conflicting emotions, anger and amusement, fought for control of her strong face. Finally, the dazzling smile won out. "You're not gonna stop busting my balls, are you Scully?"

"When you stop busting mine, I'll stop busting yours."

She considered that for a second, then waved it off.

"Okay, look—the sheriff's department doesn't spike an application on the grounds of homosexuality alone. You guys don't either."

"Not now, but what was it like in the mid- or late nineties?" I asked.

"Not sure." She tapped the folder on her thumb, exactly the same way I had. "Most likely, Doctor Emerson dinged him for all this other stuff. The sado-sexual rage, the mother problem— add that to the gender confusion, and who wants an asshole like that on the job?"

"Right. But I don't think gender confusion is necessarily homosexuality."

She thought about that and nodded, so I went on.

"And there's nothing in there about depression or suicidal tendencies either."

"It's just a quick psychological scan. This doc could've missed a lotta stuff."

"Still . . ."

Just then we heard yelling up at the site. I walked across the grass again with Jo Brickhouse at my side. The Academy cadets had found a charred lump of meat about the size of a large dog. They had scraped the ash away from the mound and were all standing around, looking happily at the object like puppies who had found a ball.

I kneeled down. The smell of cooked, decaying flesh made my throat constrict. Then I saw something glistening in the ash near the corpse. Using the tip of my pen, I pulled it away from the burnt carcass. A round piece of metal.

"Dog tag," Robyn DeYoung said. "You can touch it if you want. No prints survived the heat of this fire."

I picked it up and rubbed it with my thumb, clearing the ash. "Eichmann," I said, reading the name. "Guy named his dog Eichmann."

"Hitler was probably already taken," Jo said from behind me.

"I wonder if he really was some kinda white supremacist?"

"Goes with the survivalist training Tad Palmer mentioned," Jo answered.

I handed the tag to Robyn and stood. "Okay, that probably answers the question of what happened to the Rottweiler. Can you get us a DNA scan to match the breed, just to be sure?"

Robyn nodded. She gave an order and two cadets ran to the crime van, returning with a plastic sheet and a rubber coroner's bag. Then they loaded the charred remains onto the sheet and Robyn wrapped him up like a burrito. She instructed them on how she wanted the remains loaded into the coroner's bag, then two cadets carried him down and left him in the back of her black-and-white Suburban.

Jo and I walked back and leaned against the hood of my car, watching while the cadets again started digging where the plans indicated the basement staircase would be.

"What are we really doing out here?" Jo asked.

"Loose ends," I said.

"Look, Scully, you were right. I never worked in homicide, but in IAD I've put down a pile of officer-involved shootings. So far, this doesn't stack up as a bad shooting. Smiley brought this on himself. Death by cop. I don't see how checking this guy's background adds anything to Emo Rojas's death, or Billy Greenridge's and Michael Nightingale's."

"I'm not sure it does either," I admitted, annoyed again, but trying to stay frosty.

"Not to state the obvious here," she continued, "but you and I are at ground zero in a jurisdictional hurricane. I'm starting to get a lot of cold shoulders from my fellow deputies. They don't like it that we're investigating this. We've got heavy metal blowing around over our heads and you're out here looking for a dead dog and a bomb shelter."

"I gotta get it off my mind."

"What? Get what off your mind?" Frustration again.

"What Smiley was really doing."

"Committing suicide."

"Not according to Doctor Emerson."

"Fuck Doctor Emerson. He's just a guy in a tweed coat who never dealt face-to-face with a gun-toting psychopath. For him it's all theory and book work."

"Smiley was in Kevlar," I said for the umpteenth time, speaking slowly so somebody might finally get it. "He was building a bomb shelter. That doesn't sound like a guy contemplating suicide."

"So what?" She snapped. "Look Shane, my ass is on the line too. I'm having daily meetings with the undersheriff. My boss wants results, and all you're doing is moving backwards."

I shook my head. This was exactly what I'd been afraid of. Some silk from sheriff's IAD, who'd never worked a murder, telling me what to do.

"Is this just you wandering around on the outer edge of the crime scene again?" Jo interrupted. "Because if it is, I think we need to seriously refocus."

"There's not much we can do until we get those shell striations matched. Let's just see this through."

We both went to defense postures, leaning back and crossing

our arms. She was definitely not in agreement, her face impassive but angry. The sleeves of her gray cloth jacket bulged at the biceps.

Again, I couldn't shake the feeling that I'd seen her before. *Where was it?* I wondered.

"We found it," one of the academy trainees yelled. Jo and I pushed away from the hood of my car and trudged up the lawn again toward the crowd of young cadets.

They had uncovered a staircase that led into what looked like a basement. There was ash and rubble all the way down to a lower level door. One of the female cadets was at the bottom of the stairwell, still digging with a shovel, throwing the last spadeful of sodden debris up. It landed all around the spot where we were standing. Then she scrambled up, her face smudged with soot, but she was grinning. This was a high-profile investigation, and she was thrilled. This was why she had signed on—exactly what the recruiting poster promised.

Join the tradition. Become an L.A. County sheriff. Wear the star. Shovel shit.

We looked down the staircase. It was a mess. The ash at the bottom still soggy from the fire hoses.

"I'll take you up on that slicker now," I said to Robyn.

She smiled and instructed a cadet to run to her car and get two. He returned a minute later carrying yellow panchos with LASD stenciled on the back. I handed one to Jo, put the other over my head. Once we were rigged, we started down the steps. The door at the bottom of the stairs had burned right off its hinge. I picked it up and set it aside, then we went into the underground room.

The flashover heat from the fire had been so intense it scorched everything down there. The basement contained a laundry room, a tool area, and a few metal closets. The clothes had burned off the wire hangers. The plastic on the Black & Decker power tools had melted.

But there was no bomb shelter.

We all stood and looked at the scorched remains in the concrete block basement.

Jo said "What now?"

"I don't know," I replied. "The neighbors claimed he was pulling dirt out of here. He told them he was digging a bomb shelter in the basement. So where is it?"

"Smiley was a lying head case," Jo answered.

"But his neighbors weren't lying. Where'd the dirt come from, if it wasn't from a bomb shelter?"

Again we fell silent. Then Robyn DeYoung said, "You through with us? Can I send these 'cruits back to the barn?"

"Yeah, I guess. Thanks, guys."

They all waved, then started to pack up their gear. But something wasn't right. Just before they headed back to the academy vans, I stopped them.

"Wait. Hold on a second. Help me pull this stuff away from the walls first."

Several cadets came down and helped move the tool bench. It was heavy, almost two hundred pounds, and took three of us to slide it to the corner of the room. Next we moved a metal closet. Nothing. Last, the washer and dryer. When we pulled them away from the wall, I saw where the dirt had come from.

Vincent Smiley had dug a hole in the wall under the drainage line hidden behind the washer. It was a foot up from the floor and measured about three feet in diameter. Just large enough for a man to crawl through.

TUNNEL RAT

O F COURSE, JO Brickhouse wanted to be our tunnel rat—
the one to go through the hole.

"I'm not the CHCO, remember?" she said, her attitude temporarily replaced by excitement. "Look, Scully, I'm smaller. If that tunnel narrows down you're gonna get stuck in there."

I'm sure it was one of the few times in her life that Jo Brickhouse had admitted to being smaller. But she had a point.

"Okay, but take a Handy-Talkie. Talk to me all the way to the bomb shelter."

"Of course. You think I'd even consider doing this without you bitching in my ear and barking instructions?"

I went back to the car and picked up two Handy-Talkies and a flashlight, then jogged back to the basement area.

The female cadets were all standing around Jo Brickhouse,

staring at her. They were impressed. This buff, hot-looking lady sheriff had just backed off the big, dumb L.A. cop. She was going to crawl through that tunnel alone, prepared to face untold dangers in some underground cavern. You could feel the adrenaline and hero worship flowing back and forth among the six young women and Jo. The male cadets were harder to read, but were probably thinking, *Whatta pussy this L.A. cop turned out to be.*

Finally, Jo was ready. She triggered the Handy-Talkie.

"Radio check," her voice screamed from my belt.

I took my unit off and turned down the volume, then spoke into it: "Okay, we're hot."

She leaned toward me. "This is more like it."

She looked at her audience once, then dropped down on her hands and knees and looked into the hole.

"Better take this."

I handed her the flashlight I'd brought from the car. She eased halfway into the tunnel, paused, then continued all the way in.

After she disappeared we were left standing around looking at the mouth of the hole. Me and my two dozen disapproving helpers.

"That's one brave lady," one of the female cadets said.

"Just hope she doesn't run into the gopher who dug that thing," I said.

They looked at me for a moment, trying to make sense of it. "Kidding," I added.

That remark lost me the few remaining points I had left. It was bad enough that I was afraid to go through the tunnel, but how could I make jokes about heroic Sergeant Brickhouse at a time like this? I'm telling you, it's hard to be an enlightened male. I usually end up wrong.

I looked at my watch. Two minutes. I triggered the Handy-Talkie. "How's it going?"

I could hear the squelch as she triggered her unit, then heard her grunting with effort as she elbow-crawled along.

"Gotta . . . It's kinda . . . can see . . ."

Then static—then nothing.

We waited some more. The cadets all had worried expressions as we stared at the hole. Robyn DeYoung was sitting on the bottom step of the basement stairs looking interested but skeptical.

"I triggered the unit again. "Come in. What's going on? You okay?"

All I heard back was static.

"One of us should go in after her," a dark-haired female cadet said, starting to cinch her slicker tighter.

"No—she's okay. It's just that we've lost range on the Handy-Talkie. These units aren't too good transmitting through solid matter."

"I'll go in and look for her," a blonde cadet volunteered.

". . . find . . . in . . . light . . ." I heard Jo say through a wall of static. We were all staring at the round, dark hole like a team of anxious proctologists.

A minute later Robyn DeYoung stood. Now she looked concerned. "She's been in there over five minutes."

"I guess I'd better go in," I said, and reluctantly belted my slicker.

"Won't be necessary, Hoss."

Everyone spun around. Jo Brickhouse was standing on the stairs behind us, backlit by the morning sun, spiky blonde hair dusted over with dirt.

"How'd you get there?" I said.

We all scrambled up the stairs and back into the burned out house.

"Come on, I'll show you."

She led the way across the backyard toward a four-foot-high grape stake fence. She grabbed the top of the fence and easily jackknifed up and over—a perfect, gymnastic parallel bar move. Nothing to it. I tried to duplicate the maneuver, but parallel bars are not my event, unless they've got Coors signs in the windows.

Eventually, most of us landed on the other side of the fence and followed Jo, who was winding her way down into an overgrown gully behind the house. She stopped and pointed to the other end of the hole.

"No bomb shelter. Just a tunnel. Starts in the basement, comes out here."

Finally everybody had climbed down to where she stood and we all studied this opening with varying expressions of confusion.

"You sure you didn't miss a fork or anything in there?

"This is it," Jo said. "The tunnel follows the washer drain pipe most of the way. The last fifty feet or so, the pipe goes right, but he dug straight through to here."

One thing I had come to learn working crime investigations is that even the most confusing things usually have some kind of central logic. If they appear not to, then what you have to do is rearrange the facts until the correct pattern emerges.

As I looked down at the tunnel I knew that I was working the wrong theory. We definitely had some pieces way out of order.

TRUCE AT DUPAR'S 27

TWENTY MINUTES LATER, Robyn DeYoung and her two
dozen cadets drove off. We were standing down by our
cars and Jo Brickhouse was combing the dirt out of her hair,
with her fingers.

"Come on, let's grab some lunch," I said.

She followed me in the sheriff's black-and-white to DuPar's
Restaurant off Vista Del Sol. We found a booth by the window
and ordered. I got a hot Reuben sandwich, she had the seafood
salad and a latte. We sat staring at each other like enemy gener-
als, across a white vinyl battleground littered with napkins and
scratched flatware. This wasn't working.

Finally she leaned forward. "Look—I think we need to start
over."

"I agree."

"I took a department course in human relations once," she said. "They taught us that a good way to improve a strained relationship is by acknowledging each other's strengths."

"You first," I said, sounding petulant and small.

"Okay. You were right, checking the edge of the Nightingale crime scene. We found the shooter's position, got the casing and footprint casts. That stuff could've been missed or destroyed. And going back and finding that basement tunnel might be important. I'm not sure what it proves—if anything. But you're right, it's definitely weird."

"Okay, thanks."

"Now you," she prompted.

"Okay. You seem very organized and thorough."

"That's all?" She wrinkled her brow in disappointment.

"And going through that tunnel alone was a gutsball play. You showed a lot of courage."

She smiled. "It was kinda gutsball, wasn't it?"

I nodded, and she began tearing open half a dozen packets of Equal and dumping them into her latte. I couldn't believe how much artificial sweetener she used.

She looked up and caught me staring. "So let's hear your next big theory, Scully." Looking down again, stirring her sweetened blend. "I can hear lots of shit grinding up there in the old gear box, but nothing's coming out your pie hole."

Cute.

I took a moment, then leaned back and sighed.

"Okay, you probably won't like this, because nobody else does, but I don't buy the death by cop thing. Here's my reason and my timeline, so check me for flaws."

She pulled out her spiral notebook, flipped it open, and clicked the point down on her pen.

"Vincent Smiley has a bad childhood. He doesn't get along with his mother. Maybe she sexually abuses him, maybe she just yells a lot. Whatever the reason, he's got anger problems. For some reason, his parents pull him out of Glendale High and he's home-schooled for most of his high school years. He gets a GED, goes to junior college, then decides he wants to be a cop. Maybe so he can push people around and prove he's a real man. Next, he applies to the LAPD and fails. Emerson says he has mama problems, sexual identity problems, and can't relate to women. But somehow, even with all these deficits, he bullshits his way onto the Arcadia P.D. Finally they get wise and throw him out as a probationer, probably for all the same reasons. Now he's pissed. The cops dissed him, so he hates cops; but he also wishes he was one. He becomes a military nut and a survivalist. Hacks into a secure Marine Corps Web site called Cactus West."

She wrote that down.

"He even buys a dog and names it Eichmann. All that lines up with what Tad Palmer told us."

She nodded. "So far we're on track. But what's with the Marine Corps Web site?"

"I don't know yet. Our computer people are trying to penetrate the site." She nodded, so I went on. "After dear old Mom and Dad hit the slab, Smiley cashes in their death benefits and buys a three- to five-hundred-thousand-dollar home up on Hidden Ranch Road."

"Do we know he used his parents' insurance?"

"I'm guessing. It's what Palmer said, but you're right, we should check that out. Otherwise, where does this guy who doesn't work get enough money for a place like that? If it's not insurance, maybe it's hooked to some other kind of nastiness."

She kept making notes as I continued. "Okay, so he's up there in Hidden Ranch, walking around, pretending he's a cop, and at the same time saying he hates them. Basically acting nuts. Sometime last year ATF says they got a complaint and braced him on a suspected weapons charge. They claim when they talked to him he was docile, and it turned out he was clean. No weapons in the house. So they let him go. Didn't even bust him."

Jo was scribbling notes.

"Now, a few weeks ago something happens. For some reason, Vince goes into overdrive. He's still showing the phony badge, only now he says he's working on the antiterrorist squad. But he's such a loosely wrapped package, nobody believed him. To prove it, he takes some of his neighbors into his garage and shows them his weapons stash. Palmer and the Bellinghams get spooked, call the sheriff's department, and find out there's no Vincent Smiley on the county roster. So they make a complaint to the ATF for automatic weapons and impersonating.

"ATF looks the complaint over and says we already braced this jerk-off once and it turned out to be an air ball. Since they think he's docile, they kick the impersonating beef over to the sheriff, figuring if the LASD finds guns in there, so much the better. But on second thought, SRT isn't completely sure, so when Emo calls to tell them he's serving the warrant, they give him a little covert ATF backup and wait to see what happens. Emo walks up and knocks on the front door, Smiley opens up, and it's welcome to Dodge City. The fed SRT van is just around the corner. They hear the gunfire and roll, which explains how they got there so quick. But Smiley knows it's coming, so he's waiting for them, all dressed in Kevlar with a gas mask. Next we have Waco in the foothills."

I looked up at Jo. "So far, is all that pretty much the way you have it?"

"Pretty much," she said, putting down her pen and sipping her latte. "Eat your sandwich, it's getting cold," sounding like somebody's mother now.

I took a bite and swallowed it. "Okay, so now he's pinned in that house and he's greasing off lead-core three-oh-eights. The guy's dog is in there with him. After half the cops in Southern

California are finished raining shit through the windows and burning the place down, he ends up dead in the bathtub, looking like a pot roast somebody left in the oven. His dog is downstairs, also cooked. Roof falls in, end of incident."

I took another bite of the Reuben and looked at her again. "All of that still seem right?"

"Yep. At least as far as we know."

"Okay, then here's what's wrong."

I took a deep breath. "Smiley obviously had this all carefully planned. He shows Palmer and Bellingham the stash of bullets, the grenades, the AK-forty-sevens and boxes of C-four. Smiley's gotta know it's gonna freak these guys. They have children. He's gotta know they're gonna call the cops."

"Probably."

"He's gone to all the trouble of spending two months last summer digging an escape tunnel out of the basement to the gully below. He could have easily crawled through there and gotten away, but he didn't. He crawled into the bathtub instead and let the whole fucking house fall on him."

"Makes no sense, does it?"

"Only if we put him down as a mental. And all the rest of this is too organized, too planned for a real head case. Why go to all that trouble to build an escape hatch and then not use it?"

"Maybe he was overwhelmed by the fire," she offered. "Maybe it went up faster than he planned."

"I was under that porch with Sonny Lopez when the house was burning. Smiley was downstairs at the end, running around shooting. The house was completely ablaze. He had to know it was about to come down. I did. It was hot as hell. I could barely stand it, and I was outside. He could have easily gone to the basement, pulled the washer away, crawled through the hole, and gotten out of there, but he chose instead to die a horrible, painful death. Why?"

"Maybe he just lost it."

I frowned at her. "Come on, you don't like this any better than I do."

"Okay, you're right. But it's still a dead end. Excuse the pun. I think all the stuff about SRT, and how they got there so quick, is good. We can write that up. It adds to our investigation; but everything about the tunnel and why he didn't use it is irrelevant. Vincent Smiley is in the morgue. Where does all that take us?"

She waited patiently for my answer, so I finally told her why I couldn't let go.

"When I first started working homicide it was the last year that John St. John worked as a consultant for the LAPD. He used to come around and talk to us, tell all the new humps how to work cases, how to follow the evidence trail."

"Jigsaw John?" she said, remembering the legendary LAPD homicide detective who had retired after he took a bullet in the back fifteen years ago.

He'd moved to Oregon, but back then he still rented his services out on big cases. He especially liked to work with and train young detectives.

"John told me once, when you have a twister like this, where the logic doesn't track, it's usually one of two things that are causing the confusion. One: because you're looking at the timeline wrong. Something important is out of place. Or two: because there's a factual piece missing."

"But what if there isn't? What if he was just overcome by smoke and couldn't get down to the basement?"

"John said it was like when you reconciled a checkbook. If you're off even one dollar you can't just forget it, because that one dollar could be hiding a much bigger error."

"So, what do we do?"

"We start over. Start with Smiley's backstory again. Work it from the ground up."

"You kidding? We've probably got SEB and SRT running around killing each other. We're under heavy pressure from your chief, my sheriff, your wife, and every cop and deputy in L.A. We have to find something fast that we can take to the D.A. Something that will allow them to sack up those two units until they can get it sorted out."

"Look, I don't . . ."

"No. Listen. If any other cop gets sniped on either side, you and I both go in the bag and stay there."

"But, what if all the theories they're working on are wrong? What if we're building this investigation on a bad foundation? If we are, we'll never come out at the right place."

She studied me for a long moment, then pushed her plate away. "Are you asking me?" she said.

"Yeah. Damn right," I answered. "Since we finally agree we're in this together, just tell me where you think we oughta go from here. I'm open for suggestions, but we have a lot of stuff that doesn't line up, and I only know one way to do it, and that's to start over."

She sat for a long time, then took her wallet out of her purse, opened it, and threw ten bucks on the table.

"You don't have to buy lunch," I said.

"Don't you wish. Get your dough out, Scully. Since I guess I'm going on this dumb-ass, career-ending ride with you, the least you can do is pay your half of the food bills." She got up without waiting for an answer and walked out of the restaurant.

We had a truce. I think.

28
THE RAMS

THE WAY IT was explained to me by my stressed and emotionally frayed wife, two plainclothes lieutenants from the Warrant Control Office, along with an LAPD Special Weapons and Tactics Team, under the command of a captain from our Internal Affairs Division, drove out to 130 South Fetterly Avenue in East L.A. and served a search warrant on the captain in charge of the Sheriff's Enforcement Bureau. Scott Cook, who had commanded the Gray team at Hidden Ranch and his scout, Rick Manos, watched angrily as two LAPD SWAT team members in body armor collected five Tango 51s and seven 40-X long guns. They were put in one of the sheriff's ARVs to be driven out to Spring Ranch and test fired.

A warrant was also served on SRT by two SWAT teams about

an hour later, at 4 P.M. SRT had nine AR-15s, which were very versatile weapons that could be switched in seconds from a sniper rifle to a fully automatic carbine simply by swapping the upper receiver. All nine SRT guns were picked up and taken out to their training facility in Moorpark to be test fired.

The collection of the weapons had gone down without incident, but Alexa told me that nobody was happy about it. "An insult," is what she'd heard Scott Cook had called it.

In the past I'd found out that the best way to get the pieces of a confusing case to line up correctly was to focus my head on something else for a while. Let some fresh air in. It was five in the afternoon when I called home, and Delfina told me that Chooch had driven out to Agoura High to run his first Pop Warner football practice for the Rams. I was only a few miles away, so I said good-bye to Jo and drove over.

The high school was in the foothills, not far from where this had all started. I parked behind the athletic building and walked around the big fieldhouse until I saw the practice fields on a terraced level about five feet above me. There were fences everywhere. The Agoura High football team was also running a practice using the two full-sized fields, but the Rams were on a fifty-yard overflow field on the far right. The problem was, I kept hitting locked gates when I tried to get up there. I had to ask a student for directions.

"Gotta go around by the administration building." Then he added: "You can't get there from here."

Story of my life.

I eventually found my way onto the grass, snuck up into the bleachers a short distance away, and watched Chooch without letting him know I was here. He had a clipboard under his arm, a walking cast on his foot, and was working with two twelve-year-old quarterbacks. Both boys were wearing red no-contact jerseys, watching Chooch, with his broken foot, trying to demonstrate how to throw a quick out off a three-step drop.

Across the field, Sonny Lopez was working with the linemen—the wide bodies, such as they were. The heaviest kid on the field was still under 170.

Finally Chooch blew a whistle. "Okay, everybody over here and take a knee," he yelled.

The twenty or so members of the team surged toward him. You could spot the serious athletes from the wannabes, even from where I was sitting in the bleachers. The committed players ran all the way to Chooch, some even raced each other. The other kids, the ones who were just there for their fathers, walked. I got up from the bleacher seat, and, trying to stay unobserved, moved down closer so I could hear.

"Okay," Chooch said, "good warm-ups. In a minute we'll start walking through plays, then do a half hour of scrimmage. I'm not gonna have all of your names for a while, so when I talk to you, if I don't call you by name, you guys tell me who you are. I'll get it straight pretty quick."

I watched Sonny Lopez pulling a blocking sled out of the way, getting the short field ready for play.

"I've been studying Coach Rojas's offense, and even though I've never had much experience with a Veer, this one looks good. But I'm gonna have to put you guys through some new speed tests. Forty-yard dashes. Sorry about that, but I need to see for myself where the quickness is."

The kids were a little subdued, all of them down on one knee, helmets off, looking at the grass instead of at Chooch.

He sensed it, so he said, "On this team, anybody can say anything. I'm only a few years older than you guys. I'm your coach, but I also want to be a friend. I feel a lot of stuff going on under the surface—stuff you're thinking about me, or what happened to Coach Rojas. We gotta get that all behind us if we want to have a winning spirit."

Nobody looked at him.

"I want you guys to tell me what you're thinking. How you

feel about all this—Coach Rojas dying. If it's on your mind, let's get it out in the open and deal with it."

Still nothing.

"Can't somebody please say something?" he said, smiling slightly.

One of the larger boys in the back raised his hand. He was an African-American wearing number 58 on his jersey. Probably a linebacker.

"Yeah," Chooch pointed at him.

"How come we . . ."

"First gimme your name," Chooch said.

"Deshawn Zook."

My blood chilled a little.

"Okay, Deshawn. How come what?"

"How come we gotta play for you when your dad is trying to fuck ours?"

I almost got up and walked over to Chooch to answer that, but before I could move Chooch was talking.

"I know most of you guys have sheriffs for dads, and I know a lot is going on between the LAPD and the sheriffs right now, but whatever happens down there, it isn't part of this team. This team is about us. You and me. It's about our values and how much we want to win, for ourselves and each other. It's about that and nothing else."

Now they were listening. Most had their heads up watching him.

"I was friends with Emo Rojas. That's why I'm here. I wanted to do this for him. What happens between our fathers can't be part of what happens on this field, but I'll tell you this, Deshawn, my dad is one of the fairest people you'll ever meet. I met your dad, Darren, on an Iron Pig rally this summer. He seemed really cool and really nice. With your dad and mine working on it, I just don't think whatever's going on is gonna be that big of a problem."

Deshawn Zook nodded his head. He was smaller version of his father.

Then Chooch looked down at his clipboard and said, "Deshawn, you're playing inside linebacker, right?"

"Yes."

"You like that position?"

"Not really."

"Why not?"

"Used to play fullback. Like that better."

"Okay, then here's the deal. All positions are open again for two days. Everybody write down the position you prefer, the position you'll take, and the position you're playing now. Hand 'em in after practice. I'll work with each of you to try and get you where you want to go. I can't promise to move you, but everybody can have one tryout at any position he asks for. By Tuesday any position changes will be posted, and then we'll get back to work. Fair?"

The boys started nodding, some were even smiling.

Half an hour later, when the scrimmage started, I left, slipping out behind the bleachers. I don't think Chooch ever saw me. As I walked back to the Acura I was thinking how proud I was of the way he handled that—how smart. Throwing everything open and giving everybody a second chance was a great idea. The kids were now focussed on the future, not on Emo, or me, or any of the other angry nonsense that had washed over them.

When I reached my car I had another surprise. Scott Cook and Rick Manos were standing there with Darren Zook and Sonny Lopez. As I took out my keys, Rick Manos intercepted me.

"You know what happened this afternoon?" he asked, not waiting for an answer. "Warrants got served on us. They think we shot that fed. Your SWAT guys rolled in and took all our long guns."

I stared at him, not sure how to play it. Then I glanced over at Sonny. "You call these guys when you saw me arrive?"

"No sir," he said, leaning on the *sir* so it sounded more like a curse than anything else. "All our kids play on the team. Pickup is in half an hour."

I turned back to Manos. "I'm getting sick of this. I'm just doing a job, what do you want from me?"

Now Scott Cook leaned forward and fixed me with a level, no-nonsense stare, frightening in its focus. "You don't know where this is headed Scully. If you did, you'd play it differently."

"Then you know something," I said.

They started to walk away, but Scott Cook turned back.

"I know what those assholes at Treasury are capable of," he said. "I know whatever those casing striations show, we didn't shoot Greenridge. And I know this has just started, Scully. Nobody can stop it now."

MELTDOWN

I 'M WORRIED," ALEXA said.

I was barbecuing chicken in the backyard, basting on my beer butter sauce and nervously watching the Santa Ana winds blow briquette smoke and sparks across the fence into the yard next door. I hoped my surfboard-shaper neighbor, Longboard Kelly, wasn't watching and cursing as my embers sailed over the fence. Franco was right at my feet, purring. He liked my barbecued chicken, so he was watching carefully.

"I'm worried too—these hot embers. Maybe this wasn't such a great idea," I said, trying to refocus the conversation.

"I'm not talking about the wind or the damn barbecue," she snapped.

"I know you're not, honey."

"How long until the sheriff's ballistics lab can get us a match on those casings?"

"I don't know."

The phone rang and Alexa jumped. She was that stressed.

"Delfina will get it," I said. "It's probably just Chooch telling her he's gonna be late getting home from football practice."

I wanted to tell Alexa about what I'd seen and how proud I was of the way Chooch had handled the team, but I didn't want to compromise the story by telling it while she was this upset.

After a minute Delfina walked outside. "It's for you, Shane."

I handed the barbecue tongs to Alexa. "Don't let my little chickadees burn," I said, doing a bad W. C. Fields. Then I gave her some Groucho eyebrows, trying lighten the moment. But she was in no mood to smile.

I went into the den and picked up the phone. It was Jo.

"You want the bad news, or the bad news?" she said.

"Shit."

"We got a positive match on the three-oh-eight you and I pulled out of the apartment. The pin impression and ejection striations line up perfectly with a long gun from the sheriff's SEB armory. A Tango fifty-one. Serial number X-one-five-seven-eight. Brand new sniper rifle bought three months ago."

"Whose gun is it?"

"That's the problem. They don't assign individual weapons at SEB. They have an armory, keep 'em in the van when they roll, and pass 'em out when they hit the event."

She was right. That's what I had seen happen at Hidden Ranch Road.

"So anybody could have taken this gun out of the armory and used it," she finished.

"Great."

"Sometimes one of the snipers will check a long gun out and take it home if he's on standby. That way they can roll to a call from home. When that happens, they sign them out. I imagine certain guys get attached to certain guns. They like the way the sights line up or the way the trigger pulls, the balance—stuff like that. I figure, if this long gun kept getting checked out to the same guy, maybe that leads us somewhere. I'll get the records"

"Right. Good thinking." I tried to guess where this was going. No doubt we would now have to take the whole SEB Gray team off duty, print everybody, and hold them somehow.

"I called Sheriff Messenger," Jo said. "He's not a happy camper. ATF went out to our crime lab with a court order and took the two-twenty-three casing we found at Nightingale's house. They're doing their own ballistics match. Messenger's gonna send a print team out to our SEB SWAT house at South Fetterly. With that three-oh-eight casing match, we have enough PC to force a print check on everybody in our enforcement bureau. That's all the updates."

I stood looking down at the desk, trying to figure out what our next move was.

"Whatta you bet we also get a positive on that two-twenty-three casing from SRT?" she said.

"No bet," I replied.

"Your place or mine? We've got a lot to do here."

"Whatta we gotta do, besides wait?" I asked. "You figure we should go out and roll prints ourselves?"

"I've been working on your angle. Rebuilding Smiley's back-story—his history. Isn't that what you wanted? I've been doing computer runs all afternoon. I've got reams of county and city printouts. I could use some help sorting."

So, while I'd been at football practice Jo Brickhouse was down at the sheriff's computer information center doing runs on Vincent Smiley. I was impressed, and okay, a little embarrassed. I should have been on that, instead of watching my son coach. Figuring out priorities are a bitch.

"Your place," I finally said, because Alexa was in a foul mood and I wanted to get some air. Also, she hated my background approach, so I'd just as soon not do it right in front of her.

Just before Jo hung up I said, "Hey, Sergeant, Brickhouse?"

"Yeah?" Her voice was wary.

"Thanks for the help."

"We're partners, aren't we?"

"Yeah, but it was very thorough. The gun info, the background search—everything."

"Just doin' police work, Hoss," she said. "Nothin' special."

"Take the fucking compliment, why don't ya?"

"You sure it's a compliment, or are you finally trying to make up for being such an asshole?"

I could picture the dazzling smile spreading across her face. "See you in half an hour," I said, smiling myself as I hung up.

Outside, Alexa had her back to the house, facing the canal, talking on her cell phone. When she turned around, I knew it must have been Tony telling her about the casing match, because her face was pulled tight.

"You heard?" I said.

"They matched the casing," she said.

The chicken had been forgotten and was blazing merrily on the grill. Alarmed, Franco jumped up on the table to watch it burn. If a cat could frown, Franco was frowning. I grabbed the tongs and plucked a piece off the grill, but it was too late. Chicken briquettes.

"Now we're gonna have to get everybody on SRT off the street and printed," Alexa said.

"SRT?" I said. "Whatta you talking about?"

"Brady Cagel just called Tony. The two-twenty-three matched one of their AR-fifteens. What were you talking about?"

"I was talking about SEB," I said. "That was Jo. She said sheriffs matched the three-oh-eights to one of their Tango fifty-ones."

Alexa stood holding her cell phone, looking lost, her face a dark mask. She had always been my strength. Even though I hated to admit it, I looked to my wife for moral clarity and emotional guidance, because I was often at sea in those two critical areas. Now as I watched her I saw only confusion and fear on her lovely face. Suddenly she pushed past me and went quickly into the house, leaving me and Franco in the back yard.

"Not good, buddy," I said to the cat.

I had never seen her like this before. I turned and headed into the house after her. She was in the bedroom with the door locked. She never locked the door.

"Alexa?" I called through the wood panels. Nothing. "Alexa, please let me in." No answer. "Don't make me break this open," I said.

"Go away, Shane. Please." She sounded like she was crying. She wasn't a weepy woman. I had only seen her cry once, and that was when her ex-boyfriend and commanding officer, Mark Shephard, was murdered.

"Alexa, please. Please open up."

I heard the lock being thrown and she stood in the doorway, her face contorted, her mascara running. "What?" she said angrily.

"I'm not the problem here."

"Look, Shane, I'm having a meltdown, okay? Occasionally it happens."

She turned and went into the bathroom. Then I heard that door lock.

I sat on our bed and waited. Ten minutes later the door opened and she came out. She looked more composed, but she was still stressed. There was a tightness around her eyes. She saw me and paused, looking down without expression.

"Honey . . ." I started.

"No, look. I'm okay. I just caved in for a minute. Leave it be."

"Most of the time you're propping *me* up. Most of the time

I'm looking to you, but when *you* get down, if you won't let me be a part of it, how's that supposed to work?"

Now she had the strangest expression. An ugly mix: confusion, anger, dismay. Her eyes were swollen from crying and lack of sleep.

"It's just a job," I said.

"No—no, please don't." She moved to the bed and threw herself down on the far side—on her side. Then she grabbed the extra pillow and held it in front of her, wrapping her arms around it as if it would protect her from me.

"We need to talk about this," I said softly.

"I was always the good little sister, the one who did it right. After Mother—after she and Dad . . ."

She stopped and her eyes started welling up. Her mother and father had died in a car accident when she was sixteen.

"I know how you feel about my brother Buddy," she suddenly continued, "and part of that is justified. It's just . . ."

Where was this going? Her older brother sold supermarket products to chains all over the country. Buddy was sort of the ultimate Bubba. I didn't much care for him because, when he wasn't being self-centered he was loud and overly friendly. He also treated Alexa like a servant. But she loved him and mothered him unreasonably.

"I always wanted to do the right thing," she went on. "People counted on it. I took care of Buddy until he left for college. My life was so confusing after he left. I had nothing. It was like I'd lost my job—my reason for being alive. Then I decided to become a cop. I don't know why it surprised everybody. Police work is about order. About rules and social design. All the things I was good at." She stopped.

"This is absolutely ridiculous." She pounded the pillow savagely.

"Honey, you haven't slept a full night since we got handed this case. Is it Tony?"

"Fuck yes, it's Tony. He's putting more pressure on me than I ever would have guessed. Every morning he calls me in and shouts at me. Nothing I do is right."

"Then I'll go over to his place and dial him down a notch."

"Jesus, Shane, would you stop it? This isn't a schoolyard. He's the chief of police. He's got major pressure coming down. The press, the mayor, Salazar, the governor. The feds are all over him; so is Bill Messenger. That dickhead Cole Hatton is threatening a malfeasance lawsuit." She stopped again.

"We're being threatened constantly. Not just lawsuits—the police commission. They could fire Tony. We could both get axed. Everybody's looking for a scapegoat, and if we don't handle this right we're it. So he's been hammering on me, telling me to keep you focussed. I'm trying to hold the line for you, but . . ."

"Is this because of the way I want to work the case?" I was stunned.

"It's about that. It's about us trying to investigate two sister agencies. I'm getting threatening phone calls at Division. Can you believe it? Right in the Glass House. A whispery voice telling me I'm next."

My heart almost stopped. She hadn't told me any of this. It was just like her. Taking it all on herself, never complaining until she broke from the strain. I came around to her side of the bed and tried to put my arms around her.

"Honey, I'm sorry."

"Just—just . . ." She stopped, and the tears started coming again.

She shouted at the ceiling. "Stop crying, Alexa!" then rolled over and buried her face in the pillow.

I lied down beside her and started stroking her back, whispering to her, telling her how beautiful she was and how she was the most important person in my life. After a moment she stopped crying and turned again to face me.

"It's not just about the job. It's the way I feel about a lot of things. It's all changing."

"Come here," I said and held her close.

We embraced for a long moment, until, male libido being what it is, I started to wonder if making love would help her. Would a priceless piece of Scully ass make things right here? *Shane Scully, the Loooove Doctor.*

I rubbed her back and shoulders. She started to relax a little and cuddled close to me. I was still trying to figure out what to do when she initiated it.

We caressed each other for a long time, making the beginning moves. Then she unbuttoned her blouse and in moments we were naked.

Emotions are the basic currency of police work, yet sometimes I'm surprised at how little I understand. We made love once diligently, then a second time with abandon. The air conditioner clattered in the window, but our combined heat and the Santa Ana winds had us slick with sweat.

When we finished I lay in her arms. "You're the best," I told her. "You make all things worthwhile."

She snuggled closer and nuzzled my ear. "Sometimes I'm so lonely and afraid," she said in a voice so tiny I barely heard her. "Sometimes I don't have any of the answers I'm supposed to, and I'm just down there faking like a gypsy."

I said, "We all do that."

"I can take pressure. I'm good under pressure. It's self-doubt that I can't deal with."

"It's that way for everybody," I told her.

"Except, you always seem so sure."

I couldn't believe she said that. I always felt so unsure. Always following in the footsteps of other people, like Jigsaw John, or Tony, or Alexa.

"I'm never sure," I told her. "Every time I'm sure, I turn out to be wrong."

But then I started to work on a way to solve her problem. If it was my investigative technique that was causing trouble, I could change that. I could focus on the SWAT teams like she wanted, leave everything else, the tunnel and all my hunches, for later. Also, I had an idea how I could get Tony off her back.

I was just getting ready to lay some righteous stuff on her when she said, "I'll get past this. It's just a hitch in the road." Then she whispered, "And thanks."

"For what?"

"For just listening. Not doing what you usually do, trying to solve it."

So I scotched all my brilliant solutions and just held her.

An hour later I changed my clothes and got ready to go to work with Sergeant Brickhouse. As I was passing through the living room the phone rang. It was almost ten, and I was pretty sure it was Jo wondering where I was. I almost didn't answer it, but then changed my mind and snapped up the receiver. Immediately, I heard a whispering, threatening voice.

"You been warned Scully. Shut this down now or you pay the price, bitch."

"Wrong Scully, asshole," I said, anger and violence flaring. "When I find out who you are—and I will—I'm gonna reach down your throat and pull your asshole out."

Before I could finish the sentence he had hung up.

STAR TROUBLE

I **IMMEDIATELY HIT** star-69, but the number was blocked. Alexa was already under enough stress, so I didn't tell her about the call. Instead, I got in touch with Tony. The chief promised to run a phone check on my line and to increase the patrols in our neighborhood, keep an eye on our house.

I was almost two hours late getting to Jo's house off Alameda, in Glendale. It was in a middle-class neighborhood full of small one-story houses and duplexes. It was nine-thirty in the evening as I pulled slowly up the street, looking for her address. I spotted the number painted on a mailbox and turned into the narrow drive of a nondescript painted brick house. There was a black Navigator parked in the driveway facing the street. As I was setting my hand brake, a very pretty woman with black hair and long legs stormed out of the rear of the house, carrying a laundry basket full of clothes. She threw the basket into the back of the SUV and slammed the door. When she came around to the driver's side, I could see a mask of fury on a beautiful, structured face dominated by high cheekbones. She motioned for me to back up, then jumped into the Navigator, started the engine and blasted the horn angrily.

"Okay, okay, I'm trying," I said to my dash. I fumbled the key into the ignition and backed out into the street.

The Navigator came out of the driveway like a getaway car after a 7-Eleven robbery. She whipped the wheel right, squealed rubber, and roared away up the street.

I pulled back into the drive, parked, then went up to the front door and rang the bell.

Nobody answered. I rechecked the address. No problem there. I looked around the front yard. It was neatly trimmed, but bland. The flowerbeds were organized, but mostly planted in white. Colorless. The brick house was gray with white paint on the sparse wood trim. It was a square, uninspired structure. The whole feeling of the place was clean efficiency. No energy had been wasted on frills. *A brick shithouse*, I thought.

I rang the bell again. Still nothing. So I walked around to the rear.

The backyard was small. Two recliner sun chairs and a portable Jacuzzi with wood sides sat out on the lawn. There was a utilitarian concrete patio that held a coiled hose and a flower potting area.

The back door was ajar. I knocked loudly, then called out, "Jo. It's Shane."

No answer.

I was beginning to feel alarmed. Sheriffs were getting shot, Alexa was being threatened. Who was the angry woman who had raced out of the driveway in the Navigator, almost hitting me?

I checked my gun, but left it in the holster and entered Jo

Brickhouse's sparse kitchen. It was neat, but like everything else colorless and efficient. Lots of stainless steel.

I moved into the living room. Wood floors, plain walls, Danish Modern furniture, which always struck me as the ultimate triumph of form over function.

As I passed through the dining room, I could hear someone crying down the hall. Large, wracking sobs.

"Jo, it's Shane," I yelled out again, and the crying abruptly stopped.

"Just a minute," she called, in one of those fake brave voices. "Go wait in the den."

I turned and went into the den, which was really just an alcove off the living room. More Danish Modern furniture, gray upholstery, white walls. No art. All the warmth of a G.E. refrigerator. Her desk, on the far side of the little nook, was piled high with Vincent Smiley printouts.

I decided not to futz with it, but to let her pass out the paper. A minute later I heard her in the bathroom running water. Then her footsteps came down the hall. When she walked into the den her eyes were rimmed red and badly swollen.

First Alexa, now Jo. My female karma was in serious retrograde. "You okay?" I asked.

"Dandy," she said sharply, to cut off further discussion.

"You don't look dandy," I pressed, thinking even as I said it: *Don't get into this, Shane. Whatever it is, you can't solve it.*

"Where were you?" she snapped. "You were supposed to be here two hours ago." She was pissed at the pretty, black-haired woman in the SUV, but she was taking it out on me.

"I had to deal with something at home," I said.

"Really?" Focusing more anger. "Well, that can happen I suppose. But it never hurts to call. It's why we all carry beepers and cell phones."

"Who was that who almost took off my front bumper pulling

out of here?" I asked, thinking again: *You don't want to know, Shane. Don't get into this.*

"That was Bridget."

"Who's Bridget?"

"Somebody I'll probably never see again." She said it so bitterly that it sounded like a curse. Then, little by little her composure began to crumble. It started with a slight lip quiver, then spread upward, eventually crashing her entire face. She hiccupped a loud sob at me, spun and ran out of the den, up the hall, leaving me standing alone.

Again, I had the same strange feeling that I knew her from somewhere before, but where the hell was it? The feeling was circling close, just out of reach. I tried to pin it down. Sometime, a while back. It was something about her build, or the way she moved. What was it about those muscular arms, those developed calves and thighs?

Then it hit me.

"Son-of-a-bitch," I said softly to myself.

I went out through the kitchen into the backyard, then crossed to the small garage and opened the side door. Parked inside was a department black-and-white. I walked around to the far side and there it was.

Jabba the Slut's yellow-and-black Screamin' Eagle Deuce.

JABBA THE SLUT

IWAS BACK in the tiny den waiting for her, thinking: *She must have remembered me from the Iron Pig's rally*. But, just like me, she wanted to pretend to have emotional distance on Emo's death. If I'd known they were friends I would have questioned her objectivity, as she had undoubtedly been questioning mine. It explained some of her argumentative attitude. At least, I hoped it did.

After a while she came out of the bedroom and sat in the swivel chair across the room, maintaining a careful physical distance from me. She looked crushed. Emotionally shattered.

"Look, Jo, this is probably a bad time to work on this. I could come back tomorrow."

"No. No, we have to do it now. There's a lot at stake."

"Right. But I can see you've just—I don't want to add to your emotional problems."

She looked at me, then shrugged her big shoulders. The motion said: I don't count, I'm nothing. Don't worry about me.

Then she added, "My brother sheriffs want this solved. I'm getting threatening calls at work."

She went to her desk and sat looking down at the papers. I decided not to complicate things by telling her Alexa was being threatened, too. I needed to get her focused on something else for a minute.

So I said, "I saw your bike in the garage. Why didn't you tell me you were on that ride?"

She shrugged again. "I didn't like you. From the first moment I saw you up in Trancas Canyon you sorta pissed me off. Sitting on that big Roast King that wasn't even yours, acting like some bullshit Willie G, high-siding and countersteering every turn. You ride like a girl."

"Jesus. That bad?" I smiled at her.

"Hey, I have female issues. I won't deny it. I also make snap judgments, so I'm wrong a lot. I've befriended a lotta assholes, alienated a lotta friends." She rubbed her hand under her one green eye, taking away some excess moisture. "Look, I do the best I can. Everybody doesn't see my virtues."

"I do," I said softly.

"Gimme a fuckin' break, Scully. I piss you off. But that's okay, I piss everybody off. If you could throw me overboard ten miles out, tied to an anchor, I'd be strolling the Catalina Trench right now.

"Don't be so hard on yourself."

"Right." She shook her head in bitter frustration. "Bridget says deep down I'm cold. I don't let people in. I suppose she's right, but I never know what to expect from people. I get scared, so I play a lot of defense."

"Me too."

She spun the swivel chair around and regarded me with frustration. "Don't try and get inside my head, Shane. It'll scare the hell outta you."

"What's in your head probably wouldn't scare me, Jo. My own devils seem worse than yours, because they're mine."

"I'm sure," she said skeptically.

For some reason, at that moment I needed to get something off my chest. Maybe I was feeling guilty and isolated over Alexa, or maybe it was that I sensed that in her current state, Jo wouldn't judge me. Whatever it was, I took a deep breath and let go.

"Most of the time I feel pretty lost and unsure," I said softly. "And deep down I usually don't think I'm worth very much."

She was watching me carefully now, waiting for a punch line. But there wasn't one. This was one of my dark spots, a place I rarely go. Her mismatched eyes softened, so I went on.

"That can happen when you're left at a hospital when you're six weeks old, and the county can't give you away, even if they're paying people to take you. I'd go with somebody for a week and they'd spit me back—too fussy, too hyperactive, too old, too hard to handle. Mostly I was raised by the county. So, like you, for most of my life I never let anybody get close.

"I wanted to be a cop because cops got respect just by wearing a badge. Being a cop gave me standing in the community. It made me part of a brotherhood—a family. I stood for something important that didn't have to be explained to be understood. But there was something else—something less noble. As a cop I didn't need to have a personal relationship to affect the relationships of others. I was great at police work, but as a person I was hiding out. I was good with assholes, because at least I understood them. I knew what to expect. Nothing. And I was used to getting nothing."

She sat quietly listening, so I went on.

"But in the last few years I've been trying to change that, to take more chances and be more vulnerable. I'm learning that vulnerability doesn't have to signal weakness. In fact, it draws people to you. Little by little, my personal life is getting richer. But it's like everything is balanced on some kind of complicated teeter board. The more vulnerable I become the happier I am personally, but the more inept I feel as a cop. I'm getting played more, and I'm having trouble finding a reason to care about anything on the job. This case we're working is threatening to end my career because it is the ultimate breakdown of everything I once believed in."

"So you're taking a chance with me now. Is that what this is? Showing how open and nonjudgmental you can be?" She was sort of sneering as she said it.

"I don't care whether you're gay, Josephine. It's just a choice and it's yours to make. But if you want some unsolicited advice, don't let your sexuality define you. You're worth more than that. I have my own issues I'm working on. Nobody gets through life without getting ambushed occasionally. Stop thinking it's only you. Everybody's out there looking for their own answers."

She remained silent, her face hard to read.

"You and I are in this thing together," I said. "My wife is getting phone threats like you are. I'm worried about her safety, and now yours, too. Everybody wants us to ditch the Smiley background and start focusing on those two SWAT teams. Only, I can't shake the feeling that the answer is hiding in his past. Putting our rocky beginning aside, you've been a good partner, and I don't usually do well with partners, because trust is another one of my issues. But maybe we could develop some trust. If you wanta let down some personal boundaries, just say the word."

She didn't respond for a long moment, then finally nodded her head. "Lemme think about it. I'll get back to you."

She reached over and scooped up all of her background material on Smiley and handed me half the stack.

"Wanna get started?"

She still seemed shaken, but she had a lot of will power, just like Alexa, and I knew she wouldn't break again.

"Sure. What's this?" I said, pulling the top sheet off the stack.

She glanced at it and said, "It's a bank payout to Vincent Smiley for four hundred and eighty thousand dollars. I'm guessing it's the Firemen's Fund Life Insurance policy for Edna and Stanley Smiley. Stanley had a one-truck plumbing service, Smiley, The Happy Plumber. Both he and Edna died in a car accident in 'ninety-five. Insurance premiums were fifteen thousand a year."

"So that's where the house came from."

"Exactly."

"Fifteen thousand a year?" I said. "Isn't that a pretty big premium?"

"Why?" she wondered.

"I don't know. Guy's a plumber with one truck, pays fifteen grand in life insurance premiums? Sounds kinda high. How much life insurance would that buy?"

She scribbled a note. "I've got a friend who sells insurance. I'll check it out."

"Can't you just call the broker who handled this policy?"

"No."

"Why not?"

"You don't want to know."

I frowned. "Don't tell me you hacked this bank's computer to get this."

"Ve haff our veys," she said, using a corny German accent. "I have a friend in computer sales who doesn't mind skating the edges, and she knows how to write spaghetti codes. I'll get her to hack the insurance company's computer. Because of the medical file, all this life insurance stuff is confidential."

"Shouldn't we just serve a warrant on Fireman's Fund?"

"Smiley's dead, so whatever we find now can't hurt him. This isn't going to end up in court, anyway. You want to waste time we don't have getting a no-recourse warrant that we can't file until Vincent is buried?"

"Probably not. What else?"

She reached over and picked up more printouts. "Here's everything I could hack and track on Smiley from the county and municipal sites. Most of it's probably useless, but at least it's a start."

She divided the stack in two. "I've arranged it chronologically by date, starting with county health records, preschool, middle and elementary, his GED in 'ninety-five, on through to the shoot-out statements and death certificate. Couldn't find his birth records. What do you want, Smiley in short pants or Smiley in Kevlar?"

"Smiley in short pants."

She handed me one of the stacks. We spent the next hour reading and making notes. At midnight we were both cranking off yawns, but we had a record of his life as far as county and municipal records took it.

"I'm shot," she said. "Wanta meet first thing for breakfast? Work out a doorbell schedule?"

"Yeah. My brain is fuzzed." I closed my notebook and got to my feet. She followed me to the door. I was just starting to leave, when she reached out and took my arm, stopping me. It was the first time that she had actually touched me.

She looked earnestly at me for a moment, then let go of my arm and cleared her throat. "Listen Shane, you say you used to be a loner, that you didn't let people in, but now your personal life is richer. Exactly how did you change that? No matter how hard I try, I'm afraid to trust anyone."

"It was pretty easy once I got the knack," I said, and she leaned forward as if I was about to give her the secret of life.

"When you don't like yourself, it's damn hard to have much

of a relationship with anybody else. All you've gotta do is start finding things to like about yourself. Once you learn what they are, find somebody you care about and give those feelings away. What it boils down to is: In order to get, you've gotta give."

"That sounds like New Age bullshit," she replied skeptically.

"Some of the best answers are the easiest," I said. "But at the same time, the easiest answers can be the hardest to understand."

MATCHES

DOCTOR GOUDA CALLED Jo at 8 A.M., just as she was leaving her house to meet me for breakfast. She called me and we changed our plans. It was a little after nine when we walked into the print bay of the sheriff's old lab. Doctor Chuck E. Cheese was bent over, studying two enlarged blowups of a fingerprint through a magnifying glass the size of a hotel ashtray.

"I think I got something," he said without turning around. "Enough, at least, to have a serious talk with this guy." He straightened up, hefting his big belly off the table. This morning he was decked out in a tent-sized dashiki large enough to camp under.

"This is the comparison print we rolled at the sheriff's SWAT house yesterday afternoon." He handed Jo a blowup of a right index finger. "We think it belongs to a guy named Pat Dutton. It more or less matches that partial on the three-oh-eight you guys found. Dutton's one of the long guns on the SEB Red team out there."

"The Red team?" I looked over at Jo, surprised that it wasn't someone on Scott Cook's Gray team.

"How sure are you of this match?" Jo asked, holding the blowup and examining it carefully. She had regained her composure from last night, and looked fresh in a crisp white blouse, black slacks, and a blazer.

"As I told you before, this is not a great latent." Doctor Gouda picked up a second photograph, which was of the partial taken from the casing we'd found across the street from Greenridge's house. He laid it next to the photo of the print they'd rolled yesterday, then started pointing out similarities.

"These two tented arches are pretty good matches. Here's half a central pocket whorl that's pretty much on the money. This isle ain't a bad match. Would I take it to court? Probably not. Would I make an investigatory judgment based on it? You bet."

Gouda looked up. "That footprint you plastered was identified by the grunts in soles and holes," referring to the footprint and gunshot lab. "Follow me," he said, and waddled out of the fingerprint bay into the room next door.

The GSR lab was a windowless room given over to several large electron microscopes, used for breaking down and reading barium and antimony, the chemicals used to determine gunshot residue. There was one long table for identifying footprints. The three young criminalists working on the equipment sat, heads bowed, eyes pressed to various viewfinders.

"Hey, Ruben, you got that bootprint from Mission Street?" Gouda asked.

An African-American criminalist rose up from a microscope and handed Gouda a photograph from a stack on the footprint table. Clipped to the back of the footprint photograph was some catalogue material from the Danner Boot Company.

"Your print came from a Striker CTX Danner Terra Force jump boot, size twelve," Gouda said. "The print was pushed out a little, but it looks like a narrow foot. Maybe a double-A."

Gouda handed it to Jo, who glanced at it before passing it to me. I knew that Danner boots were big with most cops. They came in a lot of styles. Police officers bought them because they were light, durable high-tops with thick rubber soles and good traction.

Gouda took the photo back. "This one looks pretty fresh. Right from the box. No nicks, cuts, or flaws. It'll be hard to make a positive match."

Thirty minutes later Jo and I were standing in the parking lot of the old crime lab watching for Chief Filosiani to arrive. Ten minutes later he pulled his maroon Crown Victoria into the lot. He was talking on his cell phone as he got out, just closing it up as he approached.

"That was Bill Messenger," he said, holding up the phone. "He got an arrest warrant. We're staying off the scanners to keep the news crews away. Gonna meet our SWAT unit out at South Fetterly in twenty minutes and pick up Pat Dutton."

"Chief, we only have four identifiers," I said. "The criminalist inside says this print's probably not going to stand up in court. We need to polygraph Dutton, if he'll sit for it."

"That'll be up to his lawyers," Tony said.

Just then Sheriff Messenger arrived in the passenger seat of a LASD black-and-white. His face was drawn. He had the arrest warrant in his hand.

We piled into our separate vehicles and followed Sheriff Messenger out to East L.A.

An LAPD SWAT van and a support SUV, along with three black-and-white escort vehicles, were lined up at the curb across from the public library, a block down from the sheriff's SEB building. LAPD SWAT was organized, more or less, the same as SEB, only each LAPD team had ten guys, instead of eight.

Tony and Bill had elected not to tell the Justice Department about the arrest until after it was over. ATF was the agency investigating William Greenridge's murder, but both chiefs reasoned that emotions were running way too high. If they were notified, SRT would want to serve the warrant. Under these sensitive conditions, that seemed like a really bad idea. Messenger reasoned it would be far easier and less risky for him to arrest his own officer, but to keep the LAPD SWAT in reserve.

After they briefed the LAPD SWAT team leader on how they wanted to serve the warrant, the four of us got into the Crown Vic. We drove up to the corner and parked next to SEB's long driveway. Sheriff Messenger used a cell phone to call the captain in charge of his SWAT house.

"This is Sheriff Messenger," he told the switchboard operator. "Who's on the desk this morning?" We waited, then he said, "Put Captain Otto on please."

A minute later the SWAT commander came on the line and Messenger told him what he wanted.

I took my Beretta out of my ankle holster and jacked a round into the chamber, then repacked the nine on my belt.

"Okay, Captain," Sheriff Messenger said, "I want you to take Sergeant Dutton to the side door. Make sure he's not armed. Stand there with him and wait."

He paused while the captain spoke, then said, "Good. See you in five."

We drove down the winding drive. There were almost twenty sheriff's black-and-whites of all makes and sizes, along with four big SWAT vans, parked in the lot beside a one-story ranch-style building.

Tony pulled around to the side door where a middle-aged, dark-haired captain with a Marine's combat bearing was standing next to a freckled, red-haired man about twenty-five who was chewing a wad of tobacco, occasionally spitting juice into a

Styrofoam cup. This was Sergeant Patrick Dutton. He had a confused look on his Irish face.

Tony set the brake and we all got out.

Sheriff Messenger walked over to his SWAT commander and handed him the arrest warrant, then he turned to the red-haired man.

"Sergeant Pat Dutton?" he asked.

"Yes sir," Dutton replied, clearly puzzled.

I looked down and saw that he was wearing Danner Terra Force jump boots laced up over his tan, SEB Weapons Team jumpsuit. But so did the captain and probably two-thirds of the SWAT guys stationed here.

"You're under arrest for suspicion of murder," Messenger said as Captain Otto handed Dutton the warrant.

Dutton's expression barely changed. All that happened was he shifted his tobacco chaw to the other side of his lip, then spit a line of juice into the cup.

"Whatta you kidding?" he said. "Who'd I kill?"

"An SRT agent named William Greenridge," Messenger said.

Dutton looked from me, to Jo, to Chief Filosiani, then back at Sheriff Messenger. An entire new range of emotions now played like a wide-screen movie across his open face: first humor, then disbelief, followed by fear and panic. I knew a split-second before it happened that he was going to bolt.

He lunged away from Captain Otto and headed across the parking lot. I threw myself at him, low and head first, tackling him with a body block below the knees. The move took his legs out and he tumbled over my back. The cup of tobacco juice went flying, but Dutton was a commando and he hit and rolled, coming up to his feet almost immediately.

I've seen fast moves in dojos, seen plenty of black belts working out with each other on police mats, but I wasn't prepared for Sergeant Jo Brickhouse. As Pat Dutton regained his footing, he spun and Jo blocked him with her body, then threw three quick blows: A straight-hand finger strike to his neck, followed by a closed fist shot to the solar plexus. The last was a knee to the groin.

Patrick Dutton went down hard, and seconds later Tony and I had him cuffed and in custody.

"I want an attorney," Dutton gasped at Captain Otto. He was holding his balls and must have swallowed the chaw, because he suddenly gagged, leaned forward, and puked it up at our feet.

THE OTHER SHOE

THE NEXT MORNING Jo and I were unceremoniously shifted to the backwater of our own investigation.

The ABC news desk had gotten wind of Pat Dutton's arrest. Somebody at SEB or Parker Center had leaked it, along with all of the evidence we had against him. The story about two L.A. SWAT teams gone wild broke nationally on *Good Morning America*.

Alexa called me into her office at 9 A.M. and told me that, for political reasons, the U.S. Attorney was taking charge of the investigation. Jo and I could stay on background, but Cole Hatton had strong-armed the city council and Mayor Mac off the case and was using his own investigating officers. Starting this afternoon, we would report to a couple of GS-12s from the local bureau of the FBI.

There was a press conference scheduled on the fifth floor of Parker Center at 10 A.M. Jo and I were told it was not necessary for us to attend.

We were two blocks away, sitting in a back booth of the Peking Duck restaurant while keeping one eye on the TV that was on in the bar. Half a dozen off-duty dicks from the Robbery-Homicide P.M. watch were sitting in there having a 10 A.M. after-work beer and watching KTLA's field reporter, Stan Chambers, do a pre-event standup in front of an empty podium. The volume was just loud enough to hear from our booth in the next room.

"Sources inside the department indicate that these two SWAT team murders might be connected to the fiery shoot-out that occurred on Hidden Ranch Road ten days ago," Chambers announced. "We'll be waiting right here at Parker Center for this all-important press conference to convene. Back to you, Hal."

I kept one ear on the TV, but turned back to Jo while weather and sports drifted in from the bar.

Jo was saying, "This insurance guy I called says a fifteen-thousand-dollar premium on a universal life policy would pay out almost a million dollars in benefits if it was whole life, which, according to this printout my friend hacked, it was."

A Chinese waiter came over to bring us coffee. Jo asked him for some Equal and he recovered a dish from another table. She immediately began tearing open little blue packets while I sat back and took a sip from my cup. Unfortunately, the blend at the Peking Duck was watery, just like their tea. I guess it's okay when green tea is weak, but weak coffee really sucks. I'd forgotten how bad it could get in here.

I set my cup down and said, "So if Smiley buys a house in Hidden Ranch for five hundred K, where's the other half mil?"

"Don't know. Here's the exact financial picture." She looked down at her notebook. "I went through his tax returns. He deposited four hundred eighty thousand in Glendale S and L at five percent when the policy paid out in 'ninety-six. The house didn't cost five hundred K. He paid three hundred thirty thousand for it in 'ninety-nine, all cash, leaving him with one hundred fifty grand in the S and L. He's been drawing down on that to live. He still has a little under eighty thousand left."

"So, if there's eighty grand in his estate, and nobody is stepping up to collect his body, we gotta figure there's nobody left in his immediate family to claim it."

"Would seem that way. I checked all his bank accounts. No safety deposit box. So, if he did have the missing five hundred thou, maybe it burned up in the fire." She started making her gruel, mixing in the six packets. She was going to end up with brown sugar water. "Or maybe the other half mil's in a fruit jar buried in the backyard," she added as she stirred.

"I can hardly wait to ask Robyn DeYoung to head back out there with a metal detector and her trusty cadet shovel squad."

"I wouldn't do that. There's too many better ways to hide cash these days."

"So, where's the rest of it, then?"

"Don't know," she said. "Boat? Foreign investments? Unlisted house in the Bahamas? Money isn't the motive anyway. Neither was suicide. Pure, kick-ass anger got this done. Vincent was a wannabe cop and a cop-hater with deep psychological problems. He goes fruitcake and barricades himself in his house and starts shooting our troops. He was just killing cops. That was his whole program."

"So you're buying that now?" I said, looking up.

"It took me a while to get there, but yeah, I think that's the reason this all started. But we're just jerking off with all this background. The U.S. Attorney doesn't want to hear it. The case went that-a-way." She jerked a thumb at the TV in the bar.

"I'd still like to know what happened to the five hundred thousand dollars. I get nervous when half a mil is missing."

"Maybe he didn't inherit all of the insurance benefits," she said. "Maybe someone else got some of it."

"Who else is there?"

"His parents could have had debts that needed to be paid off before the insurance could be disbursed."

"Half-a-million-dollar's worth?" I asked skeptically.

She took her first sip of coffee and swallowed it. A faraway look spread across her face, followed by a slow grimace. "That is truly shitty," she said softly, looking down at her cup in disbelief.

"Welcome to the culinary environs of Parker Center. What else did you find?"

She flipped a few more pages in her notebook. "He applied to the L.A. Sheriff's Department in two thousand, like you figured, but was turned down. Nothing in here about why. Our academy doesn't include a psych package in their A-elevens. I called, but nobody there remembers him. They burned me a copy of his file app. Nothing on it looks too different. He was blown out on his preliminary interviews, same as at LAPD."

"Two for two. He must have been a pretty twitchy guy even back then."

She mimicked a high voice. "Mr. Smiley, why do you want to be a deputy sheriff?" Then, in a deep voice, " 'So I can carry a big gun and kick the shit out of people.' . . . Wrong!"

She closed her notebook and looked at me, then added, "No military service, which seems strange. They have guns, grenades, armor-piercing ordnance. Sounds like Smiley's kinda deal. In the mid-nineties enlistment had fallen off so badly that the military would take anybody who had a heartbeat and a temperature above ninety-six degrees. I'm doing a follow up to see if I can get an answer.

"Oh yeah—he also belongs to a mountain climbing club. The Rock Stars. I put a call into their president, Marion Bell. Marion's a guy, by the way. We don't need any more gender confusion on this case."

She looked up, waited for my grin, and got it. "He agreed to meet me this afternoon. Didn't sound like a big Smiley fan. Said Vince wanted to learn rock climbing as part of his survivalist training. Apparently he told some of the other members of the club that he was part of some survivalist group, but he was very secretive about which one, or where they hung out. The Rock Stars is a sports club, so Smiley didn't really fit in. Marion said he wasn't surprised when he saw the shoot-out on the news."

She took another tentative sip of her coffee, then pushed it away. "That's Smiley in Kevlar. Let's hear about his roller skate days."

I looked down at my notes. "Went to Glendale Elementary School K to fifth grade, then through Mrs. Kimble's Country Day Middle School in Eagle Rock in sixth and seventh. Then he was in high school for a year, but got pulled out and homeschooled through twelfth grade. GED in 'ninety-five. I'm still looking for his birth records, just in case there's something missing—medical problem from birth, like maybe he was born with a tail and horns and nobody thought to tell Geraldo. I put a wire out to all the county hospitals in Southern California, most should get back to me sometime today or tomorrow."

"Juvie record?" she asked.

"He's got one. But, as you know, according to California State law it was sealed when he turned eighteen."

"Man, I'd like to get my hands on that."

"I'm working on it."

"You little devil," she said. "How?"

"Ve haff our veys."

She smiled at that, so I added, "His doctor retired professionally as well as physically, so we can't get anything there, unless you wanta dig him up and try to restart his heart. That's all I could find by nine thirty this morning."

"We're really sucking wind on this thing!" She was looking at her coffee, twirling her spoon in the cup. "Now that the U.S. Attorney is in charge, we're just doing busywork." She frowned. "But to be honest, you know I never thought the answer was gonna come out of his past. Now they're just using that to keep us out of the way."

There was certainly something to what she was saying. With the murder of Michael Nightingale this case had turned into a hot grounder. I was pretty sure Alexa was looking out for my career and had put me and Jo on background checks to keep me out of the line of fire.

"Even if we come up with more questions to ask, Hatton's IOs aren't gonna be interested. They're focused on those two SWAT units. We might as well spend the day at the beach," Jo said bitterly.

"Look, we're still officially on the Hidden Ranch investigation. Let the U.S. Attorney's investigators run the Greenridge and Nightingale murders, but for the next four to eight hours, while they're all doing press conferences and organizing evidence, we can still work our case. Nobody is even thinking about that anymore.

We probably have less than a day before we're gonna be assigned to do grunt work for the FBI. Let's put the time to good use."

She dropped her spoon into her cup and looked over at me. "One thing you said doesn't track," she said, and held my gaze with those incredible mismatched eyes.

"What?"

"This is a nitpick, and it's definitely in the who-gives-a-damn column, but middle school is sixth through eighth grade, not just sixth and seventh."

"So there's a year missing," I said, waving it off. "He drops out of eighth grade, home-schools, then goes back into the ninth grade at Glendale High, drops out in tenth, homeschools again, gets his GED two years later . . ."

"That's a lot of dropping in and out. Whatta you think happened to cause that?"

"Who knows?" I said. But since she mentioned it, I guess it was a little strange. "So you think something is wrong there?"

"Look, Shane, as far as I'm concerned, we're on the sidelines. I'm just saying it sounds screwy."

I thought about it some more. I had to agree.

I glanced over at the bar TV. Tony and Bill Messenger were just stepping up to the podium, along with Brady Cagel and Cole Hatton. Mayor Mac and Supervisor Salazar, politicians that they were, knew a no-win when they saw it and elected not to attend. The press conference was starting. "Wanta see this?" I asked.

"Nope," she said. "My bullshit meter is already red-lined."

I slid out of the booth and drifted into the bar. The Robbery-Homicide detectives made room for me. One of them was a big street monster named Griff Hover, who I'd worked with way back when I was in Valley Patrol. He looked over and smiled.

"Hey, Shane. That's a good-looking pile a bones you got sitting over there." He glanced back at Jo, who had her head down, again going over her notes.

"Yep," I agreed and turned to watch Sheriff Messenger at the microphone.

"We've arrested an L.A. sheriff's deputy named Patrick Dutton and are holding him as a material witness in connection with the murder of ATF Agent William Greenridge. We have identified a shell casing that appears to have been fired from a sniper rifle belonging to the Sheriff's Special Enforcement Bureau. A partial print from that same casing appears to match Deputy Dutton's."

Then Sheriff Messenger stepped aside and made room for

Brady Cagel, who was dressed in his tan gab, with his tan face and tan, freshly barbered hair. Everything tan and perfect. A fed.

"Good morning," he said. "I am sorry to have to also confirm that one of the AR-fifteen sniper rifles belonging to the Bureau of Alcohol, Tobacco, Firearms, and Explosives Situation Response Team appears to have been involved in the shooting death of Deputy Sheriff Michael Nightingale. At this time we have not determined which ATF agent, if any, might be involved. The weapon could have been obtained by anyone with access to our armory, even civilian personnel. We are currently requesting that all agents and civilians with access to that particular SRT armory remain in the SWAT house under voluntary curfew. It is our hope that they will also cooperate with polygraph examinations."

He quickly gave way to Cole Hatton, who looked like ten million bucks in a tailored black pinstripe. Hatton cleared his throat, then spoke in his booming baritone.

"There is currently no evidence tying these two murders together. Sheriff Messenger, Agent Cagel, and I are all appalled at the suggestion that members of the ATF Special Weapons units and Sheriff's SEB Special Weapons Team might be gunning for each other after hours. However, until this investigation is complete, I urge the news media and the individual members of both the Los Angeles Sheriff's Department and ATF to please stand down and cooperate with us in every way possible. I promise that, in the end, justice will be served."

"Serve this, dickhead," Griff Hover said as he grabbed his crotch. "These humps at ATF are dirty."

"What about the sheriffs?" one of the other detectives said.

"Hey, the sheriffs might be square badges, but at least they back us up when we need 'em, and they roll on our calls," Griff said.

I went back into the restaurant and paid our bill.

"Dare I ask?" Jo said.

"Come on, don't put me through it. I saw you listening."

"This is about to get a lot messier," she said.

What happened was it got a lot deadlier.

PIECES

Jo AND I split up and I used the walk back to Parker Center
to gather my thoughts. I climbed up the stairs to the fourth
floor, taking them two at a time, using the brisk climb to clear
my head. Frankly, my spirits were a little low.

I was beginning to think maybe I *had* been wasting my time,
like everybody kept telling me. When you got down to it, Jigsaw
John retired twenty years ago. Things were different when he
was on the job. Back then, each division only had two or three
homicides per week. Now we have that many a night. With the
growing caseload, there just wasn't time to investigate this way
anymore.

In theory, you study pre-event behavior to determine mindset.
You look at the victim to see what might have been going on in
that person's life to draw the perp in.

If something didn't fit it could signal a mistake in reasoning, but it didn't have to. It was entirely possible that Smiley had just gone nuts and started shooting like Jo said, and then, because he was completely delusional, had chosen not to use his carefully dug tunnel.

What had been eluding me was a plausible alternate theory. Without that I had no line of logic to follow, nothing to work on.

I suppose it was always possible that these two SWAT teams were shooting at each other, but that was a hard concept for me to buy into. SWAT teams were supposed to be the cream of any law enforcement agency. All the evidence to the contrary, I just couldn't believe that SRT and SEB would try and settle a grudge with long guns. Was that valid reasoning, or just me trying to prop up the last vestige of a once-treasured idea? I wasn't sure any longer.

This afternoon I'd probably be getting a call from one of Hatton's federal IOs, with a new list of things to investigate. They'd treat me like a stupid lackey, ordering me to do scut work they were too busy for. They'd want me to background every member of SRT and SEB, looking for somebody with anger-management problems, or a history of unprovoked violence. There was no chance that the police union was going to let any of them be polygraphed.

I reached my cubicle in Special Crimes on the fourth floor, out of breath from running the stairs, and sank into the chair at my desk. Jo and I had divided our workload. She was going to see if she could get her computer genius to run down the insurance policy. Then she was going out to talk with Marion Bell and any of the members of the Rock Stars mountain climbing club she could locate.

We both had Vincent Smiley down as a loner. It would be worth finding out if he really belonged to some survivalist group or Nazi wilderness outfit. If that proved to be a reasonable alternate theory, it would move this investigation off SWAT and onto an antigovernment hate group. Skinheads always make convincing bad guys.

While Jo was running that down I was going to stay on the few hot trails we'd turned and work my way through Vincent's school years.

Busywork?

I looked up Mrs. Kimble's Country Day Middle School in Eagle Rock and placed a call. When I asked for the director, somebody named Rose Merick came on the line.

"Mrs. Kimble is retired," the sweet-sounding woman said.

One of my little games is to see if, over the phone, I can guess a person's age by their voice tonality. She sounded about sixty. I wrote 60 and put a question mark after it, then circled the number.

This was one of the many ways I attempt to alleviate boredom on the job. Innocent enough, I guess, but boredom, like violence, can change you. Some cops become so tweaked, they carry their emotional remedies to dangerous extremes.

Back in the late seventies, the entire night shift at Devonshire Division was so far into the ozone they devised a weird photo contest. They each put up ten bucks, then ran a monthly competition to see who could come up with the grossest photo. These guys were crawling onto beds with overdosed hookers while their partners snapped Polaroids. That's how screwed up you could get.

Humor is the shield that protects cops from the grim realities we're forced to deal with every day. As your view of life darkens you can quickly come to believe that most of humanity is primal, corrupt, and deadly. Little by little, if you're not careful, your humor becomes so sick that you're crawling into bed with a dead sixteen-year-old junkie just to get a laugh. The more death and human depravity you see, the more disillusioned you become, until one day you find yourself sitting on a toilet in some restaurant bathroom with the door locked and your service revolver in your mouth. After you pull the trigger nobody you work with even has to ask what went wrong or why you did it. They all know you just couldn't find a way to laugh anymore.

Angrily, I scratched out my *60*, thinking I had better find a more constructive way to dodge my boredom.

"I'm sorry I can't be of more help," Mrs. Merick was saying.

She was about to ring off when I had a thought.

"Do you still have records of your student body from the late eighties?"

"My goodness, no," she said. "That's over fifteen years ago. And if we do, they're in storage someplace. This is a very small facility."

"Were you teaching there during that time?" I asked.

"No. Except for Midge Kimble, I don't think anybody from the eighties is still around."

"Is Mrs. Kimble still in the area?"

"Yes she is."

"Could you give me her number?"

"I could, but I'd need to see your badge first. We can't just give out phone numbers anymore. Times have changed."

"How about you call me back at Parker Center. I'm in Special Crimes. Sergeant Scully. You can get the number out of the book so you'll know it's legit."

"I guess I could do that . . ."

Three minutes later my phone rang. Rose Merick again. She gave me Midge Kimble's number and address.

I called and reached a recording. If Mrs. Merick sounded sixty, Midge Kimble sounded a hundred. *I'm out right now*, a raspy voice shouted. *Leave your number and I'll call back.*

I did as she instructed.

I was gathering my notes, getting ready to head out, when the phone rang again. I snatched it up.

"Scully, it's Cletus."

Clete James was a friend who worked in the Juvenile Justice

Division. He was going to try to cut through the red tape and pull Vincent Smiley's early record.

"Your guy Smiley had some juvie busts in 'eighty-eight and nine, but I'm in a tug of war with the Pasadena City Attorney," he said. "She's being bitchy and set her heels on me. I'm gonna need a court order to open them."

"Pasadena?" I said, writing that in my crime book with the years '88–'89.

"Yeah, that's where all his juvie cases were filed."

"Nothing in my records about Pasadena. I have him living in Glendale, Burbank, and Agoura, going to middle school in Eagle Rock, but nothing in Pasadena."

"Well, Eagle Rock is only a few miles west of Pasadena. I think it's even in the same school district," Clete pointed out.

"Listen, in the late eighties Smiley had to have been about ten or twelve. Can you check to see if there's a bicycle license in Pasadena or Eagle Rock for a Vincent Smiley? Could be under his dad's name, Stanley, or maybe Edna."

"No problem. Hang on for a minute while I log on." Clete came back a few minutes later.

"Got it. Stanley Smiley. A Schwinn Scrambler, registered in March of 'eighty-eight—2346 Mountain Circle, Pasadena."

"Thanks, Clete. I owe ya."

I hung up and pulled a Thomas Street Guide out of my bottom desk drawer. Midge Kimble now lived on the far east side of the L.A. basin, way out in Duarte. I decided I'd start in Smiley's old neighborhood in Pasadena. Once I'd canvassed that, I'd move on east, check out Mrs. K., then head back and stop in at the hospital in Pasadena. I figured, if Vincent lived there in '88, there was an outside chance he was born in Pasadena at Huntington Hospital. I packed my stuff and headed out.

Mountain Circle is a side street off a main drag called Fair Oaks Boulevard, which runs north and south, stretching up into the Pasadena foothills. The further up Fair Oaks you go, the more sketchy and run-down it gets. I quickly found myself in a mostly black and Hispanic neighborhood. Single-story, run-down houses sat next to three-story, brown stucco project buildings that, when they were built, were heralded as the answer to urban blight, but within years had turned into urine-soaked, graffiti-marked monstrosities.

As I passed the Foothill Projects I witnessed a drug deal going down through a chain-link fence, right in plain view. The seller was a thirty-year-old banger dirtbag in a hooded blue sweat-shirt and satin basketball shorts. The buyers looked like two fifteen-year-old girls. I didn't stop. *Not my turf. Why sweat what you can't change?* I told myself.

I knew, even as these thoughts hit me, that I was wrong. Every time I see something like that and instead of stopping choose to just drive on and give it a wave, I know I'm losing a small part of myself. I become a little more jaded and skeptical with each lost opportunity. But experience taught me that if I did stop and chase that dealer and those teenagers through the projects and caught them, I'd likely face angry parents who would claim that I'd used unnecessary force during the arrest. They would file charges against me and then the crowded court system would plead the busts down to misdemeanors rather than prosecute. In the end, nothing much would have changed, except that a few more 181 complaints would be added to my IAD file.

Why bother? It won't change anything. But, of course, it does. It changes you.

I found Mountain Circle almost in the foothills, turned right, and eventually pulled up across the street from 2346. It was a small wooden house that had definitely seen better days. The long-dead lawn had been beaten into a hard dirt playground lit-tered with broken plastic toys. An old black Cadillac Brougham with a single hubcap and primered trunk was parked in the driveway.

I walked up to the door and rang the bell. The broken ringer snapped and buzzed like an angry wasp. Moments later the door opened to chain width and an angry black woman of indeterminate age glared out at me.

"Police?" she said, before I could even get my badge out. Something, some vibe had warned her that I was The Man and up to no good, even though I was smiling.

I showed her my shield and she glared at it with contempt. She'd seen dozens of badges, and experience told her it always turned out badly.

"Are you the owner of the house?" I asked.

"Got a warrant?"

"No ma'am," I said. "I'm just trying to find out if there's anybody living here who remembers Stan and Edna Smiley. They owned this house back in the eighties."

"Ain't no Smileys here," she growled.

"No—I know that. They *used* to live here. I wonder if there's anybody still in the neighborhood who might remember them from back then."

She looked at me with shrewd distrust. "What dis be about?" she said. " 'Nother nigger goin' down?"

"No ma'am, the Smileys were Caucasian."

Maybe she was glad to see some white assholes finally getting popped, or maybe she just wanted to be done with me. Either way, she blurted out the answer:

"Try the Phillips. They 'cross the street on the corner. Been here forever."

Then, without waiting for my thank you, she slammed the door in my face.

Across the street I saw a set of curtains close. You could almost feel a warning pulsing through the neighborhood. *Cop on the block.* How many eyes were watching me? Hard to say. I felt exposed, like a soldier caught behind enemy lines. I walked up on the Phillips' front porch and rang the doorbell.

"Who is it?" a high-pitched man's voice yelled.

My estimate? Seventy-five at least. Call that my last guess. One for the road.

"Police," I called through the door. "Mr. Phillips, I have a few questions about a case we're working. Maybe you can help us," trying to sound like Ed McMahon delivering a million dollars.

After a moment I heard half a dozen latches being thrown. The door creaked and a very old man was standing in front of me. His skin was so white I could see blue veins on the backs of his hands and around his temples. I'd undershot my guess by at least twenty years. A complete Magoo—round, hunched, half blind, and almost bald, he was dressed in a frayed checkered shirt, tan slacks, and old tennis shoes. A hearing aid the size of a bottle cap stuck out of his right ear, and thick, horn-rimmed magnifiers rode his bony nose.

"What was that you said?" he shouted at me, reaching for the volume on his hearing aid.

"Can I come in, sir?" I held up my badge.

He squinted at it. "Pasadena police?"

"Los Angeles."

"Fucking drugstore glasses," he mumbled.

Without saying anything further, he turned and hobbled into his living room.

I followed, breathing in Vicks VapoRub and mildew.

"Who is it, Albert?" a woman shrilled from the back.

"I got it. Go back to yer soaps," he yelled.

We sat on his uncomfortable coil-sprung sofa and he leaned forward.

"We don't give to no charities," he shouted, without warning. "Police included. Food Stamps. Social Security. You want money from us, gonna have to knock out our teeth and steal our fillings." Then he laughed. It was a strange, high-pitched, braying hee-hee.

"No sir. This isn't for money. It's about a case we're working on."

"A what?" He leaned in and again cranked up the volume on his hearing aid. It started screeching, but he didn't seem to notice.

"Sir, I think you should maybe turn that down a little."

He looked at me, blinking like a lizard on a flat, rock, but made no attempt to adjust the volume.

I plunged on. "Do you remember the Smileys?" I asked loudly. "Stanley and Edna? They lived across the street at 2346 back in 'eighty-eight or 'eighty-nine."

"Right," he said. But I wasn't sure he'd heard me.

"Edna and Stanley Smiley," I repeated.

"Yeah—that fucking plumber," he said. "I had him work on this place once. Fucked up everything. Had shit running out the overflow pipe in the backyard. We was on septics back then."

"Do you remember their child? He would've been about eleven or twelve."

"Which one?"

"What?"

"Which kid? Had two—boy and a girl."

"A boy and a girl?" I said, taking out my notebook.

"Ain't that just what I said? What's wrong? Y'deaf?" He actually said that to me while his hearing aid was wailing like an air-raid siren.

"How old was the girl?"

"Shit—how do I know? They was little kids 'bout eight or ten, both around the same age."

"Albert, who is it?" the woman demanded impatiently from the back.

He ignored her, or maybe he didn't hear her.

"Can you tell me anything else about them? What were their names?"

"The girl was Susan, the boy—can't remember what they called the little bastard. Both were assholes. Loud. Playing outside all hours. The parents were drinkers. Them kids was out sometimes riding their bikes around after ten o'clock at night, makin' noise. Edna and Stan inside, drunk as skunks."

"Was the boy's name Vincent?" I asked.

"Don't remember, mighta been. It wasn't like all I had t'do back then was watch the fuckin' plumber's house," he snapped. "If you say he was named Vincent, fine. Ain't gonna get no argument from me."

"How long did they live here?"

"One year. One year and one year only. Just one year." Why he said it four times, I have no clue.

"And then what? They sold the house and left?"

He thought about that, then nodded and sliced a withered hand through the air between us. "Good riddance. Fuck 'em."

He finally reached up and turned down the ear piece.

"You don't happen to have any pictures, do you?" I asked.

"Why would I take pictures o'assholes?" he said reasonably.

"And you have no idea where they moved to?"

"Nope."

"Albert, who is it?" the woman yelled again.

He didn't answer, but I knew he heard her this time, because an annoyed look followed.

"Well, thank you, sir. You've been a big help."

I walked to the front door then turned back to say good-bye. A strange, troubled expression appeared on his pale face. I thought he was about to say something, but he just lifted one haunch and farted. I let myself out.

Once outside I called Jo on my cell phone. She picked up on the second ring.

"I might know what happened to the other five hundred thou," I told her.

"Let's hear."

"Smiley had a sister named Susan. Maybe she got the other

half. The old man I talked to said he couldn't remember if Vincent was the boy's name or not, but the guy was ancient. Waiting for the chariot."

In light of that, we decided to scotch what we were doing and meet to reorganize at a restaurant I knew in Pasadena.

35

TWIN PALMS

THE TWIN PALMS Restaurant was developed by Cindy Costner in the mid-nineties. It's located on Green Street, just one block south of Colorado Boulevard in Old Town Pasadena. Old Town is one of the great redevelopment stories in Southern California. Back in the eighties it was a slum. Situated at the west end of Colorado Boulevard, it had become a hang out for winos, hookers, and hugger-muggers. Drug dealers hung on every corner selling bags of cut. Low-end secondhand stores were lumped in with all the urban decay, and the entire nine- or ten-block area had completely slid off the human spectrum into some sort of environmental hell.

Then a group of entrepreneurs saw an opportunity. They bought the land cheap and tore down the slums, while saving the period architecture. They lured in retail chains and designer shops and sprinkled in some upscale sidewalk restaurants with colorful Cinzano umbrellas shading decorative wrought iron tables. Presto! Four years later, Old Town became a shopper's mecca. Caffe Mocha and sushi bars, Tommy Bahama and The Gap. The winos moved east and started camping out under the freeway.

I pulled to the curb in front of the white-tented patio restaurant, then handed my keys to a red-coated valet and walked around the corner to the gated entrance. I didn't have a reservation, but it was a large place and there were enough tables so that you could be seated without too long a wait. I spotted Jo over at the bar. In one fist she had a Coors Light, the other was up to her mouth, head tilted back, tossing salted peanuts down her throat. Nothing too delicate there.

"You beat me," I said.

"Story of our short little partnership," she said, then slid off the stool and followed the hostess to a table over by the wall, taking the preferred gunfighter's seat looking out at the room, leaving me with the chair facing a slab of concrete. I settled in and ordered a Corona with a lime squeeze.

As I watched our hostess walk away to give my order to the bartender, Jo said, "So the neighbor says there were two kids. A boy *and* a girl."

"That's right. Susan and a boy, probably Vincent, both around the same age."

"Twins?" she said, looking up at me with a hunter's predatory gaze.

"I don't know. He didn't say."

"Twins would have the same DNA, right?" She was leaning forward now, a pointer on scent. "What if that was Smiley's twin sister they found in the bathtub up at Hidden Ranch Road? What if he *did* go out through the tunnel like you thought?" Loving her connect-the-dots theory, looking intently at me, waiting for me to pump my fist and go "Yesss!"

Instead, I felt myself frowning. "To begin with, we don't know if they were twins or not. Second, a girl and a boy would be fraternal twins, not identical."

"So what?" she said brushing that aside with an impatient gesture.

"We have an identical DNA match at the morgue. A boy and a girl can't have identical DNA. Fraternal twins don't look the same or have to be the same sex, because they come from two separate female eggs fertilized by two separate male sperms."

"You're sure about that?"

"No, I'm just saying it to mess up your theory."

"Look, you don't have to be copping attitude all the time. It was just a question."

"I was dealt off to a foster family in Torrance when I was seven. They had fraternal twins. Tom and Morgan Weiss. I had it explained half a dozen times. To have identical DNA, they have to be identical twins. That's the way it is."

"But all of a sudden we've got an extra kid here. Maybe his sis can fill in some of the blanks." She was jazzed. "So how do we find Susan?" she asked.

"We go back through county records. Start hunting. Of course, Susan might be married now. Different name."

She thought for a minute, then finally said, "How do you want to do this?"

"Huntington Hospital is only a mile or two from here, down Arroyo. If they lived here, maybe that was where they were born, and you can access Edna Smiley's prenatal records for the mid- to late seventies, find out for sure if they were twins, or if they were just brother and sister. Susan could have been a few years younger or older than Vincent. Mr. Phillips wasn't too sure of anything. Maybe there's other family listed on that form that we can contact."

"What're you going to do?" she asked.

"I'm gonna go see Midge Kimble. Maybe Susan went to that school with her brother and she can remember something."

Just then my cell phone rang. I looked at the readout: Jeb Calloway.

"Who is it?" she asked.

"My skipper." I turned the phone off and put it back on my belt.

"Aren't you gonna take it?"

"It's just him telling me to contact the IOs at Justice. The minute I do that we're gonna both get turned into info humpers for the FBI. Turn yours off, too. Let's be out of cell range for a while." She reached into her purse and switched off her cell.

The waiter came over and handed us menus. "Something for lunch?" he asked.

"Sorry, we're going to have to leave. Something just came up," I told him.

While we were waiting outside for our cars Jo touched my arm, and I turned to face her.

"I hate to tell you this, Hoss, but you were right. If we hadn't been reworking Smiley's background we would have completely missed this. Feels important, like it might lead somewhere."

"But let's not get carried away. So far, all we have are questions and we only have a few hours to get the answers before we're yanked in a another direction."

"Maybe you should learn to take a fucking compliment yourself," she grinned. Then she did a strange thing—she reached out and took my hand. "Don't get the wrong idea here, Scully, this is purely professional, but as partners go, you ain't half bad."

Our cars arrived. She had managed to get the green Suburban back from Vice. She got in and, without looking back, roared off toward Huntington Hospital. A few minutes later I was in the Acura on my way to see what Midge Kimble had to offer.

My nose was definitely twitching. Or, as Jigsaw John might have said, "We got our first whiff of something good here, boy."

MIDGE

ROYAL OAKS MANOR turned out to be an upscale assisted-living facility. As I pulled up the drive I saw a large expanse of rolling lawns and neo-Spanish Colonial buildings. This wasn't your standard linoleum floor and vinyl couch old folks home. There were attractive, tile-roofed buildings separated by expensive floral landscaping. The residences all had their own two-car garages. There was a large medical facility off to the east side of the property, next to a tennis court and a large common patio. I pulled in and parked between a new red Mercedes and a black Lincoln Town Car, then walked up the manicured path to the main building. Inside the spacious contemporary lobby I found a house phone, dialed zero, and asked for Midge Kimble. A minute later I heard the familiar shouted greeting from her answering machine.

I hung up and went to the front desk. An elderly man working over some papers glanced up at me.

"I'm looking for Midge Kimble," I told him.

"Today is bridge day," he said. "She's out in the Culture Center Annex."

"Where's that?"

"Through the main lobby, down the corridor. It's the pavillion on the right."

I thanked him and made the trip. If you were stuck waiting for the Grim Reaper, this was certainly the place to do it. The windows offered views of beautiful trees and flowering bushes. Purple bougainvillea trellised off latticework set up in each of the small, landscaped areas. Outside the main sliding glass doors, Brown Jordan outdoor furniture sat on a large, pebbled, concrete patio, all of it washed clean, sparkling in the afternoon sunshine.

The Culture Center Annex was an art exhibit area off the main building. I walked into a high-ceilinged room filled with older, well-dressed men and women studiously playing bridge. There were at least ten card tables, all fully occupied, everybody bent forward, intent on their cards. For a room full of people, it was strangely quiet. I didn't quite know where to start. This place seemed so upscale, I couldn't just shout out Midge's name. Sensing my dilemma, a woman seated at the table nearest me reached out and touched my arm. I turned toward a pleasant octogenarian in a pink pillbox hat.

"You look lost," she said sweetly.

"I'm looking for Midge Kimble."

"In the blue dress over by the window." She smiled, so I smiled back. "Nice to have such fine young people come visit," she said.

Right then I didn't feel very fine or young, but I thanked her and walked over to the table and waited until the foursome finished a hand and started throwing their cards into the center.

"Excuse me, are you Midge Kimble?" I asked the woman in the blue dress.

"I am." Her voice was strong and didn't even resemble her shouted message on the answering machine. She was close to eighty, but there had been a time when she would have stopped traffic. The remnants of beauty still clung stubbornly to her strong, wrinkled face.

"I hate to interrupt your game, but I have a few questions."

"In that case, you have excellent timing," she said a bit too loudly.

"I do?"

"I'm the dummy."

"I beg your pardon?"

"It's a bridge term," she said, smiling. "After the bid on the next hand I lay my cards down. Don't have to do anything after that. It's called being the dummy."

"Oh—I never played bridge."

I watched as the cards were dealt and a round of bidding started.

"Three spades," one of the women said.

"Four hearts," another answered.

"Four spades," a third said. It went on like that for a while until finally Midge said:

"Trump." Then she laid down her hand face up, rose, and accompanied me to an alcove in the adjoining room.

Midge Kimble was spry and athletic. She moved with authority and purpose. We sat down and she fixed a polite smile on her face, waiting for me to begin. She had inbred grace and refined social bearing.

"This is nice out here," I started, apropos of absolutely nothing. I hate to admit this, but, sometimes when I'm in the presence of money or culture my normal self-confidence can suddenly desert me. Another curse visited on me by my childhood. I had a sudden revealing thought: *Did I become a cop so I'd have social authority and could use my badge to gain emotional status, and to build a wall between me and my insecurities?*

"My husband was a developer," she was saying. "He actually put up two of these buildings when we moved out here. The Kimble Rec Center across from B unit was his. You can see it on the right when you drive out."

"So the school was just a hobby?" I said, putting the pieces together thinking, her husband had the gelt and she ran the country day school for kicks.

"Not a hobby—a treasured vocation," she said, fixing me with a stern look.

My smile felt hot on my face. I immediately pulled out my badge and showed it to her.

"Oh my goodness," she said. "I knew I shouldn't have borrowed Lillian's jewelry and not returned it."

"I'm sorry?"

She smiled. "I'm just fooling, Sergeant. When you get to my state in life, you need to take your laughs where you can find them." The same argument the humps in Devonshire had used.

But I liked her. Instantly I felt more at ease.

"This is about a young boy who I believe went to your school, named Vincent Smiley. It was around 'eighty-eight or 'eighty-nine. Do you remember him?"

"Yes." Her expression softened slightly, or maybe it saddened. "Vividly," she added.

"I was wondering if you could tell me a little about him?"

"It was one of the strangest things that ever happened during all the years I ran that school."

"Start at the beginning," I said, and whipped out my trusty notebook, clicked down my pen, then poised over a fresh page, all business now. Sergeant Scully on the case.

"The Smiley children first came to school in the sixth grade. Paul and Susan."

"Paul, not Vincent?"

"If you'll let me finish, I'm getting to that."

"Sorry."

I wrote down PAUL AND SUSAN SMILEY, underlined PAUL, then wrote KIMBLE COUNTRY DAY—'88.

"Paul was very bright and outgoing. His twin sister, Susan, was extremely shy. Almost never said anything."

So they were twins, I thought, writing that down.

Midge was saying, "They didn't get along, which seemed strange for twins, but they were both excellent students."

"Sixth grade—that made them about twelve."

"Yes. Twelve."

"At the end of seventh grade something very extraordinary happened."

"What was that?"

"Susan Smiley was in the girl's restroom when one of the other little girls happened to open the bathroom stall. Susan had forgotten to lock it and this other girl saw that Susan had a penis. She was standing up in her blonde ringlets and dress, urinating right into the toilet."

"Susan was a boy."

"Yes. It turned out that Susan was really Vincent. We took the child into the nurse's office and called his parents in. Stanley Smiley didn't come, but his mother Edna did. We forced an inspection in her presence so we could see for ourselves. Well, I must tell you, nobody was prepared for what happened next. Mrs. Smiley went into a white rage. I think she was a drinker and was maybe a little drunk at that meeting. She started shouting that she didn't care what I or anybody thought. She didn't want twin boys, always wanted a daughter. So she raised Vincent as Susan. She let his hair grow long and had been dressing him as a girl since he was an infant."

She sat back and looked at me, the sad memory of this rich on her face. "Once Mrs. Smiley told us that, it explained everything. Vincent's shy behavior when he was being Susan, the fact that the twins seemed to hate each other. It was an impossible situation. All over school the children were talking about it. We had to call a school assembly with everybody's parents to discuss the situation. Twelve is an awkward age, and sexuality becomes a growing concern. I knew that it would be a mistake to try and keep the Smiley boys at school. The school year was almost over, so I made arrangements for them to finish the grade work at home."

"And then they were homeschooled the following year?" I said.

"Yes. We called in Child Services. There was a major argument about taking the children away from the Smileys. But, since they weren't being physically abused, there was no way to remove them from the home, because, when you came down to it, they had only violated a school dress code. We signed an affidavit and the boys were homeschooled for the eighth grade. We supplied the curriculum, then the boys went off to Glendale High in ninth grade."

"As boys this time?"

"Yes. Vincent and Paul registered at Glendale High."

"Do you know about the car accident that killed their parents?" I asked.

"Strange you should mention that. When it happened I think the police suspected Vincent. They came and talked to me. Back then he was still a juvenile, around seventeen I believe."

"So the results of that investigation would be locked in his juvenile record," I said, making a note. This explained why the C.A. wouldn't release Vincent's file. She obviously had read all of his juvie records for Pasadena and Glendale and knew it would be used at the SWAT trial. Without a court order mandating its release, she'd have a lot of explaining to do.

"I think the police suspected Vincent of foul play," Midge was saying. "I know they picked him up and talked to him. The

Smileys had moved to a house off Cliff View in Glendale. There was a steep incline that went down from their house. One evening, Stanley and Edna's brakes failed. They went over the cliff on the last turn. The car burned, so nothing much was left for the police to examine. Eventually, it just went into the records as an accident."

Fat chance, I thought.

"He was out of high school after that—in junior college." She went on. "That was the last I heard of him, until that shoot-out two weeks ago." She frowned. "That poor boy probably never had much of a chance, did he?"

"Thank you, Mrs. Kimble. You've been a huge help." I stood to go. "If you think of anything else call me at that number." I put down my card.

"You should try and get in touch with his brother Paul. I think he lives up in San Francisco. He might be able to tell you something."

"I can't," I said. "Paul's dead."

37
UNION PARK

I COULDN'T REACH Jo on the phone, but then, like an asshole, I'd told her to keep her cell off to avoid getting called in by the FBI. My next try was Alexa.

She was in Cole Hatton's office and stepped out of a heated debate to take my call. Since the meeting was just breaking up, she agreed to get together with me in Union Park across the street from the Federal Building in thirty minutes.

I hit the gas and cut through traffic, banging on my horn, going Code 2, breaking red lights all the way to the freeway. Then I slammed the pedal down, doing almost ninety on the 110 and took the Chinatown off-ramp to Union Park. It was a little past one o'clock when I grabbed a metered parking place and got out. I saw Alexa in a great-looking black dress I'd bought her for her birthday. She was standing over by a hot dog vendor buying a foot-long, saw me coming, and met me halfway.

"Sit down," I told her. "So you don't drip mustard on my favorite outfit." We settled on a bench nearby.

"What is it that couldn't wait an hour until I got back to the office?" she said. She still looked way too stressed to me.

"If I told you that Vincent Smiley was alive, that he went out that tunnel Jo and I found under his house, what would you say?"

"That it's impossible. His DNA was crossmatched. The man's positively dead."

"Smiley had an identical twin brother named Paul. Identical twins have identical DNA."

She sat there taking this in. Then she said, "Had?"

"My bet is it was the twin who did the flambé in the bathtub. It's a long story why, but Paul and his twin brother Vincent hated each other. My theory is Vince lured his brother down from San Francisco, or maybe even kidnapped him. Either way, he gets Paul out to Hidden Ranch. He ties him up and waits. When Emo shows up he starts a shoot-out, conks his brother, and leaves him in the tub, then crawls out through the tunnel we found."

"And you think Vincent is the one murdering the SWAT team guys." She furrowed her brow, trying to fit the pieces.

"That's my guess. He hates cops because they wouldn't accept him so he arranges his death using Paul as a stand-in. Then he crawls out through the tunnel. He pops Greenridge first, then does Nightingale to get a SWAT war going between the sheriff's department and ATF, sits back, and watches it go down on TV. I've been looking at this guy's early life, and we have a very sick puppy here."

"What about the shell casings? We found shell casings at both crime scenes that match long guns at both SEB and SRT. One of them has a partial print that matches an SEB deputy."

"I've been thinking about that on the way over here. SRT does their SWAT training out in Moorpark, at a range they have there. Sheriff's do it at Spring Ranch, near Agoura. I've been to Spring Ranch. You can see the firing range from the road. How hard would it be to hide out on the road until an SEB SWAT team shows up for target practice, wait till they leave, and sneak in and pick up the brass from the long guns?

"It never quite worked for me, that Patrick Dutton was on the SEB Red team and not Scott Cook's Gray team. Now it makes a lot of sense. Smiley couldn't tell who fired which casing. He just knew it was all SWAT ordnance that would eventually be matched to one of their sniper rifles."

Alexa sat looking at me, the hot dog forgotten in her hand. "Shit," she said softly, then dropped the uneaten dog in the trash.

"My guess is Vince got the two-twenty-three casings from the SRT range in Moorpark and the three-oh-eights from the sheriff's SWAT range. He set up the phony shooting sites, the secondary crime scenes, left the three-oh-eight casing in the apartment across the street from Greenridge's house and the two-twenty-three behind Nightingale's, along with the Danner boot prints, for us to find. We all thought the shooter was making it too easy, not picking up his brass. That's why! He needed us to find them. He was setting a frame."

"I'm going to go talk to Tony and Bill. Then we need to take it to Cole." Alexa stood. "Where are you going to be?"

"I've gotta find my partner. She's disappeared."

"Okay, but turn your damn phone on. I got a call from Cal. He said he can't reach you. Who do you think you're fooling with that shit?"

"If I'd answered that call, I'd have spent the morning downtown sorting through SRT folders, and we wouldn't have any of this, so you tell me," I said.

She nodded, turned to go, then turned back and unexpectedly

kissed me. A bright smile suddenly appeared on her face. The first one I'd seen in two weeks.

"You're the best damn detective on the force," she told me.

"Wanta fuck?" I asked.

"Hold the thought. I'll get right back to you on that."

Then she spun and ran across the park toward Parker Center.

38
WHERE'S BRICKHOUSE?

Jigsaw John was a genius. No wonder the guy cleared 85 percent of his cases. I sat in the park, looking up Union Street at Parker Center, trying to pin down the last pieces of the puzzle. Smiley had used identical weapons from his own armory to shoot Nightingale and Greenridge. Mr. Magoo couldn't remember the correct ages of the twins. He'd guessed too young. They weren't eight or ten, they were twelve. An easy enough mistake for an old grump with no kids. The Smileys moved away in one year because of the fiasco at Midge's school. Changed school districts, left Pasadena, went to Glendale.

My guess was that Jo Brickhouse was still out in Pasadena at the hospital. I called and asked for someone in admitting or records, did my badge number boogie, and was told that nobody from the L.A. Sheriff's Department had been there looking at birth records.

Okay—so, where was my strong-willed partner?

I called the Sheriff's Bureau, reached Jo's office at Internal Affairs, and asked them if they'd heard from her. Nada.

Where are you, kid? Then uneasiness struck. A sense of impending disaster swept down on me. A fluttering of dark wings in my mind, stirring dead air in my empty head.

Why did I tell her to keep her cell off? Stupid.

But I'd solved it. *We'd* solved it.

From here on it was just a straight-up system bust, put out a BOLO: Be on the lookout. Wait until some passing squad car made the spot, take Mr. Smiley off to jail, or if he wanted to do the dance, plant him right where we find him. Either way, Jo and I were out of it. For us it was over. Nothing bad was headed our way. I tried to ignore my premonition of disaster.

"You got five dollars?" a gruff voice said.

I looked up at a homeless man, about fifty, with matted hair and taped-up sneakers.

"I'm starvin'. Ain't et for a day."

"I know where you can get a good meal."

I reached down into the trash and fished out Alexa's uneaten hot dog. It was still warm and wrapped in white paper. I handed it to him.

"What the fuck am I gonna do with that?" he said.

"Eat it. Nothing wrong with it."

He shook his head. His expression, a symphony of disgust.

"Ain't the way it works, asshole." He dropped the dog back into the trash, turned, and limped away.

Yeah? So, how does it work? I wondered. *I give you the fin, so you can buy more malt liquor? Keep you drinking malt 40s until your leaking kidneys finally rot? That how it works, asshole?*

I had a moment of sweeping remorse. I had been so focused

on the case for the last ten days, it had completely consumed me. Now that it looked like we had the answers, I was feeling empty and alone, sitting on a bench in a park full of strangers. Again, my case had moved on without me. I needed to clear my head, so I decided to call and see if Chooch was having football practice this afternoon. He'd said he would leave a message on the phone to give me the time and location. I called our answering machine and, sure enough, Chooch's voice greeted me.

"This is for Dad: four o'clock—same place in Agoura. It's looking up. I've got some real animals on this team."

Just as I was about to hang up I heard another voice.

"Hoss, this is Jo. I found Susan Smiley's address." She sounded jazzed. "I had someone in my office go through all the phone books. We found a listing. She lives in Inglewood, off Centinela, near Vincent Park. Three-four-six Hillside. Since we're running out of time, I'm on my way over there now. If you get this message you can meet me there. In the meantime, I'm going to go ahead and brace her woman-to-woman, see how much I can get. Wish me luck."

I hit the ground running before the message was complete. Jo didn't know that Susan was Vincent.

I reached the Acura and squealed out, jamming my finger on the GPS to bring up the map screen. The most direct route to Inglewood was straight down La Brea. It was just a little past one in the afternoon, so, with the lunch traffic, I'd probably make better time on surface streets than by trying to get over to the freeway.

I roared down Exposition, breaking lights, then hung a left onto La Brea. I don't have a MCT in my personal car, so, with no computer, I turned on the police scanner under the dash and put out a call for backup.

"This is L-nineteen. Officer requests backup at three-four-six Hillside in Inglewood. One plainclothes female officer with blond hair in a blue jacket is already on the scene. Perp at this address is a possible One-eight-seven P. Request a unit respond Code Three."

The RTO came back immediately and put out the call division-wide. Unit A-22 was assigned Code-3.

All the way down La Brea I cursed myself for having Jo turn off all her communication equipment, a complete breach of police procedure. How could I have been such a jerk?

I passed Slauson.

I was praying this was another Susan Smiley, but the way my luck had been running, I doubted it. Vincent had been Susan Smiley all the way through seventh grade. Susan was his alter ego. In trouble, hiding from the law, I was pretty sure he'd choose to be Susan again. If he did, then Jo Brickhouse was walking right into another vertical coffin.

After I passed Fairview, I heard a siren converging on my left. In the LAPD, only one unit at a time can go red-light-and-siren. The reason is, if two units both have their sirens on, they can't hear one another. As they both get close to the address, the chance of a high-speed collision grows exponentially. Way too many units crashed before this rule was in place.

I could hear the crosstalk on the scanner. One-Adam-22 was about four blocks to my right as I turned on Hyde Park. I was now inside of Inglewood. All the way down La Brea I had been trying to dial in my GPS. Finally I had the address programmed in. Hillside was about four blocks up, off Field Street.

I saw Field, hung a right, then turned right again. Finally I was on Hillside. I'd beaten the squad cars. Half a block away I saw Jo's green Suburban parked at the curb. I didn't want to come sliding in hot, squealing rubber because I didn't know what kind of a situation I had and didn't want to announce myself with a high-speed, tire-smoking stop. I pulled over half a block up, unholstered my Beretta, then made a low run across the street and up the grass onto the front porch at 346.

Nobody seemed to be home. The house was a small one-story, wood-sided number, badly in need of paint. The yard was overgrown. It looked deserted, but if Vincent had bought it as a place to hide out after the shoot-out, I didn't see him wasting a lot of time on maintenance.

Then I heard a gun shot.

Seconds later I heard a car start in the back of the house. I ran to the corner of the porch and peeked down the driveway. A huge black Ram 2500 truck, with high-suspension and dual tires on the rear, came flying right at me. Smiley was behind the wheel. At least I think it was him. He was wearing a woman's blonde wig, lipstick, and hoop earrings. Man-sized muscular forearms gripped the wheel. I jumped back as he roared past. Then I fired three shots at the fleeing truck. I broke some glass, but that was about it.

The black-and-white patrol car was just screaming up Hillside, going Code-3. Smiley steered the bigfoot Dodge right at it. In this deadly game of chicken, the huge, high-centered, pipe-grilled truck was bound to win. At the last moment Adam-22 swerved, hit the curb, and blew out its suspension skidding up on somebody's front lawn, tearing deep furrows in the grass. The Dodge disappeared up the street, smoking rubber around the corner. I knew Jo had to be in big trouble, but my first duty was to get Adam-22 back into the pursuit. I ran toward the squad car holding my badge out in front of me.

"LAPD! Take the black Acura. Go after him." I threw my keys at them. "He's a cop killer! Get it on the radio! Ida-May-Victor, five-eight-seven." I yelled the truck's plate number and immediately one of the cops was putting it out on the air while the other ran to my car. He got in my Acura, his partner finished his broadcast and dove in beside him. They squealed away up the street after the Dodge truck.

I ran back to the house with my gun drawn, heading up the driveway, moving fast, but carefully.

Jo was lying up on the back patio, a messy hole, high in her chest. I ran to her and kneeled down, put my hand on her throat to check for a heartbeat. The bullet had entered just above her heart and had gone through her lung, blowing out a large exit hole in her back.

After a minute, Jo opened her eyes, looked up at me and started to speak.

"Save your strength," I said. Then I took off my jacket and slid it underneath her, putting it over the larger exit wound in her back making a compress, pushing it tight.

She started to cough.

I grabbed my cell, dialed 911, ordered an ambulance, and put out an officer down. Then I prayed they'd get there in time.

Jo's face was turning pale and slick, her eyes were losing focus. I stroked her forehead and held her hand.

"This still ain't gonna get you laid, Hoss," she whispered softly.

39 E.R.

J O DIDN'T SPEAK again and lapsed into unconsciousness. I was holding her in my lap, watching the life leak out of her. Finally I heard the ambulance siren arrive out front, and the EMTs pulled into the drive. I yelled out and they quickly found us in the back.

The rest was a blur. I wandered around in the backyard trying to keep my wits about me as they loaded her on a gurney and set up an IV bag. I felt weak and nauseous. I was shaking, beginning to come unstrapped.

They lifted Jo into the ambulance and I hitched a ride, sitting in the front seat of the rescue unit with Jo's black leather purse in my lap.

"Get this thing moving," I snapped at the driver who was slowly edging the big ambulance out onto the street.

Then we were speeding out of Inglewood on the way to the L.A. County King/Drew Medical Center, which was only five miles away. The siren heehawed, clearing traffic all the way down Crenshaw Boulevard to the hospital.

I found a spot in the E.R. waiting room as anxious surgeons ran down from the O.R. upstairs. Finally, I opened Jo's purse and used her cell phone to call her office. I told her lieutenant supervisor what happened, then hung up and scrolled through the numbers. I found a listing for BOLLINGER, BR. *Bridget?* I pushed dial and in a moment I had Sheedy, Long, and Bollinger Advertising.

"Is Bridget Bollinger there?"

"Ms. Bollinger? Just a minute," the operator said. Then I was connected with some guy in New Accounts.

"I'm trying to speak with Bridget Bollinger," I told him.

"Who may I say is calling?"

"I'm a friend of Josephine Brickhouse's."

"Moment, please," he said and put me on hold. I was listening to an inane muffler shop jingle.

He came back on a minute later.

"Ms. Bollinger cannot be disturbed. She's with an account," he said.

"Hey, Sonny—this is Sergeant Scully, LAPD, and it's a police matter. You tell *Ms.* Bollinger to get her ass on the phone right now or I'll come down there and put the whole building in cuffs."

I was shaking, my nerves and emotions in a boil. *Calm down,* I lectured myself. *This isn't the way you get results.* I was back on hold. Then a minute later I heard a female voice that was smooth and coldly inquisitive.

"What's this concerning?" she asked.

I pictured the pretty, black-haired woman with the high cheekbones and structured face.

"Ms. Bollinger, I'm Sergeant Scully, LAPD. Jo Brickhouse

and I have been working a case together. She was shot this afternoon. She's in critical condition in L.A. County King/Drew Hospital. I thought you might like to know."

"Oh, my God!" Bridget said, attitude replaced by anguish. "Where is the hospital?"

"Wilmington Avenue, south of the one-oh-five."

"Is she . . . is she going to be . . ."

"I don't know. She was hit in the chest, lost a lot of blood. She's in a coma. To be honest, it doesn't look too good. If you want to see her, you'd better get here quick." I hung up.

They moved Jo upstairs to an O.R.

I waited on the surgical floor while the docs opened her chest and started picking out bullet fragments. The asshole had shot her at point-blank range, using a hollow point, which broke up on impact. They were desperately trying to tie off the bleeders and fix the mess inside her.

I called Alexa and told her what happened.

"Oh my God, Shane. I'm sorry," she said.

"I tried to get there to warn her. She didn't know about Vincent. She thought she was going to see his sister Susan. He came to the door in a wig, shot her, and took off in a black Dodge truck. I don't know what happened after that, whether they caught him or not. Two blues crashed their unit, so they borrowed my car and went after him.

"I'll find out. Keep your phone on." She hung up.

Ten minutes later she called back.

"You won't believe it," she said, "but the two guys from A-twenty-two tried to bust through an intersection against a red light and got broadsided by a city bus. Both of them are in Baldwin Hills Emergency. Your car is totaled."

"And Smiley got away?"

"Looks like it," she said.

Ten or fifteen minutes later people from the Sheriff's Department started showing up. Among them was Jo's boss at IAD and the undersheriff, a nice looking guy with silver hair, named Bert Clausen.

They began filtering in one by one, some in uniform, others in civvies, off-duty officers and civilian personnel. I wondered if they were sorry now that they had been dogging her all week for just doing her job. As more of them arrived, I was pushed to the side and ended up sitting alone on a vinyl sofa trying to keep my chin up.

If only I hadn't told her to turn off her cell.

Why didn't I go out there with her?

Ifs and whys. Questions that never get answered.

Twenty minutes later Bridget arrived looking drawn and nervous. I saw her come off the elevator and I went to intercept her.

"I'm Shane," I said.

"Thank you for calling me." Her voice was faint, almost a whisper.

I didn't respond. I was all out of pleasantries.

"Is she . . ."

"In trouble."

You can generally tell how bad it is by the way people move in the hall outside the operating theatre. Too many nurses were running to suit me.

Bridget looked like she was about to break.

"We were having—she and I . . ."

"Look, Bridget, that's between you guys."

"No—I mean—I walked out. I've wanted to call her half a dozen times since then. It's just—Jo can be so definite. She's not someone who lets you get too close."

She sank down onto the sofa. Her face crumpled, her eyes brimmed with tears. I reached over and took her hand.

"You're wrong. She's not definite, and she wants to let you in. She's just scared. It's how she covers it."

"She thinks I don't care, but that's not the problem. The problem is I care too much."

"Bridget, she needs you now. She needs somebody to sit with her. I can't stay. I've got to catch the guy who did this. But somebody needs to protect her from the mistakes that can happen in big medical factories like this one."

"I can do that," she said valiantly.

"And she needs somebody to hold her hand. Somebody to pray for her and—"

I stopped because suddenly I was on the verge of tears, myself.

"You really care for her, don't you?" Bridget said.

"Yes," I said. "I really do." Then I thought for a minute before I went on.

"Jo is one of a kind. She makes her own rules. You gotta love someone who walks their own trail, no matter the consequences."

"I do," Bridget said softly, and from the sound of her voice, she meant it.

Ten minutes later the surgeon came out and told us that Jo was critical and had been moved to ICU.

"The next forty-eight hours will tell the story," he said.

I decided to put them to good use. I couldn't help Jo sitting around here. I was going to even the score, get some payback for Josephine Brickhouse. I'd failed Jo just at the moment I realized how special she really was.

I was going to catch this son-of-a-bitch or die trying.

CLIMBING

AT THREE-FORTY-FIVE I was back at Smiley's hideout house in Inglewood. Since I'd left two hours ago it had become a full-fledged LASD crime scene. CSI had chalked the spot where Jo fell. She was facing the back door when he shot her. The techies from soles and holes were searching the backyard with metal detectors, looking for bullet fragments. I found the man in charge. Deputy Douglas Hennings was a fifty-year-old plainclothes drone with a vanilla personality and hair the color of poured concrete.

"You were working this thing with her?" Hennings said, after I had shown my creds and explained who I was. He started motioning to his second, another deputy sheriff in a suit, who wandered over and stood behind me, blocking my exit as if I was the problem.

"How come an LAPD Special Crimes dick is working with one of our IAD advocates?" Hennings said. "That sounds screwy."

"Look, Deputy Hennings, if you want to call Sheriff Messenger . . ."

"No, I don't wanta call the sheriff. I'd like you to answer my question."

"We were working a joint reinvestigation of the Hidden Ranch Road shooting at the request of Mayor MacKenzie and Supervisor Salazar." I saw a little shadow pass across his eyes at the mention of the politicos. "Sergeant Brickhouse left me a message that she was coming over here to conduct an interview. I arrived right after Vincent Smiley shot her. He blew out of here dressed in women's clothing, driving a new black Dodge Ram twenty-five hundred, license number Ida-May-Victor-five-eight-seven. Surely, you must already have all this." My frustration was mounting.

"Let's get this on tape from the beginning," Hennings said, motioning again to his partner, who moved in and cracked his knuckles like a gunfighter about to upholster a six-gun. Instead, he reached for a Sony minitape and placed it under my nose.

For the next twenty minutes Hennings took my statement. What I wanted to do is get past this guy and search the house before the sheriff's department criminalists bagged everything for evidence and hauled it out of there.

After I finished my statement, I asked Hennings if I could take a look around. He regarded me skeptically.

"I know how to work a crime scene," I assured him. Then, to show him I meant business, I pulled out my latex gloves. *See?* He finally nodded, so I snapped them on and went down the hall into the master bedroom.

It was immediately obvious that Smiley had been living here as Susan. The clothes in the closet were all large-sized dresses and skirts. In the bureau, women's blouses and underwear, extra large. The cosmetics in the bathroom were pancake and rouge.

His preferred shade of lipstick was Bozo-the-Clown red, something called Torche. Pinned up over the mirror were several Polaroids of Vincent in drag—close-ups of his face in full makeup. Janet Reno on steroids. I broke my promise to Hennings, and filched one, putting it in my side coat pocket. Then I stood surveying the bathroom, trying to get a grip on the methodology here. Was this just a place to run after he shot Emo and barbecued his brother Paul, or did he actually live here as Susan half the time? How long had he owned this house, or did he just rent? I made a mental note to check the local Realtors.

I left the house twenty minutes later and walked out to the driveway. I wondered if anybody had gone through his garbage yet. Not wanting to let this normally important crime-scene treasure trove get away, I moved behind the garage and opened his cans. Both empty. The sheriff's crime techs had beat me to it. Then I noticed some sheets of paper on the ground, partially hidden behind some bushes. One was an old market list, but the other was some kind of computer printout that had "YUMA TACTS" on the top. Under that was a series of columns and boxes:

7S	MECH INFANTRY REIN	1335	PG783783	N 33 13 57.1	W 115 05 16.6	LIVE ORD	1, 2
8S	MECH INFANTRY REIN	1539	PG726796	N 33 14 39.9	W 115 08 58.2	LIVE ORD	1, 2
10S	SA-6 Site	2240	PG771820	N 33 15 56.5	W 115 06 01.1	LIVE ORD	1, 2
11S	ARMORED COLUMN	2203	PG773815	N 33 15 38.1	W 115 05 54.3	LIVE ORD	1, 2
12S	SAM SITE	1348	PG735806	N 33 15 12	W 115 08 18.5	LIVE ORD	1, 2
13S	MECH INFANTRY	1444	PG718803	N 33 15 02.9	W 115 09 27.5	LIVE ORD	1, 2
14S	MECH INFANTRY REIN	2350	PG771772	N 33 13 14.5	W 115 05 57.4	LIVE ORD	1, 2
15S	NE-SW AIRFIELD W/SAM, AAA, RADAR SITES	0205	PG736809	N 33 15 23.6	W 115 08 17	LIVE ORD	1, 2
MT. BARROW	NE-SW AIRFIELD W/SAM SITES	0545	PG895707	N 33 09 42.1	W 114 58 10.8	LIVE ORD	1, 2, 5

Tad Palmer told me he'd seen this site on Smiley's computer out at Hidden Ranch, and I had tried unsuccessfully to access Cactus West on my PC. With words like INFANTRY and LIVE ORD, I knew it was some kind of military site.

I put the paper in my jacket pocket with the Polaroid and headed back toward the driveway. As I passed the garage, I noticed that the side door was ajar, so I pushed it open with my toe and walked in.

Nothing much was inside. A few recent oil stains on the pavement, but nothing was piled up against or hung on the walls. I noticed some old cardboard boxes up in the rafters that looked like they'd been broken down, folded and stored up there. Probably nothing, but most people don't go to the trouble to store broken-down boxes, so I found a ladder and dragged it over, climbed up, and started pulling at the edges. They cascaded down and landed on the floor.

I climbed down and started opening them up. The shipping labels indicated they had come from a mail order catalogue called The Mountaineer. The UPS dates indicated they were all delivered within the last week. I started to pull out the manufacturer's packing lists that had been left behind.

The first box I went into had contained a GPS—a miniunit for exact global satellite positioning. I reached into another box and found the printed instructions for installing something called "crampon metal spikes." They attached to the bottom of boots and were used for ice climbs. There was a box for an ascender and one for fifi hooks, which had a complicated set of instructions for a hanging belay. There was a box for an SLCD. The instructions indicated that it was a spring-loaded camming device, used to improve handholds on a cliff face.

What it all came down to was Vincent had recently ordered one hell of a lot of expensive mountain-climbing equipment. The boxes had been opened here, but since the gear wasn't in the house or garage, it was probably in the back of that bigfoot

Dodge 2500 that had roared out of here, almost hitting me. Detective logic at its tip-top best.

I left the garage by the side door, walked down the drive, and climbed into a slick-back D-car that I'd picked up at the motor pool downtown after leaving the hospital. I drove slowly up the block, trying to figure my most effective next move. Jo's purse was on the seat beside me. Nobody had asked me for it at the hospital, so I just held onto it. I drove up the street and found a quiet place to park, then pulled over and turned off the engine.

I opened the purse and pulled out Jo's crime book, then began flipping pages until I found what I was looking for.

IF IT'S A BELL, RING IT

I PULLED INTO the parking lot of a one-story showroom office in Sunland a few minutes past five in the afternoon. The window art advertised Sprint contracts and the latest in digital communications. The company's name and slogan were in big white letters:

BELL COMMUNICATIONS
IF IT'S A BELL . . . RING IT

I got out and walked inside. Most places that sell computer and phone equipment keep the air-conditioning on way too low. This was no exception. They hadn't wasted much thought on décor either. Like a lot of yuppie businesses these days, the trend was toward open space and hard surfaces. The color scheme was overpoweringly gray. The showroom had concrete floors and the ceilings were crisscrossed with exposed aluminum air ducts. Every kind of cell phone imaginable was displayed in glass cases.

I asked for Marion Bell and was told by a sneering pair of pleated pants that I couldn't see Mr. Bell without an appointment. I showed this arrogant dweeb my badge and cocked a suspicious eyebrow, which is the cop equivalent of "Wanta bet, asshole?"

He had an immediate change of attitude and led me into the back where the sales offices were. After a whispered conversation on the phone, I was shown into the boss's corner office. Decoratively, more of the same.

Marion Bell was one of those compact, thirtyish, yuppie packages whose stiff body language suggested a lack of grace, despite an athletic appearance. The best word to describe him was "severe." His physicality screamed no-nonsense, from the half-inch buzz cut to his ugly, Velcro-fastened shoes. His eyes were so blue, I suspected contacts.

"Police?" he asked as I entered. "I talked to Sergeant Brickhouse yesterday. She said she was going to set up a meeting, but she never called me back."

"She's my partner," I said. "This won't take long."

"About Vincent Smiley?" From his expression and tone, I could tell that Jo was right. Smiley was not a favorite.

"The cops are spending a lot of time on that guy, considering the fact that he's dead," he said.

"There are potential lawsuits surrounding that Hidden Ranch Road shoot-out," I said, electing not to tell him that Smiley was still alive. People are generally not all that anxious to rat out paramilitary psychopaths.

"Go ahead, ask away." Marion said, lowering himself behind his gray metal desk.

I took the uncomfortable gray chair across from him and

opened my casebook. "Just tell me a little about Vincent. I understand he joined your mountain-climbing club, the Rock Stars, sometime last year. What month was that?"

"June," Marion said.

I wrote it down, thinking that was about the same time Smiley started digging the escape tunnel at his house in Hidden Ranch. Important? I wasn't sure.

Marion went on. "He wanted to do some organized mountain climbing. We're an outdoor club."

"As opposed to what?" I asked him.

"That means that our climbs are on real mountains. Some clubs are strictly gym climbing clubs. They scale indoor, artificial walls, that sort of thing."

"What was your take on him? What kind of guy was he?"

"Well, on a personal level he was a jerk. Frightening, if you want to put a better word on it."

"How so?"

"He was always right on the edge of going off on you. Even when he was laughing, it could turn ugly in a second. You said the wrong thing and you'd set him off. He had real anger-management problems. We took him in originally because he said he was YDS fifth-class qualified. YDS stands for Yosemite Decimal System. It rates climbing ability. To be fifth-class rated, you have to have expertise in all forms of technical free-climbing and be proficient with specialized techniques and equipment. Once he became a member of the Rock Stars, and we took him on his first climb, we realized it was all BS."

"So he lied."

"Big time. He was basically a Gumby. His equipment was a mess, mostly second-hand stuff. His haul bag was a disaster, full of the kinda stuff mountain shops sell to newbies, but nobody ever uses. Since we do outdoor climbs, not gym climbs, we have to travel to our sites. Sometimes it's a two- or three-hour drive, so I like to get an alpine start."

"A what?" I was writing all this down.

He smiled. "Alpine start—early, like three A.M. We'd meet in a market parking lot, or some agreed-upon place, and take off from there. You go early, especially if it's a snow climb, because the hard pack starts to melt after noon and you want to be off the mountain by then. Once the snow starts melting, all your protection starts pulling loose and it can get treacherous."

"Protection?" I was still scribbling like mad trying to keep up.

"Anything you pound into a rock face, or screw into ice to tie you off, is called protection."

I nodded.

"He always escalated any disagreement past the place you were willing to go. It's how he won arguments. There was something about Vincent. You never knew what he was capable of, and you didn't want to find out."

I nodded. Pretty much exactly what Tad Palmer had said.

"On the first climb he went on, we saw how dangerous he was, so we made him a belay monkey. That's basically somebody who stays at the belay station and minds the anchors."

"I'm sorry, I'm afraid . . ."

"Somebody who stays below and holds the end of the climbing rope, keeps it from getting tangled. It's a job anybody can do. If a guy brings his nonclimbing girlfriend, we always give her the job. Make her our 'Belay Betty', so to speak, okay?"

"Right."

"But after the first time he didn't want to do that, so the next time we went, we had to take him up as a rope man. He was long on nerve and short on skill. Basically, a screamer in training."

I raised my eyebrow again.

"A screamer is somebody taking the big drop. A screamer is dangerous to everybody, because he can zipper out all the protection and kill everyone on the line with him."

"Got it."

"So we asked him, basically, to stop climbing with us and

resign from the club. As president, that was my job. I actually considered putting a gun in my belt when I talked to him. He was that unstable."

"Sergeant Brickhouse told me you'd mentioned that he belonged to some kind of survivalist club."

"That's what he said. He was always talking like some ex-military, antigovernment fanatic. But if you want my take on it, he was just mouthing off. He didn't have any tats on him, no swastikas, or any of that other antigovernment nonsense those survivalist guys like. I think it was just talk."

"Anything else?"

He thought for a moment, then said: "Well, one thing. He was always wanting us to climb the Chocolate Mountains."

"Where's that?"

"Way the hell on the other side of the Salton Sea. It's a mountain range between California and Arizona, which is, to be honest, not all that challenging. But he wanted to go up there anyway. Said there was a high altitude SEAL training camp he wanted to see. Even had maps."

"When was this?"

"All the time. He never stopped talking about it, until we threw him out. Most of the club members like the big face at Pinnacle National Monument, or, if we're going to overnight, we like Yosemite National Park. There's hundreds of great V-five climbs up there, some as high as thirty pitches, that require two or three days to complete."

I didn't know exactly what pitches or V-5 climbs were, but I more or less had the idea, so I didn't ask. "If he was going to make a climb somewhere, you think it would be in these Chocolate Mountains?" I asked.

"If he was still alive, yeah, I'm sure that's where he woulda gone. To the SEAL camp up there. It's almost four thousand feet up."

"Do you have a map?" I asked.

"Yeah, I think I have the Chocolate Mountains in a book—right here."

He crossed to a bookshelf where he had a library of climbing books. He pulled down a volume labeled Bradshaw Trail Climbs.

"The Bradshaw Trail is out past Indio by the Salton Sea in Riverside County," he explained as he started flipping pages. "It runs between the Chukwalla Mountains and the Chocolate Mountains. There's some spectacular views from the Chukwalla Bench of the Palos Verdes Valley."

Then he found the page he wanted. "There's a Navy SEAL camp known as Camp Billy Machen down here at the base camp. They used to use it for desert training. It's closed now. The other SEAL camp, the one he wanted to visit, is at altitude." He pointed at a spot on the map. " 'Bout here, above Silver Pass."

"Could I make a copy of this?" I asked him.

"You can take it, if you bring it back."

He gave me the book and I pulled out the sheet of paper that I'd found by Smiley's trash. "You recognize anything here?" I asked him. He scanned it for a moment.

"YUMA TACTS," he read aloud. "Looks like some kind of military operation."

"Yeah, but for what?" I wondered out loud.

He shrugged and handed it back. "Beats me."

I thanked Marion and walked back out to the car, wondering how to go about this.

If Smiley wanted to go to the Chocolate Mountains, then that's where I wanted to go.

My problem was, I didn't know the first thing about mountain climbing.

THE DEAL

BY SIX FIFTEEN the Rams were halfway through practice. I pulled the borrowed D-car into the upper parking lot at Agoura High School and walked through the campus. It was Friday afternoon, and the school sign announced that the Agoura football team was playing at San Marino High that night at eight, so the high school team wasn't out on the field. I stood for a minute on the top steps, looking down to where Chooch and thirty or so kids in their practice uniforms were running plays on the main field. There was still almost an hour of fall sunlight left.

Chooch was with the offense. Across the field, working on breakdown drills with the defense, was Sonny Lopez, the man I'd come to see. He was coaching the boys to come to a partial balanced stop, setting their feet, running in place before making an open-field tackle.

Chooch saw me and waved. "Hey," he yelled. "This is a closed practice."

I flipped him the bird and he laughed, then turned and limped on his walking cast back toward the offense. Sonny looked up when Chooch yelled. He was dressed in sweats and football shoes, with a towel around his neck. When he saw me, he scowled and immediately started walking in my direction. We met about midfield.

"I came to make a deal," I said.

"You got nothing I want."

I told him about Smiley's twin brother Paul, how Jo Brickhouse and I had found the tunnel at Hidden Ranch, and my theory about how easy it would have been for Vincent to steal those casings from the shooting ranges, commit the Nightingale and Greenridge murders, and frame both SWAT teams. When I was finished, he had lost the attitude.

"You and Jo Brickhouse turned all that?" he said, a little respect creeping into his voice and eyes.

I nodded, then added, "Jo was shot by that bastard this afternoon. She's in critical condition at L.A. County. She went to a house Smiley was using in Inglewood and he dumped her. It's all over the department and on the news. I'm surprised you haven't heard about it."

"I've been at practice here since two."

"I think I know where Smiley might be," I continued, "but I have a few conditions."

Sonny stood with his hands on his hips, his face a mask. I couldn't read him at all.

"First, I can't go after him alone. I need your word that if I tell you where I think he is, you'll do your best to deliver what I want."

"I'm not gonna promise anything, Scully. At least not until I know what you have in mind."

"All I want is your best effort. If you can't deliver, then you can't deliver."

"Let's hear." He took off the towel that was around his neck and dropped it on the grass. His team had stopped practicing, so he turned and yelled, "Hey! Keep that drill going. This ain't a break! We have the Chargers on Saturday!"

The boys again lined up and continued the tackling drill. Sonny looked back at me.

"I think Smiley went up into the Chocolate Mountains. It's a range out by the Salton Sea, south of Indio."

"So call the FBI. It's their case now. Turn it over to them."

"I want to arrest him myself. Two weeks ago he shot Emo, a guy I really cared about. This afternoon he dropped my partner. I really want this guy, Sonny."

"It's not like Sergeant Brickhouse was your real partner." He was hedging.

"Hey, she's my partner! And she's also my friend!" I almost shouted this at him. *Calm down*, I lectured myself for about the tenth time in two days. Then I put my hand on his shoulder. "Listen Sonny, if not for me or for Jo, then do it for Emo. You cared about him. Smiley deserves some first-person payback."

"You said you had a few conditions. I got the first one. What're the others?"

"I don't know how to mountain climb, and from what I've found out, I think he's going into some pretty rough terrain. I need help to get up there."

"How can I help you with that?" Sonny said. "I don't know how to mountain climb."

"SEB does. They teach their SWAT teams mountain rescue. I want you to get in touch with Scott Cook, tell him to bring the Gray team, or as many of those guys as he can, and have them meet me here and bring their climbing equipment. I'll call Cagel at SRT and see if I can convince him to loan me that unit too."

"SEB and SRT are barely speaking. Put 'em in the same place, and you could end up with people getting killed."

"Think about it. These are the two units that were hurt the most by all this. They weren't out killing each other, Smiley just made it look that way. What better way to bring these guys back together?"

"A joint op."

"Exactly. We work it together. Go up there and drag that asshole off the mountain."

"You oughta sell this to the Discovery Channel," he said dryly. But I could tell from his expression and the glint in his eyes, that I had him.

"Tell Sergeant Cook that my condition for giving him Smiley's exact location is that I go up there with them."

"He's not gonna go for that."

"He is if he wants to catch the guy who killed Billy Greenridge."

43
GOOD TO GO

WHATTA THEY DOING here?" Gordon Grundy said, standing in the back of the SRT SWAT truck, which was parked in the Faculty Only area of the Agoura High School lot. He was looking across the tarmac as the SEB SWAT van's headlights swept across us pulling in. It was just after sunset.

"So far, the only thing all of us are guilty of is having a stupid fight in a bar," I said. "Nobody shot anybody. SEB didn't light up Greenridge and you didn't shoot Nightingale. Maybe it's time to bottle up some of this testosterone and aim it at the real shooter."

Grundy was a tall, hard-edged man, dressed in black Kevlar. A collection of right angles and hard surfaces, his jaw jutted and his knuckles looked like unmined calcium deposits. He was flacked and jacked. His first scout, Nacho Rosano, was behind him, also glaring across the tarmac at the sheriff's van.

Grundy, Rosano, Happy Zant, and Ringo Wagner, the two other members of the ATF Situation Response Team, climbed out of their truck. They stood in a tight huddle watching the Sheriff's SEB team dismount from their van twenty yards away. From this distance, it looked like only SEB team leader, Scott Cook, and his first scout, Rick Manos had come. Then I saw Sonny Lopez jump down out of the back of their van. He was only supposed to be the messenger, so what the hell was he doing back here? Scott, Rick, and Sonny moved across the parking lot toward us.

"Let's talk to these guys," I said to Grundy.

He nodded, and along with Nacho Rosano, walked with me toward the SEB team. Once we got to within a few feet, everybody stopped. There was enough electricity here to start a power company.

The sheriffs wore tan jumpsuits with Glocks in low-slung outside rigs strapped with Velcro to their right legs. They were carrying long rifle cases called drag bags. Each one was folded up around a long gun and contained a shooter's mat and sniper's pack, with a multifrequency radio and several bullet trays. All of them, including Sonny, were wearing heavy Cover6 Plus tactical vests.

ATF was in black jumpsuits with "SRT SWAT" in gold letters on the back. They also carried big holstered sidearms, wore Ultima flak vests, and were carrying fifty-pound mission packs.

Everyone traded appraising looks. It seemed it was up to me to perform the marriage ceremony.

"Okay," I said. "We need to get some stuff behind us before we start." Nobody said anything. "I think somebody needs to own up to what happened at Hidden Ranch."

Grundy shifted his weight. "We told your warrant control desk there was a possibility of automatic weapons in there."

"Not according to them," Cook said immediately.

"Excuse the expletive, but fuck 'em," Grundy said danger-ously.

"Whatta you mean, fuck 'em? Fuck *you!* They said you only told them about the impersonating bust."

"That's bullshit." Grundy was getting hot. "Somebody, prob-ably some six-dollar-an-hour civilian in your warrant office, is covering his ass. We told them there was a weapons complaint and that there was a possibility of ordnance at that address. We also—" He stopped and everybody waited. "Okay," he went on. "We put a low assignment risk on it because we'd braced Smiley before and, quite frankly, he looked to us like a feeb. We didn't see any trouble coming. In retrospect, we shoulda assigned a higher risk to the warrant delivery. That was a mis-take. But we're not fucking mind readers. Nobody thought the shit was gonna jump off like it did. We backed up Deputy Rojas. We were just around the corner."

"Why didn't you serve your own damn warrant?" Cook asked.

"We thought it was unnecessarily provocative to roll in there with a SWAT team. We didn't think he had an AK-forty-seven, but we wanted to give your guy cover, so we parked nearby."

They were all silent for a long time.

"Look, we're sorry," Grundy said. "I know that doesn't cover the loss of Deputy Rojas, but the fact is, we feel pretty damn bad about it. We tried to come to the funeral, but you guys ran us out."

Scott Cook looked at Sonny Lopez. It was almost as if he was asking Sonny's permission to go for this. Finally Sonny nodded.

"Okay," Scott said. "We accept the apology." Then he put out his hand and Gordon Grundy shook it. After that we shook all around.

"I understand this guy is in the mountains up on rough ter-rain." Grundy was getting right to business.

"Right," I said.

"Okay, we're good to go," Grundy said. "We're all V-five-certified climbers."

"So are Rick and I," Scott said. "But Sonny Lopez couldn't climb off a whore's ass in the middle of a vice raid."

"Then what's he doing here?" Grundy asked.

"He came over to the SWAT house to give us the word, then wouldn't get outta the damn van."

"I'm going," Sonny stated bluntly.

"We can't take anybody who isn't certified. It's dangerous and it'll slow us down," Grundy said.

"I'm going," Sonny repeated.

"Me too," I said. "I didn't put this whole thing together so I could read about the capture in the newspaper."

"You're not going either, Scully," Scott Cook said. "Neither of you are."

"Then you're not getting the map," I answered. "I'm the only one who knows where on that mountain Smiley went. Those are the terms."

Scott and Gordon glowered at me. Again, I was the problem.

"Okay, if that's the way you want it, you guys can come. But we're not waiting for either one of you. If you can't keep up, we're leaving you."

"Fine," I said. Sonny nodded.

"Is that all you've got to wear?" Grundy said, looking at my jeans and cotton shirt.

"I'm sure you guys have another one of those snazzy lookin' bunny suits in the truck."

Grundy turned to Rosano. "Nacho, get this asshole suited up."

Nacho headed to the truck and I followed. As I was changing my clothes inside, putting on the jumpsuit and Tac vest, Gordon Grundy and Scott Cook walked over to the back door.

"Okay, so where the hell am I going?" Grundy asked.

I pulled the book that Marion Bell had given me out of my briefcase, and flipped it open to the Chocolate Mountains. "He's heading for a Navy SEAL camp. Right here."

I put my finger on the spot marked Silver Pass.

THE CHOCOLATE MOUNTAINS

44

WE WERE ALL in SRT's SWAT truck, because it was bigger, newer, and had better toys. Gordon Grundy drove, while Sonny, Rick, Scott, Nacho, Ringo, Happy, and I sat on the benches in the back facing each other with tight, blank expressions, dressed like Gulf War commandos. We sped along the 210 on our way toward Palm Springs, lost in our own thoughts. Too many friends had died or had been injured in the last two weeks.

I thought of Emo, remembering his easy smile, the way he had of looking at you without judgment. I had once seen him in a booking cage telling jokes to a guy he had just busted, both of them doubled over with laughter. He could arrest somebody without making a power trip out of it. He understood human weakness and always seemed to be able to communicate, even with the most hardened criminals. Emo was the kind of cop I had joined up to be.

Before we left Agoura, I had called the hospital and Bridget reported that there was no news. Jo was still in ICU and critical. Bridget sounded like she was beginning to come apart, her voice tight, verging on shrill.

As we rode toward the desert, I was feeling very alone in the crowded state-of-the-art SRT truck. I knew I had been going through a simultaneous process of growth and degeneration. I was slowly exposing the vulnerable parts of myself, taking the chance that the people I cherished the most wouldn't hate me for those weaknesses. While this helped me in my personal life and on the job, I no longer saw the landing lights, unsure of why I was even on the mission or if I would ever find the answers. Then along comes this one moment of moral certainty. Find Vincent Smiley and make the sonofabitch pay. As if his destruction would somehow restore order to my fractured value system.

Jo Brickhouse and I were coming from the same place emotionally. The order we both craved from police work had only produced confusion and disillusionment. But she was lying in a hospital close to death as a result of my bad police work, and I was in this SWAT truck roaring across the desert to avenge a shattered sense of justice, telling myself I was doing this for Jo, a woman I hadn't even liked a few days ago and had badly misevaluated, and for Emo, a man I'd admired but hadn't spent that much time with.

Was this just a big, ugly piece of street theater? Was I making a splashy move to convince myself I was still relevant? Could I put an end to my moral slide by stepping on the back of Vincent Smiley's neck and jamming his face in the dirt? Would that restore my values, make my work seem worthwhile again?

Even as I raced toward the Chocolate Mountains to apprehend him, I couldn't forget the look of hatred in that Compton grandmother's eyes. What the hell was I really looking for?

We turned off the interstate past Palm Springs at Indio, traveling south, toward the Salton Sea. Nacho Rosano stood, bracing himself in the jouncing truck, and started going through drawers, passing out communications equipment.

"Since we don't share a frequency, let's all use one of these." He handed each of us a small radio transmitter with an LCD faceplate, and pointed to the small screen. "That's a GPS. If you get lost, it'll tell you where you are, within half a meter." After he showed us how to operate it, I loaded it into my vest.

I had my cell phone on and checked the battery. It was at three-quarters, but there was no signal out here.

It was after 10 P.M. by the time we took State Highway 111 to the Salton Sea Recreation Area, then continued south. After about half an hour Grundy pulled to a stop, set the brake and came back into the rear of the truck. He filled the door to the driver's compartment, his crewcut tickling the ceiling.

"Okay, we're outside of Niland," he said, looking right at me.

I opened the map book. "Go on up Coachella Canal Road to Camp Billy Machen. The Chocolate Mountains are on the left. There should be a parking area at that old camp. There's no more road, so we hike into the mountains from there."

"Okay. Everybody saddle up now," Grundy said. "Smiley had an AK up at Hidden Ranch and he knew how to use it. I don't wanta be climbing out of this truck, hooking our shit together, while this jerk-off is up in the trees somewhere picking us off with three-oh-eights."

Everybody started buckling up vests and chambering weapons. Then Grundy went back up to the front, put the truck in gear, and we were rolling again. Scott and Nacho gave Sonny and me a short course in mountain climbing, showing us the belt harness and how to use the carabiners.

"You're gonna feel like you want to climb using your arms," Scott said. "But that's a huge mistake. Use your legs. Your glutes are much bigger muscles than your biceps. Your glutes won't tire. Most newbies try and pull themselves up. You do that, you'll burn out in less than an hour."

"In a lead climb," Nacho said, "a leader and a second go up first, set the protection, get to the top, tie off, and then bring the rest of the team up. Last up are the belay monkeys; that's you two. We change lead and seconds after each leg of the climb. Each leg is called a pitch. A pitch is a section of the climb that is slightly shorter than the rope. The ropes we use are a hundred meters long."

I remembered Marion Bell saying that some of the climbs in Monument Valley were thirty pitches.

"The first climber, or leader, wedges a piece of protection into the rock halfway up the first pitch," Nacho was saying. "We mostly use SLCDs, which are spring-loading camming devices."

He held one up. It matched the printed picture Smiley left in his garage.

"An SLCD can fit in a crevice and attaches to the rope with carabiners. We can use it for protection or for handholds on sheer cliffs. If somebody falls, the idea is the protection should catch and hold him until the rest of us can reel him back up. If the lead climber sets this thing too far down, then a fall will zipper out the protection and we're all toast. The last man on the climb is called the belayer. He holds the rope steady until the lead climbers make it to the top of the pitch. Once the lead and second have tied everything off and the others are secure up top, we pull the belay monkeys up and start all over again."

Sonny and I glanced at each other. It sounded doable.

We were all rigged and ready to go when the truck pulled into a parking area at the old Camp Billy Machen.

Scott Cook opened the door and we stepped out into the darkness. The temperature was forty degrees and dropping. We were standing in the parking lot feeling exposed under a slim slice of desert moon.

Parked ten feet away, next to a weathered maintenance shed, was Vincent Smiley's black Dodge Ram 2500 pickup. It looked evil and predatory, sitting up high with its Bigfoot suspension on huge, tractor-sized tires. We approached slowly and looked inside. There was an empty box of .308s down in the floor well.

"Looks like he's locked and loaded," Grundy said, pointing at the cartridge box. "Let's decommission this truck."

He and Nacho shinnied under the Dodge and checked the engine compartment for boobie traps. "Looks clear," Grundy shouted, and they both rolled back out.

Scott Cook popped the hood and removed the positive battery cable. "Souvenir," he said and handed it to me.

I put it into my pack.

"Now let's go get this guy," Rick Manos growled.

We all turned and walked through a gate marked "Gas Line Road," and started the long trek across the sandy desert toward the dark brown Chocolate Mountains.

THE ALPINE START

WE HIKED IN the freezing desert until midnight, picking our way across dry, sandy gullies and parched ground. Unseen cacti tugged at the bloused ankles of our jumpsuits. About a mile out we crossed a small trickling stream in a gully. In the damp sand were footprints. We all kneeled down and looked at them. Nobody had to mention that the cross-hatched sole prints came from Danner Terra Force jump boots. We continued on, then finally bivouacked at a little past midnight.

I lay on my side in the still warm sand and prayed I wasn't parked over a scorpion nest. Almost before my head hit the crook of my arm I was asleep. I was so tired I didn't dream. Before I knew it, someone was shaking me.

"Okay, we're heading out," Scott Cook said. I rolled over and looked at my watch: 4 A.M. "We need to get a jump on it," he added.

By sunup we were four miles north in the foothills, working our way up through the crevices and canyons. I won't say it was easy, but for the first hour of the climb we had no need for ropes, carabiners, or harnesses. Then we reached the first huge rock, fifty feet high with no way around it. We had to go up and over, a feat Nacho called "bouldering."

Before we started Gordon Grundy took out his binoculars and, using the first rays of morning light, focused them on the face of the giant rock, looking for the best ascent.

"There's something there," he said. "Halfway up, somebody left a piton jammed in the rock."

I took the binoculars and focused them on the metal spike. It had been pounded into the face of the boulder, and had a carabiner hanging off the threaded end.

"Probably part of his protection," Grundy said. "He had to leave it behind because he's climbing alone and couldn't yank it free."

"Time for some white courage," Scott Cook said. "Let's chalk up." The SWAT members all dug into their haul bags and broke out tin shakers full of powdered chalk. They chalked their hands like gymnasts, sharing it with Sonny and me. Then we faced the first part of the climb.

The initial boulder was surprisingly easy. We were warned again by Grundy and Cook not to pull ourselves up by our arms. The problem was, pushing up with my legs felt dangerous, as if I would fall backward off the mountain. The leg climbing technique fought all my instincts. Grundy did the first lead climb, with Nacho as his second. He put in the protection halfway up the pitch, pounding in a spike with his belt hammer, testing it by hanging from it, using all of his weight. Then he and Nacho went the rest of the way up to the top of the rock. The climbers following scrambled up using nubbins for footholds, taking advantage of the tiny flutes and chimneys, jamming the toes of their hiking boots into crevices for traction before finally reaching the top of the first boulder.

Nacho yelled, "Off belay!" which was Sonny's and my signal to climb up and join them.

Lopez went up first. I was last. My job was to yank out our protection and bring it up with me. It was a rush, making that first pitch, hanging from my harness a thousand feet up. My heart pounded while my eyes swept the landscape below. As I passed Smiley's piton, I looked carefully at it. Stenciled on the side it said MOUNTAINEER. It had come from one of the boxes in his garage.

When I finally got to the top I was expecting a lot of praise, but nobody said anything, except Nacho. "Stop using your arms," he growled. Then they all turned and started the next pitch, with Scott Cook taking over as climb leader and Rick Manos as his second.

By ten o'clock I was so wiped out that I was unable to go much further. I had spaghetti arms from pulling myself up. Sonny Lopez was in the exact same condition.

Nacho said, "I told you to use your legs. Your arms won't hold up on a long climb like this."

"I warned you guys if this happened I was gonna leave you," Grundy said. "You're gonna have to get down on your own. Here's the spare key to the SWAT truck," he said, handing it to me.

"You're not leaving me," I said.

"This was your call," Grundy responded. "The deal was, you could go as long as you didn't slow us down. This guy is just up ahead. He's killed three cops and put a fourth in ICU. We're gonna get him, but not with you two holding us back. The last two pitches, you guys barely made it."

"We'll be along in a minute," Sonny said as the two SWAT teams turned away and took off up the next boulder. Sonny and

I lay on our backs on a narrow ledge, out of breath, and watched them climb away from us. Despite the fact that the sun was out, at this altitude it was still cold. Scott and Gordon had left us some rock pitons, carabiners, and two lengths of rope for our descent.

"Let's go on up," I said, pulling myself to my feet and moving to follow. "I'm not being left behind."

I approached the boulder and tried to do a solo lead climb, scaling the rock, going up about ten feet, pounding in some protection with my belt hammer. But I was shot. My arms were shaking from the effort.

"Whatta you stopping for?" Sonny said sourly as he watched me, still on his back. I was dangling ten feet up.

Then suddenly I lost my handhold and fell, zippering out my poorly set piton. As I landed I felt a rib crack. I lay on my side moaning in pain.

"That was encouraging," Sonny said, his face strained with exhaustion. "I especially liked the eekie little scream."

"Let's get off this damn mountain," I said angrily.

Climbing down was easier, but not a complete snap. We had to tie off and belay from above. We didn't get back to the foothills until almost two in the afternoon. I was monitoring the small radio Nacho had given me and could hear the two SWAT units talking to each other as they neared the SEAL camp at Silver Pass. Once we reached level ground, Sonny and I started the long, hot hike back to Camp Billy Machen. The temperature had soared on the desert floor, so we stripped off our Tac vests in the dry hundred-degree heat and carried them.

By five o'clock we were almost there. I triggered the radio. "This is Scully. We're one or two klicks from the Billy Machen camp." Scott Cook came right back on the radio.

"We just left that SEAL camp at Silver Pass. The place was empty, no sign of him. No tackle, foot, or rope marks on the climbing faces. You want my take, this guy hasn't been up here."

"But we saw his piton," I said.

"Roger that, but he's not on this side of the mountain. We're gonna check the back side, but if he's not over there. I think we've been messed with."

I clicked the transmit button twice to indicate I understood.

Sonny and I didn't say anything but we were both walking faster, now afraid that Smiley had for some reason lured us out toward the Chocolate Mountains, then doubled back.

We got to the end of the Gas Line Road and pushed open the gate. The black Dodge was gone. Somehow he'd rewired the battery system. I wondered where he'd found a cable way out here. Then I looked over at our SWAT truck. The hood was up.

Spray painted on the side in black paint was a message:

NICE TRY ASSHOLES

CACTUS WEST

THE BACK OF the SWAT truck, where the spare ordnance was kept, had inch-thick metal doors with a bolt lock, impossible to penetrate. But Smiley had pulled the engine alarm wires and opened the hood. The emergency alarm had probably brayed until the system's battery went dead. As we approached, I could see that our battery cable was missing.

I reached into my pack and pulled out the one that Grundy had given me, then opened the truck with the spare key and found a toolbox in the back. Sonny went to work reattaching the positive cable to the engine battery.

"Yeah, nice try, asshole," he said softly as he finished. We opened the driver's side door on the truck. Sonny slid one of the keys into the ignition and started the engine, then backed the truck out while I walked over to where Smiley's Dodge Ram had been parked when we pulled in. I knelt down and studied the tracks in the gravel, as Sonny rolled up and stopped the SWAT truck behind me.

I pointed to a service road, "Cochise read many signs. Track many assholes."

Sonny grunted, and was already talking on the radio by the time I had the passenger door open. "You guys, he's down here. He got his truck going and went west, down the service road. We're tracking him in the SWAT truck. What's your ETA the parking lot?"

"We're losing light up here. It's gonna be slow going down at night. We can't get back there until around twenty-two thirty," Scott Cook said.

Not till 10:30 P.M. I looked over at Sonny and he said, "Looks like it's up to the dumb-ass arm-climbers to fix this mess."

We put our SWAT Tac vests back on, then drove along the fenced perimeter of camp Billy Machen. It had once been a tent city, but now all that was left were some poured concrete pads. It looked completely deserted. We kept going until we hit the Niland Blythe Road, which wasn't really a road, as much as a narrow dirt trail. Sonny slowed the truck to a stop and we looked to the left out across open desert. We were trying to decide which way to go, when I thought I saw something flash way out in the distance.

"What's that?" I pointed toward the spot.

We focused on the dark landscape, working on our night vision. After a minute it flashed again.

"See if they've got any infrared stuff back there," Sonny said.

"Good idea." I ducked through the opening into the back of the truck and started reading the labels on the equipment drawers, finally spotting one marked: LIGHT-GATHERING SCOPES.

Inside was a single pair of heavy-duty infrared binoculars. I brought them forward, then settled back into the seat, turned them on, and focused them through the windshield, toward the spot where the flash of light had been.

As they heated up, the picture first turned green, then slowly brightened. I was looking at the same landscape, only now I could see details, almost as if it were daylight. Something was racing around on the desert floor at least two miles away. It was still too far away to tell if it was Smiley's black truck.

"Something's out there. Some kind of vehicle," I said.

Sonny turned the wheel toward the spot and drove up the dirt road, heading deeper into the desert valley full of Joshua trees and cacti. Suddenly, the road veered right and we were running beside a ten-foot-high industrial-strength chain-link fence. Every quarter mile or so there was a large painted sign:

CHOCOLATE MOUNTAIN AERIAL GUNNERY RANGE
DANGER EXPLOSIVES!
KEEP OUT!
BY ORDER OF THE U.S. GOVERNMENT

Then under that:

PELIGRO—EXPLOSIVOS!
PROHIBA LA ENTRADA!
POR ORDEN DE LA GOBIERNA
DE LOS USTADOS UNIDOS

Sonny had his eyes on the rutted road, trying to keep from breaking an axle, when I reached over and turned off his headlights.

"What're you doing?" he barked. "Can't see."

"I have a feeling we're gonna end up going in there." I pointed at the range. "I don't think we oughta be advertising our location."

Sonny grunted, but made no move to turn the lights back on.

We were soon passing what appeared to be a massive automobile graveyard. Bombed out wrecks, old county and state vehicles, yellow bulldozers, garbage trucks, and decommissioned road-maintenance equipment loomed behind the chainlink. Most of them were scorched by fire or blown to bits, some barely recognizable, others had signs painted on the sides in large white letters: *Armored Column, Russian T-62 Tank, SAM Missile.*

"What the hell is all this about?" Sonny said, slowing to look as we passed.

"I've heard about this place. Navy and Marine pilots fly practice sorties against all this old junk."

"Is it safe for us to go in there?" Sonny said, suddenly apprehensive.

"If that's where Smiley is, we got no choice."

Then I remembered the slip of paper I'd found out by his trash. I dug it out of my pocket and opened it up. "Pull over for a minute."

Sonny stopped the truck and I turned on the map light.

"Whatta ya got?" he said.

"I found this at his place in Inglewood. I couldn't figure it out back then, but you know what I think it might be?" Sonny shook his head, puzzled.

"A Marine Corps firing mission. MCAS could stand for Marine Corps Air Station. YUMA is the Yuma air wing. TACTS could be like Tactical Air Combat Training or Combat Target Systems—something."

We both studied the sheet.

7S	MECH INFANTRY REIN	1335	PG783783	N 33 13 57.1	W 115 05 16.6	LIVE ORD	1, 2
8S	MECH INFANTRY REIN	1539	PG726796	N 33 14 39.9	W 115 08 58.2	LIVE ORD	1, 2
10S	SA-6 Site	2240	PG771820	N33 15 56.5	W 115 06 01.1	LIVE ORD	1, 2
11S	ARMORED COLUMN	2203	PG773815	N 33 15 38.1	W 115 05 54.3	LIVE ORD	1, 2
12S	SAM SITE	1348	PG735806	N 33 15 12	W 115 08 18.5	LIVE ORD	1, 2
13S	MECH INFANTRY	1444	PG7718803	N 33 15 02.9	W 115 09 27.5	LIVE ORD	1, 2
14S	MECH INFANTRY REIN	2350	PG771772	N 33 13 14.5	W 115 05 57.4	LIVE ORD	1, 2
15S	NE-SW AIRFIELD W/SAM, AAA, RADAR SITES	0205	PG736809	N 33 15 23.6	W 115 08 17	LIVE ORD	1, 2
MT. BARROW	NE-SW AIRFIELD W/SAM SITES	0545	PG895707	N 33 09 42.1	W 114 58 10.8	LIVE ORD	1, 2, 5

"I don't know what column one is, but column two is the target description," I continued. "Mechanized Infantry, Armored Column, SAM site. They drag these old garbage trucks and bulldozers out on the gunnery range, set them up to look like armored columns or a SAM missile site, then the jet jocks roll in and hit all this stuff with Tomahawk missiles. Column three is something. Numbers—I don't know what."

"Could be the coordinates of the target. The latitude and longitude." Sonny said.

"No, it looks more like military time. Thirteen thirty-five hours is one thirty-five P.M. Columns five and six look like the coordinates. That N33.13 would be longitude, W115.05, latitude. Then the next column says LIVE ORD. Means they're shooting hot ammo."

"As opposed to what?" He grinned. "Rubber pellets?"

"Inerts. We trained with the air wing when I was in the Corps. Inert ordnance is like bombs made out of concrete. They use that stuff to test for target accuracy, but it doesn't explode."

"And that last column?"

"I don't know," I admitted.

"So why did Smiley print this out?" Sonny asked.

"I don't have a clue," I answered. Again, we sat in silence. "Okay, we have a couple of ways to go here. Your choice," I said.

"Don't do that 'your choice' BS on me again, Shane. I remember the choice you gave me up at Hidden Ranch Road."

"Hey, Sonny, if we call the authorities, the Marines are gonna chopper out here in those big double proppers, bullhorn this place, and before they can catch him, Smiley will be long gone across the border into Mexico. Let's just go under the wire and get this puke."

"With no backup."

"Our backup is five miles south of this range, still up on the mountain, and we've got the truck."

He thought about it for a minute, nodded. "Okay, I'm down. Let's see if we can find where he went in."

I checked my cell phone again. Still no signal. We continued past the auto graveyard until, off to the right, I saw a wash leading away from the gunnery range with a lot of dune buggy tracks marking the deep sand.

"Turn down there," I said, "Follow those tire tracks. Somebody must live down there. Maybe we can find out more about this place and use their phone to call in the locals."

Sonny hung a right and headed into the wash. The SWAT truck was muscular but heavy, and the minute we slowed, the tires started to dig in and spin. Sonny had to keep the speed up or we'd be stuck. We followed the tracks. Then, off to the right, I spotted a small homestead. A trailer and junkyard sat next to a fenced parking area containing a bunch of radical-looking sand rails. I estimated we were about a mile east of the gunnery range.

"Pull up," I said.

"If I stop we're never gonna get dug out," Sonny answered.

"We have to take a chance. We can't off-road in this truck. Look what's parked back there. Just stop," I said.

We rolled to a stop and our tires immediately sank into the soft sand. Behind the six-foot-high fence we counted half a dozen unpainted dune buggy–like vehicles of various sizes. All were equipped with big, exposed V-8 engines and had massive tractor tires on the rear wheels, with smaller ones up front. The buggies were light and lean with open cockpits, bucket seats, and no windshields. A few had large flatbeds resting between the rear axles. None of them had headlights.

The chain-link gate was bolted shut with a large heavy-duty padlock. Off to the left an old, rusted-out silver Airstream trailer was parked under a lone olive tree. All the lights were off inside. No phone wires anywhere. Whoever lived here was some kind of recluse. I walked to the trailer, climbed up on a creaking wood porch, pulled out my badge and knocked on the front door. It didn't look like anybody was home. Sonny followed and stood behind me.

"What kinda fool lives out here, less than a mile from a live gunnery range?" he asked.

"Desert Rat," I said. "Since nobody's home to lend us one of those dune buggies, whatta you say we just borrow one and call it a police emergency?"

"How? They're all locked up," Sonny said.

"I think I saw some bolt cutters in the back."

Sonny nodded and took off running to the truck. He returned with a set of heavy-duty bolt cutters, put them on the padlock, and easily clipped through it. Then he carried the cutters back to the truck and disappeared inside.

When he reappeared he was carrying two AR-15s and four circular C-mag hundred-round clips. He reset the complicated alarm on the truck, while I swung the metal gate open. He handed me one of the AR-15s and two of the heavy C-mags. Then we surveyed the motor pool.

"How 'bout this one here?" Sonny said, checking out a two-seat racer with no flatbed. He unscrewed the gas cap and stuck his index finger inside. "Full. I can hot-wire it easy."

A few minutes later Sonny had unhooked the ignition wires, twisted them together, and we had the sand rail going. It had straight pipes with no muffler, and the roaring engine fractured the still desert night. I climbed into the passenger seat. The owner had screwed in a metal pole between the seats, about where the windshield would be. The thick mast went up about a foot above our heads and had a huge bolt welded to the top.

"What's this thing for?" Sonny said, pointing at it.

"It probably ain't for water skiing," I quipped. "Let's get out of here."

I stacked the two automatic weapons between us, then Sonny hit the gas and we careened out of the enclosure, passing our SWAT truck sitting low in soft sand.

We raced back up the wash to the gunnery range fence, turned right, and continued running on the road beside the range, which was situated in a desert valley halfway between the Chocolate and Chuckwalla mountains. We were speeding along under a quarter moon, without a windshield or headlights, the wind stinging our eyes, tears streaming down our faces, running almost blind at about forty miles per hour in a two-seat dune buggy with no suspension. I was bouncing hard and holding on with both hands. Every time we hit a pothole my cracked ribs talked to me. After this ride, I was going to need to get my prostate checked.

Up ahead I saw a spot where somebody had cut a hole in the government fence. I pointed at it and Sonny steered over and parked. I got out and peeled back the wire flap. He slowly edged the rumbling, vibrating dune buggy through the opening and I jumped back aboard.

We were inside the restricted area of the Chocolate Mountain Aerial Gunnery Range.

I still had the night vision binoculars around my neck, so I pulled them up and focused them toward the center of the vast area. There had to be thousands of acres out here. I saw burned cacti and sand charred black from Nadaum drops. It looked apocalyptic, as desolate and bombed-out as any place on earth. Then I noticed a small outcropping of low buildings a mile or two away. I pointed them out to Sonny but didn't speak, because the straight pipes on the sand rail were so loud I would have had to scream to be heard. Sonny floored it and we were off again, heading toward the buildings, flying over the sand, jumping berms, Sonny driving like a man who had lost his mind.

As we approached I saw that this was some kind of target town. There were two or three transecting streets and a main drag. The houses were all one-story, built out of adobe bricks and corrugated metal. Many of them had been leveled by past bombing runs, then rebuilt and tumbled down again. We slowed the sand rail and came to a stop on the outskirts of this little unmanned village. Our engine idle filled the night and vibrated the sand rail energetically. A hand-painted sign was posted directly in front of us. It said:

CACTUS WEST CITY LIMITS

DEADLY PREMONITION

S ONNY PULLED SLOWLY into Cactus West and drove through the little empty village once, taking each street to the end before turning around and retracing the route. After we looked the place over he turned off the engine.

"Wait here," I told him and found a building that had a tumbled down wall I could use to climb up to the roof, one story up. I stood gingerly on the flexing corrugated metal and surveyed the flat, ugly terrain. From up there I had a good view of the desert gunnery range. I could see more vast, blackened napalm drops. The few yucca trees that had survived were also scorched black. I slowly scanned the landscape with the night vision binoculars. The strong lenses pulled the eastern mountain range into focus.

The Dodge was parked about half a mile away. I saw a figure that had to be Smiley, walking around examining things on the ground. He picked up something large and loaded it into the back of his truck. It was hard to make out what he was up to, because he was so far away. The night scope bathed everything in a strange green hue but afforded me a lightened view of the area. As I watched, Smiley got behind the wheel, the truck started up, then turned and headed right toward us.

I scrambled down off the roof and ran back to the sand rail.

"He's coming this way," I shouted.

"The black truck?"

"Yep. Pull this thing around behind that bombed-out shed." I pointed to a structure that had only three sides. "Back it in so you're heading out. Gimme one of those AR-fifteens."

Sonny handed me a carbine with a hundred-round clip, then twisted the ignition wires, restarted the rail, and drove it around to the back side of the nearest building. He put the dune buggy in reverse, backed it in, and shut it down. Suddenly the desert was very still. A second later Sonny ran toward me carrying the second AR-15, jamming in one of the large C-mags and tromboning the slide.

The temperature fluctuation out here was amazing. Over a hundred degrees at noon, it was now close to freezing. The stars twinkled and winked as if somebody had punched a load of buckshot through a dark blue blanket. The quarter moon shed almost no light on the little uninhabited town.

"Let's set up a cross fire," I said.

"I'll take that wall over there." Sonny pointed to a bombed-out structure that would give him waist-high cover if he was standing, and would completely hide him when he kneeled. I picked a little square adobe shed with an open front window and corrugated tin roof. I pointed to it and we split up to take cover.

Way off across the desert we began to hear the sound of the

truck approaching, its engine growing louder, growling in low gear. It sounded like he had it in four-wheel drive to keep from sinking into the sand. Less than a minute later headlights appeared around the far end of the last building in Cactus West. The high beams shot light up the center street of the empty town. I was hunkered down under the small window, holding the AR-15 at port arms, listening to his truck engine idling. Then I rose up cautiously and peeked over the top of the window frame.

"I see you, asshole," Smiley shouted, then opened up on my position.

The walls all around me started to disintegrate. I immediately knew from the sound and fury of his weapon that this time he wasn't firing an AK-47. He was shooting at us with a .50-caliber Browning machine gun. The huge antitank exploding rounds were cutting the bricks in half, knocking my cover down around me with devastating efficiency. The .50 slugs contained exploding tips. If he kept this up, my little adobe shack would soon be dust. Sonny opened up on him trying to take some pressure off me.

Smiley laughed maniacally, then turned the weapon on the low wall where Sonny was hiding. I heard the exploding shells tearing Sonny's cover down. I popped up and squeezed off a twenty-round burst. The .223 bullets ripped into the truck, but didn't seem to be doing much damage. Before I could fire a second burst, Smiley spun back and started unloading on my little adobe shack again.

The AR-15 is a good assault rifle, but it's no match for a .50-caliber antitank weapon. Adding to the problem were the truck's high beams that were shining right at us, blinding me.

Sonny made a move away from the crumbled wall, firing the AR-15 as he ran. I popped up and gave him some cover fire. He dove behind an old burned-out van just as Smiley started ripping holes through it. Suddenly he stopped shooting and I heard his engine accelerate. The black truck sped right down Center Street. I caught a glimpse of him as he roared past. His eyes were wide, the cords of his neck bulging. Then his tail lights receded as he headed back out into the desert.

Sonny was on his feet, running toward me. "He's got us outgunned with that thing!"

"Get the rail. We're going after him," I shouted.

Sonny ran for the dune buggy and got it going, while I stood in the center of town with the night vision binoculars up, watching the truck disappear into the dark desert night, trying to see if he made a turn before I lost sight of him. Sonny skidded to a stop beside me.

I jumped into the passenger seat, Sonny popped the clutch, and we shot out into the gunnery range speeding after Smiley.

We were running at breakneck speed across the desert. The moon was almost no help. The ravines and gullies were hard to see and came up fast in the dark. Sonny was not slowing for any of it, swerving at the last minute to miss the few tall cactus plants that had managed to escape the napalm drops in this charred, bombed-out no-man's-land. Occasionally we were airborne, landing in soft sand throwing a rooster tail off both of the giant rear tractor tires. We were slowly gaining on Smiley, who was forced to use four-wheel drive and couldn't run the truck as fast.

We were only about a hundred yards behind him when he turned off his headlights and swerved right, heading down into a gully. Sonny whipped the wheel and followed. We raced along the sandy wash, narrowing the distance between us until we were so close the flying dirt from the truck tires stung our cheeks and filled our eyes with grit. We rounded a turn and roared past a line of trucks and old bulldozers situated to look like a stalled armored column. Each one was identified in large, white letters that read: T-62 or ARMORED TROOP CARRIER.

Was this out here for a reason? Why had he turned off his

headlights? Why was he leading us here? Suddenly I had a deadly premonition.

Just then, off to our right, a loud siren started blaring in the distance. I turned to see where it was coming from but couldn't locate it. Seconds later, five state-of-the-art FA-18 fighter jets dropped out of the moonlit sky, heading right at us. The Super Hornets roared down toward the column of parked trucks and bulldozers. Just as I looked up, a Maverick missile launched from under the wings of each plane. The pilots were a mile out and I doubted they could even see this little sand rail down here. Had Vincent turned off his headlights so they wouldn't see him in the low light of the quarter moon?

The air-to-ground weapons streaked toward us and five loud metal clicks sounded from above. I'd only heard this once before when I'd done cross-training with the air wing, back in the Marines.

"What's that?" Sonny screamed as we roared along.

"Detonators!" I yelled as the warheads went hot overhead.

The Mavericks vectored in over our shoulders. The first one blew an old dump truck off its axles and ten feet into the air. Little pieces of it rained down all around us. The other four hit seconds later, blowing up a bulldozer and some old trucks.

Smiley had already turned right, driving the Dodge Ram out of the gully. But Sonny and I were stuck in the middle of this night fire mission. Suddenly, five more Mavericks came streaking in. Their detonators clicked on, followed ten seconds later by huge explosions. A bulldozer on our right turned into deadly shrapnel.

I grabbed Sonny and threw him out of our speeding sand rail just as two more missiles struck, blowing up vehicles on both sides of us. We burrowed down into the sand as the four fighters screamed by low overhead, climbed into the night sky, and banked right to come around for a second pass.

"We gotta get outta here now!" I pulled Sonny up and we

started running back toward the sand rail, which had come to a rolling stop twenty yards away and was miraculously still upright with the engine idling. There were destroyed garbage trucks and bulldozers blazing all around us while the strike fighters climbed, making a sweeping turn, their wings glinting in the moonlight.

"They're coming around!" I yelled. "Listen for the sound of the detonators. They click on about a hundred yards out. You can hear it happen. Means you got about five seconds to get in a hole somewhere."

Just then, I saw the Dodge nose up to the lip of the wash, fifty yards away. The door slammed, and without warning he was firing the .50-caliber at us again, pinning us down. The huge slugs whined all around, tearing holes in the night and exploding anything they hit.

The Super Hornets had completed their turn and were coming back. Smiley saw them, dove into his truck, and backed up out of range of the missile attack. It gave us a precious few seconds to get out of there.

"Let's go!" I yelled as we jumped into the bucket seats. Sonny put it in gear. We hung a right, climbing up out of the wash just as the FA-18s leveled out and started another pass. I saw more bombs light up and streak out from under the wings heading our way again, then seconds later: click, click, click, click. The detonators snapped on.

"Now!" I yelled.

Sonny and I dove out of the rail while it was still moving and started eating sand.

The trucks and vans parked in the wash exploded like a chain of fireworks, shooting sparks high into the air. We were further out of the fire zone this time, so none of the shrapnel or falling debris landed on us.

The Hornets completed their pass and climbed out again. Our sand rail was again miraculously still unscathed. It had a low center of gravity and wasn't prone to flipping. We raced toward it as the .50-caliber started up again, chopping loudly from a sand hill on the right.

Sonny screamed and went down in a heap. His right leg was missing from the knee down. Blown right off.

"Shit!" I stopped short and kneeled over him.

Smiley's laughter rang out from a distant hillside. The jets roared low overhead, passing over us again before they careened to the left, turning for another pass. Once they were gone, climbing to come around again, I heard Vincent yell:

"Having fun, assholes?"

I took off my belt and cinched it tightly around Sonny's thigh.

"How bad is it?" he asked, lying on his back, straining to look down at his leg.

"It's fine. Just a scratch," I told him, pushing him back down so he couldn't see.

When I had it tied off, I threw him over my shoulder and made a run for the rail. I could barely see Vincent up on the sand hill. He had the big Browning thrown across the hood of his truck and was squeezing off long bursts. The massive exploding slugs dug holes all around me as I threw Sonny into the passenger seat, and jumped behind the wheel. The FA-18s were coming in again, wingtip-to-wingtip. Five more Maverick missiles launched. Smiley backed the truck away fast, out of the line of fire.

I threw the sand rail into gear and floored it, roaring back across the desert toward Cactus City. The buildings loomed on the night horizon as we approached. I looked over my shoulder, but Smiley was nowhere behind me. I needed to get back to the SWAT truck and get a first aid kit for Sonny, then radio for help. With his leg shot off, and his arteries open, even with my belt tourniquet, he would bleed out soon and die. I headed back toward the hole in the fence.

Suddenly, off to my right, another silver dune buggy was

heading right at me. Where it had come from I didn't know. The same huge rear tractor tires threw sand out behind as it closed in. The same metal mast jutted up between the seats.

A skinny man wearing a checked shirt and John Deere ball cap was at the wheel. He angled in to head me off, then pulled alongside until we were wheel to wheel, running at breakneck speed. I looked over and saw that he was driving with only one hand. The other was holding a big Army .45 pointed right at me.

He raised the muzzle and fired one shot over my head. My AR-15 was on the floor, banging around uselessly at my feet. I fought the wheel with both hands, flying along half blind at over forty miles an hour.

The man extended his arm and aimed the gun at my head. His meaning was very clear.

Stop or die.

ROYAL

I HAD TO make up my mind fast. Do I pull over for this asshole in the John Deere hat and risk Sonny's life, or keep going and pray for the best? I decided to make a run for it. Out of the corner of my eye, I saw the truck closing in from the right. Smiley had sped across the hard-pack that rimmed the edge of the gully, but now he was back in the soft sand. I heard the truck shift back into four-wheel drive and start growling. I knew he wouldn't be able to keep up if I just kept going.

Suddenly the black Dodge braked to a stop and the Browning started chattering. One of the bullets hit the metal mast in the front of my rail, blowing the large welded bolt away. The bullet ricocheted and metal fragments stung the side of my face. One piece blew a pretty good hole in my forearm, knocking my hand off the wheel. The rail spun right and finally shuddered to a stop.

I heard the .45 popping and looked back to see that the guy in the John Deere hat was now firing the large semiautomatic pistol at the truck. Impossible to hit at that distance with a handgun.

I pulled up the AR-15. With blood running down my arm and dripping off my fingers, I aimed at the truck and squeezed off a burst, holding the trigger down until the C-mag was dry. Then the man in the checked shirt spun his sand rail around in a circle and roared up on Sonny's side.

"Follow me," he yelled. Now we were teammates.

"My friend is wounded. He needs help!" I shouted over the roar of both sets of straight pipes.

He waved for me to follow, then floored his sand rail and sped out in front of me.

My arm was bleeding and the blood made my grip slick on the steering wheel. I fought the rough terrain. The hard suspension on the sand rail kept jerking the wheel from my grasp. The man in the John Deere hat roared ahead of me, back into Cactus City, but he never stopped. He exited the far end, then turned right and drove down into a sandy gully. I followed, wondering where the hell we were going and if he'd heard me about needing a doctor. I glanced over at Sonny. He was holding on with both hands, a ghastly expression on his face.

"Where's my leg?" he yelled across to me, the sick realization turning his expression into a mask of horror.

The man in front of us drove his dune buggy up to a large bush, then stopped, jumped out, and pulled it aside to reveal a metal drainage pipe about five feet in diameter. I could see from the tire tracks leading inside, that he'd used this before. He pulled his rail into the pipe, then motioned me to follow. I pulled in behind him. He ran past me and replaced the bush. As he passed back again he shouted, "Follow me! Stay close!" He jumped in his rail and took off before I could reply. It was suddenly pitch black and my tires were chattering across the ridged metal. I navigated by following sparks from his exhaust.

The tunnel angled slowly to the right. I found that the rail would almost steer itself inside the pipe. All I had to do was keep it from climbing the walls and flipping over. After about a quarter mile we came out the other side. There was an old wood shed next to a concrete, windowless building that was about twenty feet square. The man stopped the dune buggy and jumped out. He still had the .45 in his hand, but no longer looked like he was going to shoot me.

"Come on," he said and motioned for us to follow him.

"He's lost his lower leg," I said.

The man came back and stared at Sonny, who was now white and pasty, going into shock. Then without a word the skinny man lifted Sonny out of the rail, threw him over his shoulder in a fireman's carry, and ran with him across the sand to the concrete building a short distance away. He had a padlock key and was struggling to get it out of his pocket, with Sonny still over his shoulder. He finally opened the place up and carried Sonny inside. I followed, bringing both AR-15s and our two remaining C-clips.

Once we were inside, the man put Sonny on a mat on the floor, then closed the door and threw a bolt, locking us in. With no windows, it was again pitch black.

"I can't see," I said.

"Shut up," he answered. "Ya sound like a feckin' pussy."

A match was struck and a Coleman lantern hissed, throwing a dim light into the area. I looked around. We were in some kind of old water-control building or pumping station. There were rusted pipes and valves everywhere. Off in the distance I could still hear bombs exploding.

"This here's a no-impact area, inside the gunnery range," he said. "I found it three years ago. I wait here durin' fire missions."

Then the man came over and looked at Sonny's stump. "This here boy's gonna have to be tough as stewed skunk ta get through what we gotta do. But we cain't wait, gotta fix this mess now." He reached down and pulled a piece of Sonny's pant leg away, exposing the bloody stump.

"Don't touch him," I said. "He needs a doctor."

"We don't get this fixed up now, this Mexican won't need no doc. He'll be upstairs with Jesus. I was a medic. Vietnam. Seventy-fifth Army Rangers," he said. "I seen a lot worse than this. But we gotta triage the fecker now."

He had a deep cracker accent—Virginia, or South Carolina. He took off his hat, revealing a snow white forehead above a tan line on his weathered face. Gray hair, growing long, covered his ears. His teeth were a mess and he hadn't shaved in at least a week.

"Gimme yer shirt," he said.

I took off the SWAT vest, then removed my shirt, leaving me in a T-shirt. My forearm didn't look so bad, now that I saw it in the light. It had more or less stopped bleeding.

The man started ripping my shirt into strips. Then he took off the tourniquet belt I'd put on Sonny's thigh.

"Gonna let this bleed out a little, clean her out some," he said, and Sonny looked at his newly shot-off right leg in horror. Blood started spouting out onto the floor around us. Then the man cinched up the belt again, stemmed the flow, pulled a pint of scotch out of a backpack, and handed it to Sonny.

"Get this down," he ordered.

Sonny took a sip.

"Not like that. Give yerself a party, boy."

So Sonny started swallowing the scotch until the bottle was empty. The man crossed to one of the valves and turned it. When the water started to flow, he washed his hands, then brought the lantern closer. He knelt down, and picked up Sonny's stump in both hands.

"Whatta you gonna do?" I asked, feeling a little sick as I looked at what was left of the leg.

"Cain't git no lard without boilin' the hog," he said softly.

"Ain't gonna be much fun, but I gotta tie off them bleeders, or this boy's gonna be tradin' his guitar for a harp."

He crossed to his backpack, pulled out a small nylon combat medic's bag, and returned to Sonny. "Keep this handy and gimme what I ask for."

For the next ten minutes, while Sonny screamed in pain, this man, whoever he was, searched Sonny's bloody stump for the main arteries, then one by one, pulled them out, then clamped and sutured them.

Somewhere in the middle of this Sonny stopped screaming. He had fainted.

The FA-18s had completed their run and were gone. It was strangely quiet in the little concrete room. Finally, the man completed this field surgery and bound up the stump with strips of my shirt. He did it all in thirty minutes.

"Help me move him over there to the bed," he said.

We carried Sonny to a futon by the far wall, laid him down and elevated his leg. I sat on the floor next to him while the man went back and washed Sonny's blood off his hands. Then he returned and slumped down next to us.

"Who the hell are you?" I asked.

"I'm the guy you stole that feckin' sand buggy from," he said, flat southern vowels ringing on poured concrete.

"I'm a police officer," I said.

"Then ya oughta know better," he replied.

He had iridescent blue eyes—the kind of eyes I'd sometimes seen on the criminally insane. Madness glinted there. Everything else screamed hillbilly. The bony hips and the lean frame with the bulging beer belly, an Adam's apple that looked like somebody had shoved a tennis ball down his throat.

"I'm Shane Scully," I said. "This is Sonny Lopez."

"Royal Mortenson," he answered, but made no move to shake hands.

"I've gotta get him to the hospital," I persisted.

"You go back out there before the twenty-three-fifty strafing run and Blackie will drop you with that big Browning. He's pretty damn good with that thing. Knows the terrain. He'll set up over at the wall, or north a' Cactus West where he can see us coming. Before we get to any of my through-holes, mother-fecker will rip us all new assholes."

"What the hell do you do out here?" I asked, wondering why he and Smiley were wandering around at night on an active gunnery range.

"I'm a scrapper," he said. "All this shit lyin' around out here—the fins on the inerts and stuff—is worth money."

He wiped his hand across his mouth, then pulled out a can of Skoal, took a pinch, and put it behind his lower lip.

"Aluminum on them fins of the two-thousand pounders is worth plenty." He pronounced it *al-ow-min-eum*.

"Depending on the market, I kin git ninety bucks a fin on them thousand-pound inerts. Sometimes I'll disarm some of the smaller unexploded stuff. A seventy-pound fin is worth thirty-five bucks a blade. Then, twice a week them Cobra assault choppers with twenty-millimeter cannons, swoop in here, blow up some dump truck. Brass cartridges coming down all over the place. Fifty cents a round, like it's raining money." He smiled at me, his brown, uneven teeth looking like a busted-down fence.

"And Smiley? Does he scrap too?"

"Who's that?"

"The guy in the black Dodge Ram."

"Ya mean Blackie? Blackie is a big feckin' problem. I'm out here pickin' up scrap, tryin' to make me a livin'. He's bringin' the EOD down on us."

"Don't you need a permit for this?"

"I got me a permit." He held up the .45. "The EOD don't got no problem with me, on account they know I'm an ex-Ranger and I'll do the right thing, by God. Yessir!"

"I was a Marine," I said, looking for some connection.

He seemed to think about that. Then he went on.

"Blackie's a problem cause he don't give a shit. I only take fins off the inerts and the low-yield ordnance. Them's the blue bombs and the yellow stripers. But we got a lotta UHE shit out here—that's undetonated high explosives, and it's stuff EOD doesn't want messed with."

"What's EOD?" I asked him.

"Explosive Ordnance Disposal. They shut this place down once a month and go searching for unexploded JADAM two-thousand pounders and up. Hot ordnance that didn't detonate. Them's the bombs got C-four packages in 'em. Gotta disarm the warhead to get a one-pound package out, but it's worth fifteen grand or more on the black market, especially now, with terrorists tryin' to buy it. I could mine C-four easy, but I never do it. I'm an American. Ain't gonna help no sand nigger terrorist assholes get shit to blow us up. That's why EOD kinda leaves me alone. Fifteen years out here and they coulda busted me easy, but they let me be. Blackie, he's a whole 'nother story, 'cause he's in the C-four business. He's out here three times a week pullin' warheads off the reds, takin' out C-four packs. I been tryin' to catch the fecker myself, but he's tricky, and smart as a windmill fixer."

That explained where Smiley got the C-4.

The strange man spit a stream of tobacco juice across the room into a Folgers coffee can. He hit it pretty much right in the center and it rang loudly. Bull's-eye.

"With Blackie puttin' the heat on, EOD's gonna end up throwin' me out, right along with him."

"How soon till we can we get out of here?" I asked.

"Now that I got the bleedin' stemmed, yer friend's probably gonna hold up for a while, but he's gonna be needin' some regular doctorin' soon, antibiotics, a proper stitchin'. 'Course, we try to get outta here now, Blackie's gonna make some trouble. That big Browning's got some bite to it." He looked at his watch. "Like I said, ain't got another firing mission until eleven-fifty. Warthogs gonna be takin' out a phony SAM site. That's our best chance fer gettin' outta here. While they kick ass on them targets on the east ridge, he's gotta keep his head down. That's when we go."

48
THE WIRE

WE SAT ON the floor of the old pumping station, the Coleman lantern hissing loudly, Sonny lying unconscious beside us. The Warthog fire mission was scheduled to begin in an hour. Then we'd put Sonny in the sand buggy and make a run for it. Royal was talking softly, his voice droning in the dimly lit room.

"Ain't nobody comes out here much. 'Round April, it gets so dry the jackrabbits is all totin' canteens." He shook his head sadly. "After Nam, didn't have no place to go. Seemed there was no place I fit in. Folks spittin' on me, callin' me baby killer. But how do ya tell some snotty draft dodger who never served that some o' them kids over there would ask ya for a Hershey, then trade ya a hand grenade for a candy bar? After I got back, seemed weren't nothin' much to give a shit about no more. I seen my share of misery and there's no doubt it changes ya. Out here I don't gotta explain it to nobody. It's just me and the range. Takes my chances, makes my livin'. If I pull the wrong wire, it's adios, motherfecker. Nobody's even gotta come to my funeral, 'cause there ain't gonna be nothin' left t' bury."

I listened to him ramble on like that, talking about South Carolina and Vietnam. Royal Mortenson was what you became if you gave up and withdrew. A lonely, angry old man who had retreated to a spot so unforgiving and desolate that he no longer had to deal with life. As he talked my thoughts about my own future sharpened. I knew one thing: Whatever happened, I didn't want my journey to end up there.

Royal suddenly switched to current events. "Blackie, he seems t' want you dead pretty bad."

"He hates cops," I said flatly.

"I can get behind that one," he joked, then spit some more tobacco juice.

Another bull's-eye.

"Course, bein' as you're a cop, I know y'all gotta do things a certain way. You probably got some penal code tells you when t' shit and how far out in the woods to bury it. But sometimes I've found things work better when ya skin yer own possums."

He looked at me with a sharp twinkle in his eye.

"I'm listening."

"Ol' Blackie, he's clever. He hacks into the Yuma Range Management computer, just like me. Gets the time of the firing missions. Them Marines are always right on time, Drop their loads, regular as Presbyterians. So he knows, just like me, when them planes is comin'. Once they start bombin', he's ducked down in a safe place like this one. Rest of the time, he's out there on the range, prospectin' C-four."

He looked up at me, shrewdness a cagey visitor on his weathered face. "So here's the way I see our choices. We could wait for that flighta Warthogs to come in at twenty-three fifty, then make our move, get yer Mexican to the hospital. But looks to me like this boy could go inta shock. Blood pressure gets too low and his heart could just plum quit. Not wantin' that ta happen, maybe you and me oughta advance up the timetable a smidge." He started picking at a loose thread hanging off his pant leg. "I seen ol' Blackie shootin' at you in Cactus West, then lettin' you chase him out by Kill Hill, down inta Jackrabbit Creek, leading ya in there right on time, so them Hornets could have their shot at ya."

"Are you telling me he knew they were coming?" I asked.

"Yep." Royal kept picking at the loose thread. "Knew the exact time and exact coordinates. Got 'em off the range computer. Took ya down there specifically so you could French-kiss a Maverick."

He snapped the thread off, then looked over at me. "If ya wanta get Pancho to that hospital a scootch ahead of schedule and keep him from singin' in the celestial choir, then I might have a way we fix ol' Blackie. Make it so he loses his head and makes a mistake. Or, if it pleases ya, we could arrange it so that happens the other way around."

Then Royal told me why he had the metal masts screwed into the front of the sand rails. The government strung low wires at various places on the range to make it dangerous for scrappers that were running fast without headlights at night. The EOD kept moving the wires to new locations so the scavengers wouldn't know where they were. The masts on the sand rails were up front to catch a missed wire and snap it.

" 'Course, I don't hit many of them things, cause I make it my business to know when them EOD boys change a wire. But ol' Blackie, he's in that big truck with a cab to protect him so he don't pay them wires no nevermind. Maybe we can arrange it so things happen a little different tonight."

He looked up and flashed his yellow smile. Then he told me his plan. When he finished, he looked over at me, his criminal blues blazing.

"Can't shoot the fecker, 'cause if EOD finds him fulla lead, it looks like a murder, and I got a lotta explaining to do. This way it looks like he just got careless and paid the price." Then he stopped talking and a crafty look followed.

" 'Course, with you being a cop, I wouldn't want to be facin' no bullshit trial afterwards. You want my help, you and me gotta come to an understanding."

I stayed quiet for a minute, thinking. He could call it an accident, but what he was really talking about was murder.

Then I thought about the last two weeks, and about Emo and Jo. I remembered how Emo's son Alfredo, had held onto Elana's hand at the funeral, standing tall, refusing to cry, knowing he and his mother would have to go on alone. I remembered Emo up on Smiley's porch, dead in the vertical coffin. Smiley had opened the front door and shot him at point-blank range. He'd had no chance.

I thought of Jo, lying in her hospital bed, hovering near death, a victim of the same situation. Only with Jo, I had to share the blame and it weighed heavily on me. I looked down at my shirt wrapped around Sonny's stump, his life slowly seeping out, his blood staining the cloth. I needed to get him out of here before he died. Add in Greenridge and Nightingale and the score was five to zip. I was getting pretty tired of losing.

I could feel Royal's eyes on me as I weighed the decision.

"We do this right, it'll go down slick as snot on a doorknob," Royal drawled. "But you and me, we gotta swear us a oath, first. We gotta swear to both take this piece'a business to the grave."

Then Sonny coughed and moaned, helping me make up my mind.

"Let's do this guy," I whispered.

Royal looked up, smiled widely, then nodded.

I put my Tac vest back on and we left Sonny lying on the futon with the empty pint of scotch now filled with water.

Royal and I exited the pumping station and stood outside in the moonlight.

"Things're goin' so good, I might have to hire me somebody to help enjoy it," he joked, then turned to me. "You know what you're gonna do?"

"Right," I replied, thinking I shouldn't be taking tactical orders from a withered old hick who was probably half insane. But as he'd said, this was his backyard. He knew the rules and the terrain.

Royal unscrewed the mast on the front of my sand rail and leaned it against the pumping station. "Now git, and keep your head down," he warned.

I nodded, fired up the buggy, and drove back into the drainage tunnel. Royal was already removing the mast from the second rail as I pulled out. The engine echoed loudly in the metal pipe. After a quarter of a mile, I stopped at the end of the tunnel and removed the bush blocking the opening. Then I drove back out onto the desert floor heading toward Cactus West. My forearm was aching where the shrapnel hit me and my fingers were going numb, but I ignored it and kept driving.

I pulled in five minutes later, parked off the main road in a bombed out adobe structure, and turned off the motor. I grabbed the AR-15, jammed in another C-mag, then found a spot up on a roof where I had a clear view of the main street. I proned out on the cold corrugated metal, put the assault rifle to my shoulder, and waited.

Half an hour later I heard the sound of Royal's rail way off in the distance. He was roaring toward Cactus West, the straight pipes blaring faintly across the desert, changing pitch every time he shifted gears. Then slowly, an octave lower, I began to hear the distinctive sound of the black Dodge. I pulled the night vision glasses up and focused them in the direction of the noise. The sand rail was out front, jumping berms and ridges, going about forty, spewing rooster tails of sand from its rear tires. About two hundred yards behind him, the Dodge Ram growled loudly in four-wheel drive, going about thirty-five, trying to stay up. In the strange green hue of the night scope the scene appeared ghostly and surreal.

Then the truck stopped and Smiley jumped out, threw the Browning down across the front fender, and started firing. The Browning was winking death silently, then the chattering bark of the huge weapon reached me a few seconds later. But Royal was almost in town. Smiley jumped back in his truck and continued the chase. Royal flew past my position and drove right out of town, dragging the truck like a tail behind him, much the same way Smiley had dragged Sonny and me down into Jackrabbit Creek.

In a few seconds he would pass my firing position. I tromboned the slide, kicking a .223 out of the breech to make sure I wasn't jammed, then waited. The black truck sped toward me, the engine growling ominously. I had the Dodge in my sights as it sped past. Then I opened fire, shooting at the tires, squeezing off at least fifty of the hundred rounds in my C-mag.

The truck tires all exploded. The Dodge shuddered and spun to a stop. Even before it came to rest, Smiley was out with the .50-caliber cradled in both hands. He swung it around towards my position and fired, but I was already up and running, jumping down off the roof. As the exploding shells tracked me, I dodged between the disintegrating adobe buildings and quickly reached my sand rail. Royal Mortenson was in the driver's seat with the engine running.

"Where'd you leave it?" I asked.

"Right on the edge of town. Fecker can't miss it." He downshifted, popped the clutch, and the rail exploded forward, out of the bombed-out building and up the street. Royal turned right onto Main and powered out of town.

Smiley, on foot, saw us make the turn and started firing. The slugs blew holes in the last building on the street as we swerved around it and headed out into the desert. I turned around in the passenger seat with the AR-15 in both hands and squeezed off a short burst at him, aiming high.

Smiley was firing the Browning at us from the edge of town where Royal had stashed the other sand rail, but we were out of range. He finally spotted the second rail parked over to his right, and moved cautiously to check it out, not sure if it was booby-trapped. Then, without much delay, he was in the driver's seat and coming after us, the big .50-cal propped in the bucket seat next to him.

We vectored toward the north end of the gunnery range. I thought Sonny had been driving fast, but nothing like Royal was driving now. We had to be going at least sixty, maybe more, screaming across the desert. When we hit a berm or a gully, it seemed we catapulted at least five feet in the air.

"Yeeeeeaaaaahhhhh!" Royal screamed every time the rail flew. We headed toward two large fenced-off areas where it looked like they dragged the unusable bombed-out truck carcasses. The fenced lots were about fifty yards apart and filled with torched wrecks.

"There she blows," Royal screamed, slowing slightly. "Give the sidewinder a little encouragement."

I fired off another burst and saw him swerve, then speed up, closing fast. He had somehow managed to prop the Browning up on the dash and now he squeezed off a short burst. It was surprisingly accurate. The chain-link fence on the left side of us sparked with bullets.

"Keep down, wires ahead!" Royal shouted as we roared between the two fenced lockups.

Smiley was a hundred yards back. Royal had his head way down, almost between his knees. I was laid out, facing backward, holding the AR-15, the sand rail throwing sand out behind us on both sides. I could see the glint of a wire flash past inches over our heads.

Unexpectedly, Royal screamed a bad joke at nobody, yelling it into the night air: "Hey, Blackie, ever hear the one about the fecker who bought hisself a blow job but forgot his wallet so he lost his head?"

Almost as he yelled it, Vincent Smiley's head flew from his shoulders, cut off clean by a bridging wire. It sailed up into the air like a bloody jumpball and landed ten feet away. The head-less torso now drove the dune buggy, which swerved wildly, crashing into the fence.

"Yeeeeeaaaaahhhhh!" Royal Mortenson yelled. He slowed to a stop. We got out and ran back toward the spot where Smi-ley's torso had landed when his sand rail crashed. We were care-ful to duck under the taut wires that EOD had strung between the fences. They were nearly invisible in the dark.

The second sand buggy was still upright. Royal reached in and shut off the engine. Then we walked over and looked down at Vincent Smiley's head lying on the sand. The final expression on his face was a terrible, ugly grimace.

Royal leaned down and stared into the lifeless eyes. He gig-gled, then looked up with mad eyes that revealed to me, in that instant, the landscape of his tortured soul.

50
INHERITANCE

ROYAL MORTENSON HELPED me get Sonny back to the SWAT truck. He used his tractor to pull it out of the sand, but he didn't want to go with me.

"Towns're like a booger you can't shake off yer finger," he said, charming and understated to the end. We shook hands and that crazy bastard walked out of my life forever.

I raced to the hospital in Brawley with Sonny in the back of the SWAT truck. Like my other partner, Jo, he went right into ICU. I sat in the waiting room while doctors were paged and people ran back and forth. Too many nurses were running.

The two SWAT teams arrived an hour later and sat with me in the waiting room. They told me they had seen the Super Hornets bombing the desert from the mountain as they climbed down. I explained that we'd chased Smiley onto the gunnery range and that Sonny was hit when Vincent opened up with the big Browning. I told them we'd been trying to get away with Smiley chasing us when he had unexpectedly hit the wire and decapitated himself. It fudged the truth but nobody had asked too many tough questions. At least not yet.

I called to check on Jo and was told that she'd taken a turn for the worse. She was having a lot of secondary problems, low blood oxygen and a troublesome infection that was slowly taking her resistance down.

After Sonny was out of surgery the doc came back and told us that he was going to make it. The good news was they had been able to save his knee so he would eventually be able to walk with a prosthesis. I left Sonny with his fellow sheriffs, Scott Cook and Rick Manos, then caught a ride back to L.A. with SRT.

"The military really strings cable out there to stop these guys from scrapping metal at night?" Gordon Grundy asked, having trouble believing it. "Why would they want to decapitate people?"

"Because of the C-four," I explained. "They don't want terrorists to get their hands on it. The whole place is posted. You enter at your own risk."

"Well, if somebody had to lose his head, I guess Smiley's a good choice," Rosano said, putting the best spin on it.

The news treated the story and me very kindly. ATF was in charge of all investigations involving stolen C-4. That gave Brady Cagel control of the case. A good break for yours truly. Nobody seemed inclined to question EOD's description of the event. The way they told it, Smiley had been scrapping out there for months. They had tried to run him off, even got him on a radio frequency once and warned him about the wires, but he had cut off the transmission.

They had tried to apprehend him, but he worked mainly at night and had always been able to escape. EOD said Smiley had stolen the sand rail he'd been driving when he died. It belonged to a local Coachella Valley resident named Royal Mortenson, who the newspaper said was a Vietnam vet and recipient of the Silver Star.

When Smiley's truck was finally found in Cactus West, all four of the tires that I'd shot out had been miraculously replaced. I'd been worried about what questions would be asked when that Dodge was found full of .223s.

Who had done that little piece of cleanup for me? Royal? EOD? The gunnery range good fairy?

I'm not asking, so I'll never know.

Life settled, more or less, back to normal. My overweight partner, Zack Farrell, returned from Miami. He was wearing a new dark green outfit, and he filled his swivel chair across the desk from me, looking like three hundred pounds of gristle wrapped in a GLAD bag.

"Man, I leave town for a minute and all the action starts," he groused. His mother had made a miraculous recovery, so Zack was back in my life.

Jo Brickhouse continued to lose ground. I spent most of my spare time at the hospital, looking across a chipped linoleum table into the worried eyes of Bridget Bollinger.

"I know she's going to get better," Bridget said. "She just has to."

"We're not in charge," I told her. "It's in God's hands."

Platitudes. Why do people think they have to say stuff like that? I've been on the receiving end of those same remarks, and they never help.

Bridget looked more frightened every day. "Y'know, Jo really liked you," she said one afternoon, unexpectedly. "She said you were attractive. We even had a fight about it."

"You never had anything to worry about there," I told her. "Our friendship worked on different levels."

Every evening after visiting hours Bridget and I went down

into the little chapel at the hospital and said prayers for Jo's recovery.

She lingered like that for days, sometimes rallying before taking a turn for the worse. And then, slowly, we started to lose her.

Two days later she was gone.

Bridget and I were sitting in the waiting room, playing Gin, when Jo's surgeon came in and told us she had passed on. Bridget started to cry and I held her, feeling the huge, wracking sobs, realizing my own tears were mixing with hers.

...

The Rams' first game with Chooch as a coach was against the Chargers. Sonny Lopez was on the sidelines in a wheelchair with a blanket over his lap. Alexa and I wheeled him onto the field. The sheriffs who were there, and all the players, came over and shook his hand.

Darren Zook had taken over for Sonny and was coaching the defense. He and Chooch had the Rams in pretty good shape, but they were behind by seven points at the half. I walked over to the end zone where the team had their helmets off, sitting on the grass eating oranges and getting instructions from the coaches for the second half.

"Who has that middle linebacker on the inside blitz?" Chooch was saying as I joined them. "He's killing us."

"I do, Coach," a tall Mexican kid said. "But the guy's been using his hands and the refs don't call it."

"Forget that. Knock this guy on his butt. He can't sack our QB if he's seeing sunshine."

Chooch made the halftime speech. "You guys are playing great. But they have a good team, some great athletes, so we gotta dig a little deeper. Emo's up there watching," he said simply. "He'll give us the plays. He knows the game plan, and his offense rocks."

"Coach," Deshawn Zook said, and Chooch looked over at

him. "Thanks for sticking with us," the boy said softly. "We're gonna win this for Emo, but we're also gonna win it for you."

An hour later, with ten seconds left on the clock, they did.

A week after the game, on Sunday morning, we were sitting around after breakfast looking for something to do with the day. Delfina and Chooch decided to go to the park to study under the trees. I went out to the backyard with Franco and sat looking at the Venice Canal. So much had happened. So many people had died, and I had to figure out how to accept my part in it. *What could I have done differently?* I had prayed for Jo and Sonny until my knees were sore, but one had died and the other was in a wheelchair, and the answers still hadn't come. I felt culpable and out of touch with myself. I was in an emotional echo chamber—a moral cul-de-sac.

Alexa came out to join me and handed over a beer. We clinked bottles.

"Chooch was really happy about winning the game," Alexa said, smiling. "With three college coaching visits scheduled this week, his cast coming off on Tuesday, and Delfina's play about to open, things are definitely looking up in the kid department."

"Yep." I was trying to feel the upper, but not getting there.

"And Tony—yesterday he actually called me in and apologized."

"Really?"

"Yep. He said he knew that he was acting like a jerk, that he was just passing his misery down, and that it was lousy command tactics. He promised he'd never do it to me again."

"Tony's a good guy, but if he hadn't eased up on you he'd be wearing a few new knots on that shiny bald head."

She hit me in the arm. "Cut it out, tough guy."

"Sorry, some parts of me won't ever change. You gotta take the good with the bad."

She looked over, sensing the strange place I was in, seeing how uncomfortable I was with how all this had ended.

"You know, Shane," she said softly, "we can only do the best we can. If life was so easy to predict, nobody would ever get hurt. You can only view your culpability in any situation by the choices you made looking forward. If you view it looking back, it's called second guessing."

"When you look into the future, what do you see?" I asked her.

"I see things I want to do. I see Chooch in college, getting married, raising children. I see us growing old together, always being in love." She reached over and took my hand. "What do you see?" she asked.

"Nothing. I see nothing. I've always been afraid to have dreams, to look too far into the future."

"We'll just have to work on that." She smiled sadly, but I could tell she was worried about me when she said it.

"From the time I was a baby, my future only held disappointment," I said, trying to explain. "Maybe if I'd seen more, felt more, taken more chances . . . maybe I coulda changed what happened."

"Honey, don't go there. Coulda, woulda, shoulda. You're not to blame. Jo Brickhouse was a good police officer, she signed on to do a dangerous job. She made a mistake and she paid the full price. I didn't know her, but from what you've told me, she'd tell you to let it go. She'd want you to know it's not your fault."

"Okay," I said, but I was just ducking her now, and she sensed it.

"I know something happened out there on the gunnery range, because a lot of this doesn't add up. But Shane, whatever happened, whatever you had to do—you did the right thing. You reached down into a vat of goo and pulled out a rabbit. You saved this for me and for Tony, and you kept something terrible from happening. What happened to Jo and Sonny wasn't your fault. You could just as easily have been the one to get hit."

"Cut one and we all bleed," I said softly. I finally understood the full extent of that slogan.

Later that afternoon, there was a knock at my door. I opened it and Darren Zook was standing there.

"Come outside, I want to show you something," he said.

I followed him out.

Parked in my driveway was Emo's beautiful red Harley Softail. The chrome glittered, the lacquered black paint sparkled in the sun.

"Isn't that Emo's?" I asked.

"Not anymore," he said. "It's yours."

"Mine?" Looking at the bike, not understanding.

"Elana Rojas is grateful for all you did. She wants you to have it if you'll teach Alfredo to ride it when he's sixteen."

He handed me the keys.

An hour later I was riding Emo's bike through Trancas Canyon, going fast, leaning hard on the turns. Not oversteering this time—taking chances, just letting it all happen. The wind was tugging at my shirtsleeves and flapping my pant legs. The engine filled my ears with its throaty roar. Finally, I pulled into the place where we'd started the Iron Pig ride last summer. It was a spot high in the Malibu hills that overlooked the ocean. I shut off the engine, kicked down the stand, and reached into the hand-tooled saddlebag, taking out the beer I'd brought with me. Then I opened it and walked over to the lip of the hill, sat on a boulder, and looked out at the Pacific. The sun was just setting, turning the water and sky a purplish-orange.

In my heart and head I was always racing toward something I could never quite define, my ambition and ego pushing me, my final destination, unsure. Along the way, there were many places to stop. Some of them were havens where people I loved were waiting—Alexa, Chooch, Emo, and Jo—places where lessons could be learned. Others were simply hideouts. There were also dangerous spots where demons waited. Where I stopped, and what happened to me when I did, was not only controlled by fate. I had a lot to do with those decisions. They defined my destiny. All I had to do was simply own it. I had spent two hours with the ghost of the future, and knew I didn't want to end up like Royal Mortenson. In the end, life was all about choices. Alexa was right. I had done the best I could, and it hadn't quite worked out the way I wanted. I had to find a way to accept that, but not second-guess it.

I had told Jo that in order to grow she needed to be vulnerable. Maybe that's all this was. Vulnerability. Maybe I didn't have that down quite as well as I thought. Maybe vulnerability was just going to take some more getting used to.

The funerals had all been delayed by the forensics. In the next week, after the coroner finished with the bodies, I would stand at four grave sites while more empty words and hollow platitudes were spoken.

But this was my time.

I raised my beer and said all of their names softly.

"Emo Rojas, Josephine Brickhouse, William Greenridge, Michael Nightingale." Soldiers who had fallen while I marched on. It was just the way it was.

As the sun went down, I said good-bye to all of them.

God, how I hate cop funerals.

AUTHOR'S NOTE

I trust Californians will forgive me for rearranging the geography of the State a bit to suit my fictional designs, with special apologies to the municipalities of Palm Springs and Indio.

THE
TIN
COLLECTORS

Principles serve to govern conduct when there
are no rules.

—LAPD Management Guide
to Discipline

THE "CHOOCH" LETTER

Dear Dad:

Charles Sandoval, who everybody calls Chooch, arrived this afternoon as planned (actually, I picked him up). This is already shaping up as one of my biggest boners. I pulled up at the fancy private school Sandy's got him enrolled in and I had to go to the principal's office to sign the pickup permission slip. The principal, John St. John, is a wheezing, hollow-chested geek who seems to honestly hate Chooch. The way he put it was: "That child is from the ninth circle." I had to ask, too. It's from Dante's Inferno. *Apparently, the ninth circle is the circle closest to hell. Now that I've met Chooch, not an entirely inappropriate analogy. Then, this pale erection with ears hands me a packet of teacher evaluation slips. For a fifteen-year-old, his rap sheet* is impressive . . . pulled fire alarms, and fights *in the school cafeteria (food as well as fists). Mr. St. John informs me that they have notified Sandy that Chooch is not to return to the Harvard Westlake School next semester and that I need to get him enrolled elsewhere (like this is all of a sudden supposed to be my problem). But it's not as if this boy doesn't have a good reason to be angry. I think I wrote you, he's a love child with one of Sandy's old clients. Making matters worse, Sandy doesn't want him to know how she makes her living, so she's been shipping him off to boarding schools since third grade.*

Needless to say, I had no idea what I was getting into here.

3

Maybe I can last the month until Sandy takes him back or sends him to the next sucker on her list. One way or another, I'll work it out.

I'm planning to get out to Florida again sometime next year. I was thinking you and I could rent one of those fishing boats like we did last time, drink some beer and cook what we catch over a beach fire. Those memories are treasures in my life.

I know, I know, cut the mush, blah . . . blah . . . blah. I miss you, Dad. That's all for now.

Love,
Your son,
Shane

USE OF FORCE

SHANE WAS IN deep REM black. Way down there, but still he heard the telephone's electronic urgency. The sound hung over him, a vague shimmer, way above, up on the surface. Slowly he made his way to it, breaking consciousness, washed in confusion and anger. His bedroom was dark. The digital clock stung his eyeballs with a neon greeting: 2:16 A.M. He found the receiver and pressed it against his ear.

"Yeah," he said, his voice a croak and a whisper.

"Shane, he's trying to kill me," a woman hissed urgently.

"What . . . who is this?"

"It's Barbara." She was whispering, but he could also hear a loud banging coming over the receiver on her end, as if somebody was trying to break down a door.

"He's trying to kill you?" he repeated, buying time so his mind could focus.

Barbara Molar. He hadn't seen her in over two months, and

then just for a moment at a police department ceremony, last year's Medal of Valor Awards. Her husband, Ray, had been one of three recipients.

A crash, then: "Jesus, get over here, Shane. Please. He'll listen to you. He's nuts, worse than ever."

Shane heard another crash. Barbara started screaming. He couldn't make out her next words, then: "Don't, please . . ." She was whimpering, the phone was dropped on a hard floor, clattering, bouncing, getting kicked in some desperate struggle.

"Barbara? Barbara?" She didn't answer. He heard a distant, guttural grunting like a man sometimes makes during sex, or a fight.

Shane got out of bed and started gathering up clothes. He slipped into his pants and grabbed his faded LAPD sweatshirt. He snapped up his ankle gun, hesitated for a moment, then pulled it out, chambered it, and strapped it on. He ran out of his bedroom toward the garage without even looking for his shoes. He was already behind the wheel when he realized he had forgotten that Chooch Sandoval was asleep in the other bedroom. He wasn't used to having fifteen-year-old houseguests. He knew he shouldn't leave Chooch alone. The garage door was going up as he backed out his black Acura. Grabbing for his cell phone, he dialed a number from memory. He streaked down the back alley away from his Venice, California, canal house, as cold beach air slipstreamed past the side window onto his face.

Brian "Longboard" Kelly, his boned-out next-door neighbor, picked up the phone. "Whoever this is, fuck you" was the way he came on the line.

"Sorry, Brian, it's Shane. I got called out, and Chooch is still asleep in the guest bedroom."

"Chooch? Who the hell . . ."

"The kid I told you I was taking for the month. Sandy's kid. He came yesterday."

"Ohhh, man . . ."

"Look, Brian, just go over and sleep on my couch. The key is in the pot by the back door."

"Good place, dickbrain. Who would ever think to look there?"

"Just do it, will ya? I'll owe ya."

"Fuckin' A." Longboard slammed the phone down in Shane's ear.

Shane was now at Washington Boulevard. He hung a left and headed the short distance to the Molar house. When they'd still been partners, he'd made this trip at least once a day to pick up Ray, heading across Washington to South Venice Boulevard, through Gangbang Circle, where, once it got dark, the V-Thirteens and Shoreside Crips staged their useless, life-ending street actions, occasionally killing or wounding a tourist from Minnesota by mistake.

He shot across Abbot Kinney Boulevard and turned right onto California, finally coming to Shell Avenue. All the way there, he wondered why Barbara would call him. Why not dial 911? Of course, the answer was sort of obvious after he thought about it. Even though she was scared spitless, she still didn't want another domestic-violence beef in Ray's LAPD Internal Affairs jacket. He was a thirty-year veteran with a big pension, which another DV complaint would jeopardize. That pension was an asset that was half hers.

Still, Shane Scully was the last guy Ray Molar would want to see coming through his door, quoting departmental spousal-abuse regulations at two A.M. *So why Shane? Why not Ray's current partner?* He guessed he knew that answer, too. She called him because she thought she could control him, use him for protection, then keep him from talking. Also he was handy, only five miles away. . . . Just like before, he had turned up as the double zero on her slow-turning roulette wheel.

When he got to Ray's small, wood-sided house, he pulled into the driveway behind Ray's car and jumped out. The hood was warm on the dark blue Cadillac Brougham; the lights were on in the house. Then he heard muffled screaming.

"Shit, I hate this," he mumbled softly, feeling the cold grass on his bare feet. He moved toward the house, tried the front door and, to his surprise, found it was open. Reluctantly, he stepped into his ex-partner's living room.

Ray's house always seemed delicate and overdecorated. Too much French fleur-de-lis upholstery, too many knickknacks and hanging lamps. It was Barbara's doing and definitely didn't seem like the lair of a street monster like Ray Molar. Ray should live in a cave, cooking over an open fire, throwing the gnawed bones over his shoulder.

Shane could hear Barbara's screams coming from the back of the house, so he moved in that direction. He came through the bedroom door just in time to see Ray Molar hit his slender, blond wife in the solar plexus with the butt end of his black metal street baton. Then, as she doubled over, he expertly swung the nightstick sideways, catching her in the side of the head with a "two from the ring" combat move . . . a baton-fighting tactic taught to every recruit at the Police Academy. Shane stood frozen, as Barbara, her head bleeding badly, slumped to the floor, almost unconscious.

"Ray . . . " Shane's voice, a raspy whisper, cut the temporary silence like a sickle slashing dry wheat. "What's the story here, buddy?"

Ray Molar swung around. He was at least six-four and weighed over two-forty, with huge shoulders and long arms. He had bristly blond hair and a corded, muscled neck. Adding to these Blutoesque dimensions was a huge jutting jaw and almost total lack of a forehead. "Get the fuck outta here, Scully. We don't need the Boy Scouts," Molar growled, his pupils round points of focused hatred.

Shane had seen that look in the street many times before and had come to fear it. "Let's just back off, slow down, and give it a rest, Ray." Shane was moving slowly toward him, not wanting any part of the fury and craziness he saw on his ex-partner, but feeling compelled to get close enough to protect Barbara if he swung on her again. When Ray lost control, he could turn instantly murderous. He spewed white rage without thought, violence without reason.

"You got anything to eat?" Shane said, trying to refocus the energy in the room. "I'm starved. Missed dinner. How 'bout I get us a beer and a sandwich, something. . . . We chill out a little . . . Cool out . . . Talk it down . . . Get solid . . ."

"You wanna eat somethin'? Eat shit, Scully!" He was halfway between Shane and Barbara, still brandishing the black metal police baton.

"Ray, I don't want trouble, but you can't go hitting Barbara with the nightstick, man. You're gonna fuck her up bad."

Then Ray started toward Shane, swinging the metal stick in a lose arc in front of him. "Yeah? Who's gonna stop me, dickwad?"

"Come on, let's stay frosty here, Ray. Let's . . . let's—" And he stopped talking because he had to duck.

Ray swung the nightstick. It zipped through the air an inch from Shane's ear. As he was coming back up, Ray swung a fist, hitting him with a left hook that landed on Shane's right temple, exploding like a pipe bomb, sending him to the floor, ears ringing. Then Ray yanked a small-caliber snubby out of his waistband. It looked to Shane like an off-brand piece, a European handgun of some kind, maybe a Titan Tiger or an Arminus .38, definitely not standard police issue. Ray always kept a "throw-down gun" on him to drop by a body if some street character got funky and had to take a seat on the sky bus.

"Put it away, Ray."

"You fucking this bitch, too? You fucking her? 'Cause if you ain't, you should get in line—everybody else is."

"Come on, Ray, that's crazy. I never touched your wife; nobody's messin' with Barb, and you know it. Why're you doin' this?"

"She's been getting snaked by half the fuckin' department."

He turned back and glowered at her. "Am I right, baby? Tell him 'bout all the wall jobs you been doin' in the division garage."

Barbara groaned. Ray, turning now, aimed the gun at Shane, pulling the hammer back. Shane watched the cylinder begin to rotate on the center post as Ray applied pressure on the trigger. He was strangely mesmerized by the hole in the barrel; a dark eye of damnation, freezing his stomach, dulling his reactions. He was seconds from death. . . . Almost without realizing it, his right hand slipped down to his ankle, fingers encircling the wood-checked grip of his 9mm automatic. He slid the weapon free.

Shane dove sideways just as Ray fired. The bullet thunked into the wooden doorframe behind him. Shane was operating on instinct now, with no control over what happened next, going with it, not questioning, rolling, coming up prone, his Beretta Mini-Cougar gripped in both hands.

As Ray turned to fire again, Shane squeezed the trigger. The bullet hit Ray Molar in the middle of his simian brow.

Huge head jerking back violently.

Brainpan exploding, catching the 9mm slug.

Then Ray looked directly at Shane as the gun slipped from his meaty paw and thumped onto the carpet. Ray's pig eyes, bright in that instant, registered hatred and surprise, or maybe Shane was just looking for something human in all that animal ferocity.

Ray Molar took one uncertain step backward and sat on the edge of the bed. Even though his heart was probably still beating, Shane knew that his ex-partner was already dead. But the street monster sat down anyway, almost as if he needed a moment to consider what he should do next or where he should go, momentum and gravity making the decision for him, toppling him forward, thudding him hard, face first, onto the carpet.

Shane looked over at Barbara, who was staring at her dead husband, her mouth agape, her puffed lip split and bleeding.

"Whatta we do now, Shane?" she finally asked.

M-417-00

I N THE SECONDS after the shots were fired, the bedroom seemed so quiet that he could almost hear dust settle. Then the sharp smell of cordite, mixed with the coppery smell of blood, began to fill his nostrils. Barbara was still on the floor not ten feet from Ray's body. Shane moved first. He stood slowly, feeling his knees shake as he rose. He stumbled to the dresser and leaned on it heavily, propping himself up for support. They were both trying to digest it, understand what had just happened and comprehend how it would alter, in a ghastly way, events stretching before them. Then, from the floor, Ray Molar farted. Shit ran into his pants as his bowels let loose. The perfect punctuation mark for the past few minutes.

"We need to get a story, Barbara," Shane said. "This isn't going to go down smooth. You know how they all feel about Ray."

"I don't know . . . I don't know . . . He just . . ."

"Barbara . . ."

Her eyes were darting around the room in a desperate escape dance. Her face was also beginning to swell where Ray had hit her on the right side, distorting her natural beauty.

"Tell me," he prodded softly, "what set him off?"

Somewhere in the distance they could hear the faint wail of a police car.

"Already?" she said, referring to the sirens.

"You were screaming, shots were fired, you've got neighbors. Nine-one-one response time is supposed to be less than five minutes. If something more is going on here, I need to know, Babs. You and I, we're not completely clean, if you know what I mean."

"I know." She pulled herself up on the bed and sat. He could see that her hands were shaking as she brought the back of her wrist up to wipe the blood oozing from the corner of her mouth. Her hand came away with an ugly red streak on the back. "He . . . he just . . . I don't know."

"He just what? Let's go, there isn't much time. What set him off?"

"I got a call yesterday from a woman. She asked me if I'd seen the videotape yet."

"What videotape?"

"I don't know. That's the whole point. I haven't got any tape, and I told her. She sounded like she was crying. Then she said it was coming in the mail, and it will show me what a cheating bastard Ray was."

"Who was she?"

"Didn't say. I didn't recognize the voice. She just hung up."

The sirens were now less than a block away as Barbara Molar looked at Shane in desperation. "What're they gonna do?"

"They're gonna separate us. Take statements. This is our only chance to coordinate. We need the same story. Stay with me here, Babs. Keep goin'. What happened next?"

"Ray hasn't been home much since he got his new assignment.

He's been away days at a time, so when he got home tonight, I asked him where he was all the time. I told him what the woman said and he . . . he just . . . went nuts. You know his temper, how he gets. You worked patrol with him. He accused me of sleeping with his friends. He called me a whore. He started beating me. I can't take any more beatings. I can't. I told him I was going to leave him, and then he chased me into the bathroom. I locked the door and called you. Then he just—"

The sirens growled to the curb outside, and Shane quickly looked around the bedroom, taking mental pictures of the crime scene, filing them in his memory for later. Oddly enough, it was Ray who had schooled him in this technique, quizzing him at "end of watch" on what he remembered. They'd sit in some bar at EOW, betting drinks on the answers. Ray would ask questions: What was on the dresser? How many windows in the kitchen? Were there screens? Ray was violent and unpredictable, but he sure knew how to police a crime scene.

"They're gonna take me downtown," Shane said. "They'll take your statement here, then probably transport you to the ER. Just say exactly what happened. He would have killed you, Barbara. He fired first. This was self-defense. Just leave out you and me. Whatever you do, stay tight on that."

They could hear cops coming into the house through the open front door.

"We're back here, LAPD!" Shane yelled. Then, as an afterthought, he whispered to Barbara, "Call the phone company and see if you can get an AT&T printout of calls to your phone so we can try and find out who that woman is."

Barbara nodded just as a uniformed South Bureau "dog and cat" team came through the door, guns drawn. Shane had his hands in the air and his Beretta Mini-Cougar hanging down, dangling uselessly from his right thumb. "LAPD," he said again.

The cops didn't know him, and not seeing a badge, the male officer rushed him, disarmed him, and threw him down onto the floor right next to a puddle of Ray's blood. The female kept her Smith & Wesson trained on him until her partner had Shane cuffed. Then they both roughly yanked him up.

"Where's your shield?" the lady cop said. Her nameplate read S. RILEY.

"On my dresser, at home. I was asleep. She called for help. I live four miles from here. I'm Sergeant Shane Scully, Southwest RHD. My serial number is 50867."

They looked down at Shane's now-bloody bare feet, then at Ray. The male cop was a policeman III; his nameplate read P. APPLEGATE. He knelt down and looked closely at the body. "Shit. This is Steeltooth. You shot Lieutenant Molar."

Shane stood quietly as Applegate fingered his shoulder mike. "This is X-ray Twelve. We're Code Six at 2387 Shell Avenue. We have a police officer down. We need a sergeant on the scene and the coroner. Notify South Bureau Detectives we have the shooter in custody. He claims to be Southwest Robbery/Homicide Sergeant Shane Scully." Then he turned to Shane. "Gimme that serial number again."

"It's 50867," Shane said into the officer's open shoulder mike.

"You get that?" Applegate asked. The female radio-transmission officer answered quickly.

"Roger, X-ray Twelve. That's 50867. You're Code Six Adam at Shell Avenue, requesting a supervisor and a Homicide unit. Stand by." There was static, and in less than thirty seconds, the RTO came back on. "X-ray Twelve, on your suspect ident: that badge number is confirmed to Southwest RHD Sergeant Shane Scully, 143 East Channel Road, Venice, California."

"Roger. We're locking down this crime scene for Homicide and moving outside." The officer then turned to Shane. "Who's your direct supervisor?"

"Captain Bud Halley, Southwest Division Robbery/Homicide."

"You got his call-out number?"

"Just call the squad. I can do it myself if you take these cuffs off."

"Hey, Scully, you done enough already. You just croaked the best fucking cop on the force." Then he unlocked the handcuffs. "Shannon, take Mrs. Molar into the kitchen. I'll hold Sergeant Scully in the living room." They left Raymond Molar in an expanding pool of his own blood to wait for the Homicide team and lab techs.

■ ■ ■

On every unnatural death in L.A., the RHD assigns a fresh homicide number and the next team up on the division rotation gets the squeal. The numbers start on January 1 and continue sequentially until the last day of December. If the body is a male, the number is proceeded by an *M*; if female, by an *F*. On that chilly April morning, Lieutenant Raymond George Molar became M-417-00.

The RHD team got there a little after three-thirty A.M. as the crime lab was just finishing photographing the scene. The two lab techs had already done their preliminary workup. They'd bagged the lieutenant's hands, outlined the DB in tape, and were standing around, waiting for the detectives to show before rolling the body.

Both Homicide dicks were veterans and had been notified before they got there that the officer down was the legendary LAPD Lt. Ray "Steeltooth" Molar. They had both signed Patrolman Applegate's crime-scene attendance sheet and now stood in the bedroom looking down at the body with stone-cut expressions as the lab techs flopped Ray over. His face had already begun to fill with blood, causing a darkening of the skin, known as lividity. More postmortem renal jettisoning had occurred, and the smell of feces in the room was getting strong as the two detectives from Robbery/Homicide silently policed the area, making their preliminary notes and observations. They graphed the location of the body and marked the bullet in the doorjamb that Ray had fired, then instructed the lab techs to dig the slug out and get it to the Investigative Analysis Section for a ballistics comparison. They bagged Shane's 9mm Beretta; it would be booked as evidence.

Shane was waiting in the living room with Patrolman Applegate. After half an hour the lead Homicide dick, an old, wheezing department warhorse with a basset-hound jawline, came out and sat on the sofa opposite Shane. His name was Garson Welch; he and Shane had shared a few easy grounders back when Shane was still working uniform in Southwest. One case had been so simple, they solved it in less than ten minutes when Shane arrested the perp half a block away as he was trying to stuff the murder weapon down into a Dumpster. The man had confessed on the spot. Shane and Welch had gone EOW at the jail and had had a few beers in a cop bar on Central known as the Billy Club. They didn't have what you'd call a friendship, but they were at least friendly—better than nothing.

"This ain't gonna go down too good at Parker Center, Shane," the old detective said, rubbing his ample forehead with a big, liver-spotted hand.

"Yeah, Gar, you're right. I should've just stood there and let him kill her with his nightstick."

"Calm down and listen," Welch went on. "What we got here is a brown shit waffle. Lieutenant Molar had big juice with the Super Chief. People you and I only read about in the *L.A. Times* are getting phone calls right now over this piece of work. I just got a call and found out he's been Mayor Clark Crispin's police driver for the past two months. So there's gonna be big interest at the city level. We're gonna go slow and get it right."

"The mayor's driver? Shit," Shane said. He hadn't known that was Ray's new assignment.

"I'm gonna take your preliminary here, then send you to the Glass House and let your captain do the DFAR," Welch said, referring to the Division Field Activity Report that had to be filed after any incident involving violence or death at the hands of a police officer.

"I got my car. I can meet you there," Shane volunteered.

"I'll have one of the blues drive it in and park it for you in the underground garage, but you're gonna go downtown in the back of a detective car. By the book. That way, nobody gets days off for bullshit nitpicks."

"Yeah, sure, if that's the way you want it." Shane was beginning to get a premonition of disaster. Then he followed Detective Welch out of the house for the long drive to Parker Center.

DFAR

THE TRIP DOWNTOWN at four A.M. on deserted freeways took only twenty-two minutes. The black-and-white slick-back that the RHD dicks were forced to drive now finally made a wide turn off Broadway, its headlights sweeping the south side of the Glass House. It pulled up to the security station. Sergeant Welch showed his badge, signed them all in, and drove into the huge underground parking garage that adjoined Parker Center.

The building was known as "the Glass House" to everybody on the job because of the excessive amount of plate glass that draped its huge boxy shape. The otherwise nondescript building had been designed in the fifties, which had proved to be a decade of architectural blight. The parking garage next door went down nine stories underground. The detectives found a spot on U-3, and both led Shane out of the parking complex, through a security door, and into the third basement of police headquarters. They took the elevator to six and got off at the Robbery/Homicide Division, which took up half the floor and was fronted by a thick glass partition.

Garson Welch buzzed them through and found the OOD, a thin-faced sergeant in uniform, sitting at a computer just inside the squad room. "Is Captain Halley around? He was supposed to get a call out on this activity report."

The sergeant nodded and pointed down the hall. "Interview room Three," he said.

They moved single file down the linoleum-floored corridor and turned into a small, windowless interrogation room that contained a scarred desk, two wooden chairs, and Robbery/Homicide Captain Bud Halley. Halley had his jacket off and was showing the beginnings of a twelve-hour beard, having missed his shave at four A.M. He had also missed two belt loops. Other than that, he was a remarkably handsome, fit, prematurely gray man in his mid-forties. He was Shane's Southwest Homicide Bureau commander. They had a good professional relationship. In the two years Shane had been assigned to Southwest Detectives, Halley had given him two excellent evaluation reports. As Shane came through the door, Captain Halley motioned him to a chair. "You guys don't have to stick around unless you need him. I'm gonna send him home after the activity report," he said to the two detectives.

"Thanks, Cap, check you later," Welch said as they left the room and closed the door behind them.

"We only have a few minutes and then God knows what happens," Halley said.

"A few minutes? What're you talking about? You're doing the DFAR. What's the rush?"

" 'Cept I'm not doing it. Deputy Chief Thomas Mayweather is on his way in. He's doing it."

"The head of Special Investigations Division is doing my activity report? You can't be serious. Why him?"

"Chief Brewer ordered it," Halley said.

"Same question, then."

"Don't you know what Ray Molar's assignment was?"

"Yeah . . . he was Mayor Clark Crispin's bodyguard and driver. He was also killing his wife with a nightstick. He fired a shot at me. Barbara Molar is my wit. This should be a slam dunk. So what's the deal?"

"Lemme give you the secret to survival around here." Shane waited for the punch line. "Everything that's not department history is department politics. Chief Brewer was awakened by Mayor Crispin, who called the Big Kahuna from the Dark Side, who got rousted off his sailboat at the marina. He was planning to sail across the channel for a long weekend in Avalon. Now, instead of salt air and sea chanteys, Deputy Chief Mayweather is coming here, in his fucking yacht attire, looking to tear you a new asshole."

"Cap, let me say this again, so none of us miss it. Steeltooth was killing his wife. He shot first. If I hadn't returned fire, we'd both be in the county icebox bleeding from the ears. I know for a fact Ray has two spousal-abuse beefs in his IAD package. He's a regular at rage-management counseling. Aside from that, we both know he was a head thumper from way back. You don't get the nickname Steeltooth just because your last name's Molar."

"Don't convince me. Make Mayweather believe it," Halley said softly.

Shane's hands started to shake. He was coming down from a two-hour adrenaline rush. He had killed Ray Molar, his ex-partner, a man he had once respected, then came to fear, and then finally to hate. His emotions hovered just below consciousness. He knew he couldn't afford a mistake, so he pushed personal feelings aside and concentrated on his plight, his survival instincts taking precedence.

■ ■ ■

Deputy Chief Mayweather was six three and ebony black. He had a shaved head and always carried himself with the athletic grace he had shown as a first-string point guard on the UCLA basketball team in the seventies.

He moved through the predawn stillness of the Robbery/Homicide Division and looked at the tired collection of swing-shift detectives who were manning their desks, sneaking glances at the clock, waiting for the day-watch to show up and relieve them. Mayweather stuck his gleaming black head into the interrogation room containing Scully and Halley.

"Let's do this upstairs." Mayweather's voice was cold and smooth, Vaseline on ice. "We'll use the conference room on nine. Bud, see if they got some coffee down here and bring it up." Then, without even looking at Shane, he moved out of the room, leaving them there.

"Good luck," Halley said as Shane got up off his hardwood chair and followed Mayweather, who was already halfway down the hall, striding toward the elevators with a Yul Brynner elegance, his arms swinging freely, his hips slightly forward. He was not in yachting attire. He'd dressed for this gig. The suit he wore was charcoal gray, creaseless, and fit him like a second skin. Tom Mayweather could easily have made a nice living on the pages of GQ.

Shane moved along behind him like a barefoot, dark-haired, brown-eyed shadow, his own gait more the shuffling stride of a street fighter. Although Shane had always been able to attract women, he found his own looks pugnacious and off-putting. In his mirror, he saw a face marred by cynicism and loneliness. He was always surprised when he heard someone describe him as attractive.

He caught Mayweather at the elevator. Both men remained silent as they waited for the stainless-steel doors to open and take them to the ninth floor, where Tom Mayweather and the other deputy chiefs had their offices down the hall from Chief Burleigh Brewer.

"Sorry about the Avalon trip, sir," Shane said, going for a little pre-interview suck.

"Let's save everything for when we get the tape running, okay?"

"Sure," Shane said.

The door opened and they stepped in and rode the humming metal box to the light-paneled, green-carpeted executive floor. All the way up, Deputy Chief Mayweather said nothing, but he was staring at Shane's bloodstained bare feet.

Shane had been on nine only once before. He had been in Chief Brewer's office three years ago when he received a Meritorious Service Medal. He had risked his life, the citation said, freeing two children from a burning car wreck on the San Pedro Freeway.

They moved down the hall. Shane glanced out the plate-glass windows and could see the morning sun beginning to light the corners of the buildings across Sixth Street, throwing a fiery glow on the stone roofs and concrete balconies of the old brown buildings that surrounded the huge police monstrosity like tattered memories.

Mayweather opened the door to the conference room, turned on the lights, and left him there.

The room was paneled in the same light-colored wood. It was huge and windowless, being part of the interior structure of the building. On the walls were portraits of all of L.A.'s past police chiefs. The father of the new department, Chief William H. Parker, was hanging in a place of honor on the wall at the head of the table.

They had all learned about Bill Parker in the Academy. In 1934 then-Lieutenant Parker, a law school graduate, was assistant to L.A. police chief James E. Davis. From that post, Parker saw the workings of L.A. city government close-up. The Shaw brothers presided over a corrupt city, and Chief Davis was beholden to the Shaws. Mayor Shaw's brother controlled the Vice Squad and was selling sergeant's tests for five hundred dollars apiece. Working with Lieutenant Earl Cook, Bill Parker campaigned for the passage of the city charter amendment that contained Section 202, which provided for a Police Bill of Rights and administrative reviews to protect police officers from inappropriate charges of wrongdoing. That section of the city charter set the model of police disciplinary review that the LAPD still uses today. Portraits of Chiefs Davis, Reddin, Gates, Williams, Parks, and Brewer hung on the walls of the conference room and seemed to glower down at him, silently reproaching him for killing one of L.A.'s finest.

"Guy was murdering his wife," Shane muttered to himself and to the stone-faced gallery of disapproving ex–police chiefs.

Mayweather returned with a tape recorder and plugged it in. He chose the seat at the far end of the table, under the recently hung painting of Burl Brewer.

Mayweather glanced at Sergeant Scully. "You're a sergeant one, is that right?"

"Yes, sir."

"Okay, Shane, you and I don't know each other. I guess we've probably met once or twice, but we're not really acquainted. It's important you know that I'm just here to take your statement. I'm going to try and determine what happened and then make a recommendation to the department as to what our next step should be. A police officer died at your hands. His death may have been completely unavoidable, but either way, we're into a mandatory use-of-force review. I'm not here to hurt you, take advantage of you, or trap you in any way. Okay?"

"I appreciate that, sir."

The door opened and Bud Halley entered with a pot of coffee and three mugs. He poured. They each took one, blew across the steaming surface, then sipped gratefully.

"What goes on here is subject to the Police Bill of Rights under Title One," Mayweather continued, "so this pre-interview will not preempt any of your Skelly rights or privileges guaranteed by Section 202 of the city charter." The Skelly hearing was his chance to answer the charges against him before his case went to a Board of Rights, if it got that far.

"This is an administrative review and is subject to the provisions laid down in Section 202. I'm going to record the interview." Mayweather turned the tape on. "Raise your right hand." Shane did as he was instructed. "Do you, Sergeant Shane Scully, swear that all information given by you during this interview is the truth, the whole truth, and nothing but the truth, so help you God?"

"I do."

"This tape-recorded interview is for use in an Internal Affairs investigation only. For purposes of department statute-of-limitations requirements, today, April sixteenth, will be the due date of this inquiry. If no action is taken within a year of this date, the investigation will officially be determined to be closed. Is this interview being conducted at a convenient time and under circumstances you find acceptable?"

"Yes, sir."

"Are you aware that the nature of this interview is to determine if the escalated force that resulted in Lieutenant Molar's death was within departmental use-of-force guidelines?"

"Yes, sir."

"It is April sixteenth, at five-seventeen A.M. We are in the main conference room, on the ninth floor of Parker Center. Present is the interviewer, Deputy Chief Thomas Clark Mayweather. Also present is the officer being interviewed, Sergeant One Shane Scully. Witnessing the interview is Captain Bud Halley. In accordance with departmental guidelines, it is noted that no more than two interrogators are present. Okay"—Mayweather paused and glanced at a crib card in front of him—"Section 202 governs this part of the administrative process and establishes procedures for the completion of a chronological log. If you could take care of that, Captain Halley? And then if you could get us a fresh DR number to file the case under." A DR number was a Division of Records number, issued in all nonarrest reports.

Bud Halley nodded then took out a pad and pen to begin a chronology.

"Shane, if you could just start at the beginning and tell us what happened this morning . . . Don't leave anything out. Give us approximate times if you can. I want to get it all down on tape because the preliminary interview will be an important part of the record, if anything more comes of this later."

"Okay." Shane cleared his throat and began to tell exactly what had happened, starting with the wake-up call from Barbara at 2:16 A.M., followed by his call to Longboard Kelly. He told how he drove to Shell Avenue, found the front door open, saw Molar beating his wife. He related the conversation that ensued, telling how he tried to settle it down. Then how Molar, moving toward him, swung the baton at his head, hit him with his fist, pulled his gun, and fired. Shane explained how he returned fire, killing the huge LAPD lieutenant with his 9mm Beretta Mini-Cougar, just moments before Unit X-ray Twelve arrived.

When he finished, he looked up at Mayweather, who was making notes on a pad, a puzzled expression on his face.

"That's everything," Shane finished.

"Tell me about your relationship with Raymond Molar."

"Uh . . . well, he was sort of a mentor, I guess you'd call it. I met him when I went through the Academy. He was conducting a self-defense lecture. He and I were at the same table for lunch. We sort of hit it off, gravitated to each other. He did three street-combat classes while I was there, and we became friends. After I graduated, I ended up in Southwest, in the Seventy-seventh Division. He was a sergeant there. I was still just a probationer, and since we were friends, he got himself assigned as my training officer. He was my partner for the first six months of my tour. After I finished probation, we rode together for six more months."

"Sergeants don't usually ride with partners."

"Well, in the Seventy-seventh, a lot of the sergeants took a shotgun rider. It's pretty hairy down there. Anyway, we rode together for that last six months, and then I got reassigned. I went to the West Valley Division for four years, then spent six in Metro. I've been back at Southwest for the past six years and in RHD down there for twenty-eight months. Ray was in Central, then Newton, so we didn't see much of each other after that."

"I see." Mayweather made some more notes on his pad. "You see him socially during that first tour in Southwest when you were partnered?"

"Yes, sir, we were friends."

"Right about then you had an Internal Affairs complaint that wasn't sustained, isn't that correct?"

"Excuse me, sir, but I thought I had immunity from background on unsustained IAD complaints." Shane knew that since Mayweather was head of the Special Investigations Division, which supervised IAD, he had access to those old Internal Affairs records. Obviously, the deputy chief had done more than change clothes before coming in for this interview.

Mayweather looked up and lay down his pen. "I'm just trying to determine if, when you were before that Board of Rights in March of '84, you were still partnered with Ray Molar."

"Yes. That was just before we stopped working together."

"Okay." Mayweather picked up his pen. "You say Lieutenant Molar pulled a gun. Did you see it clearly?"

"I was only a few feet away."

"What kind of gun was it?"

"I think it was a European handgun, a Titan Tiger snub-nose thirty-eight is what it looked like."

"That's not a department-approved handgun."

"Well, he was at home. I suppose he can have any kind of weapon he wants at home."

"And then, after you shot him with your Beretta, what happened to his gun?"

"I guess he dropped it. I don't know, I was kind of jacked up after the shooting."

"Sergeant Scully, do you mind taking a urine test? As you know, you can refuse under the Police Bill of Rights, but I should warn you that in an administrative hearing, unlike a criminal case, your refusal can be viewed by the department as insubordination. You could be brought up on charges. If you *do* refuse, I'll have to send for a DRE to examine you anyway, and his opinion will go in the record and carry the same weight." A DRE was a drug recognition expert who would make a judgment on sobriety by observation, checking vision and reflexes.

"That won't be necessary. I'll take the test, sir," Shane said.

"I'll get the paperwork ready." He leaned over and picked up the phone. "This is Mayweather. Send somebody up from the lab for a urine sample and have whoever's on the duty desk out there dig around and get me an authorization form." He hung up the phone, having never shifted his gaze from Shane. Then he leaned back in his chair and templed his fingers under his chin.

"Barbara Molar is quite an attractive woman."

"Yes, sir, she is. The lieutenant was very lucky."

"Until tonight."

"Well, yes, that's what I meant, sir.

"Right."

They sat in silence for a few moments.

"Did you and Lieutenant Molar retain a friendly relationship after you were reassigned to the Valley Division?"

"Well, sir . . . no. Like I said, we sort of drifted our separate ways."

"I heard you and he got into some kind of scuffle one night, back in '84, just before you were separated as partners."

Shane looked over at Captain Halley for help, but the captain only nodded slightly, encouraging him to keep answering. It was now painfully obvious that Mayweather had someone in the IA Administration Section open his sealed jacket in violation of his rights under Section 202. The fight with Steeltooth had been logged because Shane had needed medical attention for his injuries. However, neither he nor Molar had pressed for a hearing, so it went into his sealed record as an unsustained incident. He couldn't prove that Mayweather had opened his file. The deputy chief could claim he had heard about the fight secondhand. Now Shane had to answer the question or face insubordination charges. He felt used and double-crossed.

"I need an answer," Mayweather said. "Was there an altercation?"

"I guess you could say that. We had a kinda problem once."

"What was that all about?"

"Shit, it was nothing. . . . I mean, shoot . . . we . . . we'd been working long hours and I was nervous, facing that Internal Affairs board. I was stressed. Molar was fucking around. We were in the detective squad room in Southwest. He threw ice water on me, so I pushed him and he went down over a chair. If you knew Ray at all, you wouldn't have to ask what happened next."

"What happened next?"

"We went down into the parking garage, and while six or seven guys from the squad stood around and watched, Ray punched out two of my teeth, broke my nose, and pretty much destroyed me."

"And you're not mad about that?"

"Well, for a while I guess, but that was Ray. He and I had just about ended our tour by then, so we unhooked. I was rotating out. He was on the lieutenant's list back then. Pretty high up. The sixth band, I think, so he was going to get his bar in a month or two anyway. We both just moved on."

"And you didn't harbor any resentment? I find that hard to believe."

"Chief, if I could ask . . . has anybody looked at the damage on Barbara Molar's face? Has anybody seen what he did to her? 'Cause if all these questions strike to some other possible motive, that's why I went over there. I tried to break it up. He fired first, and I was forced to return fire. He was seconds from killing both of us. I hope you photograph those injuries because all I was trying to do was keep us off Forest Lawn Drive."

"We'll get photographs, don't worry about that."

There was another charged silence in the room that lasted for almost a minute.

"Anything else you want to say for this record?" Mayweather said.

"No, sir. That's what happened. I'm sorry he's dead, but he gave me no choice."

"Okay, then." Mayweather looked at his watch. "This interview is concluded. It is five thirty-five A.M. This tape recording has been continuous, with no shutoffs, and it has been witnessed throughout by Captain Bud Halley." Then he snapped the machine off and rubbed his eyes. "That's it, Sergeant. I'm going to forward this transcript to the Officer Involved Shooting Section of the Robbery/Homicide Division, and they will schedule your Shooting Review Board. Don't sweat it. That board is mandatory with any incident involving firearms."

"I know, sir."

"Then get outta here. Go give the lab tech his sample and go home."

"Yes, sir."

Shane got up and moved past Captain Halley, into the hall. He waited for his CO to come out, thinking they would ride down together and Shane could get a performance critique, but Captain Halley didn't come out. The door was slightly ajar, and he could hear Mayweather and Halley talking. Then suddenly the door was kicked shut, cutting off the conversation and leaving him alone in the hall.

STREET 4 DIVORCE

SHANE WAS FORCED to wander in the Parker Center garage, looking for his car. It was six A.M. He had started on the top level, which was aboveground, and had moved slowly through the garage, heading down, deeper into the bowels of the parking structure. He had his keys in his right hand. They had been left for him at the OOD's desk in Robbery/Homicide, but the uniform who had driven his car in didn't tell the duty sergeant where in the garage it was parked. The structure was huge, and his bare feet were cold on the concrete floor. As he walked, he could occasionally see flashes of red on his feet—Ray's blood. He had stood in it, and it had seeped up, between his toes, staining his skin. After giving his urine sample, he'd been in such a hurry to get out of there and get home, he hadn't remained in the rest room to wash it off.

"Sergeant Scully. Over here," a voice yelled at him; he turned around and looked back. He could see two uniformed officers standing by the elevator. He was six stories down, and the garage was dimly lit by the neon overheads. The two policemen moved out of the darkness toward him. The overhead lighting threw long shadows under their visors, and he could not make out who they were. As they got closer, he realized he had not seen either of them before. It was not unusual for members of the LAPD not to know one another. There were over nine thousand sworn members of the department sprawled over a huge geographic area. From the markings on their uniforms, he could tell that they were both first-year officers—policemen I's.

"What is it?" he asked.

They were close enough now for him to see that they were both in their early twenties. Their silver nameplates indicated that the shorter one was Officer K. Kono, the other, Officer D. Drucker. Kono had a wide, flat face and the complexion of a native Hawaiian. Drucker was a bodybuilder. His arms bulged the short sleeves of his Class C uniform shirt. They stood in front of Shane, studying him as if he were roadkill that one of them would eventually be forced to scrape up.

"Whatta you want, Officer?" Shane asked Drucker. "I've had a long night. I wanna get home."

"That Ray's blood on yer feet?" Kono asked. He had no Hawaiian accent. He was pure West Valley, but his voice was shaking with emotion.

"Whatta you guys want?" Shane repeated.

"Why'd you have t'butt in?" Drucker asked. "Who asked you?"

Shane could now see that they were both extremely emotional. They had obviously heard about Ray's death, which was spreading through the department like a raging virus. He speculated that Drucker and Kono must have come in and waited for him in the garage.

"He was killing his wife. He was taking batting practice on her with a baton."

"So you butt in and give him a fucking street divorce," Drucker hissed. A "street divorce" was police slang for any domestic argument that turned into a murder.

"Get outta my way." Shane tried to push past the two cops, but they held their ground and he found himself bumping shoulders with them violently. They weren't about to let him through, so Shane backed up and reevaluated the situation. He didn't have his gun. It had been booked by Homicide as evidence. He was alone in an empty garage. He was barefoot and tired, and his head still ached from where Ray had hit him. The two cops in front of him were jacked up on anger and out of control emotionally. In that moment, he had a flash of how it must feel to run up against enraged, violent cops in a desolate part of the city with no witnesses and no way to prove what really happened. Here he was, a sworn officer, standing in the police garage, yet he was beginning to pump adrenaline and fear for his safety.

"Is this about to turn into something?" he asked softly, glaring at both of them.

"Ray was the real deal, asswipe," Drucker hissed. "You're department afterbirth. Ray knew we had to take this fucking town back a street at a time. Since Rodney King, we've been eating shit and smiling about it. Ray knew that had to change. He knew the war was on, knew what we had to do out there. He understood you can't just stand around while a buncha freeway-dancers put it to ya."

"If you believe that, both you guys need to take a swing through the Academy retraining program."

"Swing on my dick, Tarzan," Kono hissed.

Shane shook his head and smiled. "Okay," he said, "I guess that ends this discussion. Your move."

"This is police headquarters," Drucker said. "This is the Glass House, man. Nothing happens here. But stick around, Scully. There's gonna be some payback."

"Now you're threatening me, Drucker?"

"You killed the best cop to ever ride in this department," Kono said. "Shot him just 'cause he was straightening out his old lady? Okay, it's done. Ray's gone. But we loved him, man, we—" He stopped, and Shane thought he saw moisture in the young Hawaiian cop's eyes.

"You two guys need to go home and think this out," Scully said.

"We don't need to think nothin' out," Drucker snapped. "You think it out. We've got someone pulling your card right now. From now on, nobody's gonna take your side. Nobody's got your back, Scully. You're a walk-alone."

"I'm putting you both in for this."

"Have fun," Drucker said, touching the brim of his visor. "Your word against ours. Have a nice morning, asshole." They both turned and walked away. He could hear their footsteps echoing in the concrete darkness. Then a car started, headlights went on, and they pulled past him, going fast. The wind from their black-and-white flapped his sweatshirt as they sped away.

Shane stood alone in the garage; he suddenly felt a shiver of dread come over him. Then he turned and again started looking for his car. He found it way down on U-9, at the back of the garage, on the bottom level. When he looked at the car, something seemed wrong, it seemed lower. He knelt down in the dim light and saw that all four of his tires had been slashed. The black Acura was squatting sadly on its rims.

"Shit," he said, looking at the car. Then he suddenly remembered Chooch. He wondered how he would ever get home in time to get the boy to school.

CHOOCH

SHANE ARRIVED HOME at a little past seven, driving a slick-back he'd checked out of the motor pool. He parked the black-and-white detective's car in the driveway and entered the back door. As he walked into the kitchen, Chooch was bent over with his head deep in the refrigerator. Startled, he jerked around and glowered.

"It's fucking bleak in there, Chuck. Don't you got nothin' to eat?" Chooch was dressed in baggy jeans pulled down low, gang-style, exposing two inches of his red plaid boxer shorts. His white T-shirt read EAT ME.

"There's some strawberry Pop-Tarts in that cupboard," Shane said as he quickly headed through the kitchen, hoping Chooch wouldn't see his bloodstained feet and put him through a description of the early-morning shooting. Shane moved into the master bedroom, which was furnished in "relationship-eclectic." Nothing matched. All the furniture in his house was salvaged from broken love affairs. It had gotten to the point where every time he and a new female roommate went furniture shopping, there was some cynical side of him that would wonder which of the new bedroom or living-room ensemble pieces would become his in the post-relationship settlement. The result was a depressing mixture of colors and styles.

He stripped off his blood-spattered sweatshirt and pants, then got into a hot shower, scrubbing Ray's blood off his feet with his shower nailbrush, rubbing so hard that he was afraid his toes would bleed.

Shoot it; frame it; hang it in his gallery of defining moments. The Lady Macbeth Exhibit. He finished with his feet and then stood under the hot spray, trying with less result to cleanse his spirit. Finally he got out of the shower, wrapped himself in a towel, and looked in the foggy bathroom mirror. The face was angular and rugged. Dark eyes wore a raccoon's mask of sleeplessness. His hair hung black and limp on his forehead. He stared at himself for a long time, trying to see if he looked as different as he felt. In his thirty-seven years Shane had never killed anyone before; on the drive home from the department, that change in his life experience had started to weigh on him. Now, as he stood in his bathroom, it was plunging him into a fit of depression, which, according to the self-help psych books he had started reading recently, was self-hatred turned inward, driving his spirit down. He turned away from the mirror and dressed in slacks, white shirt, maroon tie, and a blue blazer. He slipped on socks and loafers, clipped his backup gun onto his belt, grabbed his pager, badge, and handcuffs, then went into the living room, where Longboard Kelly was snoring on the sofa.

Shane shook the twenty-eight-year-old blond-haired surfboard shaper's shoulder to wake him. Brian had turned out to be a surprisingly good friend. In the two years since Kelly had moved in next door and had started running his surfboard business out of his garage, the resinhead and the cop had surprised themselves with their unlikely friendship.

"I'm back, Brian. Thanks, man."

"Mmmmsaaakjjjjaaaawww," Longboard said, and rolled over, turning his back on Shane.

Shane smiled and headed into the kitchen, where Chooch was now seated at the small wooden table. Chooch had one of the strawberry Pop-Tarts in his hand, nibbling at the edges. He had struck an insolent go-fuck-yourself pose with one hand jammed deep down in his pants pocket. His bare feet were up on the table.

"So, how much is the upslice bitch paying you?" Chooch started, unexpectedly.

Shane knew, from years on the street busting gangbangers and pavement princesses, that *upslice* meant a cheap woman and referred to the vagina. It pissed him off that this kid would refer to his own mother that way.

"She's not paying me anything."

"So what's the deal, then? She carving you some beef?" Another gangbang sexual reference.

"I'm not sleeping with your mother, Chooch. I've got other reasons. Now get your feet off the table, we've gotta eat off a' there." He slapped Chooch's feet hard, knocking them off the wooden tabletop. Chooch exploded out of the chair, anger and violence seething.

"Don't fuckin' hit me," Chooch said, breathing through his mouth, his right hand balled into a fist at his side.

"Go on . . . take your best shot," Shane said softly, "but you better tell me where you want your body sent first."

"Oh, you're gonna swing on a fifteen-year-old?"

"Hey, son, I've seen fifteen-year-olds roll pipe bombs under taxis and peel a clip-a'-nines at a passing squad car. Being fifteen gets you nothing."

Chooch unclenched his fist and stood there for a long moment.

"Gee, look't this. I think we're really beginning to communicate," Shane said sarcastically, then moved over and grabbed a second strawberry Pop-Tart out of the box on the counter. He dropped it in the toaster and pushed the lever down. "You do your homework last night?" Shane asked, not really knowing what to say to the hostile Hispanic youth across the kitchen, glowering at him with smoldering eyes. At six feet, he was almost Shane's height, and already Shane could see he'd been hitting the weights. He had Sandy's dark good looks.

"I don't do homework. I got fly bitches do it for me."

Shane could see why Sandy had begged him to take Chooch. *"Do whatever it takes,"* she had said. *"He needs a male authority figure. He's got to see where this path he's on is headed."*

"Chooch, you and I have to get along for a month. Let's try and keep from peeling the skin off each other. Now get your stuff together, we gotta get you to school."

"I ain't goin' to school. I quit. Where's the TV? I can't find it. What kinda jerkoff ain't got a TV?"

Shane didn't answer. He moved out of the kitchen and into the guest bedroom. The house was on one of the Venice, California, grand canals, and through the side window he could see the morning sun glinting off the still water. It was 7:10; he figured if he hurried and there wasn't much traffic, he could still get Chooch across town to the Harvard Westlake School by 8:15. The school was located on Coldwater, in the Valley.

As he started to grab Chooch's book bag, he saw that there was a stash of tobacco tucked into the side pocket. He took the Baggie out and held it up. Two ounces of marijuana. He carried the book bag into the kitchen, where Chooch was standing, looking out the back door, his arms folded across his chest. He pretended not to be watching as Shane emptied the Baggie of Mexican chronic down the kitchen sink and turned on the disposal. It finally dawned on Chooch what was happening. He exploded away from the wall and made a grab for the Baggie.

"Hey, what you be doing with my bale, man?"

Shane grabbed Chooch by the collar, spun him, and backed him up, slamming him hard against the refrigerator, pinning him there.

"Hey, asshole, take this to the bank. Rule one: You're not gonna smoke grass in my house. Not today, not ever!"

"That shit was hydro, man."

"And you can stow the rap dictionary, okay? We're talking English in this house."

"Fuck you."

They were nose to nose, breathing hard. Shane was close to the edge, focusing his frayed nerves and growing depression on this angry fifteen-year-old. He took a deep breath to calm down. Then he let go and took a step back. "I don't know whether you get away with stuff like this at school, but it won't work here," he said in a calmer voice.

"I don't wanna stay here. I'm leaving," Chooch said softly.

"Okay, here's the deal. . . . One: Use any dope in this house, you're gonna get a chin-check from me. Two: You do what I tell you, when I tell you. Three: Knock off the Hoover Street attitude. Four: You're gonna do your own homework and not farm it out to girlfriends. If you live up to those four rules, here's what you get from me in return. You get room and board. You get my friendship and respect. You get a fair deal; I'll lay it out straight. I won't ever lie."

"Like I give a shit."

"And clean up your mouth."

"You think I wanna stick around and go to your bullshit white-slice Gumby boot camp?"

"You take off, I'll put the LAPD Runaway Squad on you. You'll go to juvie detention and then to a CYA camp, where you won't have to worry about some private-school geek in a bow tie who teaches chemistry. You'll be slappin' skin with the heavy lifters from south of Hawthorn."

The two of them held gazes. Even though Shane was tired and mad, he had to admit that Chooch Sandoval had been dealt a bad hand. Sandy had made a bunch of horrible choices when it came to her son. Now Chooch was full of anger and resentment. His hormones were raging, and he was looking for a place to park all that frustrated hostility. On the plus side, Chooch had not whimpered. He didn't feel sorry for himself, and he was no cupcake. Somewhere deep down inside, Shane had already begun to respect him.

"I'm through going to that school," Chooch said. "I got no friends there. It's not what I'm about."

"That's one of the best private schools in California. You're throwing away the chance of a lifetime, and for what? So you can hang with a bunch a' street characters?"

"They're my brown brothers. My home slice."

"They don't care about you, Chooch."

"And you do? Or Sandy? I ain't for sale, asshole. You can't buy me with clothes or a school or this crummy deal you got here. You ain't got what I need, Mr. Policeman."

"Get your shoes on. Where are they?" Shane asked. "And change out of that shirt." Chooch snorted but didn't move, so Shane went into the guest room, found another T-shirt and Chooch's tennis shoes. He reentered the kitchen and handed them over. "Let's go. . . . Put 'em on, or face the consequences." Chooch changed shirts, then slipped his shoes on without bothering to tie them. Then he exited the back door, insolently brushing Shane with his shoulder as he went past.

Shane followed him out into the alley behind the house, where the department Plymouth was parked. It was a detective car but looked exactly like a regular black-and-white minus the Mars-bar light on the roof.

Back in 1997, Chief Willy Williams had started making sergeants drive them instead of the preferred plainwraps. In the old days, before Chief Gates, one of the perks of being a detective had always been driving an unmarked car, but now nobody bothered to check out a department car off duty except in extreme circumstances. Trying to work a stakeout or surveillance in a slickback was absurd, so detectives ended up using their POVs— personally owned vehicles.

"I ain't gonna show up at school in this," Chooch said, looking at the car, appalled.

Shane opened the passenger door, then spun Chooch around, took out his cuffs, and slapped them on, cuffing his hands in front of him.

"What you doin', man? What's this for?"

"Comin' to school handcuffed in a squad car oughta harden your rep. You'll be chasing the fly bitches away for a week." He pushed Chooch into the front seat of the car, and he could see the boy smile slightly as he walked around and got behind the wheel.

■ ■ ■

It was 7:45 A.M. before Shane finally caught his first minor break of the day. Traffic on the 405 was unusually light. It took him only forty-five minutes to get over the hill, into the Valley. Harvard Westlake was half a mile up Coldwater Canyon, on the left side. All the way there, Chooch had remained silent. He had pulled his CD player out of his book bag and plugged himself in.

Even with the break on the traffic, Shane arrived at Harvard Westlake fifteen minutes late. He pulled past the Zanuck Swimming Stadium and the Amelia and Mark Taper Athletic Pavilion. He let Chooch off at the Feldman Horn Fine Arts Building, where his first-period class had already convened. The intended image-enhancing uncuffing ceremony passed without audience.

"I'll pick you up at three-thirty," Shane said, putting his handcuffs away.

"Whatever," Chooch growled. Then with his book bag over his shoulder, he did a gangsta lean into the building.

Shane watched him go, feeling a sense of frustration and use-lessness. What on earth was he ever going to be able to give this boy? It had seemed like a good idea two weeks ago when he'd told Sandy yes. . . . A chance to contribute to Chooch Sandoval's life in an important way. Shane had been fighting recent bouts of intense loneliness and had seen himself helping Chooch sort out his adolescent problems. Shane hadn't expected him to be such a hard case. Now that he had him, he doubted he would be able to make any deposits in Chooch Sandoval's adult experience account. This boy was already molded by the strange circumstances of his life. And now, in the harsh reality of Chooch's anger, it occurred to Shane that maybe he had just planned to use Chooch to find meaning in his own life. While Shane was pondering these thoughts, his cell phone rang and dropped him back onto an even more distressing playing field.

"Yeah."

"Shane, Captain Halley."

"What's up, Skipper?"

"I don't exactly know how to tell you this, but the Molar shooting is turning into a red ball." A red ball was any department case with such a high priority that failure to succeed threatened career advancement. "They're not going to take it to a Shooting Review Board."

"Whatta you mean, they're not gonna? They have to."

"Your case is jumping the Officer Involved Shooting Section and going directly to a full Internal Affairs Board of Rights."

"It's what?" Shane couldn't believe what he was hearing. "How can they send it to a Board of Rights without first giving me a shooting review?"

"The chief can send any case he wants to a full board on his sole discretion. He doesn't have to give any reason. Look, Shane, I don't know why this is happening, but you can't stop it. It's inside departmental guidelines."

"Sir, you gotta talk to them. I mean, I don't wanna go through another BOR. I'm gonna get time off without pay. It's career poison. It's gonna be in my jacket. This is nuts. Anybody would've done what I did. For God's sake, he fired on me. It was self-defense."

"It's what the chief wants."

"I don't even know Chief Brewer. I only met him once. He gave me a Citation of Merit."

"I've gotta go. You'd better get in touch with a defense rep. Who handled your case last time?"

"DeMarco Saint."

"You like him?"

"I guess. He got me off," Shane said dully.

"I think he's retired, but because of IAD crowding, there's a new provision for using retired officers. If you want, I can get you his address and give him a call."

"Sure, check and see if he's still living at the beach." Shane waited on the line for a few seconds. His head throbbed. His stomach churned. The captain came back on.

"He still lives in Santa Monica, on the Strand—3467 Coast Highway. I'll let him know you're coming."

Shane put his car in gear and pulled away from the shaded, tree-lined splendor of the private school, then made his way back toward the beach and the shrewd counsel of DeMarco Saint.

All the way there, he kept trying to figure it out. Ray Molar had been a black hole in his life from the day he first met him seventeen years ago. In the beginning, he'd been too green to see it. Eventually he recognized Ray for what he was and had gotten away from him. Last night, with Barbara's call, he'd been pulled back into Ray's sinister orbit. In one second he'd ended Ray's life and opened some kind of evil vortex that now threatened to destroy him as well.

6

DEFENSE REP

ANY POLICE OFFICER facing an administrative review gets to choose a defense rep to defend him. According to Section 202 in the Police Bill of Rights, that representative can be anyone in the department below the rank of captain. The charter provides that the chosen officer *must* serve as the accused's defense representative unless such service would cause undue hardship or unless the chosen officer has a current duty assignment of such a sensitive nature as to prohibit the time commitment.

Over the years, several officers had become very adept at winning Internal Affairs cases and, as a result, got chosen as defense reps time and time again. They became schooled in the legal vagaries of the department disciplinary system, and most of them viewed Internal Affairs as a black hole of intrigue that they referred to as "the Dark Side." In a way, these men and women were mavericks inside the department, seeing themselves as an important demarcation line between the accused officers and the meat-eating "politicians" who worked at Internal Affairs.

Such a man was retired Sergeant DeMarco Saint. He lived on the beach in Santa Monica. His house was run-down and desperately in need of a new roof and paint. He had made his place a hangout for a young, breezy beach crowd: everybody from surf bums and Rollerbladers to volleyball players and sidewalk musicians. They hung in clusters in front of his wood-shingled bungalow. DeMarco Saint presided over this collection of party animals like a wise, bearded guru. He had been a police officer for thirty years and had pulled the pin just last December. Then he had made an almost seamless transition from maverick cop to New Age swami.

Shane pulled his slickback into the public parking lot two doors down from DeMarco's house and showed his badge to the attendant, who greeted the free-parking move with a frown. Shane locked the car and walked to the beach bike path. He could hear loud rap music pounding before he even got on the pavement. As he got closer, he saw several young girls in string bikinis and some tanned surfers in boxer shorts sitting on DeMarco's low brick wall like prizes in a game of beach Jeopardy being played all day at high energy under a synthetic drumbeat.

Of course, Shane looked like a cop to them right off, and the conversation shriveled up like rose petals in a hot summer wind. By the time he got to DeMarco's wall, only the recorded rap of Snoop Doggy Dogg managed to ignore his presence.

"DeMarco around?" he asked the closest girl, a tall brunette in her mid-twenties.

"Inside," she said, arching a pierced eyebrow and clicking her silver tongue stud against her teeth to see if it would piss him off.

"That's nothing." He smiled. "I've got mine through my dick."

She laughed as he moved past her and through the front door of DeMarco's house.

He found the fifty-eight-year-old defense rep on his hands and knees, trying to adjust one of the blasting speakers while a teen-age boy watched.

"Fucking bass is vibrating. Sounds like shit," the young surfer with bleached blond hair and black roots said sullenly.

DeMarco kept fiddling and finally took some of the low end out. He leaned back on his knees to listen. "Whatta you think?" he asked. "Better?"

Snoop Doggy Dogg's staccato voice was bouncing ghetto hatred off the walls while DeMarco leaned forward again to screw with his woofers and tweeters.

"Gotta fuck the pigs. Gotta make da man die, if he come passin' by da pork's gotta fry," the Snoopster rapped violently.

"You got a minute?" Shane yelled.

DeMarco turned and saw him, grinned, and stood up. He was over six feet tall, and since Shane had last seen him, he'd let his gray hair grow. It was now tied in a ponytail that hung a quarter of the way down his back. He was wearing a tank top and had added a few tattoos that Shane thought looked ridiculous on his spindly arms, but not anywhere near as ridiculous as the silver cross that dangled from a chain in his left ear.

"Halley called. Been expecting you." He turned to the fifteen-year-old surfer. "You tinker with it for a while."

As the rap banged against their ears, he led Shane through the kitchen, where he grabbed two cold Miller Lites out of the refrigerator, and then out the back along the side of the house, onto Santa Monica's long, sandy beach. The waves were unusually high that morning because of a storm in Mexico. They broke energetically forty yards away, shaking the sand under the two men's feet.

"I must be getting really old," Shane said. "That shit pisses me off."

"I like having the kids around. So what're you gonna do?" He smiled, then reached into his ears and pulled out some cotton balls.

Shane couldn't help himself, he started laughing. "You're tuning your speakers with cotton in your ears. No wonder your low end is vibrating."

Shane and DeMarco sat in the warm sand and ripped the tabs off. The beer cans chirped and hissed foam. They clinked aluminum, and both took long swallows.

"I need help," Shane said.

"I know. Captain Halley already filled me in. He thinks you're being schmucked."

Shane looked at DeMarco. Sixteen years ago, a much younger DeMarco had saved him at a BOR. He was praying the newly ponytailed defense rep could do it again.

"Alexa Hamilton is back down there," DeMarco continued. "I figured she'd've transferred to some cushy job in administration by now."

"She's still there after sixteen years? I thought an average tour at Internal Affairs was only five years."

"She used to be their number one tin collector," DeMarco said. "They brought her back just to get you." A tin collector was an advocate who got convictions that resulted in an officer losing his badge. Sergeant Alexa Hamilton was the department prosecutor who tried him all those years ago, only she had failed to get his tin.

"They're all a bunch a' ladder-climbing suck-ups," DeMarco said, his hatred for the Dark Side spewing out of him unchecked. "Everybody in the fucking division is looking to get to the top floor of the Glass House. It sucks, the way it's set up."

Shane had heard DeMarco's complaints before and knew the old defense rep was talking about the fact that most of the captains and deputy chiefs on the ninth floor at Parker Center had also spent time as tin collectors in Internal Affairs. That made assignment as an IAD advocate a coveted post. It was a club. Lieutenants and below were selected by virtue of their test scores and oral boards, but to make captain, you had to be picked by the chief of police. The fact was, it was hard to be picked if you hadn't spent some time on the Dark Side. This phenomenon had the effect of making Internal Affairs a catcher's mitt for every hot dog and ladder-climbing politician in the department.

"Why did you mention Alexa Hamilton? What's she got to do with this?" Shane asked, thinking of the attractive but overly severe woman who sixteen years back had prosecuted him with such fanatical enthusiasm. She had quite a reputation, both personally and professionally, leaving a long trail of busted careers and broken hearts. More than one Parker Center Romeo had moved in with her, only to discover that her personal demands matched her professional compulsions. Shane wondered if her apartment was furnished in relationship failures as his was.

He had grown to despise her in the few months that his case was going through the division. One of his best moments on the job was seconds after his not-guilty verdict had come in. He looked over and saw such distress on Alexa's face that it gave him a moment of pure, soul-cleansing vengeance. When she caught him looking, he smiled and surreptitiously flipped her the bird.

"I thought you knew," DeMarco said, interrupting his thoughts. "She's got your case. She put in for it."

"You can't be serious," Shane groaned.

"Yeah. If at first you don't succeed, and all that good shit." DeMarco took another long pull on his beer and let out a deep belch. "Maybe you shouldn't've flipped her off."

"Wouldn't matter, she hates me anyway."

DeMarco went on. "It's not good that they hopped over your Shooting Review Board and went straight to a BOR. It shows the department is going to war."

"Why? Barbara Molar is my witness. She'll say what happened."

"I made a few calls down to my old crew at the Representation Section in Parker Center. The rumor down there is, this whole railroad train is coming right out of Mayor Crispin's office. He wants your balls in his trophy case."

"Why?"

"Lemme take a wild guess. . . ." He drained his beer. "How 'bout 'cause you lit up his bodyguard. Blew his arithmetic all over that bedroom wall."

"You gotta help me, Dee. You gotta get me off."

"I'd like to, Shane. I really would. But frankly, I can't get into that rat race again. Alexa Hamilton is one tough, nail-chewing piece of business. I faced her fifteen or twenty times. Lost more than I won. I don't like it one bit that she's volunteering for this case. That tells me there's a big political payoff somewhere. Maybe lieutenant's bars and a transfer to something sexy like Organized Crime or Special Investigations. Mayweather could set that up for her, no sweat."

"You're telling me I'm cooked before we even get a hearing?"

"Tell you what . . . you know Rags Whitman? He's a good defense rep, smarter than me. I used to ram my dick up their asses and piss on their hearts. Ragland, he's mellow, he plays the game—Mr. Wheel of Fortune. They like him at Parker Center. I was you, I'd get him to take your case. Ask him to plead you out, see what kinda deal he can get. My bet: maybe he gets you a six-month suspension without pay and no termination."

"For defending myself from that crazy bastard? What kinda deal is that?"

"You shot Ray Molar. Not a good move, but you got an eye-witness who, we hope, backs you up. You got Ray's bullet in the wall, proving he fired before you got him. You also got Molar's record of spousal abuse. All this is good. On the bad side, you got the fuckin' mayor of L.A. tail-gunning you. You got Chief Brewer with his ears back, and you got some tricky 'undue use of force' statutes that could go against you. Your best bet is to see if Rags can spin the big wheel and plead it down."

"You won't help me? Come on, Dee, you're off the department. They can't threaten you; they can't get to your pension. What's the problem?"

"I'd do it if I could, man. I just can't. I've got no stomach for it anymore. I go down there, and my guts start churning. I'd choke. I hate those pricks worse than the National Anthem. You wanna know why I pulled the pin? It wasn't 'cause I had my thirty in. It was ulcers. My stomach lining looks like a Mexican highway. I can't put myself back in that mess. Go talk to Rags. Get him to negotiate a kick-down."

Shane stood up and handed DeMarco his half-empty beer. "Okay," he finally said. "Sorry to take up your morning." Then he turned and walked away, his shoes filling with warm sand as he went.

"Hey, Scully," DeMarco called, and Shane turned around. "Whatever you do, don't volunteer to take a polygraph. I think the IA poly is rigged. They use it to get confessions. I've had more than one case where I think I got a bum test."

"Okay," Shane answered. "Thanks for the warning."

. . .

Shane pulled out of the parking lot and back onto the Coast Highway. As he started toward the Santa Monica Freeway, his stomach was churning and he could taste bile in his throat. Then he heard a siren growl and saw a black-and-white behind him with its red lights on. Since he was in a black-and-white slickback, it surprised him that he was being flashed to the curb like a civilian. He pulled over and got out.

A young uniformed cop with two stripes on his sleeve moved up to him.

"What's up, Officer?" Shane asked.

"You Sergeant Scully?" the man asked.

"Yeah."

"I'm Joe Church. I was ordered to accompany you to Parker Center forthwith. Apparently your mobile data terminal is turned off."

"They get the gallows up already?" Shane quipped.

"I'm sorry, what, sir?" Officer Church said, deadpan, maybe with a tinge of cold anger.

"Why?" Shane asked. "What do they want?"

"Chief Brewer wants to see you immediately." He sort of barked it at Shane.

"Did I do something to piss you off?" Shane asked.

"You wanna follow me?"

"I can make it. You afraid I'll get lost?"

"Why don't you wait till I pull around. Since you haven't got a bar light, I'll put on the flashers and siren. It gets us there faster."

"You got a siren, how cool. I can hardly wait."

Shane got back into his unit and waited until the squad car pulled around in front of him. Joe Church growled his siren once, then raced out into the fast lane with Shane behind him.

The two police cars shot up onto the Santa Monica Freeway, heading back to downtown L.A. and Parker Center, Code Three.

SUPER 7 CHIEF

TRAFFIC WAS JAMMED UP because some jackass had issued a motion-picture permit to an Arnold Schwarzenegger movie that was now shooting on Wilshire at Spring Street. The film crew had moved in downtown, parking their honey wagons, dressing rooms, and sixteen-wheelers up and down the curb on Third, laying out barricades and blocking traffic for ten city blocks. Shane couldn't believe that some dummy in city government had signed a film-location permit that would tie up all of downtown L.A. Twice, Patrolman Church had to get out of his car and talk to an off-duty policeman working for the movie company so they could get through.

After struggling for over forty minutes, they finally drove into the parking structure next to Parker Center. They both found a spot on the top level. Shane got out of his car, and Joe Church immediately joined him.

"Damn movie has this town tied up worse than my colon,"

Church growled as they looked at a low-flying helicopter that was hovering half a block away. There was a cameraman hanging out of the side door in a harness. Suddenly the rotors changed pitch, and the silver-and-red Bell Jet Ranger took off after a car that was speeding down barricaded Main Street after a motorcycle, Arnold Schwarzenegger kicking ass on celluloid.

"Let's go," Church said, getting back to business, taking Shane by the arm.

"I can make it. Even go to the bathroom now without Mommy's help."

"Don't be an asshole, Scully. I've got orders."

Shane decided not to push it, but he pulled his arm free and followed Church into the building.

For the second time in four hours, he found himself back on the ninth floor. They moved off the elevator, onto the thick, sea-foam green carpet, past the blond paneling and executive furniture, until he was finally standing in front of a massive woman who sat behind an oak desk the approximate size and shape of a Nimitz class carrier. She was parked directly outside Chief Burleigh Brewer's office.

Joe Church had shifted gears. No longer the stern centurion, he was now wearing an ingratiating, apple-polisher's smile. "Patrolman Church," he effused. "I was called specifically by Chief Brewer for this assignment. I've brought Sergeant Scully in. It was a 'forthwith.' "

"Thank you, Officer," the linebacker-sized woman said. Her heavy body wasn't helped by the shoulder pads in her tan suit coat. The name on her desk plate read CARLA MILLER. "You can sit down over there, Sergeant," she said to Shane, pointing to a chair. Joe Church took a position of advantage, guarding the exit.

"Jeez, Church," Shane growled, "I'm not Clyde Barrow. I'm not gonna shoot my way outta here. Try giving it a rest."

Carla Miller nodded to Church. "We'll be okay."

Church shuffled his feet, flashed a gee-whiz smile, and a few seconds later backed out of the office and was gone.

Carla buzzed Chief Brewer and talked to him softly for a second, then hung up the phone.

Shane waited in the chair for almost thirty minutes, watching the efficiency with which Carla Miller fended off appointments and people. She was a tough, competent goalie, crouching in the net, deflecting problems. She never looked at him once. Outside, he could hear the distant drone of the movie helicopter as it whirled and turned, its rotors whining above the streets of L.A.

Suddenly the intercom buzzed. Carla picked up the phone, listened, then looked at Shane. "You can go in now."

He got up and moved into Chief Brewer's office. The first thing that struck him was that the movie helicopter seemed to be almost inside the office. The chief had a huge expanse of glass. You could see all the way down Main Street to the Financial Center. The Bell Jet Ranger was hovering loudly only fifty feet from the chief's plate-glass window. It was a startlingly eerie effect.

Chief Brewer's back was to him. He was looking out the window at the chopper and the movie company in the street below. The camera ship hovered, stirring air gusts against the window. The rotor sound inside the office was almost deafening. Shane could see the pilot's features clearly. The cameraman hanging from straps inside the open side door was still hunched over the eyepiece. It occurred to Shane that while he had been outside, waiting with his heart in his throat, his police commander had been watching them shoot this fucking movie.

Then Chief Brewer turned. Making it worse, he was holding a pair of field glasses. He set them down on his desk and motioned to Shane to come forward.

"You wanted to see me, sir." Shane's voice was lost in the noise from the helicopter. Somewhere in the pit of his stomach he knew that what he was about to be told was not going to be good. Sergeants get summoned to the COP's office for only two reasons, and Shane was pretty sure he wasn't about to get another Meritorious Service commendation.

Then the chopper turned and flew away abruptly, photographing some part of the movie in the street below. The silence that ensued was a blessing.

"Sergeant Scully, you've had a busy morning," the chief said. He was a stout forty-five-year-old red-haired man with cheeks that always seemed to have a ruby blush. He had his suits carefully tailored to hide a growing midsection. Recently he had added rimless glasses that blended a touch of severity into an otherwise unremarkable face.

"Yes, sir. Busy morning, sir," Shane said, trying to read where this was going.

"Movies," the chief said. "Boy, they use a fuck of a lot of equipment. They've got four whole blocks tied up down there. Three helicopters. That one there is the camera bird. God knows what the other two are for. We let 'em use one of the police choppers for a picture ship."

"That's very generous, sir. I'm sure they're grateful."

"It's a Schwarzenegger flick called *Silver and Lead*. He plays a cop who breaks up an armored-car robbery. It's a silver shipment, but it turns out the robbery is just a decoy to pull the cops away from a presidential assassination. Arnold signed a copy of the script for me," Chief Brewer bragged.

"Bet that'll be worth a few bucks." Shane felt like a moron, standing there with his asshole puckered, talking about the movie business.

"People would feel a lot better about you, Sergeant, if you were more of a team player."

No segue. One moment it's show biz, the next it's team ball.

"Oh?" Shane said. "I think I'm a good team player, sir. Check with my captain, my watch commanders."

"I'm not talking about your field performance, Scully. I'm sure you're a good detective. That's not what this is about. What I'm talking about is attitudinal."

"Attitudinal?" Shane was lost. He didn't have a clue.

"Sometimes a guy will find himself in a position where he thinks maybe he's got an advantage. He thinks maybe he got lucky, stumbled into a piece of good fortune, but the fact is, he's not lucky at all. Fact is, he's stepped in a vat of shit and doesn't even know it. Then he's isolated—a marked man. That's not a good thing. It's better if you're a part of the team."

"Exactly what is it we're talking about, sir? I'm kinda lost."

"Are you? How come I knew that's what you were going to say?" Chief Brewer stood there, looking at Shane as if he were a grease spot on one of his new silk suits. Then he let out some more line. "Sergeant, there are items missing from Lieutenant Molar's case files. According to his duty logs, they were in his house before you shot him. They are no longer there. We questioned his wife. We believe she knows nothing. That leaves you. You were in a position, after you killed him, to remove those items."

"And you think I have them?"

"These items might appear to you to be some kind of windfall or perhaps something an ambitious person might think he could use to his advantage. They aren't what they appear to be. Lieutenant Molar was involved in something very sensitive, and he had the full cooperation of this office. This material could easily be misinterpreted if it got into the wrong hands. It needs to be returned now!"

"Sir, I don't have anything of Ray's. *Nothing.*"

"I fully expected you to deny this because we both know it's against departmental regs to remove another officer's case material. You could be terminated if you admit you took it. However, Sergeant, there are things in this life that are worse than job termination. I expect that you're going to continue to deny it until the full gravity of the situation becomes clear to you, but by then it may be too late. There may be nothing I can do to help you."

"What items?" Shane's heart was pounding now. He was feeling as if he were trapped in a nightmare and couldn't find a way to wake up. "I didn't take anything," he repeated.

"In which case, you probably wouldn't object to taking a polygraph test."

"A polygraph? I . . . I don't even have a defense rep yet. I . . . I'm not sure I want to submit to a lie detector test without legal advice."

"Again, exactly what I thought you would say. Believe me, Scully, you're making a horrible mistake."

"Sir, I'm not saying I won't take a polygraph. It's just . . . I'm having a hard time figuring out what's going on. I shot a man who was trying to kill me. He'd been beating his wife with a nightstick. Since that happened, my shooting review was canceled. I understand my case is being directed to a full administrative hearing, and now you're telling me I'm supposed to have stolen something from Lieutenant Molar's house? I took nothing, sir. I'll swear an affidavit to that fact."

The chief made a waving motion, brushing all this aside. "Here's my deal, Scully—and if you know what's good for you, you better take it. You've got four hours to turn over what you took. Drop the material off here. If you think you can use it to extract either money or career advantage, then you're going to find out that the entire city of Los Angeles, from Police to Sanitation, will go to war against you. It won't end well. By way of example, the district attorney, right now, is seriously considering filing murder charges against you for killing Lieutenant Molar."

"What?" Shane couldn't believe what he was hearing.

"Sergeant, do yourself a big favor and turn the material over."

Shane stood across from Chief Brewer with his knees shaking. He tried to collect his thoughts, then he took a breath to calm down.

"Let's suppose I have what you want and I turn it over," he

said. "What happens to the charge of removing case materials and my Internal Affairs Board of Rights?"

"Maybe something gets worked out there. We look the other way on the case material. Your undue-use-of-force gets sent back to the Officer Involved Shooting Section, they look it over. Maybe it gets disposed of in a few hours, the district attorney decides there's no case."

"So you're using the BOR and this murder charge to try and scare me into doing what you want?"

There was an awkward silence, then the chief took a step toward him and changed the subject.

"Sergeant, there are only three places that material can be, and we've already looked in the other two. You've got four hours. Your career, and maybe the way you spend the rest of your life, depends on your decision. That's all I have to tell you." Then he turned his generous backside on Shane and looked out the window again, at the movie company.

Shane hesitated, wanting to continue to try convincing him, but it was obvious he had been firmly dismissed. Shane turned and walked out of Burl Brewer's office, closing the door behind him.

When he got into the waiting room, Alexa Hamilton was sitting in the same chair he had been warming a few minutes before. She stood when she saw him. Alexa Hamilton was in her mid- to late thirties and was beautiful in a severe, hard-charging way. Coal-black hair was pinned up on the back of her head. High cheekbones and slanted eyes gave her an exotic look that Shane didn't think fit her no-nonsense, ball-busting personality. She had a tight, gym-trained body. He thought her beauty was badly overpowered by a raw will to succeed that made her sexually unattractive to him. He saw her as one of the new breed of LAPD ladder-monkeys, moving fast through the department, eating her dead, leaving a high-octane vapor trail behind her.

"We meet again," she said, arching a tapered brow and smiling without humor.

"This isn't a meeting, it's an ambush."

"Call it what you like, I'm ready. I don't usually have to take two swings at such a slow pitch."

"I'll try and put a few more rpms in my routine." He looked down at the folder in her hand. "That my package?" he asked. "My sealed background records seem to be making the rounds. Will I be reading about my confidential history in next month's newsletter, or is it just going up on the division bulletin board?"

"I'm not reading secure files, Scully. I don't need to cheat to hammer you in. The infield fly rule's on. We have a play at any base."

"If you say so." He walked out of the office and was heading down the hall when she stuck her head out and called to him.

"Hey, Scully."

He turned and faced her.

"I didn't 'peel the nine' at Ray Molar, you did. You go around shooting your ex-partners, you're bound to pick up a little grief."

"Lemme file that under 'shit to remember.' "

He stabbed hard at the elevator button, missed, and stabbed again. Thankfully, it opened almost immediately and he got on, stepping out of her black-eyed stare. It whisked him mercifully away, down to the traffic-jammed reality of downtown Los Angeles and Arnold Schwarzenegger.

TOKING

AFTER PICKING UP his Acura at the Spring Street Tire Center, Shane got back to the Harvard Westlake School at
three-thirty to retrieve Chooch. He waited in a long line of British
and German cars driven by Beverly Hills soccer moms. When he finally pulled to the curb where the students waited to be picked up,
there was no Chooch. Then he saw him, off to the side of the
crowd, sitting on a curb by himself. His CD player was hooked in
his ears; he was lost in the music. Shane tapped on the horn to get
his attention. Chooch picked up his book bag and ambled over to
the newly shod black Acura now sporting four Michelin radials
that Shane couldn't afford at a hundred dollars a tire.

As Chooch was sliding into the front seat, a tall, reed-thin man
with a lipless mouth, curly hair, and heavy, dark-rimmed glasses
stuck his head into the car. "Mr. Sandoval, I'm Brad Thackery,
head of the Latin department and high-school assistant dean of
admissions."

"I'm not his father," Shane said.

"Oh . . . uh, well, I'm sorry. I just got the job two months ago, and I'm still trying to get all the names and faces straight. Will you be talking to Chooch's parents today?"

"Whatta you need, Mr. Thackery?"

"We need to schedule a teacher's conference immediately. Chooch has some severe problems that need to be addressed, *ad summum bonum.*"

Off Shane's puzzled expression, he translated, "For everyone's good."

Shane looked at Chooch, who seemed not to be hearing any of it as he bobbed his head to the beat of some alternative rock leaking at high decibels from his earphones.

"I'll call his mother. Thanks."

Parents behind him were beginning to tap their horns impatiently, so Shane put the car in gear and pulled out onto Coldwater.

Shane said nothing until they were on the Ventura Freeway. "Hey, Chooch," he said, looking over at the boy slumped down in the seat beside him. "Chooch, you wanna take off the headset for a minute!? We need to talk."

Chooch paid no attention. He was bobbing his head to the music, oblivious.

Shane suddenly reached over and ripped the jack out of the CD.

That got his attention. Chooch spun around and glared. "What!" he said angrily.

"They want a teacher's meeting."

"I heard him. Thackery's a dick. Who the fuck cares? I hope they kick me out."

"Whatta they wanna talk about?" Shane asked. "I've gotta call and tell your mother."

"Whatta they wanna talk about? They wanna accuse me of dealin' drugs at school."

"Of what!?"

"You heard me. They think I'm dealin' drugs."

"Are you?"

Chooch didn't say anything, he just shrugged.

"You're not gonna tell me?"

"You're a fuckin' cop. Don't I get a lawyer and my Miranda rights first?"

Shane pulled the car off the freeway, down the Sepulveda ramp, and parked on the busy cross street. Then he turned to face Chooch. "Listen, Chooch, I'm not a cop where you're concerned. I'm your . . ." Shane couldn't think of the right word. What was he?

"My what?" Chooch challenged. "My fuckin' guardian? My baby-sitter? My spiritual coach? What the fuck are you?"

"How 'bout your friend," Shane finally said.

"You're not my friend. I don't have any friends. Not one."

"Chooch, if you're selling drugs to kids at school, we've got a big problem. They could go to the LAPD. They could file criminal charges against you."

Chooch leaned back in the seat, not sure what to do.

"I'm not gonna bust you," Shane continued, "but I've gotta know what the deal is if I'm going to help."

"Not gonna bust me, huh? Where'd I hear that before?"

"Tell me. Were you selling drugs?"

"No. I didn't sell nothin'." He leaned back and closed his eyes. "Once or twice, maybe . . . I loaned some Rasta weed to somebody. And then maybe once or twice I found some cash in my locker that I don't know where it came from. . . ."

"Shit," Shane said, not sure how extreme his response to this should be. "You're in deep shit if they can prove it. Is anybody there gonna talk?"

"You mean, will my dickhead clients roll over and give me up?" Chooch asked. "In a fuckin' heartbeat. You want my opinion? They're not gonna go to the cops. That school doesn't want some newspaper story about drugs on campus. Since I'm Mexican, they're also probably scared shitless somebody will charge 'em with race discrimination. They're just gonna demand I go quietly, something I'm real prepared to do."

Shane looked hard at the teenager, still sitting with his head back on the seat, his eyes closed.

"It isn't your problem anyway," Chooch said. "You're just this month's paid jerkoff."

"Right. That's me." Shane put the car in gear and headed back up onto the freeway. They didn't speak all the way back to Venice.

Finally, Shane pulled into his house at 143 East Channel Road. He parked in the garage and got out. Chooch grabbed his book bag and slouched along after him as they opened the back door. The two of them walked into the kitchen, and Chooch slung his book bag angrily onto the counter.

"Take that into your room and start doing your homework."

"Homework? Ain't that a little off the point?"

"Do it anyway," Shane said. Then he moved out of the house into his small backyard, which looked out onto one of the narrow channels of Venice. What had been a cold April morning was now turning into a surprisingly pleasant California afternoon.

From Shane's small backyard on Venice's East Channel, he could see all the way down the intersecting Howland Canal.

Venice, California, had been the brainchild of Abbot Kinney in 1904. Kinney had wanted to create a luxury community in the style of Venice, Italy. He supervised the design of channels to carry water in from the ocean two blocks away. He designed his development around four long canals, intersected by a series of concrete, arched Venice-like driving bridges that spanned each canal. He added small walking bridges and brought some scaled-down gondolas over from Italy. It had been quite a place in the early 1900s but had seen hard times ever since. The canals still had a sort of rustic charm, but the once-grand houses of the thirties had been knocked down or subdivided and in their place were smaller, cheaper structures. The architectural style ranged from antebellum to trailer-park modern. The people who now lived on the canals were an even more interesting mix. Young doctors who smoked dope lived next door to disapproving retirees. New Age musicians and mimes competed for hat tips on the boardwalk, while four blocks inland, on Fifteenth Street, gangbangers and unaware tourists fought and died over wallets and watches. Jammed in with all of this confusion, next to a longhaired surfboard shaper, was LAPD Sergeant Shane Scully. There was something about the canal blocks of Venice, California, that suited him; something offbeat and sad. Venice seemed as misplaced as her residents.

Less than half a mile to the south were the yuppified environs of Marina del Rey, where young ad executives and airline flight attendants took sexual aim at one another in the crowded waterside bars and fish houses. A mile to the north was Santa Monica, with its population of trendy superagents, junk bond salesmen, and Hollywood power brokers. Halfway in between, sitting on its silly three-foot-deep canals, trying to be something it could never duplicate, was the other Venice, sinking into the mud of social indifference as surely as Venice, Italy, was sinking into the sea.

But Shane Scully was at home there, like no place else on earth. Venice, California, defined him.

As he watched a hummingbird hang energetically over the still East Channel, he opened his cell phone and dialed Sandy.

She answered after the tenth ring and seemed out of breath. "Yes," she said. "Hello." She also sounded angry and impatient.

"Catch you at a bad time?" he asked sarcastically.

"Shane, I can't talk now. I was already out the door. I'm late."

"Then let me make it quick. I think they're going to throw

Chooch out of Harvard Westlake for dealing grass. Some guy named Thackery wants a teacher's meeting with you. I told him I'd let you know. That's the whole message. Nice talking to you."

"Wait a minute. He's dealing what?"

"Grass . . . Mary Jane, Aunt Hazel, African bush, bambalacha. You pick the cool name. He's selling shit to his classmates, and Mr. Thackery ain't one little bit amused about it."

"Well, what am I supposed to do? I can't . . . I mean, can't we . . . ?"

"Unfortunately, I don't think there's much *we* can do. But *you've* gotta call and set something up. As Thackery says, 'It's for everybody's good.' *Ad mumble bubble gum.* And before you ask, lemme say that as this month's paid jerkoff, I'm not up for the teacher's conference."

"Come on, Shane, it can't be that bad."

"Sandy, I'm in some very big trouble myself right now. Big enough that I could end up getting fired or, worse still, even prosecuted by the DA."

"But—"

"No. Listen. I can't handle this problem. I didn't know what I was getting into with Chooch."

"He sounds worse than he is. He's not that bad. You just have to be patient with him."

"You're sure about that? 'Cause I think he's one very confused, very angry kid. I think he's in the diamond lane to Juvenile Hall, and not that you care, Sandy, but I think you need to pay more attention to him. This kid is being passed around like a hot rock. Nobody's giving him what he needs."

"Including you?" she said darkly. "I thought you told me you *were* up for it, that you wanted to make a one-on-one investment in something with lasting dividends."

"What the fuck were we drinking, anyway?"

"Shane, look, I hear you. Unfortunately, I'm working for the DEA right now. I'm up to my ass in a dangerous sting that is days from going down. You know from the jobs we've pulled together that my biggest jeopardy is right before I drop the dime. If I get made now, I could end up the captain of a fifty-gallon oil drum at the bottom of the Catalina Channel. I can't take Chooch. I can't take a chance he'll get hurt, and I can't divert my energies or my concentration at this point in the sting. You said you'd take him. You promised. Otherwise, I wouldn't have left him there."

"Okay, Sandy. I'll do the best I can. But you wanna know something . . . ?"

"Not if it's gonna be a lecture."

"It's an opinion, baby. This boy is hurting bad. He's on fire. He's so self-destructive, I'm heartsick for him. But I'm up to my ass in department bullshit. I shot my ex-partner."

"That was you? It was on the news." Shane didn't answer. "Well, good," Sandy finished. "Ray was a son of a bitch. He deserved to die."

"No, he didn't. But if this goes like it's been going, I'm not going to be available for Chooch, either. So start figuring what you're gonna do and call this prick Thackery and get him off my ass."

"Okay, okay, sugar. I'll call him. Gotta run. Bye." And she was gone.

He slumped down in his rusting metal lawn chair, and then someone cleared his throat. Shane turned and realized that Chooch had come out the side door and had been sitting in one of the other metal chairs at the side of the house.

"Well, she's probably got a lot more important shit on her mind," Chooch said. "Want me to roll you a number? It's pretty fine Jamaican ganja."

Chooch had some Zig-Zag papers and a small cloth drawstring bag in his hand. Shane hadn't had a hit of marijuana since the Marine Corps, but he was so tight, so frayed, that he was worried about his imploding psyche. "Yeah, sure, roll me up one."

"No shit?" Chooch said, "What about Rule One: No smoking grass in my house, not now, not ever?"

"I gotta do something to bend the energy in this day. Rule One is temporarily suspended."

Chooch rolled a bud, fat and short. Then he handed it over. Shane sat there, holding the jay, wondering what kind of example it was going to be for him to blast a joint in front of Chooch or, worse still, get high with him. But then he thought of the events of the day, starting with his shooting Ray Molar at 2:30 A.M., all the way through to his disastrous meeting with Chief Brewer. Somehow, in the light of all that, passing grass with an angry fifteen-year-old just didn't seem all that important.

"Fuck it," he said, then reached back and grabbed one of Chooch's matches, fired up, took a hit, and passed it to Chooch.

The two of them sat in metal chairs in the small, green-brown garden behind Shane's house, sharing the joint and trying to unwind their separate but equally devastating problems.

THE "FUNERAL" LETTER

Dear Dad,

Boy, do I wish you were here so we could sit down and talk this one out like the old days. I'm really in the shit this time, Pop, and no matter which way I turn, I'm faced with a new set of terrible options.

Where to begin?

I guess Ray's funeral is my biggest unanswerable right now. The department is going to give him a full-dress good-bye: honor guard, speeches, everybody wearing black ribbons across their badges. To-day we got a department directive demanding that all officers not on day watch attend in dress blues. There's going to be a parade led by two hundred Mary units (motorcycle cops), followed by a hun-dred black-and-whites. The damn thing forms up at the Academy training field and will wend its way out of the foothills to Forest Lawn. Full TV and press coverage, of course.

Part of me wants to go. I feel like hell, and going to Ray's funeral might help me through it. Another part of me is scared to death. They're going to have this giant turnout of my brother officers: a twenty-gun send-off, with everybody mourning Ray Molar, "the Po-liceman's Policeman" and double Medal of Valor winner.

My problem, of course, is I'm the asshole who shot him.

I don't know if I can bear to stand there under all the hatred I know will be directed at me.

What would you do, Dad? I could really use the advice. I remember you told me once that, in matters of the soul, the thing that is the most difficult to do is generally the thing that you must do. You said that in order to grow spiritually, one must not turn away from emotional hardships. But, still, I feel so isolated, so alone, so out of the loop.

Having you so far away has made things difficult. I know you can't get around much and having emphysema makes flying difficult, but I need help, Dad.

I guess one of my problems is I always tried to make the department my second family. All that bullshit they preach up at the Academy . . . the long blue line, fraternity of police, brothers in blue . . . I wanted to believe all that. I think maybe it's why I decided to become a cop. And now, despite almost seventeen years on the job, I've found a way to fuck it up. I'm alone again.

If you have any thoughts, gimme a ring. I'm still undecided about Ray's funeral.

I wish I had your strength, willpower, and sense of honor. I'm trying to do what I think would make you proud but, damn it, I'm panicked to go to that funeral.

You're probably saying I should just bite the bullet and go. So, that's the answer. You always did know what was best.

I miss you and love you. I know, enough already, blah, blah, blah.

> *Your loving son,*
> *Shane*

WARRANT 9

SHANE DIDN'T GO to the funeral.

He put in for a sick day and, mercifully, it was approved. He hated himself for not having enough guts, but he just couldn't make himself attend. Chooch, showing more backbone, had not objected that morning when Shane loaded him into the car, took him across town to Harvard Westlake, and dropped him at school. They barely exchanged words as Chooch got out of the car.

Shane drove back to Venice, trying hard not to think about his emotional cowardice. He arrived home and busied himself cleaning the small house. He did some deferred maintenance, fixing a sprung hinge on the back screen door, then managed some idle conversation with Longboard Kelly, both of them talking over the back fence. But he couldn't keep his mind on what Kelly was saying . . . something about Hawaiian North Shore supersets and the merits of a stubby board compared with a nine-foot Hawaiian classic. As he walked back inside, his recollection of the conversation hovered over him like a dream barely remembered. Then he checked his answering machine, something he hadn't done for almost ten hours. There was only one message:

"Shane, it's Barbara. I know it might be dangerous, but we need to meet. I assume you'll be at the funeral, but obviously we can't talk there. How about 'our spot'? I could be there by one. The funeral is scheduled to be over by twelve-thirty. Don't contact me, I'm worried about my phone. I'm calling from a pay booth. Just be there. I have news. I love you." *Beep.*

Their "spot" was the outdoor restaurant at Shutters Hotel on the beach in Santa Monica. Once or twice, when they'd been dating, they'd taken a room there. The place was picturesque, and most of the units overlooked the water. Back then they'd both been in their early twenties and single. Having lunch together on an open patio before going up to a rented love nest was fine. Now, after shooting Ray, the last thing he needed was to be seen hunched over a table, in whispered conversation with his widow. Still, Shane was drawn to her in a way he couldn't describe. Maybe it was guilt, or maybe the feeling that she had been the one, and he had lost her through bullheaded pride, or maybe she had become just a fantasy in his memory. He had saved her from Ray, setting up, God help him, possibilities for some sort of future together. Or maybe it was just that he hadn't been laid in almost three weeks. Whatever the reason, he decided to take the chance and meet her there. After all, he rationalized, she said she had "news."

He dressed with more care than usual and even used the hair dryer on his dark, unruly mop. Then he got in the Acura and drove the short distance up the coast to Santa Monica.

He arrived at Shutters at about quarter to one and selected a table near the back of the patio. He ordered her favorite bottle of wine, a French Montrachet. While he waited, he tried to justify the meeting in his guilt-ridden conscience. Maybe her "news" would shed light on his problems. Maybe it would be something that would help dig him out of the mess he was in. Of course, lingering always, like a sour aftertaste, was his desire for her and the knowledge that he wanted to sleep with her again. It was another picture for his gallery: guilt-ridden lust . . . presenting a portrait of carnal self-hate. Hang it in the Virginia Woolf exhibit.

She arrived at 1:25 and stood in the doorway of the patio restaurant, wearing a black dress with a single strand of pearls. She wore large dark glasses to cover a black eye. The swelling from the nightstick was gone, and miraculously she no longer appeared to have any bruises. Her blond hair shimmered in the bright afternoon sunlight. She looked around the patio, spotted him, waved off the maître d', and walked toward him with her athletic dancer's step. She had once performed in the chorus of several musicals at the Dorothy Chandler Pavilion. She slipped gracefully into the vacant chair, puckered her lips, kissed the air, and smiled. Now that she was across the table from him, he could see that she had expertly covered the effects of the beating with Dermaplec, an over-the-counter makeup that is the best product available for hiding bruises. Every patrolman answering a spousal-abuse complaint quickly learned to check the medicine cabinet for Dermaplec. If it was there, it was almost as good as a confession by the husband that he had engaged in wife battering before.

"Hard day," she said sadly. "I thought you'd be at the funeral."

"Truth is, I chickened out."

"I can hardly blame you. It was a real Hollywood layout. Chief Brewer made a speech. Said Ray exemplified commitment to community and police honor. Mayor Crispin talked about his courage. Said he set a new standard for police excellence. They had a twenty-one-gun salute, gave me the flag off his coffin. There was a helicopter flyby, the whole police air unit."

"I'm surprised Schwarzenegger could spare the bird."

She cocked her head.

"Nothing," he said, not wanting to go into it.

"Anyway, Ray's in the ground. Lots of ceremony, lots of news crews and crocodile tears. Jeez, you wouldn't believe what a big deal it was."

Shane poured her a glass of Montrachet. She sipped the wine and looked out over the sandy beach and the ocean a hundred yards beyond. A light wind ruffled her perfectly streaked blond hair. She seemed to be working up to something. He waited and let her get at it in her own way. Finally she turned back to him, a small, sad smile on her face. "This is strange, sitting here again after all these years, isn't it?" He nodded his agreement. "God only knows why I chose to marry him, Shane. All day I've been trying to figure what was going through my mind. You were always the one."

"You don't have to explain it," he said, shifting awkwardly under the weight of the conversation and her penetrating stare.

"You were what I was looking for, but Ray told me *you* had beat that kid half to death in Southwest Division. He told me horrible things about you and I just . . . got mixed up. It wasn't until after we got married that he told me one night when he was drunk that he did it and that you had just taken the blame so IA wouldn't kick him off the job. He thought it was funny. 'Scully's just a dumb fuck,' he said."

"It's okay. It's done. Forget it." He felt his self-respect washing away like water rushing back to the sea, taking the sand beneath his feet, altering his stance, threatening his balance. It seemed wrong to be discussing this on the day that Ray went into the ground. Wrong to feel desire for his widow, wrong not to have found the courage to go to the funeral.

Barbara went on, in a hurry to rid herself of her own painful memories. "Back then, when I told you not to call me anymore, I cried for a whole night. I thought you had done what Ray said, you were on trial at Internal Affairs for it . . . and I . . ." She stopped and shook her head. "Ray started coming around a month later, and he seemed so strong. At first he could be so sweet, so tender. It was sort of touching, a huge brutish guy like that with an inner softness. I was looking for something, I don't know what. Then he kept at me . . . calling . . . gifts . . . it went on for years before I said yes. My dancing career was going nowhere, and I just thought . . ." She shook her head in exasperation. "Whatta mistake, huh?"

"Barbara, you don't have to explain it to me. Please. I understand."

"I want to, Shane. I need to. I know this is a shitty day for it, but frankly, in the twelve years we were married, I'd come to despise Ray, and I had come to despise myself for getting into such a mess with him. He drank, he cheated, he didn't come home sometimes for a week. Then a few years ago, he started hitting me. At the end, I was so frightened of him. I swear, it was a relief to see that casket go into the ground, almost like his grave was the doorway to my future." She took a deep breath. "If that seems coldhearted, I'm sorry. It's how I feel."

Shane looked at her for a long time. Under the dark glasses he knew she had beautiful aqua-blue eyes, the exact color of tropical reef water. She had a luscious body and chiseled features. More than once, in the old days, he had walked into rooms with her and felt the gaze of every man in the place undressing her. She was a physical trophy, but it went beyond that. He thought she had intense feelings and a depth of personality that this conversation betrayed. God help him, Shane still desperately wanted her, wanted to hold her and make love to her, but the feeling diminished him. Making it worse, he could tell that she was reaching out to him, asking him for forgiveness and inviting him to try again.

"Barbara, I think, no matter what eventually happens between us later, this needs to wait."

"I know. I know. It's just . . . I've been thinking about what it would have been like if things had been different. Sounds like a sad Barbra Streisand flick, doesn't it?"

He sat there looking at her, afraid to mention the number of times he had lain awake with the same thought. They'd really fucked it up. Ray had given it a nudge, but it had been the two of them, accelerated by Shane's pride and anger, who had pushed something special over the cliff. Now any future relationship was destined to be a reclamation project. Ray's memory would forever be between them.

"You said you had news," Shane said, changing the subject.

"I got the phone printout like you asked, from AT&T. I got the number that woman called in on."

"Great. Lemme see it."

She handed over a slip of paper and he frowned. "This is a Venice exchange."

"I know."

"Why would somebody send an important package through the mail, where it might get lost, when they could just drive by at midnight and stuff it into your mailbox?"

"I don't know. Doesn't make much sense."

He pulled out his cell phone and dialed the number. He got a recording. "Disconnected," he said as he snapped the phone closed. "When you gave your statement, did you tell the police about the woman who called and the videotape she said was coming?"

"Yeah. I told them everything." Then she added with a strange smile, "I told them Ray fired first, that it was self-defense."

Shane sat, thinking for a long moment. "We need to take a look through your house. I want to do a thorough search."

"There's nothing there. Robbery/Homicide looked already when they did the crime-scene investigation."

"I wanna look anyway. Maybe they missed it. I think that tape the woman was talking about may be what this is all about. Can we skip lunch and go there now?"

"What if they have someone watching the house? They'd see us together."

"With two-thirds of the department taking the day off for Ray's funeral, I doubt there's any spare manpower for a stakeout. Now is the best time. Let's go. If it's there, maybe we can find it."

He paid for the wine, and they walked out of the restaurant. On the way through the lobby, Shane had another thought. "Barbara, do you know Ray's cell phone number?"

"No. It was strictly a business phone. He told me never to use it, but I think he had it written down somewhere. Why?"

"When we get there, see if you can find it."

"Okay." She got into her red Ford Mustang convertible. The parking attendant stared openly as she pulled away, her blond hair streaming in the wind. Invisible in her wake, Shane got into his Acura and followed.

■ ■ ■

When they got to Barbara's house on Shell Avenue, the front door was ajar. Shane pulled up to the curb as Barbara pulled into her driveway. They both got out of their cars and looked at the half-open door with concern. Shane pulled his gun and handed Barbara his cell phone.

"Call nine-one-one if I'm not out in two minutes," he said. Then he moved up the steps and onto the front porch. He could see that the front-door lock had been drilled. Part of the tumbler mechanism was lying on the porch at his feet. With his toe, he edged the door open, staying to one side, out of sight. Then, when he had determined it was clear, he slipped into the house.

He could hear drawers being opened and closed in the back. He moved silently in that direction, finally looking into the bedroom where, seemingly a lifetime ago, he had killed Ray Molar.

There were two uniformed police officers going through dressers and closets. Shane decided to retreat. He didn't want to be caught in this house with Barbara standing outside. As he took a step back, the floor squeaked; both policemen spun and saw him standing there, gun in hand.

"What the fuck're you doing going through Ray's house?" Shane snarled, switching to offense and glaring at the two officers.

They were both first-year patrolmen. One of them he recognized as John Samansky, Ray's last probation partner. He was almost too short to be a cop, probably barely reaching the LAPD five-seven male height requirement. He had made up for his short stature by lifting weights. His wide trapezius muscles were straining his uniform shirt collar. The other police officer Shane had never seen before. He was also young but prematurely balding, with a narrow, pockmarked face. His nameplate read L. AYERS.

"Whatta you doing here, Scully?" Samansky asked. He had the blown voice of a pack-a-day saloon singer or a throat-punched club fighter.

"You got a warrant?" Shane asked, ignoring the question.

"Show him, Lee," Samansky said. Patrolman Ayers pulled a folded slip of paper out of his pocket and waved it under Shane's nose. "Not that you got any rights in this house, least not that we know about."

Shane ignored the comment, turned, and moved out of the bedroom, back to the front door. He waved to Barbara, who closed the cell phone and walked into her house. He didn't need more cops added to this party.

"Give her the warrant," Shane demanded as she entered the living room.

Lee Ayers handed it to Barbara.

"Why?" she asked. "Why are you searching my house?"

"That's none of your business, ma'am," Samansky said, his sandpaper voice gruff and irritating.

"You two are patrol officers," Shane said. "Long as I've been on the job, it's always detectives who administer warrants and paw through the dressers. Shouldn't you guys be parked on a corner somewhere, writing greenies?"

"You're the asshole who's headed for Traffic Division," Ayers said with a smirk. " 'Sides, we got this squeal direct from the top of the Glass House. You got a problem with that, take it up with the warrant control officer at Parker Center."

Shane took the warrant out of Barbara's hands and looked at it. It had been signed by Judge José Hernandez, known by police and trial attorneys around the municipal courthouse as "Papier-Mâché José" because he was willing to hang all the paper the cops wanted: subpoenas, arrest warrants, wiretaps. If they wrote it up, Hernandez signed it. Defendants had their own moniker: "The Time Machine," because the judge was infamous for passing out maximum sentences. He was a Mayor Crispin ally.

Shane handed the warrant back to Barbara. "You guys about through?" he asked.

"Yeah, we did the whole place," Ayers said. "You need to vacuum behind the furniture, lady. You got a fuckin' butterfly collection back there."

The two cops moved out the side door. Samansky had Barbara's garage-door clicker, and he opened her garage, exposing their black-and-white. They had parked it there to avoid calling attention to their presence.

While Lee Ayers got into the patrol car and backed it out of the garage, Samansky turned to Barbara. "You should be ashamed of yourself. Scully is the guy who shot your husband."

"That's none of your business," she said weakly.

" 'Cept it is my business. Ray was my friend, my partner. He was special. A guy like Ray comes along once in a lifetime. You had the best, lady. I'm fuckin' dyin' here . . . can't even believe he's really gone. You're his wife, and you're walking around with the shitwrap who dropped him. You should be ashamed." Then he turned, moved to the squad car, and got in. He glowered at them from the passenger seat. "I wonder what Robbery/

Homicide's gonna say about you two bein' together. Wonder how that's gonna play downtown." Samansky cleared his raspy throat, hawked up a spitball, and shot it in their direction. It landed two feet from the step they were on. Then he threw the garage-door opener at Shane, who snatched it out of the air.

They backed out of the driveway, around Barbara's Mustang convertible, and onto the grass. The squad car bounced over the curb, banging hard into Shane's black Acura, caving in the front fender with its pipe bumper, knocking Shane's car away from the curb. Then Lee Ayers cranked the patrol car's wheels and sped off up the street.

"It just keeps getting better," Shane said softly. "I can hardly wait till the tin collectors find out you and I were spending time together."

They turned and walked back into the house. Shane stood in the living room. It was probably a waste of time, but he decided to make his own search anyway. He checked the living-room furniture first. The carpet indentations were exposed, proving that the two cops had moved the sofa as promised. He pulled off some of the seat cushions and saw that they had all been stabbed with a kitchen knife that had been left on the floor under the sofa. That meant they had been looking for something that was small enough to be hidden inside a seat cushion. Something about the size of a videotape, he thought.

As he moved through the house, it was obvious that Samansky and Ayers had done a thorough job. It was also obvious that whatever was missing was still missing. The whole house had been searched. If they had found what they were looking for, they would have stopped when they recovered it.

Shane kept looking anyway, but he was getting dispirited. He ended up in the bedroom closet. He carefully went through the top shelf. Nothing. He checked the shoeboxes. Nothing. As he was getting set to close the closet doors, something caught his eye. He looked again and saw that there were half a dozen white shirts in plastic cleaner bags. What stopped him was that several of the shirts were on white hangers with printed plastic that read BAYSIDE CLEANERS, while two others were on plain hangers with light green cellophane over them. He took all the shirts off the rod and held them up.

"What is it?" Barbara asked.

"I don't know. Why do you use two different dry cleaners?"

"I don't. I just use Bayside, here in Venice."

Shane held up the Bayside Cleaners shirts. The covers indicated that Bayside was located at 201 South Venice Boulevard. He put them on the bed, then examined the other shirts with the plain hangers and greenish cellophane covers. There was no printing to indicate the name and address of this second cleaner. He pulled the laundry tag off one of the Bayside shirt collars. It was a small yellow strip with a number and bar code. Then he found the laundry strip for the unknown cleaner: a purple square stapled through the bottom buttonhole.

"You say Ray was away a lot. Maybe he had these cleaned somewhere else." Shane took the shirts with the purple square strips and folded them over his arm. "We have a database for laundry tags. Sometimes, when we get a John Doe with no ID, the laundry mark helps us identify the body. I'll drop this at the Scientific Investigations Section and see what they come up with. I better get out of here. Did you find that cell phone number?" he asked.

She snapped her fingers. "Forgot," she said, and went digging around in one of Ray's drawers. She found the box the phone had come in. Inside, with the warranty and sales slip, Ray had written the number. She handed it to Shane.

"Same number as on the AT&T printout," he said, holding up both sheets of paper. "Whoever she is, she was using Ray's cell phone."

"So we can't trace it."

"Guess not."

Shane moved toward the front door but stopped in the entry as Barbara put a hand on his arm. She looked at him softly with her beautiful blue-green eyes.

"Can we see each other?"

"Barbara . . . that's gonna get us nothing but grief."

"Tell me you don't want to see me. Just say it, and I won't bring it up again."

"I can't say it, 'cause I do. It's just . . ."

"If we're careful?" she said. "I feel so lonely, so frightened."

Why is this happening this way? he wondered. Finally he put a hand up to her face and held it there for a moment. "I'll think about it. I guess if those two cops notify RHD, the damage is already done," he heard himself say stupidly. Of course, he knew he could probably explain away one incident. He could say he'd come over to apologize or pay his respects. All he needed was to start seriously fooling around with Ray's widow in the wake of this shooting. A first-degree murder charge would probably be his reward for that behavior. *How could he even consider seeing her again?* His heart was beating fast, slamming in his chest like a broken cam shaft, his breath coming in rasping gasps. Loneliness swelled. He looked at her and wondered again how this had gotten so fucked up.

"Buy a cell phone," he said impulsively, "a new one. Leave the number on my home machine. You have mine. Since these cells aren't secure, don't use my name if you call me."

"Okay," she said. Then she reached up to kiss him, and he found his lips brushing against hers. He started to put an arm around her but then pulled away and quickly left her house without looking back.

Samansky was right. They should be ashamed, but a hard-on was stuffed sideways in his Jockey shorts. He reached down and adjusted it. Another work of art, *The Pagan Love God*; hang it with the others. The Shane Scully Gallery was filling fast.

He got to his car and knelt down to survey the bashed front

fender. It was hard to tell whether he or his poor black Acura had been taking more hits recently. He reached over and tugged the fender slightly off the new radial front tire. Then he got behind the wheel, and with the front fender rubbing badly, he turned the car around and drove back to his house on the East Canal in Venice.

Two hours after he got home, another uniformed patrolman showed up. He hand-delivered the PERSONAL AND CONFIDENTIAL envelope Shane had been dreading. Inside was an LAPD Letter of Transmittal.

THE
LETTER OF
TRANSMITTAL

POLICE DEPARTMENT

LETTER OF TRANSMITTAL
APRIL 21, 2000

ADJUDICATION
Complaint filed by Robbery/Homicide and IAD. Place of Complaint: 2387 Shell Avenue, Venice, CA. Complaint Investigation CF no. 20-4567-56. This complaint form contains allegations of misconduct against Department employee:

SERGEANT I. SHANE SCULLY   SOUTHWEST DIVISION
Serial No. 8934867   RHD

Allegations are listed below with recommendations for classification and supporting rationales.

ALLEGATION ONE: That on April 16, at approximately 2:30 A.M., Sergeant Scully inappropriately involved himself in an incident of domestic violence.

ALLEGATION TWO: Sergeant Scully drove to the house of his ex-partner, Lieutenant Raymond Molar. He did not use his police radio to call uniformed police, instead electing to inject himself into a potentially dangerous incident where uniformed personnel would have been in a better position to contain the situation.

ALLEGATION THREE: Sergeant Scully arrived on the scene and used inappropriate and out-of-policy escalating force. (Force may not be resorted to unless other reasonable alternatives have been thoroughly exhausted.)

ALLEGATION FOUR: After engaging in an inappropriate escalation of force, Sergeant Scully fired his police weapon, which resulted in the death of Lieutenant Raymond Molar.

ALLEGATION FIVE: Sergeant Scully removed from the Molar residence certain related case items that he believed would reflect badly on him in the subsequent investigation. (Note: The confidential nature of these materials prohibits notification and description of same in this letter of transmittal, but such notification will be made available to the accused upon discovery.)

CLASSIFICATION

It is recommended that all allegations be classified as *sustained*.

RATIONALE

It has been determined by investigating officers that Sergeant Scully had a prior relationship with the wife of the deceased. As a result, Sergeant Scully should have known that his involvement in this domestic dispute would not produce a favorable outcome. His reckless attempt to intervene in a family dispute where he had an emotional history, and his refusal to call for uniformed assistance, produced a situation that resulted in an undue escalation of force and the death of Lieutenant Molar. Further at issue is Sergeant Scully's prior relationships with both the deceased, Lieutenent Molar (ex-partner), and Molar's wife (former girl-friend). This throws doubt on his use of force and gives rise to questions of personal motive. It is also noted that on February 12, 1984, then-Patrolman Scully was involved in a physical alter-cation with the deceased in the underground parking structure at Southwest Division. This altercation resulted in the breakup of their partnership and Scully's transfer to West Valley Division.

COMPLAINT HISTORY ANALYSIS

Sergeant Scully's use-of-force history has been examined, and it has been determined that this officer has had six complaint in-vestigations in ten years (none sustained). However, he has re-ceived one departmental admonishment due to a nonsustained Board of Rights involving the severe beating of a nineteen-year-old Hispanic gang member in Southwest Division. (It was deter-mined by the board that some eyewitness accounts of the beating were perjurious, and this perjury resulted in the subsequent not-guilty verdict. However, in the estimation of Sergeant Scully's commander, some undue force had taken place.) In reviewing his complaint history, it has been decided that this officer has shown a pattern of failure to exercise good judgment. Additionally, he has received admonishments for two separate (preventable) traffic accidents. There are no negative-comment-card entries from his current commanding officer.

RELIEF FROM DUTY CONSIDERATION

It is recommended that this officer be relieved from his duty in Southwest Robbery/Homicide and that he be suspended without pay until further notice. Note: The complaint copy and Relief from Duty Suspension Form (1.61) issued by Internal Affairs Di-vision and signed by Deputy Chief II Thomas Mayweather is be-ing faxed to Sergeant Scully's CO, Captain Bud Halley, in accordance with departmental regulations. Upon receipt of same,

Sergeant Scully shall surrender his gun, badge, and identification card to Captain Halley for safekeeping.

RECOMMENDATIONS
The chief of police has directed this case to a full Board of Rights, said board to commence ten days from the date of this letter.

COMMANDING OFFICER'S RESPONSE
None.

Respectfully submitted,
Alexa Hamilton
Internal Affairs Division

PANEL

A LETTER OF TRANSMITTAL is always delivered to an accused officer and is, in essence, a summons and complaint. It gives the preliminary results of the IAD investigation and the determination by the department of the appropriate form of adjudication.

Shane had received the letter just before going out the door to pick up Chooch from school. He ripped open the brown envelope with trembling fingers. He had figured it would be bad, but this was even worse than he had expected. He shook with rage as he read the allegations. Then he stuffed the document into his side pocket and headed out the back door. *Fuck 'em,* he thought, *I'm not gonna plead this out. I'm gonna fight it.*

He pried the crushed front fender farther away from the tire, using the Acura's tire jack. Then as he took the 405 over the hill to Coldwater, he turned on his cell phone to call his new defense rep, Rags Whitman. He had talked with him once yesterday, but

Rags was in the middle of defending another BOR, so they had agreed to meet at six that evening.

He punched the number into his cell phone.

Rags Whitman was on a break outside hearing room three when he answered the phone. Internal Affairs had rented the top three floors of the Bradbury Building in downtown L.A. It was a beautiful turn-of-the-century structure with a glassed-in courtyard and black wrought-iron banisters. Because Parker Center had become so overcrowded, the entire Advocate Section of IAD, as well as its four main hearing rooms, had been moved to this architectural treasure at the corner of Broadway and Third.

"Yeah," Rags answered in his surprising soprano voice.

"It's Shane. I just got the Letter of Transmittal."

"Bad?" Rags asked.

"They suspended me without pay. They're alleging I shot Ray because I used to date Barbara. It's total bullshit!"

"You'll probably do much better with DeMarco, if that's the way they're going. He fights gladiator-style."

"DeMarco won't take the case."

"He changed his mind. Your machine was turned off. He's been trying to reach you all afternoon. He didn't have your mobile number, so I gave it to him. The way this is going, you better start leaving your cell phone on."

"Oh," Shane said. He'd turned his answering machine and cell phone off because he was afraid that Barbara would call. He'd been having second thoughts about seeing her and wanted to put some distance between them for the time being. "You got his number handy? I don't have it with me."

Rags Whitman gave it to him, and Shane dialed.

"Go," DeMarco said when he answered. Shane could hear a mellower brand of rap being played in the room behind the conversation. This time he thought it was L. L. Cool J.

"It's Shane."

"Where've you been? I changed my mind. I gotta get one more swing at that bitch advocate Alexa Hamilton. I've been trying to reach you all day."

"I had my cell off by mistake. I'm glad you reconsidered. I got this fucking Letter of Transmittal. It's a complete load a' shit. They're fuckin' me over, Dee."

"Meet me at the beach as soon as you can."

"I've gotta go pick up a friend's kid at school. I promised his mother. Okay if I bring him?"

"Sure, I'll meet you at the Silver Surfer. It's a bar-restaurant on the Strand, about six doors up from my place. How 'bout an hour?"

"How 'bout an hour and a half?"

"See ya then."

"Hey, Dee . . . thanks. I feel better with you on this. I wanna go to war. I don't wanna plead out this bullshit. I wanna fight it."

"We'll talk in an hour."

When he arrived at Harvard Westlake, Brad Thackery was waiting for him. Thackery followed Chooch to the car and immediately came around to the driver's side.

"We still haven't heard from Chooch's mother," he said angrily, shoving his thin, pinched features and wiry hair down into Shane's face.

Chooch got in the passenger side and pretended to pay no attention, looking out the side window at the football field.

"Whatta you want me to do about it?" Shane said sharply.

"I want you to have Mrs. Sandoval get in touch with my office."

"I told her to call you two days ago."

"Obviously, neither you nor she have any idea of the seriousness of Chooch's situation. This is about his future here at Harvard Westlake."

"I told Sandy. I can't do more than that."

"*Facta non verba*," Thackery said with a smirk, then added, "Actions speak louder than words."

"*Gobbelus feces*," Shane replied, and after a second to figure it out, Chooch burst into laughter.

Shane put the car in gear and pulled out onto Coldwater. He was smoking mad. Of course, he knew it wasn't Thackery, it was his whole damn life that was pissing him off.

"*Gobbelus feces*. Eat shit—pretty fuckin' good," Chooch crowed.

"Calm down, will ya . . . it wasn't that funny."

Chooch looked at him carefully, then turned off his headset and put the rig back into his book bag.

"Don't worry about Thackery, okay? It doesn't matter that Sandy didn't call. They're gonna throw me out anyway. It's a done deal. I'm not even in regular classes anymore. I'm in detention. They don't care if I do my homework or not. They're just sitting on me till they can tell her I'm dust."

"Shit," Shane said. "Good goin'."

"I don't care, so don't sweat it."

"Yeah, that's right, I forgot. I'm just this month's paid jerkoff."

"That was before. You're not a paid jerkoff anymore. You've been promoted."

"To what?" Shane was barely paying attention. His mind was spinning, a kaleidoscope of horrible, career-ending problems.

"You're my doobie brother," Chooch said with a grin, "my ganja gangtsa and Rasta weed warrior."

"Listen, Chooch, you gotta forget about that. Okay? I'm having a rough time right now, I'm not thinking straight. That was a huge mistake."

"Shit, it was the first thing you did that I liked. Showed me some stones, man. No other cop I know would sit around with some kid and bogart a fatty."

"Chooch, if you tell anybody about that, I'm gonna kill ya."

"No sweat. I can keep a secret." He smiled, then put his head-phones on again and cranked up the tunes. He stayed plugged in until Shane made the turn onto the Santa Monica Freeway. It was the wrong way home, so Chooch took off his headset and looked over. "Where we going?"

"I gotta go to a meeting down at the beach. It should only take an hour, maybe less. You can hang for a while, okay?"

Chooch cocked an eyebrow. "Something's going on, right? You're in the soup, just like me, aren't ya?" he said with surprising intuition.

"It's okay. I can handle it."

They shot off the end of the freeway, back onto the Coast Highway. Five minutes later Chooch and Shane were walking through the front door of an almost empty bar-restaurant with a sawdust floor and a neon sign that read SILVER SURFER.

It was 4:15 in the afternoon.

. . .

They found DeMarco seated at the bar. He was wearing cut-offs and a blue-jean vest with no shirt, working on his third beer. The other two empty brown glass longnecks were lined up on the bar beside him.

When Shane introduced DeMarco to Chooch, the teenager looked at the longhaired defense rep and smiled. "Cool fuckin' earring, dude."

"I like your friend, Scully. You're finally kicking." The defense rep smiled at Shane.

"Is it okay for him to be in here?" Shane asked, referring to the fact that they were in a bar that served hard liquor.

"Yeah, he can go play the video games over there. Technically, that's not in the bar area."

Shane dug into his pockets and gave Chooch some change.

The boy moved over to a small alcove in sight of the bar, sat on a stool, and began feeding coins into one of the machines.

Shane slid the Letter of Transmittal over to DeMarco, who read it carefully, then set it on the bar between them. "Mark, gimme another Lone Star," he yelled. "How 'bout you?" he asked Shane.

"Slow down on the brewskies, will ya? I'm on fire here."

"Then you're in luck. With this bladder, I can piss it out for you," DeMarco quipped. "In your telephonic absence, I went ahead and covered some pro forma ground. Tell ya this much, Alexa Hamilton doesn't let much grass grow under her magnificent gym-trained ass. She already got the rotation list for your judging panel and faxed it to me. Seven names: four sworn members of the department above the rank of captain and three civilians. If you remember how it works from before, you get to throw off two of the cops and two of the civilians, leaving you a panel of three judges: two sworn, one civilian." He reached into his blue-jean vest pocket and pulled out two slips of paper. "This ain't much of a beauty contest," he said, sliding both slips over to Shane. "In my opinion, all of these department guys are douche bags. Tell me who you like. I hate the whole bunch." DeMarco read the names aloud while Shane studied the list. "Captain Donovan McNeil, West Division; Commander Mitchell Van Sickle, Ad Vice; Deputy Chief Laurence Gadsworth—he's the chief's administrative staff officer, so forget him; and Captain Bernard Cookson."

"Jesus," Shane said, "except for Donovan McNeil, who I used to go fishing with occasionally, aren't these guys all in Chief Brewer's golf foursome?"

"Yep. But it gets worse. Look't the civilians: all lawyers from South Temple Street; one's a retired judge, a Crispin crony, of course. I checked the others—all work at the municipal courthouse and all have strong political ties to Mayor Crispin. This guy here, Knox Pooly, actually chaired his committee to reelect."

"What's going on here, Dee? This isn't right."

"No shit. You're getting screwed without the Vaseline. If Donovan's an old friend, I'm surprised he made this list of suckfish."

"He figures. A year ago he was the chief's community affairs officer. They probably picked him not knowing he was a friend of mine."

"Okay, so we keep him on the list and hope that he'll at least have divided loyalties. Who else?"

"Not Deputy Chief Gadsworth, of course. I'll take Commander Van Sickle." Shane looked at the list of three civilians and cocked an eyebrow at DeMarco for help.

"Beats me," DeMarco said. "Throw 'em out alphabetically or just drop 'em over your shoulder and the one closest to the door stays. Good a way as any."

"I'll take Clifford Finch. At least he's a defense attorney."

"Okay, then your panel is Captain Donovan McNeil, Commander Van Sickle—he'll be the chairman, based on rank—and Cliff Finch. Good fuckin' luck. This bunch would convict Santa Claus of home invasion, but I'll notify Alexa that these are our choices."

Shane sat and brooded as DeMarco was served his fourth beer, then started to gulp it down. "Go easy, will ya?" Shane murmured.

"When I'm being fucked, it feels better if I get a little loaded first," DeMarco said dourly. He picked up the Letter of Transmittal and reread the Rationale Section. "Two things here; let's take 'em in order. One: they think you took something from Ray's home."

"It's bullshit. I don't know anything about it."

"You wouldn't hold back on me again, would you, Shane? You did last time."

"I don't know what they're talking about."

"Okay, so what's with this old fistfight in the garage at Southwest Division?"

"Nothin', just frayed nerves. It was way back in '84, for God's sake. You and I were just going through the BOR. I was uptight. I boiled over, that's all."

"Shane, you gotta tell me the truth, the whole truth, and nothing but the truth; otherwise, we're gonna get blackjacked at that board. I'm gonna ask you again. What the fuck was going on between you and Ray and Barbara? Why did you get into that fight?"

"We never talked about it, but you knew who really beat that Hispanic kid half to death."

"My guess—it was Ray."

"Right."

"So, not that it matters all these years later, but why don't you do me a favor and finally spit it out. Tell me what happened."

"I was in a gas station, taking a leak. I came back to where our patrol car was parked, and Ray was beating this kid with his baton. I broke it up. If I hadn't stopped it, Ray would have killed him. Then, after the complaint got filed by the boy's family, Ray begged me to take the blame. The kid's head injuries had him blank on the incident. He couldn't remember who hit him. Since I was just a probationer and had no complaints on my record, Ray convinced me I would probably get only a few weeks' suspension. He said he'd make up my lost pay out of his own pocket. I was his partner—real young, impressionable. Back then I was just like some of these rookies today. I thought he was the best cop on the streets of L.A. He had a way of getting to you, making you believe in him. And he was brave. More than once he risked his life for a brother officer. His two Medals of Valor were not bullshit. So I said okay. I took the complaint for him. But later, while you and I were going through the hearing, I started having nightmares. In those dreams, Molar and I would both be beating that kid. We'd be taking turns. I'd wake up sweating, hating myself. I was under a lot of stress back then, and I guess it was the beginning of my seeing Ray for what he really was—a vicious, violent son of a bitch who wasn't a cop so he could protect and serve. He was a cop so he could kick ass and hold court in the street. . . .

"It boiled over that night in Southwest. Barbara had just broken up with me. I was under investigation at IAD, and I just snapped. I yelled at him. He went into the coffee room, got a pitcher of ice water out of the refrigerator, told me to cool off, and threw it on me. I pushed him; he fell; we ended up in the parking garage. It wasn't much of a fight."

"You were way out of your weight division," DeMarco said softly. "He had almost a hundred pounds on you."

"That's the whole story."

Again, DeMarco swigged on the beer. He put the bottle down and began making Olympic rings on the varnished bartop, stamping them out with the bottle's wet bottom. Finally he wiped his artwork away with his palm. " 'Nother longneck, Mark," he shouted.

"Listen, Dee . . . I hate seein'—"

"Give it a rest. Okay?" DeMarco said sharply. "Don't tell me how to lead my life. While you were running around with your cell phone turned off, I've been working this thing. I'm not through filling you in yet, so shut the fuck up." Shane nodded. "This morning I wrote up a standard petition to overturn the 1.61 and requested your return to duty. It's kinda pro forma when a police officer has been suspended without pay, like an automatic appeal, only I've never seen one get approved before. Guess what? You're the exception." He reached into his back pocket and shoved a fax over to Shane. "Signed by the Big Noise himself." Shane looked at the document. It was as DeMarco said, signed by Chief Burleigh Brewer. "The whole shebang, from application to acceptance, took two hours. Now go figure that."

"I can't," Shane said, staring at the fax in disbelief. The document put him right back on duty with full pay. It didn't make sense in the face of everything else.

"I called Bud Halley and asked him about it. He told me Tom Mayweather walked it through the system personally. However, Halley also told me where they've reassigned you. You're not in Southwest Detectives anymore."

"Where am I?"

"You ain't gonna believe it. . . ."

"Oh, shit. What is it this time, the grain and drain train at the city jail?"

"You've been assigned to the chief advocate's office at Internal Affairs."

"I've been what?!" he said, his voice so loud that Chooch momentarily turned away from the video game he was playing and looked in their direction.

"You report to the tin collectors at the Bradbury Building at eight-thirty A.M. tomorrow."

"That's nuts. I've never heard of an officer awaiting a Board of Rights being assigned to the very division that's trying to terminate him."

"Me neither. But after thinking it over . . ."

"They want to keep me where they can watch me," Shane said.

"A winnah. Give the man something from the top shelf. You is da new Dark Side kick-me. I guess Chief Brewer doesn't want you running around looking for whatever it is they think you took out of Ray's house. They want you on a tight leash."

The bartender brought DeMarco his new beer. He took three long swallows, then set it down with the others. "All in all, not a good start, Shane, but rigged boards are my specialty. These tin-collecting assholes can be had 'cause they all got target fixation. Just go down there and keep your nose clean. Let me do the grunting and groaning."

As he sat on the barstool, looking at the old defense rep, his heart sank, taking his hopes down with it. He had no choice. He had to go down to Internal Affairs. He'd been ordered, and failure to comply with a direct order was also a termination offense.

The only bright spot was that he was still on the payroll. He'd still collect his bimonthly base salary of $2,170.20, plus his ten-year longevity compensation of $60. In return, he'd be working down at IAD, forced to endure the biggest collection of milk-fed assholes on the planet. As he sat there, he decided that he would devote all of his nonworking hours to finding out what was missing from Ray's house.

"Yes! Kick ass!" Chooch yelled suddenly as his game buzzed victory and he was advanced to the next level.

"Don't worry, Shane. I'll unwind this for you. I'll get you off," DeMarco said, causing Shane to look back at him.

"*Factus non verba*," Scully said darkly.

THE PEOPLE RULE

AS SOON AS Shane got home, he called Sandy. She said she was sorry she hadn't gotten in touch with Thackery, but promised she would. She said she'd had a tough two days.

"What'm I supposed to do with Chooch tomorrow?" Shane asked. "They've got him sitting in detention all day. He's not even going to classes."

"That guy Thackery is a complete ass," Sandy said. "He's on Chooch for smoking dope? What a hypocrite."

"Not smoking it, Sandy, selling it."

"I was there at the school two months ago when Chooch enrolled. Thackery was just driving out. He put down the window of his crummy, rusted-out van to talk to me, and the smell of old pot was so strong in that thing, I got a contact high."

"Sandy, lots of people smoke pot, okay? It's a sad social truth, but there it is. It doesn't matter what Thackery does in his off-hours. You've gotta call him and set up an appointment."

"Right. Okay, I promise, sugar."

"You promised yesterday."

"This time I pledge it. I *swear* it, okay?" She changed gears. "You go ahead and take him to school tomorrow. Forget Thackery. I'll have already called that snooty headmaster, Mr. St. John. I'll square him away. That guy is always leering at me. Wants to get in my pants."

"You always put things so delicately," Shane said, beginning to wish he'd never met the beautiful raven-haired informant.

"Don't be such a prude. When I get through with St. John, he'll be at Camp Fantasy, pitching a tent in his Jockey shorts. Don't worry about Chooch."

After she hung up, Shane went outside. Chooch was already out there in one of the metal chairs. Shane dropped his tired ass in the vacant seat beside him. They looked out at the still canal, both lost in separate thoughts. Finally Shane jerked his mind off his department problems and focused on the boy sitting sullenly beside him.

"If your mom and I could keep you in school," Shane started slowly, "would you go there and really give it a try?"

"Moot point, 'cause you can't. I already got the scarlet *E* for 'expel.' I'm gone, brother."

"Chooch, I've been thinking about it. You're really smart. You've got a great head on your shoulders. You could be something important in life. You have it in you to be anything you want."

"Like a cop?" he smirked.

"Better than a cop. You could go to college, pick any career. Your mom has money; she'll pay for anything. That's a big advantage for you. It's a chance most guys never get."

They sat in silence, looking at the still canal water, both of them rocking slowly in the old metal chairs.

"I know you're trying to help, man," Chooch finally said, "but it ain't about having a career. Y'know . . . it's just not what it's about. It goes much deeper than that."

More silence, then Shane turned in his chair to look at the teenager. "Wanna know something?" Chooch didn't answer. "I believe in you, Chooch," he went on softly. "I know that whatever you want, you've got the ability to get it. You've got what it takes. I think you're special."

"That's bullshit," Chooch shot back.

"No, it's not. I've been watching you . . . how you handle stuff. You've got guts. You stand up. You walk your own trail. That's very rare. It takes strength of character. Most people can't do that." More silence. "Listen. I told you I wouldn't lie to you— not ever. So this is the straight stuff. It's what I see in you, and it's impressive."

Chooch turned his face away from Shane. His breathing had changed. His right hand darted up and brushed his cheek under his eyes. Then he stood up, and anger flared. "Don't fuck around with me. Okay? I can't take any more bullshit. Just leave me alone." He moved quickly into the house.

Shane sat in his garden until the setting sun began turning the still canal bright yellow, then orange and purple, and finally black. After the sun surrendered its hold on the day, a cold evening wind came off the ocean, blowing marine air across the coastline. Shane was getting a chill, so he got out of his chair and walked back inside the house.

■ ■ ■

"It's fucking forty minutes too early!" Chooch glowered as Shane pulled up in front of the Harvard Westlake School the next morning. There were no waiting lines of foreign cars as Chooch opened the door and dragged his book bag from the front seat.

"I've got a new duty assignment downtown, so I need to get there early. Live with it," Shane said.

"Sure, no problem. Live with it. That's my fuckin' motto anyway." Chooch angrily moved away from the car and sat alone on a bench near the athletic pavilion.

Shane pulled out of the driveway and drove two miles to the Valley Division HQ. He figured if he hurried, he'd be able to get everything done before eight-thirty.

Fifteen minutes later Shane was back in the Harvard Westlake faculty parking lot waiting for Brad Thackery. After ten more minutes the assistant dean of admissions pulled his rusting Ford van into his parking stall and got out. Shane moved to him. "Good morning, sir," he said pleasantly.

"Maybe for you, but it's not a good morning for Chooch. I saw him sitting out front when I drove past. Since I still haven't heard from Mrs. Sandoval, you can just go right back around and pick him up and depart the premises, *ad quam primum*. He is no longer welcome at this school," Thackery said harshly, then added brusquely, "and remove your vehicle from faculty parking. This is a restricted area."

"How do you say that in Latin?"

"I'm through talking to you, whoever you are. Good-bye."

Shane pulled out his badge and held it up for Brad Thackery to read. Thackery looked at it, surprised, readjusted slightly, then with less anger said, "Big deal."

"You're right, it is a big deal, 'specially since your van there is crawling with vehicular irregularities. You wanna put that blinker on? Seems to me it wasn't working when you turned in here."

"I'm about to get it fixed."

" 'About to' doesn't cut it," Shane said. "Put it on, please. I want to check it out."

Thackery glared at Shane. "This is what really gets you guys off, isn't it?"

"Yep. Can't get enough of it."

As Brad Thackery opened the van, Shane moved to his Acura and opened the back door. A black Labrador jumped out and, with his tongue lolling, followed Shane back to the van. Thackery was leaning into the front seat, fiddling with the blinker and trying to get it to work, when the dog started barking and pacing back and forth along the side of Thackery's van.

"Whoa . . . whoa . . . whatta we got here?" Shane said with mock surprise. Thackery jerked his head out of the van.

"Get that dog away from me."

"This isn't a dog, Mr. Thackery, this is a drug enforcement officer. His name is Krupkee. It looks like Officer Krupkee's got a noseful. Where is it, boy? What ya got?"

The black Lab had moved to the rear of the van and now had both paws up on the spare tire, which was hooked by a locked bracket to the back of the van. Then the black Lab started barking and pawing at the tire.

"Oh boy, this ain't good, Mr. Thackery. You wanna give me the key that releases that back tire?"

"No. No, I don't."

"Lemme put it another way, sir. Gimme the key, or I'll pry the fucking thing off with my tire jack. Officer Krupkee just gave me probable cause for a search."

After a long moment, Thackery reluctantly dug into his pocket and produced the key that unlocked the tire bracket. Shane swung it away from the van and looked into the tire. There, attached by magnets to the inside of the tire drum, was a small metal box. Shane pulled it off and opened it. There were about four ounces of grass in a canvas bag and a bottle with a few pills. Shane opened the bag and poured some low-grade pot into his palm.

"This is not good, Mr. Thackery. As a matter of fact, you're under arrest, *regnat populus*." He poured the dope back into the bag. "So you won't get the wrong idea about me and think I'm some overeducated, Latin-quoting blowhard, that's just the state motto of Arkansas. I was stationed there in the Marines. It means 'the people rule,' and the people of Los Angeles don't like this one bit and are about to rule that you go to the city lockup."

Shane pulled out his handcuffs, spun Thackery around, and put them on.

"You can't do this," Thackery protested.

"Somebody should tell that to my watch commander. In the meantime, you're gonna sit this one out downtown. Don't worry, I'll call the principal for you and tell him his assistant dean of admissions is gonna be at County Jail riding the pine in the detox box."

"Is this about Chooch? Is that what this is all about?" Thackery's eyes were darting around, hoping no other member of the faculty would come driving in and witness this debacle.

"You bet it's about Chooch. But it's also about you, Brad. If you weren't such an insufferable asshole, I probably wouldn't have gone so far out of my way to knock your dick in the dirt."

"Look, Chooch has problems. Okay? He's got deep emotional difficulties. Besides, he's selling drugs."

"Bet he didn't sell you this crummy bag a' bird food," Shane said, holding up the bag of thin, seed-ridden grass.

"You think this is funny, is that it?"

"It's about as funny as prostate surgery. How do guys like you end up teaching school?"

"What do you want?"

"I want you to cut Chooch some slack. I want you to go to bat for him."

"I can't change the course of events. It's too late. They've already had a faculty meeting about him."

"I'd think the assistant dean of admissions would have a little pull around here," Shane said. "Of course, after this bust, you'll be lucky to be in charge of school bus schedules."

"Look, okay . . . maybe . . ."

"Maybe what?"

"If I . . . if I said to them I'd work with him separately, maybe do some drug counseling or something . . ."

"I don't think you're exactly the right guy for that, but go ahead, keep talkin'."

"Maybe if I really try, I could get him another chance. Just one . . ."

"Okay, that sounds more promising. You give him another chance, I give you another chance."

Just then, two other faculty cars pulled into the parking area and slowed as they passed Thackery's van. He was standing there with his hands cuffed behind him. A woman put down her window.

"Is everything okay, Brad?" she asked, looking at the handcuffs.

"We're fine." Shane said. "I'm the magician Mr. Thackery hired for next month's high-school assembly. Just showing Brad here how I do my handcuff escape." Shane smiled and she drove on, not looking too convinced.

"I want immediate results, Thackery. I'm looking for Chooch to get outta that detention hall this morning and back into regular class. If he gets goofy about anything in the future, don't bust him. Call me."

Shane shoved his business card into Thackery's shirt pocket and then unhooked the cuffs. He put the dope and pills in his jacket pocket, gave Brad Thackery back his car keys, then he led Officer Krupkee over to the Acura.

The Lab jumped into the backseat, Shane put the car in gear, pulled out of the faculty parking area, then drove back to Valley Division and returned the dog to the Valley Bureau Drug Enforcement Unit. He shot back onto the freeway and got to Internal Affairs downtown with ten minutes to spare.

THE DARK SIDE

THE BRADBURY BUILDING never failed to amaze Shane. He felt that it was the most magnificent building in Los Angeles. Only five stories high, it had been designed in the late 1800s by Gregory Wyman, a draftsman with no architectural degree. It sat bravely on the corner of Broadway and Third while slovenly men leaned forward to piss against her or curled up to sleep, rubbing the grime from their clothes on her magnificent yellow bricks.

Shane pulled into the modern concrete parking structure that had been built next door, took the ticket, then found a spot on the second tier. He rode the elevator down and came out onto a brick patio with umbrella tables that served as a lunch area. It was located directly behind the old building. Along the concrete wall adjoining the patio was the historic fresco depicting the life of an African-American woman named Biddy Mason. The wall chronicled her odyssey, from her birth as a slave in 1810, through her incredible life journey, all the way to her final heroic years of service as a nurse delivering babies in Los Angeles hospitals in 1870.

The fresco had been placed there to show the early African-American commitment to the quality of life in L.A. Shane found it strange that in post–Rodney King L.A., this monument was behind the Internal Affairs building, in a patio where mostly cops accused of misconduct would ever see it.

He pushed through the back doors of the Bradbury, through a section under reconstruction on the first floor, into the building's magnificent covered courtyard. He looked up at the five floors stacked above him. Light brick contrasted with the intricate black wrought-iron railings. They wrapped around the interior hallways that surrounded the open atrium. Polished oak banisters snaked along the top of the ornate black-painted iron. On each side of the building's courtyard were beautiful, antique turn-of-the-century open elevators. They ran on exposed counterbalances that carried the filigreed boxes up and down. They moved slowly, stopping carefully at each floor as if time had not sped up in modern L.A. or had not fallen into desperate conflict with elegance. Over it all hung a glass roof five stories up, supported by black metal grates.

Shane stood there for a long time. He had been here for a week during his last BOR and had learned the rituals of the place. He knew about the waiting-room silence that followed the bustle of echoing voices in the atrium just before the nine o'clock commencement of the boards. He remembered the tense posture of witnesses and police officers as they leaned over the metal railings near the fifth-floor hearing rooms, waiting nervously to testify. There were the subtle, silent signs that were read only by the people familiar with the activity in the building and who spread the word on each board's outcome. The elevator operators watched carefully as accused officers left their penalty hearings, checking to see who was carrying the accused's gun. If it was in the advocate's hand, it meant the officer had been terminated.

The administration of LAPD justice churned relentlessly in the building, leaving bits and pieces of its victims' lives bobbing like scattered garbage in its wake. Like the Tower of London, it was way too beautiful a place for all the beheadings that occurred there.

Shane got on the elevator, rode to the third floor, and moved up to the heavy glass-paneled, wood-frame door of the Advocate Section. After taking a deep breath, he pushed it open and walked inside.

He was back in the narrow, gray and brown space fronted by three reception desks, where secretaries directed business to the twenty advocates seated behind them. Across the hall, on the opposite side of the open atrium, were the investigating officers, known as IOs. They were regular detectives assigned to IAD who did background interviews and took affidavits from "wits." All of Shane's memories of the place came rushing back. From where he was standing, he could see back to the advocates' cubbies located on the far side of the office. The advocates were all sergeants or lieutenants and worked in five-by-five clutter at small desks, cardboard "case" boxes filled with affidavits and IO reports clustered at their feet.

Shane remembered the chief advocate, a tall, vanilla milkshake named Warren Zell. Shane moved to one of the secretaries, a black woman with a remarkable body, and smiled at her.

"I'm Sergeant Scully. I've been assigned here. I'm supposed to report to Commander Zell."

"Hi," she said, "I'm Mavis. Take a seat. I'll tell him you're here."

While she buzzed in, Shane sat and picked up the LAPD newsletter, *The Blue Line,* that was on the table along with a stack of Chief Brewer's newsletters, a glossy white four-sheet called *The*

Beat. He assumed *The Beat* was required reading in this political squirrel cage. He was looking down when he heard the female voice that distressed him the most.

"Mavis," the voice said, "can you send all these 301's on the Scully deps out to the subpoena control officer and tell him I need them served as soon as he can get them issued? Also, make sure this charge sheet gets sent to Pam Davis in the District Attorney's Office. They're monitoring his board for a possible murder indictment."

He looked up and saw Alexa Hamilton standing with her back to him, wearing one of her severe, tailored gray suits. Her shapely calves and tight, rounded ass were only a foot from his face.

"Work, work, work," he said softly.

She turned abruptly and, for the first time, saw him sitting there.

"It's not work when you're having fun," she replied.

"Don't forget to subpoena Barbara Molar; she's an eyewitness and supports my statement word for word."

"We always include exculpatory evidence, despite what you think, Scully. This division exists to try and keep the department clean. We're not down here doing hatchet jobs."

"This division exists to destroy hardworking cops so people like you can get an E-ticket ride to the top of the department. You know it. I know it. Everybody on the job knows it. But don't take it from me, go ask any uniform sitting in the front seat of a Plain Jane."

Alexa stood there and tapped her thumb against a file folder. "Y'know, Scully, you mighta been an okay cop, except you've gotta do everything your own stiff-necked, jackoff way. You're always trying to be the smartest guy in the room, always cutting corners and blaming others. This is a division that is set up to defend the rules and mandates of this department. Since you have your head so far up your ass, you only see things through your navel; it's understandable your view is clouded. That's your problem, not mine." She turned to Mavis. "On second thought, Mave, I'm gonna walk this stuff over to the subpoena control desk personally. Nothing's too good for Sergeant Scully." She turned away and, carrying the paperwork, moved back to her desk behind the counter. Her hips swayed seductively as she walked. Shane felt nothing. She had turned his balls to ice.

The phone buzzed, twice.

"You can go in now," Mavis said.

Shane got up and headed down the long rectangular space between the east wall and the three reception desks. He entered Zell's office at the end of the room.

Seated behind a slab of oak was Commander Zell. He had his jacket off; a huge Glock automatic in an upside-down shoulder holster hung under his arm like a sleeping bat. It is a proven LAPD street-cop axiom that any officer in plain clothes who wears a shoulder rig is, by definition, an asshole. If it's upside down, then he's a puckered, purebred asshole. Zell looked up and pushed a stack of signed papers away as Shane entered.

"Sergeant, don't bother to sit, you won't be in my office that long." It was starting out worse than Shane had expected. "You're under my direct supervision," Zell went on, but while he spoke, he turned his attention to another stack of papers. "I expect you to report for duty at eight-thirty every morning, without fail. You have only half an hour for lunch, so I suggest you bring it. You punch out at five. It's a straight eight. No overtime will be approved. Questions?"

"Well, sir, I have to drop a fifteen-year-old boy at school every morning. I have to get him there by eight-fifteen. Eight-thirty is going to be pretty tight."

"Then here's your solution, Sergeant. You drop him off at eight instead of eight-fifteen." Zell finally looked up, fixing his gaze on Shane, as if to determine what sort of lame idiot wouldn't be able to figure that out by himself.

"Sir, if I might ask, what will I be doing?"

"You're the unit discovery officer."

"I'm sorry?"

"On every case going through here, the accused officer has the right to look at all statements and affidavits taken by our IOs. It's called *discovery*," Zell said, his voice dripping with sarcasm. "In order for the accused to get those documents, somebody has to Xerox the material, or make tape copies if it's a voice or video recording. The discovery officer works at the Xerox machines located on the second floor. There are four machines and some audio/video duplicating equipment. You make copies of everything, including personnel investigations, addenda, and any supplemental findings of proposed disciplinary action. Also include the response of the accused and the reply of the commanding officer, photographs or laser reproductions, rough field-interview notes, chronological records, case summaries, and the department wit list." He was ticking them off from memory, showing off. "Every case folder will tell you how many copies and where they are to be sent. They go out by registered mail to the accused officer's defense rep."

"I'm a Xerox machine operator?" Shane asked. He couldn't believe this was his new job.

"You are the unit discovery officer. Your job is to operate Xerox and electronic duplicating equipment. That's it. That's the job. You're excused."

"Wasn't there a crummier job you could have given me?" Shane asked, anger creeping into his voice.

"If you don't want the job, just tell me."

"Why? So you can hit me with a negligent-duty slip and put me in for insubordination?"

"Then go do what you've been asked to do."

"Yessir."

Shane moved out of the room and walked back down the hall. He stopped at Mavis's desk. "What room does the discovery officer use?"

"Room 256," she said. "It's locked. Here's the key." She handed him a key attached to a square wood block. It reminded Shane of a gas-station lavatory key. Appropriate. He was definitely in the toilet. As he moved out of the Advocate Section into the open corridor, he saw Alexa Hamilton coming back from the ladies' room. She passed him, her gaze straight ahead, as if he didn't exist or, more to the point, as if she knew he was about to disappear.

He punched the button for the beautiful old wrought-iron box. The elevator arrived and he got on. An elderly black gentleman in a dark blue blazer was running the lift.

"You must be new here," the old man said. "Whatchu gonna be doin'?"

"I'm the new discovery officer."

"Boy, good goin'. That sounds pretty darn important."

"Yeah," Shane said sadly. "No doubt about it. I am de man."

UNIT DISCOVERY OFFICER

13

AFTER CALLING Harvard Westlake and leaving a message for Chooch that he'd be late picking him up, Shane spent the morning Xeroxing cases in the narrow one-window office on the second floor. It was the only office that Internal Affairs had rented on two. Except for the occasional secretary who came in and dropped more cases on his stack, he was alone with his thoughts while the Xerox hummed and coughed up copies, passing its white light over the endless pages.

Shane wondered how much longer he should stay on the job. He'd pretty much run out of police department highway. He couldn't believe that the district attorney would ever bring murder charges. That was just being orchestrated by Chief Brewer to put pressure on him. But being terminated by Alexa Hamilton at his upcoming board was a distinct possibility. Except for Bernie Cookson, the judges were stacked against him. He would probably lose his tin and be kicked out, his seventeen-year pension going down the drain with the verdict.

He thought about Barbara Molar, how he wanted to hold her and make love to her, but this was immediately followed by a puzzling feeling of dispirited grief for something he couldn't identify. Moments later he was aware of a thickening depression. As the Xerox machine hummed and kicked pages into a tray, he tried to work it out.

He knew that pursuing a relationship with Barbara was stupid under these circumstances. Beyond that, something else was nibbling at his subconscious. He finally slapped it down and held it up.

It was a simple five-word question.

Why had Barbara married Ray?

What had led her to walk away from him and find solace in the arms of the most brutal cop on the force? She said that it was sweet to see tenderness in such a huge, seemingly brutish man.

Shane had known Ray almost from the day he'd joined the force, and he had never seen tenderness. Ray Molar was buffalo meat. His temper was always close to the surface, hiding there, waiting to explode. So why had Barbara married him? Why had she made such an obviously miserable choice?

With that question came another.

What weakness in her had caused her not to see Ray for what he was? Of course, Shane had also been fooled at first. But he'd had Ray as a partner. Having a kick-ass partner was considered a life-insurance policy in police work. Shane had misevaluated for reasons of his own survival. Why had Barbara been fooled?

His mind left that half-chewed thought and began on another. He had physical desire for her. He had once thought he loved her, but yesterday afternoon at Shutters, she had seemed to be trying to start up their relationship on the heels of Ray's death. He could understand cerebrally why this might be: she was lonely and scared, and Ray had been abusing her. She had come to hate him, but . . .

Ray had been her husband for twelve years. She had once slept in his arms. Yet his death seemed to hold no consequences for her. Shane had despised Ray, but he had not felt the same way since he'd squeezed off the round from his Mini-Cougar and watched his bullet explode in Ray's head. The picture of that death was on a macabre bulletin board in his psyche. He could not do anything without walking past it. Yet Barbara had no remorse, no guilt, no misgivings. To her, Ray's death was the doorway to her future. *What did that say? What did it mean? Had he been too young, immature, and blinded by lust to see any of her shortcomings back then? Had she changed . . . or had he?*

Shane looked at his watch. He was surprised to see that it was just a few minutes to twelve. He finished the case he was Xeroxing, then, following instructions, he put the copies in a manila envelope and addressed them to the defense rep involved. Then he put the packet in the OUT basket, where it would be picked up and sent off by registered mail.

He shut off the Xerox, locked the office door, dropped the key with Mavis, and headed out of the Bradbury Building on his lunch hour—make that *half hour.*

Shane wasn't hungry, so he decided to check on his Scientific Investigation Section request. He began to walk the four blocks to Main Street, where Parker Center was located. He needed to clear his mind. He made it a brisk outing, his arms swinging hard, his stride even and quick. When he got halfway there, he ran into another movie barricade. He badged his way through, walking along the sidewalk while wary assistant directors with head-mikes and walkie-talkies clipped on their belts glared at him. He was ignoring their barricades, trespassing on their superiority.

"You're in our shot, sir," one of them yelled.

Shane hurried along. Arnold was across the street with the

director, engaged in an animated discussion. There was a lot of gesturing and arm waving. Tourists and downtown office workers stood behind the barricades, holding their cameras at port arms, hoping for a shot while streetpeople angrily cursed this invasion of their living space.

Shane got to Parker Center and moved quickly to the Scientific Investigations Section on the seventh floor. He went down the corridor, hoping to remain invisible. Occasionally somebody would look at him, grab the arm of a companion, and start whispering. Shane could write the dialogue: *"That's him, right over there. Can you believe it? He shot Lieutenant Molar . . . they used to be partners."*

He got to SIS and asked for the results of his laundry tag analysis. A middle-aged woman with thick, red-rimmed Sally Jessy Raphaël glasses leaned across the counter with the results. "We got lucky. Most of the laundries in the database are local; this one is a ways away, but was still inside the sample area."

Shane looked at the printout. "Mountain Cleaners, Lake Arrowhead," he read aloud.

"That's what the computer says," she replied. Then almost as an afterthought: "I don't know if you missed it, but on the inside of the tag is a date, April tenth."

"Thanks," he said. "You're right, I missed it."

He moved away from the desk with the printout. The address was on Pine Tree Lane in Lake Arrowhead. He left Parker Center for the walk back to Broadway and Third, wondering why Ray Molar was getting his shirts done in Lake Arrowhead, and whether it really mattered.

Arrowhead was a two-hour drive up in the mountains. Shane had been there once or twice before. He remembered that the town sat in wooded splendor, around the ten-mile circumference of a beautiful freshwater lake. The community was picturesque, catering mostly to artists, writers, and L.A. refugees. A lot of old

Hollywood royalty had built huge mansions on the lake in the thirties, and some of these houses still existed—out-of-place old European-style homes with their stone walls and slate roofs.

When he got back to IAD, he picked up his key and trudged back down to the Xerox room. He unlocked the door and saw that a new case had been shoved through the mail slot. He picked it up and glanced at it as he walked across the room to drop it on the IN pile. Just as he was setting it down, he saw the name on the face sheet: PATROLMAN I JOSEPH CHURCH.

Shane stopped and looked at the sheet again. Joe Church was the patrolman who had escorted him yesterday morning, red light and siren, to see Chief Brewer. He flipped through the file, reading quickly.

According to the charges, three weeks ago Patrolman Church had been in a Code Thirty burglary car. He had accepted a call on a "hot ringer" in Southwest. A Hoover Street jewelry store was being robbed. It was a "There Now" call. Church had "rogered" the transmission but had not shown up for almost forty-five minutes. His Mobile Data Terminal showed him as being three blocks away. When he finally got there, the owner of the store had been beaten almost to death, and was still in the USC Medical Center. The IOs on the case stated that Church claimed he had never received the call, despite the fact that he had rogered it, and all of his communications and times were logged on his MDT as well as in the Communications Center.

Shane dropped the case back on the pile, not attaching much significance to it, except for one stray thought: *Why would an officer whom the chief of police had just personally directed to an IAD Board of Rights be given a special assignment by the chief to pick up and escort Shane to his office?* It didn't make sense. But then, nothing that had been going on lately made much sense.

He turned on the Xerox machine and spent the rest of the day burning copies in the hot, narrow room.

Shane punched out at five-thirty, walked back to his car next door, and headed to Harvard Westlake.

Chooch was sitting alone on the curb. Everyone else had been picked up. He stood slowly, then dragged both his book bag and ass over to the car and got in.

"Sorry. We're gonna have to make new arrangements for the pickup. I can't get back here till five forty-five. I sent you a message. I hope they gave it to you."

Chooch was strangely quiet. He just nodded.

Shane put the car in gear and headed up onto the freeway, back to Venice.

"Did you have some kinda talk with Mr. Thackery?" Chooch finally asked after almost ten minutes of silence.

"No, why?" Shane said, glancing over at him.

"I don't know. He pulled me out of study hall. It was like he was a different guy, wants to be my bud. He said I was gonna get another chance, that he had gone to bat for me."

"I'll bet your mom called and set him straight. Sandy did pretty good, huh? I'm telling ya, you got your mother down in the wrong column, Chooch."

"Yeah . . . What column is that, the 'Don't bother me, I'm always busy' column? She's had me in boarding school since second grade. Up at Webb School in Ventura, I never even got to come home at Christmas. I was the only kid left in the dorm over the holidays. I was being watched by custodians . . . had to eat at the headmaster's house. Sandy's some mom, all right. We gotta get her a Mother's Day award."

"People aren't always what they appear to be," Shane persisted. "Your mom has reasons. Her job takes her away a lot. She's trying to give you a great education. She wants you to have a good start in life."

"Thackery said if I have any problems, or if I want to talk, I should look him up," Chooch said, changing the subject. "As if I'd even tell that dickhead which way was due north."

"Look, Chooch, if he's changing his tune, don't hawk a lugie at him."

"He's a prick."

"Yeah, maybe. Or maybe he's had a change of heart. If he's trying to cut you some slack, take it."

"And you believe him?"

"Yeah. Yeah, sure, I believe him. Hey, look, Thackery may be okay underneath all that Latin he quotes. Maybe he's just a guy who's scared, like us."

"I ain't scared a' nothin'."

"Then you're the only one on the planet, Chooch. Everybody is scared."

"Were you scared when you shot that guy?"

Shane looked over. He had not discussed the incident with Chooch, and he didn't have a TV. He was foolishly hoping it would never come up.

"It's all over school," Chooch said, reading his look of dismay. "So tell me. When you offed him, were you scared?"

"Yeah. Yeah . . . I was scared to death. I was shitting bricks."

Chooch sat there for a long moment thinking. "Physical stuff doesn't scare me. I'm not afraid a' getting bombed on or fucked over that way. But"—he hesitated for a moment, his eyes on the road ahead—"sometimes I'm afraid that what I believe in isn't true, that everything I think is true was just set up by somebody to fool me."

Shane nodded. "Yeah, I've been getting some of that myself lately."

"And sometimes, just once in a while, I want to be the most important, instead of the least. . . ." He paused for a long time, his face in a wrinkled frown. "Sometimes I'm scared I'll never have anybody who gives a shit."

They rode in silence.

Finally they got back to East Channel Road. Shane pulled the car into the garage, and they went into the house. Shane closed the door and watched as Chooch dragged his book bag into his room, to sit there with desperate, lonely thoughts that probably matched his own.

A.K.A.

SHANE SAT in his living room listening to an occasional siren, which always seemed to come from the east, where the gangbangers held their nightly life-ending turf parties. It was six o'clock and the sun had just gone down. He put his mind back on his problem.

Any police detective worth his salt always started a case by arranging known or probable facts in chronological order. Shane took a piece of paper off the table and began making notations:

1. Late Feb. or early March, Ray Molar gets a job driving for Mayor Crispin.
2. March, R.M. begins not coming home.
3. April 2, Joe Church fails to respond to Hoover St. robbery (related?).
4. April 10, R.M. gets shirts done at Mountain Cleaners.

5. April 14, B.M. gets phone call from mystery woman/tape coming.
6. April 16, 1:30 A.M., R.M. gets home, beats B.M.
7. April 16, 2:35 A.M., R.M. shot (no tape found in house).
8. April 16, 5:17 A.M., T. Mayweather does DFAR (S.S. secure files in IAD possibly accessed).
9. April 16, 6:00 A.M., S.S. threatened by Kono and Drucker, police garage.
10. April 16, Joe Church escorts S.S. to C.O.P.
11. April 16, C.O.P. threatens S.S. with murder indictment. Wants case material returned.
12. April 18, Samansky, Ayers break in and search B.M.'s house (no tape found). Warrant signed by Hernandez, Crispin appointee.
13. April 18, Letter of Transmittal arrives. S.S. suspended. S.S. motive for murder mentioned.
14. April 18, T. Mayweather walks 1.61 appeal through department. S.S. back on duty.
15. April 19, S.S. reports to IAD (DA intends to audit BOR).

He stopped writing and looked at the list. It was his first chronological log. There were huge holes in his time line. Aside from the missing tape, there was Ray's increasingly violent behavior toward Barbara. Also, the list made it even more obvious that there was some kind of link between Ray and the top floor of the Glass House, and that it might have to do with Mayor Crispin. The list directed him to where he had to look next. He needed to find out why Molar had his shirts done ninety miles away. He looked at his watch—seven o'clock. Shane turned on his desk lamp and picked up the phone. He got the number for the laundry on Pine Tree Lane in Arrowhead and dialed. After a few rings, a man's voice came on the line.

"Mountain Cleaners," the voice chirped.

"Yes. Who am I speaking to?"

"This is Larry Wright."

"Mr. Wright, I'm Sergeant Shane Scully, with the LAPD. I'm working a case and I have some dry-cleaned shirts that were done at your laundry. I'm trying to find out who dropped them off."

"I see, well, without looking at the tags, I wouldn't know. They're bar-coded; I'd have to run them through our scanner."

"This case is pretty important. If I got in my car, I could be up there in two hours. I know it's an imposition, but do you think we could make an appointment to meet about nine tonight?"

"No problem. I'm usually stuck here till nine-thirty."

"Great. I'll bring the shirts with me." He hung up and dialed Longboard Kelly.

"Yer tappin' the Source," the surfboard shaper answered. Kelly believed "the Source" was a magical place where great waves came from.

"It's Shane. You think you could come right over and keep an eye on Chooch for a couple of hours?"

"I'm busy crankin' off an eight-ball, dude. After I finish, I could make it."

"You're doing what?" Shane asked.

"I'm on the throne, takin' a shit. Gimme five."

"Great. I'll pay you."

"What for, man? One day, if I get busted, you play the 'Get Brian out of jail' card."

"Right. Only we took that card out of the deck. How 'bout I play the 'Put in a good word for Brian' card instead?"

"Agreed, dude! I'll be right over."

Shane hung up.

He went into the guest bedroom. Chooch was hunched over the desk, doing his homework. Shane had a momentary stab of "parental" gratitude. "It's great you're doing your studies," Shane said proudly.

Chooch looked over at him, and Shane saw that he had a Game Boy on his lap.

Shane's expression of gratitude was replaced with exasperation. "I'm gonna run out for a few hours. Kelly is coming over to be with you."

"Cool. He's kickin'."

"Right. When are you gonna get back to your studies?"

"I'm just takin' a break, man. You don't get breaks down at that duck farm where you work?"

"Yeah, I get breaks. I'll be back before midnight."

"Solid."

Shane left the room, got his coat, collected his badge, and grabbed one of the bagged dry-cleaned shirts, which he had hung in the closet. He headed out the back door.

As the garage door was going up, a car's headlights pulled in right behind him, blocking his exit. He put a hand on his belt holster and cautiously moved toward the driveway. As he rounded the back of his car, he could see Barbara Molar's red Mustang convertible. When she turned off her headlights, he saw her behind the wheel, a scarf tied around her hair.

"Shit, Barbara, whatta you doing here?"

"I had to come over. I couldn't reach you. Your machine was off and your cell phone is out of service."

"If they catch us together, *I'm* gonna be out of service," he said quickly.

"Shane, I'm getting phone calls at the house. Spooky calls. I'm being threatened."

"Go park a few blocks away. Lock up. I'll drive over and pick you up."

She nodded and followed his instructions. Shane got behind the wheel and backed the Acura out. He drove up East Channel Street to where Barbara was standing, her arms wrapped around her, shivering slightly in the cold marine air. She had put up the

Mustang's top and, he hoped, locked the car. Shane reached over and threw open the passenger door. Barbara got in. He put the Acura in gear and pulled off East Channel to a side street, keeping one eye on his rearview mirror.

"Who's calling?" he finally asked. He could tell she was panicked. Her features were drawn; she seemed even more pale than normal.

"It's a man's voice. He just says, 'If you've got what we want, turn it over, or you'll pay the consequences.' Stuff like that. Then a couple of calls where there was just breathing first, then somebody said, 'Do the right thing, bitch,' and hung up."

Shane pulled to the curb and parked. "That means they still haven't found what they're looking for."

"I'm scared."

"So am I."

She looked at the shirt between them on the front seat. "Is this one of Ray's?"

"Yeah. The laundry is in Arrowhead."

"Arrowhead?"

"You got any idea why he'd have his shirts cleaned all the way up there?"

"None."

"It doesn't make much sense," Shane said. "He was driving the mayor. Arrowhead is two hours out of L.A."

"Maybe the mayor had personal business there."

"Maybe."

"What are you going to do?"

"I was just heading up to Lake Arrowhead to talk to the cleaner. I wanna see what I can find out from the guy. They have customer information on the bar code of this laundry tag." He held up the shirttail with the purple tag attached.

"I wanna go with you. And don't tell me no. I'm scared. I can't go home. Those calls are terrifying me."

"Barbara, the DA is contemplating indicting me for murder.

My motive, they think, is that I killed Ray to be with you. If we get caught riding around together, I will be trying to explain it in court."

"Take me with you," she said again. "Please. I need company. I'm shaking."

Kinetic thoughts were buzzing around, bouncing off unanswered questions with pinball energy. Then without really weighing his answer, he just nodded.

"Okay," he said impulsively, and put the car in gear. They headed up the street.

Shane turned right onto Washington Boulevard, which took him to the 405, then north to the 10, which would lead them east toward San Bernardino and Lake Arrowhead.

■ ■ ■

The road was narrow and winding. His headlights swept across shadowy tree trunks that lined the two-lane highway in the Angeles Mountains. Shane had his eye on the road, but his mind was on Ray Molar.

Barbara sat silently beside him. She had started the trip with a lot of chitchat, then had tried to swing the conversation to her future, what she would do with her life now that Ray was gone. Then she made the leap to how Shane was feeling, how he felt about her and about them.

Shane had deflected it all, keeping his answers short. He was beginning to suspect that Barbara had some hidden agenda, but he couldn't yet tell what it was. Maybe it was just his cop instincts that distrusted everything. But something was telling him to pull back—to defend his perimeter.

While she talked, he had been thinking about the night of the shooting: the two critical minutes from the time he'd gone into that bedroom to the moment he had peeled the Nine at Ray. Something in his Letter of Transmittal had stuck in his mind. The department had accused him of inappropriate use of force, of bad judgment, which had escalated the situation out of control. *Had he fucked up? Why had he taken his gun? Had he anticipated shooting Ray? Had he acted out of policy? Was there a way he could have prevented Ray's death?* The only other witness to the event was sitting next to him, so after weighing the consequences, Shane gingerly broached the subject.

"Barb . . . the night I shot Ray . . . how well do you remember it? You looked almost unconscious, as if he had stunned you with that blow to the head."

"I remember it all. It's indelible. It's branded in my memory," she said bitterly.

"Do you think I had any other choice but to shoot him?"

"What are you talking about?"

"If I'd called in some uniforms, would it have made a difference?" he asked.

She turned in her seat and looked directly at him. "You mean, if you had called in a 415? Would it have changed things?" she said, using the cop's radio code for a general disturbance, the majority of which ended up being domestic disputes.

"Yeah. What if two blues had come through that door instead of me, Ray's ex-partner, your old boyfriend . . . do you think it would have changed anything?" He was straining to hear her answer as he drove, straining to evaluate any nuance in her voice.

"Are you joking?" she said, snorting the words derisively. "He was insane." She was incredulous now. "Ray was crazy. *You* know it. *I* know it. He went nuts on spec. Once he snapped, he didn't care what he did or who he did it to. It wouldn't have mattered if Robocop or Pope John Paul himself had come through that door."

"Do you think if I'd held fire that he—"

"If you'd held fire, Shane, you and I would both be dead, and somebody else would have the fucking coffin decorations. You can't be serious."

He looked over at her and could see that she was almost angry about it. Finally he nodded. "Yeah, okay," he said. "I was just wondering."

She shook her head in amazement, and they remained silent the rest of the way to Lake Arrowhead.

The two-lane highway led into a small, lush, wooded valley and then descended into the beauty of Lake Arrowhead. A-frame houses and log-cabin architecture dotted the roadside.

The buildings on the main street were rustic, the sidewalks narrow. They found Pine Tree Lane, and Shane pulled up to Mountain Cleaners. He and Barbara got out, entered, and found Larry Wright.

After Shane showed his badge, he gave Mr. Wright the shirt. The man walked into the back, leaving Shane and Barbara standing alone in the neon overhead lighting, looking into the area where the finished dry-cleaning hung on a moving conveyor belt. In less than two minutes, Mr. Wright returned.

"Got it." He smiled at them. "These were done for Jay Colter. He lives at 1276 Lake View Drive.

"Then they're not Ray's?" Barbara said.

Shane waved her off, then reached into his pocket and pulled out an old photograph he had brought of himself and Ray when they were both working together in Southwest. The picture had been taken in a bar. They were EOW in plain clothes and had their arms around each other's shoulders, grinning drunkenly at the camera. "Is this Jay Colter?" Shane asked, handing the picture to Mr. Wright.

He looked at the shot and nodded. "Little heavier now, but that's him."

"You know what he was doing up here?"

"Well, I only talked to him once. Seems to me he said he was a builder, or in construction, maybe. . . . A builder, I think it was."

"Okay, thanks, Mr. Wright. That's a big help."

They moved out of the cleaners and stood on the curb under

a streetlight. "What's going on?" she asked. "Jay Colter? Why would he change his name?"

"When we were partnered, Ray told me once that if I ever worked undercover and was going to use an alias, I should choose a name that sounds close to my own. So if somebody calls out to you using your assumed name, you will react to it, instead of forgetting it's your alias. For instance, a good a.k.a. for Shane Scully might be Lane MacCully."

"And Ray Molar would be Jay Colter. But why?"

"Let's go see who lives at 1276 Lake View Drive," he said.

BADGER GAMES

THEY FOUND the address on Lake View Drive. Shane drove the black Acura slowly past the house. The small cabin-style bungalow was lit up. They could see men moving around inside.

"What do you think they're doing?" Barbara asked as Shane slowed the car but didn't stop. He pulled up the street and turned left at the first intersecting road. He drove half a block up, parked, and turned off the headlights.

"Who are they? What're you gonna do?" Barbara pestered as Shane got his zoom-lens camera out of the trunk.

"Stay here," he ordered, and quickly moved down to Lake View, then crept along the sidewalk toward the target house. He heard something behind him and spun around. Barbara was hovering nearby.

"Go back. This could be dangerous."

"Maybe I know one of them," she said.

Shane realized that it was a good thought, so he nodded, then put a finger up to his mouth for silence. They crept along, slower this time, finally getting to a position of advantage behind a hedge across the street from the lake cabin. Shane put the zoom-lens camera to his eye and adjusted the focus, bringing the small house closer.

Through the front window he could see men moving around, carrying boxes and emptying drawers. He snapped a few pictures with the flash off, hoping that if he pushed it in the lab, he would get adequate resolution in spite of the low light. Through the viewfinder, he could see the men clearly. He didn't recognize any of them.

"What d'you see?" she whispered in his ear.

"They're tossing the place, looking for something, same as at your house," he said softly, handing her the camera. "You recognize anyone?" After a minute she shook her head and handed the camera back.

They continued to watch the house for another twenty minutes. Several times one or two of the men carried a cardboard box out and set it near the back door. Shane used up an entire roll of film, and then finally the men turned off the lights, locked up the house, and carried the boxes down to the little dock on the lake.

Shane moved out from behind the hedge, with Barbara at his heels. He ran in a crouch until he got to the side of the house, in time to see the men load the boxes into a small, old-style, wooden reproduction Chris-Craft, with varnished sides and teak decking. They all jumped aboard, and the boat's engine roared. It pulled away from the dock and sped off across the lake, leaving a white-foam wake that glistened in the mountain moonlight.

"Shit," Shane said, "I was hoping they had a car parked around here so we could follow them."

He turned and moved back to the house. He tried the doors. They were all locked. Then he took out a pocketknife. He crept onto the wooden back deck that overlooked the lake, and inserted the blade into the sliding glass door. Slowly he pushed the latch up, then slid the door open. He and Barbara stepped cautiously into the small two-bedroom house.

Shane moved to the back hallway and turned on a light. It threw a low glow into the front room and would slightly illuminate most of the rooms in the small house. He didn't want to light up the whole place and call attention to their presence.

"What're we looking for?" Barbara whispered.

"Evidence that Ray lived here or used this place," he said.

"Y'mean like this," she said, picking up a small framed photograph off the living-room TV. It was Ray with his arm around a very pretty dark-haired woman. They were both laughing, holding up glasses of champagne. Slightly out of focus in the background was a small wooden church with a sign that read:

THE MIDNIGHT WEDDING CHAPEL
LAS VEGAS, NEVADA

Barbara looked at the picture, and her expression turned dark. "Is this what I think it is?" she asked sharply. "Is this a fucking wedding photo?"

"I don't know." He removed the picture from the frame and put it in his pocket.

They moved through the house. The cottage appeared to be some kind of party pad. Both bedrooms sported huge king-size waterbeds, complete with ceiling mirrors. Shane looked around, opening drawers, searching closets. All were now empty; everything had been removed. When he got to the guest bedroom, he noticed that the closet seemed very shallow, with no hanging rods. He tapped on the back wall. It sounded hollow. He searched around the edges of the closet wall until he found a small kickplate near the floor. He touched it with his toe, and the back wall of the closet opened on a spring hinge. He pushed "the wall" and found that he was in a small, dark area, about six by ten feet. From where he was standing, he was looking through a glass window, directly into the master bedroom.

"Barbara," he called to her, "go into the master bedroom and stand by the bed."

"Okay," she called from the kitchen, where she had been searching the cupboards. She went into the bedroom, and he could see her clearly through the window in the wall in front of him.

"Go to the mirror over the dresser," he said. She walked to the dresser and was now standing only a few feet away, looking directly at him through a one-way mirror.

"Where are you?" she asked.

"In here, in the guest bedroom."

She moved away from the mirror, exited the master bedroom, and in a minute was pushing the wall open and entering the small back closet he had discovered. Shane found the overhead light and flipped it on. The room was empty except for a vacant bookshelf.

"What is this?" she asked.

"Glory hole," Shane said, using the cop term for any opening used for sexual spying. He began looking around the secret room. Finally he pulled an empty bookshelf away from the wall. He found two videotape boxes that had slipped down behind the shelf and had been missed. He picked them up—they were empty. One of the boxes was not labeled, but the other had a name written on the spine:

CARL CUMMINS

"What were they doing?"

"Looks like some kind of variation on the Badger Game. They get a guy up here, have a party, videotape the funny stuff, then blackmail him."

"Ray was doing this? Ray and that girl?"

"I don't know. I'm not sure. Early in an investigation, it's best not to jump to any conclusions," he said. "Are there any Baggies in the kitchen?"

"Yeah, that kitchen is completely stocked," she said.

They moved out of the videotape room and into the kitchen. Barbara found a large Baggie, and Shane dropped the videotape box into it while she held it open. Then he pulled the photo out of his pocket and dropped it in, too. Suddenly they heard the back door open, and froze.

"In there," he whispered, pointing to the pantry.

A breathless moment, then the light Shane had turned on in the back hallway went off. The house was thrown into darkness.

As they crouched in the darkened pantry, Shane slipped his service revolver out of his belt holster and pulled the hammer back. He held the Smith & Wesson .38-caliber roundwheel out in front of him with both hands, using a two-hand Weaver grip. He could hear three, maybe four men conducting a careful search, looking for them. One of the men moved into the kitchen.

"In here, Cal," the man called out. The kitchen lights went on, exposing Shane and Barbara cowering in the back of the pantry. Shane aimed his revolver at the overhead light and put a round in the fixture, shattering glass and throwing the kitchen back into blackness.

Then all hell broke loose.

Gun muzzles flashed in the darkness. Shane pushed Barbara down, grabbed a can off the pantry shelf, and threw it out into the kitchen. It landed on the counter across the room, and where it hit, shots rang out, breaking glass.

Shane grabbed Barbara's hand and pulled her out of the pantry, into the kitchen. He ran full into one of the men, knocking him down, then heard the man's gun hit the floor and slide on the linoleum. Shane dove into the dining room, pulling Barbara. When they landed, two more shots lit the kitchen with their muzzle flashes as the slugs slammed into the dining-room wall over their heads. Shane rolled off his back, came up into a sitting position, and blindly fired all five of his remaining shots into the kitchen. He heard somebody yell in pain, then there were footsteps running. The back door was thrown open. He could hear people fleeing along the side of the house.

"Barbara, you okay?" he whispered.

"Uh-huh," she replied.

Shane got to his feet. His gun was empty, so he knocked open the revolver, tilted it up and dropped the hot brass into his palm, then quickly dumped the shells into his jacket pocket. He pulled his quick-load off his belt and pushed the six-slug package into his open revolver, then snapped it shut. A speedboat at the dock started, and he heard it roar away.

"Stay there," he said, and stepped into the kitchen, his gun out in front of him, combat-style. He moved slowly across the room and finally found the light switch in the pantry. He flipped it on. Whoever he had hit had left about half a pint of blood behind, but somehow had managed to escape. Then he heard a siren's distant wail across the lake.

"These bohunk sheriffs have even better response time than we do," Shane said. "Let's get outta here."

He had dropped the bagged videotape box in the gun battle, and it took him almost half a minute to find it. On his way out of the kitchen, he saw an answering machine sitting on the counter. He grabbed the entire unit and yanked it out of the wall. Then, leading Barbara, he ran out the side door of the house.

The siren was dangerously close. Shane ran up the street, pulling Barbara along. Suddenly he stopped, reached down, and stuffed the videotape box, camera, and answering machine into an overgrown hedge, wedging it way down, out of sight.

Shane and Barbara sprinted to his car. He got behind the wheel, and they took off. As he streaked out of the side street, he ran right into the headlights of the arriving sheriff's car. Shane jerked the wheel, hit the gas hard, and powered past the black-and-white. The sheriff's car spun a U-turn and came after them.

"What're you doing? Why don't you stop? You're a cop!" Barbara shouted.

Shane didn't answer. He had his hands full and his foot on it, trying to take as many corners as he could to get out of sight of the pursuing police unit.

Finally he made a skidding right turn and accelerated down a narrow street. Bad choice. He had picked a residential cul-de-sac and slammed on the brakes. He started to turn around when the sheriff's car squealed in behind them. The two cops were out instantly, crouching behind their squad-car doors. One had a shotgun resting in the window frame.

"On your stomach, assholes!" the shotgun officer yelled. "Do it now!"

"Do as he says," Shane ordered Barbara. He opened the door, dropped his revolver, and kicked it across the pavement toward the sheriff's car. "LAPD!" he yelled.

"On your stomach, now!" the man repeated. Shane and Barbara did as they were told. In seconds he could feel a sheriff's deputy's hot breath on his neck, and cold steel handcuffs on his wrists. They were ratcheted down hard. In L.A. it was what they called an "adrenaline cuff." His hands were pinned painfully behind his back, then he and Barbara were jerked up onto their feet and shoved into the back of the sheriff's car.

COP SHOP

THE ARROWHEAD SHERIFF'S DEPARTMENT was wedged in between a gas station and a small country market. The parking lot behind the station had three empty Plain Janes.

Shane and Barbara were unloaded from the back of the patrol car and shoved angrily into the station. The two arresting officers were still burning off their chase adrenaline.

Shane was pushed into a chair at the booking desk while Barbara was taken into another room. Separate interviews were always the rule in any half-decent police department. All cops quickly learned that most criminals never expect to get caught. As a result, they rarely have a cover story. One would tell you he was going to the market to get beer; the other would say they were picking up a sick aunt. Separating suspects to take statements was pro forma.

Shane was pissed at himself for making the same dumb mistake as every deadhead felon he had ever busted. He didn't know what Barbara would say, so he planned to tell them the exact truth.

The Arrowhead Sheriff's Department was in turmoil. Earlier that day they had found a dead body in the lake. From what Shane could pick up, it was so decomposed that they hadn't been able to make an ID. In L.A., a dead body was no big deal, but up here an unexplained death was the kind of unusual tragedy it should be everywhere. Shane watched as the tall, balding, fifty-five-year-old sheriff of Arrowhead made multiple calls to the coroner's office. After five minutes he hung up and walked over to Shane. His nameplate read SHERIFF CONKLYN.

"Sorry to add to your problems, Sheriff," Shane said pleasantly.

"What's your story?" Conklyn asked angrily.

"I'm LAPD. I'm up here working on a case."

The sheriff nodded to one of the deputies, who handed Shane's leather ID wallet to Conklyn. He opened it and looked at Shane's tin.

"If you're a cop, why did you run?" the sheriff said, looking at him critically.

"I'm out of my jurisdiction and I didn't take the time to check with you guys like I should have, so I just decided to get small," he said. "Bad choice. Your guys were magnificent."

"Put away the jar of Vaseline," Conklyn said. "You got a CO we can call?"

"I'd really appreciate it if we didn't have to do that," Shane said. "He's not going to be happy."

"It's a big club. I'm not happy." He pointed to his deputies. "They're not happy. You're up here on Lake View Drive, busting caps, and now I've got lots of unhappy people in houses up there. All of a sudden it's like Mexican New Year."

"My captain is Bud Halley," Shane relented. "He's in Southwest Division Robbery/Homicide."

The sheriff took one of Shane's business cards out of his wallet and went to the phone. He talked softly for a minute, waited, then hung up and dialed another number. The second call was taking entirely too long, and Shane's danger lights started flashing. After another minute Sheriff Conklyn moved back and unhooked Shane's cuffs.

"He wants to talk to you," he said.

Shane went behind the counter and picked up the phone. "Captain?"

"It's Tom Mayweather," the deputy chief said in his resonant baritone voice. "Halley transferred this to me 'cause you're in my division now. What the fuck are you doing in Arrowhead, Scully?"

"Sir, something is definitely not right. Ray had a second house up here and another identity, maybe even a second wife."

"Says who?"

"Sir, a dry cleaner identified his picture and gave us the alias he was using. His picture was inside the house, on top of the TV."

"Scully, you are really pissing me off. Read your fucking badge; it says LAPD. You're ninety miles out of your jurisdiction with Ray Molar's widow, engaging in a gun battle with who the hell knows who. Then you have the stones to try and tell me Lieutenant Molar had two identities and a second wife. He was assigned to the mayor, for God's sake."

"Sir, I—"

"Shut up!" Mayweather said. "Here's what you do. I'm gonna alibi your fucked-up story with Sheriff Conklyn. He'll cut you and Mrs. Molar loose. Then I want you to leave Arrowhead and drive directly to Los Angeles. I want you to park your car in the Parker Center garage, then turn yourself in to the Homicide Division duty officer. Send her home in a cab. I want this all to happen in less than three hours. Are we straight on this, Sergeant?"

"Yes, sir."

"Put the sheriff back on."

Shane motioned to the sheriff, who took the phone, listened for a minute, then nodded. "No problem," he said, and hung up.

Fifteen minutes later Shane and Barbara were back in the parking lot behind the sheriff's station. Barbara rode in the front seat as one of the arresting deputies drove them back to the Acura and let them out.

"Good luck solving your John Doe murder," Shane said pleasantly.

"Want some advice from a fellow badge carrier?" the deputy said.

"You bet." Shane smiled, trying to be as nonconfrontational as possible.

"Don't ever come back up here."

"Okay, sounds reasonable." Shane put out his hand, but the cop just looked at it.

"All right, then. Good deal," Shane said, pulling his hand back.

He and Barbara got into the Acura and drove away, staying five miles below the speed limit. Shane kept his eyes on the rearview mirror. The squad car was going to follow him all the way out of Arrowhead. He drove slowly down the mountain, until the black-and-white finally turned off and headed back toward town.

Shane pulled over and parked. He looked at his watch.

"What're you doing?" she asked.

"Giving this guy fifteen minutes to forget about us."

"Only fifteen minutes?"

"Small-town cops have short attention spans," he answered, then added, "I hope." They sat and listened to the motor cool.

"What is it?" Barbara said, noticing a frown on Shane's face.

"Those guys in the speedboat? I was thinking, how did they know we were in the house?" Barbara shrugged. "I think the place is bugged. They heard us searching, then they came back, maybe drifted back to the dock, then jumped us."

■ ■ ■

Fifteen minutes later Shane started the Acura and turned around. This time he constructed a cover story.

"Here's the deal. We came back to get gas. We only have half a tank." He pointed to the gauge, and she nodded.

He drove quickly through town, made remembered turns, then found himself back on Lake View Drive. He drove up to the bushy hedge, jumped out, and retrieved the videotape box, camera, and answering machine. He locked them in the trunk, then got back behind the wheel and drove quickly out of the mountains, returning to L.A.

ELECTRONIC EVIDENCE 17

SUSAN AND I can't come to the phone right now, but leave your name and number and, as soon as we can, we'll return your call." *BEEP*. Ray's voice sounded happy and unthreatening. Then there was another beep. "Ray, it's Calvin. Where the fuck are you, man? You gotta call me now." *BEEP*. Then: "Ray, it's Calvin again. The powers that be are asking questions. Don't fuck with love, man." *BEEP*. "Ray, it's Don and Lee. We're on for Saturday night. The Web after dark. Bring the jerseys." *BEEP*. "Ray, it's Burl. Call the special number." Then there were two hang-ups without messages.

Shane and Barbara were listening to the tape in his kitchen. He turned it off after the last message played.

"Burl—that's Chief Burleigh Brewer. . . . He knows about the house in Arrowhead. Shit," Shane growled. "Ray was the mayor's driver; I guess it makes sense that Brewer would be close to what

Ray was doing." Shane was looking down at the answering-machine tape.

"Who are all these other people, and who the hell is Susan?" Barbara asked angrily.

"I don't know. . . . Don, Lee, and Calvin. I never heard of them, either." He thought for a minute. "There were two cops who braced me in the Parker Center garage at six A.M. the morning I shot Ray. I think one of them was named D. Drucker—maybe that's Don. The other was a Hawaiian guy named Kono. Maybe he's Lee or Calvin. I don't know. 'Don't fuck with love.' And 'the Web' . . . 'Bring the jerseys' . . . What's all that?" he said as they traded blank stares.

They stood over the kitchen counter, where the answering machine was plugged in. Finally, Shane changed the subject. "Barbara, look . . . you gotta go home. I'll drive you down to where your car is parked."

"I'm afraid to go home. I can't take any more of those calls."

"There's a good hotel a few miles south of here, in Marina del Rey. I can't remember the name, but you can't miss it. It's on Admiralty Way. Why don't you go check in there?"

"I get the feeling you're throwing me out."

"I'm not throwing you out. I've got Chooch in the guest room. Longboard is sawing z's on the sofa. It's like a men's dorm around here. Just check into the hotel. I'll talk to you in the morning."

She turned her face up and kissed him on the mouth. When he didn't fully respond, she pulled back and looked at him carefully. "Are you sending me a message, friend?" she asked with an edge in her voice.

"Barbara, let's not confuse this more than it is. We need to focus on what's going on—who's behind this."

"If you promise that you'll let us happen again, once it's over."

"Of course I promise," he said, forcing it. "You know how

much I want that." His words hung in the kitchen, bright and empty, like a broken piñata.

"What're you going to do?" she finally asked.

"I'm gonna get this tape analyzed by the Electronics Section at SIS."

"You don't need a voice print. It's Ray's voice, believe me. I recognize it."

"I know it's Ray. I'm more interested in seeing what else is on here. Answering-machine tapes are used, erased, and rerecorded on. Sometimes there are old messages hiding there. I'm gonna see what the ESIS can pull off the erased portions," Shane said, referring to the Electronics Scientific Investigation Section.

"Oh," she said softly. Then she squeezed his hand for luck, and they headed out the back door of the house.

He drove her to her red Mustang, parked a block away. She got out of the Acura and unlocked her car door, then leaned down into his open passenger window and smiled at him sadly. "Why do I get the feeling this is over?"

"It's your imagination, Barbara. It's not over. It's on hold."

She kissed her fingertips and gently put them on his cheek. "Night," she said sadly, then got into the red Mustang and drove away.

. . .

Shane drove back to his house and locked up. He decided not to wake Longboard, who was snoring loudly on the sofa. He turned off the light and moved into his bedroom, stripped off his clothes, and wearing only his Jockey shorts, dropped heavily onto his bed. His head felt like a forty-pound medicine ball, worn, seamed, full of cotton and lead. He looked up at the ceiling, closed his eyes, and fought a wave of intense self-pity: *Why can't I catch a fucking break?*

"When did you get home?" Chooch's voice sounded suddenly,

pulling him up from useless thoughts. He opened his eyes and saw the teenager standing in the doorway, wearing a Lakers shirt and baggy shorts.

"I thought you were asleep," Shane said.

"I woke up."

"Well, go back to sleep. You've got school tomorrow."

Chooch didn't move; he had an expression that seemed both frightened and sad.

"What's wrong?"

"Nothin'. It's just . . ."

"What?" Shane turned on his side and looked at Chooch carefully.

"Sandy called. She wants you to call her first thing in the morning."

"Why? What's up?"

"She didn't say."

"She probably just wants to tell me how she smoked your geek principal."

"She didn't call St. John, I asked her. She said she's been involved in a big deal and hasn't had time to get in touch with him yet."

"Right. Well, okay." He lay back on his pillow. "So I'll call her in the morning."

"That means old Thackery musta talked to you, not her. You made him keep me in school."

Shane looked over at Chooch again, then rubbed his eyes and sat up on the bed. "Let's go outside for a minute. I can't sleep with this fucking headache."

"We could light up, toke some bang?" the teenager said hopefully.

"We're through getting high together. I wanna talk to you."

Chooch shifted his weight uncertainly, then nodded. "Okay, sure."

Shane got up, put on his pants and an old sweatshirt, then the two of them moved quietly past Longboard into the backyard. Shane pulled up chairs, and they both sat under a fruitless tangerine tree, looking out at the still canal. The reflection of an almost full moon wavered on the glassy surface.

"What is it?" Chooch asked cautiously.

"I'm in a lot of trouble," Shane started.

"Trouble's the exhaust of life," the fifteen-year-old said surprisingly.

"The trouble I'm in could get dangerous. Some of the people I'm sideways with could decide to make a play. I don't want you to get hurt."

"I'm not afraid." Chooch smiled. "Got your back, bro."

They were silent for a moment, then Shane continued. "I also think it's time for you to get to know your mother. Maybe you haven't given her a chance."

"I hate her," Chooch said softly. "Let's drop this, okay?"

"You can't stay here. When I talk to her tomorrow, I'm going to make arrangements for her to take you back for a week or so."

There was a long silence. Suddenly some crickets started up in the hedge between Shane's and Longboard's yards. They sawed holes in the silence with their back legs.

"I think it's time you gave your mother a break," Shane persisted. "Make me a promise, give it a week. Just five days."

"You're fulla shit, just like Thackery and all those other dickwads. I thought you were never gonna lie to me. I thought we had a deal."

"I'm not lying to you, Chooch. I'm trying to keep you from getting hurt."

"I'm not stupid. I get what's going on here. I've become a problem, an inconvenience, so you wanna throw me out, simplify things for yourself."

"Just one week, till I can get my problems sorted out."

Chooch got up and started into the house. Shane grabbed his arm to stop him, but Chooch yanked it free.

"Look, it's not . . . I'm not trying to get rid of you."

"Eat me!" the boy said, defiance and pain shining in his black eyes.

"I care what you think," Shane said. "It matters to me. We need to talk this out."

"You came close. You almost had me fooled, but I got it straight now. I finally got it . . . nothing's changed. It's just like it always was—I can only count on myself. So fuck off."

Chooch walked back into the house. Shane's head was still pounding. No matter which way he turned, he saw disaster. He didn't know what to do next, so he went inside and wrote a letter to his father.

THE
ARROWHEAD
LETTER

Dear Dad,

I hate to admit it, but I'm really scared. Something big and dangerous is going on, and I have the feeling if I don't figure it out soon, I will be destroyed by it. The answer is in that Lake Arrowhead house. Why would Chief Brewer call a location where Ray was committing some kind of sexual blackmail? Who is Carl Cummins? That name isn't in either the Arrowhead or the L.A. phone book. I need to get the answers to some of these questions fast. I'm running out of time. Why do I feel it all closing in? Dad, I'm losing it. I sense disaster coming. I need to talk to somebody.

I know my problems are the last thing you need right now, but please give me a call.

I love you, Dad, and miss you. I'm scared and lonely. You're all I have left.

Your son,
Shane

CLERICAL DIVISION

THEY PULLED UP in front of the Harvard Westlake School at eight the next morning. It was half an hour before the other students would arrive. Chooch got out, dragged his book bag off the front seat, and walked away from the car without looking back. He hadn't spoken all the way there. He had completely tuned Shane out.

Three times before leaving the house, Shane had tried to get through to Sandy but had reached only her machine. As he pulled away from the school, he dialed her number again.

"Hi, you've reached 555-6979. I'm not in, but you know what to do," announced the recording in her furry contralto voice. Shane didn't leave a third message. He closed his phone and headed back to Internal Affairs.

He pulled into the parking structure adjacent to the Bradbury and used his newly issued employee-parking card. The arm went up, and he found his assigned space on the third level.

He was just getting out of his car when he saw Alexa Hamilton five spaces away, removing a heavy cardboard case-file box out of the trunk of her plainwrap. A few Metro sergeants and special players in the department still had these prized vehicles instead of the hated slickbacks. Alexa's was a new dove-gray Crown Victoria with blackwalls and red velour upholstery. Crown Vics were senior staff vehicles, and hers was prima facie evidence that Sergeant Hamilton had top-shelf department "suck."

She slammed her trunk lid and started carrying the box to the elevators. Shane didn't want to ride down with her, but she had seen him and they were both heading toward the elevators, destined to arrive within seconds of each other. For him to veer off now or pretend he forgot something and divert back to his car would be a chickenhearted admission of weakness, so he kept walking and arrived a few seconds behind her. She had balanced the heavy cardboard box full of case files on her knee so she could push the elevator button with her free hand. She looked over at him with those slanted, exotic chips of laser-blue ice—poker player's eyes that cut holes through him but revealed nothing in return.

"Need help with that?" he asked, hating himself for even offering, the question inadvertently slipping out of him in an anxious attempt to fill the awkward silence.

"Wouldn't that be sorta like asking a condemned man to carry his own ax to the chopping block?"

"Hardy-har," he said sourly. It surprised him that the box was so full. She'd been on the case for only forty-eight hours. "That can't be all me."

"All you. And this is just '92 to '96. 'Ninety-four seemed like a fun-packed year, all those civilian complaints . . . the second unit-destroying traffic accident coming in April after the first-of-the-month kick down to Southwest Traffic."

"You had to be there."

The elevator arrived and they got in. The door closed, and as they rode down, Shane kept looking into the open box with the morbid curiosity of a freeway rubbernecker passing a fatal accident. All of his mid-nineties career pileups were collected there. He spotted a bunch of his old 7.04 ADAM control cards, which were identification sheets for radio-message logs. It shocked him. She was actually reading his old radio transmissions. He couldn't believe it. He also saw two manila envelopes from the Traffic Division that he assumed detailed the two unit-wrecking collisions he'd had while he was in Southwest Patrol. Wedged down in the side of the box were dozens of 8.49 out-slips, which were like library cards from Records and Identification. She was pulling all of his old arrest reports. The rest of the box was littered with field-interview cards and DR numbered witness statements filed by the IOs working his case. He was staring down into the box with growing dread.

"Jesus Christ, what's with the fucking rectal exam?"

"And you don't even have to grab your ankles," she said, shifting the box away from his stare. She was still balancing the heavy box on her knee as the elevator door opened.

Shane moved out without looking back at her. He had a tinny taste in his mouth as he pushed open the double doors at the back of the Bradbury Building and hurried through. He heard them swing closed behind him, right in Alexa Hamilton's face. She must have been trying to slip in with the file box before the doors closed and mistimed it, because he heard the heavy oak frame hit her hands, which were clutching the leading edge of the box.

"Shit!" she said as the door bounced off her knuckles.

Shane now had his own key to Room 256; he let himself in and turned on the stark neon overhead lights. They blasted a harsh, unfriendly blue-white glare down on the three Xerox machines. He dropped his coat on the back of the chair and glanced at his watch. It was 8:32. Since no deputy chief ever got in before nine, he took a chance and picked up the phone, dialing the number for Parker Center.

"LAPD Parker Center," a cheerful woman's voice greeted him.

"Deputy Chief Tom Mayweather," he said, and a few seconds later got Mayweather's secretary.

"Is he in?"

"Who's calling, please?"

His heart was beating fast. Once he identified himself, if Mayweather was in, he'd either have to talk or hang up; neither was an acceptable choice. What he wanted was just to leave an ass-covering message. "It's Sergeant Shane Scully," he finally answered, holding his breath.

"I'm sorry, Sergeant, he's at a breakfast meeting."

"Breakfast meeting" was department bullshit for "not in yet." Shane let out a chestful of air.

"It's really important that I talk to the chief," he lied, laying it on a little.

"I'm sorry," she said. "Can I give him a message?"

"Will you tell him I've been trying to get in touch with him, please? Tell him I was unable to get to Robbery/Homicide last night as he ordered because I fell asleep driving down from Arrowhead. Crashed the car, broke my front fender. It was dangerous to drive when I was that tired, so I stopped in a motel. I just woke up. I have some errands to take care of when I get home, so tell him I'll get in touch with him later."

"I'll be sure he gets the update." She hung up.

Shane hoped the phone call would give him a little cover.

He looked at his IN box and found half a dozen new cases that had been left for him to copy. He started to pull them out, and as he was arranging them in stacks on the worktable, his eyes scanned each face sheet.

He was surprised to see that Don Drucker had made this morning's lineup. Apparently Drucker was scheduled for a full board as well. Under the face sheet was an internal notification slip that informed Drucker's defense rep that his board had just been postponed from April 20 until April 23, as requested. The face sheet had the IAD case number and had been signed by the head of Special Investigations Division, Deputy Chief T. Mayweather.

"What the fuck?" he said softly, thinking, *Why was the head of the division signing these charge sheets instead of Warren Zell, here at IAD?* Then he picked up his phone and dialed the Clerical Division. He asked for and was transferred to a civilian employee who was a longtime friend.

Sally Stonebreaker was nothing like her name . . . a sparrow of a woman with a Transylvanian complexion, translucent skin, and thin white hair. Shane had met her in municipal court nine years ago. He'd been testifying in a robbery case, and she was getting a restraining order against her ex-husband in the courtroom next door. Al Stonebreaker had beaten her twice and had been threatening her over disputed alimony payments. That same night Shane had looked him up and explained the new rules. The "discussion" had taken place in the alley behind a neighborhood bar and required Al to get half a dozen stitches and some new bridgework. After that, Al Stonebreaker had left Sally alone.

Shane got Sally on the line. Once he identified himself, he could hear a little pause before she went on.

"I'm sorry about what's going on," she finally said. "Ray Molar was some piece of work."

"Sally, I need you to do a computer run. I'm sort of locked off the system now, and I don't want a record of this search anyway."

"Shane, I'm busy right now." She paused, then added, "Besides, they've got new DataLocks on our consoles and it's real hard to access the mainframe without a case clearance number," she said, trying to shake him. He was already department poison.

"Sally, I need this favor. You've gotta come through for me."

Another long pause, during which he could hear her breathing. "Okay, but only this once. After that, I can't do it again."

"Thanks. I've got an IAD complaint investigation CF number for a Board of Rights on a policeman one in Southwest, named Don Drucker. I need to find out what IAD is trying him for. The number is 20-290-12."

"Just a minute."

He could hear computer keys clicking, then she came back on the line.

"He's been charged under a 670.5 of the PDM," she said.

"What is that? Six hundred codes are like booking and prisoner-escape violations, right?" There were hundreds of numbered codes listed in the five-hundred-page LAPD manual.

"Yeah. Escaped juvenile. Drucker lost him in transit, prior to booking. Gimme a minute to read this," she said. Then a moment later she came back on the line. "Okay. Prisoner was a teenage Hispanic named Soledad Preciado, arrested in Southwest. According to Drucker's Internal Affairs complaint, he left the arrestee unattended in the back of his squad car while he went into a drugstore. Drucker claims he was having a migraine and needed to fill a prescription, said he couldn't drive with the headache and was getting nauseous. While he was in the drugstore, Sol Preciado got out of the unit and walked away."

"Was this kid, by any chance, a Hoover Street Bounty Hunter?"

"Just a minute," she said, and her computer keys were clicking again. She came back on. "A suspected Bounty Hunter, age fifteen. He claimed he's not in a gang, but he's listed in the Gang Street Alias Index under the name Li'l Silent, so at the very least he's a TG or a known associate." TG stood for "tiny gangster" and was basically a killer in training. Shane knew you didn't usually get a street name unless you'd already been "jumped in the set," so it figured he was probably a full member.

"Can you punch out another name for me?"

"I gotta go, Shane. My supervisor's a great white. All he does is swim and eat. Right now, he's cruising this floor."

"Sally, I need help. I hate to put it this way, but I helped you once, now you gotta do this for me." He could hear her sigh loudly on the other end of the phone.

"Okay, gimme it." She was getting mad.

"A policeman one, his name is Kono. I don't have his first name. Check him to see if he's got an Internal Affairs complaint." He was shooting with his eyes closed, firing on instinct.

"You got a CF number?" Sally asked, frustration in her voice. "It'll make it a lot easier."

"I'm sorry, this is just a hunch. There may not even be a board pending on him."

He could hear keys clicking again, then: "Yeah. Kris Kono. He's got a CF number, 20-276-9."

"No shit," Shane said, his heart beating fast now. He wasn't sure what was tugging on the end of this line, but he'd definitely hooked something. "What's IAD got him for?"

"It's . . . lemme see . . ." She was quiet as she scanned the file for a few minutes, then: "It was a gang fight, also in Southwest. Two bystanders got shot. A store owner died. Kono got the BOR 'cause he lost some key evidence. In this case, the murder weapon disappeared from the trunk of his squad car. The case got pitched by the judge at the prelim. The dead store owner's wife complained, and this complaint has a bunch of community affidavits attached. A city councilwoman in that district is on a tear. I process Southwest complaints on my terminal. The division started heating up about six months ago. Gang-related crime is soaring. The community is getting pissed down there."

"Was the Kono blown bust also H Street Bounty Hunters?"

"Yeah . . . same as Drucker."

"Two more names: Lew Ayers and John Samansky. I think they're operating in Southwest, too."

"I can't. I gotta go. I'm gonna get in trouble."

"Just tell me if these guys all worked on the same patrol shift or if you see any other common denominators."

"It's Southwest. That's all I can tell you. Look, Shane, I can't—"

"Okay, thanks, Sally. You've been a big help."

He hung up and sat silently in the Xerox room. His mind was chewing it, looking for the connection. Joe Church, Don Drucker, and Kris Kono were all first-year cops, emotionally distraught over Ray's death, and all had fucked up on cases involving the Hoover Street Bounty Hunters, a Hispanic gang in Southwest Division. Ayers and Samansky were policemen working Southwest, but had searched Barbara's house in Harbor Division, using a warrant supplied by a Mayor Crispin–owned judge. They were also highly emotional over Ray.

He sat in the wooden chair and tried to put it together. *What had he stumbled into? Was this just a bunch of stupid coincidences, or something much more sinister?* His phone rang. He looked over at it as if it were a coiled snake. Finally he picked it up.

"Yeah."

"Chief Mayweather calling Shane Scully," the chief's secretary said.

"Scully just left. He wasn't feeling good. Got the flu, I think. If I see him, I'll tell him the deputy chief was trying to reach him," he said, and after she bought it, he hung up quickly. He grabbed his coat and left the Internal Affairs Xerox room, locking the door behind him. He passed up the slow-moving elevators and hurried down the stairs. In less than a minute he was back in his Acura and driving out of the parking structure on his way to the Records Division on Spring Street.

DEN

O N HIS WAY across town, Shane dropped off the roll of film he had taken at Arrowhead. He told the man at the Fotomat that he wanted one set of normal prints and, if they didn't come out, a set with the negative pushed two stops. He was told that pushing the negative could permanently destroy the film, but he okayed it. The man behind the counter told him the film would have to be sent out and wouldn't be ready for six to twelve hours.

Shane drove to the Records Division and parked in the big asphalt lot on Spring Street. He locked the Acura and moved around the front, trying hard not to look at the bashed-in fender. He walked through the door of the large three-story brick building and climbed the stairs to the Criminal Division, where he sat at a table and filled out a records release request.

In order to access Soledad Preciado's criminal offender record information (CORI), Shane had to fill out a right-to-know/need-to-know CORI release form. Those persons defined in the California penal code with right- and need-to-know authorization included the juvenile court, Social Services, and members of the Special Investigations Section, which now, technically, included Shane Scully, its new unit discovery officer. Since it is specifically mandated that automated and manually stored CORI information not be electronically distributed, Shane had to be at the Spring Street building to tender his request in person.

Juvenile records are further restricted by the Department of Public Social Service (DPSS) and can be reviewed only by order of a juvenile court judge or the Los Angeles County Children's Services Department (LACCSD). However, the Special Investigations Division was exempted. . . . Shane was beginning to view his transfer to Internal Affairs in a more favorable light. Since Sol's case was part of Don Drucker's Internal Affairs investigation and had a Special Investigations CF number, Shane included that number and fraudulently listed himself as the case IO. He handed the paperwork to the clerk, a small, narrow-shouldered man with wispy blond hair combed over a yarmulke-sized bald spot. Shane hoped that the man was too bored to check the request against his badge number.

A few minutes later a manila envelope was passed over. Shane unwound the string tie, pulled out Soledad (Sol) Preciado's Criminal Records folder, and opened it. For a fifteen-year-old, Soledad had a very extensive yellow sheet. His arrest record included two CCWs (carrying a concealed weapon), one assault with intent to commit, and one attempted murder. He'd been down twice: once for a year at the Pitchess youth camp on the attempted murder, once for six months at CYA on a parole violation. Sol Preciado had definitely been out there flagging with the homies. Shane kept reading and finally came across the incident involving the escape from Drucker's patrol car, which was there by virtue of the department's Alpha Index Criminal History cross-reference system. He scanned Drucker's commanding officer's review. At the end of the page he saw that Preciado had not been originally arrested by Don Drucker. He had been called in later only to handle Sol's transport to Los Padrinos Juvenile Hall, which was all the way across town at 2285 East Quill Drive, in Downey. It was unusual for the arresting officer not to transport his own prisoner. Shane wondered why it had happened. He started flipping back, looking for the original arresting officer's report. He finally found it; Preciado had been arrested on November 12 by Sergeant Mark Martinez. Shane scanned the arrest report.

Sol Preciado, a.k.a. Li'l Silent, had been alleged to be committing multiple assaults outside the L.A. Coliseum (court appearance pending). The crimes occurred at about 12:30 P.M. as people were streaming in for the USC–Oregon State football game. He had assaulted several women, knocking them down and snatching their purses. Events escalated when a man trying to stop him was knifed in the abdomen, allegedly by the enraged fifteen-year-old. Preciado had been apprehended by Sergeant Martinez, a member of the Coliseum Division police unit.

Since Martinez was working a duty station and could not leave, Drucker had been dispatched to the Coliseum to pick up Soledad Preciado, then subsequently lost him on his way to the city jail with the ill-advised stop at the drugstore for a headache prescription. The report said that Preciado had somehow managed to open the handcuffs and escape.

There was a statement by Drucker describing his chronic migraine headaches, which had become unbearable and had caused him to stop for medication. He had listed several police officers who could attest to his medical problem. At the very top of that list was Lieutenant Raymond Molar, whom Drucker identified as his LAPD den leader.

Shane put down the arrest report and picked up the phone on the scarred wooden desk. He redialed the Clerical Division and, after a moment, had Sally Stonebreaker back on the line.

"Aren't you happy it's me again," he said, trying to put a friendly smile in his voice. It didn't work.

"Good-bye, Shane."

"Sally, don't hang up. This will just take a minute. Nobody else can help me."

"You've gotta leave me alone, for God's sake. I can't do this."

"One little, teeny favor. Just one. Take you thirty seconds. Take you fifteen."

"Oh, shit," she groaned, but he knew he had her.

"I just found out Ray Molar was a den leader, and I need to know who was in his den." He could hear a loud sigh for emphasis.

"Okay, but this is absolutely it. You call me again, I'm hanging up."

"Thanks, Sally, and don't get hit by the flower truck 'cause it's on its way."

"Don't send me flowers, just stop calling."

He heard the keys clicking as she entered Ray's name into the computer. After a moment she came back on the line. "He had a den in Southwest. Get a pencil, these are his cubs . . ."

Shane grabbed a pen out of his pocket and turned over the manila folder. "Go."

"A full pack. There's six: Lee Ayers, John Samansky, Coy Love, Joe Church, Don Drucker, and Kris Kono. Don't call again." And he was listening to a dial tone. No good-bye, no good luck, just a click and a buzz.

But he'd hit the lottery. The connection between all these first-year officers was Ray's police den.

A few years back, the LAPD had instituted an innovative concept called den policing. The department had discovered that it was difficult to go from civilian life into police work. After graduation from the academy, rookies were assigned a den leader to help them make the transition. As civilians, many of them had never experienced the discrimination and hatred that some elements of society aim at its sworn badge carriers. Often, particularly in the first year on the job, officers were totally unprepared for the abuse heaped on them. It was difficult not to respond when someone called you a pig and spit on you or your police car. Many cops ended up losing their tempers and resorting to violence. The idea of a den was to have a veteran officer who had perspective on the problems of police work assigned as a kind of emotional coach to help these rookies through their transition year. Den leaders were not commanding officers or watch commanders; they were not responsible for the officer's performance, only for his emotional stability.

Suddenly Shane could understand why these cops were hovering over Ray's death. He had been their coach; their confidant, their police department godfather. It was a piece of connective tissue that jerked the hostile emotional attitudes of the six officers into focus.

But it still left several more difficult questions unanswered: Why was Chief Brewer using Ray's old den to lean on him, and why were they all facing charges at Internal Affairs? What was the Hoover Street Bounty Hunter connection, and why were these six officers all involved in broken cases concerning that one Hispanic Southwest Division gang?

Shane sat there at the table, deep in thought. After a minute the narrow-shouldered wisp of a man who had given him the folder was hovering again. "You through with that?" he asked.

"Yeah." Shane handed back the folder, with the names of Ray's den still scribbled on the back. The clerk hurried away with it.

Shane was not sure what to do next or where to go. He couldn't return to IAD; he was dodging Mayweather. He didn't want to go home and just sit, taking the chance that the deputy chief would send a patrol unit out there to arrest him.

Finally, because he couldn't think of a better course of action, he decided to check in with DeMarco Saint.

...

It was not even ten-thirty in the morning when he got there, and DeMarco was already drunk. Shane was standing in the defense rep's living room, watching him struggle to get up off his sofa. He almost made it but fell awkwardly, catching himself painfully by an elbow on the coffee table.

"Whoa . . ." the defense rep said as he tried once more, this time managing to stumble to his feet. Two young boys, about fifteen, were lounging on the sofa on each side of him, watching the proceedings with glazed indifference.

"The fuck's wrong with you?" Shane asked, looking at his teetering defense rep. "How can you be wasted? It's not even noon."

"Had a few bubblies. Hit me harder'n I thought." DeMarco grinned. "Shane, meet the guys—Billy an' Mark. Guys, meet Shane. They just moved in. Been sleeping under the fuckin' pier. I'm helpin' 'em out."

They looked right through him, no change of expression. He wasn't even a blip on their radar. Anybody in a tie over thirty was in a parallel dimension and didn't exist for them.

"We gotta talk. Let's go." Shane grabbed DeMarco's arm and tried to drag him out of the house. The two fifteen-year-olds rose up to protect their new landlord.

"Sit down!" Shane growled menacingly, and they did.

"S'okay," DeMarco slurred. "Lez go . . . jus' don' yank on me."

They left the house and walked out onto the sand. It was a bright Southern California day. DeMarco groaned painfully as the sunlight hit him, and he shaded his eyes, wavering badly as he walked. They were twenty yards away from the house when Shane spun him and faced him.

"How can you be fucking drunk, man?"

"Relax, will ya? I was up half the night workin' on your case.

Haven't even been t'bed yet. No food . . . s'why the brews snuck up on me."

"Have you interviewed Barbara, prepared a witness list, contacted Mayweather or Halley to get their sworn affidavits and a copy of the DFAR, sent anything to the subpoena control desk?"

"I . . . I'm . . ."

"The answer is no, 'cause I've been with Barbara and you haven't even called her yet. She's gotta be priority one 'cause if she changes her statement, I'm dust. You gotta lock her in with an affidavit, secure her testimony before you mess with the rest of it. Since I know you know that, you've done nothing."

"Hey, Shane . . . will y'calm down? Okay, just calm down." DeMarco took a step forward and lost his balance and fell down. "Oops," he said, grinning. "Somebody's moving the beach."

"Dee, I was down at IAD this morning. I bumped into Sergeant Hamilton, who is running through my life with spikes on. She's got a box full of every mistake I ever made, even down to my old Patrol Division TAs. She's giving me a fucking sigmoidoscopy, while you're out here getting hammered. We only have eight more days, then we go in front of the board."

"Relax. Okay?" He was trying to get up and not having much luck, so Shane knelt down beside him.

"How can I relax? I'm on the block."

"I don't think Alexa Hamilton really wants to prosecute you. Okay?" He was smiling stupidly.

"That isn't what you said before. You said she'd been in Southwest supervising a patrol watch and came back to Internal Affairs specifically to take my case, that she volunteered for it."

"When I said it, I was trying to duck the case, but now that I have it, I think otherwise."

"She's the queen of the Dark Side. Whatta you mean, she doesn't want to prosecute me?"

"Why d'you think ya won the BOR sixteen years ago?"

"We won because you caught her key witness lying."

"We won 'cause Alexa threw the fuckin' case." He belched and then tried to stand, but again didn't make it.

"She what?"

"She threw th' fuckin' case, went in the tank, intentionally bricked it."

"You never said that before. If she dumped it, you would've told me."

"Hey, winning cases was how I kept my rep hard back then. I din' wanna share the glory. Wha' good's it to win a tough board if the prosecuting advocate throws the fuckin' case? 'Sides, she swore me to secrecy. . . . Said she'd get busted if I tol'."

"I want facts, Dee. I want the whole story. If you're bullshitting . . ."

"Not shitting." He sat back and took a deep breath to clear his head, then went on. "She comes to me like two days 'fore the board and tells me the chief advocate himself, the fuckin' Dark Prince, got a statement from Ray that was devastating to your case."

"Wait a minute. Ray was on my side."

"Grow up, man. Ray was on Ray's side. He didn't wan' any part of your problem, and his statement contradicted yours. Since he was your training officer, it was gonna flat fuckin' sink you." He took a deep breath and rubbed his eyes. "Alexa said she wasn't gonna include Molar's affidavit in the discovery material. Said since the DA took Ray's statement personally, he would insist Ray be called to testify, but Zell wouldn't be aware that Ray's affidavit had accidentally on purpose been left out of discovery." Now he was grinning stupidly again. "She said I should object an' get his testimony stricken, because she had failed to include it, makin' Ray's testimony inad . . . inad . . ."—he belched—"inadmissible at the hearing. Thas wha' happened."

Shane was confused. It didn't add up.

"Then she tells me she thinks the gas-station attendant was lying," DeMarco continued. "Tells me to polygraph him. She impeached her own fuckin' guy, and he was the best part of her case."

"Why? Why would she do that?"

"Maybe she wants your bod."

"Get up." Shane pulled DeMarco up to his feet.

He stood there, weaving drunkenly. "I'm figurin' there's a good chance she's gonna come across again." He grinned.

"You mean you're sitting around, sucking down beers, waiting for her to throw this case, too?"

"I'm not waiting around. I'm bustin' tail, bud. I'm all over this puppy. . . ."

"Okay, Dee, I'm stuck with you because they fast-tracked my board and nobody else will take it on such short notice. Right now I've got something to do, but I'm coming back, unannounced. You better be fuckin' clear-eyed and sober. Next time I'm here, I want a full review of this case, blow by blow. I want your subpoena list and I want to know who you're interviewing. I want to hear your case strategy."

"Done," he said, giggling slightly, shading his eyes, squinting into the sun.

Shane couldn't believe what he was seeing, couldn't believe what DeMarco had just told him. Alexa, with her box full of his career glitches, was hardly going to throw this board, regardless of what happened the last time. He glowered at the wavering defense rep. "We've gotta get our helmets on. If I catch you drunk again, I'll beat the shit out of you. Don't fall down on me, man." Then he turned, leaving the longhaired defense rep teetering badly in the bright sunlight.

THE BLACK WIDOW

AFTER HE LEFT DEMARCO, Shane sat inside the hot Acura in the beach parking lot with the driver-side door open and called Sandy. Surprisingly, this time he got her; she picked up on the third ring.

"Sandy, it's me."

"Shane, it wasn't anywhere near as bad as you thought. I called the school, and they told me there's no problem. Chooch is back in classes."

"Yeah, no problem. What an alarmist I'm becoming. I need to see you today. We need to work out some stuff. I'll be there in half an hour."

"Today's really shitty for me."

"The whole week has been shitty for me," Shane growled. "You're meeting me at noon."

"Can't. I have a lunch engagement."

"Cancel it." He was pissed at DeMarco but taking it out on Sandy.

"It's not that easy," she hedged.

"Cancel the fucking lunch date. I'm gonna be there at noon." He hung up on her. It was eleven-thirty.

Sandy lived at the Barrington Plaza in Brentwood, in one of two gorgeous penthouse suites. Shane got there in thirty minutes. He pulled up to the overhanging porte cochere and handed the keys for the busted-up Acura to a doorman who had enough braid hanging off his uniform shoulders to lead a Latin American country or the University of Michigan marching band.

"I'll need to announce you, sir," the doorman said, frowning at the bruised Acura parked on his brick entryway, subtracting elegance like a turd on a serving platter.

"Shane Scully for Ms. Sandoval."

The doorman picked up the phone, had a short conversation, then walked with Shane into the lobby and key-carded the elevator for the penthouse level. "You can phone down before you return and I'll have the vehicle brought up." He pronounced the word "vehicle" like an ancient curse.

"Thank you," Shane said. The doors closed and he was alone in the fragrant oak-paneled luxury of the Barrington Plaza elevator, listening to a selection of orchestrated show tunes.

Shane marveled once again at what Sandy had been able to accomplish. When he had met her, he'd been on the job only a little over a year. It was just after he'd been separated from Ray and moved to West Valley Division. The first month in that division he'd been a floater, and because he was a "new face," he had been temporarily assigned to detectives working a bunco scam as an undercover. She had been a top-line L.A. call girl, working an executive clientele. The bunco detectives had been investigating a counterfeit bond trader, and Sandy happened to be balling the guy for a thousand a night. Shane, working UC, had arrested her for prostitution, but then instead of booking her, the bunco squad instructed him to try to "flip" her. He did, and she worked the case for him as an informant. Shane was her contact. She had skillfully pillow-talked the bond trader, allowing Shane and the Valley detectives to expand their investigation. When the bust went down, fifteen bond traders hit the lockup and Shane protected her, managing to keep her from being prosecuted. During that operation she proved that she had guts and savvy and could be counted on in a pinch. Shane became her friend, and one night, a week later over dinner, she suggested that she might be willing to work for the police if the price was right.

"How much do you guys spend to get a big player into court?" she had asked him. "How much overtime and special duty gets approved to bring down a big vice lord or drug kingpin?"

The truth was, often hundreds of thousands of dollars were spent trying to collar a predicate felon, and sometimes even then they failed to come up with an indictment.

Sandy's proposal was shrewd; it showed her keen business mind. She told Shane she would work any target they pointed her at and charge LAPD nothing up front. Despite the upscale nature of her clientele, she was tired of working one-night stands and wanted to expand her horizons. She had two conditions: if successful, she wanted half the amount of money the department had spent on that criminal investigation in the preceding year, and she would not work a target who had an annual police budget of under a hundred thousand dollars. She said she would trust Shane to divulge the correct amount. After almost a month of negotiating with her over terms and conditions, the department finally agreed.

Sandy proved to be exceptional in this new line of work. She was thorough and totally prepared herself before ever moving in on her target. First, she would study the criminal, research him like a doctoral thesis. If he liked Russian literature, she would memorize passages of Solzhenitsyn. If he was interested in Impressionistic art, she would become an expert on Gino Severini's essays, *From Futurism to Classicism*. Then she would set up shop somewhere in his field of vision. One day Mr. Big would be at his favorite country club bar and he'd look across the room and see a dusky, raven-haired goddess sitting at a table alone, reading an art pamphlet detailing the next Impressionist auction at Sotheby's. A conversation would ensue, and this unsuspecting criminal would find that, lo and behold, he had a soul mate, a drop-dead ten on the libido scale who miraculously liked everything he did, from van Gogh to ocean catamaran racing. She became so tuned in, she could finish his sentences.

Before long they would become intimate. Here, Sandy was on her home field. She was a Hall of Fame sexual acrobat. Mr. Big would think he'd won the quiniela. Then Sandy would slowly begin to work him for information. After sex he'd start bragging. He'd fill her beautiful head with his criminal exploits. She'd coo and tell him he was a genius. Once she had his criminal operation down, she would start looking around for a patsy. She knew that when the cops made the arrest, Mr. Big would know he'd been sold out. He might turn violent from his cell, might figure her for the informant and order her killed. To protect herself, Sandy would look around at Mr. Big's criminal companions for a stand-in who could fulfill this unrewarding role.

Before dropping the dime to the police, she would set up the patsy as the informant. She was careful to always pick someone worthy of execution, so the unsuspecting police department wouldn't put too much time into the scumbag's murder. Once she had selected her patsy, she would begin flirting with him, setting up a romantic triangle. Mr. Big would get furious at the patsy: "Stop hitting on Sandy. I catch you putting the make on her again, I'll drop you where you stand." But Sandy was worth the risk, and she'd work both men into steamy jealous rages.

When the bust came down, it didn't take Mr. Big long to figure out who had fingered him. The patsy would end up strolling the tidal basin in concrete loafers while Sandy sat in the jail visitors' room, crying her eyes red and promising Mr. Big that she would be there when he got out.

Because she always destroyed her targets, and a patsy always died, her nickname in the department was "the Black Widow." Like her namesake, she was a great but deadly piece of ass.

She would then present her bill to Shane for this valuable service, and he would be her bagman for the department's payoff. She was L.A.'s most successful consignment concessionaire. It was a fair deal. If she didn't get the goods, the LAPD didn't pay.

In the beginning Shane was the only cop she would trust to be her intermediary. The cases went down smoothly in court because the tip that led to the bust was always anonymous, so it couldn't be traced back to the department. Naturally, the arresting officers didn't even know about the arrangement. Since Sandy never testified in court or told anybody what she had to do to get the goods, it was, strictly speaking, legal. She was paid as an informant—something police do all over the country. It was a very efficient and profitable deal for everybody.

Inevitably, the feds got wind of her and, in their typical, claim-jumping fashion, moved in. Since their budgets were larger and she could make more money with them, they started poaching on the LAPD, and now she was working mostly federal cases.

■ ■ ■

The elevator doors opened, and Sandy was standing in the hall waiting for him. Every time he saw her, he was knocked out all over again. It was as if his memory wasn't able to retain her remarkable physical perfection. She was tall, almost five-ten, and had a spectacular, trainer-sculpted body. She had told him once that her mother was Mexican and her father Colombian, which was responsible for her Latin coloring. She had raven-black hair and coffee-colored skin. Her brown eyes twinkled and danced and said "Take me." She was one of the most attractive, sensual women he had ever laid eyes on. Although she was in her mid to late thirties, she could have easily passed for twenty-nine.

She was standing before him, wearing designer heels and a tailored white dress that revealed just enough knee and breast to cause him to lose concentration, but she was never overtly sexy. She was a strange, exotic mixture—classy yet seductive, expensive yet available—and somehow Sandy carried it off with incredible ease.

"Shane, you look tired. I hope you're not doing stakeouts, sleeping in your car," she said, reacting to the circles under his eyes.

"You always know how to make me feel so special," he said darkly as she took his hand and offered her cheek to kiss.

"Come on, stop it, you know I love you. I made us sandwiches." She was smooth, working him now, making him feel important. She was good at it. Men were her business.

The penthouse was huge, beautiful, and all white. White walls on white carpet, with white drapes framing an acre of plate glass. The antiques were all real. A black and goldleaf Louis XV desk and matching secretary unit were on opposite walls; white sofas and European accent pieces immediately caught the eye. Sandy stood in the middle of the entry with her hands on her slender hips, the most exotic decoration in the room by far.

"I think, now that I see you, you need some alcoholic CPR. How 'bout a beer?" She moved into the kitchen without waiting for a reply, got two Amstel Lights, and brought them back, along with the sandwiches on bone china plates. All of it was carried on an expensive antique silver serving tray. She set everything down on the white marble-top table near the windows.

The mirrored glass skyline of Century City twinkled in the clean air blowing in from the ocean a few miles away.

"You have to take Chooch back," he said without preamble.

"I can't, Shane, I told you, I'm on this thing for the DEA. I'm working almost every night. The target is a hitter. I stumble—I'm gone. Honest to God, this guy's a vampire . . . he plays all night."

"Sandy, I'm going to say this again, 'cause it's important. You need to spend some time with your son. I blew it. I almost got through, but I blew it. Now I'm afraid he's gonna take off, then we're gonna be out there looking for him. He's got some gang-bang friends in the Valley; he'll hang with bad company. He's pissed off, ready to run. I'm worried about him."

They sat with the beers and untouched sandwiches between them as Sandy bit her lower lip in concentrated thought. "I know you think I've just dumped him, that I sent him off to boarding school or left him with friends . . . but I'm trying to make enough money so he can go to Princeton or Yale. I want him to get the best education, maybe be a doctor."

"To begin with, it doesn't matter what I think. It only matters what Chooch thinks. You've gotta show him *you* care. You've gotta make room for him in *your* life, make him feel like he belongs somewhere, like somebody truly gives a shit. Forget about Yale, 'cause the way he's going, he's gonna be doing his postgrad study at Soledad State Prison."

"My plan is to get ten mil in tax-free munis and blue chips, stuff that will grow and throw off cash, then I'm gonna retire and move with Chooch to Arizona—Phoenix, I was thinking—settle down, be a regular mom. I'm a year away, maybe less."

"You don't have a year. You may not have a week."

"Shane, the sting on this drug deal goes down in two days. I'm right at the critical point, creating my exit strategy."

"You mean setting up your dead man," he corrected.

"Boy, are you in a shitty mood. Stop being so contentious. I'll take him once this sting is over. I promise. But I'm not taking him today, or tomorrow. . . . Maybe this will be over by Monday. Let's shoot for Monday."

Shane got to his feet, without having touched the sandwich or the beer. She didn't beg him to stay, either.

"By the way, who the hell is his father?"

"His name is Carlos Delmonica. I got careless with my pills. He was a drug dealer in Simon Boca's operation, and he's currently a resident of Leavenworth, Kansas, doing twenty-five to life in the federal pen."

"Jeez, no help there, I guess."

"The best thing we can hope for is that Chooch never meets his father. And don't tell him who he is. I don't want Chooch writing Carlos, who doesn't even know he has a son."

"Monday," Shane said with finality.

He started for the door, and Sandy scooped her purse off the sofa table. "I'll go with you. Maybe I can still make my lunch." She picked up the phone and dialed the bandleader with the braided shoulders in the lobby. "Darling, it's Sandy. I'm coming down with the gentleman who just arrived. Be a dear, will you?" She hung up and smiled brightly. "Our cars will be right up. Magic."

They exited into the hall. As she punched the elevator button, a phone rang. Both Sandy and Shane dug for their cells. It was Shane's. He popped it open.

"Yeah," he said.

It was Luanne McDermott, of the Fingerprint Analysis Unit at SIS. "The print lab lifted a set of pretty good latents off the videotape box," she said. "They came back to Calvin Sheets, 2329 Los Feliz, apartment sixteen."

"Calvin Sheets," Shane said, taking a pen and his small spiral notebook out of his pocket. "Spell it *ea* or *ee?*"

"Sheets—*ee*. Also, he used to be one of us."

"A cop?"

"Yeah . . . got terminated by Internal Affairs six months ago."

"Anything else?"

"That's it."

"Thanks." He closed the phone and tapped the pen on the spiral notebook, deep in speculation.

The elevator arrived at the penthouse level, and he and Sandy got aboard. This time they were listening to an orchestrated version of "Eleanor Rigby."

"I know Calvin Sheets," Sandy said, surprising him.

The doors closed and they rode down.

"You do?"

"He works for Logan Hunter—at least he used to."

"The movie producer?"

"Actually, Logan runs his own independent studio now, Starmax. Calvin Sheets is head of his security."

"How do you know Logan Hunter?" Shane asked, always surprised by the level of people Sandy knew. "Isn't he a big social deal, always doing some major fund-raiser or civic project?"

"Actually, that's how he keeps his reputation. He only works on stuff that will keep him in the press. Right now he's in the paper 'cause he's trying to get a pro football team to come to L.A. He's a football fan like I'm a microbiologist, but it's popular, makes him look good. If it's a news story, he's up for it."

"I hesitate to ask you how you met him."

"I was working Logan for U.S. Customs about two months ago. It went nowhere. He just wouldn't give me any play. One of my few wipeouts. I found out a few weeks later that he's a closet gay. To each his own . . ."

"What did U.S. Customs want him for?"

"They thought he was smuggling heroin into the country, using film magazines being shipped back from a production he had shooting in Mexico. They thought he was unpacking loads of Mexican Brown in the film lab, but like I said, I never got close enough to find out."

"And Calvin Sheets works for him now?"

"Yeah. And is he ever an asshole. A blister, that one. I'd hate to get caught alone with him in a dark place."

They got to the lobby and stepped out of the elevator. The doorman had already called up the cars; two Spanish-speaking men in white coveralls with BARRINGTON PLAZA stenciled over their pockets delivered the keys and stood by the cars waiting for their tips.

Shane slipped his man a dollar, while Sandy tipped hers five, then rattled some Spanish at him. He smiled and bobbed his head energetically up and down like a sparrow digging for worms. She got behind the wheel of her new bottle-green XJB convertible. They both drove off, heading their separate ways: Sandy in her Jag, to arrange some poor asshole's funeral; Shane in his battered Acura, to pick up her only son at Harvard Westlake before Mr. Thackery threw a shit-fit and started threatening expulsion, *ad summum bonum.*

B&E

IT WAS JUST after ten P.M. when Shane left a brooding Chooch Sandoval with Longboard Kelly. He was driving across town to the Bradbury Building, dressed for a burglary in 211 colors: a black LAPD sweatshirt, black jeans, and Reeboks. He had his .38 backup piece snug against his belt. His badge and ID card, picklocks, and penlight were stuffed in all available pockets.

He pulled off the freeway and drove down Sixth Street, right into the hovering helicopter lights of the Schwarzenegger movie. They were back downtown doing night work, barricades in place, assistant directors and klieg lights glaring. He had hoped he would be able to sneak into IAD, rifle the chief advocate's files, and get out unobserved. The last thing he needed to deal with was this fucking movie.

He got stopped two blocks from the Bradbury by a motorcycle cop, now a potential witness who could put Shane at the location.

He considered turning around and going home but then decided, *fuck it,* he was running out of options. He had to take the chance.

"Sorry, Sergeant, we're almost on a take," the old motorcycle cop said after Shane badged him. He had outgrown his uniform, which stretched over his belly like a Mexican bandit's faded guayabera.

The LAPD supplied movie companies with police assistance to control crowds and traffic on location, and many of the retired old-timers made some money by working movie gigs. Shane didn't know this officer. He never had many friends in Motors because the officers assigned there were basically "hot pilot" types—attitude junkies known on the job as "mustard cases."

"I need to get to my office," Shane explained.

"Lock up traffic. This is picture," the assistant director's voice came over the motor cop's walkie-talkie.

The officer was in his late sixties and looked slightly ridiculous in his too-tight shirt and worn leather knee boots. He held up his hands as if to say there was nothing he could do. The god of cinema had just spoken. "Sorry, we have to wait for the shot," he said.

"It's a good thing the corner bank isn't being robbed," Shane muttered.

They waited while the helicopter hovered loudly overhead. Suddenly a car squealed around the corner of Spring Street, roared down Sixth, skidded sideways, then disappeared around another corner.

"Cut. Release traffic," the AD said over the walkie-talkie, and Shane was finally waved through.

In L.A., movies had their own hallowed place in the subculture. God forbid anybody should fuck with a unit production schedule.

When Shane got to the Bradbury Building, he was greeted by another surprise. The entire north side of the building was flooded by a huge condor light suspended forty feet in the air from a crane. It lit almost the entire city block.

"Shit," Shane muttered. This was getting ridiculous. He was dressed in black, trying to do an illegal entry while a movie was shooting, and the fucking building he was burglarizing was lit up like City Hall. He had already decided not to use the parking structure, because he was pretty sure that the gate had a common security feature that would read his key card, then time-log it, so he parked in a private lot next to a string of honey wagons and dressing rooms.

He locked the Acura and walked past a line of chattering extras, out onto the brightly lit sidewalk. Hugging the bricks of the Bradbury, turtling his head down into his collar, he tried to hide, feeling stupid and exposed like a cockroach scuttling along a kitchen baseboard.

The building was open, as he knew it would be. Advocates often worked late, so the department kept civilian guards on at night. Usually they slept somewhere on the fifth floor.

He walked into the huge lobby and stood in the atrium. The guard desk was empty. He looked up at the advocates' windows on the third floor. The lights were off. He climbed the stairs, his tennis shoes squeaking on the tile floor. When he got to three, he headed down the corridor and stood for a moment in front of the advocates' offices, looking through the windows, past the reception desks to the cubbies beyond, where any late-working advocates might be sitting. The place looked empty, and the lights were all off. He knocked loudly on the door.

Shane had a cover story ready. If anybody was inside, he was going to abort and say that he had come back to finish some Xeroxing but first needed to pick up his key.

He knocked again, but nobody answered. Everyone had gone home. He looked up and down the exterior corridor, then pulled out a small leather case and removed a set of picklocks.

Ironically, picking locks was a criminal specialty he had learned from Ray Molar. A good set of picklocks contained an array of long, needle-shaped tools and one long, thin, notched metal strip. Shane slid the notched strip into the lock and jiggled it to find the first tumbler by feel. Then the smaller picks slid in behind it. The idea was to fill as many of the lock's keyed openings as possible so that you had enough leverage to turn all the tumblers inside the bolt. It was not as easy as it looked on TV, where some guy would just slide a credit card into a door and, bingo, he was in. It took Shane almost ten minutes before he could turn the lock and let himself inside.

He stepped onto the gray carpeted area just inside the door, then slowly withdrew the picklocks and returned them to the case. He closed the door and locked it from the inside. He moved down the carpeted hallway between the reception desks and windows, heading quietly toward the chief advocate's office. Shane knew that all of the active IAD cases were in a file cabinet there. He got to the end of the long reception area, pushed open the door to Warren Zell's office, took two steps inside, and stopped to adjust his eyes to the low light.

He had stood right in this same spot yesterday, when Zell had informed him that he was IAD's new Xerox machine operator.

He saw the file cabinet at the far end of the room. As he moved to it, he prayed that the cabinets weren't locked. He didn't want to spend any more time there than necessary. As he crossed the room, he took the small penlight out of his back pocket, turned it on, and stuck it in his mouth, gripping it between his teeth. The narrow light hit the top of the metal cabinet, reflecting the beam off its burnished gray finish. He put his hand on the top drawer handle and tugged on it. It slid open. The sound of the little metal rollers filled the room.

He looked down into a file crammed full with case folders; each one had a yellow tab with the officer's name and CF number. He cocked his head to aim the light on the tabs and, working alphabetically, quickly went through the cabinet. In the middle of the top drawer, he found a tab marked L. AYERS. He pulled the file out and opened it. Inside was a single slip of paper with the typed words:

FILE RELOCATED TO S.I.D.

He looked in the second drawer for Joe Church, the second name on the list, and found a file for him as well. It contained the same slip, indicating that the contents had been sent to the secure files over at Special Investigations Division in Parker Center. He glanced at several of the other case files in that drawer and found that none of them had been relocated, only Ayers and Church.

He knelt down and opened the bottom drawer, where he figured he would find Samansky's file, if there was one. It was right in the middle of the drawer, also empty, except for the same note.

What the fuck is this? he thought as he began looking for the Drucker and Kono files. He found both folders empty; the same note was in each. Coy Love didn't have a case pending. He was the only one of Ray's den not facing a Board of Rights.

Shane closed the drawer and stood up. He was just taking the penlight from between his teeth when he heard a gun cock behind him.

"Don't move," a woman's voice said. Then the lights were switched on.

He turned and saw Alexa Hamilton framed in the doorway, a black automatic gripped in both hands, her arms triangled out in front of her in a shooting stance. "You sure are one rule-breaking son of a bitch," she said.

"I'm just trying to—"

"Shut up, Scully! Where's your piece? Where're you packing?"

"Huh?" His mind was spinning, looking for a way out.

"Turn around. Put your hands behind your neck."

"Come on—this Dirty Harriet thing isn't working. I'm assigned down here, same as you. Put the gun down."

"Do what I say, asshole. Do it now!"

He turned his back to her and assumed the position; she quickly patted him down. She removed his clip-on holster, took a step back, and put it on the desk.

Shane assumed she didn't cuff him only because she didn't have her handcuffs handy. She was dressed in a blouse and jeans, her hair was slightly mussed, and he guessed she'd been working late, then fell asleep on the sofa in the back of the advocates' section. He'd awakened her when he'd broken in.

She shifted her gun to her left hand and held it on him while she picked up the phone, locked the receiver under her ear, and dialed three digits. "This is Sergeant Hamilton . . . requesting a Code Six Adam at 1567 Spring Street, third floor. I'm in the chief advocate's office. Notify the responding unit that they will be transporting a police officer under arrest to Parker Center, and notify Chief Mayweather, head of Special Investigations, to call me at 555-9878." She listened for a moment, then hung up the phone.

"You've gotta hear me out before you do this."

"It's done, Scully. You've just been yanked."

"I wasn't looking at my file—"

"I don't wanna hear it. I'm prosecuting you, so we're not having an ex parte conversation. Just button it till the backup gets here."

Shane was down to his last chance. She would either have to shoot him or listen to him, but he was not going to just stand there, mute, waiting to be arrested.

"Ray Molar was supervising a den of six guys. Five of them have cases going through IAD."

"Shut up. I don't wanna hear another word outta you."

"All of their case files are missing. They've been relocated to the secure files at SID. Why? I've never heard of that before, have you?"

"I said be quiet."

"Alexa, I need you to listen to me. Those files are missing because they contain dangerous information."

"Those files could be missing for a lot of reasons."

"Only the files on the guys in Ray's den are gone," he said incredulously. "Why only those guys?"

"I don't care. It doesn't matter. The chief advocate can relocate files anywhere he wants. They're his. Maybe he knows what a loose cannon you are, figured you'd pull this dumb-ass burg."

"Ray has a second home in Lake Arrowhead," Shane went on. "He had a second identity up there: Jay Colter. The house is owned by a real estate company, Cal-VIP Homes. I don't know who owns the company yet, but I have a search being done by the Corporations Commission. When I was up at Ray's Arrowhead house last night, I caught four guys cleaning the place out. After they left, I broke inside."

"So, you're averaging one illegal entry a night. This some kind of sideline for you?"

"Listen to me, will ya?" He was getting impatient. He told her about the one-way mirror, the glory hole, and the videotape box with the name Carl Cummins on it.

"None of this ties to anything," she said. "You're rambling, Scully."

"What're you talking about? A lot of it ties together. Ray's old den had some kinda deal going with the Hoover Street Bounty Hunters, possibly to blow arrests and let them off. Chief Brewer was on his answering machine at the party house. I can play the tape for you if you don't believe me. I think maybe even the mayor, who Ray was driving, is somehow involved."

"In what? Involved in *what?* You think it's some kinda buy-down? Some bullshit collars-for-dollars scheme?" she asked, referring to a situation in which a criminal shares his take with the arresting officer in return for a chance to walk. "Why would the chief of police and the mayor of L.A. be involved in some two-bit street hustle like that? You're delusional."

"I don't think it's a buy-down. I think it's something else, something much bigger. I got called into Brewer's office yesterday. He threatened me with this ridiculous murder charge, told me he thought I stole a videotape out of Ray's house, and if I gave it back, maybe all my problems would go away. If Ray was videotaping sex parties, maybe this Cummins character or somebody else was getting blackmailed, and if I lean on him hard enough, maybe he'll tell me what's going on. That is, if I can find him." He *was* rambling now, his own voice sounding desperate to him.

"This is weak shit, Sergeant—delusional and paranoid."

"Gimme some time. I've only been working on it for two days. Whatever is going on, it's sure got the top floor of the Glass House worried. They're threatening me with a murder indictment to get some tape they think I have."

"They're threatening you with murder because Ray's wife was your eighty-five. You used to date her, and my IOs say, like the stone-ass moron you're proving to be, you're still actually seeing her."

"Eighty-five" was police slang for girlfriend. Shane ignored it and went on: "All of these IAD cases involve the Hoover Street Bounty Hunters. Some ex-cop named Calvin Sheets is involved. His fingerprints were on the Carl Cummins videotape box I found up at Ray's house in Arrowhead."

When Shane mentioned Calvin Sheets, suddenly Alexa's body posture turned rigid. Her jaw clenched and her expression darkened. "Calvin Sheets is now head of security for the Starmax movie studio," he continued. "It's an independent studio owned by Logan Hunter, who U.S. Customs suspects of drug smuggling."

She was looking at him differently now. So he took a wild guess, trying to reel her in. "You know Calvin Sheets."

For a minute, he didn't think she was going to answer him.

"Another advocate, a good friend of mine, terminated him," she finally said. "He was a rogue officer, a dirty sergeant. How was he involved with Ray?" Shane had *finally* piqued her interest.

"I'm not sure. I've got his voice on that same answering-machine tape from Ray's house in Arrowhead. He said, 'Don't fuck around with love.' At first I thought they were talking about love in the romantic sense, but now I know they were talking about Coy Love."

He waited for her to respond, but she didn't, so he went on. "I'd like you to explain to me why my case jumped over the Shooting Review Board and went straight to a BOR, and why the district attorney is setting me up for this bullshit murder charge, when I have an eyewitness who backs me up."

"Barbara Molar is a shit witness. She's the motive for the murder. I should've punched your ticket sixteen years ago."

"Okay, since you brought that up, why didn't you?"

Her ice-blue eyes were sparking anger. "Why didn't I what?"

"You threw my board sixteen years ago. Why?"

"Who told you I threw it? That's ridiculous."

"DeMarco told me. He said you impeached your own witness and withheld Ray's sworn affidavit."

Now they could hear men's voices downstairs; they echoed in the hollow atrium. The backup unit had arrived. The elevators were shut down for the night and, after a minute, they heard footsteps marching up the tile stairs.

"You might have me on this low-grade B and E, but I'll get you for throwing that Board of Rights sixteen years ago," he threatened. "DeMarco will testify that you gave the case away. You'll probably be getting your own CF number down here. Give you a look at this division from the other side."

"I wish I'd never laid eyes on you," she said sharply.

He could see the beginning of indecision in her eyes. She was a career cop, high on the lieutenant's list.

There was a rattling at the front door of the Advocate Section.

"Anybody in there?" a cop's voice called into the office.

"What's it gonna be, Sergeant?" he asked. She stood frozen, holding her gun in one hand. Finally she lowered her weapon, turned, and walked to the door, then opened it.

Two uniforms moved in. Shane could see them through Warren Zell's open office door.

"It's okay, Officer. My mistake," he heard Alexa say. "It was just one of our sergeants. He works here."

To punctuate the point, Shane pulled out his badge and flashed it at them.

"Sorry for the call," she said. "If you could do me a favor . . . Cancel my Code Six A and ask Communications to cancel my call to Deputy Chief Mayweather."

The cop nearest to her touched his shoulder mike and started broadcasting a Code Four, which was a stand-down. Both uniforms turned and left. Alexa closed the door and walked back to where Shane was standing. "We're even. Get outta here," she said angrily.

"Not until you hear the rest of it," he said softly. "And not until you tell me why the hell you threw my board sixteen years ago."

EX PARTE
COMMUNICATION
22

THEY WALKED DOWN Third Street, through the glare of the movie lights, and settled on a small, dingy bar called the Appaloosa, two blocks south of the Bradbury. The proprietor had made a half-assed decorating attempt at a Mexican motif: table candles with corny glass sombreros, badly painted pictures of Appaloosas with stoic Mexican cowboys or dusty regal hombres from Santa Ana's army looking across prairies or valleys, their heads held high, reeking Hispanic nobility.

"That fucking Schwarzenegger movie is driving me nuts," she said as they slid into a cracked vinyl booth and waved at a Mexican waiter wearing a dirty white coat about the same color as the gray linoleum floor. Mariachi recordings hissed and popped through a bad speaker system. The place was a refried dive.

"Scotch and water," she said.

"Two," he added.

The waiter left and they sat there, each waiting for the other to start. She was pushed back on the ruptured red vinyl seat, as if she were trying to get as far away from him as possible.

"This is your party," she finally said.

"I want to know why you threw my board."

"Ancient history."

"I wanna know, just the same."

"I wanna know why Christie Brinkley can't keep a husband. It's a mystery. Leave it at that."

"You threw my board sixteen years ago, and now you volunteer for this one?"

"I didn't volunteer. I was ordered. I've been out of Internal Affairs for ten years, running a patrol shift down in Southwest. I wanted to stay in the field, but because of you, I ended up getting called back by Tom Mayweather to handle your board. Don't ask me why."

"Tom Mayweather?"

"Yeah. Heard of him?" Cutting sarcasm now, laying it on with a trowel. "He's head of Special Investigations Division. Read your department administration list."

"I heard you volunteered."

"Look, Scully, for whatever it's worth, you don't even remotely interest me anymore. I'm gonna try your BOR in seven days because the Glass House wants me to. Then I'm going back to Southwest Patrol, where I can actually do some honest-to-God police work."

"Why would Tom Mayweather pull you back to handle my board?"

"If I tell you what I think the reason is, it'll just piss you off."

"I'm already pissed off."

"Because I hold the record. I'm the best advocate they ever had down there. I only lost your case and a few others in the time I was in that division. Mayweather wanted the best, so he ordered me back. If that seems egotistical and self-serving— tough. That's what I think."

"You know what I think?"

She didn't answer, but sat staring at him with those remarkable laser-blue eyes.

"He pulled you back because you tried me before. Sparks flew back then, and he knew it would piss me off. He's trying to pressure me to turn over that videotape he thinks I have. He thought putting you on the case would up the stakes." He paused while the waiter set down their drinks and left.

"That's your take, because you always put yourself at ground zero," she said. "To everyone else, you're marginal business, just another dumb mistake that needs to be handled in due course. This has been fun. We've had our one drink. Meeting's over, see ya." She took a long swallow, then set the glass down and started to leave.

"Hey, Lexie, I'm not through yet."

"I don't go by 'Lexie,' asshole. The name's Alexa."

"I don't go by 'asshole,' Alexa. The name's Shane."

They sat in silence for a moment.

"So, why did you throw my board?"

"You won't get off that, huh?"

"It's pretty unusual. You're the best advocate down there, the Black Witch of the Division, yet you intentionally let me slide? I want to know why."

"Because I knew Ray Molar was using you. In the years I'd been at IAD, I'd seen a handful of probationers take violence beefs for him . . . guys he'd handpicked out of the Academy and teamed up with. It became pretty obvious what was happening. He was busting heads and holding court in the street, then getting you dummies to take the heat for him if complaints came down. It was starting to piss me off. Then, when Ray gave the chief advocate that bullshit statement behind my back, saying that you had emotional problems and that he'd been worried about your mental stability, I sorta lost it. Furthermore, I was sure my key wit, that gas-station attendant, was dirty. Ray musta threatened him to get him to say he saw you beat that kid, because he flunked the poly I gave him. The case was an air ball, so I called DeMarco and told him where the holes were."

Shane sat there for a long moment and looked at her. She seemed different, somehow softer, more vulnerable. Maybe it was the low light, or the scotch, or maybe it was what she'd done for him sixteen years ago at some risk to her own career. But he was being compelled to view her in a different way, so he sat there, turning dials, trying to regain some focus on her.

"You just throw cases if they seem wrong to you?"

"Listen, Scully, I know you think Internal Affairs is a sewer full of ladder-climbing politicians who don't care how many cops' careers they wreck."

"And it's not?"

"No, it's not. Don't you think we're drowning in all the politically correct bullshit that goes through this division? The Gay and Lesbian Alliance gets pissed because some cop gets tough trying to bust a two-hundred-pound angel-dusted bull dyke who's brandishing a hammer. The arresting officer ends up putting the bracelets on but has his head opened up in the process. Instead of filing a resisting-arrest charge on the hammer-wielding debutante, the cop gets accused of gay bashing. It's a big news story. Lots of angry meetings in West Hollywood. The L.A. *Times* does a blue-death dance on the front page, and our fearless leaders dump the whole thing into our basket. . . .

"Or some gangbanger caught standing over a dead body with a smoking MAC-Ten accuses the arresting officer of beating him in the station I-room. The EMTs are called, and the banger doesn't have a mark on him. But the special-interest groups take it to the press—racial violence, forced confessions, cops on the rampage. It's a big deal, and everybody knows all the banger is doing is getting back at the cops who busted him. It's total bullshit. My own IOs are telling me the board won't float, but the perp's a minority. The Glass House and the mayor fold like deck chairs, and the whole mess is back in my office.

"After a while you start to sort out the really bad ones, maybe drop a few key pieces of manufactured evidence overboard, impeach one of your own lying wits if you have to, lay back a bit, try and even things out so good cops don't end up paying the price for somebody's political agenda.

"Then along comes a Rodney King, where the cops were dead wrong, and you gotta go to war, kick some ass. The police need policing. A department without self-investigation is bound to become corrupt."

She drained her drink, the ice cube clinking on her teeth. She set the glass down hard on the table, telling him the lecture had ended. "Is that all? Can I go now?"

"Tell me about Calvin Sheets."

"I told you. Calvin was terminated by a good friend of mine, a current advocate named Susan Kellerman. Susan and I were both sergeants in Southwest Patrol, and I recommended her for Internal Affairs. She's not there two weeks and she gets Calvin's board. He was threatening her life with anonymous phone calls all during the investigation, but she couldn't prove it was him. She called me and asked what she should do. I took a ride out to Calvin's house and gave him a heads-up talk. It wasn't pleasant."

"What happened?"

"I just said it wasn't pleasant. Okay?"

"Did Susan tell you everything about his case?"

"In detail. As a matter of fact, I got so mad at Sheets, I worked it for free. Did some IO work in my off-hours to help her."

"What was he charged with?"

"He was shift commander on the Coliseum detail and was keeping bogus time sheets. He had officers listed as 'on duty' who weren't even there. They were kicking back salary and overtime to him. It was a mess—more than ten cops involved. His whole shift was signing their own arrest reports 'cause Sheets wasn't around. On top of all that, he was off working a second job at the movie studio, doing security work."

"For Logan Hunter."

"Yeah. The cops on his detail called him Dream Sheets because he was so tired when he finally got to the Coliseum, he would just sleep in his office. He was running the sloppiest PED team I ever saw. His Prostitution Enforcement Detail at the Coliseum was watching the games while the hookers were running wild. There were more blow jobs going on in the parking lot than at a swingers' convention. The Coliseum Commission was enraged. We had dozens of letters from those guys. Calvin's board took two days, and Susan got his tin. Eight of the ten cops he was supervising got terminated with him. Two rookies survived but were given six-month mandatory suspensions. It was a disaster for the city. Calvin called me up after he got terminated . . . told me he would pick a time when I wasn't looking and pay me back with interest. I can hardly wait for him to try. Total sleaze."

Shane sat across the table, absentmindedly twirling a red swizzle stick between his fingers.

"Stop playing with that, will you? It's making me nervous."

He put the stick in the ashtray. "Doesn't any of this seem strange to you? Add what I have to what you just told me, and it starts to reek. All these Internal Affairs cases, Ray's den and the H Street Bounty Hunters . . . a banger named Sol Preciado was doing assaults at the Coliseum; Calvin Sheets was failing to supervise his PED team down there, his fingerprints were on that videotape box, in an Arrowhead house where I think prostitutes were screwing guys that Sheets and Ray were blackmailing . . ."

"You've gotta connect the dots, Shane. You haven't done that. It's called police work."

"I know, but don't you think a lot of this is damn strange?"

She sat looking at him for a long moment. Finally she nodded her head slowly. "Drucker's case is going to a board tomorrow."

"No, it's not. Mayweather just got an extension pushing it back to the twenty-third. If you're so concerned about policing the police, why not work on this?"

"Because I'm on the other side of *your* case. I'm prosecuting you. How on earth can I help you?"

"I won't tell if you won't." He grinned.

"Tell you what, tomorrow I'll ask a few questions, just for the hell of it."

"I think we should talk to Sol Preciado. He's a witness in Drucker's case. Why don't we go out to juvie and sit him down."

"When were you planning for us to do that?"

"Now. Let's do it now. You've got an advocate card; the jail warden won't question it. Let's get him in an I-room at juvie hall and play 'I've Got a Secret.' Bluff him, see what he knows."

She sat looking at him, not answering or reacting to the suggestion.

"If we get nothing, I promise I'll leave you alone." Then he added, "You won't have to see me again till my board."

"We've gotta get one thing straight first," she said. "I want an unequivocal promise that you're not gonna use what I just told you about your old BOR against me."

"Alexa, I was never gonna use that. You may think I'm an asshole, but at least I'm an asshole with principles. You did me a favor. I won't forget it. Whatever you decide now, as far as I'm concerned, nothing happened back then."

"Okay, then let's go do some jailin'," she said.

They each took a car and followed each other all the way out to the juvenile jail in Downey.

Trouble was, once they got there and asked that Sol Preciado be brought to an interrogation room, they found out he was no longer a guest of the city. Earlier that afternoon a door had been mysteriously left open in the back of a court transport vehicle and the fifteen-year-old gangbanger had escaped again.

Shane and Alexa took the creaking elevator back down to the lobby and walked out of juvenile hall into the harsh Xenon lights of the parking lot.

"This kid has more jailbreaks than Dillinger," she said.

"They pushed Drucker's board back to get time to arrange for this. They let him go so he wouldn't be around to testify," Shane said. When she looked over at him, he added, "I'm telling you, it's been like this ever since I shot Ray. Somebody is pulling strings, making shit happen. It's been orchestrated better than the Philharmonic."

"You're being paranoid," she concluded.

"I'm being framed," he corrected.

CROSSROADS AND CROSSFIRE

I'M MAKING ARRANGEMENTS for you to go back to your mom on Monday," Shane said.

They were sitting in his backyard chairs, Chooch with his feet up on the low picket fence, leaning way back, trying to look as though he couldn't give a shit. "Make any arrangement you want, but I won't be here on Friday," Chooch snarled. "You can go quakin' about it with the cave bitch all you want, don't matter, 'cause I'm gone."

"You think that I'm dumping you, that I don't want you here, but you're wrong. I'm telling you the truth, Chooch. I feel shitty about this."

No response.

"Tell you what. I should be clear by the end of next week. Whatta you say you and I get outta town, go do something together."

"What're we gonna do? Score some tasty together? Do some

jay?" He was smirking now, letting Shane know he was back on the other side.

"I told you no drugs. How 'bout a weekend at Disneyland?" Shane said. "We'll stay at the hotel there, ride the Matterhorn, Space Mountain; do the Log Ride, all that stuff."

"You think I'm some little kid? You can't bribe me with a trip to Disneyland."

"You ever been to Disneyland?" Shane asked.

Chooch shrugged, not answering.

"If you've never been, you don't know what you're turning down. And if you wanna score some tasty, there're girls all over Disneyland," letting Chooch know he understood rap lingo.

But Chooch said nothing.

"You told me once that you wanted to be the most important instead of the least. And I get that, man. I really do. But lemme ask you something. If I let you stay here, knowing that I was in some real danger and that you might end up hurt, what kinda guy would that make me? And how important would you be to me if I just flat disregard your safety?"

"Whatever . . . You're gonna do what you wanta."

"You want me to understand, to care about your problems, but you don't want to understand or care about mine."

"Is this gonna take much longer?"

"You're going to Sandy on Monday. Sorry you and I can't talk about it."

"You say you're in danger, that someone's gonna ride on you? And I'm supposed to believe this?"

Now it was Shane who didn't answer.

"Well, I don't. Okay? I see it as total doo-rah. You're a fuckin' liar."

Shane got up and moved toward the door. Before going in, he turned and talked to Chooch's back. "There are defining moments in a man's life, Chooch. You're at one. You can deal with this like a man, or you can run from it like a kid. If you run—if you take off and go hang with a buncha street bravos, you're gonna regret it."

" 'Cause why? You're gonna get me booked on a juvenile court detaining order?" he said, surprising Shane that he knew the exact document, and further proving he'd been hanging with some very unsavory people.

"You're at an important crossroad. Read the signs carefully before you choose what direction you want to go. You're fifteen. Nobody can tell you what to do anymore, certainly not me. You're gonna make your own decisions, no matter what Sandy or I say. You're almost a man now, so you stop getting the juvenile discount. But you also gotta pay adult rates—be careful."

Shane went inside and undressed for bed. It had been a strange night. He had left Alexa not knowing what she would do, or whether she believed any of what he had told her. Then he had come home to this draining conversation with Chooch. He lay on his pillow, looking at the cracked ceiling, wondering where it was all heading.

In his wildest imagination, he never would have expected what happened next.

■ ■ ■

Shane heard something outside the house.

It woke him.

He didn't know whether it was part of a dream or someone in his yard. He lay still, his heart pounding, his senses tingling; then he rolled out of bed and crept slowly to the dresser, where he had put his gun. He retrieved it, snuck out of the bedroom, padded down the hall in his underwear, and checked the guest room. Chooch was asleep in the bed next to the wall, so Shane went back up the hall.

He wasn't two steps into the front room when a machine gun opened up, blowing out the entire front window. Glass rained in on him, taking part of the drapery with it. Shane dove for the floor as the machine gun kept firing, stitching holes in the wall behind him, breaking plaster, shattering pictures. He worked his way toward the front door on his stomach.

Another burst from a second gun came through the side window. Nine-millimeter slugs tattooed the living room's east wall. He was pinned in a deadly cross fire. Shane rolled over and sat up, firing blindly out the broken side window with his .38. Then he heard a car start in the alley.

Chooch ran into the living room, and Shane launched himself at the teenager, taking him down seconds before another barrage of bullets screamed just above their heads, breaking a lamp and turning an end table into splinters. Shane pinned Chooch under him, protecting the boy with his body.

"Let's go. Let's get outta here!" somebody shouted.

A car door slammed; an engine roared. There was the chirp of rubber and then the sound of a car speeding away.

"Stay here. Stay down," Shane ordered Chooch. He wormed his way out the front door, slid down the front steps on his belly, and rolled behind a low wall. He didn't want to risk sticking his head up until he had a chance to check out all possible lines of fire. He strained to hear in the dark, to identify any warning sound, trying to be sure all of them had left. Then he rolled up and scooted back on his ass until he could feel the side of the house against his shoulder blades.

His neighbors were starting to shout: "What's going on!?" "What the fuck's happening?!" "Call the police!"

Shane couldn't remember how many shots he had squeezed off, so he flipped open the cylinder . . . three cartridges left. He snapped the revolver shut and got to his feet, quickly making a lap around the house. He ran into Longboard in the backyard and almost shot him.

"Get back inside, Brian," he ordered.

The surfboard shaper turned and ran back into his house.

After Shane was certain the house was secure, he went back inside.

"Let's go," he said to Chooch.

"Where?"

"You're going to your mother's. You can't stay here. Get your clothes, now! Meet me in the garage. We're outta here!"

They could hear sirens approaching, way off in the distance.

"Let's go. I don't wanna be here when the cops arrive. Move it!"

Shane grabbed his clothes out of the bedroom and, not waiting to put them on, bolted for the garage. He was already pulling the Acura out when the teenager arrived, carrying his shirt, shoes, and pants; Chooch jumped into the passenger side. The police sirens were now only a few blocks away.

Shane shot up the alley behind the east canal, made a left away from the water, and floored it. Miraculously, he didn't choose the same streets as the arriving squad cars. Five minutes later they were on the freeway, both clad only in their undershorts, heading toward Barrington Plaza.

Chooch sat quietly in the passenger seat, shaken by the experience. Finally he looked over at Shane.

"I thought it was bullshit," he said.

"Now you know," Shane answered, but he hadn't been prepared for the ferocious machine-gun attack. He had never imagined that somebody would stand outside his house pouring lead into his living room. His hands were shaking; he was glad he was gripping the steering wheel so it didn't show.

"Who were those guys?" Chooch asked. "They ride down on you with fucking machine guns. . . ."

"I'm not sure. Bad cops, I think."

When he looked over at Chooch a second time, he saw a strange expression on the boy's face, too complicated to read.

They got off the freeway at Sunset. Shane found a dark spot

and pulled to the curb so they could change into their clothes in the car. Then they drove around the corner and pulled in at Barrington Plaza. Shane badged the doorman with the braided shoulders. Sandy was standing in the living room wearing a silk robe belted around her slender waist. Her hair was tousled. She looked composed but concerned, an actress playing a scene.

"I can't believe it," she said after Shane filled her in.

"This isn't going to be a discussion, Sandy. You're taking Chooch."

"My God, who do you think they were?"

"I'm not sure, but I have a few hunches." He stood there, feeling a wave of fatigue. Then he looked at Chooch, wearing the same strange expression Shane had seen in the car. In the better light of Sandy's apartment, it looked a little like regret, or maybe it was guilt.

"Okay, here's the deal, Chooch . . ."

The boy jerked to attention and faced Shane.

"Disneyland, next weekend. You stay here till then, and I'll be back for you. It's a promise."

Chooch nodded.

As Shane moved to the door, he heard Chooch call his name, and he looked back. "I'm sorry," the boy said. "I thought you were lying, but I was wrong."

THE POLICE
BILL OF RIGHTS

24

WHEN SHANE GOT BACK to his house on East Canal Street, it was sunup. Five black-and-whites and a crime-scene station wagon were blocking the street. He edged the Acura past them and pulled into the garage.

There were ten cops standing in his living room. When he entered, they turned, clearly surprised to see him.

"Where the hell you been?" Garson Welch asked. The fact that the old detective had been called out on this told Shane that he was still a murder suspect in the criminal investigation surrounding Ray's death.

Welch had been given this call because he was investigating Molar's shooting and this machine-gun attack was most likely connected. The old detective looked at Shane with his basset-hound expression and tired brown eyes. "We just put a bulletin out on you."

"I had something personal to take care of," Shane said.

"What the fuck *was* this?" Garson said, pointing at the destroyed wall where Crime Section techs were busy digging 9mm slugs out of the plaster and bagging them as evidence for a ballistics comparison later. That is, if they ever found the weapon, which was right up there with the odds on Shane's next promotion.

Shane was sure that the machine guns were illegal street sweepers: AK-47s, maybe MAC-10s, most likely taken from the vast array of confiscated weapons held in the Firearms and Ammunition Section's secure property room, destined for eventual burial at sea.

"Who did this?" Garson asked.

"Don't know," Shane said. "The lights were out, and I was flat on my stomach eating carpet."

"Okay, let's go. You got an appointment at Parker Center."

"Shit . . . do we have to do that again?" Shane asked. The remark was greeted by a flat stare.

Shane was taken from his house and again made the early-morning ride across town to the Glass House. Garson Welch stayed quiet as they drove. He had the case but didn't want it. As far as Welch was concerned, the brass at Parker Center could ask the questions. They pulled into the parking garage next to the huge lit police building, then rode the elevator up to the ninth floor. This time Shane found Deputy Chief Tom Mayweather standing in the hallway waiting for him, looking very GQ in his black pinstripe suit, white shirt, maroon tie, and matching pocket accessory. His bald head was gleaming, his handsome face theatrically troubled. He didn't say anything but motioned Shane down the hall. Garson Welch stayed in the lobby, glad to be out of it.

Shane followed Mayweather into his office. The room was not as large as Chief Brewer's by half but had a picture window with a Spring Street view. The shelves were littered with Mayweather's old basketball trophies, game balls, and team photos, along with the more standard police memorabilia: his Academy class picture, civil-service awards, and plaques attesting to his superiority as a police officer.

Mayweather stepped behind his desk, using the large, light oak piece of furniture as a barricade to separate them and define their roles. Shane stood while Mayweather sat in his tan executive swivel chair. The overhead ceiling spot kicked white light off his shaved head.

"You are an amazing piece of work, Sergeant," the deputy chief finally said.

"Thank you, sir."

"I wasn't complimenting you. Why the hell didn't you come back from Arrowhead and report in here, as instructed?"

"I left you a message."

"Right . . . the 'I had an accident/fell asleep at the wheel/stayed in a motel' message, left with my secretary at eight-fifteen A.M." He shook his head in wonder. "You must think I'm one stupid son of a bitch."

"How would you like me to respond to that, sir?" Shane was getting mad now, wanting to fire back but on tender ground professionally.

Mayweather leaned back in his chair, the knife-sharp creases in his pants now visible over the desktop. "Take off your gun and hand me your badge. You're suspended from duty without pay pending your Internal Affairs Board of Rights."

"Don't you have to write up a 1.61 before you can suspend me?"

"Consider it written."

"The Police Bill of Rights really seems to have its limits where I'm concerned, doesn't it?"

"The 1.61 will be in your hands before nine o'clock. Take off your gun and give me your badge and ID card."

Shane removed the clip-on holster from his belt, then pulled his badge and ID in the brown leather fold-over out of his pocket.

"Put them on the desk, please," Mayweather commanded. Shane did as he was instructed. "Now what?"

Mayweather seemed puzzled by the question, so Shane added, "Doesn't the district attorney show up about now with a murder warrant and cart me off to the lockup?"

"You really have an active imagination."

"I didn't imagine the nine-millimeter machine-gun slugs in my living-room walls. Chief Brewer has been threatening me with a murder indictment. Since you're not doing that, something else must be happening. Maybe you just want to leave me on the street without my gun and badge, where I'll be easier to get at?"

"You are a sick, paranoid man, Sergeant Scully. There are other ways to view what just happened."

"Let's hear."

"I think you're involved with the wrong people, vice or drugs . . . some other street action. You were taking a 'patch' and you took too much." A "patch" was police argot for a payoff to a cop for letting a crime happen, differing from a "buy down," which was a bribe to turn an arrestee loose or book him for a lesser crime. "People you thought you had fooled, or had under control, got tired of paying and threw you a party," Mayweather added.

"You surprise me, Tom," Shane said, using the deputy chief's first name to show he had lost respect for him. "The word in the department is you're a good guy, a smart guy, but what's happening here right now, between us, isn't smart at all. If you really don't know what's going on, then you're being used—played for a patsy. Either way, it marks you."

"I see." Mayweather seemed to consider this, sitting still, thinking, his big trophy-filled office and black Armani pinstripes dissing Shane—making him small. Then the deputy chief seemed to make up his mind and sat upright. "Get out. Check in every day with Captain Halley. Go home and leave this alone."

"Go home? Should I sit in the window?"

"That will be just about enough of that. Go home. Stay put. If you know what's good for you, you'll stop making trouble."

"You can suspend me, but you sure as hell can't tell me not to work on my own defense. Somebody made a big mistake. They thought I took something out of Ray's house and they over-reacted. Now they're pretty sure I don't have it, but Chief Brewer leaned too hard and got me looking in the wrong places. Suddenly I have too much of it and have to be neutralized. Whoever's be-hind this had one easy shot and missed. I won't be stumbling around, half asleep in my undies, next time. It's gonna be much harder."

Shane turned and walked out of the office without looking back, leaving his badge, gun, and career in police work behind.

Once again, he was stranded downtown without his car. He didn't trust anybody enough to ask for a lift, and as a suspended officer, he couldn't check a slickback out of the motor pool . . . so he walked four blocks east to the Bradbury Building and waited in the parking garage for Alexa Hamilton to arrive.

PRINT HIT

S EVEN THIRTY-FIVE A.M. Alexa pulled the gray Ford Crown Victoria into the parking structure and parked in her spot. She was early, as usual, getting a jump-start on the day while DeMarco slept late.

She got out of the car, dressed for success in a dark charcoal pantsuit tailored to her trim, twenty-three-inch waist. She was carrying another cardboard box full of files, her bulging, faded leather briefcase hanging from a strap over her shoulder. She headed toward the elevators and stopped when she saw him standing next to a concrete pillar in the shadows of the huge, underlit parking garage.

"You shouldn't be here," she said.

"I know, I should be in a slumber room at Forest Lawn."

She walked toward him now, closing the distance, stopping two feet away. He could smell her perfume. He'd never thought of her as wearing perfume.

"What happened?" she asked. "The chief advocate called me at six. He said somebody shot up your house."

"Shot up . . . My house was massacred. I got enough lead in the walls to go into strip mining. On top of that, I got suspended this morning by Mayweather. He took my gun, badge, and ID, kicked me loose. So I'm back on the street running around, a moving target. It's been way too entertaining. I was expecting to get hit with a murder one indictment, but for some reason it didn't happen. I guess things were bound to slow down sometime."

"The warrant's coming. The writ got signed. I saw it yesterday. Looks like they're holding it in reserve. . . . Let's go back and sit in my car," she said unexpectedly.

They walked to her car. She put the box in the backseat, then they both slid into the Crown Vic and closed the doors.

"Look, I don't understand what's happening. I agree, something's going on. I don't get it myself . . . but I'm compromised here," Alexa said with some anxiety.

"Lemme see if I got this straight," he said. "I've been threatened by Chief Brewer and most of Ray's old den. Somebody blew the shit out of my living room, Mayweather just suspended me, I got a murder warrant pending, but we're worried *you're* 'compromised'?"

She sat quietly, deep in thought. He sensed there was something she wasn't telling him.

"What is it? You know something else," he said.

Finally she opened her briefcase and pulled out a sheaf of papers.

"Those are the missing files from the Chief Advocate's Office. On my way in this morning, I stopped by the Office of Administrative Services. They supervise the Officer Representation Section at Parker Center. I have a friend down there. She pulled the duplicates on all missing case folders from the discovery files and made copies for me."

Shane took the missing files and looked through them. "Jesus, look't this, it's just what I thought. All of them involve Hoover Street Bounty Hunters. Lee Ayers was beefed by a store owner just like Drucker; slow response to Code Thirty calls. Kris Kono is also accused of a slow response. Joe Church failed to Mirandize a banger after a street homicide. The case got pitched." He looked up at her and, for the first time, saw indecision on her chiseled face. "Why would Ray's old den be kicking gangsters loose?" he asked.

"I don't know, but it's not my case. You're my case. I'm supposed to be prosecuting *you*."

"Well, excuse me," he said, anger filling the space between them.

"Look, Shane, I just said I agree you may have stumbled into something, but—"

"But you don't wanna see your career go in the bucket with mine."

"What do you want me to do? If I start messing with this, they're going to pull me off your case. The district attorney will file against you anyway. It won't change anything."

"Yes, it will, because you'll be doing the right thing. Alexa, I'm down to just you. Nobody else in the department will even talk to me. With no badge, I'm locked out. I can't even access the computer system."

"And you want me to sacrifice myself for you?"

"All that righteous shit you were giving me last night, the Rodney King speech about IAD policing the police, kicking ass when there's corruption—that was just bullshit. Sounds good, but what you really meant is, as long as you can do it without hurting yourself or putting yourself in jeopardy."

"That's not fair."

"Then help me."

"I can't help you. I'm prosecuting you. Don't you get that?" She sat in the car, glaring at him. Shane wondered how it happened: this woman he had despised so recently now seemed like the only chance he had left.

"I'll resign from the department, okay? I'm gonna get terminated anyway, so I'll save you the trouble. I'll send a letter of resignation, and then you won't have to prosecute me. You won't have this monumental ethical problem."

"Don't resign," she said softly.

"Why not?"

"Because . . . just because."

Then her beeper sounded, and she pulled it out of her purse. She looked at it, then quickly put it away.

"What is it?"

"Prints and Identification. I dropped off one of those empty folders from Zell's files. They're calling me back."

Shane didn't say anything, but he thought it was a good move to see whose fingerprints were on those empty file folders. He was surprised he hadn't thought of it.

She pulled her cell phone out of her briefcase and dialed a number. "This is Sergeant Hamilton, serial number 50791. I got paged to this number. I have a fingerprint request, number 487, April twenty-third," she said, reading off a slip of paper from her purse.

They sat in the still air of the parked Crown Vic as she waited. Then: "Okay . . . right. Okay, I've got it." She hung up and put the phone back in her purse.

"What?" he asked.

Indecision was tightening her lips, bending them down. "I've been a cop for seventeen years. It's all I ever wanted to do," she said sadly.

"Alexa, whose prints were on the file? They weren't Commander Zell's, right?"

"Zell's were on there, of course. But there was another set, fresh ones."

"Whose were they?"

"Why is the fucking head of Special Investigations Division personally clearing active case folders out of the Chief Advocate's Office?"

"Mayweather?" Shane said.

They sat in the Crown Vic, both realizing the answer was obvious. Mayweather had been doing damage control. There was no way she could ignore it, he thought. Mayweather was actively involved. The deputy police chief was personally emptying sensitive files because he didn't trust anyone else to do it. Shane looked at her and waited. Would she finally admit he was right? Whatever was going on, it was frightening and went straight to the top of the department.

26
ESIS

ALEXA HAMILTON sat in the Crown Vic for another minute, saying nothing. Then she opened the door and stepped out, retrieving her box of files from the backseat. She kicked the back door closed with her foot and stood looking over the roof of the car at Shane, who had also exited the vehicle.

"I don't know what you expect me to do," she said, her voice ringing in the cold, empty structure.

"I don't, either," he said. "If the district attorney files that 187 warrant, I'm going to be sitting this out in jail. I've got a lot of ground to cover, six cops to check out."

She stood there, reluctant to stay, unable to go. The heavy box was balanced on her slender knee. "What're you gonna do?" she asked, finally sliding the box up onto the trunk so she wouldn't have to hold it.

"On the tape in Ray's Arrowhead house, Don and Lee left a message. It said, 'We're on for Friday night, the Web. Bring the jerseys.' I don't have a clue what that means, but it's Friday, so tonight I thought I'd tail Drucker or Ayers, see what and where the Web is."

She listened but said nothing.

"Then I've gotta find out about Cal-VIP Homes . . . research who owns that company."

A car came up the ramp in the garage and pulled past them.

"I can't stand around here talking to you. Give me your cell phone number. I'll call you," Alexa said impatiently.

"When?"

"*When I'm through*. I've got six affidavits scheduled for today, starting with Bud Halley at eight-fifteen this morning. I've gotta go to the Patrol Division and dig out your old TA reports, then over to the Traffic Coordination Section and pull the reckless-driving sheets. You sure busted your share of city vehicles."

"You can't be serious?"

She pressed the alarm activation button on her car key, and the Crown Vic chirped loudly, cutting him off, ending the argument. Then she pulled the file box off the trunk and headed away from him toward the elevator. He watched as she stood in front of the elevator, balancing the heavy box; then the door slid open and she stepped inside. Just as it started to close, she stuck her foot out and stopped it.

"Meet me at the Appaloosa after work, five-thirty. We'll follow Drucker and Ayers together." Before he could answer, the door closed, taking her from view.

■ ■ ■

Shane spent the morning getting himself settled. He rented a room in a building called the Spring Summer Apartments, picking it because it cost only two hundred for one week. It was also within walking distance of the Bradbury.

The room was small but clean. He sat on the faded blue bedspread and dialed Budget Rent-a-Car. He reserved a Mustang from the rental agency located a few blocks away on Third, and walked over to pick up the car.

As he started down Third Street, he could see signs posted on telephone poles and buildings that notified residents and store owners that there would be no parking permitted on Saturday, by order of the LAPD, as a motion picture would be shooting on these streets. Schwarzenegger, no doubt.

When he got to Budget, they showed him to a red Mustang convertible, a year or two newer than Barbara's but totally unacceptable for a tail job. He turned it down in favor of a dull-brown four-door Ford Taurus.

He drove the Taurus back to the Spring Summer Apartments, parked, went back up to his room, and checked in with the Corporations Commission on his request for a printout of corporate ownership of Cal-VIP Homes. He was informed by a cold female voice that his request was in line but had not been processed yet. Maybe sometime after noon. He gave his cell phone number to her, stressing the urgency, and the woman promised to call back.

He hung up and sat in the room, feeling restless and caged. After pacing for almost half an hour, he called the Electronics Scientific Investigation Section (ESIS) to check on Ray's answering-machine tape analysis. He got a clerk there, somebody named Boyd Miller, who told Shane that ESIS had picked up fragments of old voices on the tape.

"Some of this is kinda jumbled," Miller said. "On one message, our best fragment sounded like 'If this is Susan Burbick or Burdick, we have your . . . something.' I couldn't make out the rest."

"Anything else?" Shane said, writing it down.

"No. That's it. You want to pick this up or shall we send it back to your office?"

"Hold it for me. I'll pick it up."

He hung up and sat there for several moments before reluctantly calling Barbara Molar at her house. He got the machine, so he tried her new cell phone. After he identified himself, she brightened.

"Hi, stranger. How you doing?"

"Terrible. How 'bout you?"

"Well, actually, pretty good. It's nice you finally called. I was worried."

"Have you ever heard of someone named Susan Burdick or Burbick?" he asked.

"What do I get if I say yes?"

"You get to find out if Ray was actually married to her or not."

"Oh . . . well, I'll have to think about it. I'll look in Ray's address book. How 'bout we get together for a drink, talk it over?"

"I can't, I'm meeting someone at five."

"Don't play hard-to-get with me, Shane. I don't like being dumped."

"Neither did I," he said softly, and hung up.

He sat in the transient apartment with its chipped, broken bathroom fixtures and fly-speckled wallpaper and wondered what to do next. Finally he got the number for the Arrowhead Sheriff's Department, called, and asked for Sheriff Conklyn. After a few minutes the tall, middle-aged sheriff was on the phone.

"Sheriff, it's Sergeant Scully. Remember me?"

"Whatta you want?" He was angry now, or maybe just impatient.

"When I was up there, you had a murder, a body you pulled out of the lake and couldn't identify. I never heard if it was a man or a woman."

"Woman."

"You ever ID the corpse?"

"Nope, still a Jane Doe." There was a sliver of interest in his manner now.

"Check out a woman named Susan Burdick or Burbick. I don't

know which. I also don't have an address, but maybe you can get a line on her through her marriage license. I think she was married to Ray Molar using the name Jay Colter. They tied the knot at the Midnight Wedding Chapel in Vegas six months ago. If that checks, you could get a dental match and maybe pin it."

"Why do I get the feeling I'm doing your footwork?"

"Hey, Sheriff, I'm trying to help you. If you don't wanna ID your icebox cases, don't bother with it."

"But if I do, you'd probably be interested in who she is and where she came from."

"I'm a curious guy."

"Okay, this will probably take a day or so. Call me back."

After he hung up, Shane drove back to the Fotomat to pick up the Arrowhead pictures. He was told by the clerk that they had to push the negative four stops to get an exposure. Shane opened the envelope and looked at six grainy snapshots of the men inside Ray's house. He could see most of their faces but didn't recognize any of them. He wondered which one was Calvin Sheets. Since his camera was in the Acura back in Venice, he bought a new Canon with a zoom lens and some film. He was loading the film when his cell phone rang. It was Sandy.

"Chooch ran away," she told him straight out.

"I was afraid of that."

"You've gotta find him."

"How'm I gonna find him, Sandy? All I can do is put a 'runaway juvie' out on him, and he's gonna get arrested. Then you'll be fooling around with the LACCSD—that's children's social services. If they find out what you do for a living, they'll take him away from you. Then he's gonna be a ward of the court."

"Well, what can we do?"

"I don't know. I'll try and find him, but I don't even know where to start. It's not going to be easy."

But it was easier than he thought. As soon as he hung up from Sandy, his phone rang. It was Chooch.

"I'm in a phone booth over by UCLA, the Texaco just off the freeway on Sunset," the teenager said. "I gotta see you."

"On my way." Shane got into his rental car and headed back to West L.A.

DEAL

H E WAS SITTING on a low wall that framed the perimeter of
the Texaco station one block west of the 405. He seemed
small sitting there, diminished by events, his head down, staring
at the sidewalk as if the answer to his life might be hiding in the
scrub weeds growing between the cracks.

Shane pulled the rented Taurus into the gas station and tapped
the horn. Chooch got off the wall, moved to the car, and slid in,
pulling the door shut. He sat there, silent, looking like he'd lost
something he couldn't replace.

"Your mom's worried."

"Yeah. Okay, let's go," he said.

"You had lunch? There's a good place in Westwood, over by
UCLA. Got subs and a great deli."

The boy shrugged, so Shane put the car in gear and headed
that way.

The place was called the Little Bruin. Shane and Chooch got a booth in the back surrounded by chattering college students and lunch-break shopkeepers. Chooch ordered the special; Shane, pastrami on rye. They both had Cokes.

"I thought we had a deal. You were gonna stay put, and I was gonna try and get my stuff settled, get back to you by next weekend at the latest."

Chooch was looking out the window at the passing traffic so he could avoid Shane's eyes. "I been thinkin'," he said. "I know it's like a problem all the time havin' to have somebody look after me, but like you said, I'm a man. I make my own choices now, right?"

"Right."

"So, if I moved in with you, you wouldn't have to baby-sit me anymore or have Longboard come over and sit. I don't need to be supervised. I'm sorta beyond that. Like you said, right?"

"Yeah, I guess," Shane said. "But I got guys shooting up my place. We'd have to get Kevlar jammies."

"You're not sleeping there, either. I'll go wherever you go."

" 'Cept I'm not your legal guardian. I can't make that choice for you. Sandy has to."

"Yeah, well, the thing is, Sandy and me, we're not gonna happen."

"You sure of that?"

"Yeah. I'm sure. It didn't work."

"You gave it a whole nine hours."

"You know what she does for a living?"

Shane didn't know how to answer that. "Do you?" he finally said.

"Yeah. She's a hooker. I found her trick book. She has over fifty guys in there. It lists what they like, what kinda sex." He was having trouble talking about this, watching the traffic out the window, studying the street with manufactured interest.

"She's paying for my school and shit by fucking guys. She's a whore." He turned back, and Shane could see the anger in the boy's black eyes.

"Chooch, your mom—"

"Yeah?"

"When I first met her, she was young, alone in L.A. She made a bad choice, but she doesn't do that anymore. She's an informant for the police department. Federal, as well as LAPD."

"How does that pay for anything?" he challenged. "The private school and that penthouse."

"She dates guys that law enforcement wants to bust, works 'em for information, then sells it to the cops. She does real well. She's trying to save up enough to retire, live with you in Phoenix, be a regular mom."

"Some real mom."

The waitress, a college girl in shorts and a UCLA T-shirt, delivered their lunches, set down silverware wrapped in paper napkins, and left. Shane unwrapped his knife and fork and put the napkin on his lap while Chooch continued to look out the window, brooding.

"Whatta you want, man?" Shane finally said. "It is what it is. I can't change it; neither can you. You've gotta move past it."

"Easy for you. I got nobody now. Least you've got somebody you can talk to."

"Yeah? Who's that?"

"I found all the letters you write to your dad. They were in the desk drawer in the living room. I was looking for paper for my homework."

Shane put down his half-eaten sandwich. Chooch watched him closely, focused on him hard.

"You shouldn't read other people's mail," Shane said softly.

"You write them but you never send 'em."

"He's sick. They were downers. I didn't want to distress him. I don't want to talk about this with you. It's not right you reading my private mail."

They sat in silence for a moment, then Shane's cell phone rang, interrupting an awkward moment. It was the guy at Parker Center checking the Cal-VIP Homes with the Corporations Commission.

"Go," Shane said, grabbing a pencil.

"Spivack Development Corporation, Long Beach, California, owns Cal-VIP and paid the real estate taxes on the Arrowhead address you gave me."

"Anthony Spivack? That Spivack Development? The big corporate developer?"

"It just said Spivack Development, 2000 Lincoln Ave., Long Beach, California."

"Thanks," Shane said, and folded the phone.

"I can't go back to Sandy's place. I won't do it," Chooch protested.

"Okay, okay, I'll work out something. But I've gotta call and tell her you're okay."

"Fine. I don't care. I just don't wanna go back."

"Okay. We can try, but I can't promise that's gonna stick."

They sat quietly in the booth and ate their sandwiches. Chooch, still deep in thought, only picked at his.

"Shane," he said, and Scully looked up at him. "Did she ever tell you who my father was?" The question had been waiting there building up pressure, needing to be asked.

"Yeah," Shane said, "but she didn't want you to find out who he was."

"Because he was one of those guys, one of the crooks she plays to the cops?"

"Chooch, come on . . ."

"I wanna know. Was my old man a criminal?"

"She'll have to tell you. She made me promise, but it's not really gonna change anything, because he's not coming back for a long time."

"He's a crook . . . I know it. Some legacy, huh? No wonder I get into so much trouble."

"Hey, Chooch, criminal behavior isn't genetic. You don't pass it on, father to son, like blue eyes and freckles. You can make whatever you want of your life. It's up to you. Your father's mistakes are his. Everybody gets to make their own."

"That's what you keep telling me," the boy said. Then he gave Shane a rueful smile. "And you don't ever lie, right?"

"Right," Shane said. Then without really knowing why, but realizing it was the right thing to do, Shane finally unburdened himself of something he had kept hidden for years. "You wanna know why I never mailed the letters?"

Chooch nodded.

" 'Cause I don't know where to send them."

"It says Florida."

"I don't know where he is, or even who he is. I was left at a hospital. 'Infant 205,' in 1963. I got named by City Services. It's silly. I write the letters when I need to get my thoughts down. And my father . . ." He stopped, unable to finish for a second. "My father is an idea I can talk to."

"Somebody you wish you had, who can be whatever you want him to be," Chooch said, knowing exactly what Shane meant, feeling all the same things . . . the loneliness, the disenfranchisement, the emptiness coming from the same hole in their personal histories.

"Yeah." Shane's voice was husky.

"I wondered why you agreed to take me. That's why."

"I don't know why, Chooch. I don't know what I was looking for."

The waitress came to the table and asked them if they wanted anything.

"Yeah," Chooch said. "But I don't think you've got it in the kitchen."

Shane smiled. "Let's get going. I've got an errand to run. You want, you can come with me."

He paid and they left the Little Bruin and headed to the brown

Taurus parked at a curbside meter, dazed by what had just happened.

"Thanks for telling me about your dad," Chooch finally said.

"I won't tell about your dad if you won't tell about mine," Shane said.

"Deal," Chooch said, and smiled. They got in the car and left Westwood, both wondering what this strange new connection held for them.

CONNECTING THE DOTS

THE FIFTEEN-STORY steel-and-glass building on Lincoln Boulevard was named the Two Thousand Building by a large monument sign that marked the entrance. Under that in gold letters:

A SPIVACK DEVELOPMENT

It was also on top of the building in five-foot-high lit letters, leaving no doubt about who owned the place.

Shane and Chooch parked in the underground garage, got out, and moved to the elevator, taking it up to the management floor at the top of the building. They exited into a huge architectural lobby decorated in monochromatic colors, dominated by too many sharp edges and angular lines. Steel-and-glass furniture dotted the interior. Futuristic recessed lighting laid down a cold blue-white glow. A huge gold sign behind the receptionist again announced that this was:

SPIVACK DEVELOPMENT
CORPORATE HEADQUARTERS

Shane left Chooch by the elevator and approached a striking, unfriendly white-blond receptionist who looked cold enough to have been delivered with the furniture. Shane opened his wallet and took out his police business card. Since he didn't have his badge, the business card was the best he could manage. He was hoping it would get him past the blond goddess who was guarding the floor, stationed behind her huge, semicircular, two-inch-thick green glass desk, like a turret gunner.

"What's this regarding?" she asked, speaking coolly, not intimidated by his card or manner.

"Police business," he replied.

"Mr. Spivack isn't here. Perhaps someone else can help you?"

"How about Calvin Sheets?" Shane said, wondering if Logan Hunter's head of security was also working for Spivack.

"He's down at the city council meeting with Mr. Spivack. Sorry . . ."

"The Long Beach City Council?"

She ignored his question and smiled an icicle at him. "Would there be anybody else . . . ?"

"Coy Love."

"We don't have a Coy Love."

"I'm not doing too well, am I?"

"Sometimes if you make an appointment in advance, it works wonders." Freon.

"I may just have to get a search warrant and start emptying everyone's desks. . . . Do a couple of body searches."

"Anything else?" She had grown tired of him.

"Pamela Anderson Lee wouldn't happen to be around, would she?"

"Just left." But at least this earned him a smile.

He picked up his business card, tucked it into his wallet, then took a Spivack Company brochure off the glass desk and walked across the lobby, the ice-blonde watching him all the way. He retrieved Chooch, got into the elevator, and went down. He left the teenager in the lobby, then found the staircase to the basement. It took him five minutes to find the service utility room. Inside was a huge gray panel box with a dime-store lock that took Shane less than thirty seconds to pick. Now he was looking at a startling array of colorful wires. "Shit," he said, then slowly went to work unraveling the building's complicated alarm system.

■ ■ ■

"I wonder where the city council meets. Probably city hall," Shane said as they settled back into the Taurus. He picked up his almost fried cell phone, called Information in Long Beach, and got the address for city hall on Front Street just before the phone quit.

They drove away from the Two Thousand Building and, with some help from a gas-station attendant, found Front Street. The huge domed city building loomed two blocks ahead. . . .

As they pulled up the street, they could see quite a demonstration in progress—thirty or forty pickets were congregating around in front of city hall. It was a strange mixture of people. Some were old men in American Legion uniforms, holding duplicate hand-lettered signs that read:

VETERANS AGAINST LONG BEACH
LAND-FOR-WATER DEAL

Other pickets carried more traditional union placards:

**AFL-CIO OPPOSES NAVAL YARD WATER SWAP
THEY GET THE DOUGH, WE GET THE HOSE**

Others protested with:

**GIVE US JOBS, NOT SOBS
SPIVACK-EVACK—WE DON'T WANT YOU HERE
WE SAVED THE WHALES—YOU SAVE OUR JOBS!**

Shane and Chooch had to park a block away in a city parking lot and, after locking up, moved across the shimmering, heated asphalt to where the demonstration was taking place.

"What's going on?" Shane asked a tough-looking woman with inch-long hair wearing a plaid shirt and carrying a sign that read:

**BEACHFRONT FOR H$_2$O?
OUR CITY COUNCIL SUCKS!**

"These idiots are trading the Long Beach Naval Yard to Los Angeles County for a bunch of fuckin' water rights," she growled.

"Naval yard? I thought the navy shut it down years ago."

"Yeah, they did, and now we're giving it to L.A."

"Isn't it federal property?" Shane persisted.

She shot him a withering look. "Where you been, buddy? This is all over the fuckin' news."

"I don't have a TV," Shane answered.

"It was leased land. Now Long Beach's gonna trade it for some dumb water rights."

Shane moved past her and, along with Chooch, climbed up the steps and entered city hall.

The Long Beach Municipal Building was a large brick structure that had been built in the forties. It had a high, two-story rotunda, now overflowing with TV news crews who had set up there for a press conference.

"I'm gonna try and find this guy Spivack," Shane said to Chooch. "Stick close, okay?"

"Got it."

Shane moved past the news crews but got stopped at the door to the City Council Chamber by a uniformed Long Beach police officer.

"Sorry, we're maxed out. Fire regs," the cop said.

"LAPD, I'm working." He handed the cop his business card.

"Okay, Sarge, but it's a madhouse in there."

"He's with me," Shane said, indicating Chooch; then they entered the meeting hall.

The council room was a theater-sized, cavernous hall with a sloping floor and raised dais. The room was packed. They could hear a contentious argument being staged over microphones:

"How the hell can you say that the property can't be used by Long Beach?!" a woman yelled from the floor. "I worked at that yard, I was an employee of the Metal Trades Council for thirty years. I thought we were being reamed in '94, when the government closed the only profitable shipyard in the navy. But that's nothing compared to what's going on here. You're taking a huge city asset and trading it for chump change!"

The crowd shouted its approval. The president of the city council banged his gavel for order, then replied, "To begin with, the yard was closed in '94 because it was badly situated, too close to the big refitting yard in San Diego. What's going on here now is *good* for the city of Long Beach. Mr. Spivack is going to clear all the old military buildings off the site, regrade the property, and develop it. Okay, it's going to be ceded to the city of L.A., but I might remind you that the shipyard borders L.A. on the north and Long Beach on the south, so it's contiguous with them as well as us."

"Who cares? I'm not talking about geography. I'm talking about jobs!" the woman fired back, to a chorus of cheers.

The city council president was prepared. "Long Beach residents *will* get the jobs because the yard is much closer to our main workforce than to L.A.'s. There'll be hotels, shopping malls, restaurants—all employment for Long Beach citizens. And we don't have to float bond issues or construction loans to develop the site. We won't have to pay for its construction; L.A. will. But we will get the major work benefits, plus much-needed water from L.A."

Shane was looking for Anthony Spivack somewhere down front, not paying much attention to the argument going on between the Long Beach City Council and its angry residents. He had the Spivack brochure open to a picture of the CEO. Spivack was a heavyset man with a thick head of close-cropped, curly gray hair. The woman at the mike raised her voice in response, cutting through the background noise with electronic shrillness. "And who, may I ask, gets the municipal tax revenue on all this commercial property, Mr. Cummins?"

Shane spun around and looked up at the president of the Long Beach City Council. He was a slender, hollow-chested man with horn-rimmed glasses, identified by a plaque in front of him on the elevated dais:

CARL CUMMINS
PRESIDENT, LONG BEACH CITY COUNCIL

"Son of a bitch," Shane said.

Chooch looked at him. "What is it?"

Just then, some kind of disturbance seemed to be taking place in the back of the hall. A chant began: "AFL-CIO . . . Tony Spivack, you must go."

About thirty protesters had broken into the hall and were trying to march down the aisle, carrying placards. The agitated audience soon picked up the chant.

Carl Cummins started banging his gavel, trying to regain order. "We can't conduct this hearing under these conditions!" he said, screeching it into his mike, getting loud boos and electronic feedback. "The discussion period on City Resolution 397 is concluded. The board will retire to chambers to take its vote. We're adjourned." He angrily banged his gavel and rose.

The chorus of boos grew louder. Suddenly people in the front rows stood up and started throwing fruit at the stage; pulling oranges and plums out of carry-bags, brought in anticipation of this demonstration.

Carl Cummins and the nine other members of the city council bolted from their chairs as they were pelted with fruit, making a hurried exit from the stage.

The pushing and shoving was getting increasingly intense in the auditorium, threatening to turn into a riot.

"Let's go!" Shane said, grabbing Chooch. "Stay close to me. Hold on to my belt."

He felt Chooch grab hold of his belt in the back, and then Shane pushed through the melee to the fire exit on the same side of the room that Carl Cummins and the city council were using as a retreat. By now most of the frightened council members had left the stage.

Shane got to the fire exit, but it was guarded by another Long Beach cop. "Sorry. This is an alarmed fire door," the policeman said.

"Long Beach Fire Marshal," Shane bullshitted. "I'm authorized to open it under Regulation 1623. Excuse me."

He handed the startled cop his official LAPD business card and jostled him, hoping he couldn't read it in the commotion. In that moment of hesitation, Shane pushed down on the silver bar and opened the door. The alarm bell sounded. People were panicking as fruit continued to fly. Shane pushed past the Long Beach cop, dragging Chooch into the hot sunshine.

Up ahead, he could see a black limousine waiting with several chase cars. Then Shane spotted Anthony Spivack beside the limo. With him were several of the men Shane had photographed in Arrowhead. He assumed one of them must be Calvin Sheets. The people with Spivack started piling into cars. Carl Cummins arrived with one of the other council members and jumped into Spivack's limo. Like the last politicians leaving Saigon, they slammed car doors and squealed away from the angry mob pouring out of the doors behind them.

"Stay with me!" Shane said, trying to get an idea which direction the fleeing cars were headed while simultaneously sprinting for the Taurus, parked almost a block away.

He and Chooch finally reached the car. Both were out of breath as they jumped in. Shane put the car in gear and sped across the lot, cutting between parked cars. He bounced over the curb, shot out onto Front Street, and took off heading south, after the speeding limo and its four chase vehicles.

"What's going on?" Chooch asked.

"Some of these guys were in the house up in Arrowhead," he said, fearing he couldn't catch up with them.

Shane had lost sight of the cars but was now driving along a frontage road that bordered the Long Beach Airport. On a hunch, he turned into one of the executive terminals, past an open bararm at the end of a ramp, driving out onto the tarmac that bordered the runway. As he sped along past a row of FBOs (flight base operators) that lined the west side of the field, several ramp attendants and cargo loaders started screaming and waving their arms at the brown Taurus. Shane just ignored them, racing past parked Lears and Gulfstreams.

He thought he saw the black limo in the distance parked near a large Sikorsky helicopter, idling with the rotor turning slowly.

He drove around more executive jets—transportation necessities of the megarich.

Finally he could see the helicopter more clearly. Spivack and Cummins were getting into the idling chopper with the rest of the men from the Arrowhead house. He was close enough to the helicopter to read SPIVACK DEVELOPMENT on the side door as the huge green-and-white nine-passenger Sikorsky lifted off.

Shane got there half a minute too late. He watched in frustration as the chopper hovered for a minute a few feet above the tarmac, then the rotor changed pitch, and the helicopter streaked away, climbing to the north. Soon it was just a speck in the bright blue cloudless sky.

TAIL JOB

A T A FEW MINUTES before five in the afternoon, Shane was back inside the Appaloosa, watching a cockroach trying to hide under the molding that framed the tabletop, one feeler reaching out, tentatively tapping the Formica. He was in the same cracked vinyl booth in the back, nursing a Coke grudgingly supplied by the same greasy-coated Mexican waiter. "Das all chu gonna haf?" the man said.

"Yep," Shane said. "Working." The waiter left. Shane kept a wary eye on the barricaded cockroach and while "Malaguena" played through ruptured speakers, he was thinking about Chooch, whom he had left ten minutes earlier at the Spring Summer Apartments with the TV blaring. Shane had convinced Longboard to stop by the Venice house, get Chooch's book bag with his homework assignments, take it to the apartment on Third, and stay with the boy until Shane got back. In return for this service, Shane had given up his Lakers-Trailblazers tickets for the weekend. He made a mental note to call by six to make sure Longboard had gotten there okay.

Surprisingly, with trouble and chaos swirling around his own life, Shane found himself worrying about Chooch's back homework assignments as well as his emotional well-being. Something about this newly found concern for someone else's future seemed to settle his own emotions in a way he couldn't understand. Underneath the boy's grumbling and bitching about the extra supervision, Shane suspected that he appreciated the concern. Earlier in the hectic day, when Shane had turned around unexpectedly and caught Chooch staring at him, the expression on his face was one of wonder. It said more than any words could convey.

Perhaps Shane could work out something more permanent with Sandy. She had her hands full right now with the DEA, but after that, she'd change teams and be on to some other predicate felon. He, on the other hand, was in the checkout line. If he didn't end up in prison or the grave, he was certainly through being a cop. Once he was off the force, he could devote more time to Chooch, stop farming him out to Longboard. Chooch didn't know who his father was, and although Shane couldn't fill that role, he sure as hell could be a big brother. Then he looked up, and she was coming through the door.

Alexa stood backlit in the late-afternoon sunshine, holding her briefcase under her arm, the shoulder strap tucked inside. She let her eyes adjust to the cavelike darkness of the windowless bar-restaurant. Finally she spotted him and moved across the room, her hips swaying seductively with the motion.

She slid in and smiled wanly at him. "Our spot," she said dryly.

"If it is, we've gotta either train these cockroaches or start killing them." She looked puzzled, so he lifted the sugar shaker, and the eight-legged German roach took off like a shot.

She let out an involuntary feminine squeal, then returned to form, slapping at it bare-handed and missing. The roach dodged, shooting across the table as Alexa slammed her palm down again—the only thing she hurt was her hand. The roach went off the end of the table, hit the floor, and was gone.

"Sign him. Good broken-field run." Shane smiled.

She checked around the perimeter of the booth, looking for relatives, then glanced at Shane. "Strong survival instincts. We should take lessons."

He took out the Arrowhead pictures he'd had developed and slid them across the table to her. "Know any of these guys?"

She went through them while he waited.

"Yep. All of 'em. This one is Calvin Sheets." She pushed a picture over and showed it to Shane. It was of the medium-built man with the ash-blond hair, setting a box down at the back door. Shane realized he'd been right, that Sheets had been the man standing with Tony Spivack at the limo.

"This is Coy Love," she said, sliding another photograph over to Shane, who could see why you wouldn't want to "fuck with Love." He was large, over six feet, with a huge, jutting jaw and a cruel, angular face. He had a thin, lipless mouth, straight as a ruler.

"These other two guys were cops on Calvin's Coliseum detail. They both got terminated with him on his bullshit time-sheet hustle." She pushed those shots over. "Lon Sherwood and Carter something, I can't remember his last name."

She looked up, and the waiter was back, hovering like a dragonfly over a lake, waiting for her order.

"I'll have what he's having."

"Chu makin' my day." He left, grumbling.

"Cummins is president of the Long Beach City Council, and I found out Spivack Development Corporation owns Cal-VIP Homes." Shane filled her in on the Long Beach City Council meeting; the dispute over the transfer of the naval yard to L.A. for water; the chase through Long Beach trying to catch Sheets,

Spivack, and Cummins; and their eventual helicopter escape. She was holding her briefcase on her lap in both hands, ready to strike in case another cockroach took off on an end run around the Mexican condiments.

"You had a busy day," she said.

"I won't ask how your day went, for fear it'll severely depress me."

"I hope DeMarco is staying busy, 'cause I'm getting good prima facie stuff," she said, needling him.

"Don't worry about DeMarco. The Saint's all over this. He says with what he has, we'll probably want to to file a civil action."

"Good. 'Cause I'd heard he'd become an alcoholic—a blackout drunk—and that's why he pulled the pin."

"Don't worry about Dee. He's kicking ass."

Blackout drunk? I'm fucked, Shane thought.

She looked at her watch as the waiter set down her Coke and left. "I ran both Drucker and Kono through the Office of Administrative Services at the Personnel Group," she said. "Drucker just got reassigned from Southwest to Hollenbeck. He's working street patrol—day shift. Kono has a worrisome nickname. They call him Bongo. I'm hoping that's because he's of Hawaiian ancestry, and not because he beats people like a drum."

She picked up her Coke and drained it. "Thirsty," she apologized. "Anyway, Kono's still in South Bureau, but now he's working day watch in University Division. That means we're going to have to split up if we want to follow both guys." She glanced at her Timex. "We better get moving. Day watch breaks in forty minutes. Which one a' these raisin cakes do you want?"

"Ladies first."

"Chivalry always knocks me out," she said drolly. "Okay, since he's closer, I'll take Drucker."

He put some money down on the table for the two Cokes, and they both stood.

"Let's communicate on a tactical frequency," she said. "One of the high ones nobody uses. Organized Crime is on tac ten, and that division doesn't have much going now. Let's use that."

"I don't have a police radio; my car's in Venice. I'm using a rental."

"You really bring it all to the table, don't you, Scully," she said sarcastically.

He needed her help, so he let it go.

"We can pick up a handset at IAD. I saw a whole bunch of them in a box in the IO's section," Shane suggested

She nodded. "We better move it, or they'll both be EOW before we get there."

■ ■ ■

The University Division station was an old concrete four-story building located on South Adams Boulevard, near USC. Shane left the Taurus in the only available spot he could find, half a block up the street. He fed the meter, moved away from it, and sat on a bus bench across from the station. From there he had an unobstructed view of the station parking lot. He had on an L.A. Dodgers cap, pulled low over his eyes, and a dull green-and-brown camouflage windbreaker he had picked up that afternoon at a surplus shop downtown for fifteen bucks.

Shane felt invisible and ready for action: Mr. Brown-and-Green in his camo jacket and dirt-brown Taurus. He had the police handset in his lap and was watching as the day watch started streaming out in civilian clothes, on the way to their private vehicles. It was 5:45.

"Six to Five. Target D is in motion." He heard Alexa's voice coming over the radio on tactical frequency 10. They had chosen their radio code numbers in the parking lot outside the Bradbury while doing a quick equipment check. He picked up his handset.

"Copy, Six. I'm still parked and waiting."

"Roger that," she said. "Target D just left Hollenbeck, heading up onto 91. He's westbound."

"Roger. Standing by on tac ten." He laid the radio on his lap and sat on the bus bench waiting for Kris "Bongo" Kono.

Officer Kono was one of the last ones out the station side door. He was dressed in jeans and a T-shirt and was carrying a duffel bag. He sprinted to his car, obviously late. He jumped into a blue '76 Camaro with racing stripes and a primered left front fender, then pulled quickly out of the lot, burning rubber.

Shane was caught leaning. He was half a block away from the Taurus and late getting back to it, fumbling to unlock the door as the Camaro made a sharp turn out of the parking lot. The 455-cubic-inch engine and blown mufflers on the muscle car roared angrily past and sped up the street.

"Shit," Shane said, finally piling into the Taurus and starting it up. He found a hole in traffic and pulled out, already danger- ously behind. He watched, frustrated, as the Camaro went through the intersection up ahead on the yellow light. Shane tried to make up ground, spinning his wheels, chirping rubber, trying to get around slower traffic. When he got to the cross street, the light was against him, so he leaned on his horn and broke reck- lessly through the intersection against the red light, causing an eastbound truck on Atlantic to slam on its brakes. The angry traffic started screaming at him, blaring their horns and flipping him off.

As Shane shot through the red light, he could see the blue Camaro one block ahead, speeding through another light on the yellow.

"Slow the fuck down!" Shane yelled at the Camaro as he was forced to stop at the second light, trapped behind a row of cars, unable to get around them. He could see the Camaro a block ahead, turning right, heading up onto the 110.

"Come on, come on, come on . . ." Shane begged the five-way light that was trapping him. Then it turned green, but an old woman in a rusting Subaru was making a cautious left, blocking traffic, afraid to go. "Come on, lady. You got the fuckin' right-of-way!" he shouted at his windshield.

"Six, I'm on 91, heading west, passing Olive," Alexa's voice announced. Static, then: "Six, do you copy?"

Shane had his hands full as the woman finally completed her turn. He was flooring it, illegally passing a city bus on the right, shooting past the line of traffic, hanging a right, going up the on-ramp. His tires squealed on the sun-hot asphalt.

He hit the 110 going way too fast for the flow of rush-hour traffic that loomed before him on the packed freeway. He had to hit his brakes to keep from plowing into the right side of a Ford Escort, startling the two hard hats inside.

"Six, this is Five. Do you copy?" Alexa's voice persisted. "Six, you are Code One. Copy, please." Code One was a command to respond and was given only when a unit did not answer a radio call and was perceived to be in difficulty. It was imperative to respond to a Code One, if at all possible.

Shane impatiently snapped the radio up off his lap. "I copy. I've got my hands full, for Chrissake. Gimme a minute." He threw the radio back down on the seat and managed to get around the Ford Escort. He couldn't see the blue Camaro anywhere. "Fuck!" he said, but kept heading west on the 110, going as fast as he could, dangerously passing cars, trying to make up lost distance, driving on the right shoulder, getting angry horn blasts from a whole line of drivers.

"Six, Target D is transitioning to the 710. I'm making that freeway change now." Alexa's voice, pissing him off, was cool and in control. *Fuck her.*

Shane was sweating. A river of perspiration ran down under his arm, slicking his shirt and rib cage. People around him were screaming through their car windows as he passed them on the shoulder illegally. He was running out of room, so he veered back into the right lane, forcing the Taurus between a sixteen-wheeler Vons Grocery truck and a green Chevy van. Both drivers yelled obscenities at him. The grocery truck blew its heavy six-tone air horn, scaring the shit out of Shane, but he forced his way in, now catching a glimpse of the blue Camaro in the far left lane. Kono was transitioning off the 110 to the 105.

Shane was fucked. He slammed the heel of his hand on the steering wheel. He was fenced off by four lanes of bumper-to-bumper traffic and was pushed helplessly along by the slow flow, past the 105 transition, heading uselessly in the wrong direction. The tail was completely blown. He snapped up the radio.

"Five, this is Six," he said.

"Roger," she said.

"I lost K. He was on the 110. I got trapped, missed the transition. He's southbound on the 105, running clean." Shane waited for Alexa to curse him out or belittle him for losing his man. But she didn't do either.

"Okay, I copy," she said. "My guy just left the 710 at Ocean. We're down by the water. I'll talk you in."

"Roger that, coming your way," he said, feeling like a complete rookie.

For the next ten minutes she was silent, then: "I'm Code Six at 2300 Ocean Boulevard. Take the 710 to the end of the freeway and turn left. I'm in a gas-station parking lot."

"Copy that," he said.

It took him another ten minutes before he pulled up Ocean Boulevard and saw Alexa's gray Crown Victoria parked in a Texaco station across the street from a vast piece of fenced property.

Razor wire ran for miles in both directions. He could see two big gates, each with a private security guard. The sign over the drive-through arch had been torn down.

Shane pulled into the darkened gas station, parked near the Crown Vic, got out, and slid into the front seat next to Alexa.

"Sorry, I got totally jammed on the 110."

"It's okay," she said. "All roads lead to Rome."

"Huh?"

"Your boy just pulled through that gate five minutes ago. A blue Camaro with racing stripes and a bondoed front fender, right?"

"Yeah."

He looked through her windshield at the five-hundred-acre piece of land across Ocean Boulevard next to the bay. On the east side of the property, the buildings were still standing, but to the west there were piles of rubble where the structures had already been knocked down. It looked a little like pictures of Berlin after the bombings in '45.

"Is this place what I think it is?" she asked.

"Yep," he said softly. "The Long Beach Naval Yard."

CHOIR PRACTICE

THE SUN SET slowly and magnificently over the Pacific Ocean. Scattered clouds that were strung across the horizon in steel-gray formations suddenly turned deep purple, riding above the dark blue sea like a colorful celestial armada until the sun was gone and night claimed its final victory.

Shane retrieved his new camera from the trunk of the Taurus, grabbed the heavy lens and some film, then walked with Alexa along busy Ocean Boulevard, across the street from the old naval yard. They were both looking for a good place to climb the fence. With cars streaking by in both directions, they picked a hole in the traffic, sprinted across the busy four-lane street, then continued west, looking through the fence at the property beyond.

There were security lights located inside the old naval yard every block or so, illuminating sections of the torn-down facility. This part of the huge yard had already been completely razed.

Behind them, on the east end of the property, the surviving naval buildings loomed.

Shane reasoned that they had a better chance of getting inside unobserved if they went west, where there were no structures left standing and, hence, nothing to steal and less need for security.

"Where do you want to try?" she suddenly asked.

He pointed to a place up ahead where the razor wire had come down, making it possible to get over the fence without ripping their hands and clothes.

"With all this traffic on Ocean, we'll be spotted; somebody's gonna call it in," she said. "Let's try over there." She pointed to the far end of the property, where the fence seemed to turn a corner and head south toward the bay.

There was a huge lit structure looming down there that Shane didn't like the looks of. "Except, what the hell is that?" he asked, pointing at it, but she didn't answer.

They kept walking and finally got close enough to see that it was an active Army Reserve post, with its own entrance located at the far end of the naval yard. A bunch of weekend warriors were standing around in the parking lot, milling in front of the post HQ.

"Okay," she said. "You're right. Let's go back and try your place."

They returned to the spot Shane had seen, and then waited for the line of traffic to pass. Once the light down the street turned red, Shane touched her arm.

"Now," he said.

He and Alexa hit the fence simultaneously. It was an eight-foot-high chain-link; Shane scrambled up and over fast, surprised to see that they hit the ground on the other side at about the same time.

They sprinted away from Ocean Boulevard as the light down the street turned green and the headlights of the approaching cars came toward them. They crouched in the dark unobserved as the traffic streamed past on the far side of the fence.

"When Drucker and Kono went in, you sure you couldn't see which way they turned once they got inside?" Shane asked.

"They were stopped by the plastic badge guarding the east gate, but once they drove through, I lost 'em. I was half a block away, across the street. I didn't want to chance getting spotted."

"If they went in there, then they're probably still on the east side of the property," Shane reasoned.

"Probably."

They took off along the paved road inside the fence, this time heading east, back the way they had just come. The two-lane base road they were on was identified by a sign as COFFMAN STREET.

They were both struck by the vastness of the old shipyard. Shane had heard about the property ever since he was a kid growing up in L.A., but he'd never been down there before.

"This place is huge," he said, stating the obvious as they quickened their pace, doing a speed walk. "No wonder those people at the city council hearing were pissed. This place has gotta be worth billions of dollars. Prime waterfront, right on the border between L.A. and Long Beach; the *Queen Mary* is half a mile from here, Fisherman's Village a stone's throw away."

She nodded but said nothing.

They were coming to a part of the yard that had not been demolished yet. They began passing huge covered docks, once used to refurbish naval vessels. Faded signs hung on every kind of structure, from wood-frame officers clubs and enlisted-personnel mess halls to poured-concrete warehouses and five-story-high covered sheds. They passed blast foundation plants; the compressor boiler plant loomed next to an air compressor building; then some hazardous-waste staging areas. There were mammoth towers leaning against a dark sky, marked COLLIMA-

TION TOWER and PUMPING STATION TWO. Neither Shane nor Alexa had a clue what they were used for.

They passed the old naval credit union building, the sheet metal shop, and the asbestos removal headquarters, which was part of the current demolition operation and consisted of a flock of portable trailers.

The property was beyond anything that Shane had ever imagined. Now they were at the end of Coffman Street, where it turned into Avenue D.

Up ahead they could see some bright light streaming out of a huge warehouse. They were moving slowly now, trying to hug the shadows created by the occasional streetlamps.

They finally got close enough to see ten or twelve cars parked in front of a huge lit warehouse. Shane and Alexa could see the open loading door with a sign overhead that read:

BUILDING 132
MACHINE SHOP—PIPE AND COPPER

They crept across Avenue D and found cover behind a two-story-high cylindrical tank. When they looked around the rusting tank, Shane and Alexa could see directly into the mouth of the warehouse through the raised loading door.

A party with more than thirty people was going on inside. Some tables had been set up full of food and buckets of beer. Men and women were dancing on the cold concrete floor, which was lit by lights from two gray police plainwraps that had been pulled inside. Both Crown Vics had the doors open; stereo music was coming from the car radios tuned to the same FM station.

Shane was looking through his telescopic lens at the partyers. "Most of these guys are cops. . . . I know some of the girls. I busted a few when I was in West Valley Vice."

"Hookers?" Alexa asked. "Gimme it."

He handed her the zoom-lens camera, and she squinted through the eyepiece, panning around inside the lit building. "You're right, it's a regular coyote convention in there," she murmured. "Those are Beverly Hills pros—thousand-dollar girls— Angelica DeBravo, Deborah Kline, Donna Fleister, plus the rest of our police-department cast of characters." She was referring to Ray's den: Joe Church, Lee Ayers, John Samansky, Don Drucker, and Shane's blown tail, "Bongo" Kono. Calvin Sheets and Coy Love were not there, but the other guys he'd photographed up at Arrowhead were. Alexa identified them as ex-cops terminated from "Dream" Sheets's Coliseum detail. Then she caught her breath. "Shit—don't like this," she said, her eye pinned to the camera viewfinder.

"What?"

"There're two guys from the mayor's staff in there—his legislative assistant, Mark somebody, in the suit by the door; and Rob Lavetta, his press-relations guy, the one standing next to Drucker." She handed the camera back to Shane, who took a picture of both men.

The party was in full swing, everybody drinking beer and dancing to the music, although "dancing" was a conservative description of what was going on. It was more like a group grope in 4/4 time. Dress was optional, with the thousand-dollar girls opting for maximum exposure.

Shane wanted to photograph everyone, keeping a mental count of whom he had already shot and whom he still needed, waiting for the right moment when the dancers would spin, giving him a good angle of one or both. When he finished, he sat next to Alexa, leaning back against the rusting cylindrical tank.

"They oughta put these shots in the departmental brochure," he finally said. "We'd end our recruiting problem."

Alexa volunteered a slogan: "Not just long hours and cold coffee. Police work—a changing profession."

"Whatta you wanna do?" he asked.

"I don't know. . . ." She winced, then pulled something out from under her. It was a sign she'd been sitting on. They both read it:

ABRASIVE TANKS
MAINTAIN 50-FOOT SAFETY PERIMETER

They both looked up fearfully at the old rusting tanks they were hiding behind. Then Shane realized that his hand was in something wet, pulled it up, and looked at it.

"Shit," he said, shaking it dry.

"Let's move back, get outta here," she said.

Suddenly they heard laughing nearby. A man's voice: "You're on. Let's do it."

Shane and Alexa cautiously leaned out and looked at the party. It had now spilled out of the huge building; people were standing around the back of one of the cars parked outside, while Drucker pulled two cardboard boxes out of the trunk. He ripped them open and started handing out shirts to everybody.

"What the hell are those?" Alexa asked.

"The jerseys," Shane replied.

Black football jerseys with red numbers and letters on the back that read:

L.A. SPIDERS

The shoulder trim was done in a pattern resembling a red spider web. The cops started moving in a pack up the street with handfuls of beer and their arms draped casually around the hookers.

"I gotta see this," Shane said.

He and Alexa followed from the shadows, staying at least a hundred yards behind the group, which was drinking and grab-assing its way along Avenue D until finally they came to the old base athletic building and adjacent field. Shane and Alexa found themselves at the far end of the old field, the grass long dead from lack of water.

Someone had brought a football, and after more drinking and groping, a very fundamental game of tackle ensued. Slow, looping passes drifted to giggling hooker wideouts who gathered the spirals in without too much interference. The playful tackles were short on violence but long on rolling around on the ground and piling on. The beer kept flowing. The game looked to Shane like a hell of a lot of fun.

"How do you get a jersey and a place in the lineup?" he wondered.

"You don't want in that game, Shane. You'd get tired of all the AIDS testing."

He nodded and smiled. He realized it was the first time she'd used his first name.

They watched for quite a while and finally decided that everybody was so drunk, this was where the evening would end. They backed out, got over the fence, and returned to the gas station.

"I hate spiders," she said once they got to their cars.

"So the jerseys are football, but is this place the Web?"

"I don't know, must be," she said. "But I can tell you this much: these cops are having choir practice with first-string girls and two guys from the mayor's staff." "Choir practice" was an after-hours police drunk, usually in a park or some deserted place.

"Gimme the film," she said. "There's an all-night drugstore half a block from my apartment. I'll have the proofs back in two hours."

He hesitated, then unloaded the camera and gave her the two other exposed film containers.

They got into their respective cars and started to pull out when Alexa sounded her horn. Shane rolled down his window. She leaned across her front seat, talking through her passenger window. "For whatever it's worth, I believe you. Something big and shitty is going on here. I'm in."

"Thanks," he said gratefully. Then she waved at him and drove off. It had been more than a week, and she was the first one.

THE PITCHES
31
MOTION

SHANE WAS ON the 405 on his way back from Long Beach when he saw the transition ramp for the Santa Monica Freeway. He wondered whether DeMarco had been working on his case or whether he'd spent the day drinking and listening to rap. He decided to find out. He put on his blinker and made the turn onto the 10. Seven minutes later he was standing on the bike path outside DeMarco's house.

He hesitated a moment, almost afraid of what he would find. Finally he pushed open the gate, walked up to the front door, and knocked. One of DeMarco's new surfer roommates opened the door. He looked right through Shane and, without saying a word, stepped back and let him in. The boy was wearing surf trunks with no shirt and had an athlete's build. The eyes were where the problem was: empty, hollow tunnels of distrust.

"DeMarco around?"

The boy didn't seem to want to waste even one syllable on Shane. He jerked a thumb in the direction of the hallway, then flopped back down on the sofa, where his buddy was lounging with the TV remote. MTV's *Real World* was on the large Sony. Two teenage girls were on the screen arguing about their gay male roommate's new rottweiler, who apparently was shitting all over their London flat. One of life's smelly little problems. Shane moved through the hall and knocked on the end door. His defense rep called out angrily: "What?!"

Shane pushed the door open and looked in. For the first time, Dee was hard at it. He had law books and police department manuals open on the cluttered desk in front of him, his half-glasses perched on the end of his nose. He was a blue and gray vision in a faded LAPD sweatshirt and jeans. He had taken his long gray hair out of the knot in back, and it now hung on his shoulders, Cochise-style.

"How's it goin'?" Shane asked.

"Don't you wanna give me a Breathalyzer first?" he groused.

"Come on, Dee, gimme a break."

The defense rep leaned back in his squeaking swivel chair and swung around to face Shane. "Basically, it ain't getting any better," DeMarco said.

"You talkin' about the 1.61 Mayweather sent through this morning? I haven't seen it yet. I haven't been home."

"Copy right here," DeMarco said, picking up a fax and waving it at Shane. "But it's worse than just the 1.61. I found out this afternoon that Donovan McNeil, the only friendly face you had on your judging panel, is no longer able to attend the hearing." DeMarco rooted around his paperwork, found another fax, and held it up. "He's been transferred as of yesterday to the command chair at Administrative Vice in Central Division. Big fucking job. And since that transfer is effective immediately, it has been determined by the Special Investigations Division that, under these extreme circumstances, he does not have the time available to serve on your board. He's been replaced. I guess these Dark Side pricks finally found out you two used t'sling bait together."

"Who'd we get this time? The chief's brother-in-law?"

"Nope. The chief's old driver, Leland H. Postil."

"Fuck," Shane said. "Don't we still get to throw one out?"

"Yeah, they gave me two choices. The other was Peggy York, former head of IAD. In your absence, I chose Postil."

"Things can't get much worse," Shane growled.

"Wanna bet? Check this. I've been trying to restrict Alexa Hamilton's demands for your personal background file. It's full of a buncha unsustained complaints, CO's tardy slips, ridiculous stuff that every cop gets the minute he starts hooking up scumbags and dealing with this nitpick four-hundred-page LAPD Manual. The stuff in those background files is always just unproved bullshit, but it looks bad if you string it out in front of a board hearing."

Shane was pissed. "Old, unsustained complaints can only be used *after* the board convicts, *if* they convict, and then it can only be used as part of the penalty phase of the hearing to help determine past history and state of mind," he said.

"I see you've been reading Section 202," DeMarco said.

"I sleep with the fucking thing, for all the good it's doing me."

"Well, buddy-boy, once again, the powers that control the Special Investigations Division have ruled against you. Alexa filed a Pitches motion to overturn that section of the Police Bill of Rights. The panel granted her motion, and the package went over to her at four this afternoon."

They sat quietly in the room. Finally DeMarco got up, went to a small refrigerator in the corner of the office, and pulled out a beer. "You want one?"

"Dee, you've gotta stay off the Bud Lights. Okay?"

"Fuck you. I'm through listening to that shit from you." He ripped the tab off and took a swallow.

"I'm hearing around that maybe you have an alcohol problem," Shane said. "I hear that's why you pulled the pin."

DeMarco looked at him and smiled, then took a long fuck-you swig. "I won't even favor that with an answer."

"Look, Dee, I'm into something here. I think I've got the mayor tied into a blackmail scheme to trade billions of dollars' worth of property from Long Beach over to L.A. Ray and his den were blackmailing people in Arrowhead so this would happen, most notably Carl Cummins, who's president of the Long Beach City Council. I followed some guys out there to the old naval yard. I've got—"

"You got shit," DeMarco interrupted, slamming the beer can down on his desktop. "Maybe if you'd stop running around, accusing all these high-profile guys of bullshit crimes, we wouldn't be facing all this administrative flack. We wouldn't be losing the Pitches and all our other motions."

"But—"

"No! Don't 'but' me. Ever since I took this fucking case, you've been accusing me of not trying. The reason we're getting hosed here, buddy, is that you have proceeded to piss off the chief of police, Deputy Chief Mayweather, Ray's rookie den, and everybody in between. Add to that the fact that you're acting like you're fucking guilty. What kinda asshole breaks into Warren Zell's office and goes through his files?"

"Who told you that?" Shane asked.

"It's all over the department that Alexa Hamilton caught you in there, you dumb shit!"

Shane stood there, feeling slightly dizzy and stupid as hell. *Had Alexa lied? Had she told the department what he'd done?* "I . . . I don't see how—"

"On top of all that, you're about to get arrested for first-degree murder," DeMarco interrupted. "I got a call from the warrant control desk today. They wanted to know if you were here. They've been checking your house and said you're not living there. I think you'd better get in touch with them—turn yourself in."

Shane spun and moved out of the office, back into the hall. DeMarco followed him through the living room and out the front door.

"If you run, you're making a huge mistake," DeMarco said, standing in his doorway, peering over his half-glasses at Shane on the sidewalk.

"What else can I do, huh?" Shane answered. "I got nobody but me. If I get arrested, I'm gone without a ripple. Nobody will try and find out what's happening here. If I don't figure it out, I'm gonna go down in front of this rigged murder case." Then he turned and walked up the path. When he arrived at the parking lot two doors away, he got into his car and pulled out onto the highway.

He decided to go up the coast and cut across town on Sunset, afraid that DeMarco might call the cops down on him. He tried to get his head clear and to organize the facts. But one thought kept coming back.

Why would Alexa tell about his break-in at Zell's office? Shane could end her career with the information about her throwing his old BOR. Something had to be wrong.

Less than an hour ago, Alexa had said she believed him.

Now Shane needed to decide if he could believe her.

THE MONEY SHOT

I T WAS TEN-THIRTY when Shane got back to the 110, heading downtown toward the Spring Summer Apartments. His pager buzzed. He pulled it off his belt and read the printed message on the LED screen:

911 to IAD

A.H.

A.H.—Alexa Hamilton. She wanted Shane to go to the Bradbury Building immediately. He wondered what she wanted, or whether he should even trust her. Maybe the warrant was there and she was drawing him in so he'd be served and end up spending the night in jail. He picked up his cell phone, dialed her cell number, and got a not-in-service recording. He tried her apartment, no answer. Despite his suspicions, he had almost no choice. He had to take a chance on her. He knew the switchboard at the

Bradbury was closed, so he fumbled in his pocket for the number of the Spring Summer Apartments. He dialed and after a minute got Longboard Kelly on the phone.

"Yeah," the surfboard shaper said softly.

"It's Shane. Everything okay?"

"Yeah." Again, a whisper.

"What's wrong? How come you're whispering?"

There was a long moment, then: "Chooch is asleep."

"Look, I've gotta go run an errand on my way home. It's only a few blocks outta the way. Are you guys cool?"

"Yeah."

"See you in about an hour. If that changes, I'll call."

" 'Kay," and then Longboard was gone.

Longboard Kelly sounded strange. He was usually a nonstop talker. Shane wondered whether he and Chooch had started toking together. He almost called back, but then he had to change lanes to make the off-ramp on Sixth Street. In a few more minutes he was downtown.

It was just before eleven and Schwarzenegger was back.

■ ■ ■

"Sorry, absolutely nobody gets through on Sixth. We're shooting a big stunt," the motorcycle cop said. "Back up, go four blocks over to Wilshire."

"I gotta get to Spring and Third," Shane said.

"Can't. It's inside the restricted area. You'll have to park it here and walk. This area has been posted for three or four days." The cop was another old-timer, a forty-year veteran, in his mid- to late sixties. He was standing on Spring Street, behind his yellow barricade, glowering in his knee boots and dark blue shirt with its thirteen hash marks, each one representing three years of service. The entire eight-block section from Wilshire to Seventh had been closed. There was a helicopter sitting in the middle of Sixth Street; klieg lights and a condor had the buildings lit up almost like daylight. Stunt people were milling about. A Brinks armored truck was parked in the middle of the street, near a camera on dolly tracks. The director and some assistant directors were pointing at extras with briefcases, directing them where to stand.

"When are you guys gonna be outta here?" Shane said darkly.

"Don't know," the motor cop replied. "But we got special permission tonight for this big shot, 'cause we had to land the bird in the middle of the street and then do the chase with the armored car down Spring. It's some lash-up," he said proudly, eager to display his film expertise. "We're using Tyler mounts on the camera ship to photograph the stunt exchange from the picture bird to the roof of the speeding armored truck. Arnie is gonna be on top of the moving truck, do the fistfight with the stunt captain while they're heading down Spring. Then Arnie jumps and catches the bar under the picture chopper and does the car-to-helicopter exchange. We cut, rerig, and the stunt double hangs there on the flyaway. It's a money shot," he said proudly. Everybody in L.A. talks the talk. Arnie had to be Schwarzenegger. It never even occurred to the bragging cop that half of downtown L.A. was ready to strangle this entire cast and crew.

Shane got out of the car and started to move past the barricade, toward the gathering of assistant directors and stunt people standing near the idling helicopter.

"Hey, you can't just walk through here, buddy. It's restricted," the cop warned.

"I'm not parking here and walking a mile."

"You gotta go around. This is a danger area. Nobody can be in there who's not cleared or been to the stunt safety meeting."

"Sarge, I'm on the job. I gotta get to Internal Affairs at the Bradbury." Shane dug into his pocket, pulled out his last business card, and handed it to the cop.

"You got a badge?"

"Left it at home. I was out on a boat when I got the call."

" 'Cept you could a' got this card from anybody," he said suspiciously.

"When did you stop being a cop and start being a movie PA?" Shane was getting pissed. He started around the barricade, and the old cop reached out and grabbed Shane's arm just as an assistant director came running up.

"What's the problem, Rich?" he asked the motor cop.

"Guy says he's a cop. Wants t'drive through." He handed Shane's card to the assistant director, who looked at it.

"We're still a bit away from the shot," the AD said to Shane. "Lemme see if I can set this up. Hang on." He turned and ran back to the group of men huddled near the armored car, handing the card to a tall man in a safari jacket. The man looked at the card, then up the street to Shane, and nodded.

The assistant director waved his arm at Shane to come ahead. The motorcycle cop was pissed off and didn't look at Shane as he moved the barricade.

Shane got back in the Taurus and pulled up the street, right into the activity of the movie set. He was trying to get around the idling helicopter when a man stepped out from the group by the armored car and motioned him to stop, then leaned in his passenger window, smiling.

"Hang on a minute," he said.

Suddenly Shane felt something cold and hard press on the left side of his head.

"Howdy-do," a low, soft voice said with a country twang. "Y'all wanna slowly get out of the car?"

Shane tried to look back, but the second man had positioned himself to the left of Shane and behind him, pointing the gun through the driver-side window, placing it against the left side of his head. Shane didn't have to see the gun to know what it was.

"This is pretty dumb, whoever the fuck you are," Shane finally said.

"Hey, dipshit, we been lookin' all over for you. You're the dummy. I sent you the nine-one-one. We was down here anyway, and you stumble right on in here, nice as can be." Then the man with the gun suddenly shouted at the man in the safari coat.

"Dom," he yelled. "What if, when Arnie leaves the car, we stage Sandra's abduction like this. Lookee here." Then he opened the door to the Taurus. "Out," he growled at Shane. "We're gonna get in that chopper. You're sitting in the back right side."

"You're gonna kidnap me in front of all these people?"

"This ain't a kidnapping, it's a rehearsal," he said. "You're gonna be Sandra Bullock. Don't fuck with me, pal. You make trouble, I'll clock you and carry you over. It'll look like blocking to these idiots." Then he pulled Shane out of the car, led him twenty feet to the helicopter at gunpoint, and shoved him into the back. Shane saw that it was Calvin Sheets.

Waiting in the helicopter was another piece of muscle Shane had never seen before. He was holding a gun low, out of sight. Shane settled in, and the man's cold eyes never left him. Calvin looked back down at the director, who shouted, "Yeah, maybe that could work, Cal. But I gotta deal with this first."

Calvin shouted back, "Hunter just called. We'll be back in half an hour, if that's okay."

"Go ahead," the director shouted. "We're an hour away, but we need the chopper back by eleven."

Calvin waved, climbed into the helicopter, and motioned to the pilot, who revved up the motor.

They lifted up off the pavement, hovered, then veered over the street and climbed away from the movie company.

Shane looked out the window and saw the fully rigged and lit street with the hundred or more movie people who had just witnessed his kidnapping without realizing it. They became miniatures as the chopper rose.

"So this is a Logan Hunter film," Shane said.

"Huh?" Calvin shouted back over the roar of the chopper.

"Forget it," Shane said.

Then the helicopter turned north and flew toward the mountains, picking up altitude, leaving the L.A. basin far behind.

THE HAT

I'M GONNA PUT her down in the Valley of the Moon," the pilot yelled over the rotor noise. "I'll call the house; they can meet us there."

Calvin responded with the okay sign. They were flying low, streaking through the San Bernardino Mountains, following a river-cut canyon about fifty feet off the ground. Occasionally Shane could see the moon shadow of the helicopter against rock outcroppings of the granite cliffs on the west side. Suddenly the helicopter rose and veered right, then flew around a mountain peak.

"Arrowhead Peak!" the pilot yelled at Sheets, pointing at the pinnacle, acting like a tour guide instead of a fucking kidnapper.

They skirted the mountaintop and cleared the east face. Shane could see Lake Arrowhead shimmering off in the distance directly ahead. A few miles closer was a smaller body of water five or six miles west of Arrowhead, which Shane remembered was Lake Gregory.

The helicopter streaked low, skirting the shore of Lake Gregory, until finally they were hovering over the appropriately named Valley of the Moon . . . no trees, no rocks, just acres of brown dirt.

The helicopter engine picked up rpms as it hovered. Out of the window below, Shane could see a late-model Land Rover streaking along a dry riverbed, its headlight beams bouncing against the ground. The pilot pointed to the black four-wheel drive racing toward them, and Sheets nodded.

They found a flat spot in the center of the riverbed, and the pilot lowered the chopper until it was just a few feet above the ground. The black Land Rover came to a stop a few hundred feet away. Dirt flew out in every direction, sandblasting the shiny new vehicle, pitting its ebony surface. Then the helicopter touched down its skids. The pilot didn't kill the engine; the turbine whined and the rotor flashed overhead as Sheets and the man sitting opposite Shane opened the door.

"Out!" Sheets commanded. Shane looked out of the helicopter at the desolate terrain, wondering if he was going to get a seat in the Land Rover or become an eternal resident of the Valley of the Moon.

Before he could protest, he felt cold steel on the back of his head as Sheets pushed the weapon against his skull. Shane didn't move.

"Just gimme a reason, and I'll put one through your wet wear."

"This hard-ass routine you got ain't working, Sheets."

"You know who I am?"

"Everybody in Southwest knows you. You ran the French embassy in the Coliseum parking lot."

"Get the fuck out," Sheets snarled.

"Calm down," Shane growled, but he got out of the chopper before Sheets could sucker punch him. He ducked his head reflexively as the rotor spun safely above him and the silent man. Sheets got out last, and they pushed him toward the Land Rover. Dust was flying, getting into everybody's eyes.

They scrambled to the SUV, driven by a shorthaired, bull-necked man. Before they could get the Land Rover turned around, the helicopter revved its engine and lifted off, pelting them with sand and destroying what was left of the paint, starring the back window near Shane's head with a flying rock.

"Shit. Fucking guy . . ." Sheets said, glowering at the chopper as it spun around and flew away, hurrying back to Spring Street, Arnold Schwarzenegger, and the money shot.

Shane was glad to be in the SUV, moving out of the Valley of the Moon. The fact that they were taking him anywhere gave him some hope. If he was being brought here to be disposed of, they probably would have gone ahead and chilled him in this desolate valley.

Calvin Sheets sat next to the bullnecked driver, looking out the front window, the .38 snubby still in his right hand. The silent man from the helicopter sat in the backseat next to Shane, never taking his eyes off him.

They raced along the creek bed in four-wheel drive, bouncing through rain ruts, and after five tire-pounding minutes, shot up onto the paved highway. The driver shifted out of four-wheel and sped past a weathered sign that identified the road as North Drive.

Soon they came to Bay Road, which Shane knew went all the way around the perimeter of the Lake Arrowhead shoreline. He watched the shimmering lake appear and disappear, peeking out from behind buildings and trees as the Land Rover sped around the lake, finally turning onto Peninsula Road, making a left onto Long Point.

They pulled up to a dock at a deserted camping area. Shane

could see a man with his left arm in a sling standing next to the same classic reproduction Chris-Craft inboard that had delivered his assailants to Ray's dock two days before. The varnished sides glistened against soft teak decks.

Sheets went through his rough-guy routine again, poking at Shane with the gun. "Let's go, asshole," he growled. Shane got out of the Land Rover and moved ahead of the ex–LAPD sergeant, toward the boat.

Now he was struck by another gruesome possibility: maybe, instead of a dirt nap, he was about to go swimming with a forty-pound anchor. He didn't have much time to worry about it, though, because as he stepped up to the boat, the man with his left arm in the sling stepped forward as if to help him aboard, then, unexpectedly, threw a right hook, knocking Shane back against Sheets. His vision starred; he bit his tongue; his mouth filled with blood.

"Cut it out, Marvin," Sheets growled. "Rich, get the lines."

"Motherfucker," Marvin said, snarling at Shane, who was trying hard to clear his vision. The blow had landed high on his cheek. His eyes started watering badly. This was probably the guy who stopped his bullet and left the two pints of blood on Ray's linoleum floor.

"You know what they say, Marv. The kitchen is the most dangerous place in the home," Shane said.

"Fuck you," Marvin growled.

Rich untied the boat as Marvin got behind the wheel and turned the key; while the engine burbled and growled, they all took a moment and listened like teenage boys to the throaty rumble of the blown 257 flathead. Shane was pushed into the enclosed backseat of the boat, which was separated from the front by a teak deck and a second chrome windshield. He found himself wedged in tightly next to Sheets and the silent man named Rich from the helicopter.

Marvin angrily slammed down the throttle with his good hand

caught the wheel, and the boat roared away from the dock, picking up speed as they headed across the lake in the shimmering light of a three-quarter moon.

Shane could see Arrowhead Village twinkling across the water, about half a mile to the right. Finally Marvin slowed the boat and turned the wheel. Ray's party house and dock were ahead, about a hundred yards away. Seconds later they were slowing down, and Shane could feel the heavy inboard bumping softly against the wood dock.

"Out," Sheets ordered, again jamming the pistol in Shane's ribs.

They walked up onto the porch. The door was unlocked and they went inside.

Coy Love was waiting in the living room. Shane had only seen his picture, and the photo didn't begin to capture the essence of him. At least six foot six, he towered over all of them, wearing a blue windbreaker and jeans. His thin, lipless mouth, oversize head, and stringy, muscled neck dominated an overpowering physical presence. He stood Lurch-like and speechless until they all got inside and closed the door. "This doesn't have to end badly," he said. His voice was rough—hard and dusty, like boots marching through gravel.

"That's good news," Shane replied.

"I want to show you something," Love said. "Follow me." He turned abruptly and led them through the hall into the master suite.

The lights were all on in the room. Shane tried not to look at the mirror, which, he knew from before, fronted the hidden room with its glory hole. A small suitcase was open on the bed, and it was full of cash. The used bills were stacked and banded. As soon as he saw the money, Shane was sure that he was being videotaped.

It seemed that Coy Love was in charge, which momentarily

surprised him, because Love had been only a rookie patrolman when he'd been terminated. Sheets had been a sergeant, a watch commander. Yet Sheets seemed content to stand in the background and do his funky gun-poking routine while Love ran the show. Shane figured the shift in roles was primal—the law of the jungle. Love was more dangerous and brutal and, therefore, the alpha male. "Don't fuck with Love" the message machine had said. Love was the hammer.

"We need to come to terms," Coy Love said, his bloodless lips stretched tight across tombstone-shaped teeth.

"Good," Shane said. *A one-word answer—keep it thin; don't volunteer anything.*

"That's yours," Love said, indicating the cash in the suitcase on the bed. "A hundred grand in tens and twenties."

"Lucky me. Did I win the lottery?" Shane asked.

"Yeah, you were down to your last ticket, and then you got lucky, hit the number. If you start acting smart now instead of just running around like a hard-on with dirt for brains, then maybe there's another suitcase like that one in your future."

"I like this so far."

"We got some rules that go with giving you this hat." Police terminology for a bribe.

"Rules? Okay."

"One. You go home, you sit in your house, and you stay there."

"Trouble with my house is, it's full of nine-millimeter federals. The Major Crimes dicks have been digging them out of the walls like fruit seeds."

"That was a mistake. We apologize."

"I accept." Shane was beginning to think that maybe he might actually get out of there alive.

"Two. You stop messing around in Long Beach. Stop going to the naval yard."

"No problem there. I didn't like it much anyway."

"Three. Whatever you think you've figured out about Mayor Crispin or the top floor of the Glass House—forget it."

"Okay . . . it's forgotten."

"Let me explain to you why you are being offered this hat instead of a plot at Forest Lawn."

"Okay."

"Since you shot Ray, you have been in the press a lot. We're trying to keep a low profile. You get to live as long as you play ball." Love moved around Shane, forcing him to turn sideways to the mirror while keeping his own back to it. This was definitely being videotaped. Shots of Shane Scully taking a suitcase full of cash. Damning evidence if he ever changed his mind. On the plus side, it also probably meant the murder one charge wasn't coming. If the DA had what he needed, these guys wouldn't be doing this.

"Okay, since we're playing ball, I assume I'm the catcher," Shane said.

"That's what you are. You just caught a break. If you're smart, you won't catch a bullet."

"I'm gonna be smart. I'm gonna just take my suitcase of untraceable cash and go home and sit in my bullet-riddled living room until you tell me it's okay to come out."

Love closed the suitcase, snapped the clasps, and handed it to Shane, spinning him slightly so that he was looking more toward the glory hole. Love kept his back to the bedroom mirror the whole time.

"Is that it?" Shane asked. "Is our business concluded?"

"Not quite yet. Come in here." Love moved out of the bedroom and back into the living room. Shane followed him, carrying the suitcase, thinking the hundred thousand in small bills was surprisingly light. Sheets, Marvin, and Rich stayed behind him.

In the living room Coy took a videotape box off the TV, opened it, slid the tape into the VCR, then turned his frightening, bloodless smile on Shane.

"I think it's important that you do not mistake kindness for weakness," Love said as he grabbed the remote off the TV and turned the set on. He punched PLAY.

Suddenly Shane was looking at Chooch and Longboard Kelly on the videotape. They were tied to wooden chairs in Shane's rented apartment on Third Street. He recognized the faded wallpaper and frayed blue drapes. Both Brian and Chooch had silver duct tape across their mouths. A man was offscreen holding a shotgun, the barrel of the weapon sticking about an inch into the frame.

Shane felt his guts tighten into a knot. Bile instantly flooded the back of his throat. "He's a fifteen-year-old kid," he protested weakly. "Brian Kelly is just a surfboard shaper. He doesn't know shit."

"You go home and stay quiet for two or three days. Then, if everything goes right, you get them both back. Otherwise, I'm gonna put these cowboys on the ark," Love said.

On the tape Chooch was struggling against his ropes. Longboard looked dazed and had blood on the side of his head.

"Seen enough?" Coy said, and when Shane nodded, he turned off the TV and handed Shane a set of car keys. "There's a department car parked in the driveway. Take it back and leave it in the motor pool at the Glass House. Then take a cab home and pull the grass up over your head."

Shane took the keys and the suitcase and walked on wooden legs out of the house. They all followed. There was a gray Crown Victoria with blackwalls in the drive. He got behind the wheel, started the car, and pulled out of the driveway. The headlights swept across the four ex-cops as he backed into the street, turning right. He was operating on autopilot . . . his mind on the sickening video images of Chooch and Brian tied to the chairs.

He drove down Lake View Drive, the black suitcase full of cash jiggling on the seat beside him. He took the correct turns from memory and found himself back on I-7, heading out of Arrowhead toward L.A.

As he drove, he could picture Chooch's black Hispanic eyes staring out at him from the recesses of his memory. He remembered the boy's swarthy, handsome features as he sat in the Little Bruin deli in Westwood, looking out at the traffic, his gaze averted so Shane wouldn't see his pain.

"Do you know who my father is?" the boy had asked. *"Did Sandy ever tell you?"* Hurt and longing in the question.

Shane had wanted to fill the void in Chooch's life, just as he had wanted to fill it in his own. But he had been slow out of the blocks and running two steps behind, a clown in swim fins, flapping along, heels down while the rest of the field breezed past him.

Almost without thinking, he picked up his phone and for the second time in twenty-four hours asked Alexa for help.

By the time he got to the San Bernardino Freeway, he had explained to her in detail what had happened and what was on the videotape. "I'll meet you at the Spring Summer Apartments," she said. "Maybe we can pick up something there."

An hour later he was back in downtown L.A. He found a spot at the curb on Third Street, across from his rented room. He could see Alexa's gray Crown Vic at the curb across the street. He quickly got out of his borrowed car and hurried into the building, afraid of what he might find in the cramped rented single on the third floor of the dingy rooming house.

THE THREE-FLUSH RULE

34

H E FOUND HER kneeling by the toilet in the bathroom, wearing latex gloves and brushing black granite powder from her field-investigation kit onto the toilet handle with a fine bristle brush. Every detective and patrol officer carried a crime-scene investigation kit in the trunk of his or her car.

"You got gloves?" she asked, glancing back at him, not bothering with a greeting.

"No," he replied woodenly. Alexa reached into her open kit and pulled out an extra pair. "I'm gonna need a set of elimination prints from you. We've also gotta get a set of Chooch's and Longboard's from somewhere."

"Right," he said, and looked around the bathroom. "You get anything yet?"

"Hard to tell. A lot of this is junk, smudged or overlapped. I got a partial palm off that kitchen chair, where somebody must've grabbed it by the back and carried it. I think, from what you described on the phone, the videotaping took place in the center of the living room. They moved the chairs back to the kitchen, but there are fresh indent marks on the living-room carpet. I marked 'em with chalk, so don't step on 'em. I'm gonna take pictures. I emptied the kitchen trash into a towel in the sink, but I haven't gotten to it yet."

Shane moved out of the bathroom and looked at the small living room. "You try the TV?" he called out to her. After a minute she came out of the bathroom with a yellow four-by-five fingerprint identification card in her hand. She leaned down on the dining-room table and labeled a partial print she had just lifted off the toilet flush handle.

"We'll never get a print run with these," Alexa said. "They're mostly partials and smudged. The best we can hope for, if we even catch these perps, is maybe a match on a few of the basic Galton classifieds—maybe connect up on some of these ridge endings. The loops, arches, and whorls are pretty smudged."

"Chooch used the TV; maybe the remote has a set of his you can use for elimination," he said.

She took the channel changer, holding it by its side, and started dusting it, dipping the brush into the glass vial of black powder, then softly brushing the fine camel-hair bristles across the remote, looking for graphite residue that would indicate the oil of a fingerprint. She found a few good latents on the underside of the channel-changer, then took the clear tape out of her field kit and lifted the prints, stuck them on the card, and pressed them down, labeling the back of the card, "Channel Changer Right Index and Middle Finger."

While she worked, Shane moved through the apartment. There were no signs of a struggle, no blood, but lots of dirty black powder. She had been working there for quite a while and had left graphite everywhere—on the doorjamb at shoulder height, where somebody might lean with a palm, against the wall, on the cupboard doors, on the countertops.

Shane put on his latex gloves and began, halfheartedly, poking through the trash collected on the towel lying in the deep kitchen sink. He found a cardboard roll about an inch in diameter and plucked it out, using a pen from his pocket. Then he saw an empty bag of M&M's. Longboard was an M&M's freak. He pulled it out as well and took both items back into the living room. He handed the cardboard roll to Alexa. "Looks like the core from the roll of silver duct tape," he said.

"I saw that, too," she said. "We can try, but there's so much gummy shit on it, I doubt we'll lift anything." She took the powder and brushed it on the cardboard core, but as predicted, it was too sticky. Powder clung everywhere, turning the core graphite black and revealing nothing.

He told her about Longboard's candy addiction, so she went to work on the M&M's wrapper.

"Was there anything on the videotape you can remember that might be helpful?" she asked as she brushed the surface of the wrapper.

"No," he said. "Except there was a shotgun in the side of the frame . . . a riot pump. Looked like an Ithaca."

"Department issue." She said what he'd been thinking. "I don't think we're gonna find anything. If those guys were cops, they wouldn't leave evidence behind. They were probably all wearing gloves and picked up or flushed everything."

"Speaking of flushes, did you check the trap in the toilet?" he asked.

"No," she said, looking up. "I always hate that job, but I guess we oughta give it a try." She finished with the M&M's wrapper, lifting three good prints. "We're gonna need wrenches to get to the toilet trap," she said.

"I'll go see the manager."

"Don't bring him in here," she said sharply.

"Don't worry, I'm not a total idiot," he snapped back, then

went down to the front desk, rang the night bell, and got the manager out of bed.

"Trouble with the toilet," Shane lied to the bleary-eyed man, who looked as if he hadn't shaved in two days. Rumpled, tired, and angry, he glowered at Shane from under the harsh light above his desk.

"Shit," the man said.

"You got a pipe wrench? I used to be a plumber. I can clear it for you."

The manager looked at him and computed the odds that Shane might break his toilet against the cost of calling a regular plumber. Money won . . . South of Main Street, it usually did. The manager moved into the back room and returned with a toolbox.

Shane took it up to the third-floor apartment. He closed the door and put on his gloves, then he and Alexa moved to the bathroom and removed the commode. He took off the porcelain top and plugged the flush valve with toilet paper. Then they began to remove the metal elbow from the back of the toilet.

One of the little-known truths about modern plumbing is that it takes at least two, sometimes three flushes to completely get rid of a bowl load. On more than one drug raid, the perps had flushed the dope with the cops coming through the door, not bothering to repeat the procedure, then were shocked to learn that two or three grams of cocaine remained in the water in the elbow and trap. Liquid samples had rolled up more than one drug dealer. The Drug Enforcement teams called it "the Three-Flush Rule."

They got the elbow off, and toilet water spilled onto the floor. Shane kept from kneeling in it by squatting as he worked. The elbow looked pretty clean, so he went after the trap, which was below the elbow and was there to keep larger obstructions out of the plumbing lines until they dissolved or softened.

"The things one learns in law enforcement," he muttered as he finally got the trap out and took it to the sink, emptying the four-inch cylinder into the basin. The last thing out was fat, round, and dark brown. It landed on the white porcelain like a turd on a wedding cake. The object had a shiny gold band around it.

"Cigar," he said triumphantly, picking it up with his latex gloves. It was a three-quarter-smoked panatela. The gold band said DOMINICAN REGAL.

"I think this is what's commonly called a clue," she said, smiling. "We have us a cigar smoker." She was holding out an evidence bag.

He dropped the mushy stogie inside the glassine pouch, then washed his gloved hands.

Five minutes later they had replaced the toilet fixture, taken the living-room crime scene photos, and were sitting on the cigarette-burned sofa, trying to figure it all out.

"There was no forced entry, so Longboard must have just let the guys in. If they were cops, they probably just flashed a potsy," she said.

"Maybe." His mind was circling a worrisome thought, but he pushed it aside. "Coy Love told me to go home and wait for two or three days. That means whatever it is they're worried about, it goes away after that."

"Makes sense," she answered.

"He also said to forget about the Long Beach Naval Yard and Mayor Crispin."

She nodded, but said nothing.

"These guys aren't gonna turn Longboard and Chooch loose, are they?" he blurted, putting the distressing thought into words. "They're gonna kill 'em."

"Probably," she said. "They'll hold 'em for leverage in case you get restless, but once this is over, they can't leave a kidnapping charge and two vics on the table."

"Shit," he said, rubbing his eyes. "I've fucked this up so bad. It's always like . . . if I knew yesterday what I know today . . ."

"Shane, I think we need to tell his mother."

"Yeah. I guess I've been putting that off." He looked at his watch. "It'll be sunup in an hour. Sandy is having sleepovers with some DEA target. She won't be there till sometime after eleven. I'm whipped, but I can't sleep here. How's your place sound?"

"I got a couch you can use," she said, then gathered up all of her stuff and stood in the doorway, looking at the dusted room. "If we leave it like this, you're gonna forfeit your security deposit."

"Fuck it. Let's go."

They closed the door and locked up, heading downstairs. Shane deposited the toolbox behind the counter without ringing the night bell, and they walked out into the street.

"I gotta drop this department car back at the Glass House. I don't wanna disobey any of their instructions. Follow me, then later we can go to Sandy's in your car," Shane suggested.

"My car's at home. I was with a friend when you called. I had him drop me off here. I figured we'd use your car."

"Then who owns that plainwrap?" he said, pointing to the gray Crown Vic across the street. "That's gotta be department issue. No civilian is gonna buy a stripped-down gray sedan with no air and blackwalls."

They moved across the street and looked through the windshield of the locked car. They could see the telltale wires hanging down under the dash, identifying the recessed police radio.

"Yep," she said, "but it's not a detective car. No coffee lids on the dash."

She was right. Since detectives had to do lots of stakeouts, they drank gallons of coffee. The cars were department-owned, so the cops had no pride of ownership. The common practice was to peel the plastic lids off the Styrofoam Winchell's cups and throw them up onto the dash. Shane had never been in a detective's plainwrap that didn't have half a dozen or more plastic lids up there. If the motor pool ever cleaned the interiors, the old, wet rings from the tops stained the dash and remained behind as a permanent testament to the practice.

"Staff car?" he said hesitantly.

They both walked around the Crown Vic, looking through the windows. It had beem immaculately cleaned. All the cars in the staff motor pool were automatically washed and vacuumed once a day by inner-city gangsters dressed in jailhouse orange.

Alexa took out her cell phone and punched in a number. After a minute she got the Communications Center.

"This is Sergeant Hamilton, serial number 50791. I found one of our plainwraps parked in a bad spot. It's a 548E," she said, giving the radio code for a vehicle parked illegally across a driveway. "It should be moved. Could you give me the officer's name so I can contact him to move it?" She listened, then said, "City plate, DF 453." Another wait, then, "Thanks," and she closed the cell, a troubled look on her face.

"Shit, I don't even want to ask," he said.

"It's a Triple-O staff car," she said.

Triple-O stood for the Office of Operations, which reported directly to the chief of police. Shane remembered that the administrative staff of the Office of Operations contained about five men and women, all captains and above. The office acted as an adviser to the chief of police and exercised line-of-command oversight in all divisions. In short, Operations was Chief Brewer's right hand.

"It could have been left here because of the movie," she said hopefully. "Triple-O handles press relations."

"You packing?" he asked.

"Yeah, of course."

"Gimme it. Mine's gone. I've been losing guns faster than winos' teeth."

"What're you gonna do?"

"Break into this thing. I don't wanna fuck around with the lock, standing on a street corner. Lemme have it."

She dug her Beretta 9mm out of her purse and handed it to him. He dropped the clip and handed it back, then tromboned the slide to make sure the chamber was clean. He held the automatic by the barrel, looked both ways for potential witnesses, then broke the side window of the car, shattering glass onto the maroon velour upholstery.

"Dominican Regals are expensive smokes," he said. "I don't know many line cops who can afford ten-dollar cigars."

He opened the door, leaned inside, and started rummaging around. The ashtray was clean. He opened the glove box. There were three objects inside: the departmental registration, indicating that the car was indeed the property of the Los Angeles Police Department; an L.A./Long Beach Thomas street guide; and in the back of the compartment a sealed Baggie containing three fresh Dominican Regal cigars.

THE COURTESY
REPORT

THE UNOFFICIAL NOTIFICATION of a crime to a civilian was known in police work as a courtesy report.

Shane had revealed Sandy Sandoval's identity to Alexa over breakfast in her neat duplex apartment on Pico, two blocks east of Century City. He had slept fitfully on her living-room couch, and now, marginally refreshed, they left her place and drove across town. It was Saturday morning, and Barrington Plaza loomed, a tower of sunlit granite.

Shane pulled up, and Alexa badged the shoulder-braided bandleader who announced them, then keyed the elevator. Show tunes from the Boston Pops serenaded their arrival at the penthouse level. It was eleven-thirty A.M.

"So this is the famous Black Widow Nest," Alexa said, looking at the magnificent hallway on the eighteenth floor.

Most of the LAPD knew about her and knew that Shane had once been the Black Widow's handler, but her real name had been in the possession of only two Special Crimes detective commanders. Shane had deliberated hard before telling Alexa. In the end, it was the fact that Chooch's life was involved that made the decision for him.

Shane rang the doorbell to Sandy's penthouse apartment, dreading the job of telling her what had happened. He was sweating, but it was flop sweat, cold and clammy as wet clothing.

The mahogany door opened, and Sandy was standing there in a tailored black sheath that fit her size-four frame like a second skin—skin that was dusky, the color of dark sand; her eyes, golden-brown amber; her long raven tresses swirling around her shoulders with planned abandon. A single strand of pearls dangled with fuck-you elegance. She was dressed to party. She stood in the doorway, a questioning look on her gorgeous face. Then she shot a quick glance at Alexa.

"What is it? This is a terrible time, Shane. I'm bushed, I just got home."

"Chooch is gone," Shane said. "He's been kidnapped."

"I . . . I thought you said you had found him," Sandy finally stammered, her liquid amber eyes losing focus, clouding like a fighter hit too hard.

"He's been kidnapped, Sandy. By men who are trying to stop an investigation. I'm afraid . . ." He stopped. "I think by cops," he finished.

"Cops?!" she said, and involuntarily her hand went up to her mouth.

"This is Sergeant Hamilton. She's my—" He looked over at Alexa. *What exactly was she? His department prosecutor? His only believer? His nemesis? What the hell else was she?*

"I'm Shane's partner," she said, answering his question and filling the void.

Sandy spun abruptly and headed back into her apartment. Alexa and Shane followed. She walked slowly ahead of them, fluid as a dancer, her hips swaying seductively. Shane would have preferred a more leaden gait. Even in the face of this news, she radiated sexual grace. When she turned and faced them, he saw distress bordering on hysteria in her eyes. Instantly his heart went out to her, and guilt overwhelmed him.

"Why? Where did it happen?" she asked.

"An apartment on Third Street, a safe house I was renting. I guess they followed the sitter over from my place in Venice. I can't think of any other way they could have found him," Shane said.

"We aren't exactly sure who," Alexa said. "But it appears to be high-ranking police officers who are calling the shots."

"You should go to the chief. Go to Burl. Tell him what you suspect."

When Alexa hesitated and looked at Shane, Sandy sank down on the sofa. "You're telling me you think Burl's—"

"We don't know exactly who is involved," Shane said. "But it goes way up. Maybe all the way to the mayor. It involves Logan Hunter, Tony Spivack, and the Long Beach Naval Yard."

"The 'why' is easier to understand. They took Chooch to keep us from continuing an investigation into it," Alexa said.

Sandy looked down at the white plush pile to hide her devastation.

"Sandy . . . I'm sorry. I'm really sorry. I didn't see it coming. If I could change this, I—"

She waved this away with her slender hand, sat absolutely still for a moment, then looked up. Her expression had hardened, the vulnerability had vanished. "How can I help? There must be something we can do." He watched in fascination as she tucked the loose strands of panic away, grabbed hold of her plummeting emotions, pulled hard, and darted up quickly, climbing hard, like a kite in a strong wind.

"Do you know any of these girls?" Alexa asked as she reached into her purse and handed over two packets of pictures from the party at the naval yard. Sandy spread them out on the white marble coffee table. She picked up a small antique magnifying glass with a carved ivory handle and examined each picture.

"I know one or two of these girls," she said, looking at them slowly, studying the shots, separating out the pictures of the two girls she knew. "Scarlet Mackenzie is the red-haired one. This one here—this blonde—changed her name from Gina Augustina to, what the hell was it . . . Avon Star. Used to have black hair. I think some of these others used to work with Madam Alex until Heidi took over the L.A. market. They all work the executive trade."

"What about the men? We know a lot of them are cops," Alexa said.

Sandy looked through the pictures again but shook her head. "To be honest with you, I'm not working much with LAPD anymore." She shoved the pictures of the two girls she knew toward Alexa, never once looking over at Shane. "I only know these two."

"These girls might know what's going on," Alexa said. "We need to find somebody who can help us, somebody who can tell us who took Chooch."

Sandy studied Alexa for a moment, then looked back at Shane. "I'm going to have to shut down this thing I'm doing for DEA. I'll tell 'em I need two days, that my brother got sick in Connecticut." She got up, moved to the phone, then punched in fourteen or more digits, which Shane knew was probably a number for a satellite beeper that the feds all used now.

After she finished, Sandy hung up and returned to the table. She sat down and looked at them, biting her lower lip. "Maybe I could convince Scarlet to duke me in with this crowd."

Duke me in, Shane thought. Sandy was even beginning to talk like a cop. It was definitely time for her to get out of the business.

"I could call Scarlet, say I just got out of a bad marriage and want to get back on the stroll. Nobody knows what I've been doing all these years. I haven't seen these two girls in ages."

Shane had to get out of there. He was starting to feel trapped. He got up abruptly. "Here's my beeper number," he said, giving Sandy one of his cards. "It's on all the time."

Alexa took out a pencil, wrote hers down, and handed it to Sandy.

"Okay," Sandy said. "I'll check back with you tomorrow. I should be able to get in touch with her by then. I'll set something up. If she knows anything that will help us get Chooch back, I'll find it."

"Good," Shane said.

They all walked to the front door. Sandy seemed cool and in control again. After she opened the door, she looked hard at him, and Shane knew he had to say something.

"I was trying to do you a favor when I took Chooch," he said. "It didn't work out, and I'm sorry."

What she said next was very strange. "You weren't doing me a favor, Shane, I was doing one for you."

He saw the dark, strange look again, and then her amber eyes opened for a moment and he was seeing her uncovered core . . . a self-loathing and sadness deeper than he could have ever imagined. Then the look was gone, replaced in a heartbeat by shrewd cunning and the cold gleam of sexuality. She closed the door, and he found himself looking at brown mahogany, the exact color of her eyes and almost as hard.

S AND J

IT WAS NOON, and they were back in Shane's borrowed Crown Vic. Alexa had turned on the police radio, and they were listening to staccato radio calls detailing the menu of violence and death, all of it described numerically in a flat monotone: "One X-ray twelve. A 415 at 2795 Slauson. Handle Code Two." Human carnage was a day-and-night routine.

"I don't know what the next move is," Alexa admitted.

Shane looked over at her. He knew what he was going to do, but it was a felony and he didn't think he should confide in her, for fear she'd hook him up on the spot.

But she was good, and she read the look in his eyes. "Let's hear what you're planning," she said suspiciously.

"You don't want any part of it. I'll drop you home."

"Lemme guess. You wanna go pick up Drucker or Kono or one of Ray's other hamsters . . . then go give them some S and J."

S and J stood for "sentence and judgment." Cops used to call it "holding court in the street." Either way, in this case it would be kidnapping and assault, both Class A felonies.

"Right idea, wrong guys," he said. "Kono and Drucker are small players; they may not even know what's really going on. I think they're just getting envelopes."

"It doesn't matter, 'cause we aren't going to kidnap and threaten anyone. That's a bonehead play." She stared hard at him in the dim light. He didn't look back. "Who, then?" she finally asked, her curiosity boiling over.

"You're gonna hate it." And then for some unknown reason, he told her.

After he had finished explaining his idea, she sat silently in the car for almost five minutes. The police radio underscored their separate thoughts, broadcasting misery while each of them pondered the personal cost if his dangerous plan went wrong.

Shane knew he had nothing more to lose. Any way he looked at it, odds were, he was headed to prison, where as a cop in the joint, he would last about as long as ice cream on a summer day.

Alexa, on the other hand, was only on the edge of this. She hadn't been put in play yet. Nobody except Sandy knew she'd been helping him. She could still go home and sit it out, saving her career and maybe her life.

He finally looked at her and saw those chips of blue staring out the front window, her brow furrowed in stubborn concentration, frustrated and confused like a fifth-grade algebra student.

For Shane, it was only about Chooch. It was his fault the boy was gone, and if he had to end his own life behind the secure perimeter of Vacaville State Prison, at least it would be for trying to put this mess right. Deep down he had formed a fraternal attachment to Chooch Sandoval. He couldn't exactly explain why, but it had happened.

Then he felt Alexa's weight shift on the seat beside him. He looked over at her. She had turned to face him.

"Okay," she said slowly, "I'm in."

■ ■ ■

The marina was strangely quiet for a Saturday afternoon. Shane thought the boat was a ketch or a yawl—whatever the hell they called them when the second mast was taller than the first.

"Schooner," Alexa said, reading his thoughts perfectly. The stern of the fifty-five-foot sailboat carried the boat's name.

"*Board and Cord*—cute name for a sailboat," she said.

He assumed she was thinking it stood for the wood of the hull and sail lines, so he set her straight. "It's a basketball expression. Means a bank shot off the backboard and through the net."

"Oh." She smiled. "In that case, he should have called it *Cheap Shot.*"

They were parked in the lot next to the slips at D Dock in Marina del Rey, looking out the front window of the car at the boats tied up forty or fifty yards from them, baking in eighty-degree sunlight. Both were wearing drugstore baseball caps and wraparound sunglasses—a minimal disguise.

"I heard he's down on this thing every weekend," Shane said, focusing a new pair of binoculars he'd found under the seat at the boat's portholes, looking for movement inside. "He's probably sleeping late."

Shane shifted his field of vision, concentrating on the yachts to either side of Mayweather's schooner. It appeared that most of the boats around the *Board and Cord* were empty.

"You sure you want to do this?" he asked. It was hard for him to believe she was about to risk her career and maybe even her freedom for Chooch Sandoval, whom she didn't even know. Of course, he had completely missed the point, so she set him straight.

"You claim I didn't believe what I said about keeping the job free from corruption, that I didn't want to risk it when the chips were down, and maybe there's some truth there. This is hard for me, I admit it, but these guys are committing crimes. They're kidnapping children. So, if I know this is happening and I walk away, that makes me as guilty as they are."

"Still, we're talking about committing a Class A felony."

"Shane . . ."

"Huh?"

"Shut up, will ya? Let's go roll up this shitwrap."

She opened the door and got out of the car. He followed her to the concrete path.

"I hope he's here. I wish I knew what his POV looked like," she said, changing the subject so he wouldn't pursue it, looking out at the twenty or thirty parked cars in the marina lot.

"Listen, you've gotta hear me on this," he said, turning her around, holding her arm as he talked, feeling the tight muscles in her biceps. "This means a lot to me—Chooch has become important—Brian, too, but Chooch . . . Chooch and I, we . . . it's like he's the piece of me that got lost growing up. It's hard for me to explain exactly, but I'm never gonna be able to pay you back."

"No shit, Sherlock." She smiled, then turned and moved off toward the slips.

They walked quietly along the concrete path and down onto the dock, light-footing it. They had already decided how they would do it, and as they got to the stern of the boat, Shane found some cover one boat away as Alexa moved up to the cockpit.

"Hello, anybody there?" she called out. "Anybody home? Chief Mayweather? Request permission to come aboard."

The back cabin door opened, and Deputy Chief Thomas Mayweather stuck his gleaming black head out. "Yes?" he said. "What is it?" He had on a striped polo shirt and white pants.

"You alone, sir? It's Sergeant Hamilton, IAD. I need to talk to you."

"My wife and kids will be here in an hour. What is it, Sergeant?" he said impatiently.

"It's about the Scully prosecution, sir. I've got a big problem, but I don't think we should talk about it out here. May I come aboard?"

"Okay." There was some hesitancy in his voice, almost as if he smelled deception. He came out of the cabin, reached up, and helped her down into the cockpit, then into the main salon. Once they were inside, he closed the rear hatch.

Shane had been hiding, lying flat on the dock one slip away. Now he got up and moved around until he was standing behind the schooner. They had planned to take Mayweather in the main salon, where they could control the capture and not be observed. Shane knew that he had to be very careful getting aboard. Mayweather would feel the sway of the boat if he rocked her when he stepped on.

Shane slowly lowered himself down and hung his feet carefully over the deck, gradually getting his footing on the upholstered cockpit seat. But to his dismay, the moment he put all his weight down, the boat shifted with the load, and a few seconds later the salon door flew open. Mayweather glared out at him.

"Permission to also come aboard?" Shane said stupidly.

"What the fuck?" Mayweather blurted.

Then they both heard Alexa chamber her 9mm behind the deputy chief. The sound froze Mayweather.

"Assume the position, asshole," Shane snarled, switching to street demeanor. They would have to take him out in the open. Shane moved farther onto the boat.

Deputy Chief Mayweather glanced back at Alexa in the middle of the salon, holding her gun, glaring blue ice over the barrel.

Shane was unarmed and presented Mayweather's best avenue of escape. Suddenly the deputy chief charged. Shane had been ready for it and had already screwed his heels awkwardly into the padded seats for traction.

Mayweather was coming at him fast, lunging from the cockpit. Shane swung a right hook, missing the shot, bouncing his fist off the top of Mayweather's head. The ex–UCLA point guard was fast, his quickness and athleticism on full display. He grabbed Shane's legs and took him backward over the rail onto the wooden dock. While Shane clutched him tightly and held on for all he was worth, Alexa clamored off the boat and screwed the barrel of her 9mm into the deputy chief's ear. She pulled the hammer all the way back; the gun "snicked" dangerously in the still air.

"It won't be pretty," she warned him.

Mayweather stopped struggling. Alexa grabbed her cuffs off her belt and hooked him up. Shane got untangled and yanked the deputy chief to his feet. A few people on the next dock turned to look at them.

"You people are fucking crazy! You have any idea what you're doing?" Mayweather protested.

"Do you?" Shane replied.

Three minutes later they had pulled him off the dock, past some startled onlookers, then pushed him into the trunk of the Crown Vic with his own socks stuffed into his mouth.

They drove fast, up the 405, back to the Bradbury to pick up a videotape unit. Then they headed out to a deserted spot Shane knew about in the Pavia Aqueduct of the L.A. River.

THE ULTIMATE FIELD
INTERVIEW

They parked the Crown Vic off the road in Glendale where the 134 and 5 freeways intersect, then helped a stunned and blindfolded Thomas Mayweather down the paved concrete levee that bordered the riverbed. Their hard leather shoes fought for traction on the forty-five-degree slope. They finally got the deputy chief to the floor of the wash, where a narrow trickle of water flowed down a spillway cut into the center of the paved concrete riverbed.

Black metal drain caps, thirty feet in diameter, each with two triangular cutouts on the top, faintly resembled the heads of huge black cats. Glendale taggers had completed the impression by spray-painting the metal with white noses, eyes, and whiskers.

They moved in single file, in broad daylight, under the leaden stares of the painted drain covers. Shane led the way along the wash, under several bridges, until they got to a huge metal drainage pipe, tunneling deep into the side of the hill. As they entered the mouth of the seven-foot-high sewer, they could hear things slithering and rustling in the inky darkness ahead of them. When they had gone far enough so that there was only a dim residue of sunlight from the tunnel's mouth behind them, Shane stopped.

"This is good enough," he said, and spun Mayweather around.

The deputy chief started to gurgle and wheeze around his sock gag, but Shane paid no attention. He knew there was a ladder about where they were standing that led to the surface a few hundred feet above.

Shane had been in this sewer drain two years before on a tip that it contained the body of a dead rape victim, a ten-year-old child. He'd found the girl's mutilated corpse in the tunnel, her blond hair and tiny body caked with mud and covered with feasting rats. He had had nightmares about it for a month afterward. He never caught her killer.

Shane found the ladder, more or less by feel. He uncuffed Mayweather's right wrist, dragged the disoriented deputy chief over, and hooked him to the ladder with both hands behind his back through the metal rail.

"Gimme the nine," he said to Alexa. She handed it to him, and he stuffed it into his belt. Then they set up the video camera. It was a Sony compact with a sun gun on the front. The telescoped tripod was fitted neatly into the bottom of the video carrying case. Mayweather, blindfolded and terrified, harrumphed and squirmed at the ladder. Shane secured the camera on the tripod, then turned on the sun gun. The single beam of harsh light hit the deputy chief in the chest. Shane adjusted it until it was right in Mayweather's face, then stepped forward and yanked the blindfold off the startled deputy chief.

"Welcome," Shane said softly, making his voice loony but also cold and hard as a steel blade.

"Scully?" Mayweather said, blinking his eyes frantically. Shane knew his prisoner couldn't see much, forced to look directly into the bright light.

"*Mr.* Scully! Let's have some respect for your host."

"You're gonna go away forever," Mayweather said angrily. "This is the most outrageous thing I've ever heard of. You're history. You'll both rot in jail for this. Sergeant Hamilton, you're smart, there's still a chance for you. Just turn me loose, I'll do what I can—"

"Shut up and *listen!*" Shane said. "If I don't get exactly what I want, this is where you check out, Tom."

"You can't possibly be serious."

"Hey, asshole, *think about it!*" Shane screamed, performing now, trying to sound demented and out of control. "You think I'd pull this if I weren't desperate? You've got a fucking life-ending problem here!"

Mayweather's eyes darted around right and left, then back to center. All he could see was the blinding light of the sun gun and occasionally Shane's silhouette as he paced. Bathed by the intense glare, his pupils had closed up like a Main Street junkie's.

"You screw up down here, Tommy, and you're on the lobby wall." A place just inside the huge double doors at Parker Center where they put pictures of all the dead policemen, under a huge gold emblem of the department and the letters EOW—end of watch.

"Now, here's how it goes. You tell me everything. I already know a lot, so if you even leave out one little shred, I'm gonna . . . I'm gonna park a nine between your eyes." Adding a little insanity into his routine, some Mel Gibson *Lethal Weapon* madness.

Street cops had to learn to play different roles to get confessions. "Loose-cannon homicidal maniac" was a favorite. Trouble was, once you'd seen the show, it rarely worked twice. Shane didn't think Chief Mayweather, with his shelfful of basketball trophies and high-profile sports background, had ever spent much time on the street. He probably went right from the Academy to Press Relations or the Chief Administrative Staff. Hopefully, he would be disoriented and frightened enough to buy the act.

"You wouldn't dare kill me. You wouldn't dare," Mayweather said, but he sounded now as if he was trying to convince himself, not Shane.

"You don't think I'll kill ya; watch this, asshole." He pointed Alexa's Beretta at the wall beside the deputy chief's shaved head. He aimed it wide so that the shot would ricochet off the concrete a few inches from Mayweather, then fly harmlessly up the tunnel, into the dark. But he wanted the bullet to be close enough for Mayweather to feel its draft.

Shane fired the gun. The echo of the 9mm pistol was deafening in the enclosed space. Chief Mayweather actually yelped when the gun fired. The slug hit inches from the side of his head, throwing plaster and dust in all directions, then whined away up the tunnel into the dark. Speckles of blood suddenly appeared on Mayweather's face where some flying concrete chips had hit his left cheek.

"Shit, Alexa, this thing pulls right," Shane said, keeping it loony and loose.

"Whatta you doing?" she shouted. "Are you nuts? Stop it! You can't kill him. . . . *You can't!* I don't wanna go down for murder!" Picking up her cue perfectly, she turned on the camera without having to be told. Shane heard it whir softly behind him, and just like Coy Love, he stayed to the side, out of the frame.

"Okay, okay . . . I won't. You're right—you're right. Jesus, what's wrong with me. . . . It's just . . . Ahhh, fuck it! This guy is *going!*" Shane pointed the gun at the chief and pulled the hammer back. The metallic *click* echoed in the silence.

"Don't, Shane. Please!" she shouted, in standard Actors Studio over-the-top fashion. Mayweather was too panicked to spot their bad performances.

"Please . . . please stop him. Don't let him shoot me," the deputy chief begged Alexa. This was a new Tom Mayweather; no longer the officious' police commander, this one was shitting his pants, pleading for his life.

"How can I stop, Tommy? You're such a hopeless prick. I can't believe all the worthless shit you've been pulling, starting with screwing me for Ray's death, going all the way up the penal code to double felony kidnapping."

"What're you talking about?" he said, his lips quivering, blood beginning to run down the side of his face where the cement chips had cut him, staining his collar.

"What I'm saying, Tom, is I want answers. Don't you get it? *I'm fucking pissed off!* I'm through taking your *shit.* You don't walk away from a bad FI down here. You get buried in this fucking wash!" Shane was taking time on his performance now, first working on his loony sound, then screaming, making it unstable and completely out of control.

"Look, I don't know what's going on," Mayweather blurted.

"Come on, you think I'm a fucking moron? You're the deputy chief, *asshooole,*" he said, dragging the word out, leaning on it. "You're Burl's guy. You think I'm gonna believe that? You took all those files outta Zell's office. Your fuckin' prints are all over the folders." He was pacing madly back and forth, strobing the floodlight, keeping his head turned from the lens but throwing a moving shadow against Mayweather and the sweating concrete tunnel wall. The effect was eerie.

"I just get money. I don't ask questions. I do what I'm told." His voice shook badly.

"Is that how you can afford that shiny new sailboat?" Shane asked.

"I . . . I . . . Yes."

"And you know what? You know what? You know what I'm feeling?" He was rolling his words around like marbles in a tin dish. "I'm thinkin' you and Brewer and Ray and his whole fuckin' den are just *scum-sucking pieces of shit!* You sold out the fuckin' job for a fuckin' sailboat."

Mayweather was breathing through his mouth now. His fear was so pronounced, he'd forgotten to swallow; drool started coming out the right side of his mouth, running down his chin. He was close to snapping. Close to the edge of temporary insanity.

"Hey, Shane, calm down, for Chrissake. Whatta you doing?" Alexa said, seeing the dangerous change in Mayweather, not wanting him to snap and start babbling. "The man wants to talk—why don't you let him?"

"Tom, you gonna talk?" Shane said, sounding a little more in control. "You talk, maybe you could live to go sailing again. . . . Maybe—just maybe. But I need answers, man. I can't take no more shit! I can't . . . I just fucking can't." A little insane exasperation.

"Let him talk, for Chrissake," Alexa persisted. "Go ahead, Tom. Just tell us."

"What . . . what is it you wanna know?" His voice was close to tears.

"I wanna know what's going on with the H Street Bounty Hunters. How come Ray's den was letting those bangers run free in Southwest?" Alexa asked.

"I don't know."

"This is just more fucking *bullshit!*" Shane screamed, and cocked the gun again.

"No, no . . . Please . . . Please stop it. What I'm saying is, I know they're being allowed to rob down by the university." His words tumbling out now . . . "The gangbangers were told to do whatever they want from Exposition Boulevard to the freeway, and the police would look the other way."

"Down by USC?" Alexa said.

"Yeah, the old University Division."

"Why?"

"I don't know. For the love of God, I'm telling you all I know, I swear it."

"*Why* are those Gs being told it's okay to caper south of Exposition?" Alexa continued.

"I don't know. I don't . . . All I know is Brewer, once when I asked him, said that he wanted to drive the crime stats up in that part of town."

"The chief of police wants to drive the crime stats *up?*" Alexa asked from the darkness behind the camera. "Why? His job performance depends on driving the stats *down.*"

"I don't know. It's all he said."

"Tommy, this is all fucking, runny yellow *bullshit.*" Shane shoved the gun out in front of him, right into Mayweather's face, the barrel pressed against his right cheek.

"Shane—NO!" Alexa shouted.

"Stop it," Mayweather sobbed, his eyes bugging, straining to get away, the cuffs rattling against the metal ladder. "I don't know—I swear it! All he said was he was trying to increase the number of uncleared crimes in that section of the city. Molar's den was setting it up, running it. They transported the H Street bangers after the arrests and turned them loose. Sometimes they blew the busts by not reading the Miranda or by losing evidence." He was glistening with sweat under the floodlight. Shane didn't answer, but recocked the gun. The sound echoed menacingly in the concrete tunnel.

"Scully . . . Calm the fuck down," Alexa ordered.

There was a moment when all Shane could hear was the three of them breathing. Then Alexa moved out from behind the camera.

"Stop him. . . . Make him stop," Mayweather pleaded. Tears were suddenly running down his cheeks.

"Tell me about Calvin Sheets," Alexa said. "He worked the Coliseum detail down there. He was letting hookers and petty thieves run wild. Was he part of it?" She was taking over "point" on the interview because Mayweather had begged her. She probably seemed like his only chance. Shane let her have him, taking a step back.

"I don't know why, but yes, I heard Sheets was in on it."

"So that's why all Ray's den members have cases going through IAD," Alexa reasoned. "But why send them to full boards where they'd be tried in the open, in public hearings? The chief could have disposed of the charges on his own, in private, under Section 202."

"Because the community down there was getting pissed. Their shops were being held up, people beaten or killed. They were filing complaints. That city councilwoman, Alicia Winston, is making a big fuss, her and Max Valdez. They want the bangers stopped, so the chief sent all those cases to open boards to appease the community. The panels were gonna be rigged. I was in charge of picking them. The officers were all gonna be acquitted or get modulated penalties—days off without pay, but no terminations. If that happened, they'd get envelopes to make up the difference. Burl wanted to control the timing of the boards so they wouldn't fall one on top of the other."

"And that's why Drucker's board was just postponed?" she asked.

Mayweather now seemed uncomfortable. He shifted his weight, averted his eyes.

"Something wrong with that, Tommy?" Shane asked, stepping in again. "Did I get that wrong? *Spit it out!*"

"Uh . . . uh . . . uh . . . please . . . please . . . make him . . . I'm trying to . . ." the deputy chief said inarticulately.

"Was Li'l Silent making trouble?" Alexa persisted. "Did he want something that you couldn't give, so you couldn't trust him on the stand in Drucker's case? Was he shaking you down?"

"Look, I've told you all I know."

"Are we ever gonna see Sol Preciado again?" Shane asked softly. "Or did Li'l Silent break jail and dive into a pit full of lye?"

Mayweather licked his lips and said nothing, but it was as good as a confession.

"How did you ever get to be a deputy chief?" Alexa said softly.

Mayweather was sobbing heavily now, standing there, psychologically stripped, cuffed to the ladder and sweating like a field hand, his chest heaving, tears streaming down his handsome face. "My dad was a cop, y'know. He was a uniform in Lake Falls, Illinois. When I went to UCLA to play ball, he used to save up, come to the games. . . . He loved watching me play. He was proud. . . . He was . . . he . . . he . . ." Mayweather was so lost and out of control, he couldn't get the words out.

Shane closed his eyes. He didn't want to hear this man's bullshit story.

"When I didn't make it in the pros, I wanted to make my dad proud . . . so I . . . so I . . ."

"Shut the fuck up, or I'll kill you just for being a pussy," Shane shouted, not performing now, truly pissed.

"You kidnapped a boy named Chooch Sandoval. With him was my next-door neighbor and friend, Brian Kelly. I want them back. If I don't get them back, you die."

"Honest, honest . . . I know nothing about that. I told you, I know nothing about any kidnapping."

Shane took the cold barrel of the gun and again laid it up against Mayweather's cheek and held it there. The man's eyes got wide, trying to look down to see it.

"Why should I believe you?" Shane asked softly. "Make me a believer, Tom."

"Sol Preciado is dead," he whispered. "They let him out of

that jail-transport vehicle, then took him out and shot him. That makes me an accessory before the fact in a first-degree murder. You think I'd confess to that with a tape running and withhold information on a kidnapping?"

Shane took a deep breath and a moment to get level, turned away, then shut off the videotape and sun gun, packing up the camera. Alexa reached out and uncuffed Mayweather. Shane could barely see him but knew the deputy chief would not make trouble. He was beaten.

"Go home, Tom," Shane said softly. "Think about what you've done, the lives you've hurt or destroyed. Not just mine or Sol Preciado's, or Chooch Sandoval's or Brian Kelly's, but all the shop owners who had their brains kicked loose or were murdered. Think about all the old ladies who got knifed or beaten for their welfare checks so you could have that pretty new sailboat. If you believe in God, you better start working on a good excuse, 'cause you're gonna need it."

He turned and, carrying the video box, walked out of the tunnel with Alexa.

When they were outside, he paused and handed her gun back to her. They could hear Tom Mayweather splashing around in the tunnel, slowly making his way out.

"You wanna drop him somewhere?" she asked.

"Let the prick find his way home. Maybe some H Street gangster will pick him up and finish the job for us."

They scrambled up the concrete incline and finally got back to the car. Shane locked the video box and tape in the trunk. Tom Mayweather's confession was obtained illegally and under duress. It would be useless in court but would surely keep him on the sidelines. The last thing the deputy chief wanted was to see it on the six o'clock news.

They sat in the front seat of the Crown Vic for a long moment, both changed by what they had just done.

"That was brutal," Alexa finally said. Shane nodded, and she added, "What now?"

"What now? We've just pulled off a pretty successful kidnapping and felonious assault," he said. "Wanna try your hand at forced entry and burglary?"

A BEGINNING?

S HANE DIDN'T WANT to attempt a B&E in broad daylight, so they went back to Alexa's apartment to wait for the sun to go down.

He felt dirty and tired as he sat on her snow-white sofa. Mayweather's confession had darkened his mood, driving his spirit down without producing Chooch.

Shane had always considered police work a noble calling, where Blue Centurions defended the public, upholding society's laws. The slogans reverberated in his mind: *Protect and Serve; Reverence for the Law; Integrity in Word and Action.* His oath made seventeen years ago while holding his head and right hand high now seemed hollow and meaningless. "*I recognize the badge of my office as a symbol of public faith and I accept it as a public trust to be held so long as I am true to the ethics of police service.*"

Years on the job had shown him that police work was a flawed occupation at best, its participants on a narrowing, cynical path toward destroying the very thing they had pledged to uphold. Mayweather's crimes made Shane as dirty as if he had committed them himself.

"Is it okay if I take a shower?" he asked Alexa, hoping that maybe a long, hot soaking would wash the feeling away.

"Sure," she said. "I was just thinking the same thing, but you go first."

Shane heard a sadness in her voice that matched his own. He got up and walked into the bathroom, closed the door, and looked at himself in the mirror. The face staring back at him was tired and craggy and didn't resemble what he'd come to expect. The change worried him. He stripped off his shirt, pants, shoes, socks, and underwear, then turned on the shower and waited for it to get hot. Shane stepped in and stood under its steaming spray. He looked up at the nozzle, his eyes squinting as the spray bounced hard off his face and hot water filled his mouth. He was dirty in places it could not reach.

"You want, I'll do your laundry. I'll throw it in the machine with mine," he heard Alexa call from outside the bathroom.

"Good. Thanks. I tossed 'em next to the sink," he shouted back. Then, through the frosted shower door, he saw her step into the bathroom, retrieving his clothes. He turned his back, pinching his eyes shut, trying to blank out his troubled thoughts, when, almost before he knew what was happening, the frosted glass door opened and Alexa was in the shower with him, standing there naked, the steam turning her beautiful body slick with its moisture.

"Move over, you're hogging the spray," she said.

"What're you doing?" Shane's mind was doing flip-flops.

"I feel . . . I feel . . ."—she stopped, then looked up at him— "like I don't exist . . . like I don't even want to."

"Me, too," he said softly.

"I thought if we . . ." She stopped. "Bad idea . . ."

Shane didn't say anything, just took her into his arms and held her. As her wet body slid up against him, for the first time in days he felt the tension disappear; the knot in his stomach released as they stood locked in a cathartic embrace. They remained like that for a long time—holding each other, feeling each other's comfort and warmth. Then Shane felt his desire for her swelling and pushing between her legs, proving that he was still alive, still a man; perhaps all his failures of the past week could somehow be forged into a new beginning. He desperately wanted to start over. Then he felt her clutching him, pulling him closer, and was overtaken by a desire for her that was so intense, it brought tears to his eyes. "Is this right?" he said, asking for absolution, permission, and maybe directions all at the same time.

"Shut up," she whispered.

And then they were caressing each other in the steaming shower, Shane's mouth covering hers, his body pushing her back against the wet tiles on the wall of the small shower, kissing with abandon, feeling each other's warmth. Suddenly she pulled herself up, wrapping her arms around his neck, bringing her legs up around his waist. While she clung to him, he entered her, slowly at first, then thrusting more deeply. As her moans of pleasure washed over him, he felt changed and reborn.

Shane didn't know how long it lasted; time, in that small place, had become endless. They were in a wet cocoon of human ecstasy, and then he heard her cry out as he released inside her. She kissed him hard on the mouth, her breath mixing with his in the steaming shower.

Shane finally set her down, and they remained under the hot spray in a desperate embrace, almost afraid to let go, afraid to return to their individual fears and loneliness. Finally she took the bar of soap and began to wash his back, his arms, lathering him in erotic places. After she was finished, he did the same for her. They held each other in a sweet fragrance of body and soul. Shane felt different, stronger, more alive.

He looked down into her laser-blue eyes, which now seemed softer and filled with caring.

"Now we can start over," she said, putting his exact thoughts into words.

■ ■ ■

Later she made dinner and they sat at her kitchen table. She was wearing a white terry-cloth robe; he was wrapped in a towel.

After dinner she handed him his clothes, fresh from the dryer; they felt soft and were still warm as he put them on. When he walked into the living room, he noticed that there was renewed energy in his stride and a spring in his step.

They said very little, but as they locked her front door and headed to her car, she reached out, took his hand, and squeezed it.

THE HOT PROWL

HE WAS BACK in the parking lot, studying the fourteen-story steel-and-glass building in Long Beach. They had waited for the sun to go down. It was 8:05 on Saturday night, and they were still using the staff car Shane had been given up in Arrowhead. Across the street, roof letters announced Spivack Development Corporation in five-foot-high blue neon.

"I feel like Bonnie and Clyde. Do you have this effect on everybody?" Alexa said. She was sitting in the Crown Vic next to Shane, putting on a pair of latex gloves so she wouldn't leave her prints behind, both of them feeling a sense of awkwardness from the passionate lovemaking they'd engaged in a few hours before.

"Y'know, you're the last person I would ever have thought I'd be pulling a second-story job with," he finally said. She ignored it.

"You said you were here before. Did you scout it? You got a way into this place?" She was all business, putting that memory out of reach, taking the binoculars out of the glove box, unwinding the strap and training them on the building.

"Look, things have changed. We both know it," he said softly.

"Yes, but . . . Shane, it's dangerous. We have to be either cops or lovers. We can't be both. You've seen what a mess that turns into when it happens. . . . For now, we gotta do the job."

He knew she was right and finally nodded.

"So, did you scout it?" she asked again.

"Yeah . . . we can get to the roof by way of the fire stairs. Go down through a special staircase up there for the helicopter pad. It leads right down to Spivack's floor. The fire doors have interior bolt locks except on the first floor."

She nodded. "Y'know what pisses me off?"

"Ummmn," he answered, putting on his own pair of gloves.

"These binoculars piss me off—Bushnell 16x35s with a waterproof case. I worked Southwest Patrol for three years with a cracked pair of six-power prewar Lens Masters with one side out of whack. Couldn't focus the right eyepiece, asked for new binocs ten, twelve times, was told it wasn't in the budget. And here, in this staff car, they leave 'em under the seat like throwaways."

"Yeah, and we don't get sailboats, either."

She didn't answer but continued to focus the binoculars on the building. "You think we try for the roof? Go up through the fire stairs, pry the lock up there, then go down one floor, hope the interior doors aren't wired?"

"You're a fun date," he said, finishing with his gloves, snapping the wristbands while she lowered the glasses.

"Spivack builds shopping centers and commercial real estate all over the place, right?" she said.

"Yeah, malls, sports complexes, city buildings—anything where you've got high budgets and low administrative supervision costs."

"Tony Spivack, Logan Hunter, Chief Brewer, Mayor Crispin, and Ray Molar—quite a five-man team," she said.

"With Tom Mayweather still at point guard. Seems pretty obvious they stole this land in Long Beach—the naval yard—to build something. Hotels or a huge resort would be my guess. It's right on the bay. . . ."

"Why would Logan Hunter be part of it? He's a movie guy."

"I don't know. He likes press . . . maybe it's gonna be his new studio, with a theme park like Universal's . . . call it the Web. Lotsa rides, lotsa fuzzy cartoon characters greeting you at the gate in chipmunk costumes. Who the fuck knows?"

"Let's go," she said. "This isn't gonna get any easier the longer we wait."

They got out of the car and moved across the parking lot.

"If we get stopped, flash your tin," he said.

"Always *my* tin, *my* gun."

"You collected mine already, remember?"

"Stop bitching," she said, but they were both smiling.

Strange how that can happen, in the midst of losing Chooch and Brian. Despite feeling devastated in the face of that loss, he had first had a moment of uncontrolled sexual passion with her and now he was grinning like an idiot, adrenaline driving his emotions, skewing his senses while keeping his vision bright . . . both of them acting like kids snatching a pie off a bakery-shop windowsill.

They got to the side of the building and began walking around it, looking for the fire door. There were several private security guards inside. Shane and Alexa could see them in the lobby looking out through the glass at them.

"Gimme your hand," he said.

She immediately reached out and took his, strolling lazily beside him, putting her head on his shoulder. They looked like two lovers going nowhere special, nuzzling and feeling it again: a new sense of closeness.

Shane was acutely aware of her perfume, and in that moment, while they were pretending to be lovers, he felt something strange and confusing and powerful stir inside him. The feeling was undeniably strong but totally inappropriate in the middle of a hot prowl, so he bundled it up, stowed it on a top shelf in the back of his mind, slammed the cupboard shut, and saved it for later. He turned his thoughts instead toward the fire door coming up on the left.

She took her latex-gloved hand away from his and tried the door. It was locked.

"I have keys," he said, removing his little leather pouch of picklocks.

"No way," she said, looking askance at the burglar tools.

"Stand back. I'm not as good as Ray was, but I'll have this open in a sec." He went to work on the lock while she turned and watched the terrain behind him, making sure no slow-moving Long Beach patrol car came upon them unexpectedly.

After a moment he manipulated the last pick in the lock and felt it hook down into the tumbler inside the door. He was ready to turn the knob. "Okay, all set," he said.

She turned back to him. "What about the alarm?" she asked.

"What about it?"

"Won't it go off when we open it?"

"Here's the way I have this figured," he said. "If there's an alarm on this door, then when I open it, it will damn sure go off. If there isn't one, then my thinking is, it won't."

"Asshole."

"Of course, if it rings, we need to fall back and think up a new strategy. I'm not good with alarms; I haven't had time to perfect that talent yet."

"Let's go. Do it," she said, and watched breathlessly as he put his hand on the knob.

He felt the lock turn and then pushed the door open.

Nothing!

They ducked into the dimly lit concrete stairwell and closed the exterior door.

"That's amazing," she said. "Why wouldn't they have this door rigged?"

"They did. I unplugged it yesterday afternoon when I was here. The unit box is in the sub-basement." He smiled while she glared. "Come on, lighten up. I wanted you to experience the whole thrill."

Then he turned and ran up the stairs, taking the first flight two at a time.

It took them almost five minutes to get up to the roof, then they were standing in the reflected glow of the five-foot blue letters while Shane went to work on the roof door.

"This leads right down to the lobby on the top floor," he said.

"Is this alarm unhooked, too?"

"I hope so. The panel was a little confusing down there. I had to straight-wire a lot of shit."

"So you *are* an expert on alarms."

"Ray always said the picks are worthless if you set off alarms."

"Some probation training you got."

He finally had the door open, and the two of them went down the one flight to the fourteenth floor. The interior door to the helicopter stairs was unlocked, and in another minute or so, they were inside the steel-and-glass offices of Spivack Development Corporation. The only thing missing was the blond ice goddess behind the reception desk.

They moved through the lobby into the back, where they found themselves in a long, narrow hallway decorated with artistic schematics of past Spivack developments. Huge hotels and major airport buildings hung in stainless-steel frames. The renderings were crisp line drawings with pastel watercolors. They passed out of the corridor into a huge drafting area. "I wonder where Tony Spivack lives," Shane said.

After a few more minutes of searching, they found his office, fronted by a vast secretarial area and a set of mahogany doors with ANTHONY J. SPIVACK engraved on an antique silver plaque.

Shane turned the doorknob and pushed it open. They entered an ornate, palatial office: red carpet, embroidered drapes, and a mixture of furniture styles; French armoires and steel-and-glass tables populated the room. Shane moved to the immense plate-glass window that overlooked the city of Long Beach. He could see the domed city hall and, way off to the west, the *Queen Mary* sparkling with lights. Beyond that, he knew, was the Long Beach Naval Yard, which was magnetic north because everything pointed to it.

"We've gotta go through his files, see if we can find the project drawings," he said, still looking out the window, struck by the view: the shimmering Pacific Ocean beyond a ribbon of moonlit sand.

"Shane, look at this," he heard her say.

He turned, and she was no longer in the office.

He found her standing in the adjoining conference room. There was a magnificent 1:16 architectural model on a ten-foot-long side table. It covered the entire tabletop and was ten by five feet. Shane approached the huge model and saw that it was the architectural layout for the five-hundred-acre Long Beach Naval Yard project.

The plaque read:

THE WEB
A NEW CONCEPT IN ENTERTAINMENT

The centerpiece of the development was a football stadium with two rings of luxury suites. It was perched on the property, a big concrete oval, its escalators arching away from the perimeter like eight long spider legs. It dwarfed everything. Engraved over the stadium's modern entry was a tiny sign:

THE WEB

"The L.A. Spiders. A football team," Shane said. "Sandy told me Logan Hunter was trying to bring an NFL franchise to L.A."

"This is about *football*," she said, appalled, sounding exactly like every housewife in America.

"It's really not about football, it's about real estate." He studied the rest of the development. The thirty or more architectural models placed on the site plan were beautifully made and exquisitely detailed. They dotted the five-hundred-acre site. There was an amusement park with roller coasters and Ferris wheels; five luxury hotels, each one next to the water; shopping malls and restaurants. Little catamarans were stuck in the "water," racing along motionlessly up on one pontoon, their tiny sails billowing orange and red against aqua-blue plaster waves.

Shane was trying to put it together. "Okay," he said slowly, using her words. "It's called police work. . . . Connecting the dots . . . Ray Molar and his den blackmail the Long Beach City Council with hookers at the party house in Arrowhead. A video festival occurs that forces Carl Cummins and the embarrassed city officials of Long Beach to give the naval yard over to L.A. and Mayor Crispin in return for some bogus water rights. The mayor gifts the property to Spivack in return for Spivack's promise to develop it for the city of L.A. as a home base for a new sports franchise. Spivack funds the actual physical development in return for the property. Logan Hunter gets the NFL to award L.A. a new football franchise, and everybody, from top to bottom, gets silent ownership in the deal and walks away multimillionaires."

"And the H Street Bounty Hunters were just a fun idea that got included for ethnic diversity?" she said.

"Okay, that's a wild piece. I don't have that connection yet, but I like the rest of it."

"Could be . . ." She sounded less sure.

"I remember reading once that the real money play on these

sports franchise deals is the land, not the team. These guys get billions of dollars' worth of land from L.A. for free in return for financing the project and building this thing. Most of the public doesn't bitch, 'cause they don't care about the land; they want the team and a class A stadium to go with it. Sure, you end up with a roomful of environmentalists and hotheads protesting, but it's on page ten of the Metro section. . . . Nobody gives a damn about them because pro football is coming back to L.A.!"

"They can do that? Just give the land away?"

"Yeah, happens all the time. Years ago the city of Anaheim gave Georgia Frontiere hundreds of acres around Anaheim Stadium to get her to move the Rams there. Then, even when she carpetbagged the team off to St. Louis, the land was still hers. The O'Malleys were given Chavez Ravine for Dodger Stadium— the city condemned it, moved out all the Hispanics who lived there, then gave the O'Malleys the property, free and clear, in return for building Dodger Stadium. That way they wouldn't have to try and float a bond issue."

"Do you mind if we get out of here?" she said. "This is all quite fascinating, but I'm not as comfortable doing hot prowls as you are."

"One more thing first," he said, and moved out of the conference room and over to Spivack's desk. He opened the center drawer and took out Tony Spivack's appointment calendar while Mrs. Spivack and two dark-haired children eyed him suspiciously from behind a silver frame on the corner of the desk.

He opened the leather-covered book and started flipping pages.

"What're you doing?" she asked.

"Wanna see if he's in town. Last time I saw this shitbird, he was flying off in a green and white helicopter." Shane flipped the calendar to April. "Here it is; Sunday, April twenty-sixth, Miami Beach, NFL, eight-thirty A.M."

"Lemme see that," she said, and he spun the calendar toward her.

"Alexa, he's in Miami Beach right now, meeting with the NFL at eight-thirty tomorrow morning. You likin' my theory any better?"

They moved out of the office, but she stopped at the secretary's desk and looked around at the slips of paper that Spivack's secretary had pasted up neatly on a bulletin board: lots of yellow Post-its, reminders, important numbers and addresses.

"I thought you wanted to leave."

"If we're gonna do this, let's do it right," she said, still looking. "I worked as a secretary once, during a summer vacation in college. You keep the boss's temporary numbers up near the phone if he's traveling." She reached up and pulled a Post-it down. " 'Coral Reef Yacht Club.' That sound like Miami to you?" she asked.

"Take it. Let's go," he said.

Seconds later they were on the roof, then back inside the concrete fire stairs; a few moments later they were in the Crown Vic and gone.

BACKGROUNDING

DON'T WORRY, I'll get us there."

It was just after ten P.M. and the last flight to Miami had departed LAX, so Shane drove to the Long Beach Airport. He found the executive jet area and drove along Executive Terminal Row until he found a busy-looking FBO called Million-Air Charters. He pulled into the parking lot next to the mostly glass one-story building, then he and Alexa got out.

"Private jets cost big money," Alexa said

"I've got a hundred thousand in small bills, but we're gonna look like drug dealers, so get your tin ready."

He opened the trunk and retrieved the suitcase with Coy Love's cash bribe inside. They walked into Million-Air Charters, and Shane plunked the leather bag down on the counter.

"We'd like to charter a jet to Miami," he said.

The girl behind the counter was young but no dummy. She took one look at Shane and Alexa's off-the-rack clothes, stole a quick peek at their fourteen-dollar Timex watches, and knew these two were not customers.

Alexa pulled out her LAPD identification and laid it on the desktop. "If you need to talk to a manager, this is police business. We're with the Drug Enforcement Task Force and we have got to get to Miami before morning."

Shane snapped open the suitcase and spun it around, revealing the stack of cash.

"Confiscated drug money," Alexa explained. "We'll need you to receipt it for us." All bullshit, but comforting words when a civilian is looking at a suitcase full of used bills.

"Let me talk to Mr. Lathrope," she said.

Mr. Lathrope wanted to be called Vern; he had hunched shoulders, wireless granny glasses, and hair that had the general shape and texture of a number-nine paintbrush. He looked at the cash and Alexa's badge speculatively, then made a few calls. His weary attitude said he didn't like them, but business was business. "I can have two pilots here in half an hour, then I'll put you in 868 Charlie Papa," he said to Shane.

"What's 868 Charlie Papa?" Shane asked, showing total ignorance of jet charters.

"Tail number. It's the white Gulfstream Three with green stripes," he said, nodding his head toward the window where three or four executive jets were parked.

Shane didn't know a Gulfstream 3 from a palomino pony, but he nodded anyway. " 'Bout how much is that gonna run?" he asked.

"It's fifteen each way, thirty for the whole trip. We won't charge you for hangar time up to five hours; after that, the ground rate is one-half the hourly."

"Not giving us much of a break here, are you, Vern?" Shane said.

"Our prices are competitive. Make as many calls as you want—check it out. However, if you're interested in an opinion, it is a bit unusual to be getting paid with used bills out of a suitcase."

Stalemate.

Shane moved to the sofa, put the open suitcase on his lap, and began counting out stacks of banded cash. Each packet had fifty twenty-dollar bills in it. Shane counted out thirty stacks, snapped the suitcase shut, then walked up and handed the money to Vern Lathrope, who couldn't get his right eyebrow down from the middle of his forehead.

"I usually have a brown paper bag for transactions like this," Shane said as he shoved the cash over.

Shane and Alexa sat and waited on the expensive calf-leather couches, now clients of Million-Air Charters. Shane made two calls to Sandy, but she didn't pick up and her answering machine was off.

Half an hour later two young pilots in uniforms led Shane and Alexa to the Gulfstream 3 that Shane now realized was the biggest plane sitting on the flight line.

"Vern didn't like taking used cash, but he sure didn't mind renting us the most expensive piece of iron he had," Shane groused.

They stepped on a small rectangular red carpet before climbing the ladder and entering the jet. Then the copilot quickly rolled it up and stuffed it in a luggage compartment, with a "so much for that" smile on his face. He climbed up the stairs and pulled the door up after him. A few minutes later the Gulfstream jet, with Shane and Alexa and nine empty seats, was out on the end of the Long Beach runway, waiting for the tower to green-light the takeoff.

Shane found a beer in the refrigerator and brought one back to Alexa, who had kicked off her shoes and was reclining in the seat.

The plush interior was heavily scented with the smell of English leather. Rich, polished burlwood glistened in the Trivoli lighting. There were Baccarat crystal glasses in slots over a full bar.

"Okay, Shane and Alexa," Bob, their friendly pilot, said. "We're cleared for takeoff, so we're gonna do our thing now. Anything we can get you along the way, we're on channel three on the intercom."

"Thank you," Shane said to the empty cabin.

"I think you have to pick up a little receiver first," she said, smiling at him.

"For thirty grand, Bob can come back here when I want to talk to him." Then he kicked off his loafers and put the seat back. He had chosen to sit across the aisle from Alexa, facing backward so he could look at her.

Suddenly the plane was hurtling down the runway, its wheels coming up immediately on takeoff, climbing fast. They flew out over the ocean, then the pilot made a slow turn and headed east.

Shane and Alexa sat in the luxurious executive jet, sipping imported beer while the plane climbed to altitude and the lights of Long Beach gradually slipped away below the starboard wing.

"I'm gonna try to get some sleep," she said, putting her head back and closing her eyes.

Shane could smell her perfume again; it drifted across the aisle like a carefully thrown net.

"Mayweather's dad was a cop in Illinois," she said unexpectedly, without opening her eyes. "I didn't know that."

"Yeah," Shane said. "Just another grunt in a blue suit, out there hookin' and bookin' assholes for the city."

"My dad was a cop in Hartford, Connecticut," she said, her eyes still closed. "He was a patrol cop but never made sergeant. Couldn't take tests. He froze every time he went up for the exam."

"Oh," Shane said, trying to picture her father. What must he and Mrs. Hamilton have been like to have produced this iron-willed yet exotic-looking creature?

"Did you have brothers or sisters?" he asked, hoping she would open up. After a long moment:

"Two brothers." She started slowly, then it seemed important for her to tell him more. "I was the youngest. My mom died in childbirth. For a long time I thought that was my fault. We had pictures of her all over the house. It was like a shrine. My brothers and I, we tried to imagine what it would have been like to have her around. I used to wonder if she was in heaven looking down, mad at me for causing her death, so I tried to make her happy by doing all the chores: cleaning up after Dad and my two brothers, doing dishes, washing clothes, trying to take her place but knowing I never could." She stopped, the memory somewhat painful, then went on. "Dad remarried when I was fifteen, and we got Karen, who was nice but kind of distant. It was like Dad's three kids were some sort of mistake that she was forced to accept in the deal. I went to college on a track scholarship at UCLA— sprints and hurdles. I was there about ten years after Mayweather, but they still talked about him on Bruin Sports Radio, particularly during Bruin basketball games. He was a big deal, even years after he graduated. They all said he should have made the pros, but he ended up on the police force instead. . . .

"It felt shitty watching him plead and beg down there. . . . Somebody special that everybody looked up to turns out to be a self-centered shitball. Down there in that tunnel, I lost something. I don't know why it should affect me, but it does."

He was looking at her, wondering if she was ever going to open her eyes.

"Is that enough personal history?" she said, shining her blues at him again.

"Are you mad at me for some reason?" he asked. "You seem pissed off."

She sat still for several moments.

"Yeah . . . I guess I am. I wanted this career, wanted to believe in it. I wanted Mayweather to be stand-up. I actually liked him once. Respected him. Life is full of disappointments. I'll get over it. I wanted Santa Claus to come down the chimney with toys made at the North Pole especially for me."

He studied her, his dark, intense eyes trading her amp for amp.

"But just so you don't get the wrong idea, Shane, I don't think it's your fault this is happening. You just got put in the soup. You didn't ask for this any more than I did. It happened to you, and I'm in this with you because to do anything else is unthinkable."

There was a long silence. He was trying to think of the right thing to say. Finally he just smiled.

"Thank you," he said.

"You're welcome."

They didn't speak again until they landed.

Before he closed his eyes and tried to sleep, he glanced over at her. Her shoes were off, feet up on the seat facing her, those restless ice-blue lasers sheathed now. She was breathing rhythmically, sleeping peacefully.

He tried to picture her as a child, a little girl wondering if she'd killed her mother during her own birth, carrying that burden around with her. Just as he'd carried the idea that he had not meant enough to his own parents to have them hold on to him even for one day. He'd been left at the hospital like trash put out by the back door.

He had often tried to picture his parents. . . . Who were they? Did they go to college? Were they just teenagers who got careless and conceived him in a drive-in movie and decided to run? Were they hicks from Alabama, driving a pickup and drinking sour mash from a jug, with no money to raise him? Was he part Jewish or Italian or Irish? Did his mom and dad ever think about him and feel bad about what they'd done?

Why had they left him without even a first name pinned to his shirt?

He'd spent his life struggling to move past it, struggling to overcome it, finally using Chooch as a way to pull himself up, until he discovered that Chooch had become more important to him than the whole tired problem that had been weighing him down in the first place.

Alexa had been struggling, too. Internal Affairs was the perfect place for her. Weeding out the bad ones, making another house clean, all the time looking up, wondering if her mother hated her . . . wondering if she was good enough to be forgiven.

He admired her for it, but it also made him sad.

The sound of the huge jet engines hypnotically hummed in his ear. *I wonder if, despite all that's happening, I'm actually beginning to feel something important for this woman.*

Then Shane Scully, whose first given name was Infant 205, finally closed his eyes and went to sleep.

Shane dreamed about Chooch. The boy was on a vast beach, flying a kite over the ocean, but the kite was all black and dipping dangerously, diving toward the surface before straightening up again. Each time it seemed to get lower and lower.

"Shane, help me!" he was yelling. "It's going to crash!" Shane was moving toward him, but the faster he ran, the farther away Chooch seemed to be. If Shane didn't stop the kite's wild flight, he knew it would all end in disaster.

THE 41 LAST DOT

MIAMI WAS BAKING in heat, the temperature in the mid-nineties, the humidity intense. They walked down the steps of the Gulfstream 3 into an invisible wall of moisture. A rent-a-car arranged by the FBO in Miami was waiting for them—a bright yellow Thunderbird. Shane signed for it; then, after locking the suitcase containing the rest of the money in the trunk, he got the map of Miami out of the glove compartment and looked for the Coral Reef Yacht Club. It was a large piece of property marked on the map in orange, located east of Highway 1, south of the wealthy town of Coral Gables.

"You navigate, I'll drive," he said to Alexa, getting behind the wheel.

The car was a hardtop, and somebody had been chain-smoking in it. The unpleasant smell of old tobacco hung over them, wet and onerous. The air conditioner needed Freon and put out a stream of tepid air. They pulled out, and she directed him to Seventh Avenue, which turned into Cutter Road.

The sky was that special tinsel-blue that you can only get in Miami, where the land is so flat that no pollution can stay trapped above the city, instead blowing across the state, dissipating in the ocean breeze, leaving Miami glistening in bright sunshine and mirrored glass architecture.

Clouds floated by intermittently, huge white formations of indescribable beauty moving slowly across the flat horizon like whipped-cream galleons.

The Coral Reef Yacht Club was just down the road from the U.S. Department of Agriculture's Plant Introduction Station. The yacht club sat on man-made levees and fronted a dredged ocean cut that was enclosed on three sides. Nestled among this lush marine setting were clusters of old Florida-style buildings made of coral bricks, with overhanging eaves. Boats of all shapes and sizes were moored at dock fingers in front of the exclusive club.

Shane pulled through an open gate with a guardhouse but no guard. The parking lot was jammed; he finally found a spot way down by the docks. There were several news vans parked a hundred yards away, by the main building.

Shane and Alexa got out of the Thunderbird and moved up a crushed-gravel drive, where they found a man leaning against one of the mobile units, having a smoke.

"They inside?" Shane asked vaguely.

"Yep. It's going down right now."

"Yeah? The . . . uh . . . NFL owners' meeting?"

"No. The owners' meeting was in July. This is the new team announcements," the man corrected, taking a closer look at him.

"Right, that's what he meant," Alexa said; then they moved past the man into the yacht club.

There was a large hall off the entry called the Trophy Room, and it was packed. There were a dozen news teams—network as well as local Miami stations—with cameras and mikes marked

CNN, ESPN, and WNS (World News Service). There were also radio and print media. Close to two hundred people were milling about in the room under exposed beams and slow-turning paddle fans.

Without having to discuss it, Shane and Alexa separated. If one got thrown out, the other probably wouldn't. They took up positions on opposite sides of the room.

There was an NFL banner behind a makeshift stage. All around the room were yachting trophies and pictures of past commodores of the club, smiling out of their lacquered frames, wearing their captain's hats with too much braid on the visors. The room was elbow to elbow. Shane's cop mind noted that they were dangerously over the fire regs.

Up on the stage, a man was droning on. Shane tried to catch the flow of his remarks:

". . . as they said . . . which, of course, made us very sure we had embarked on the right course as far as that program was concerned . . ."

Shane looked around for Tony Spivack or Logan Hunter, whom he remembered as a slim, somewhat handsome blond man from pictures he'd seen in the newspapers.

". . . So, Don and Fred, who will be speaking to you in a minute, took all of those factors into account. These decisions, at their core, are difficult at best, because community pride is always involved. That's why we have been so deliberate on this issue."

Shane waited, crushed in between a florid-faced man in a Hawaiian shirt and a news crew from WKMI-TV.

". . . That having been said, I'd like to present, with great pleasure, our very own commissioner of the NFL, Mr. Paul Tagliabue."

There was a smattering of polite applause. Shane was scanning the podium now. There were twenty-nine men and two women seated in leather club chairs behind the main speaker. He was beginning to recognize some of the faces from TV or the sports pages: Wayne Huizenga, owner of the Miami Dolphins; Alex Spanos of the San Diego Chargers; Jerry Jones of the Dallas Cowboys. All the owners of the thirty-one NFL teams were up there.

"Thank you, Lee," the commissioner said. "Okay, now for the moment we've all been anticipating. We have, as you all know, decided to award three new expansion franchises to three deserving cities: Houston, Los Angeles, and Oklahoma City. We have picked three facilities and ownership structures to be the homes of these new franchises. In Houston, we are proud to announce that we are awarding the NFC expansion franchise to the syndicate headed by Keith Fowler and Martin Fisk."

There was a gasp from the room, and then a whoop went up from the back of the hall. Shane turned and looked as the two men went up onto the stage.

The Houston winners had named their new expansion team the Houston Blaze and were holding up uniform jerseys and doing their photo op as news crews swarmed.

Shane looked over at Alexa on the far side of the room, just as a gray-haired man with a belt buckle the size of a small serving platter stepped to the mike and started throwing out Texas homilies:

"Now that we got this here thing safe in the corral, guess it's time ta wash off the war paint and throw us a shindig," he said. "We're set up like pigs in a mud bath over at the Four Seasons Hotel, so y'all come on over and help us raise the roof." He went on to thank half a dozen people.

Shane finally spotted Logan Hunter. He was dressed in a tan suit tailored to his wispy frame, without one sag or wrinkle. He had an abundance of too-blond hair and was wearing a mint-green shirt with no tie. There was something exotic in his carriage. Logan Hunter wore his millionaire film-mogul status like imported cologne; it wafted around him. He was boyish and, except for the wrinkle lines around his eyes, would have appeared to be in his mid-thirties instead of the fifty that Shane had read he was.

"In L.A. we had a terribly difficult choice." The commissioner was now back at the mike. "We had two competing franchises— one from Bill Kaufman, who proposed a restoration of the L.A. Coliseum. Bill has made a wonderful presentation, showing how that grand old lady could be brought up to millennium standards. And I've gotta say, a lot of incredible thought went into that plan. The other group, headed by Logan Hunter and Tony Spivack, have proposed a fresh site, a new development at the now-deserted Long Beach Naval Yard, which has recently been ceded to the city of L.A. I'm pleased to add that the mayor of Los Angeles, Clark Crispin, is with us today, and I'm going to let him announce the winner of the new L.A. expansion franchise. Clark . . . ?"

A door opened at the side of the room, and Clark Crispin came onto the stage. Shane had seen him at many official L.A. gatherings and had even worked his security detail one weekend during his second election campaign. He was tall and angular, and when he smiled, his face always radiated warmth. He was dressed in hit-man black, his Armani pinstripe relieved by a festive red tie.

"Thanks, Paul. What a day for L.A. We, of course, have missed having a pro team in our city since you took the Raiders back north, Al." He smiled at Al Davis, who barely returned it. "Or since Georgia moved my beloved Rams to St. Louis and won a championship . . ." She smiled warmly, but there seemed to be a definite "fuck you" in the mixture.

"So now we have a new opportunity. Will it be the Coliseum, with Bill Kaufman, or the Web, with Tony Spivack and Logan Hunter? The envelope, please," he said, grinning, and there was a mild groan in the room.

"It is my honor to announce that the new Los Angeles AFC expansion franchise, and soon-to-be Super Bowl football team, will be the L.A. Spiders, playing at the Web. Tony? Logan? Come on up. Tell us how it feels."

Suddenly, as the two of them made their way to the stage, a side door opened and ten Spiderettes, dressed in their new black and red minicostumes, came onto the stage. Music played through a speaker system as they began to dance, waving black and red pom-poms. The crowd loved it.

The TV crews were circling, gunning footage, and then as the music stopped, the girls fell back, and Logan Hunter went to the mike.

"Thank you, Clark. Well, who would've thought this day would come?" More cheering and applause.

"Please," Shane said derisively under his breath; then the nickel dropped, and he knew what the missing piece was.

"I'm delighted we're going to be bringing football back to L.A.," Logan Hunter said. "We're going to deliver a top-flight product. We'll spare no expense to build a first-rate franchise at the Web. If you buy season tickets today, we'll guarantee you a spot in the stands when we kick off in our new stadium in the fall of 2001. We're gonna be up and ready. We break ground tomorrow. Tony, you wanna say a few words?"

Spivack, who had just put on a new Spiders football jersey over his suit and tie, came to the mike. "I don't have much time to talk. I better get back and grab a shovel if I'm gonna meet Logan's date."

There was a ripple of laughter.

"Commissioner Tagliabue . . . one question!" Shane shouted. "How come you didn't choose the Coliseum? That's a national historic landmark, built for the '32 Olympics. . . . Plus, the people with businesses in that neighborhood count on Coliseum events to survive."

The room fell silent. Spivack stepped back and handed the mike to Paul Tagliabue. "There were other factors involved. It was a complicated decision," the commissioner said. "We don't want to get into that right now."

"Was it the high crime stats down there?" Shane persisted, rolling the idea up to the stage like a live grenade.

"The growing crime rate around the Coliseum certainly entered into our decision," he said. "But there were many factors. We'll have a question-and-answer session after the announcements are concluded. Now, moving on . . . We come to the last franchise, in Oklahoma City—"

"Why do you suppose crime in that neighborhood rose so dramatically?" Shane was pulling the pin now.

A police officer appeared at his elbow. "May I see your pass, sir?"

"Don't have one," he replied.

"Whatta you doing here?"

"I'm a mental patient. We sorta wander around."

"Not funny. Let's go." He led Shane out of the room, walking with a firm grip on his elbow. They moved past Alexa, who was standing next to a WMI Radio team. She caught his eye and smiled as he was ejected from the room.

Once they were outside, the cop glowered at Shane. "You can leave, or you can take a ride with me. Your choice."

"Why don't I just leave . . ."

"Why don't ya," the cop said.

Shane walked to the yellow T-bird, took a piece of paper out of his pocket, and wrote Alexa a note. He shoved it under the car, got behind the wheel, and rolled over the note, then drove out of the parking lot, up the winding driveway, and parked on the street outside. He sat in the front seat in the oppressive heat, with the lousy air conditioner blowing a foul tobacco smell, until he couldn't bear it any longer. He got out of the car, threw his coat off, and looked down at his sweat-soaked shirt. He tried to get cool under a Japanese banyan tree while he contemplated what he had just learned. It was maddeningly simple once you had all the pieces:

The NFL wouldn't put a team in an area where violent crime and prostitution were out of control, so they awarded the franchise to Logan Hunter and the new entertainment/stadium complex being built at the old Long Beach Naval Yard. That was the last dot. He didn't know what he was going to do about it, but after ten days of eating everyone's exhaust, Shane had finally caught up.

For the first time since this all started, he actually knew what the hell was going on.

42

H ALF AN HOUR LATER she came out of the Coral Reef Yacht
Club and, shading her eyes with a four-by-five card, stood
amidst milling news crews.

Shane could see her from the road, a slender figure standing
defiantly in the entryway, looking toward the empty space where
the yellow T-bird had been parked.

Shane had just tried to get Sandy on the phone again, but with
no luck. He folded his cell and watched from the road, three
hundred yards away, as Alexa walked uncertainly to the empty
parking spot, reached down, and picked up his note. Then she
turned and headed toward the main road, quickening her pace
when she saw him, walking out the main gate and approaching
the car. She frowned when she saw Shane's sweat-plastered shirt.

"Did you decide to take a swim?"

"I can't handle this steam bath they got down here." She nodded and handed him the card in her hand.

"What's this?"

"Logan's having a barbecue. He borrowed Elton John's house to celebrate. I'm invited. I can bring a guest, but I'll be damned if I'm showing up with a guy who looks like he's been playing in the sprinklers."

"I'll stop on the way and buy a new shirt. Let's go." They got into the T-bird and drove off.

They actually made two stops, first at a drugstore for deodorant and a razor, then at a small department store, where Shane bought a new white shirt and Alexa bought a simple cocktail dress. After he washed up and shaved in the employee bathroom, Shane felt 50 percent better.

He walked out and got into the idling T-bird, joining Alexa in the lukewarm stream of tobacco-scented air. "That looks good on you," he said, glancing appreciatively at the way the short pale blue dress fit her trim, athletic body.

"Thanks," she said noncommittally.

They drove up Cutter Road, back toward Coral Gables.

The beautiful Japanese banyan trees hung overhead, strobing leafy shadows across the T-bird's hood. They turned right on Casuarina Concourse and drove east, toward the water.

Elton John's house was not hard to spot. The press was already there. Shane turned into the winding drive and waited in a long line of cars while the guests showed their numbered invitations and were checked off a list.

"By the way, I'm Whitney Green, WMI Radio. Whitney does the noon show and couldn't make it."

"How the hell did you get invited?"

"I promised Whitney's husband, Don, I'd have a drink with him later."

"Yuck."

"Double yuck. You haven't seen him."

They pulled up to the man checking invitations. Alexa leaned across Shane and handed over her engraved card. "Whitney

Green and guest," she said as the security guard wearing a tailored blazer checked the invitation, then nodded. Two valets opened both doors. Shane and Alexa got out as a man in a red jacket ran up, jumped into the car, and pulled away.

As they joined a line of people heading up the drive toward the house, they could hear a band playing. They walked under a large balloon arch stretched across the driveway, done in red and black Spiders football colors, with a large sign that read:

L.A. SPIDERS 2001

Waiters in white coats circulated with trays of champagne and hors d'oeuvres. The grounds were magnificent. The huge Florida antebellum house stood at the end of the drive like a turn-of-the-century dowager; lace curtains and wicker chairs framed a sloping porch.

"Do you get the feeling that winning this franchise wasn't much of a surprise to Mr. Hunter?" Shane said.

"Even Martha Stewart couldn't lash this together in two hours," she agreed.

They got to the house and climbed the wooden steps, moving inside.

People were clustered in the magnificently furnished living room, but the flow of the party was being directed through the house and into the backyard, where the bar and the band were set up.

Shane and Alexa walked under more slow-moving Florida paddle fans out onto the veranda and stood for a moment on the back porch, looking out at the sparkling aqua-green water of Biscayne Bay.

There was a huge hundred-foot yacht called *Rocket Man* moored at the concrete dock. Palm and banyan trees hung over the grassy lawn. The twenty-piece orchestra was dressed in white tuxedos.

"Some barbecue," she said.

He nodded, but his eyes were wandering, checking out guests.

"How do you want to do this?" she asked.

"The play's at any base."

They moved down and joined the line at the bar. Four or five mannequins dressed in Spiders football uniforms, complete with helmets, had been set up in different parts of the yard in the Heisman Trophy pose. When they finally got up to the bar, Shane ordered a ginger ale; Alexa had a glass of Evian with a lime twist. Just as Shane was turning away, the bartender smiled. "Cigar to celebrate the franchise, sir?" and held out a box of Dominican Regals.

"Got anything else?" Shane asked, looking down at the box suspiciously.

"Mr. Hunter owns this company, so we only have Regals."

"In that case, give me one." He took a cigar, and they moved away from the bar, stopping a few feet away, looking at the panatela identical to the one they found in the toilet trap at the Spring Summer Apartments.

"You don't really think Logan Hunter was at your little fleabag on Third Street, supervising that videotaping and kidnapping . . . ?"

"No. But somebody who works for him was, and as far as I'm concerned, this stogie ties him in directly."

"That's theoretical, not evidential."

"Fuck evidence. I'm way past worrying about that."

As Shane moved toward the house, Alexa grabbed his arm and pulled him back. "We gotta worry about that. We're hanging out a mile here. We gotta get something worth taking to the DA, or we're dust."

"Yeah, sure."

"I'm not kidding, Shane. I'm in this with you, but you've gotta run everything past me first."

"I think we oughta find Mr. Hunter, invite him to a quiet spot in the garden, and have a little talk," Shane said, changing the subject.

"*Find? Invite?* Define your terms."

"I'm gonna kidnap the little prick, stuff this stogie up his ass, and make him smoke it rectally until he tells me where they're holding Chooch. It worked with Tom Mayweather."

"We got lucky with Mayweather. That doesn't mean we can throw a bag over Logan Hunter in the middle of this soiree and get away with it."

"Sure it does. All we've gotta do is find a good quiet interview room before we take his statement. Don't worry, you don't have to do it. I'll pick this daisy. Believe me, he's gonna tell me what I want to know."

"Shane, he's got forty security guys here, most of them packing."

"If you wanna wait in the car, go ahead. . . ."

"Shit! You are one stubborn son of a bitch," she said angrily, but he just looked at her for a long moment and nodded. "Let's stop arguing and do it, then," she relented.

They moved slowly around the party, looking for an appropriate spot. Shane recognized one or two of the girls they had photographed at the naval yard. They were dressed in slinky evening gowns, wearing hostess tags and escorting the press. Shane thought the main house looked too crowded. The gardener's shed was too close to the pool. Finally they found themselves down by the dock, where the hundred-foot yacht was tied to the wharf. There was a rope across the boarding ramp that warned: OFF LIMITS.

Shane removed the rope and they walked up onto the fantail of the yacht, where they were screened off from the party by the huge triple-deck superstructure.

"Some barge," Alexa said as she looked inside the main salon. Shane had already tried the door and had his picklocks out.

"Not again," she said.

"Unless you can find a key, this is the best I can do." He worked for a few minutes while Alexa stood on the fantail, out of view of the party on the grassy lawn. They could hear the band playing an instrumental selection of Elton John hits. The music was mixed with the low murmur of party conversation.

Shane got the door open quickly and looked back at her. "I'm getting better at this, refining my technique," he said.

"I'll add it to your charge sheet."

"I'm gonna find a nice quiet place below. Why don't you see if there are keys in that thing? We may need to make a fast exit," he said, pointing over the rail at a small red-hulled Scarab speedboat tied to bumpers against the side of the yacht.

"How'm I supposed to get down there?" she complained, looking over the rail at the Scarab ten feet below.

"Climb over the side, stand on the rub rail, then lower yourself down. Lotta people keep the spare ignition key in the engine compartment, hanging on a hook. Lift the cowling and take a look."

"The nautical equivalent of the back-door flowerpot?"

"Exactly."

He paused inside the main salon while she pulled up her short dress to climb over the side. Her toned, shapely legs were straddling the rail. She glanced up and caught him staring. "What're you looking at?"

"Nothing," he said too quickly, then ducked inside. He heard her drop down into the small boat as he moved through the magnificent yacht. Beautiful antiques and silk fabrics adorned the classic interior. He went below to the crew's quarters.

A few moments later he found the engine room behind a pair of soundproof double doors. It spanned the whole width of the boat. He turned on the lights. White-painted machinery glistened in the strong bluish neon. A hook, used to winch up heavy equipment so it could be worked on, hung between two large 2300-horse Caterpillar engines. Shane found a coil of rope on the engineer's bench, stowed it nearby, turned off the lights, and left.

When he got back to the rear deck, he found Alexa with a strange expression on her face. "You find the key?" he asked.

"Yeah, it was there, right where you said." She held up the ignition key.

"What's wrong, then?"

"I think I just saw Sandy. I went off the boat for a minute. I was trying to spot Logan Hunter . . . and I think I saw her with Calvin Sheets, walking up the path. She didn't look too happy about it."

"Sandy must've hooked up with her friend Melissa," Shane said. "Got herself invited to this party. But how the hell did she get all the way to Florida in ten hours?"

"Logan Hunter has his own jet," Alexa volunteered.

Shane nodded and walked out onto the fantail. "Let's see if we can find her."

They moved off the boat, rejoining the party, then walked along the carefully manicured path across the lawn, toward the house. Shane and Alexa were both scanning for familiar faces. Shane spotted Tony Spivack with a group of men and women, still wearing his quarterback jersey. He saw Coy Love over by the bar and grabbed Alexa's arm, turning her away.

"What?"

"Coy Love."

They got to the path that Sandy and Calvin Sheets had taken moments before, then started down it. The path wound around and finally ended about a hundred yards from the dock, down by a chauffeur's stone house on the east side of the property. The two-story stone house was connected to a six-car garage and separated from the rest of the property by a stand of mango trees. As they moved around the side of the house, they heard moaning. Shane stopped and looked at Alexa, who raised her eyebrows.

They couldn't determine the nature of the sound yet, so they stood by the house and listened. Suddenly they heard a hard slap, and a woman cried out in pain. Shane recognized the voice.

Alexa pulled her Beretta as they moved toward the front door. Shane, without a gun, felt vulnerable and exposed. He paused by the back door.

"Okay," he whispered. "Standard SWAT kick-down. I'm going right—on three. One . . . two . . ."

Then he stepped back, kicked the door, and dove inside to the right, sideways and low. He hit the floor and was unable to see the room as he rolled, but he heard Alexa dive in behind him, going left and yelling, "Freeze, asshole!"

Then two shots blasted from the opposite side of the room. Shane finished his roll and came up behind a couch. The bullets thunked into the wall over his head. Alexa rolled to the left, then fired twice. Her first shot took Calvin Sheets high in the chest. He flew backward and hit the far wall, leaving a streak of blood on the white plaster as he slid down.

Shane came up in time to see Don Drucker move into the room, pulling his gun. Sandy was darting right just as Drucker fired. She passed through his sight and was hit in the back, screaming in pain. Shane watched in horror as the bullet went directly through her abdomen, exploding out the front, leaving an exit wound the size of a softball. Sandy looked down in abject terror as blood and stomach contents streamed out of her, staining her light-green cocktail dress. Then she slumped to the floor, groaning.

Drucker turned his gun on Shane, who dove right just as the rookie cop fired. Shane felt the 9mm whiz by, inches from his head. He heard Alexa's gun discharge twice more, then Drucker flew out of Shane's field of vision and hit the floor. It was quiet for a second, but as Shane came up, he could see Drucker lying on his back, his mouth gaping open, dead. Alexa had hit him in the center of his forehead.

She was still low against the wall on the left side of the door, grim-faced and sweaty. Suddenly they heard footsteps on the path.

"Bolt the door," he ordered.

Alexa slammed it shut and threw the latch while Shane checked Drucker and Sheets. "These two are history," he said.

Shane snatched up Calvin Sheets's Smith & Wesson and tucked it away in his belt, then moved to Sandy, who was lying in an expanding pool of her own blood. It was widening beneath her, staining her dress a dark crimson, soaking the sides around her waist. He knew instantly that she probably wouldn't make it. The wound was fatal; she was already shivering, turning cold as her blood left her.

"Sandy . . . Sandy . . . it's me. Can you hear me?" he said, kneeling beside her.

When Sandy looked up, her face had lost its shape; her eyes were dimming as blood pumped out of her onto the tile floor. "I know . . . where . . . Chooch . . . is . . . Calvin told me . . . after we . . . we had sex and . . . and . . . he told . . ." She was shaking badly, struggling for breath. "Then . . . Clark Crispin came . . . seen my file . . . knew I was . . . Black Widow . . ." She started to choke, blood flowing from her mouth now, running down her chin.

"Shit," Shane said. "Let's get you outta here, to a hospital."

"No. . . ." she said as he tried to lift her. "No . . . Please . . . listen. In Arrowhead . . . Sheets said . . . they're holding him there . . ."

Sandy's strained words were overwhelmed by a heavy pounding on the front door.

"Open the fucking door, Cal! Open up!" Coy Love shouted.

"Give that asshole something to think about," Shane barked. Alexa turned and fired her fifth shot through the bolted wood door.

"Shit," they heard Coy say angrily from the porch outside.

"Shane . . . you've gotta listen . . ." Sandy whispered.

When he looked back down at her, she seemed smaller than she had just a moment before, as if she were losing volume, a pint at a time.

"Shane . . . you get him back . . . you take . . . take care of Chooch . . ." she rasped.

"I'll get him."

"He's yours . . . Shane . . . yours and mine." She was almost whispering now, her voice so small that he had to bend down to hear her.

"I was wrong . . ." She reached up and clutched his collar, pulling him down closer. "I didn't think you'd want him. . . . I wanted him but couldn't raise him. . . . You gotta do better." Her voice was so weak now, he placed his ear almost on her lips to hear. "He needed . . . his father . . . It's why . . . I made you take him . . . It's why . . . it's why . . . I . . ." And then she was looking at him, but her gaze had turned empty. Her heart had stopped beating. Those flashing black eyes went dead and stared up at him, damp and blank as licked stones.

Shane slowly lowered her to the floor. When he looked up, he saw Alexa staring at him from the door.

"Shane, we've gotta get outta here," she said.

Suddenly, Coy Love's face appeared at the window. Then his gun came up, aiming at Shane, who snatched Calvin's .38 out of his belt and fired twice just as Alexa peeled her last two rounds at the ex-cop. The window shattered as four bullets hit Coy Love, blowing him backward into the brush outside the chauffeur's cabin.

"Let's go!" Alexa screamed, and Shane got to his feet.

They could hear more voices screaming outside. They found the back door and threw it open. It led into the six-car garage. A black Lincoln Town Car was parked inside. Shane grabbed the keys off the pegboard, then he and Alexa jumped into the car; he started the engine, pulled the garage-door opener off the visor, and pushed the button. The door opened while Alexa was digging into her purse for a spare clip. She jammed it into the grip of her Beretta just as he floored the Lincoln, hurtling out of the garage and onto the driveway.

Armed men in black suits blocked their path but scattered as he plowed through them.

Out the front window, he could see security men running at them from several directions, all digging under their coats for weapons. Shane yanked the wheel and bounced the car up over the curb and onto the newly sodded front lawn. They shot across it, taking the direct route to the front gate, tearing up chunks of grass before finally bounding back over the curb onto the main driveway.

With four men chasing them on foot, they sped out the front gate, Alexa holding her gun at port arms. The Town Car skidded onto Casuarina Concourse, then a mile and a half later rounded the corner onto Cutter Road. Soon they were speeding under the leafy banyan trees, heading toward the airport.

"Get Bob at the flight center. Tell him we gotta get moving."

While Alexa turned on her cell phone and dialed, Shane got a Miami all-news radio station. It had been only five or six minutes, but the story was already breaking.

"Our field news team covering the plush NFL party Logan Hunter is throwing at Elton John's Coral Gables mansion has reported a shooting," the announcer said. "We're still awaiting more details, but as we have it so far, several people have been gunned down. A man and a woman are identified as the shooters and have fled the scene in one of Elton John's personal vehicles. Stand by as we get more information."

Shane let Alexa off at Million-Air Charters, then parked the car around the corner and up the street in a dense growth of oleander bushes, out of sight of the road. He wiped their prints quickly, using his old shirt, not forgetting to do the back of the rearview mirror, the place most car thieves miss. Then he walked around the corner and met Alexa. They entered the office and found Bob in the pilot's lounge, filing his FAA flight plan.

"Ready to go?" Bob said. "That was quick."

"Can't afford the hangar time." Shane smiled, but the grin felt wide and shiny and about as genuine as an Amway salesman.

"Be right out," Bob said.

They quickly boarded the plane, this time without waiting for the red carpet. Shane and Alexa sat in tense silence as the two pilots finally got aboard, shut the door, and smiled warmly. "We've got a slight tailwind for a change," Bob said happily. "Should get us back in four and a half hours or so." He settled into the right seat and wound up the engines.

Moments later they were rolling down the runway, taking off, leaving Miami and four dead bodies behind.

Shane sat stoically in the cabin, unable to deal with his thoughts. Alexa reached over and took his hand. "You okay?" she asked. "What did Sandy say to you?"

"Nothing," he answered. He couldn't tell her yet, couldn't quite admit it to himself.

His mind went back almost sixteen years, recapturing a memory long forgotten: it was his second summer on the job, right after the first arrest Sandy had arranged on the Valley bond trading case. They'd gone to dinner several nights later, to celebrate. Sandy had made her pitch to him, offering to work for the police as an informant. They'd had too much to drink, and in the car outside her apartment, he had shucked her out of her dress, then in awkward, thoughtless passion had entered her. There had been no tenderness in the coupling, and surely no love. It had been pure sex for him, raw and unadorned, an act he thought held no consequences. For Sandy, it was like a handshake to close their new deal. He had been just twenty-two years old.

The next morning he had felt cheap and ashamed of himself. She was a prostitute, and since he had always demanded more from his intimate relationships, he had never made love to her again. Instead, they'd gone into business together. Over the years he had managed her informant's career, making her rich while getting his share of class A busts in the bargain. The drunken romp in the backseat of his car was all but forgotten.

All these years later, the consequences of that mindless act had finally come due. If what Sandy had told him was true, she had changed his life forever with her one dying sentence.

Then he remembered what she had said in the doorway of her Barrington penthouse two days before. It had made no sense then, but now it spoke volumes: "You weren't doing me a favor," she had told him solemnly. "I was doing one for you."

DEAD END

THE ROAD was dark and winding, and he was going too fast, overdriving his headlights.

"For Chrissake, slow down. We're gonna die on one of these curves," Alexa barked at him.

Shane momentarily lifted his foot off the gas and then, without realizing it, slowly sped up again, impatient to get there.

They had turned off the car radio because he and Alexa had just been named as the shooters at Elton John's Florida home and were now dominating every national newscast. Somebody at the party in Florida had made them, probably one of the ex-cops from Sheets's old Coliseum detail. They were the subjects of a national manhunt. Shane knew it was only a matter of time before their sleeping pilot would get up, turn on his TV, and see the story. He would inform the police that Shane and Alexa were back in L.A., thereby narrowing the manhunt.

The national news story was snowballing, becoming as big as

when Andrew Cunanan shot Gianni Versace, each broadcast digging deeper into their pasts. Shane was now being described as a rogue cop prone to violence. His moment of self-defense when he protected Barbara and himself from Ray's insanity was now being called the cold-blooded murder of an exemplary police officer that launched a coast-to-coast crime spree. The news media was having a party with Alexa's involvement, calling her his Internal Affairs prosecutor, accomplice, and partner in crime. Her Bonnie and Clyde joke had come true.

Shane had chosen to take the back road up to Arrowhead. They were on I-18, known as "the Rim of the World Highway," heading through the mountain town of Snow Valley. There were patches of snow visible at the highest elevations, distant reflections glimmering faintly in the moonlight.

Shane took another turn too fast, and the tires on the Crown Vic screamed in protest.

"For Chrissake, Shane, slow down!" she repeated, then reached out and switched on the police-band radio but got only static. They were too far up in the mountains to get anything, so she turned it off.

They slowed down to drive through the small town of Running Springs. At Crest Park Drive they took 173 along Burnt Mile Creek and finally dropped down into Lake Arrowhead. Shane knew the route to Ray's house and quickly found his way there.

He drove slowly past the party house on Lake View Drive. It looked dark inside. If they were holding Chooch and Brian, he reasoned, they would probably try to make it look deserted. Shane turned the car around before parking it. He wanted no cul-de-sac mistakes this time.

Shane had found a sporting goods store in South Central on the way in from Long Beach. The owner-manager made it a point to mind his own business as Alexa bought a box of FMJ 9s and Shane a box of .38 hollow points. She had changed back into the clothes she wore to Miami: jeans, tennis shoes, and a turtleneck.

Alexa pulled her handcuffs and reload case with the extra clip out of her purse and slid them into her belt with her cell phone. Then she and Shane got out of the Crown Vic and moved down the street toward the Arrowhead party house.

As they approached, his heart was beating fast. Shane knew he had to do this just right. He couldn't take a chance that Chooch would end up in a cross fire as Sandy had. He pledged to rescue Chooch and Brian, or die trying.

The problem right now was that Shane and Alexa couldn't get backup. If they showed their faces in any police station, they'd be arrested on the spot. Nobody would listen to them, and Chooch and Brian would simply become part of the untold history of the new L.A. football franchise.

They were across the street from the house, crouched down behind the low hedge, looking at the property carefully. "I hate to say this, Shane, but that place looks empty. No cars out front, nothing," she whispered.

"They use a boat to get here. A Chris-Craft inboard."

"Okay, let's go, then," she said.

They moved like shadows across the street, their guns out in front of them, staying low as they went.

They got to the side of the house, creeping through the old rose-bushes, trying to ignore the thorns. When they were within view of the dock, they could see that there was no Chris-Craft tied there. They made their way to the back porch, where, after checking the windows and seeing nothing, Shane shimmied up under the porch rail, then wormed his way across the deck on his stomach. Alexa covered his approach, her gun at port arms, looking right, then left, scanning the area, straining her night vision.

Shane was finally at the sliding glass door. He looked into the living room but could still see no lights or movement inside. Then he knelt, taking out his pocketknife, and pried open the door as he had done before. He motioned for Alexa, who came quickly and lightly up onto the porch, using the steps on the far side.

They entered, breathing the stagnant air of an empty, shuttered house. They went through the place efficiently, moving fast— Shane going one way, Alexa the other, no longer creeping silently but throwing open doors SWAT-style, training their guns through the thresholds, calling out to each other.

"Master bedroom and bathroom clear," he heard her call from the back of the house.

He threw open the guest bedroom and was looking at another empty room. "Guest room clear," he shouted. Then he made his way to the secret room. He pushed the door open, hoping—praying—that Chooch would be there, alive, waiting. But the room was empty.

"Kitchen and pantry clear!" he heard her shout from the back of the house. Then she yelled, "We're secure!"

The entire house was empty.

They met in the living room and looked at each other. Shane's face was pulled tight. "You think they got here ahead of us and moved him?" Shane asked.

"No. There's no sign of anybody having been here. No garbage in the kitchen trash. Nothing. This isn't the place."

"Sandy said he's in Arrowhead," Shane protested.

"But not here. He's someplace else. . . ."

"Alexa, we've gotta find him." His voice was thin. Even he could hear it screeching in the still house.

"I wanna find them, too. It's how we get out of this. But ever since Miami, you've been different. You're not right, Shane. You're not thinking straight. You gotta calm down." And then she asked softly, "What did Sandy tell you? Whatever it was, your face dropped when she said it."

When he didn't answer, she took a guess. "Did you used to sleep with her?"

He still wouldn't answer.

"He's your son, isn't he?"

When he looked up at her, his expression told her it was true.

"Okay. But you've still gotta calm down, okay? Calm the fuck down. We can figure this out, but we gotta think it through."

" 'Kay," he said softly.

"All right. You said they owned an old boat—that they used a boat to get here. *Who* owned it?"

"I don't know. It's not really old. It's a reproduction of one of those classic Chris-Crafts with two windshields like they used to make in the thirties or forties."

"Maybe there's a dealer. . . ."

"Shit, that's gonna take forever. They know we talked to Sandy in the chauffeur's house and that she got the location out of Calvin Sheets. That's gotta be the reason they were hitting her, trying to find out how many people she told. If they know Sandy knew where Chooch was, they're gonna move him. He won't be up here anymore."

"We've gotta take this one step at a time," she said evenly. "Let's start with the phone book. There's one in the kitchen." She walked away from him, into the kitchen, turned on the light, and grabbed the Arrowhead directory. Then she started looking in the Yellow Pages, under "Boat Dealers." "Here. Butterfield Boats, an authorized Chris-Craft dealership."

"It's nine o'clock at night, Alexa. They're closed."

She was already flipping to the *B*s in the white pages. "Leo Butterfield, Lake View Drive. Can't be too far from here. We can call him or pay him a visit. Connect the dots. . . . What's it called?"

"Police work," he said dully. "Our faces are all over TV. We'll probably do better on the phone."

"Okay. Who makes the call, you or me?" she asked.

"The head of the department up here is a guy named Sheriff Conklyn. Let me. . . . Let's hope these guys don't go fishing together."

Shane had pulled the phone out of the kitchen four days ago, so they returned to the one in the living room. He dialed the number and after a minute a woman answered.

"Mrs. Butterfield? This is Sheriff Conklyn at the substation. I need to talk to your husband," he said.

"Just a minute." Her voice sounded puzzled.

So far, so good. She didn't seem to know Conklyn personally. Chances were her husband didn't, either.

"This is Leo Butterfield. What is it, Sheriff?" a baritone voice said.

From his tone, Butterfield didn't seem to know Sheriff Conklyn. "Mr. Butterfield, sorry to bother you at home, but I'm trying to run a trace on a classic reproduction wooden Chris-Craft. You deal in that line of boats, I understand."

"That's right."

"I can't be too specific, but I'm looking for somebody who lives up here who may have bought one of those classic designs in, say, the last two or three years."

"We got a few of those boats on this lake. It's a rare item. They're beautiful, but not for everyone. I service most of them myself."

"Can you give me the owners' names from memory?"

"Think so . . . Let's see . . . Carl Nickerson bought one last June. . . ."

Shane made a writing sign in the air, and Alexa grabbed a pen.

"Carl Nickerson," Shane said. "Go on."

She jotted it down on the back of the phone book.

"Bert Perl has one. . . ."

"Bert Perl," Shane repeated, and she wrote it down.

"Logan Hunter," Leo said. "The movie producer."

"Logan Hunter," Shane said, and Alexa closed the book and looked up.

"Does he have a dock? Where's he keep it?" Shane asked.

"It's the old mansion on Eagle Point Drive on the Shelter Cove side. The one built by Clark Gable in the forties, looks like a Transylvanian castle."

THE CODE SIX MARY

44

THEY PARKED off the road and got out of the car. The house was down by the water, two blocks away.

Shane and Alexa walked down Mallard Road to Eagle Point Drive, where they found the public dock that accessed Shelter Cove. They walked out on the wooden float and stood on the blue and white platform, looking back across the moonlit waters to the huge house that loomed majestically against the distant snowcapped mountains. Its slate roof was glistening in silver light, its four roof turrets, each crowned with metal spikes, punching holes in the cloudless sky. The twenty-thousand-square-foot mansion had been designed in the forties and resembled a medieval castle, complete with stone arches and dormer windows.

The lights were on downstairs, and from the distance, across the cove, they could see occasional movement inside. From time to time people passed in front of the first-floor leaded-glass windows. Parked on the grass, near the water, was the same Bell Jet

Ranger that had brought Shane up to the lake after he'd been kidnapped in front of an entire movie company on Spring Street.

Tied to the dock was a classic reproduction wooden Chris-Craft.

"Sandy told me that Logan Hunter was a closet gay. This must be his getaway house. Good place for slam-dance weekends."

"Boy, do I hate this layout," she said, still studying the mansion carefully. "The house sits on high ground, acres of grass all around. Porches and too many windows . . . Tactically, we're fucked."

"Come on . . . don't be so negative. We lickety-split across the lawn, slip through an open window, find Chooch and Brian, make the rescue, bust ass, and we're gone—zim, zam, zoom."

"Shane, we need backup."

"Who did you have in mind, the Power Rangers?"

"If Chooch Sandoval and Brian Kelly are being held here and we get them out, they make the kidnapping case for us, and we're halfway off the hook. If we get caught, we're dust anyway. I think we need to call in a Code Six Mary." She was referring to the LAPD radio designation for officer assistance required due to extreme militant activity. "We'd have to time it right, but once we know Chooch and Brian are there, let's just dime ourselves out, let Sheriff Conklyn sort the frogs from the princes."

"What if Chooch and Brian aren't here," he said, "and we don't get killed, but arrested? Then we're sitting in jail, trying to talk our way out of four killings in Florida."

"No plan is without some operational deficiencies."

He shot her a withering look.

"Okay, let's go in, scout it, then back out to a safe spot and do a nine-one-one," she said, revising her idea.

He thought about it for a long moment, then said, "I'd rather take it one step at a time and see what develops. But, either way, I think we should tee up the Code Six Mary before we call it in."

"Good idea . . . but how?"

"Gimme your phone."

She handed the cell phone to Shane. He got Information, then called the Arrowhead Sheriff's Department. After asking for Sheriff Conklyn, he was transferred, then got the tall, balding man on the phone. "Guess who?" Shane said.

"I don't have the faintest idea. . . ."

"Turn on your TV. I'm starring in every newscast."

"Shit . . . Scully?"

"I'm looking for you to take me in, Sheriff. I want you to make the bust. You'll be famous. It's probably at least good for a shot or two on Oprah, but I have a few conditions. . . ."

Conklyn paused, and then Shane heard a *click*, so he knew the rest of the conversation was being T and T'd—taped and traced.

"Why me?" Conklyn asked.

"If you're tracing this call, it's just gonna come back to a cell station in Arrowhead. I'm up here now, but I'm not quite ready to turn myself in yet. I want you to make the arrest because I've got problems with some of my brother officers in L.A. and I don't want to stop a stray bullet by mistake."

"Not to mention all the dead bodies you left in Florida."

"There's a story that goes with that, Sheriff. Extenuating circumstances."

"If you're smart, Scully, you'll tell me where you are now. Otherwise, this will go down hard."

"I want you to call Bud Halley, my old CO in L.A. He's a good cop. Tell him what's going on. Tell him I need to see him and to get his ass up here."

"Where are you, Scully?"

"Stick by your phone. I'll let you know." Shane hung up and looked at Alexa.

"Pretty good," she said, nodding. "He'll have his flak vest buttoned and be ready to roll."

They moved off the dock and skirted the water's edge until they got to a wire fence that went ten feet out into the lake and separated the castle's property from its neighbors. Shane climbed out on the fence, U-turned around the end post, then came back toward shore, and dropped off onto the sand inside the grounds.

After a minute Alexa repeated the maneuver, landing on the sand beside him.

They crept away from the shoreline and ran up toward the house, both silently cursing the full moon as they sprinted under its silvery glow. They hurried across the vast expanse of lawn, then hugged the wall, moving around the castle house slowly. They could see a row of ground-level windows throwing streaks of light out across the dew-wet lawn. They moved in that direction. Once they got to the windows, Shane dropped to his stomach and looked through a narrow glass pane into what looked like a huge billiards room.

"Uh-uh," he whispered, rising again and moving on. Alexa followed quietly in his footsteps.

On the south end of the house, he found the ground-level window he was looking for. When Shane glanced inside, he saw that it opened into a basement laundry room. He took out the .38 S&W and tapped loudly on the window with the gun butt.

"Whatta you doing?" Alexa hissed. "Why don't we just ring the fucking doorbell?"

"If somebody's down here, I'd rather find out now. Better to be outside than trapped down there in the basement. I'm gonna break the glass. If we get a ringer, get small."

She nodded, then watched as he slammed the gun butt hard into the pane, breaking it. The sound of tinkling shards hitting the cement floor froze them. They lay prone on the grass for several long minutes, waiting.

Nothing.

Shane reached through the glass, unhooked the latch, and swung the window open. They slipped into the laundry room and dropped onto the basement floor. Once inside, they could hear the faint sounds of opera music playing upstairs.

"Okay, let's work our way through this place, starting with this side, then moving east," he whispered.

She nodded, and they opened the laundry-room door and found themselves in a narrow, concrete-walled corridor with a vaulted ceiling. The corridor had no carpet, windows, or wall decorations. They crept along the tile floor, trying to keep their shoes from echoing on the polished surface. They checked doors as they went, mostly storage rooms and a basement bathroom. Then they were back at the poolroom Shane had seen from outside. The room was medieval in design, with old lances and shields on the walls. Two full, man-sized suits of armor on stands stood guarding a pair of double doors.

Movie posters hung on every wall, each one featuring a well-known Logan Hunter film. A red felt pool table loomed like a mahogany crypt in the center of the huge rectangular room.

They slipped out of the poolroom through a side door, still heading east. Shane and Alexa found themselves transiting through a part of the basement that was beginning to resemble a dungeon—bars and studded steel doors, ornate metal hinges with brass church locks. At the end of the center hall was a wooden door with a small, eight-by-ten-inch barred window set at eye level. Shane looked through the bars into an even narrower, underlit hallway. The door was locked. He reached in his pocket for his picks.

"What would we ever do without those?" she quipped.

It was a simple two-tumbler lock, designed more for looks than function. He got it open quickly. The door creaked ominously as he pushed it wide.

They crept down the three-foot-wide stone-block hallway. The first door on the right was unlocked, so he pushed it open and found that he was standing in a replica of a medieval torture chamber, replete with fourteenth-century stretching racks, wall restraints, and steel wall hooks holding every imaginable kind of leather apparel.

"This kink is into S&M," Alexa said.

Shane felt a chill go through him and prayed that Chooch and Longboard had not been subjected to a dose of that madness.

He passed through the dungeon toward a door on the far side of the room, opened it slowly, and found a hallway that ran farther underground. It stretched for about forty or fifty feet on a gentle slope. At the end of the corridor was another large wooden door with metal trim and steel studs.

"Hold my back," he said, then ran down the concrete tunnel. When he got to the end, he tried the door. It was unlocked.

He pushed it open and found himself looking at Chooch and Longboard. They were blindfolded, gagged, and handcuffed to pipes in a small room that contained three giant water heaters. Shane ripped the blindfold off Chooch, then pulled the wadding out of his mouth. "You okay?"

"Shane," the boy said; tears started flowing from his eyes. "I knew you'd come. . . ."

"Shhhh . . ." Shane said. As Brian *umph*ed behind his gag, Shane checked Chooch's handcuffs before quickly turning and removing Brian Kelly's blindfold and fishing the gag out of his mouth.

"Shit, am I glad to see you," Longboard said weakly.

"You guys okay?"

"I guess," Longboard said. "Frickin' scared, but okay."

"Stay quiet. I'll be right back. Gotta get a key for those cuffs. They look like standard LAPD issue."

Shane sprinted back up the ramp to the dungeon room, where Alexa was guarding the hallway.

"They're down there. They look all right. I need your cuff key."

She reached to her belt, pulled it off, and handed it to him.

Shane hurried back to the heater room and unhooked both sets of cuffs.

"How many guys are here? How many guns?" Shane whispered.

"There's about four guys who are packing," Brian said.

"Shane, that movie producer is here," Chooch said. "He owns the place."

"That kink didn't put you on any of those tables up there, did he?" Shane asked.

"No. They just cuffed us to those pipes," Brian said. "Seems like we been here almost two days."

"Okay, listen up. We're on our way out. There's a woman with me. She's an LAPD sergeant. Once we're out of this dungeon, I'll go first, she'll bring up the rear. Stay close. Don't make any noise. What I want to do here is just disappear. I don't wanna fight our way out." Shane's words echoed softly against the walls of the stone room.

He led Brian and Chooch up the corridor, rejoining Alexa. Silently they retraced their footsteps out of the dungeon and back into the connecting hallway. Shane paused by the door, looking into the billiards room. It was still deserted, so he pushed the door open and they headed out across the tile floor, past the suits of armor, and back to the laundry room at the far end of the house.

They slipped inside; then Shane locked the door and turned to Alexa. "You're first. Once you're out there, scout both sides. We need a good exit line."

"Got it," she said.

He put his hands around her slender waist and lifted her up to the open window. She grabbed the ledge and shimmied out. She was amazingly light, which surprised him. Her intellectual weight had become so huge, it didn't seem possible that her physical weight was only 115 pounds.

Next he lifted Chooch. Once the boy was out of the window, Shane turned to Longboard and cupped his hands. "Hop aboard. You're outta here."

Longboard stepped in, and Shane boosted him out the window. Then Shane grabbed the ledge and pulled himself up and out onto the wet grass.

The cold, moist lake air filled his nostrils as he regained his feet and looked at all of them.

"Somebody just pulled in. They're in a truck in the drive. There're people in the big front room now. They'll see us moving across the grass," Alexa said. "Our best bet outta here is that speedboat. We need keys, but if they aren't in the boat, we could get trapped down there on the dock, out in the open."

"Don't need keys," Chooch whispered bravely. "I'll hot-wire it. Car theft is my Vato specialty."

"Okay then, that's the plan," Shane whispered. "Alexa, you look for the keys. If they're not aboard, Chooch, you get it going. Brian, you're on lines. I'll hold the back door and lay down cover fire if we get spotted. Everybody straight?"

They nodded, their faces grim.

"Okay—let's do it."

They slipped away from the house, staying close to the west side of the property, moving like shadows against the fence line.

They finally got to a spot where, in order to reach the dock, they had to make a final dash across an open stretch of moonlit lawn. They huddled down in the dark and checked the house. There were a few people visible in the windows. Nobody was on the porch.

"This is as good as it's gonna get. Let's go," Shane whispered.

They started running in a group. They moved fast and low, across the open area, but quickly spread out. Alexa, the sprinter, took the lead, with Shane a few steps behind. Chooch and Longboard were losing ground. They all finally reached the pier and headed out to the dock.

"Who's out there?!" a male voice yelled from the house.

"It's blown. Move it! Move it!" Shane shouted. He was out on the small dock, standing by the ramp leading down to the float, motioning to Chooch and Longboard, windmilling his arms, trying to get them to go faster. They ran by him heading for the boat.

Now all but Shane were on the boat.

Alexa was looking for the keys when Chooch and Longboard got aboard.

"No key in the ignition," Alexa shouted. She was pulling the engine cover up, looking for a key on a hook inside, when the first shot rang out. The bullet pinged off the top of the concrete piling next to Shane's head, then whined angrily away into the night.

Shane, still holding his position on the dock, fired blindly up at the house. He couldn't see anyone, so he popped only one cap—firing for effect—turned, and ran to the boat.

Chooch was under the dash pulling out ignition wires, and Longboard ducked down low in the backseat. As Shane jumped into the boat, two more shots rang out from the sloping lawn. One of the bullets thudded into the boat's hull. Alexa pulled her pistol and returned fire.

"Save your rounds!" Shane yelled. "Unless you can see 'em, don't fire."

Suddenly the boat engine started, and Chooch backed out from under the dash. Longboard came up from his hiding place and started throwing off lines.

They could now see two men running down toward the dock. Both stopped halfway out on the wooden pier, aimed their pistols, and fired down from a position of advantage. Shane felt a bullet tug at the sleeve of his sport coat. He dropped into the seat behind the wheel and slammed the throttle all the way forward.

The Chris-Craft roared away from the dock amidst a hail of gunfire. He heard Alexa's Beretta bark near his left ear, then the distant sound of return fire from the dock.

"Shit," she said, and dropped onto the seat beside him. He glanced over at her, alarmed.

"I took one," Alexa said, looking at her side. She couldn't see the blood in the moonlight because of the dark turtleneck.

"How bad?" Shane shouted over the roar of the engine.

She pulled up her shirt and checked the wound. "Looks like a through and through. The right oblique. Just drive. If I start fading, I'll let you know," she shouted.

They heard two more shots, but they were distant popping sounds. One bullet ricocheted off the metal windshield, and then they were out of range.

Longboard and Chooch were lying prone on the backseat. "Did we make it?" Longboard asked tentatively as he sat up.

Shane looked back at the dock, a receding structure in the distance.

"They're out of range," he said. All of them had wide smiles on their faces. It was a well-known police axiom that nothing is more exhilarating than being fired on without serious result.

The little speedboat streaked across the lake, its metal-tipped bow parting the moonlit water, leaving a frothy, expanding wake behind them as they headed toward the lights of Arrowhead Village two miles away.

"We've gotta get to a place where Sheriff Conklyn won't panic making the arrest. Someplace out in the open. I don't want one of his trigger-happy deputies ruining this perfect rescue," Shane shouted to Alexa over the wind and engine noise.

"How 'bout the main dock in town?" she suggested. "It's open from all sides. He can make an arrest easily there."

"Good idea," Shane agreed. She pulled out her cell phone to call, but before she could dial, the odds abruptly changed.

It was coming at them low and fast across the water, its rotor blade flashing streaks of reflected moonlight. The blue and green helicopter was ten feet off the surface, approaching quickly. By the time they heard it, it was way too close. The throaty roar of the speedboat's engine had camouflaged its deadly approach.

The Bell Jet Ranger swept low across their speeding bow. Two men leaned out the open door with police shotguns aimed down at them, and seconds later the men let loose. . . . The teak deck and left windscreen were peppered with buckshot. Exploding safety glass flew back in pebble-sized pieces. Chunks of pellet-riddled teak flew up, caught the air, and were whipped away over their heads.

Shane jerked the wheel right, to change the angle, taking away the Bell Jet's point-blank line of fire. Now the speedboat was heading west, away from the town. The chopper banked, its engine whining as it turned, and in seconds it was behind them again, closing in. Two more blasts from the shotguns, and the rest of their windshield was gone.

Shane felt sharp pain on his ear and cheek where several pellets from the widening shot pattern had nicked him. Blood started running down the right side of his face. He spun the wheel again.

Alexa turned and was now facing back. She had her knees on the leather seat; her body was prone across the center deck. She had her 9mm Beretta in both hands, aiming up at the approaching helicopter. She took her time sighting. "Slow down, you're bouncing too much!" she shouted.

Shane eased the throttle back, slowing the boat and subtly drawing the chopper in closer. Then, sighting carefully, she fired twice. Suddenly the chopper veered right and pulled up fast, exposing its belly. She fired again. The pilot, feeling the hits, banked the helicopter away. He pulled back to avoid further gunfire, but was now also way out of shotgun range.

Her shots had not disabled the Bell Jet Ranger.

Shane sped up. The chopper paced along a hundred yards to the right, skimming low across the water, tracking the speedboat from the side at about forty miles an hour.

The boat was bouncing badly, hitting the larger chop in the center of the lake. The waves slammed against the varnished hull, throwing water wide to each side.

"Don't shoot! Don't waste rounds—we're pounding too

much!" Shane shouted. "They can't reach us with those twelve-gauges—save it for when they come in close."

Alexa nodded as they sped across the center of Lake Arrowhead, the chopper flying sideways now, the nose aimed at them. Four faces were staring out from behind the bubble-glass windshield.

Shane was headed toward Blue Jay Bay.

Alexa pushed redial on her phone. A moment later Shane heard her shouting at Conklyn. "Sheriff, it's Alexa Hamilton. I'm with Shane Scully and two others. A male Caucasian and teenage Hispanic. We're Code Six Mary in a speedboat heading across Lake Arrowhead, taking gunfire from a helicopter above us. We're at Blue Jay Bay. We need help. Get here fast, or notify the coroner." She threw the phone down on the seat without waiting for a reply, then aimed her gun at the tracking helicopter.

They streaked past a sign marking Village Point, then past two poles planted in the lake that warned:

SHALLOW WATER—SANDBAR

"Shit," Shane said. He was going almost forty. If he went aground at that speed, they would all end up as part of the dashboard. He pulled the throttle back, slowing to about twenty. The helicopter veered again, vectoring toward them. They could see distant flashes of fire from both shotgun barrels, then heard the slower sound of the blasts. Simultaneously the varnish on the side of the boat exploded and turned chalky white as the pellets tore holes in it.

The body of water narrowed abruptly ahead; they were running out of lake. Shane saw Totem Pole Point coming up on the right, marked by a hand-painted sign. Suddenly they were in the narrow and unforgiving waters of Paradise Bay, heading for the mouth of Little Bear River.

"Fuck," Shane said. If he turned back now, he would be forced to slow way down to make the turn in the narrow inlet, making them vulnerable to a withering shotgun attack. So he eased back on the power, cutting his speed to ten miles per hour, then headed up the narrow mouth of the river. Occasionally he could feel the boat hesitate as it scraped bottom.

The helicopter came in close now, making another pass. Two men were leaning far out of the door of the chopper. Alexa fired three more times. One of the men screamed, his voice faint and distant, barely audible over the racket of the competing engines. Then the man tumbled out of the helicopter door and splashed into the shallows below.

Shane could see the end of the ride coming up ahead. A sandbar was stretched across the narrowing river. He sped up momentarily so he could run the heavy boat up onto the sand.

The Chris-Craft shot up onto the bar. He felt the sand scraping beneath, heard the propeller pin shear. The engine screamed as the propeller flew off. As soon as the boat slammed to a stop, it leaned right against its bottom, white smoke and a high-rpm whine coming from the exposed shaft.

"Out! Out! Get out!" Shane shouted, and yanked the .38 out of his waistband. He trained it on the helicopter that was now hovering and watching, waiting for them to run away from the grounded speedboat, where they would be easy to pick off.

"Stay put. Use the boat for cover!" Shane yelled. They all huddled behind the beached hull, keeping the Chris-Craft between them and the chopper. The overheating inboard engine finally coughed and quit.

Then the nose of the Bell Jet Ranger dropped and, like a bull in an arena, made its deadly charge. Shane unloaded the .38 as the chopper streaked over them. He could hear the shotguns firing, in a steady *ka-boom, ka-boom, ka-boom!* He knew they were using police-issue, Ithaca pump-action 12-gauge riot guns. As the shots continued, the engine compartment on the beached boat blew open . . . the last shot hit the exposed gas tank.

The next thing Shane knew, he was flying through the air, the sound of the exploding gas tank ringing in his ears. He landed ten feet away and saw that Alexa, Chooch, and Brian had also been blown off their feet by the blast.

Shane had been nearest the tank, and he now realized that his clothes were on fire. He got up and made a stumbling run for it, then dove into the shallow Little Bear River. While he was rolling in the water, trying to extinguish the flames, the helicopter turned back and made a low pass at him. He was now sitting upright in the middle of the shallows, an easy, stationary target, when the shotguns started again. The first pattern went wide, turning the river water to the left of him foam white with the pellets. In his peripheral vision, he could see Alexa splashing across the open ground toward him, limping slightly, favoring her right side. She was slamming her last clip into the Beretta, chambering it as she ran.

The helicopter flashed over her now, getting closer to him. As it went over, she peeled the full clip straight up into the belly of the chopper, hitting the Bell Jet Ranger with all nine shots.

Shane didn't know what the hell she hit, but it was certainly something vital, because the helicopter immediately began spinning on its axis, wobbling around like a slowing top, going out of control. Then it slammed, nose first, into the water and went down fast.

Shane got up out of the river, his burnt clothes steaming in the cold night air. He joined Chooch, Longboard, and Alexa at the water's edge. They looked out at the spot where the chopper had crashed. The engine housing and rotor were all that was still above water. There had been no explosion and no attempt by anyone to get out. Then it disappeared, sinking quickly.

"Fuck you," Shane said softly to a bubbling spot in the water where the helicopter had been.

A few minutes later, while they were still watching the Bell Jet's last air bubbles rising to the surface, exploding trapped air, they saw the black-and-white Hughes 500 approaching, coming in low over the lake. The belly-light on the sheriff's chopper snapped on, and they were caught in its blinding glare. Shane and Alexa immediately threw down their guns and assumed the position, placing both hands behind their heads. Shane instructed Longboard and Chooch to do the same.

They were all standing out in the open as the sheriff's helicopter hovered overhead, churning up rocks and river water. "On your stomachs. Facedown on the ground!" they heard Conklyn's voice shout over the bullhorn.

All of them proned-out on the sand and waited.

It was only moments before the first squad cars arrived. They drove off the road, their tires squishing on the wet river sand, their cherry-colored bar lights flashing. Then, as patrol officers swarmed them, the police chopper landed.

"Watch it, she's been wounded," Shane said as sheriff's deputies cuffed Alexa and dragged her to her feet. They ignored his instructions and pushed her roughly toward the squad cars. Shane was cuffed and pulled to his feet, then found himself looking at the jacked-and-flacked Sheriff Conklyn. "Glad to see you, man," Shane said.

"What the fuck? What chopper? She said there was a chopper shooting at you. . . ."

"There was," Shane said, nodding to the spot in the river where the Bell Jet Ranger had gone down. "But you're gonna need to come back with divers, a crane, and some body bags if you wanna see it."

Shane watched as Chooch and Longboard were roughly cuffed, then put into squad cars. "They're victims. You don't need to throw them around like that. They were kidnapped," he complained, but Conklyn didn't seem to care.

"You're really some kinda jerkoff, Scully. This is a quiet town. Every time you come up here, I gotta throw a fucking cherry festival." Conklyn pushed Shane toward the squad car. "I can hardly wait to hear this one."

"Right," Shane said softly. "But you better send out for pizza, 'cause it's a long and complicated story."

EXCULPATORY EVIDENCE

POLICE MISCONDUCT is defined under Section 805 of the LAPD Manual and falls into one of four categories:

1. Commission of a criminal offense
2. Neglect of duty
3. Violation of department policies, rules, or procedures
4. Conduct that may tend to reflect unfavorably upon the employee or the department.

After their arrest, Shane, Alexa, Chooch, and Longboard Kelly were taken to the Arrowhead substation. Alexa's bullet wound was stitched up and bandaged by EMTs in Sheriff Conklyn's office. Then she was returned to a holding cell.

A pissed-off Bud Halley arrived at two A.M. and reluctantly

did Shane's DFAR. They were in one of two windowless FI rooms.

After he heard it all, Halley leaned back in the wooden chair and glowered. "Shit, Scully, I'm supposed to believe that the mayor of L.A., the Super Chief of our department, and one of the largest developers in the state of California, along with a dozen or more sworn or terminated LAPD personnel, are involved in murder, blackmail, kidnapping, fraud, and a buncha other criminal misconduct," Halley said, looking at Shane through tired eyes. He didn't want any part of it. This was the ultimate red ball.

Shane had asked for Captain Halley for three reasons: One, with Tom Mayweather sure to get indicted, he was Shane's most recent CO. Two, the captain was well respected in the department, and Shane needed a trusted "rabbi" as his advocate. And three, he knew that Halley was deeply religious, with a highly developed sense of morals and ethics. Underneath all the police bullshit, he was a stand-up guy. If Halley could be made to believe Shane's story, he would come aboard, regardless of the consequences.

Shane had started his DFAR talking about the kidnapping of Chooch and Longboard, finally convincing Halley that they had been hit over the head, tied up, videotaped, and abducted from his Third Street apartment. They had then been taken to Logan Hunter's mansion in Arrowhead and held there for two days by current and former LAPD officers.

Shane, Alexa, Chooch, and Longboard all volunteered to take lie-detector tests, and after Halley agreed, Conklyn rolled a big, new Star Mark polygraph machine into the FI room. One by one they were given the test, and one by one they passed.

Shane could see the building frustration in Bud Halley's hazel-green eyes as night turned to day.

By ten o'clock the helicopter had been pulled out of the Little

Bear River. Inside were the remains of the pilot, as well as Logan Hunter and Joe Church. Kris Kono had been found in the shallows with Alexa's 9mm slug buried deep in the Hawaiian officer's chest.

It was all exculpatory evidence, further sustaining Shane's statement.

Alexa and Shane described the events that occurred in Miami, starting with their attempt to rescue Sandy Sandoval and ending with the attack by Drucker, Love, and Calvin Sheets. Alexa handled their escape from Elton John's Biscayne Bay estate, then Shane explained about Ray's Arrowhead house and how Molar had been blackmailing the Long Beach City Council so Los Angeles could get control of the naval yard. Halley listened, took notes, and groaned as the scope of the corruption grew larger, reaching all the way up through the chief of police to the mayor's office.

Halley kept the startling events under wraps as best he could, but of course Logan Hunter's death had leaked out. News crews from L.A. were arriving in vans and helicopters. The newsies were already picking up other shreds of the story, sharking for details, sensing that much more was at stake.

"I don't know what to do with this," Halley admitted to Shane and Alexa after he'd heard it all. They were no longer being kept in holding cells and were seated in Sheriff Conklyn's office. He had promoted them from suspects to witnesses.

Out the window they could see a small TV uplink antenna farm being constructed on the vacant property across from the police station.

"I'm gonna call in Erwin Epps," Halley finally said, referring to the Baptist minister and political activist who had just been elected head of the L.A. Police Commission. "Under Section 78 of the city charter, the board of commissioners has the power and responsibility to supervise, control, and regulate the department." Halley quoted the section from memory.

"Good idea," Shane said.

Shane asked for and was given a chance to talk to Chooch. The boy was staying in the Arrowhead Motel with a sheriff's matron. Shane was driven over and let himself in.

Chooch was watching the news, his legs stretched out on the bed. He snapped off the television as Shane came through the door.

"Man . . . can you believe the coverage this is getting?"

"Chooch . . . I wanna talk to you about your mom."

"I know about Sandy . . . it's on the TV." His voice was guarded.

"I'm sorry you had to hear it that way. I wanted to tell you, but they wouldn't give me a chance until now."

Chooch nodded, his black eyes showing little. "I'm sorry she's dead," he said. "I didn't want that to happen. . . . I just wanted her to . . ." He stopped, then shook his head in frustration. "You know what I mean." He looked up. "You and me are the same, Shane. I got nobody, same as you." The way he said it, Shane couldn't tell what he was thinking. Chooch, like Shane, had become good at hiding his emotions.

"I want you to know something—something important about your mother."

"That she loved me?" the boy said, but his tone said he found it hard to believe.

"Yeah, she loved you, and she died trying to save you. She gave herself up for you, Chooch."

Chooch got up off the bed and moved to the window, his muscular body silhouetted in the morning sunlight streaming past him into the room.

"You were the one who saved me," he said softly.

"I never would have known where to look if your mother hadn't gotten that information for me. She gave up her life to get it."

There was a long moment, then finally Chooch turned and

faced Shane. "I want to cry for her. . . . It seems like I should. Am I being an asshole?"

"No, Chooch. I just wanted you to know. Whatever you feel about Sandy, in the end, when it counted, she was there for you."

Chooch nodded; suddenly his eyes filled, and he moved quickly to the bathroom and closed the door.

■ ■ ■

At two that afternoon, Chooch was picked up by the Child Protection Section of the Social Services Department and whisked away. Shane was back at Sheriff Conklyn's office and found out about it an hour after it happened. They said that since Chooch had no mother or father, he was being remanded to Juvenile Hall.

Shane knew he couldn't claim Chooch without a DNA test, and that would take time. Besides, the more he thought about it, the more he was beginning to suspect that Sandy had lied about his being Chooch's father. It was just what she would do—just like her to say that to get Shane to look after Chooch once she was gone. Either way, he couldn't get a DNA analysis up in Arrowhead, so it would have to wait until he got back to L.A.

Three hours later, Reverend Epp arrived and conferred with Bud Halley. He was a tall, dignified African American in his fifties who had tremendous credibility in the black community and had been put on the L.A. Police Commission to help deal with the charges of racism that had plagued the post–Daryl Gates department.

The two devout Christians listened all over again as Shane, Alexa, and Longboard Kelly retold their story.

Slowly, over a period of hours, it became distressingly clear to both Captain Halley and Reverend Epps that much of what Shane and Alexa had been describing was undoubtedly true.

The two tired sergeants were finally allowed to move into the Arrowhead Motel to get some sleep. They had rooms right next to each other but were too exhausted to even say good night.

One by one, other members of the L.A. Police Commission quietly arrived in town. They had decided to hold their meeting in the Arrowhead Lodge, away from the sheriff's department and the hovering press corps.

At the end of their first meeting, after Shane, Alexa, and Longboard had retold their stories, Sheriff Conklyn got a district judge to issue a search warrant.

On Monday evening they broke the front-door lock and entered Logan Hunter's lakeside mansion. What they found in his office files pretty much confirmed everything Shane and Alexa had been saying.

At ten o'clock on Tuesday morning, Reverend Erwin Epps chaired a meeting in his Arrowhead Lodge hotel room. Shane and Alexa were both present, along with Captain Halley, Sheriff Conklyn, and the entire seven-member L.A. Police Commission.

"I think we now have to consider Section 79 of the L.A. city charter," Epps said gravely. Then he took that bound document out of his briefcase and opened it to a paper clip marking the section.

"Let me read this to refresh you: 'A simple majority of the Police Commission is necessary to enact the provision of Section 79, which grants the commission the right to *appoint,* as well as to *remove,* the general manager of the department. However, the chief of police shall only be removed under the terms and conditions in city charter, Section 202.' " He flipped to that section and read the paragraph pertaining to the removal, suspension, or demotion of sworn police officers, then:

"I think we need to instruct the head of the Internal Affairs Division to draft a resolution to suspend the duties of Chief Brewer and bring him up on administrative charges. The head of IAD should further notify the district attorney of the possibility of criminal misconduct."

Shane couldn't help a small smile thinking of the panic that "resolution" would bring to the vanilla features of Commander Warren Zell.

The news was leaking from Lake Arrowhead to Los Angeles, and, little by little, shreds of it were showing up in the press and on TV.

The case went further into frenzied hyperspace when Tom Mayweather's body was found in the main salon of his boat anchored off Avalon Harbor in Catalina. He had put a police-issue shotgun into his mouth and blown his head off.

The subpoena control desk at Parker Center was flooded with paperwork issued by Warren Zell and the fifteen IOs he had assigned to the case. John Samansky and Lee Ayers, the two surviving members of Ray's den, had hired criminal attorneys and were both clamoring to cut a deal.

Samansky won that ugly contest and became the department's star witness against Chief Brewer, Tony Spivack, Mayor Clark Crispin, and the surviving officers. The district attorney petitioned the department for the right to sit in on the upcoming BORs under Section 21.2 of the L.A. city charter—a sure sign that criminal charges would be forthcoming.

One day after Logan Hunter's helicopter was fished out of the river, Mayor Crispin was arrested at the airport on his way to a "vacation" in Mexico.

Chief Brewer staged a press conference after his subpoena was served. He denied any wrongdoing had taken place and promised a victory in court. Nevertheless, at the district attorney's request, two detectives from Special Crimes were assigned to his house, and he was ordered to remain at home, pending further investigation.

A day later the district attorney finally filed murder one charges against them all.

Alexa and Shane had been released, then went back to L.A. and watched the rest of it on her TV, since he didn't have one. She had cooked a remarkably good Italian dinner for them, and after they had two glasses of red wine, Shane was lying on the sofa in her anally neat living room, watching Dan Rather talk about him. Alexa was in the kitchen doing dishes, hoping her mother was watching over them all.

Shortly after the news ended, an investigator from IAD knocked on the door to pick up the files Alexa had gathered for Shane's BOR. The IO notified her that she was no longer the advocate prosecuting Scully's case.

"What case?" Shane asked, coming up off the sofa like a Harrier jet. "You mean, after all this, they're still planning to terminate me?"

"Just because you two turned this department upside down doesn't mean your unnecessary use of force on the Molar shooting goes away," the IO said. Then he took the four crammed case-file boxes and left.

"When will it end?" Shane growled.

"Shane . . . you'll prevail at that board. With all this going on, believe me, their case won't stick."

He looked at her and again felt something stir inside him. She saw it in his eyes. "I know, but this time let's wait," she said. "Let's not do anything again until all this calms down and we know if it's real, or if we're just pulsing 'cause we're glad to be alive."

"It's real," he said. But she was right, now was not the time.

Shane had heard that Chooch was being held under IDC—Intake and Detention Control—at Juvenile Hall. So he called Captain Halley and had Chooch moved to PNP—USCMC, which was the patient-not-prisoner section of the Juvenile Detention wing of the USC Medical Center. They were talking about assigning him to a foster home.

Shane slept on Alexa's couch, and the next morning, after she cooked him breakfast, he had her drop him off at the police impound garage, where he reclaimed the rented Taurus he had left on the movie set the night he got kidnapped. Then he drove down and gave blood at the USC hospital. He couldn't see Chooch, by order of the district attorney, who was still interviewing him as a witness, so Shane found an old friend named Ellen Webb, who worked in PNP as a nurse. He gave her his blood sample number and asked her to get a match from Chooch.

"How come?" Ellen asked, brushing a wisp of honey-blond hair out of her eyes. "According to the news, he's Hispanic."

"His mother was, but I think I may be the father."

She looked at Shane for a long moment and smiled. "Can't keep the little head from controlling the big head?" she said playfully, so Shane stuck his tongue out at her and left.

He had one more stop to make before he went home and slept for a year.

The freeway was crowded, and he was locked in bumper-to-bumper five o'clock traffic. He finally got to the end of the 10 and found himself back on the Coast Highway. He didn't have his badge, so this time he had to pay for parking. He left the Taurus, walked onto the bike path and up to DeMarco's house.

For once it was quiet out front. The blond beach ornaments were all gone, off playing with somebody else's mind. Shane passed through the gate and walked up to the front door. He tried to look through the front window, but the blinds were pulled and he couldn't see anything. Finally he reached into his back pocket and fished out his trusty collection of picks. The lock was an old brass Yale and was a bitch to open, but after five minutes he turned the tumblers, went into the house, then closed and relocked the door behind him.

He stood in the living room, looking around, remembering his trip here two weeks days ago. . . . He had stood in this very same spot, watching DeMarco play with his speakers while Snoop Doggy Dogg spewed race hatred. It seemed as though that had been in another lifetime. He walked softly through the place, looking into each room. No one was home, so he entered the office at the end of the hall, walked across the room, then sat at DeMarco's desk. His defense rep's case material was sitting there in one half-filled file box. DeMarco had been on Shane's case for almost ten days, and as Shane went through the material, he was surprised by the lack of evidence he'd collected to support Shane's position. The defense rep hadn't yet received all of the discovery items, and there wasn't even a copy of Barbara Molar's statement. There was a halfhearted, half-full spiral notebook. . . . It was all damned puny compared with the mountain of stuff that had been carted out of Alexa's house.

He finally stopped looking at the case files, leaned back in the chair, and waited.

An hour later he heard the front door open; DeMarco was talking to someone. He heard a young boy's laughter, and then the music came on. Shane waited for a minute, then got out of DeMarco's chair and continued silently down the hall, into the living room.

What he saw didn't surprise him as much as it sickened him. On the living room sofa, DeMarco Saint and one of the fifteen-year-old surfer boys were lying in a romantic embrace. They were both naked.

"What a total shitbox!" Shane said.

DeMarco snapped his head around and glowered up at Shane. Then he scrambled up into a sitting position and grabbed for his underwear. The boy made no move to cover himself. Instead he remained lounging on the sofa, glaring his indifference.

"You didn't get thrown off the job for drinking. You got thrown off for pedophilia," Shane said.

"Nobody ever proved anything," DeMarco said, now reaching for his beach shorts.

"I should've seen it. First you turn me down, then a day later, all of a sudden, you're taking on my case. Mayweather got you to do it, didn't he? He wanted somebody on the inside of my defense. He wanted to find out what I was up to. He knew about this thing you've got for underage boys. He could've still filed criminal charges and gone after your pension. He forced you to reconsider."

"That's nonsense," DeMarco sputtered as he got his shorts on and rose to his feet. He was flushed, his complexion a ruby red. Sweat was slick on his skinny white chest.

"Nonsense?" Shane said reflectively. "I only told one person that I went to the Long Beach Naval Yard. Two hours later I'm kidnapped and taken up to Arrowhead, and Coy Love knows about it. The person who told him was you!"

"Whatta you . . . whatta you . . . gonna . . ." DeMarco's lower lip was quivering.

"Do?" Shane finished the sentence for him. "I'll show you." He grabbed DeMarco's arm and jerked him off balance. As his defense rep fell forward, Shane swung, landing a left hook square on the side of Dee's face.

DeMarco went down in a slump and began to weep. The naked teenager was on his feet now, his hands up, fists balled.

"Don't try it, Jocko. I'll make fucking hash outta you." Shane walked to the door, then turned. "By the way, Dee, you've got a subpoena coming. I'm putting you in the mix." Without saying another word, he left.

Shane drove back to Venice. The incident hung with him and poisoned his mood.

He worked hard to shift his thoughts and finally tried to contemplate his future. He thought about his life, about Chooch, and whether he was truly the boy's father. Shane had been looking for a deeper meaning in his life. Chooch had begun to fill that emptiness.

In the past two weeks, Shane had had two big surprises, both from unexpected places. Chooch had been one; Alexa, the other.

He was paralyzed with fear that the blood test would prove that his one intimate moment with Sandy would turn out to be just what he'd always believed it to be—a mindless mistake—instead of what he hoped it was now, a chance for a different kind of future. He parked the Taurus in the garage at his Venice house on East Canal Street, walked past his ruptured Acura, and went into his kitchen. Longboard had slipped a note under the door:

> *Shane,*
> *I got some cold beer and steak.*
> *I'm tapping the Source.*
> *You're invited.*
> *Longboard*

He put the note on the counter and slowly walked through the house, taking stock of his minimal emotional and physical existence: the furniture—remnants from broken love affairs; the bullet-riddled plaster walls in his front room, reminders of his fragile mortality. He picked up a pen and paper, then went outside and sat in one of the old rusting metal chairs.

He looked out at the setting sun just dipping below the horizon, dragging the last vestiges of the day across the shallow channels like a burnt orange memory.

He was in a new place, starting a new chapter in his life. He was not sure where he was going or how long it would take to get there, but for the first time in a long time, he was looking forward to the journey.

Then he uncapped the pen and wrote a long, personal letter to Chooch.

46

THE NEWS VULTURES were on the sixth floor of the Bradbury Building, leaning over the rails, blowing white streams of cigarette smoke into the huge glassed atrium. The ancient wrought-iron elevators went up and down, making unhurried stops, measuring each trip with a tailor's precision.

Shane was seated in the witness room on the fifth floor because he didn't want to stand out in the corridor and be pestered by news crews asking about the whole breaking Long Beach story. The NFL had just rescinded the L.A. Spiders' franchise along with the Web, and the Coliseum was now the likely choice to get the nod.

Burl Brewer was awaiting trial in County Jail, and the LAPD had a new chief named Tony Filosian, from New York. A short, round man who wore huge pinkie rings and spoke with a Brooklyn accent, he showed up for work in a shiny suit and was instantly dubbed "the Day-Glo Dago," but he seemed like an excellent choice because of his background of turning around troubled departments.

Barbara Molar got off the elevator and walked down the hall. Shane saw her through the window. He hoped she wouldn't come into the witness room, but when she saw him, she smiled and quickly came through the door, her blond hair shining, smile radiant, dancer's calves flexing as she took a chair next to him in the empty room.

"Boy, talk about a cluster fuck," she said, opening the conversation in typical in-your-face Barbara fashion.

"Yep, it's assholes on parade," he said, not showing her much.

"I'm here to back you up. I did the IO interview last night. I've been out, so I stopped by and signed it this morning on my way over."

"That's good. Thanks."

"So who's your new DR?" she asked. "I heard you canned DeMarco Saint."

"I'm gonna try my own board," he said.

"Is that smart?"

"I've been getting that question a lot, so I'm beginning to wonder." He smiled at her.

She fished a cigarette out of her purse, lit up, and started smoking in the small room. Shane wished she wouldn't; he'd never completely gotten over his desire for cigarettes.

"I figured I know the case better than anybody," he went on. "Since the department didn't want to give me more than a four-day postponement, I figured, what the hell . . ."

"Right. What the hell," she said. "Are we finally at a place where we can talk about the future?" she asked, smiling through the smoke.

Shane thought it'd be bad timing to piss her off just before she was going to testify. On the other hand, the IO had told him that she'd backed his story in her deposition, and he knew she pretty much had to stick to her statement.

He turned and faced her. "Y'know, Barb, I don't think we're gonna get a chance to see that happen." He watched her as her expression turned sour. "I've got some new responsibilities," he continued. "I took a blood test to see if I'm Chooch Sandoval's father. I'm expecting the results today. Then I'm picking him up and taking him home for the long weekend. We're gonna talk it out. After that, who knows? I may decide to raise him. I mean, if everything works out."

"Y'know, Shane, our timing was always pretty damn shitty, but you're not giving this a chance. Now that Ray's gone, it can work. And a kid? You wanna raise a kid?"

"Well, yeah, I sorta do," he finally said. "He and I hit it off."

"Kids are a drag," she said, stubbing out her cigarette. "Ray and I never wanted kids. You never said anything about wanting kids . . . baby-sitters, homework, car pools . . . You can't be serious?"

"Listen, Barbara, thanks for being there for me."

"Yeah. Well, I'm gonna see if they've got coffee. See you inside." She got up and left.

Over and out.

Then Commander Van Sickle arrived, and a uniformed police officer announced the commencement of the Scully Board, in hearing room one.

Shane walked out of the witness room and entered room one. It was the largest of the hearing rooms, and there were news crews in all the available chairs in the back. Internal Affairs Boards were public hearings, so there was no way of keeping the press out. They would have to suffer through his clumsy presentation of the defense.

The room was rectangular, with large arched windows that streamed in sunlight and backlit the three-man judging panel. The two sworn and one civilian panel members were seated in leather swivel chairs at a long table at the head of the room. The American and LAPD flags decorated opposite ends of the stage. A court reporter was in a chair off to the side.

Warren Zell was prosecuting the case for the department, and there were four IOs clustered around him. Shane was alone at the defense table; his one assigned investigating officer was still out, taking statements and collecting last-minute depositions. Hopefully he would be back by noon.

Commander Van Sickle opened the proceedings. "Sergeant Scully, are you ready to proceed?"

"Yes, sir."

"To start with, I'm going to read you your rights, from the Police Disciplinary Manual. Okay?"

"Yes, sir."

"You have the right to appear in person and present a defense to the charges against you. You have the right to be represented by a department defense representative. You may produce witnesses to testify on your behalf, including character witnesses. You may cross-examine witnesses testifying against you. You have the right to testify in your own defense. You have the right to be present when board members examine your personal history and records. You also have the right to have all sworn testimony at this hearing reported and transcribed by a hearing reporter. You shall be entitled to a copy thereof." He looked up. "Do you understand your rights?"

"Yes, sir."

"This board has been convened to determine if unnecessary and escalating force was used in the fatal shooting of Lieutenant Raymond Molar. There are five counts of misconduct, all listed in your letter of transmittal."

The door in the back of the room opened, and Alexa Hamilton walked into the hearing. Everybody turned to look at her. She was wearing a tailored black suit coat and skirt over a white silk blouse. A red scarf decorated the collar.

"Excuse me, Sergeant Hamilton. You've been replaced as the advocate on this case," Warren Zell said. "I thought you'd been told that."

"Could I have a moment with Sergeant Scully, Commander?" she asked the board chairman.

Commander Van Sickle heaved a sigh and nodded. She moved briskly across the room and sat down in the empty chair beside Shane, resting her purse on the defense table. She leaned in to whisper to him.

"Since I can't prosecute you, I'd love to defend you," she whispered in his ear.

"Are you serious?"

"You can choose anybody in the department below the rank of captain; the last time I checked, that included me. I know this case from top to bottom. I prepped it for ten days. I know where every piece of bullshit is. Warren Zell is a mediocre administrator and a worse trial advocate. Just say the word, and I'll kick his vanilla-milkshake ass."

"Alexa, will you please represent me?" he whispered softly.

"Honored."

"If you're through with your little discussion?" Van Sickle asked with irritation. "I'd like to get started."

"And I'd like to notify the board that I'm taking over as Sergeant Scully's defense rep," Alexa announced.

"I'm afraid you can't do that," Zell said, rising to his feet. "She's a member of the Advocate Division and, as such, is prohibited from acting as a defense rep."

"To be precise, I'm currently assigned to Southwest Patrol," Alexa said. "I was brought back to try this one case. Once I was replaced as the advocate, I was immediately reassigned to my Southwest Patrol commander, freeing me to fulfill Sergeant Scully's request that I represent him."

Commander Van Sickle looked over at Zell.

"It's completely improper, sir," the chief advocate protested.

"But not outside of department guidelines," Van Sickle said. "Sergeant Hamilton is accepted as defense rep."

"I'd like a recess for fifteen minutes to get my files on this case out of my car and up here into the hearing room. I reproduced the entire case history and have been working on it all night. Maybe you could get a few officers to help me? There's a bunch."

• • •

They adjourned, then reconvened fifteen minutes later. For the rest of the day, Alexa shredded every piece of evidence that Zell put forward.

The board had been scheduled to go for two days, but by five o'clock that evening, Commander Van Sickle had heard enough.

"If you have something substantive to add that will make your case, would you put it on now, Commander Zell? Otherwise, I'd like to entertain a motion from Sergeant Hamilton to dismiss this case."

"Sir . . . Due to obvious circumstances, this case has been fraught with monumental difficulties."

"This case should never have been brought here in the first place," the commander scolded. "It should have gone to a Shooting Review Board, which would have resulted in a finding of appropriate use of force. So, unless there is some statement or evidence to the contrary, I'm suggesting that this board immediately dismiss the proceeding. And let Sergeant Scully get back to work."

Alexa so moved.

• • •

He stood in the parking lot outside of the Bradbury Building and waited for her.

She came down at about six-thirty, carrying a stuffed briefcase and a box of paper supplies. He took the box and walked her to her car in the adjoining parking structure. They stopped at the trunk of her Crown Vic, and he put the box inside.

"I have something that belongs to you," she said. Then she reached into her purse and retrieved his badge, gun, and ID.

"I want to get to know you better," he said awkwardly.

"We killed half a dozen guys together . . . what does it take with you?" She smiled and then saw that he was serious, so she nodded her head. "I'm free most evenings unless I'm on night watch."

"Tonight I'm barbecuing dinner for Chooch. I'm picking him up at the Med Center and we're going home. We'd love to have you join us."

"No . . . that would be wrong. You should do this one alone."

"Tomorrow night, then?"

She nodded, and he stood there in the garage, not sure what to do. Then he reached out and took her hand.

"Are you going to kiss me?" She smiled.

"Probably not good form for the accused to kiss an advocate in the IAD parking garage. . . ."

"But it's okay for him to kiss his defense rep," she said.

So he took her into his arms and kissed her. The electricity that he felt again surprised him. It made him feel warm inside. His breath got short, his legs weak.

They finally separated, and she looked up at him. "Wow, you're a good kisser."

"Let's find another verb," he said, grinning.

Then he turned and left her standing there, looking after him, a smile on her beautiful, exotic face.

THE
LETTER TO
CHOOCH

Dear Chooch,

I told you once that you were an adult and that you were in charge of your life.

A man makes his own decisions but is also forced to live with the quality of his choices.

Your mother wanted a lot for you. She wanted to see you grow up to be strong, valuable, full of integrity and vision. Unfortunately, wanting something isn't the same as achieving it, but her heart was in the right place. Everything she was doing, she was doing for you. I know that's hard to envision when you're spending Christmas vacation alone in the prep school dorm, but I believe she wanted the best for you.

Sandy had parts of it right, but maybe she didn't have the whole deal figured.

Now she's gone. She died in my arms, asking me to take care of you. Making me promise that I would.

Even before that moment, I've been wanting you in my life, but I've also been wondering if I'm the right person to attempt it. Is it fair for me to mess up, when you've been given so little up to now?

And, of course, in the long run, as an adult, it should be your decision anyway. These questions have been on my mind. Since you've come to mean a great deal to me, I want you to carefully consider my offer to move in and live here, before you give me your answer.

I'm not skilled at sharing. My life has been about grabbing and holding. It's a long way from the back door of the community hospital to this house in Venice. It doesn't represent much wealth or status, but it's the best I could do, and I feel blessed to be here.

You asked me once if I knew who your father was, and I told you that you would have to find out from your mother, that she had sworn me to secrecy. She once told me that your father was a criminal, a drug dealer that she had helped to put in jail.

Before she died, she told me why she had asked me to take you for this month. She said she felt it was finally time for us to get to know each other.

They say that things are never the way they appear, and I guess in this case that is certainly true. Sandy loved pulling all our strings, and now we're both faced with her last request.

I know the responsibility of looking after you goes much deeper than advice or guidance or suggestions to do your homework. It's about being a worthwhile role model. I'm not sure I can do that well.

Sandy had dreams of glory for you; she wanted you to go to Princeton or Yale, to be an attorney or a doctor. I have different goals. I want you to be a man of substance. I want you to know how to be a good friend and how to love without reservation. I want your word to be your bond.

So, Sandy and I have different goals now, just as we did when she was alive.

If you decide to take a shot with me, I will try hard to make this part of your life enriching. Can't say we won't argue or that I won't be wrong, but I can promise I'll try to always be honest with you.

Chooch, it's a much shorter journey we're on than it appears to be at its beginning. You can accept this ride or flag down another. It's all choices. It always will be.

> Love,
> Your father,
> Shane

■ ■ ■

He heard the door open behind him and sat quietly on the metal chair. After a moment he heard footsteps coming across the grass. Then Chooch sat in the metal chair beside him. He was holding the letter and looking out at the still water. The three-quarter moon was coming off the horizon, hiding behind a drifting cloud, lighting its lacy edges. They sat in silence and watched it float slowly by.

Shane was almost afraid to speak; his heart was beating fast in his chest. "So, whatta you think?" he said softly.

Chooch sat looking at the still canal, his face strangely set, breathing deeply. Then he dropped the letter on the grass, reached out and took hold of Shane's shoulder, and squeezed it.

"I want to stay here," he finally said. "This is where I belong."